There was a boom behind him as the brute dropped down from the gantry. Fulren backed away, keen to keep both his opponents in view.

They paced across the warehouse, trying to gain flanking positions. Fulren knew he had to keep moving. He couldn't let them outmanoeuvre him.

He feinted left toward the woman, who backed away, then dashed at the brute, swinging his sword at head height. The axeman raised his weapon to parry, but instead of striking with his sword, Fulren barged into him with a shoulder. Off balance, the man went sprawling. Somehow Fulren managed to stay on his feet as the brute fell backward, and he turned quickly to parry the woman's rapier. Her attack was relentless, and he only just avoided a thrust that still sliced a smile in his shirt.

Fulren wasn't thinking now, the forms he had learned from long hours in the training yard came to him instinctually. They danced their deadly two-step until the woman was struggling to block his counters, and after one final strike at her head, Fulren kicked out. He caught her in the hip, his full weight behind the blow, and she let out a winded cry as she fell backward.

Fulren ducked.

The axe once again hacked wood beside his head. Fulren's blade came up in a clean, precise arc and would have severed the brute's arms had the man not abandoned his weapon and staggered back. His left foot caught on a loose pile of rope, his right slipping on the greasy floor, and he fell in a heap.

Fulren couldn't help but grin at the sight of the thickly muscled specimen lying there in the straw and dirt, his waxed moustache all askew. The levity didn't last long as he felt the cold edge of a rapier blade at his throat.

He froze, letting his sword arm slowly drop to his side.

"You're finished, son of Hawkspur," the woman whispered in his ear.

By R. S. Ford

THE AGE OF UPRISING

Engines of Empire

WAR OF THE ARCHONS

A Demon in Silver
Hangman's Gate
Spear of Malice

STEELHAVEN

Herald of the Storm
The Shattered Crown
Lord of Ashes

ENGINES OF EMPIRE

BOOK ONE OF
THE AGE OF UPRISING

R·S·FORD

orbitbooks.net

Cover design and illustration by Mike Heath/Magnus Creative

Map by Tim Paul

Orbit
Hachette Book Group
1290 Avenue of the Americas
New York, NY 10104
orbitbooks.net

First Edition: January 2022

Orbit is an imprint of Hachette Book Group.
The Orbit name and logo are trademarks of Little, Brown Book Group Limited.

Library of Congress Cataloging-in-Publication Data
Names: Ford, R. S. (Richard S.), author.
Title: Engines of empire / R.S. Ford.
Description: First edition. | New York : Orbit, 2022. | Series: The age of uprising ; book 1
Identifiers: LCCN 2021022688 | ISBN 9780316629560 (trade paperback) | ISBN 9780316629553 (ebook)
Subjects: GSAFD: Fantasy fiction.
Classification: LCC PR6106.O757 E54 2022 | DDC 823/.92—dc23
LC record available at https://lccn.loc.gov/2021022688

ISBNs: 9780316629560 (trade paperback), 9780316629584 (ebook)

Printed in the United States of America

LSC-C

Printing 2, 2023

For Iona

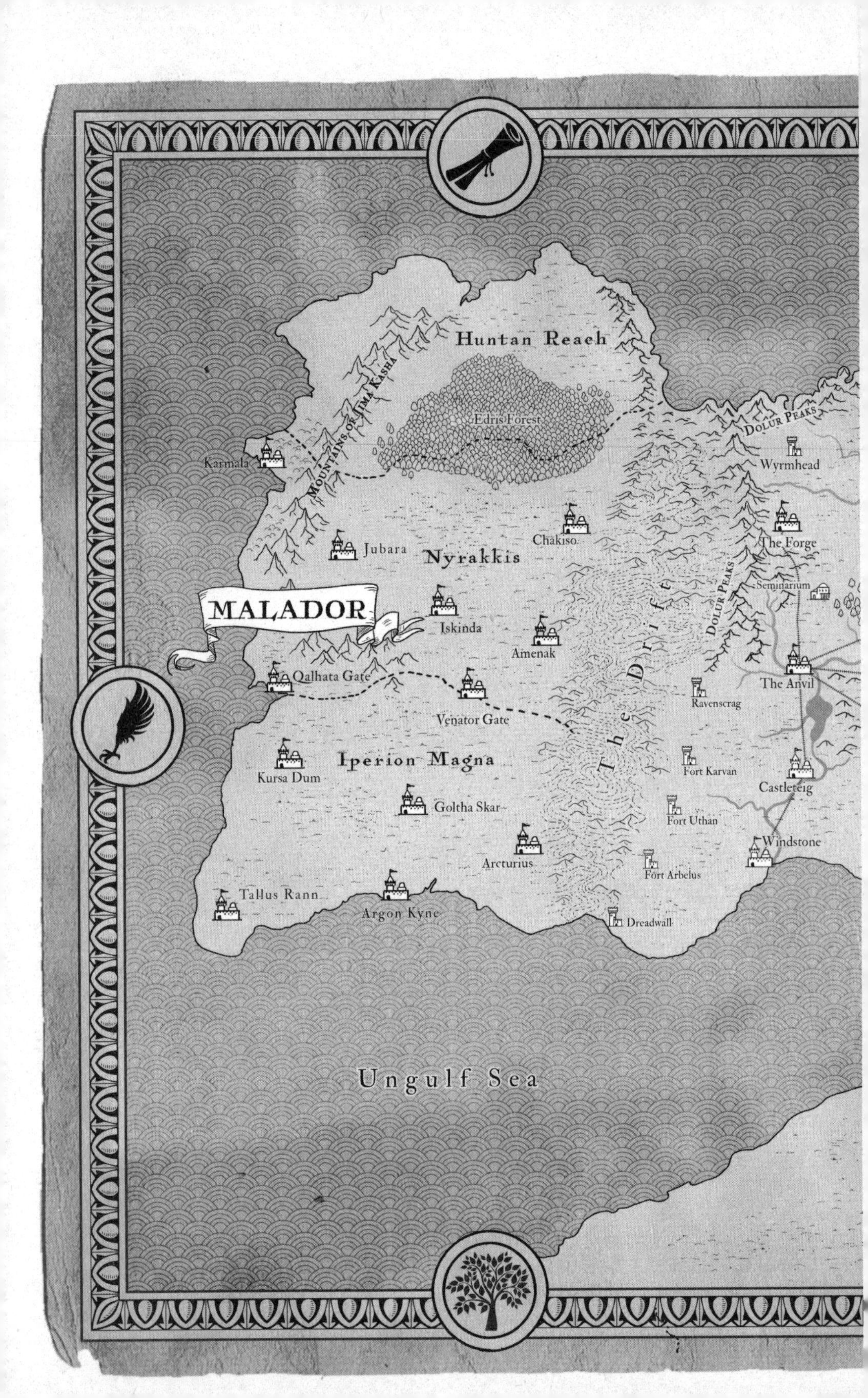

Huntan Reach
Mountains of Jima Kasha
Edris Forest
Dolur Peaks
Karmala
Wyrmhead
Chakiso
The Forge
Jubara
Nyrakkis
Seminarium
MALADOR
Iskinda
Amenak
Dolur Peaks
The Drift
Qalhata Gate
The Anvil
Ravenscrag
Venator Gate
Kursa Dum
Iperion Magna
Fort Karvan
Castleteig
Goltha Skar
Fort Uthan
Windstone
Arcturius
Fort Arbelus
Tallus Rann
Argon Kyne
Dreadwall
Ungulf Sea

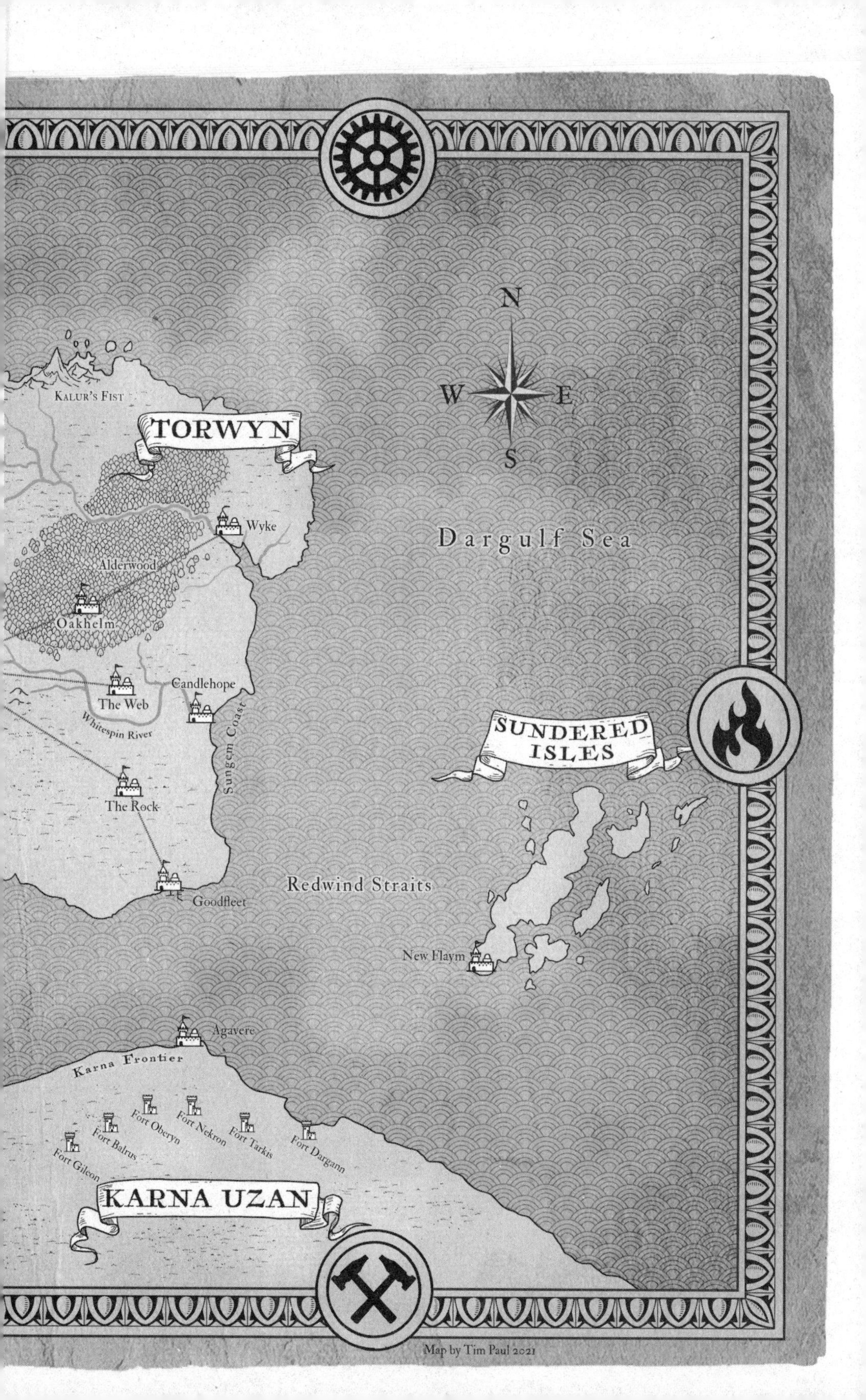
N
W
E
S
Kalur's Fist
TORWYN
Wyke
Dargulf Sea
Alderwood
Oakhelm
The Web
Candlehope
Whitespin River
Sungem Coast
SUNDERED ISLES
The Rock
Goodfleet
Redwind Straits
New Flaym
Agavere
Karna Frontier
Fort Oberyn
Fort Nekron
Fort Tarkis
Fort Dargann
Fort Balrus
Fort Gileon
KARNA UZAN
Map by Tim Paul 2021

DRAMATIS PERSONAE

THE HAWKSPURS

Athelys Branwell—Rosomon's handmaid.

Conall Hawkspur—Son of Rosomon. Captain of the Talon.

Darina Egelrath—Sister of Melrone. Mother of Sanctan Egelrath.

Fulren Hawkspur—Son of Rosomon. A skilled artificer.

Melrone Hawkspur—Husband of Rosomon. (Deceased.)

Rosomon Hawkspur—Guildmaster. Mother to Conall, Fulren and Tyreta.

Starn Rivers—Swordwright of the Hawkspur Guild.

Tyreta Hawkspur—Daughter of Rosomon. A webwainer.

THE ARCHWINDS

Arten—One of the Titanguard.

Cullum Kairns—Imperator of the Titanguard.

Dagamir—One of the Titanguard.

Lancelin Jagdor—The Hawkslayer. Swordwright of the Archwind Guild.

Lorens Archwind—Eldest son of Sullivar and Oriel.

Mallum Kairns—Imperator Dominus of the Titanguard.

Olstrum Garner—Sullivar's consul.

Oriel Archwind—Wife of Sullivar.

Sullivar Archwind—Emperor of Torwyn.

Treon Archwind—Father of Rosomon and Sullivar. (Deceased.)

Wyllow Archwind—Youngest son of Sullivar and Oriel. A webwainer.

THE CORWENS

Rearden Corwen—Guildmaster.

Wachelm—A junior actuary of the Corwen Guild.

THE IRONFALLS

Maugar Ironfall—Swordwright of the Ironfall Guild. Brother of Wymar.

Wymar Ironfall—Guildmaster. Brother of Maugar.

THE MARRLOCKS

Donan Marrlock—A minor member of the Guild.

Emony Marrlock—Youngest daughter of Oleksig.

Isleen Marrlock—A minor member of the Guild.

Oleksig Marrlock—Guildmaster.

Serrell Marrlock—Lord of New Flaym. Distant cousin of Oleksig.

THE RADWINTERS

Becuma—A senior representative of the Radwinter Guild.

Jarlath Radwinter—Guildmaster.

Mincloth Radwinter—Wife of Jarlath.

THE HALLOWHILLS

Ingelram Hallowhill—Guildmaster.

Keara Hallowhill—Daughter of Ingelram. A webwainer.

THE DRACONATE MINISTRY

Ansell Beckenrike—Knight commander of the Drakes.

Gylbard—Former Archlegate. (Deceased.)

Hisolda—High Legate of Vermitrix.

Sanctan Egelrath—Archlegate.

Willet Kinloth—A junior legate.

KARNA UZAN

Beringer—Frontier marshal of the Phoenix Battalion.

Nevan Ulworth—A scout serving under Conall in the Talon.

Stediana Walden—Sted. Conall's lieutenant in the Talon.

Westley Tarrien—Captain of the Phoenix Battalion.

NYRAKKIS

Ak-Samtek—Grand vizier to Queen Meresankh.

Amosis Makareth—Head of Meresankh's cabal of arcanists.

Assenah Neskhon—Emissary of Queen Meresankh.

Bekis Katanen—The Overseer. Queen Meresankh's bodyguard.

Gaddis Rekhmire—A disgraced centurion of the Medjai.

Kosma Khonos—An agent of Torwyn.

Meresankh—Queen of Nyrakkis.

Nimlot—Lord of House Hamaket.

Serapion—General of the Medjai.

Tiaa Sakhopenra—Witch of the Silent Key.

Torrianus the Hydra—Infamous bandit leader.

Wenamun Surero—Disgraced merchant.

Wenis of Jubara—Arcanist.

THE HUNTAN REACH

Henakor the Butcher—A warrior of the Skull Kin.

Indoneth the Flayer—A warrior of the Skull Kin.

Saranor the Bleeder—Warchief of the Skull Kin.

THE SUNDERED ISLES

Amanisa—A warrior of the Lokai.

Crenn—An old artificer.

Edana Larkin—Wife of Lavren.

Eremand—Chancellor of New Flaym.

Gelila—A warrior of the Lokai.

Lavren Larkin—A pyrestone trader.

Ozoro—A warrior of the Lokai.

Shabak—War leader of the Chul.

Suma—A warrior of the Lokai.

Yeki—Matriarch of the Lokai.

ORGANISATIONS OF TORWYN

Armiger Battalions—*Military legions that defend Torwyn from foreign threats and protect its interests abroad. The eleven battalions are Auroch, Bloodwolf, Corvus, Griffin, Kraken, Mantid, Phoenix, Raptor, Tigris, Ursus, Viper.*

Draconate Ministry—*The ecclesiastic power in Torwyn, led by the Archlegate, which worships the five Great Wyrms:*

Ammenodus Rex—Great Wyrm of War.

Ravenothrax the Unvanquished—Great Wyrm of Death.

Saphenodon—Great Wyrm of Knowledge.

Undometh—Great Wyrm of Vengeance.

Vermitrix—Great Wyrm of Peace.

***Guilds**—The ruling power in Torwyn. The six major Guilds are:*

Archwind Guild—Most powerful Guild in Torwyn, specialising in artifice. Its military arm is known as the Titanguard.

Corwen Guild—The nation's administrators. Its military arm is known as the Revocaters.

Hawkspur Guild—Controls transit. Its military arm is known as the Talon.

Ironfall Guild—Works the forges. Its military arm is known as the Blackshields.

Marrlock Guild—Mines for ore and pyrestone.

Radwinter Guild—Responsible for farming and lumber.

PROLOGUE

Courage. That ever-elusive virtue. Willet had once been told a man could never possess true courage without first knowing true fear. If that was so, he must be the bravest man in all Torwyn, as fear gnawed at him like a starving hound, cracking his bones and licking at the marrow.

He knew this was not courage. More likely it was madness, but then only the mad would have walked so readily into the Drift. It was a thousand miles of wasteland cut through the midst of an entire continent, leaving a scar from the Dolur Peaks in the north to the Ungulf Sea on the southern coast. A scar that would never heal. The remnant of an ancient war, and a stark reminder that sorcery was the unholiest of sins.

Willet glanced over his shoulder, squinting against the midday sun toward Fort Karvan as it loomed on the distant ridge like a grim sentinel. Had there ever been built a more forbidding bastion of stone and iron?

Five vast fortresses lined the border between Torwyn and the Drift, each one garrisoned by a different Armiger Battalion, the last line of defence against the raiding tribes and twisted beasts of the wasteland. Fort Karvan was home to the grim and proud Mantid Battalion, and though Willet hated it with every fibre, he would have given anything to be safe within its walls right now. Instead he was traipsing through the blasted landscape, and the only things to protect him were a drab grey robe and his faith in the Great Wyrms. Well, perhaps not the only things.

"Pick up your feet, Legate Kinloth," Captain Jarrell hissed from the head of the patrol. "If you fall behind, you'll be left behind." The captain scowled from within the open visor of his mantis helm, greying beard reaching over the gorget of his armour.

Willet quickened his pace, sandals padding along the dusty ground. Captain Jarrell was a man whose bite was most definitely worse than his bark, and Willet wasn't sure whether he was more afraid of him or of the denizens of the Drift. The only person he'd ever known with sharper teeth was his own mother, though it was a close-run thing.

By the time he caught up, Willet was short of breath, but he felt some relief as he continued his trek within the sizeable shadow of Jarrell's lieutenant, Terrick. The big man was the only inhabitant of Fort Karvan who'd ever offered Willet so much as the time of day. He was quick to laugh and generous with his mirth, but not today. Terrick's eyes were fixed on the trail ahead, his expression stern as he gripped tight to sword and shield, wary of any danger.

At the head of their patrol, Lethann scouted the way. In contrast to Terrick she was the very definition of mirthless. She wore the tan leather garb of a Talon scout, travelling cloak rendering her almost invisible against the dusty landscape. A splintbow was strapped to her back, a clip of bolts on her hip alongside the long hunting knife. Every now and then she would kneel, searching for sign, following the trail like a hunting dog.

Three other troopers of the Mantid Battalion marched with them but, to his shame, Willet had no idea what they were called. In fairness, each of their faces was concealed beneath the visor of a mantis helm, but even so they were still part of his brood, and he their stalwart priest. Willet was charged with enforcing their faith in the Great Wyrms, and when would they need that more than now, out here in the deadly wilds? How was he to provide sacrament without even knowing their names? It reminded him once again of the impossibility of the task he'd been given.

Since his first day at Fort Karvan, Willet had been ignored and disrespected. The Draconate Ministry had sent him to instil faith in the fort's stout defenders, and Willet had gone about that role with all the zeal his position demanded. It soon became clear no one was going to take him seriously. Over the days and weeks his sermons had been met with indifference at best. At worst outright derision. The disrespect had worsened, rising to a tumult, until the occasion when he had drunk deeply from a waterskin only to find it had been filled with tepid piss when he wasn't looking.

Had Willet been posted at another fort in another part of the Drift, perhaps he would have been received with more enthusiasm. The Corvus at Ravenscrag or the Ursus Battalion at Fort Arbelus would have provided him a much warmer welcome. For the Mantid Battalion, it seemed faith in the Guilds of Torwyn far outweighed faith in the Ministry. But what had he truly expected? It was not the Draconate Ministry that fuelled the nation's commerce. It was not the legates who built artifice and supplied the military with its arms and armour. It was not Willet Kinloth who had brought about the greatest technological advancements in Torwyn's history.

His sudden despondency provoked a groundswell of guilt. As Saphenodon decreed, those who suffer the greatest hardship are due the highest reward. And who was Willet Kinloth to question the wisdom of the Draconate?

"That lookout can't be much farther ahead," Terrick grumbled, to himself as much as to anyone else. It was enough to shake Willet from his malaise, forcing him to concentrate on the job at hand.

They had first spied their quarry four days ago from the battlements of Fort Karvan. The figure had been distant and indistinct, and at first the lookouts had dismissed it as a wanderer, lost in the Drift. When they spotted the lone figure again a second and third day there was only one conclusion—the fort was being watched, which could herald a raid from one of the many marauding bands that dogged the border of Torwyn.

Raiding parties had been harrying the forts along the Drift for centuries. Mostly they were small warbands grown so hungry and desperate they risked their lives to pillage Torwyn's abundant fields and forests. But some were vast armies, disparate tribes gathered together by a warlord powerful enough to threaten the might of the Armiger Battalions. No such armies had risen for over a decade, the last having been quelled with merciless violence by a united front of Guild, Armiger and Ministry. But it still paid to be cautious. If this scout was part of a larger force, it was imperative they be captured and questioned.

The ground sloped ever downward as they followed the trail, and the grim sight of Fort Karvan was soon lost beyond the ridge behind them. Willet stuck close to Terrick, but the hulking trooper provided less and less reassurance the deeper they ventured into the Drift.

Willet's hand toyed with the medallions about his neck, the five charms bringing him little comfort. The sapphire of Vermitrix imparted no peace, the jade of Saphenodon no keen insight. The jet pendant of Ravenothrax did not grant him solace in the face of imminent death, and neither did the solid steel of Ammenodus Rex give him the strength to face this battle. His hand finally caressed the red ruby pendant of Undometh. The Great Wyrm of Vengeance. That was the most useless of all—for who would avenge Willet if he was slain out here? Would Undometh himself come to take vengeance on behalf of a lowly legate? Not likely.

Lethann waved from up ahead. Her hand flashed in a sequence of swift signals before she gestured ahead into a steep valley. Willet had no idea how to decipher the silent message, but the rest of the patrol adopted a tight formation, Captain Jarrell leading his men with an added sense of urgency.

Their route funnelled into a narrow path, bare red rock rising on both sides as they descended into a shallow valley. Here lay the remnants of a civilisation that had died a thousand years before. Relics from the age of the Archmages, before their war and their magics had blasted the continent apart.

Willet stared at the broken and derelict buildings scattered about the valley floor. Alien architecture clawed its way from the earth, the tops of ancient spires lying alongside the weathered corpses of vast statues. He trod carefully in his sandals, as here and there lay broken and rusted weapons, evidence of the battle fought here centuries before. Cadaverous remnants of plate and mail lay half-reclaimed in the dirt, the remains of their wearers long since rotted to dust.

Up ahead, Lethann paused at the threshold of a ruined archway. It was the entrance to a dead temple, its remaining walls standing askew on the valley floor, blocking the way ahead. She knelt, and her hand traced the outline of something in the dust before she turned to Jarrell and nodded.

Terrick and the three other troopers moved up beside their captain as Willet hung back, listening to Jarrell's whispered orders. As one, the troopers spread out, Jarrell leading the way as they moved toward the arch. Lethann unstrapped her splintbow and checked the breech before slotting a clip of bolts into the stock, and the patrol entered the brooding archway.

Willet followed them across the threshold into what had once been the vast atrium of a temple. Jarrell and his men spread out, swords drawn, shields braced in front of them. Lethann lurked at the periphery, aiming her splintbow across the wide-open space. At first Willet didn't notice what had made them so skittish. Then his eyes fell on the lone figure perched on a broken altar at the opposite end of the temple.

She knelt as though in prayer. Her left hand rested on a sheathed greatsword almost as tall as she was, and the other covered her right eye. The left eye was closed as though she were deep in meditation. She wore no armour, but a tight-fitting leather jerkin and leggings covered her from neck to bare feet. Her arms were exposed, and Willet could make out faint traces of the tattoos that wheeled about her bare flesh.

"There's nowhere to run," Jarrell pronounced, voice echoing across the open ground of the temple. "Surrender to us, and we'll see you're treated fairly."

Willet doubted the truth of that, but he still hoped this would end without violence. This woman stood little chance against six opponents.

Slowly she opened her left eye, hand still pressed over the right, and regarded them without emotion. If she was intimidated by the odds against her, she didn't show it.

"You should turn back to your fort," she answered in a thick Maladoran accent. "And run."

Lethann released the safety catch on her splintbow, sighting across the open ground at the kneeling woman. With a sweep of his hand, Jarrell ordered his men to advance.

Terrick was the first to step forward, the brittle earth crunching beneath his boots. Two of the troopers approached from the flanks, closing on the woman's position. Lethann moved along the side of the atrium, barely visible in the shadow of the temple wall.

"I tried," the woman breathed, slowly lowering the hand that covered her eye.

Willet stifled a gasp as he saw a baleful red light where her right eye should have been. Stories of demons and foul sorceries flooded his memory, and his hand shook as it moved to grasp the pendants about his neck.

Terrick was unperturbed, closing on her position with his sword braced atop his shield. When he advanced to within five feet, the woman moved.

With shocking speed she wrenched the greatsword from its sheath and leapt to her feet, blade sweeping the air faster than the eye could comprehend. Terrick halted his advance before toppling back like a statue and landing on his back in the dirt.

Willet let out a gasp as blood pooled from Terrick's neck, turning the sand black. The other two troopers charged in, the first yelling in rage from within his mantis helm, sword raised high. The woman leapt from atop her rocky perch, sword sweeping that mantis helm from the trooper's shoulders. Her dance continued, bare feet sending clouds of dust into the air as she sidestepped a crushing sweep of the next trooper's blade before thrusting the tip of her greatsword into his stomach beneath the breastplate. Willet saw it sprout from his back in a crimson bloom before she wrenched it free, never slowing her momentum, swift as an eagle in flight.

The clacking report of bolts echoed across the temple as Lethann unleashed a salvo from her splintbow. Willet's lips mouthed a litany to Ammenodus Rex as the woman sprinted around the edge of the temple wall, closing the gap on Lethann. Every bolt missed, ricocheting off the decayed rocks as the woman ate up the distance between them at a frightening rate. Lethann fumbled at her belt for a second clip, desperate to reload, but the woman was on her. A brutal hack of the greatsword, and Lethann's body collapsed to the dirt.

"Ammenodus, grant me salvation that I might be delivered from your enemies," Willet whispered, pressing the steel pendant to his lips as he did so. He found himself backing away, sandals scuffing across the dusty floor, as the woman casually strode toward the centre of the atrium. Captain Jarrell and his one remaining trooper moved to flank her, crouching defensively behind their shields.

They circled as she stood impassively between them. For the first time Willet noted the white jewel glowing at the centre of her greatsword's cross-guard. It throbbed with sickly light, mimicking the pulsing red orb sunk within her right eye socket.

This truly was a demon of the most corrupt kind, and Willet's hand fumbled at the pendants about his neck, fingers closing around the one made of jet. "O great Ravenothrax," he mumbled. "The Unvanquished. Convey me to your lair that I might be spared the evil propagated by mine enemies."

In the centre of the atrium, the three fighters paid little heed to Willet's prayers. The last trooper's patience gave out, and with a grunt he darted to attack. Captain Jarrell bellowed at him to "Hold!" but it was too late. The woman's greatsword seemed to move of its own accord, the white jewel flashing hungrily as the blade skewered the eye socket of the trooper's helmet.

Jarrell took the initiative as his last ally died, charging desperately, hacking at the woman before she ducked, spun, twisted in the air and kicked him full in the chest. Willet held his breath, all thought of prayer forgotten as he saw Jarrell lose his footing and fall on his back.

The woman leapt in the air, impossibly high, that greatsword lancing down to impale the centre of Jarrell's prone body, driving through his breastplate like a hammered nail.

It was only then that Willet's knees gave out. He collapsed to the dirt, feeling a tear roll from his eye. The pendants in his fist felt useless as the woman slowly stood and turned toward him.

"Vermitrix, Great Wyrm of Peace, bring me a painless end," he whispered as she drew closer, leaving her demon sword still skewered through Jarrell's chest. "And may Undometh grant me vengeance against this wicked foe."

She stood over him, hand covering that sinister red eye once more. The jewel that sat in the centre of the greatsword's cross-guard had dulled to nothing but clear glass, but Willet could still feel its evil from across the atrium.

"Your dragon gods will not save you, little priest," the woman said. Her voice was calm and gentle, as though she were coaxing a child to sleep.

Willet tried to look at her face but couldn't. He tried to speak, but all that came out was a whimper, a mumbled cry for his mother. He could almost have laughed at the irony. Here he was at the end, and for all his pious observance he was crying for a woman who had made his life a misery with her spiteful and poisonous tongue.

"Your mother is not coming either," the woman said. "But the voice is quiet, for now. So you should run, little priest. Before it speaks again."

Somehow Willet rose to his feet, legs trembling like a newborn foal's. He took a tentative step away from the woman, who kept her hand clamped tight over her eye. The white jewel in her sword, still skewered through Jarrell's chest, shone with sudden malevolence. It was enough to set Willet to flight.

He ran, losing a sandal on the rough ground, ignoring the sudden pain in his foot. He would not stop until he was back at the gates of Fort Karvan. Would not slow no matter the ache in his legs nor lack of breath in his lungs. He could not stop. If he did, there would be nothing left for him but the Five Lairs. And he was not ready for them yet.

PART ONE

THE EMISSARY

TYRETA

The journey from Wyke to the Anvil was over five hundred miles of undulating land. It would have taken longer than two weeks by wagon, with regular stops and changes of horse. Tyreta Hawkspur would complete the journey in less than three days.

From the viewing deck of the landship she could already see the rising minarets of the Anvil in the distance, growing ever larger as the open fields and rivers glided by. The vessel was elevated on rails, engines growling, the sound bellowing over the wind as it rushed into her face. It was an ingenious feat of engineering. The Hawkspur Guild had established a network of such lines across the length and breadth of Torwyn, on which the long trains of steel and iron snaked. Tyreta was heir to this legacy, one that had seen the Hawkspurs rise from simple couriers to one of the most powerful Guilds in the land. It should have made her proud. All she felt was bored.

"Try to look more enthused. Your uncle will have gone to a great deal of trouble to greet us. I'd rather you didn't look like you've just eaten a bag of lemons when we arrive."

There it was.

Tyreta's mother, Rosomon, stood at the rail beside her. A constant reminder of what Tyreta was to inherit. Of her responsibilities.

"Oh, there's a big smile on the inside, Mother," Tyreta replied.

She said it under her breath, but as usual Lady Rosomon's hearing was almost preternatural.

"Well, when we arrive, see if you can conjure one on your face."

Her mother moved away, off to prepare herself to greet the emperor. It wouldn't do for Rosomon Hawkspur to look anything less than resplendent when she was met by her brother, the great Sullivar Archwind.

As she left, Tyreta contorted her face into a twisted semblance of a smile. It was a pointless act of defiance but at least one she could get away with—Rosomon's hearing might have been keen as a bat's, but she certainly didn't have eyes in the back of her head. As her mother left the viewing deck, Tyreta saw she'd not been quite as discreet as she'd anticipated.

Her elder brother Conall was watching her from across the deck, wearing a mocking grin. He was tall, handsome, sharp-witted, impeccably dressed in his blue uniform—all the things an heir to the Hawkspur Guild should be. Conall never put a foot wrong, in contrast to Tyreta's constant missteps. He was the future of their line and a captain in the Talon, the military arm of the Guild. All her life she'd been trying to live up to his example and failing miserably. He was the last person she would want to catch her acting like an infant. Well, if her mother and brother thought her so feckless, maybe she'd demonstrate just how talented she was.

Ignoring her brother's smugness, she moved from the deck and made her way below into the cloying confines of the metal carriage. If the sound was deafening on the viewing deck, it was much worse inside. The roar of the engines resonated throughout the length of the landship, the walls of the carriages trembling with the power of it. Tyreta could feel the energy coursing through the vessel, propelling it along the rails. For everyone else on board, she guessed it was just about bearable. For Tyreta it was a drug to the senses.

They were almost at their destination now, the Anvil no more than a few miles away. Surely this was the time to indulge? If her mother chided her, what was the difference? What was the worst that could happen?

Tyreta made her way forward through the carriages. Past the

soldiers of the Talon, busy polishing their hawk helms and ceremonial blades, past the servants and staff, to the engine room, the head of the snake.

The steel door was shut, a wheel at its centre keeping the engine room locked away from the rest of the landship. Tyreta turned the wheel, hearing the clamps unlock, and swung open the door. She was greeted by the growl of the engine and the hum of the power core within, feeling it nourishing her, energising her.

When she entered, the drivers immediately stood to one side and bowed their heads. There were some advantages to being heir to a Guild.

The men were masked to protect them from the smoke and dust of the engine, but Tyreta ignored the cloying atmosphere as she approached the power core. She could feel its hum, a sweet lamenting tune sung only to her. Reaching out, she placed a hand on it, sensing the energy emanating from the pyrestones within—those precious crystals pulsating with life.

This was her gift. As a webwainer she could control the pyrestones, imbuing them with life, and at her touch they responded, glowing hotter, agitated by her presence. The drivers gave one another a worried look, though neither dared offer a word of complaint.

"Is this the fastest this crate can go?" Tyreta shouted above the din.

One of the drivers pulled down his mask. "It is, my lady. Any faster and we risk—"

"I think we can do better," she replied.

She pressed her palm to the core and closed her eyes. A smile crossed her lips as she felt the pyrestones respond to her will, the core growing hotter against her palm. The engine whined in protest as the stones urged the pistons and hydraulics to greater effort.

"My lady, this is against regulations," shouted one of the drivers, but Tyreta ignored him.

The landship began to accelerate. She opened her eyes, seeing through the viewing port that the landscape was beginning to shoot past at an alarming rate. Still she did not yield. Tyreta wanted more.

She pressed the core further, communing with it, talking to it in a silent whisper, urging it to greater and greater effort. This was what her webwainer gift was for, and for too long she had been forbidden to use it. What did her mother know anyway? Lady Rosomon had never experienced the privilege of the webwainer talent. This was Tyreta's right—and besides, what harm could she do?

The landship bucked, the wheels momentarily sliding on the rails. She glanced across the cab, seeing abject terror on the drivers' faces. Before she could release her hand, there was a yell behind her.

"Tyreta!"

She snatched her hand from the core as though she'd been bitten, turning to see her mother's furious face in the doorway. The train immediately slowed, the rattling and bucking relenting as the landship slowed to its former speed.

Lady Rosomon didn't have to say a word. Tyreta removed herself from the engine room, moving back through the carriages and past the chaos she'd caused. Baggage had fallen from the securing rigs, garments and trinkets were scattered about the floor. The Talon soldiers were picking themselves up from where they lay, their arms and armour strewn all about.

Tyreta reached her cabin and closed the door, resting her back against it and breathing heavily. There might be a price to pay for this later. Lady Rosomon had never been a tolerant woman. Whatever that price was, Tyreta thought as a smile played across her lips, it had been worth it.

The rest of the journey was mercifully short and without incident. Tyreta considered it best not to push her luck, and she dressed as one might expect of an heir to the Hawkspur Guild, her blue tunic displaying the winged-talon sigil on her chest. Despite the tailored fit, it still felt as if it were throttling her, but it would be best to endure it for now. At least until her mother had a chance to cool down. As the landship pulled to a stop, Tyreta couldn't keep herself locked away any longer.

Lady Rosomon was waiting for her when she debarked. On her right stood the imposing figure of Starn Rivers, swordwright to the Hawkspur Guild. He was a bull of a man, thick moustache drooping down past his chin. Tyreta had never liked him or the looks he occasionally gave her, and the fact that he barely spoke was a small mercy.

While their cortege was busy unloading the landship and Conall joked with his cronies from the Talon, Rosomon led the group up through the terminal. Once out beyond the great arched entrance, Tyreta could see the city proper.

The Anvil was a testament to the power of the Guilds. Soaring towers clamoured for space, linked by raised walkways. Everything stank of opulence, and even the lowliest of the citizenry were adorned in fine silk and velvet. A thunderous rattle peeled down from overhead as a skycarriage rumbled by on its elevated tracks. Tyreta marvelled at the perfect union of artifice and architecture, conveying people from one side of the city to the other with such automotive efficiency.

It was a short walk to the main promenade, at the end of which stood the magnificent Archwind Palace. The way was lined with statues that crossed the Bridge of Saints, prominent members of the Guilds from the annals of history given pride of place along the Anvil's main thoroughfare. Between those icons stood an honour guard of giant stormhulks, pistons hissing as their vast mechanical frames suddenly stood to attention. Each was piloted by a webwainer—someone who could manipulate pyrestone and instil life in the huge engines. For a moment Tyreta felt a pang of envy—what a privilege to control an invention of such power—but her focus was quickly taken by the palace, rising up in the midst of the city like a vast mountain.

As they crossed the bridge, Tyreta saw that a reception party was already awaiting them. She could make out Sullivar standing front and centre, his red uniform of office pristine, breastplate of brass shining in the sun. Her uncle had recently proclaimed himself emperor of Torwyn—an affectation Tyreta found a little ridiculous. Sullivar might look the part, but it was widely known he fell far short of being the great ruler her grandfather Treon had been.

Before they reached the foot of the vast stairway that led up to the palace, Tyreta caught up with her mother.

"Just wanted to say—" she began.

"Not now," Rosomon snapped.

"But I thought I'd—"

Her mother cut her off with a glance, and Tyreta thought it best not to push it, moving back and letting Lady Rosomon lead the way once more. Maybe it would be wise to let her calm down a little more before trying for an apology again.

When they'd almost reached the stairs, Sullivar could hold himself back no longer. He walked down the last few steps, hugging Rosomon to him in a bearlike embrace.

"It's been too long," he said to her.

"Indeed it has," she replied, smiling through the indignity.

"And you brought my niece and nephew," he said, opening his arms to hug Tyreta.

She embraced her uncle, feeling his perfumed beard soft against her cheek. Sullivar squeezed her a little too tightly, crushing her against the cog sigil embossed on his breastplate, but there was little she could do to stop it. Once he'd released her, Conall reached forward to shake Sullivar's hand, but he too was met with a bear hug.

"Lady Oriel," Rosomon said, bowing before Sullivar's wife, who had come to join them. "Or should that be Empress?"

"Nonsense," Oriel replied, taking Rosomon's hand and leading her up the stairs. "We are family. No need for such affectations between us."

They might have been sisters by marriage, but the difference between them was stark. Where Oriel was dazzling in a gown of red and gold, her hair tied up in an intricate bunch fastened with elaborate pins, Rosomon wore a skirt and cloak of plain blue, brown hair falling straight and unadorned about her shoulders.

Tyreta followed them up to the palace, passing the heavily armoured Titanguard who lined their route. Each one was a behemoth, glaive in hand, bulky armour powered by ingenious artifice. She noticed there was no sign of Lancelin Jagdor, swordwright of the Archwind Guild, but then it was best if that man didn't show his face in front of the Hawkspurs. But Lancelin wasn't the only one conspicuous by his absence.

"Where's Fulren?" Tyreta asked.

"Your younger brother wanted to come and greet you," said Sullivar. "But he is busying himself in his workshop. He has almost made a breakthrough with his studies, so I am told."

"He always was dedicated," said Rosomon, glancing momentarily at her daughter.

Tyreta bristled at the insinuation. Her younger brother couldn't even be bothered to come greet them, yet still he was lauded. Once again she was reminded who the favourites were.

"He's been a great asset," said Sullivar. "His skills have improved beyond measure. You should go see him at work, Tyreta," he added.

She was about to protest, but a look from her mother made her realise she should probably do as she was bid. Best not to push things too far, considering she had still to face her punishment for toying with the landship.

As Rosomon and Conall were led away through the palace by Sullivar and Oriel, Tyreta was taken by a sullen-looking footman down into the bowels of the huge building. Here were foundries by the dozen, smelting works, rows of benches upon which artificers worked on minuscule inventions. The farther down she got the more the place stank of industry—oil and rust permeated the air, the heat of the forges making the atmosphere sticky. Tyreta felt the essence of the pyrestones that lay all about, making her tingle right to her fingertips.

The footman led her to the lowest level. A door stood ajar at the end of the corridor, and the servant stopped, beckoning Tyreta inside. She pushed the door open to see a small workshop. It was in disarray, spare parts of machinery lying all about, and in the centre of the room, hunched over a workbench, was her brother Fulren.

"Hello, Tinhead," she said to his back.

"Hello, Ratface," he replied, without turning around.

She walked toward him, picking up some piece of artifice from a bench. It looked intricate, wires and pins protruding from every surface. Tyreta had no idea what it was for.

"Too busy playing with your toys to greet our beloved mother?"

"I've been busy," he said. "I'm sure she'll forgive me."

"For you, Lady Rosomon would forgive anything."

Fulren turned to face her. On his head was strapped a contraption that supported a lens over one eye to magnify his work. He would have looked every inch the artificer—studious, serious—were it not for the fact that he was broad about the shoulders and lean about the waist. A fighter in body, inventor in mind. The perfect combination of skill and intelligence. She couldn't help but resent him for that.

"I'm sure she's forgiven you plenty," he said. "How was the journey?"

"Let's just say it could have gone more smoothly."

Fulren flashed her a toothy grin. "Just can't stay out of trouble, can you, Ratface? You're supposed to be the responsible one."

"I'm older than you. That's pretty much where my responsibility ends."

"Not for long," said Fulren.

And he was right. Though Conall was to inherit their Guild's title and obligations, Rosomon had demanded that Tyreta also take on the responsibilities of the Hawkspur Guild. Conall would see to military matters, and Tyreta would be in charge of transportation all across Torwyn—by air, land and sea. She would administer trade routes and supply chains and keep her nation moving. It was a daunting prospect, and one she would gladly delay for as long as possible.

"No," Tyreta said. "It won't be long. I'm to travel to the Sundered Isles after the reception. Mother thinks it will build character."

"So soon?" Fulren seemed genuinely concerned. "I won't see much of you, then."

"You'd see more if you came with me. We could do this together. You could take up Father's mantle yourself. You could—"

"We've been over this a thousand times. My place is here." He gestured to the junk that lay strewn all around him. "Uncle Sullivar has granted me an apprenticeship. I am to become a master artificer. It's all been settled."

"So I'm doomed then?"

Fulren laughed at that. "You'll just have to live up to your responsibilities for once. Who knows, maybe you'll like it. You'll get to see the world."

The prospect of that did excite her, but thinking on the burden of controlling an entire Guild only filled her with dread.

"What about you?" she asked. "Are you going to live out your days cooped up in here, playing with your toys?"

"Who knows? Maybe I'll get to see the world too, one day."

Tyreta glanced around the windowless workshop, then shook her head. "Not you. You'll never leave this place."

"Thanks for the vote of confidence." He winked at her. "Anyway, get lost, I'm busy." With that he turned back to his machinery.

"See you at the reception, Tinhead," she replied before she left him to his labour.

The footman was still waiting for her outside, and Tyreta asked to be taken to her chamber. It had been a long journey, even for her.

Obediently the servant led her back up through the vast workshops until they reached ground level. There they took the elevator, steam pumping and gears grinding until it had juddered all the way to the upper levels of the palace. As she followed the open walkway toward her chamber she could see out onto the vast city. Huge stormhulks walked the streets, but they looked tiny from the heady heights of Archwind Palace. Not even the highest spires of Wyke could rival this place for majesty.

When finally she opened the door to her chamber, Tyreta was brought back to earth with a crash. Her mother was waiting patiently inside, her back to the door as she gazed from the window.

Tyreta closed the door, shutting herself in, bracing for what was coming.

"Mother, I—"

"We won't speak of it," Rosomon said.

That was unexpected. Tyreta had prepared herself for a tirade followed by yet another lecture on responsibility and duty to the Guild.

Rosomon turned from the window. Her hands were clasped in front of her, face a mask of calm. She was far from the raging harpy that usually manifested after one of Tyreta's frequent misdemeanours.

"Your first public engagement is coming." She gestured to the bed, where lay a dress in the deep blue of the Hawkspur Guild. "You'll wear that. You'll fix that." Rosomon pointed at Tyreta's hair, which, as usual, was worn up in a messy knot on top of her head. "And you'll do your best to act in a manner befitting an heir to the Guild of Hawkspur."

Tyreta wasn't sure what was worse—her mother's raging or her clinical orders.

"Of course," she replied. This was no time for defiance.

"And, if you wish, you can wear this."

Rosomon opened up her hand. In her palm was a silver pendant inlaid with a single gem. Tyreta recognised the nightstone immediately. It was the rarest of pyrestones, one that was useless for artifice but valued for its beauty nonetheless.

"Mother, I don't deserve—"

"No, you don't," said Rosomon. "But it was your father's and you should have it."

She took the pendant from her mother's hand. Tyreta had never been one for jewels or trinkets, but the fact that it had been her father's made it more precious than anything she had ever owned. She was about to thank her mother, to tell her she would do better from now on and live up to her father's legacy, but Lady Rosomon was already on her way through the door.

"And don't be late," Rosomon said before closing the door behind her and leaving Tyreta alone.

She held the pendant in her hand for a moment, feeling the nightstone cold against her palm. It could not be imbued with any power, could not be used for any practical purpose, and yet she suddenly felt more connected to it than she had to any pyrestone. She would wear it with pride.

Glancing down at the gaudy blue dress, she realised there was other attire she would just have to get used to.

FULREN

Gatherings like this made him want to be sick. He stood in the corner, clutching an empty goblet, wishing he were back in his workshop. Give him a bench laden with artifice, or even a sword in the training circle, but by the Great Wyrms spare him a social event.

They were in a huge rotunda at the summit of Archwind Palace. The hall was adorned with the pennants of the six most powerful Guilds, the great and good wandering the place in a twisting dance of feigned smiles and clutching handshakes. Of course his uncle Sullivar and aunt Oriel were at the centre of it—the newly proclaimed emperor and empress of Torwyn. And around them milled their obedient subjects, though you wouldn't have known that to look at them, flush with self-importance as they were.

At the other side of the rotunda Fulren could see his mother and sister as they mixed with the other guests. He couldn't help but be surprised at how well Tyreta took to the job, smiling warmly and greeting her peers with what could only be described as charm. Clearly his mother had prepared her accordingly. Fulren was happy in the shadows. Let them carry the mantle of the Hawkspurs—he had his own ambitions.

As for the other guests, he recognised few of them. He spied Rearden Corwen looking imperious as he moved through the crowds in a robe of stark yellow. Of course he would be here. The Guildmaster of Corwen had to register and document every event and transaction that went on in the empire. The arrival of a foreign emissary would not be something he'd miss.

Lord Wymar Ironfall stood in his dark-armoured regalia emblazoned with the forge fire symbol of his Guild. His brother, the Guild swordwright Maugar, stood beside him as always. The two weren't twins, but one could be forgiven for making that assumption, both their faces being buried beneath thick black beards, long hair greased back into topknots.

Jarlath Radwinter and his wife Mincloth seemed more concerned with sampling the food Sullivar had laid on than mingling with the crowd. Since they were heads of a Guild that oversaw Torwyn's agriculture, it seemed odd they'd need feeding at a time like this. The burgeoning waistlines that strained against their green velvet tunics were testament to the fact they were both amply nourished.

Fulren's eye eventually fell on a lone figure also standing at the periphery of the rotunda. He recognised Emony Marrlock immediately, her family having visited Wyke on a number of occasions. She stood alone, ash-blonde hair concealing most of her face, her dress looking sublime despite its being cut from cloth of drab Marrlock grey. It seemed curious she was here on her own to represent her Guild since she was only the youngest daughter of Guildmaster Oleksig, but Fulren couldn't see any of the other Marrlocks.

He moved from his position in the shadows. If he was to get a decent conversation out of anyone, it would be Emony. He navigated his way through the crowd, shifting past the perfumed parade, but wasn't halfway before he saw someone who removed all thoughts of Emony from his head.

Lancelin Jagdor was no more than ten feet away. He was tall, bearing the broad shoulders of a swordsman, a thick curved scar down one side of his lean face. He wore the Archwind Guild's red uniform, embellished with polished brass pauldrons. At his waist hung his sword of office, the pommel in the shape of the Archwind cog, his hand never straying far from it. Fulren had seen him only once since his arrival at the Anvil, his workshop keeping him cloistered away for the most part. This man was the reason Fulren had trained himself with a sword just as vigorously as he had studied the trade of artifice.

Jagdor had slain his father.

It had been a duel of honour by all accounts, though no one had ever known the slight that caused it. Melrone Hawkspur had chosen to fight the duel himself rather than have his swordwright Starn fight for him. Fulren had been in his mother's belly when the duel took place. Not yet born when Jagdor had stripped him of the father he'd been raised without. Some called him Hawkslayer to this day, but Fulren would see that insult redressed.

The swordwright still had his back turned, and Fulren's hand strayed down to the knife at his belt. A vendetta blade, they called it. The weapon that would see him avenged. Fulren had crafted it himself, as was tradition. Perhaps he should draw it now. Perhaps he should plunge it into Lancelin's back and the debt would be paid.

A hand grasped his wrist, holding it tight and the blade along with it.

"You should be careful. Don't want to cut yourself on that thing."

Fulren looked up into the blue eyes of his brother, Conall. He was smiling, but the strength with which he held Fulren's arm conveyed the seriousness of his intent.

Fulren loosened his grip on the blade. "I was just..."

Conall glanced over to where Lancelin Jagdor was mingling into the crowd.

"Yes, little brother. I'm sure you were."

Conall let go of Fulren's arm, then gently laid a hand on his back, guiding him to a quiet corner.

"One day, Conall," Fulren said, feeling his rage waning.

"No," Conall replied. "That's not for you."

"It's just..." Fulren tried to put it into words but failed. He had never known his father. Never known the reason for his feud with Jagdor, but still it was his duty to avenge his family. Wasn't it?

"I understand," said Conall. "But if anyone's going to end that bastard it'll be me. And it won't be with a knife in the back."

Fulren looked up at Conall. He had always been more a father to Fulren than a brother. It would be foolish to ignore his counsel now, but Fulren yearned for justice. Or was it just a selfish need for vengeance? Either way, he was determined that this was not the end of the matter.

"How long are you here for?" Fulren asked, changing the subject as deftly as he could manage and unclenching his bunched fists.

"Not long," his brother replied, placing a consoling hand on Fulren's shoulder. "I've been posted to Agavere. I'll find out which battalion I'm seconded to once we arrive."

"So you're leaving too."

Conall smiled down at him. "It's only for a few months. When I get back to the Anvil we'll have all the time in the world. I'll have some stories to tell, for sure."

The crash of a gong pealed throughout the rotunda, making the chatter suddenly ebb away, and Fulren saw an equerry standing in the huge archway that led out onto the pier.

"My lords and ladies," he announced, his voice quaking slightly, the auspiciousness of his audience getting the better of him. "If you would like to step out onto the promenade, our honoured guest is about to arrive."

"He's here!" shouted Sullivar, smiling through his well-appointed beard.

Fulren's uncle led the way up the stairs and through the archway. Immediately a line of courtly figures followed him. Fulren and Conall hung back, watching them all clamour after their emperor, a procession of sycophants eager to follow in Sullivar's wake.

As the crowd began to thin, Fulren started to make his way outside. Turning, he saw that Conall still waited in the rotunda.

"Are you coming?" he asked when Conall made no move to join him.

"I've got better things to do," his brother said. "Preparations for my trip. But don't let me stop you."

For a moment Fulren considered leaving with Conall. They'd not see each other for months, and it would be good to spend some time with him, but he knew that if he did not attend the greeting ceremony he would be missed.

"I'll see you later?"

"Bet on it," Conall said with a smile before turning and making his way from the empty hall.

Reluctantly Fulren followed the procession up the stairs and through the arch.

The wind whipped up as he stepped out onto the vast promenade of Archwind Palace. A pier jutted from the tower, stretching a hundred yards due west. Along it was arrayed the might of the Archwind Guild. Stormhulks stood beside Titanguard, flying flags bearing the golden cog of Archwind. Thick iron roosts jutted from the tower, atop which perched the giant war eagles of Torwyn, their riders sitting proud, lances festooned with cog-symbol pennants. It appeared Sullivar wanted this foreign emissary to see exactly which Guild was in charge when he arrived.

The crowd had gathered outside, wind blowing cloaks and carefully styled hair into a fury. Fulren peered into the distance, and in the west, beyond the mountain range that marked the border with the Drift, there was a dark spot in the air. It was little more than a blot on the horizon, hovering just above the mountaintops.

A pall of silence fell over the crowd as they watched, bewitched by the approaching spectacle. Fulren spied Tyreta in the crowd and pushed forward to join her. She looked as unenthused as he felt.

"Cheer up, Ratface," he said. "Apparently this is a great day. Could be the start of a new age."

"Yes," she replied. "If Uncle Sullivar has his way."

"I'm sure he will. A treaty with Nyrakkis will mean a new trade route. It could be your time to shine."

Tyreta looked thoroughly unimpressed by the prospect. "I can't wait."

Fulren glanced down at her attire. It was the first time he'd ever seen her in a gown of any kind.

"What are you wearing?" he said.

Tyreta rolled her eyes in that way she often did when pressed into something she hated. "Don't. This was Mother's idea. I wasn't in a position to refuse."

"Ah yes." Fulren grinned. "I heard about your little trick on the landship. Just can't help yourself, can you?"

Tyreta had no answer to that. Fact was, she'd never been able to help herself. Fulren would have thought it a curse if he believed in such things.

"What's that noise?" asked a voice in the crowd.

It started a murmur among the onlookers, and Fulren turned his attention back to the approaching spot in the sky. It was closer now, growing larger above the mountains, and as Fulren listened he could hear something on the wind. A whisper carried on the breeze, bringing a sense of foreboding with it.

"That doesn't sound good," said Tyreta.

Fulren could discern an outline now. The approaching vessel was some kind of airship, black in the pale sky. The closer it got the more the sound of it increased, as though someone were being tortured in the distance.

A disquiet settled on the crowd, and some of the guests began to back away, fearful of whatever dark magics approached from the west. The guards who lined the promenade gripped their splint-bows with white-knuckled trepidation. Each of those weapons was a mechanical marvel—more accurate than a crossbow and faster loading than a longbow, the breech fed via a clip containing half a dozen bolts. Developed by the artificers of Archwind, the basic design had not changed for over a century, and they were used widely throughout Torwyn in one form or another. Nevertheless, watching that ship draw ever nearer, Fulren doubted even a hundred of them could hold back what was coming.

Sullivar was unperturbed, walking to the head of the crowd, eager to greet the vessel heading their way. Fulren saw Lancelin Jagdor at his side and bristled once more. This time he left the knife where it was, but still he could barely quell his hate.

"That bastard," he heard Tyreta say, and he was pleased that she felt the same.

"Now's not the time," he replied, placing a hand on her shoulder, remembering Conall's words.

The other Guild representatives moved forward. Rearden Corwen stood beside Sullivar, not wishing to be outdone by his emperor. Wymar and Maugar Ironfall also strode to the front, though they shuffled uncomfortably all the while. Fulren's mother came to stand among them, and even Emony Marrlock took her place with the other Guildmasters.

The airship was clearly visible now. It cruised through the sky like a great ark, a black pirate battleship ready to enslave them all. The fell sound of its passing had grown louder, more a scream than a roar, as though the engines themselves were being tormented to the point of madness.

The crowd was spellbound, and Fulren along with it. He wanted to run from this behemoth but he couldn't move. All he could do was gape, openmouthed, as it approached the far end of the vast platform.

The giant war eagles atop their perches ruffled their feathers nervously, one of them beating its wings in an attempt to take flight as the vast ark came to land. Its descent was smooth, the engines producing a strange heat haze as it touched down on the platform, landing gear slamming to the ground like black metal talons. The engines hissed, smoke and steam billowing from vents along the dark iron of the hull. Then, after a final tormented breath, the ark fell silent.

Fulren watched from the crowd, seeing the airship glaring ahead like the face mask of an iron helm. No one seemed to know what to do. Not even Sullivar wanted to walk down the jetty to greet the new arrivals.

The sound of grinding metal was carried across the promenade by the wind. Chains clanked as the ramp at the front of the ark yawned open like a huge maw. It crashed to the marble floor with a boom, revealing the dark interior.

Two columns of warriors marched from inside, down the ramp and onto the pier, before turning to face one another and raising their spears in salute. Each one was tall and thickly muscled, their upper bodies naked but for the rings and chains that pierced their flesh and the tattoos that adorned their backs and arms. Then a single figure walked from within the ship.

She was taller than any woman Fulren had seen. Even from a distance he could see her flame-red hair matched the crimson of her long flowing cloak. Beneath she wore the close-cut leather of a warrior rather than the formalwear of an envoy. She moved between the ranks of the honour guard, her rangy gait swallowing up the distance as she approached. Sullivar stood awestruck, watching her draw ever nearer until she finally came to stand before him.

A smile played across her pale lips, dark eyes regarding him with amusement. Before either of them could speak she bowed low, sweeping her cloak aside theatrically.

"Emperor Sullivar," she said, her voice easily carrying across the platform for all to hear. There was but a trace of a foreign accent, and if Fulren hadn't known better he would have thought her schooled in one of Torwyn's own academies. "I am Assenah Neskhon of Jubara, emissary to the Queen Meresankh of Nyrakkis, Daughter to the Crimson Moon and Keeper of the Silent Key."

There was a pause as Sullivar composed himself before he said, "Welcome." His voice was quiet, subdued. Then he spread his arms, though he fell short of hugging the tall woman. "Welcome," he said louder.

Assenah responded with a wide smile, displaying her impossibly white teeth.

Sullivar guided the emissary inside, introducing her to the other members of the Guilds, who seemed all but spellbound.

Fulren glanced back at the tall warriors who stood rigid on the platform.

"She left them behind," he whispered. "Like she has nothing to fear."

Tyreta watched as the rest of the crowd followed the emissary inside. "Only thing she has to fear is Uncle Sullivar talking her ear off. Are you coming?"

Fulren dragged his eyes away from the exotic warriors. "I think I've had my fill," he replied.

"Nonsense, Tinhead. You need a drink."

"I don't think—"

"Then don't think, little brother. Just try and enjoy yourself for once. We should at least try and make the most of this pompous spectacle. And Uncle Sullivar will have opened up his very extensive wine cellar."

She took his arm with a grin and led him back into the rotunda.

There was a ring of activity around the emissary, and Fulren decided it best to take his position on the periphery once more as Tyreta fought her way through the crowd to find them a drink. He far preferred the anonymity the shadows granted to being subject to the indignity of a fawning crowd.

"Never were one for public events."

Fulren turned to see his mother standing behind him, taking her own place in the shadows. She wore a gown of blue and red, straight brown hair pinned with a Hawkspur brooch. They had spoken briefly the night before, but exchanged only a quick greeting before she went to rest after her journey from Wyke.

"I know you don't enjoy them either, Mother," he replied.

"No. But sometimes events like this are good for diplomacy. And some people live for them."

She glanced over at Sullivar, who was loudly regaling the emissary, and the surrounding crowd, with one of his tedious anecdotes.

"Uncle Sullivar is a force of nature."

They both laughed at that. It was short-lived, as Fulren saw two figures approaching them from the throng.

Lady Darina Egelrath was five feet of spite, and Fulren's aunt. She wore a long flamboyant dress that made it look as though she were gliding along the tiled floor. Her wrinkled neck was adorned with expensive jewels, earrings so heavy they made her lobes droop. There was little love between her and Rosomon, despite them being sisters by marriage. She approached with her son, Sanctan, now bedecked in the white robes of the Archlegate. Fulren's cousin was approaching his middle years but looked much younger. His handsome face and open smile would have suited him perfectly were he a diplomat or merchant. Instead he now held the highest seat in the Draconate Ministry and was one of the most powerful men in all Torwyn.

Lady Rosomon stiffened at their approach, gripping Fulren's elbow as though for support.

"Rosomon, how nice to see you again," said Darina, holding out her hand, a garish ring adorning each and every finger.

Rosomon took her sister-in-law's proffered hand and gave it a limp shake. "And you, Darina."

"Cousin," said Sanctan, smiling at Fulren. It had been some years since they'd seen each other, and he appeared to have lost none of his charm.

"Archlegate," Fulren replied, with a bow.

"None of that," Sanctan replied, taking Fulren by the shoulders and hugging him close. "The Ministry hasn't forbidden me from embracing my family."

Fulren felt the anxiety leak out of him. He had always liked Sanctan, and the two had played together as children, even though his cousin was some years the elder.

Lady Rosomon bowed. "Archlegate. I was sorry to have missed your ordination."

"It was a quiet affair, Aunt Rosomon. We are all still grieving after Archlegate Gylbard's loss. He was taken from us too soon."

"The youngest Archlegate in the Ministry's history," said Darina, missing no opportunity to laud her son. "We are very proud."

"I'm sure you must be," Rosomon replied.

"And what about you?" Darina said to Fulren. "I hear your uncle Sullivar has taken you under his wing."

"Fulren is progressing very well," Rosomon replied, before Fulren could speak for himself. "A full apprenticeship is guaranteed."

"Ah, that warms the heart. And what about Tyreta?"

That question lingered in the air. Tyreta's reluctance to adopt her responsibilities was no secret.

"Rest assured the future of the Hawkspur Guild is in good hands," said Rosomon.

"Yes, I hear Conall is a captain now. A credit to the family name. I'm sure with him in charge, our Guild's future prosperity is assured," Darina replied.

"*My* Guild's future prosperity."

The two women regarded one another with looks of feigned amusement. It was widely known that after the death of her younger brother, Darina had coveted control over the Hawkspur Guild, but her marriage into the Egelrath family had made that impossible. But it seemed those old desires lingered still.

Before Fulren could interject, Sanctan took Lady Darina by the arm.

"Mother, we must introduce ourselves to the new arrival." He gave both Fulren and Lady Rosomon a nod. "It's been good to see you again. Fulren, we must catch up later. You can show me those legendary sword skills I've been hearing so much about."

He led Lady Darina away toward the centre of the room, where the envoy was still surrounded.

"Sword skills?" Rosomon said when they were alone once more. "I hope you're not still harbouring those ambitions, Fulren. There's no future in it."

"I was just—"

"I thought we'd talked about this. The military is your brother's calling, not yours. You're no warrior, Fulren, this lingering obsession with the blade will do you no good. Your duty is to your uncle Sullivar and the Guilds."

Fulren felt all the old frustrations creep back again. It was the whole reason he'd left Wyke in the first place—the burdens piled upon him; the need to please his mother, to live up to his father's reputation. A father he'd never known.

"I know, Mother," he replied, suddenly feeling the need to escape. "Now if you'll excuse me, I'm not feeling all that well."

Before his mother could question him further, Fulren squeezed his way through the crowd. It was cloying in the great hall, and he had to get out for air, to get as far from Rosomon and her expectations as he could.

When he finally managed to escape the hall, he was struck by a sudden pang of guilt. Somewhere Tyreta would be on her way to him with a stiff drink. Not that it mattered. He was sure she'd have no trouble drinking enough for the both of them.

ROSOMON

She watched from a balcony above the aerie. Tyreta was checking the tack of one of the war eagles. They had a habit of snapping and hissing at riders they didn't trust, but Tyreta always had a way with the beasts. It was calm under her ministrations, allowing her to adjust the martingale with little fuss. She could be so capable when she wanted to be. Wilful? Yes. Rebellious? Most certainly, but Tyreta's strength of character was something Rosomon had always loved. It reminded her of how she'd acted as a younger woman. All she had to do was give her daughter a chance to shine and she would become the woman the Hawkspurs needed. A leader. A master of the Guild.

Conall approached along the walkway. He was smiling his usual easy smile, the one that reminded Rosomon so much of his father. Thankfully that was largely where the similarity ended. Over one of his shoulders was slung a rare and precious pyrestone weapon—a longbarrel of masterful design.

"Where did you find that?" she asked.

Conall took the weapon from his shoulder and held it reverently. It had clearly taken an artificer weeks to craft. "Isn't it beautiful? A parting gift from Uncle Sullivar."

The butt plate and muzzle were wrought with intricate metalwork, stock and barrel crafted from finely polished red oak. Pyrestones were set in the lock mechanism, which could propel steel shot over two hundred yards. The Armiger Battalions would have paid a Guildmaster's ransom for such a treasure.

"Sullivar was always far too generous with you," she said.

Conall acknowledged the fact with a nonchalant shrug as he slung the longbarrel back over his shoulder. "Aren't you due for the meet in the Guildhall, Mother?"

Rosomon nodded but still didn't move. This might be the last she saw of her son and daughter for some weeks. Let the Guilds wait.

"I will miss you both," she said. Conall had been seconded to Agavere on the northern coast of the Karna Frontier. It was a tradition that dated back over two centuries. When they were old enough, the eldest sons of the Guildmasters were given a commission on the farthest frontiers of Torwyn to serve with one of the Armiger Battalions. Sullivar's own son, Lorens, was even now at Ravenscrag with the Corvus.

Though Conall was a capable leader, he lacked experience. A posting at one of the forts would give him that in abundance. He was to accompany his sister to the port of Goodfleet, and there they would go their separate ways.

"We'll be fine," he replied. "And it will be good for Tyreta to see the islands. She's more than ready."

Rosomon shook her head. "Are any of us ready when we're called upon? She's not ready yet, but she will learn. Tyreta needs to see something of the world. I just hope this will also help open her eyes to the weight of her duties."

"She may well surprise you," Conall replied. "You took on the responsibility of an entire Guild not so many years ago, with little experience. And look what you've built."

"What choice did I have?" Rosomon replied, remembering all too well she'd had none. After Melrone's death she'd had to take over mastery of the Guild. What alternative had there been? Hand it over to Darina? No, that would never have stood.

"We all have our duties," said Conall.

"We do. And mine are calling me away. I'll return before you set off so I can say goodbye."

"We'll be waiting," said Conall with a reassuring wink.

The gesture warmed her, but Rosomon still felt the distance between them. Conall had once been her sweet boy, but he hadn't needed her for the longest time. As much as she wanted him to take on the responsibilities of a Talon captain, she couldn't help but wonder if the eagerness with which he'd pursued the distant posting in Agavere was because he wanted to escape from something. Perhaps even escape from her.

She left the sounds and smells of the aerie behind and tried to put thoughts of Conall and Tyreta far from her mind. This was an auspicious day, and she could not allow herself to be distracted.

Starn Rivers was waiting with a contingent of the Talon as she left Archwind Palace. The Guildhall was not far, but still it would not do for the head of the Hawkspur Guild to travel there unaccompanied.

They marched the short distance, taking the Bridge of Saints over Whitespin River, which flowed through the heart of the city. Rosomon could see trading boats chugging up and down the waterway, bringing ore, lumber and textiles from the four corners of Torwyn.

At the other side of the Whitespin, the Guildhall stood like a huge monolith, though it was still dwarfed by the majesty of the palace. It had been decades since her father, Treon Archwind, had decided to construct his palace to overshadow the symbolic home of the Guilds. This was supposedly a place where all the members of the Guilds were equal, but her father had decided that his own base of operations would be the most prominent edifice in the Anvil.

Rosomon approached, and the Titanguard at the entrance dutifully moved aside. The Guildhall's lobby was a colossal affair, vaulted ceiling rising a hundred feet above her, every wall painted with a mural showing the history of the Guilds and their rise to supremacy. Rosomon could only hope the emissary would not spend too much time examining them, with so many depicting the wars fought between Torwyn and the demon lords of Malador in centuries past. They were far from flattering to the Maladorans.

As she approached the central chamber she could hear voices and felt a sudden sting of embarrassment. It would do her reputation as head of the transportation Guild no good if she couldn't even manage to transport herself to a council meeting on time.

Once in the chamber, she felt relieved when there was no sign of the emissary. The heart of the Guildhall was circular, surrounded by tiered seating. Sullivar had taken his place on the great throne that sat at one end. Beside him was Sanctan Egelrath in a conspicuously smaller seat. In years past the place reserved for the Archlegate had been more distinguished than any other, but Rosomon's father had seen fit to erect his own throne in a position of prominence. It was still a point of contention.

In their appointed places about the room sat Wymar and Maugar Ironfall, Jarlath Radwinter, Emony Marrlock and Rearden Corwen. All eyes turned to Rosomon as she entered.

"Glad you could join us," sneered Rearden, staring down his beak of a nose at her.

"My apologies," Rosomon replied, in no mood for an argument with the old scribe.

"No matter, Aunt," said Sanctan. "The emissary has not yet arrived, as you can see."

Rosomon acknowledged her nephew's gallantry with a nod before taking her place beneath the Hawkspur sigil on the wall.

"Some of us were just wondering as to the purpose of this," said Wymar. "We have not yet had a chance to state our position."

"Our position," Sullivar interrupted, "is to listen to what the emissary has to say. This meeting has been a long time coming. The least we can do is accept this as a show of good faith."

"Good faith? What good faith is that?" Wymar asked, his brother Maugar nodding his agreement. "We are the ones who have been threatened these past centuries. We are the ones who have had to fight to defend our borders."

"All the more reason for us to entertain this emissary."

Before the Guildmaster of Ironfall could argue any further, two Titanguard entered the chamber. All went silent as more footsteps approached behind them.

Assenah Neskhon walked into the room, her long legs and confident stride reminding Rosomon of some exotic feline rather than a woman. She regarded the room with a look of insouciance but at the same time managed not to look arrogant. She knew she had been expected and now presented herself like some prize the Guildmasters had all won.

As she had the previous day, Assenah swept back her scarlet cloak and bowed low. When she did so, Rosomon noticed a smaller woman had entered behind the emissary. She had short black hair and a mousy appearance. Rosomon hardly noticed her in the shadow of such a striking figure as Assenah.

"Apologies for my tardiness," Assenah announced. "But it seems I don't quite have as much tolerance for your strong eastern wine as I'd expected."

She flashed her wide, white smile at the gathered congregation. It seemed to disarm them all, particularly Sullivar.

"No apologies needed," he said. "And please accept my own apologies for such a formal setting."

"I am your guest," she replied. "You may choose whatever setting you wish. It is indeed a magnificent one."

She gazed around at the solid granite walls and the murals that adorned them.

"Thank you," said Sullivar. "This place is—"

"If we may begin," said Sanctan impatiently. "Might I take the opportunity to speak for everyone when I say we appreciate your visit. Even if the reasons for it have not been made clear."

If Assenah was rattled by Sanctan's abrupt interruption, she didn't show it.

"Of course, Archlegate," she replied, smile never slipping. "And allow me to fill in the particulars. Queen Meresankh hopes to strike up a lasting peace between our two nations. An accord that would see the establishment of trade routes across the Drift. We hope this will lead to an exchange of not only goods but also knowledge. A diplomatic union that would be beneficial to both our countries."

"Pah," Wymar laughed. "And what of the constant threats to our borders? Pirates still harry our southern coastline, raiders still creep up from the Drift. And you talk of trade routes."

"Lord Wymar, Nyrakkis cannot be held responsible for the pirates in the south. The lawless coast of Iperion Magna is troublesome to both our nations. And I can assure you any bandits remaining in the Drift will be dealt with before trading routes are established."

Assenah's words seemed to calm Wymar's anger before it even began. Indeed, as the woman spoke Rosomon hung on her every word.

"We appreciate the efforts you have gone to already," said Sullivar. "But you mentioned an accord. What details would be contained within it? Does the queen of Nyrakkis envision some kind of treaty between our nations?"

"Why, of course," Assenah replied. "And Queen Meresankh has already taken the liberty of drafting such an agreement." She held out her hand, and the mousy assistant produced a sealed scroll from within her cloak. "Details of the proposal are held within. Of course you may view it at your leisure, and we would be happy to consider any amendments you wish to propose."

This seemed to satisfy Sullivar. "You see, Wymar," he said. "Peace and trade. What more could we ask for?"

He made to stand, but Sanctan placed a hand on his arm to stop him.

"I would just ask," he said, "what has brought about this sudden change of heart? For a thousand years we have heard nothing from Malador. No words have been exchanged. No entreaty for peace. What has happened to elicit this visit?"

The smile was gone now from Assenah's face, and she regarded Sanctan with grave sincerity. "For too long our nations have lived alongside one another with little contact. This has bred fear and suspicion between us, which has in turn led to the border skirmishes of which Lord Wymar speaks. We can no longer live in isolation. It is important for the future of both our realms that we extend the hand of friendship."

Sanctan nodded at her response. "Then I'm thinking famine? Or disease, one of the two. You need our resources, our technology, but all-out conquest would be too costly."

"What the Archlegate means to say," said Sullivar, rising to his feet as though it might nullify Sanctan's accusations, "is that we are sure there is much we can share."

"The Archlegate is right to question our motives," Assenah replied. "Had an envoy come from Torwyn to the borders of Nyrakkis, we too would have treated them with suspicion. And so, as a show of faith, we have brought a gift to demonstrate our goodwill."

Assenah's young vassal had already left the room. At the emissary's words, two of her warriors entered the Guildhall carrying a huge chest between them. The men looked like brutes, flesh painted and pierced as it was, but they also bore a strange nobility.

They placed the chest down and took a step back.

The Guildmasters sat in tense silence as Assenah opened the clasp to unlock the chest and pulled back the lid. Rosomon heard someone gasp as they saw what was inside. The chest was piled high with pyrestones, red, blue and yellow jewels winking in the torchlight of the Guildhall.

"As you can see," Assenah said, "we are serious about our commitment to this accord."

Sullivar stepped down from his throne, eyes locked on the chest.

"Indeed. And we appreciate the gesture."

"But do not let this sway your decision," Assenah continued. "Please consider what Queen Meresankh has written. I will wait for your answer." She handed the scroll to Sullivar.

With that she bowed again, then, with a sweep of her cloak, marched out of the Guildhall followed by her tattooed guardians.

"It would take a month to mine that much pyrestone," said Wymar, taking a step toward the chest.

"There's enough to run an entire city for a year," Rearden breathed.

"Indeed," said Sullivar. "It seems we have little choice but to accept the emissary's generous offer."

"Quick to make up your mind, aren't you, Sullivar?" said Sanctan. All eyes turned to him as he stood before the Guild throne. "Are you so easily swayed by riches? Don't let your greed overcome your reason. We must still study this treaty. Send emissaries of our own to Nyrakkis. Rushing headlong into this will only serve us ill."

"But look," said Sullivar, gesturing to the bounteous contents of the casket. "Look at what we could gain."

"Sullivar, you are blind to the danger."

"I am your emperor," said Sullivar, suddenly glaring at the priest. "And you forget yourself, Sanctan. You are here by invitation, not by right."

Rosomon could see Sanctan growing furious at the notion the Ministry no longer had a rightful seat within the Guildhall. Both men had gone too far.

"My nephew is right," she said. "We cannot be swayed by the offer of pyrestone, no matter how valuable it may be."

Sanctan gave her a nod of appreciation.

Sullivar still seemed spellbound by the contents of the casket. "But Rosomon. Look at this gift."

"Read the treaty," she replied. "See what terms they have proposed. I can always arrange for heralds of the Hawkspur Guild to travel to Nyrakkis and see if what they are offering is real."

"Not without the smiths of the Ironfall Guild to join them," said Wymar.

"Of course," Rosomon replied.

"Nor the actuaries of the Corwen Guild," put in Rearden.

"All the Guilds may send representatives," Rosomon replied, before anyone else could make further demands. "We will unite in this as we have in all things."

"Of course," said Sullivar. "You see. My sister speaks truth as always. Does that satisfy you, Sanctan?"

The Archlegate bowed in acquiescence. "Of course, my emperor." Sullivar didn't seem to notice the lack of sincerity in his tone. "As ever, Lady Rosomon offers wise counsel."

"Good. Then perhaps we should celebrate our good fortune?" He turned back to the casket of riches.

As the Guildmasters examined their bounty, Rosomon left them to it. There would be time enough later to thrash out the details, and for now she had other things to take care of.

Starn and the Talon accompanied her back to the palace, and she quickly made her way to the aerie. Conall and Tyreta were ready and waiting, their war eagles saddled and ruffling their feathers, impatient to be off.

Rosomon embraced her eldest son. Conall was strong and

capable—he always had been. Even though he was bound for the Karna Frontier, she knew he would be fine. When Rosomon stood before her daughter, the two of them regarded one another, neither sure of what to say. Doubt had suddenly crept into Rosomon's heart. Was this the wisest course of action? Was Tyreta ready?

But, of course, she had to give her daughter a chance to prove herself if Tyreta was ever to become the woman she needed to be.

"A Hawkspur functionary will meet you at Goodfleet," Rosomon said. "You have everything you need?"

Tyreta rolled her eyes. "Yes, Mother. And I know the ship will be waiting to take us to New Flaym. I have the full itinerary."

"The Marrlock Guild are expecting you. And cousin Wyllow will be there to greet you, I'm sure."

"Mother, don't worry. I'll be fine, I know what's expected of me."

Rosomon took Tyreta by the shoulders and pulled her close. "Just take care," she whispered.

At first Tyreta stood, frozen in her mother's embrace, but then she placed her arms around Rosomon and the two held each other. It had been a long time since Rosomon and her daughter had shared such affection. She had missed it.

When they parted, Rosomon was pleased to see Fulren had come to join them.

"Weren't going to leave without saying goodbye, were you, Ratface?" he said to Tyreta.

"I'd forgotten you were even here, Tinhead," she replied.

As they hugged, Rosomon thought for the thousandth time how much she hated the names they'd picked for one another, but on this occasion she chose not to comment.

"Take care of yourself," Fulren said.

No sooner had they finished than Conall picked his younger brother up and hugged him like a bear. The two were different in every way, but to see them show such fondness warmed Rosomon's heart more than she'd ever thought possible.

"See you on the other side, Tinhead," said Tyreta, approaching her mount, which dutifully bowed its head so she could climb atop the saddle. "Take care of Mother."

Rosomon smiled at that. Whether Tyreta was being sincere or not, it still meant the world to her.

She watched with Fulren as her daughter strapped herself to the eagle's saddle, checked the harness, and then nudged its flanks. The eagle spread its vast wings and bore her aloft, the displaced air blowing Rosomon's hair from her face. Conall's mount likewise spread its wings and followed, the two of them soaring off into the clear afternoon sky. Neither of them looked back.

"They'll be fine," Fulren said.

Rosomon realised her eyes had suddenly filled with tears.

"They will," Rosomon replied. "I'm sure they will."

FULREN

The axe missed his head by an inch, maybe less. The sound of it splintering the wooden beam behind made his ears ring. It was only now that Fulren thought he'd perhaps bitten off more than he could chew.

The axeman was a brute—six feet of muscle, brawny arms bulging out of his sleeveless jerkin, teeth gritted beneath a pristinely waxed moustache. He wrenched the axe free, pulling it back for another swing. Fulren leapt from the warehouse gantry, hitting the ground and rolling deftly on one shoulder before coming up on his feet. Instinctively he adopted a defensive stance, sword raised at shoulder level. It was a perfect move and very timely.

His second assailant was ready and waiting for him. She was dressed in the same style of jerkin as the brute, but she cut a much lither figure. Her rapier stabbed in with clinical precision, but Fulren blocked her attack and their swords rang, the sound filling the riverside warehouse like a dinner bell.

She jabbed in again, a probing strike that Fulren was at pains to parry, then a third time. Fulren swept his sword in a flat arc, four feet of Novik steel that knocked the rapier aside. He kept the momentum going, swinging the sword in an arc to cut in again, but she had already ducked and danced beyond the range of the blade.

There was a boom behind him as the brute dropped down from the gantry. Fulren backed away, keen to keep both his opponents in view. They paced across the warehouse, trying to gain flanking positions. Fulren knew he had to keep moving. He couldn't let them outmanoeuvre him.

He feinted left toward the woman, who backed away, then dashed at the brute, swinging his sword at head height. The axeman raised his weapon to parry, but instead of striking with his sword, Fulren barged into him with a shoulder. Off balance, the man went sprawling. Somehow Fulren managed to stay on his feet as the brute fell backward, and he turned quickly to parry the woman's rapier. Her attack was relentless, and he only just avoided a thrust that still sliced a smile in his shirt.

Fulren wasn't thinking now, the forms he had learned from long hours in the training yard came to him instinctually. They danced their deadly two-step until the woman was struggling to block his counters, and after one final strike at her head, Fulren kicked out. He caught her in the hip, his full weight behind the blow, and she let out a winded cry as she fell backward.

Fulren ducked.

The axe once again hacked wood beside his head. Fulren's blade came up in a clean, precise arc and would have severed the brute's arms had the man not abandoned his weapon and staggered back. His left foot caught on a loose pile of rope, his right slipping on the greasy floor, and he fell in a heap.

Fulren couldn't help but grin at the sight of the thickly muscled specimen lying there in the straw and dirt, his waxed moustache all askew. The levity didn't last long as he felt the cold edge of a rapier blade at his throat.

He froze, letting his sword arm slowly drop to his side.

"You're finished, son of Hawkspur," the woman whispered in his ear.

"Bollocks," Fulren said.

Eudon climbed to his feet, not bothering to dust himself off before he straightened his moustache. "Bollocks is the word," said the big man. "But you're getting better."

Elva removed the razor-sharp blade from against Fulren's neck. "Much better," she said. "But your concentration is still lacking."

The two of them moved toward the huge gates of the warehouse that opened out onto the Whitespin River. Eudon picked up a flask and took a long draught as Elva sat on a crate, taking an oiled rag and wiping the length of her rapier.

Fulren came to stand by them, looking out onto the river as a barge floated by on the current, its crew busying itself with the sail.

"How long before I'm good enough?" Fulren asked.

"You're good," Eudon said, wiping the sweat from his brow with a meaty arm. "One of the best we've taught."

"But how long before I'm swordwright good?"

The two fighters looked at one another. Then they laughed.

Fulren had been training with Eudon and Elva Kartia almost since the day he'd arrived in the Anvil. They were the best weapon masters he could find. The fact that they weren't cheap was a testament to their skills. The only thing about them Fulren couldn't work out was whether they were husband and wife or brother and sister. He'd never summoned the courage to ask.

"How many times must we tell you, Lord of Hawkspur? No one is swordwright good," Elva said. "Not unless they've trained in the Seminarium."

Eudon fixed him with an amused look. "If that's the only thing you've been after all this time, then you're wasting your money."

"I need to be good enough," Fulren replied, though as much to himself as to his teachers.

"And I need a villa on the Sungem Coast," said Elva. "But we can't all get what we want."

Fulren picked up his scabbard and sheathed his blade. He handed it back to Eudon, who took it carefully and wrapped it in a linen cloth. The man was as attentive with his weapons as with his facial hair.

"You'll have to accept the fact that we can only teach you method and form," said Eudon. "We can't teach you how to be a swordwright. They're a breed apart. And what would a highborn heir like yourself want with such skills anyway?"

Fulren wasn't about to go into the whys and wherefores. "I have my reasons."

Eudon shrugged. "Whatever they are, if all you're in this for is to become a swordwright, I'd consider a different hobby. You're one of the best students we've ever taught, but even we aren't that good. I once saw a tourney in Castleteig. Lancelin Jagdor was—"

"All right, I believe you," Fulren interrupted, in no mood to hear another tale about that man. He fished for the bag of silver at his side and tossed it to Elva. "Same time next week?"

"We'll be here," she said, putting the coin purse away without bothering to count the contents.

Fulren made his way from the warehouse back through the river district that lined the Whitespin. Most of the warehouses were huge affairs, storing grain, wood and textiles ready for transportation to some corner of Torwyn. Much of the time this place was deserted, and consequently it served his purposes perfectly. It wouldn't do for the son of Rosomon Hawkspur to be caught sparring with two lowly street brawlers. More importantly, Fulren could learn his craft, or at least one of them, in anonymity. He looked forward to the prospect of taking on Lancelin in single combat. Seeing the look of surprise on his face when the bastard realised he had met his match. Not that it sounded a likely outcome—from what Eudon said, Fulren wasn't now, nor would he ever be, ready to take on a swordwright.

Well, he'd see about that. Fulren wasn't just becoming a decent sword; he was also learning his trade in the Archwind workshops. He might have more than one surprise up his sleeve for Jagdor, no matter what his brother said. Conall might want the honour of slaying Jagdor himself, but Fulren wasn't about to just stand aside. Avenging their father was his right as much as it was his brother's.

A twisting stairway brought Fulren out onto the river market—a wide, flat expanse covered in podiums and wooden stalls. It was empty now, but once every tenday it transformed into a bustling hub for trade from all over the nation. Fulren had made sure to attend every time the market was on. As well as the usual livestock and fabrics, there was every chance he would spy a piece of ancient artifice or some foreign trinket. He had amassed several pieces that were hidden in his workshop, though he'd not managed to get any of them working. Time would tell whether he'd reach the level of skill required to make them sing.

The closer to the centre of the city he walked the busier the crowds got. The Anvil buzzed with life, with conversation. These people were a far cry from the provincial citizenry of Wyke, and that was the reason Fulren preferred it here. Wyke was quaint enough, but Fulren had always wanted to be in the centre of Torwyn, in the house of his uncle. It was the beating heart of the nation and a centre of innovation. He wouldn't have been anywhere else.

Walking the Bridge of Saints toward Archwind Palace, Fulren spied a man he recognised up ahead. He looked agitated, craning his neck to see if he could spot someone or something among the throng. When Fulren drew closer, the man locked eyes with him, raising a hand and waving. As he made his way through the crowd, Fulren realised he was the equerry who had so clumsily announced the emissary's arrival at the recent welcome banquet.

He approached Fulren, quite breathless. "My lord, your presence is required."

Fulren waited for him to fill in the details, but the equerry seemed more intent on regaining his breath. "By whom?" Fulren asked finally.

"Oh, Emperor Sullivar, my lord. It is a matter of the utmost urgency."

Fulren's mind began to roil with possibilities, but he guessed asking the equerry the reason for his uncle's summons would be pointless.

He pushed his way along the bridge, past the crowd to the gates of the palace. The Titanguard moved aside, pistons hissing as the intricately engineered hydraulics in their armour responded to their movements.

Fulren ignored the elevator, taking the opportunity to vault the stairs three at a time until he reached the throne room of the Archwinds. The equerry came huffing after him, desperate to do his job but struggling to keep up.

At the end of the vast chamber, illuminated by an ornate pyrestone chandelier, Fulren could see his uncle in conversation with the emissary. Assenah Neskhon was as striking as he remembered, her easy manner clearly charming Sullivar like a bird from its perch. Behind her stood two of her towering bodyguards. Even without their wicked-looking spears they were a formidable sight.

Fulren walked slowly toward them, wondering what this could be about. When Sullivar saw him, a grin spread across his face.

"Ah, here he is. The man himself."

Assenah turned to greet Fulren as he made his way toward the throne. Her smile was beguiling, and Fulren couldn't take his eyes off her as he approached.

"Uncle? You summoned me?"

"I did," Sullivar replied. "I don't think you've been formally introduced to our guest."

Assenah bowed. "A pleasure to meet you, my lord."

"The pleasure is mine," Fulren replied, not sure what else to say. Officious pleasantries most definitely weren't his thing.

"Assenah has requested a tour of the city," said Sullivar. "She requires someone to show her the sights."

Fulren took a moment to process what was being asked of him. "And you chose me? But I am not a native of the Anvil, Uncle. Surely there is—"

"I requested you personally," Assenah said. "You are a descendent of both the Hawkspur and Archwind Guilds, no? Who better to teach me of Torwyn's great history than someone born into the Guilds that helped build it?"

Fulren still wasn't sure he was the right man for the job, but this was too good an opportunity to refuse. "Of course. It would be my honour."

"That settles it, then," said Sullivar. "My guard will accompany you."

"Oh, that won't be necessary," said Assenah. "My own bodyguards will be more than sufficient. I would like to view the Anvil just like any ordinary visitor."

"But your safety is paramount," Sullivar said. "I could not let you wander the city without—"

"I'm sure I will be quite well protected." She laid a hand on Fulren's shoulder. "Now, if you'd like to lead the way, my lord."

Sullivar made no further word of protest and, still a little nonplussed, Fulren led the woman and her two escorts from the throne room. All the while he wondered how she would ever pass herself off as an "ordinary visitor."

"I appreciate you lending your time to this, Lord Fulren," she said as they came out into the palace courtyard. "I imagine you are kept busy on official business."

"Not at all, my lady," he replied, though in truth he was due in the workshop. "And please, call me Fulren."

"Then you must of course call me Assenah," she replied.

She swept her red hair from her shoulder, and Fulren caught a scent on the air that made him feel light-headed. When he glanced at her, he couldn't remember having seen a more beautiful woman.

They walked together through the palace gates and out onto the Bridge of Saints. As they made their way along it, past the statues of Guild heroes, Assenah seemed captivated by the crowd, who were equally fascinated by her and her tattooed bodyguards. They gawked as she walked by, as though Fulren were accompanying some bizarre animal rather than a foreign emissary.

"These people seem a curious bunch," she said.

"We don't receive many foreigners," Fulren replied. "Certainly none from Nyrakkis."

"Something I hope we can rectify. Our countries have been enemies for too long."

That was true enough. Fulren had heard much about border raids from the Drift. To the west the Armiger Battalions occupied huge forts to see off any threat of invasion. Fulren realised how little he knew of this woman's land and customs, and her friendly manner seemed at odds with all he did know.

"I've heard a little about your Maladoran religion," he said. "That your gods demand frequent offerings."

That was a polite way of putting it. In truth, Fulren had been taught the Maladorans offered human sacrifices by the thousands.

"You mean our demon worship?" Assenah replied.

Fulren hadn't wanted to suggest that. "Well...I guess that's what we'd call it. Perhaps you have a different word?"

"Our gods are fierce. Unforgiving, certainly, but we wouldn't call them demons. But then in Torwyn you still pay reverence to dragons, so I think we have as many similarities as differences in our theologies. Although I have heard there is little credence paid to the Great Wyrms in these modern times."

"Oh, but there is," Fulren replied. "Let me show you."

He led her and her men west away from the bridge. As they walked, he noted that heads were turning, small crowds chattering as word of the emissary spread. Fulren was relieved that Assenah was greeted with curious interest rather than any outright aggression.

They eventually came to a wide-open plaza. Sitting in its midst was a huge construction of white marble, a tower sprouting from each corner of the hexagonal building. Each bore the head of a dragon, one of the five Great Wyrms.

Pilgrims and worshippers were filing in and out of the vast marble arch that led inside, along with various priests of the Draconate.

"We call it the Mount," he said. Fulren had never considered himself pious, but even he felt a swell of pride at the sight of the huge edifice. "The seat of the Draconate Ministry in the Anvil. Rivalled only by Wyrmhead in the north."

"It is an impressive building." Assenah didn't sound particularly impressed. "But isn't it still true that the Ministry's power is dwindling?"

She seemed to know a lot considering there had been little contact between their nations for a thousand years.

"It's true, the Ministry isn't revered in the same way it used to be, but times have changed. The Guilds protect Torwyn now."

"Yes. The great machine that has consumed your Great Wyrms."

"This is a new age," said Fulren, keen to defend his heritage. "It's a time of reason over blind faith."

Assenah regarded the many worshippers ambling in and out of the Mount. "And yet the people still need something to believe in."

Fulren had never given it much thought before. Though the

Guilds had brought much prosperity to Torwyn, many of its people still clung to the teachings of the Draconate.

"That may be true. The people of Torwyn have not yet abandoned their ancient gods. The Great Wyrms are still held in high regard, but it's not the Draconate Ministry that keeps the land fruitful."

"Then what does?" she asked.

Fulren thought he was perhaps revealing a little too much, but he immediately dismissed the suspicion. There was nothing he could tell her that any citizen of Torwyn didn't already know.

"Come. I have something else to show you," he said.

He led Assenah and the bodyguards on, past the throng of pilgrims and deeper into the city's industrial quarter. Dozens of manufactories teemed with activity. Here the ringing of hammer on steel resounded, the smell of forge fires thick in the air. Master artificers barked their orders above the noise of industry, and Fulren felt a swell of pride at the sight.

"This is the beating heart of Torwyn," he said, gesturing to a vast construction yard where a stormhulk was being built. Panels were being riveted to the colossal chassis and joints welded shut by hissing blowlamps. "This is what people believe in now. This can be seen and smelled and touched."

Assenah nodded, an amused expression on her face. "*Smelled* is the word," she replied.

"But don't you see? This is our future. The old gods are not revered as they were. We are done with that past. Inventions like this will ensure that famine and hunger are eradicated from Torwyn. They offer so much potential."

"I see that," she said. "And you are a credit to your nation, Fulren. It is people like you who will take Torwyn forward into a new age."

"Is that why you asked for me? Why you wanted me to show you the city?"

Assenah smiled her wide, beguiling smile. "Your intuition serves you well, son of Hawkspur. So where next? For all the wonder this place holds, it is something of an attack on the senses."

"Of course," Fulren said. "My apologies. Perhaps now I could show you the city gardens. There are more species of flora there than anywhere else in all Hyreme."

Assenah raised an eyebrow. "A bold claim. How could I possibly refuse?"

She took his arm, and Fulren led the emissary on, keen to show her as much as he could.

TYRETA

The war eagles had carried her and Conall from the Anvil to Goodfleet in less than two days, and she had revelled in every second as if it were a dream. The sea crossing to New Flaym was more of a nightmare.

Tyreta had tried to persuade Conall to let her take the eagle over the Redwind Straits. It would have been much quicker than a ship, but he was having none of it.

"Mother wants you to appreciate every aspect of the Guild's network," he had said. "Ships are integral to its web of trade routes. The experience will do you good."

She had argued, and he had resisted. She had lost. But there had never been any arguing with Conall. They had said their farewells at Goodfleet and she had embarked that very day.

As the ship cruised across the straits, Tyreta had been forced to suffer all the indignities that went along with the trip. The sailors were coarse, their language straight out of the gutter. Not that Tyreta was opposed to the odd profanity, but these gruff mariners used it as punctuation. The rations were so degraded she began to wonder where the weevils ended and the food began, and the choppiness of the sea made her want to vomit every morsel she'd managed to keep down. Mercifully, the crossing was a short one.

After three days at sea, Tyreta saw the Sundered Isles appear on the horizon. She stood at the prow, looking out across the calm waters, tasting the salt on her lips. Despite this whole sojourn being made under duress, she had to admit she was excited at the prospect of exploring a new land.

By the time she had collected her meagre belongings and made her way back onto the deck, the ship was docking in the harbour. She could see the bustle in the port. New Flaym spread out from the coast, cutting through the surrounding jungle. Buildings were packed tight to one another, as though the land had fought back against the urban encroachment, squeezing the city in a leafy fist.

Once the ship sidled into port and the sailors began securing the moorings, Tyreta wasted no time in making her way down the gangplank and across the jetty. She had not yet reached the harbourside when a sudden warm feeling started to grow in her chest. She raised a hand to the nightstone pendant beneath her shirt, feeling its warmth intensify till it was almost burning her flesh. The heat grew unbearable, but before she was compelled to tear open her shirt and fling the jewel away, it ceased as suddenly as it had begun.

Before she could think any more on the strange sensation given off by the nightstone, she was greeted by a shrill voice from the dockside.

"Tyreta!"

Isleen Marrlock cut an insignificant figure, despite the gaudy gown she wore. Her hair was piled up on top of her head as though she'd been invited to an official dinner but had run out of time getting ready. Although she was a member of the Guild responsible for mining across the whole of Torwyn and its foreign colonies, she barely looked the part.

"How nice of you to meet me in person," said Tyreta, affecting a smile and trying to sound as much like her mother as she could. "Really, there was no need."

"Nonsense," Isleen replied, walking forward to embrace Tyreta in a hug of false affection. "It was the very least we could do, considering how far you've travelled."

She wasn't wrong—it was the *very* least the Marrlock Guild could have done. Isleen was a minor member of the family, a distant cousin to Guildmaster Oleksig Marrlock. They might as well have sent one of their housemaids.

"I'm looking forward to—"

"Yes, yes," Isleen interrupted. "Let's get you to your villa. You must be tired from your journey."

The last thing Tyreta felt was tired, but she allowed Isleen to lead the way from the port.

New Flaym was a bustling hub of industry. All the pyrestone mined in the Sundered Isles came through the port for transportation back to Torwyn. Tyreta passed crates containing ore from the mines at the edge of the colony. She could feel the power, like a distant call, her webwainer instincts kicking in. Pyrestone was in such abundance here that Tyreta began to feel dizzy.

They left the busy harbour behind them, passing the ramshackle buildings closest to the sea, which grew more and more opulent the farther they walked. Eventually they came to an estate of whitewashed villas, blue and yellow birds perched atop their eaves, singing a sweet tune. The place was humid, so much so that the relatively short walk had left Tyreta with a sheen of sweat across her body.

"You'll be staying here," Isleen said as they reached a two-storey building at the edge of the walled complex. "Everything is prepared. We'll be dining this evening at sundown. It's the villa right next to this one, so try not to be late."

"Thank you, Isleen," Tyreta said, but the woman was already on her way back toward the port.

She entered, and inside the villa there was some relief from the oppressive heat, as mechanical fans spun on the ceiling to cool the air. On the top floor were two rooms, and Tyreta chose the one with the best view. Through the window she could see the entirety of New Flaym as it rolled down to the sea, flanked on either side by thick jungle.

After dropping her bags in the corner of the room, she sat on the bed.

"Well, here you are," she said to herself. "Now what?"

The room didn't give her any answer.

Tyreta fished in the top of her shirt, pulling out the nightstone pendant. It was cold to the touch now, no sign of the burning heat it had emitted when she debarked from the ship. She stared at the dark facets, wondering if it had been some strange kind of reaction to this new place. Normally when she held a pyrestone she could feel it throbbing with life, but this one was dead. She might as well have been holding a pebble from the beach.

There was a noise behind her as someone made their way up the stairs. Tyreta stood, expecting Isleen to appear and give her yet more instructions about decorum or dinner etiquette, but she was pleasantly surprised when it was a young man she recognised.

Her cousin Wyllow Archwind was a bundle of mischief. It was part of the reason Tyreta liked him so much. Despite being Emperor Sullivar's second son, he looked anything but regal. His hair was a ruffled ginger mess, and he managed to look scruffy despite his expensive attire.

"How is it, Ty?" he asked, smile beaming.

"It's good, Wyl," she replied. "How long you been here?"

He entered the room, glancing around at the bare walls. "Oh, a few weeks. You know the old man, wants me to get a feel for every aspect of Guild business."

"That's exactly why I'm here." She felt some relief in knowing that finally there was someone in the same boat.

"Then later I must introduce you to the local colour."

"I have no idea what that means," she replied. "But I'm in. Although I do have a dinner to attend."

"Ah, one of Lady Isleen's dinners," Wyllow said, rolling his eyes. "We're sure to have a scintillating evening."

"You're coming?" asked Tyreta.

"Wouldn't miss it." He mimed sticking his fingers down his throat. "I have some business to attend to, but I'll see you there."

"Don't be late," she pleaded.

"Would I leave you to suffer alone?" he asked before skipping out of the room.

The prospect of his attendance made the idea of dinner with Isleen much less daunting. He was also a webwainer, a gift that rarely manifested in boys, and their shared talent had bonded them as children. He'd been more of a brother to her than Conall or Fulren ever had.

Tyreta set about preparing for dinner. There was water to wash with and several dresses in one of the wardrobes. She took some time looking through them—after all, her mother would have wanted her to be presentable. In the end she donned her travelling clothes instead. She was determined to make her mother proud, but one thing at a time.

Just as the sun started to fall she made her way to the adjoining villa. The garden was afire with yellow pyrestone lights, and crickets chirruped enthusiastically in the shrubbery. Inside, a quartet of minstrels were playing a lilting tune on various stringed instruments. Their skill was spellbinding, and Tyreta was pleasantly surprised at the welcome, but it didn't last long.

"Ah, Tyreta." Lady Isleen stood at the entrance, wineglass in hand. "Please, come and meet the other guests."

Isleen led Tyreta into the dining room. It was dominated by a huge pinewood table, places set neatly, intricate ironwork candlestick placed as a centrepiece. All but two of the chairs were occupied.

"Let me introduce you," Isleen said as Tyreta took her place. "Wyllow Archwind I think you know."

"Of course," Wyllow said, offering his hand. "It's been too long."

Tyreta had to bite back a laugh at his feigned charm.

Isleen introduced the three others. Lavren Larkin was a pyrestone trader from the mainland. His wife Edana looked stunning in a blue-and-red gown, though she didn't have much to say. Then there was Eremand, the chancellor of New Flaym, whose pale, pockmarked skin gave him the look of a plucked chicken.

The meal was served in several courses, and Tyreta was full after the third. Conversation flowed between the other guests, but talk of trade and ledgers and trouble with labourers didn't really interest Tyreta, to the point where she gained more amusement from Wyllow pulling faces at her across the table. Eventually Wyllow had eaten his fill and suddenly lurched to his feet, cutting Isleen off midflow.

"That's enough for me." He held out a hand to Tyreta. "Shall we?"

"You're leaving?" asked Isleen.

Tyreta stood, glad of the excuse to escape. "Wyl promised to show me the sights. I think now's as good a time as any."

Before Isleen could complain, Wyllow and Tyreta made a break for the door.

"It's been a pleasure," Tyreta cast back before they reached the porch.

Isleen moved after them. "Lady Rosomon has charged me with looking out for your welfare. I don't think—"

"I'll be back later," she said. "Don't wait up."

"This is not..."

Tyreta and Wyllow didn't wait to hear what she had to say. They were still giggling as they left the villa and rushed across the gardens to freedom, not slowing till they were halfway to the harbour.

"You're going to land me in so much trouble," said Tyreta.

"Ha!" Wyllow replied. "That makes a change."

"What's that supposed to mean?"

Wyllow stopped and fixed her with a bewildered look. "You were always landing me in the shit."

Tyreta thought back to her childhood visits to the capital. Wyllow had always been the mischievous one and she his unwitting foil.

"Who was it who made me steal Aunt Oriel's bath lather so you could put engine oil in it?" she asked.

Wyllow shook his head. "What do you mean? That was your idea."

"No it—" Tyreta thought back, beginning to doubt her own memory of events.

"Whatever. That wasn't the only time." Wyllow skipped on down the road toward the harbour lights and the rising sound of mariners. "Clearly you need your memory jogged."

"Where are we going?" Tyreta asked as she followed him.

"I promised you some local colour, didn't I?"

He broke into a run, and Tyreta sped after him. The two of them rushed down the street as the sound of chirruping crickets was replaced by the lap of waves against the dock. They came to a row of buildings that looked out to sea, and Tyreta could see men and women sitting out on verandas. Sailors were drinking, the songs they sang competing with one another on the night air and mixing in a cacophony of drunken voices. Women laughed, high and shrill—so loud Tyreta wondered what could possibly be so funny.

As Wyllow led them toward the entrance to one of the bawdy houses, she stopped.

"We're going in there?" she asked, her mother's words about responsibility coming back to haunt her like a troublesome spectre.

"What's the matter?" Wyllow replied. "Scared you might enjoy it?"

He didn't wait for her answer, turning and walking through the door to the drinking house.

Tyreta stood out on the dock. Wyllow had always known just how to play her. Of course she wasn't scared, they both knew that. But now she had to prove it.

"Wyllow Archwind, you're such a shit," she said, and she followed him inside.

She could have sliced the air with a knife, it was so thick with the fug of pipe smoke and the sound of profanity. The room was packed to the rafters with the roughest bunch of louts she had ever seen, some of whom she recognised from the ship that had brought her here. Wyllow was already at the bar, the man behind it pouring his drinks.

"Knew you couldn't resist," he said as she came to join him.

Tyreta took the proffered glass. "See, you are the one who always got us into trouble."

"Let's agree to disagree on that," he said, raising his drink. "To adventure."

Tyreta glanced around the room at the dangerous-looking crowd. "To not getting stabbed," she replied, raising her own glass before downing its milky contents.

Whatever it was burned its way down her throat, and they both screwed up their faces. After three more rounds of the stuff it started to taste almost pleasant, and the rough crowd in the drinking hole began to look a lot friendlier.

Tyreta felt all the pressure of her obligations slough off her shoulders as they drank, and she laughed loudly as Wyllow began to remind her of all the things they'd gotten up to in their younger days. She almost felt comfortable in this place, and it wasn't until she glanced toward the door that she felt the cold clutch of reality.

Lady Isleen stood in the doorway, surveying the room, and it was an easy guess as to who she was looking for.

"We need to go," she told Wyllow.

He looked over, seeing Isleen, who was ignoring the awkward stares she was getting from the other revellers. Her intricately styled hair and extravagant dress made her stand out like a pansy in a dung heap.

"Why don't you just tell her to get lost?"

"It's not as easy as that," Tyreta replied. "She's my mother's eyes and ears. If she finds out I'm in here, there'll be repercussions."

"Not to worry," Wyllow replied.

He closed his eyes, and she could feel a sudden thrum of energy as he summoned his webwainer's gift. The pyrestone lamp suspended from the centre of the ceiling suddenly shone brighter, bathing the room in yellow light, before it exploded into shards. The room was cast into sudden darkness.

Wyllow took her hand. "I know a back way out," he said over the sudden panicked din.

Tyreta shuffled after him through the shadows as he led her to the rear of the drinking house and out into the warm night. The alcohol hit her as soon as they were in the fresh air, and she almost fell as they ran from the sound of the inn. She had no idea where they were or where they were going, and she was giddy with excitement and drunkenness. Eventually they came to a stop outside an old storehouse. It looked abandoned, but something inside had piqued Wyllow's interest.

"What is it?" she asked.

With a sly grin on his face, Wyllow gestured through the open doorway. The moon shed its light on two giant stormhulks, rusted and forgotten in the shadows.

"Looky looky what I found," he said, excited as a child on festival day.

"These things are ancient," she replied, moving forward and laying her hand on a worn metal carapace. Both engines stood over ten feet tall, lost and forgotten like a pair of antique statues.

"I know. Beautiful, aren't they?"

Tyreta could see the conversion chambers lying open and empty where the pyrestones had previously sat and powered these behemoths. An idea formed in her head.

"We could get them working," she said. "Go on a jaunt."

"Nah, these things haven't walked for years."

She fixed him with a determined stare. "Don't be so defeatist. Bit of work and we could have them up and running in no time."

"Not a chance," he said.

"What's the matter? Scared you might enjoy it?" she shot back.

Before he could answer, she heard someone shout her name.

Isleen was close.

Without another word they snuck out of the warehouse and ran all the way back to her villa. Wyllow left her there after shooting that cheeky wink of his, and she made her way inside, jumping into bed and hoping Isleen wouldn't give her too much of a grilling when she returned.

Before she could even try to formulate an excuse for her behaviour, Tyreta was asleep.

FULREN

The workshop was Fulren's sanctuary, and he cherished being alone among his tools and his artifice. His days were spent productively—solder and weld, temper and forge—and the sum of his work was spread across the bench. He had studied hard for the past year to attain his current level of expertise, and his tutors had described his work as prodigious. Fulren was confident it was only a matter of time before he would graduate to being a fully fledged artificer, perhaps only a couple more years until he attained the rank of journeyman and then master. He had never understood what other apprentices found so difficult about the craft; the principles were simple enough.

By placing a number of pyrestones inside small conversion chambers, a webwainer could use them to imbue any piece of artifice with life. The real skill was creating artifice that could be used without the webwainer's gift.

It was a straightforward concept: create a circuit of steel to conduct the pyrestone's power and a switch that would activate it. By combining different-coloured pyrestones, an artificer could produce varying types of energy—blue for electricity, yellow for heat, red for storage and regulation. So far Fulren had been able to craft simple devices, but his area of study was beginning to expand. Soon he would create artifice that didn't require the red regulator stone—an engine that could work independently, controlled purely by machinery rather than the sorcery of a webwainer.

He had a selection of the different-coloured stones with which he could experiment, tiny samples that contained little power but would allow him to practise and hone his craft. A conversion chamber lay open on his workbench, and he placed a bright-yellow pyrestone into the housing. With a click, eight conductor arms snapped shut, holding the pyrestone in place, ready to transform its core into raw energy.

Fulren lit the wick of a burner connected to the artifice by thin copper wires and waited as the flame's heat was conducted to the chamber. The pyrestone began to pulsate with life, its power radiating along yet more copper wires.

At the opposite end of the bench was a blue pyrestone, already connected to identical apparatus. Fulren pulled a switch, connecting the channelled energies from both pyrestones to a central bell jar. Immediately sparks began to fly, tines of light dancing and coruscating within the glass. A smile crossed his face... until the glass shattered.

Lightning danced across the room, singeing papers, turning the air bright with voltaic energy. Fulren dived for the switch, flipping it to break the circuit. Immediately all went dark.

He stood to view his broken apparatus, unperturbed at his failure. After all, it was a natural step in his progression.

Before he could begin to set up his experiment anew, a slow hand clap resounded behind him, and Fulren turned to see someone silhouetted in the doorway of his workshop.

As the pyrestone bulb that lit his workshop winked back to life, he saw Olstrum Garner was watching him with amusement. He stopped clapping and moved closer, his eyes flitting here and there as though he'd never seen such marvels before.

"You get better every day, my lord," said the consul.

He was Sullivar's closest adviser and a man of great power within the Anvil. What he was doing down in the workshop was anyone's guess.

"Thank you, Consul. Although that could have gone slightly better." He gestured to the mess. "To what do I owe the pleasure of your visit?"

Olstrum straightened the red doublet he wore tight to his lean frame. "I understand you have grown close to our visitor from Nyrakkis over these past days?" he said, getting straight to the point.

Fulren nodded. "The emperor requested I show her the city, yes," he replied.

"That is... diligent of you," he replied, running a hand through his greying goatee. "And how have you found that duty?"

"Most enlightening," said Fulren. "In fact I am due to meet her today." He glanced at the timepiece that ticked away on a nearby shelf, realising he was already late.

"Good, good..." Olstrum said, absently picking up a piece of unfinished artifice and examining it.

"Was there something else, Consul?" Fulren asked.

Olstrum put the machinery down and fixed Fulren with a serious look. "The emperor is keen for relations between Torwyn and Nyrakkis to improve. And improve quickly. He has been advised that such a rash attitude might prove detrimental to the Guilds, and to the country at large. We have warned him that bestowing too much... trust on our visitors may not be as beneficial as he thinks."

"You mean we should keep the emissary at arm's length?" Fulren suggested, though in truth he knew exactly what Olstrum was saying: that the Maladorans were still enemies of Torwyn and he thought Assenah Neskhon was a spy sent on some reconnaissance mission. It was an obvious assumption, but one Fulren found hard to accept.

"I mean be careful what you say to her. Where you take her. What you reveal to her."

"I understand, Consul. But the emissary has only shown interest in our culture and traditions. I have taken her to facilities and exhibits open to any ordinary visitor. And of course I have carried out my duties with the utmost discretion."

That seemed to please Olstrum. "Of course you have. I am led to believe you are a very shrewd young man. A credit to your Guild.

And clearly your talents are myriad." He gestured around at the disorganised workshop.

"Good of you to say, Consul," Fulren replied. "If that's all, I have an appointment with the emissary now."

"Perhaps just one more thing," said Olstrum. "As much as you're doing an excellent job in introducing the emissary to our way of life, it might also be pertinent to make that a reciprocal arrangement."

"Consul?" Fulren wasn't entirely sure what Olstrum was suggesting.

He fixed Fulren with a serious look. "It would be expedient of you to share any information you can about this emissary. We know little about her and her country. See if you can't get her to open up about Nyrakkis and what its intentions are. Since you've built up such a bond of trust over the past few days."

"You want me to interrogate her for you?"

"I wouldn't use such a crude term," Olstrum replied. "Consider it an exchange of information."

"You want me to spy for you." Fulren didn't like the proposition one bit.

"Call it what you will, Lord Fulren. But remember, all we have seen from the Maladorans is aggression for a thousand years. We have no reason to believe their current position is an altruistic one. They want something from us. You may be our best way of learning what that is, before it's too late."

"I have to go, Consul," Fulren replied.

"Of course," said Olstrum. "Please don't let me keep you."

Fulren left Olstrum behind in his workshop. On his way from the palace all he could wonder was what the consul meant by "before it's too late." Was he expecting some kind of invasion? Did he suspect Assenah Neskhon of being a scout sent to gather information to make that possible?

The prospect seemed implausible. Assenah had been charming, allowing Fulren to show her the Anvil with nothing but grace. He had revealed no great secrets regarding the country or the Guilds. Fact was, he didn't know any. He was a lowly apprentice artificer with little access to the inner workings of the Guilds.

Nevertheless, when he finally met up with Assenah at their

meeting place, he couldn't shirk the seed of doubt Olstrum had planted.

Assenah was waiting beneath the statue of Saphenodon in the city's western plaza, and this time she was alone and unaccompanied by her towering escorts. The green jade dragon reared up above the crowds, watching over them with its jewelled eyes.

"An impressive monument," Assenah said when Fulren reached her.

"Yes. One of the Great Wyrms," Fulren replied, trying his best to clear his head of the conversation he'd had with the consul. "She's said to have imparted her wisdom to all humanity. Bringing us out of the forests with the knowledge to build and farm. She is revered by the scribes most of all." He rattled off the words without really thinking about them.

"Fascinating," Assenah said. "Where can I learn more?"

Immediately Fulren was on his guard, the words of Olstrum coming back to him in a wave. "Learn more?" he replied. "For what purpose?"

Fulren hated himself as soon as he'd said it. The consul had turned him from a willing guide into a suspicious cynic.

"You know why, Fulren." She smiled that disarming smile at him. "I am here to learn as much as I can."

"Of course," Fulren replied. "Then I must take you to the Great Library."

Assenah seemed to find that amusing. "An excellent decision."

"What's so funny?" Fulren asked as he began to lead her from the plaza.

"Nothing," Assenah said, and then she turned to him. "Only you seem to have many great things in your country. Great Wyrms, a Great Library. Is anything merely mundane?"

Fulren had never really thought on it before, but when she said it, he had to admit it did sound pretentious.

"Yes, the library was called the Annalium some years ago, but my grandfather Treon decided *the Great Library* had a better ring to it."

"He changed it just like that?" Assenah clicked her fingers.

"Pretty much," Fulren replied. "No one seems to have complained."

"Your grandfather was a powerful man. And as part of his family, so are you. It seems odd to me that you should walk about the city unguarded."

Fulren looked around at the few people on the street. "It's quite safe here."

"Even for me?"

Though some of the city folk they passed looked on curiously, they had grown used to the sight of a foreigner in their midst over the past few days.

"Especially for you," Fulren replied.

They continued on into the scribes' district. Here the embassy of the Corwen Guild stood, the plaster cracked and crumbling on its facade. Old Rearden Corwen was so tightfisted he had not seen fit to pay for the much-needed renovations.

"You never mention your family," Assenah said. "Other than your uncle, Sullivar. He is your mother's brother, yes?"

"He is," Fulren replied. "Though there's not much of a family resemblance."

"Quite. Your mother is very beautiful. Your father must have been equally fetching."

The thought of his father stung Fulren. A host of suppressed emotions suddenly rushed to the fore.

"I wouldn't know. He died before I was born."

"Ah yes," said Assenah. "A duel of honour, I am told."

"So they say," Fulren replied, not wanting to get into the details. Not wanting to mention his father was all but murdered by Lancelin Jagdor.

"It must have been difficult for you, growing up without him."

It had been difficult. He had been raised with a seed of resentment that had only grown in the years since. "I don't really think about him," he replied.

"I am sure he would have been proud of you," Assenah said. "You have grown into a very capable man."

"We're here," Fulren said, gesturing to the Great Library ahead. In truth he was relieved to change the subject.

Assenah seemed suitably impressed by the huge building. It was a testament to the masons of the Anvil, a circular edifice of granite hewn to look like a single piece of rock. A mountain rising up in the centre of the city.

"A thing of beauty," she said, staring up at the colossal monument.

"Not just that," Fulren replied. "The Great Library is the sole repository of all Torwyn's knowledge. Scribes work tirelessly to log and file every element of history and ensure it is kept safe for all to see and study."

He led her to the main doors, crowned by the symbols of the six Guilds—cog, winged talon and scroll. Hammers, oak tree and forge fire. The custodian at the entrance bowed in respect as they entered, recognising Fulren from the many visits he'd made before.

If the building looked magnificent from the outside, its interior was truly a wonder to behold. Even Assenah, who had reacted to every other sight with underwhelmed politeness, looked up in awe at the rows upon rows of leather-bound tomes. Racks had been erected in intricately carved oak, housing scrolls of yellowed vellum. Thousands of shelves were arranged in tiered columns that crawled up to the ceiling a hundred feet above. But the Great Library did not house only the written word.

"It's as much a museum as a library," Fulren said as they made their way past a corridor of glass cabinets, each one filled with artefacts both ancient and modern. Treasured pieces of artifice sat alongside relics from every age of Torwyn's history.

They walked about the place in silence, and Fulren was pleased he had finally shown her something she seemed truly impressed by. As they came to the centre of the library, Assenah stopped at the huge relief map of Torwyn set into the floor, looking over the myriad cities connected by a spiderweb of rivers, roadways and landship lanes.

"This place is a true marvel," Assenah said. "A valuable resource of knowledge and history."

"It is," Fulren replied proudly. "And it is open to all."

"And yet the place is bereft of visitors."

Fulren hadn't really paid it much attention, but as he looked about the library he saw she was right. A couple of custodians were busying themselves at the bookshelves, but other than that he and Assenah were the only people here.

"That's unusual," he replied.

At the other side of the library he heard the sound of the wooden doors being slammed shut, the snap of their bolts resonating across the abandoned interior. It was strange, but perhaps they were closing early. Fulren turned to one of the custodians.

"Is there some kind of—" he managed to say before the custodian shuffled off hurriedly, ignoring his enquiry. The second custodian also disappeared behind one of the shelves before Fulren could ask what was going on.

"Perhaps they don't know your pedigree," Assenah said.

"I'll have them flogged," Fulren joked with a smile.

Assenah laughed at that, a tinkling sound that filled Fulren with a moment's satisfaction. Then the mirth fell from her face.

Fulren turned to see someone appear from behind a huge shelf of books. His shoulders were broad, face covered by a blank ivory mask, piercing blue eyes peering from within. He held a sword in his hand—a short stabbing blade that could be easily concealed.

To the right another man appeared, same type of mask, same type of blade.

Fulren moved to stand protectively in front of Assenah as two more assassins revealed themselves. He and Assenah were surrounded.

Fulren's hand strayed down to the vendetta blade at his side, but it wasn't there. In his haste to escape his conversation with Olstrum he had left it in the drawer of his workbench.

"Stand aside, Hawkspur," said the biggest of the men, his voice muffled behind his mask. "We only want the witch."

"Gentlemen," he replied. "Perhaps we should talk about this before someone gets hurt?"

"Someone getting hurt is inevitable," said the man.

"Really?" Fulren saw the keenness of the man's weapon. For a moment he wondered what Conall might say in this situation. "Because by the look of it someone's going to get dead."

No more words as the big man advanced.

Fulren rushed to meet him. Those endless hours spent training with the Kartias came rushing back in a flurry as he moved to disarm his opponent, the weapon masters having taught him a dozen ways to defend himself in this very situation. He slipped in low, keeping his eyes on the masked man's sword, ready to dodge the inevitable thrust and immobilise his arm, using his own attack against him. Fulren didn't anticipate the assassin's feint, or his consequent punch to the jaw.

As he fell, the assassin went for Assenah. His strike was swift and true, stance demonstrating he was a veteran of the blade, but the emissary was quicker. She moved with preternatural speed, her lips moving in a silent incantation as she dodged the blow, her hand coming up to grip the man's face. As she grasped the mask, her hand turned black as night, steam rising where she gripped her attacker's jaw as though her flesh were white-hot to the touch.

The assassin's scream was deep and throaty. He dropped his weapon, pulling away from Assenah's grip and staggering back, wrenching the mask from his face. He would have been handsome but for the blackened imprint of Assenah's hand marring the flesh of his mouth and chin.

Fulren shook his head to clear the fug. He ignored the pain in his cheek, scrambling across the floor to grab the dropped sword. The other three assassins were rushing toward Assenah, and he managed to pick up the blade and rise to his feet as the first one attacked.

He parried the assassin's strike, countering at his midriff, but these were trained men, even more skilled than Fulren, and the assassin deflected the counter with ease. Fulren sliced at head height, but his opponent ducked, striking forward, blade aimed at Fulren's chest.

There was a noise in Fulren's ear, an unearthly bark that desecrated the air like a corrupt wind. The assassin was knocked backward, flying into a bookshelf, scattering tomes and scrolls in every direction.

Assenah reeled back, black ichor spilling from her lips. Whatever dark magics she had conjured had taken a toll on her body. It looked as if these assassins may have been right when they'd claimed she was a witch.

She turned to face another assassin, arm held out to strike him with blackened fingers. The emissary didn't see the masked man approaching her flank. With a swipe of his blade he hacked Assenah's arm off at the elbow.

Fulren cried out, rushing forward to help, but the men were already on her. One thrust his blade into her shoulder, the other finishing with a strike that sank into her chest up to the hilt.

Fulren couldn't get close before he felt someone punch him in the back.

Everything slowed, his vision suddenly darkening at the edges as the energy was sapped from his body. Looking down, he saw a blade protruding from his side just as his legs gave way. His attacker grabbed him from behind, halting his fall and gently lowering him to the ground.

It was the one with the burned face, his blue eyes peering down from above a blackened chin.

"I tried to warn you," he said as he wrenched the blade from Fulren's side.

Without another word the assassins left Fulren bleeding on the ground. The last thing he saw before darkness took him was Assenah's face staring lifeless amid the fallen tomes.

TYRETA

The harbour of New Flaym was abuzz with the sound of commerce. Tyreta watched as a dozen ships were loaded—sunburned mariners lugging all manner of goods across the jetty like a trail of ants.

Of course the most valuable export was pyrestone. The Sundered Isles was a virtually untapped resource, its bounty having been discovered only a decade previously, and there were many other goods to be stripped from this land. Meat and skins from giant reptiles were piled high, limed and bated for transportation, the stink of the tannery wafting across the entire outpost on windy days. Exotic fruits were heaped in crates, their bright blues and yellows contrasting starkly with the drab walls of the harbour. A group of labourers were levering stacks of lumber aboard one ship, its deck already heavily laden with logs.

Tyreta spied the harbourmaster and his gaggle of assistants as they noted every last commodity in their ledgers, issued permits, logged dockets. She couldn't think of a more tedious existence, but then this was Guild business. This was the machine. And she was destined to be a part of it, whether she liked it or not.

"Frog?"

She turned to see a charred amphibian glaring at her from one end of a blackened stick. Holding the other end was Wyllow, his face beaming at her as always.

She gingerly took the grilled frog from him, holding it at arm's length as Wyl took a bite of his own, tearing the rubbery meat from the stick with his gritted teeth.

"Good?" she asked.

"I've had worse," he replied, chewing for all he was worth.

Tyreta held up the frog next to his head. "I can't work out who's better looking."

Wyllow winked at her. "But you know who's sweeter."

She looked back at the dead frog glaring at her limply. "I'm not entirely sure."

For the most part Tyreta hadn't gotten on with the food. She was willing to give most things a try but had drawn the line at the fried insects that seemed so popular among the sailors and traders who populated New Flaym's bustling markets. She steeled herself as she opened her mouth to take a bite, then thought better of it, flinging the skewered creature aside.

"Never were very adventurous, were you?" Wyl said, mouth still full of frog.

"As adventurous as I was allowed to be," she replied, bristling at the insinuation. "It was all right for you. Lorens is the one marked for rulership, and you were left to run riot. Lady Rosomon had different ideas. None of us were ever allowed off the leash."

"I don't know about that. We got into our fair share of trouble back in the day."

That brought a smile to her face. Tyreta remembered those early days of visiting the Anvil with fondness.

"True," she said, glancing about the harbour and suddenly feeling the weight of her responsibilities creeping up like a phantom. "But it's unlikely we'll get in much mischief here. Before long I'll be pawing through ledgers and dockets and drowning in invoices."

Wyl offered a consoling pat on the shoulder. "At least you've got a purpose. Half the time, I think the only reason I was sent here was to get me out of the way."

Though she would never have admitted it to him, that thought had crossed her mind too. "Maybe I should just leave. Before it's too late."

"Yeah, right," Wyl chuckled. "Just march up to Lord Serrell and tell him you've decided the Hawkspurs no longer want to pursue their interests in the Sundered Isles, and his Guild can have the lot."

Tyreta glanced across the harbour toward the Marrlock embassy, where Lord Serrell resided. He was a not the Guildmaster of the Marrlocks, but in New Flaym his word was law. As cousin of Lord Oleksig Marrlock, Serrell was the most powerful man on these islands, and the thought of telling him she was leaving this place was both terrifying and exciting all at once.

"Maybe we should all leave," she said. "Let whoever owned this place before have it back."

"No one owns this place. The only thing on these islands with a hint of intelligence is the kesh, and they're little better than animals."

"The kesh?"

"Yeah." Wyl raised his hands and curled his fingers like claws. "Fierce beasties living in the jungle. Though they can't have been that fierce. When we first came to these islands ten-odd years ago they were all over this area, but they've been moved on since then. Apparently the Marrlock Guild tried to use them as a labour force in those early years, but they weren't suited to it. Too dumb, I guess."

"Or too wild?" Tyreta said. She had never heard of these kesh before, but they sounded as if they'd been given a raw deal.

"Whatever," Wyl replied before jumping down from the wall.

"Where are you going?" she called after him as he made his way across the harbour toward the tightly packed streets.

"I think it's time we checked on our project," he replied.

With sudden eagerness she followed Wyllow away from the market. Since he'd revealed the stormhulks to her a few nights before, she hadn't been able to stop thinking about the possibilities. As a consequence she'd persuaded Wyllow they had to get the things working again. He hadn't taken much coaxing.

They reached the old storehouse, its doors open to the humid afternoon air. Wyllow had easily discovered who owned the place and its ancient contents—an old merchant who was long gone back to Torwyn. He'd purchased the deeds to the storehouse and the stormhulks for a pittance. It would cost them a little more to get the decrepit machines in working order, though, which was where old Crenn came in.

Tyreta entered the building, hit immediately by the stink of oil and burning metal. Crenn sat atop his makeshift scaffold, goggles tight to his hairy face, hammer raised and about to swing. Tyreta resisted the urge to put her fingers in her ears as Crenn began beating frenetically against the stormhulk chassis, easing out a dent, though it looked as if he was just making it worse. The hammer rang out, filling the storehouse with a deafening cannonade.

"You know these things were expensive, Crenn," Wyllow lied, raising his voice above the din.

Crenn looked up from his labours. On seeing them both a wide gap-toothed grin spread across his dusky face. "I'm being more gentle than it looks, young master. But sometimes teasing these old beauties just won't do."

"Well, remember we're trying to get them working. Not reduce them to scrap."

Crenn put down his hammer and took off the goggles. His eyes were wide set, nose a broken mess. He jumped down from the scaffold with all the agility of a monkey. There was certainly something feral about him, but after a brief search, he'd been the only artificer they could find in New Flaym. At least the only one they could afford.

"Working, you say?" Crenn's grin grew wider.

Tyreta looked up at the stormhulk, then back at the old artificer. "You mean..."

Crenn nodded with vigour. "Wanna see?"

"Does a fat baby fart?" Tyreta replied.

Crenn turned back to the stormhulks with a guffaw. "Indeed it do, young miss. Indeed it do."

He reached up to the arm of one of the stormhulks, opening a panel in its elbow and revealing the conversion chamber. Then he produced something swathed in a dirty cloth from his waistcoat. Reverently he unwrapped the item, showing them both the small blue pyrestone. With uncharacteristic care, Crenn placed the stone into the chamber, closing the clips to hold it in place before shutting the panel.

"Ready when you are," he said, stepping back from the stormhulk.

"Do you mind?" Tyreta asked Wyllow.

"Be my guest," he replied.

Tyreta focused on the stormhulk, feeling the dormant power of the pyrestone within its chamber. All that potential energy was immediately at her beck and call, and she closed her eyes, convening with the pyrestone as only a webwainer could. It responded to her mental touch, and she sensed its response as though she were feeding it, nurturing it to life.

With a shudder the stormhulk's arm moved. It bent at the elbow with a grinding of gears, the ancient hydraulics whining after years of inaction. Its hand opened up, three fingers splaying before it snapped shut, tightening into a fist.

"There it is," squealed Crenn, dancing from one foot to the other. "Just needs a bit of oil, tighten up a few nuts, and it'll be good as new."

"It needs more than that," said Wyllow.

"Yes," Tyreta agreed, releasing her communion with the pyrestone. "We're not going to get far with just one stone."

"I can't help you with that," Crenn replied with a shrug. He opened the panel in the stormhulk to retrieve his precious power source. "This is the only one I got."

"It shouldn't be too difficult to get more," Wyllow said. "I'm sure I can requisition something from the Archwind stores."

"You mean steal," Tyreta said.

"I mean borrow," Wyllow replied, his face a picture of innocence. "Anyway, don't you worry about that. What we do need to work out is what we're going to do with these things when they're operational."

Tyreta looked at the stormhulks, sitting there as they had for so many years. There was so much potential. So much untapped power.

"We're going to do anything we bloody well want," she said.

Wyllow's trademark grin grew all the wider. "I like the sound of that."

ROSOMON

She woke in an unfamiliar room, a fug of confusion all that remained of a dream fast fading from memory. Her hair was matted, and she still wore the same gown she'd had on for three days. Lucid thoughts began to replace the haze—the fear and worry returning after a few hours of sweet release. Her mouth was dry from the wine she'd drunk the night before—a strong southern vintage she'd guzzled down to help her sleep.

Rosomon sat up, feeling guilt draw over her like a wave. What was she doing? Her son needed her, and here she was, wallowing in a comfortable bed.

She walked to the basin, splashing cold water on her face, trying to rub some sense into her befuddled head. This was the last thing Fulren needed—his mother in a bloody stupor. Her mind had to be clear. It just had to be if she was going to get him out of this.

The palace had been in upheaval since Fulren was found in the Great Library. The emissary murdered. Her son the only witness... the only suspect. But he was wounded and unconscious, unable to speak for himself. The draughts and embrocations they'd administered had put him in a deep slumber. She should be there at his bedside. Should be holding his hand, praying for all she was worth, for all the good that would do him.

Rumour had already started to infest the palace. Talk of conspiracy. Talk of betrayal. Fulren was some kind of spy. Some insurgent. What nonsense. Fulren was her son and loyal to the Guilds and to his uncle. There was no way he would have become embroiled in—

A knock at the door.

Rosomon dried her face on a towel, doing her best to fix her wayward hair before opening the door. Starn stood there, a grave look about his dull features.

"Well?" she demanded when he didn't speak. She feared the worst. Fulren's wound was deep, the apothecaries uncertain if he would live.

"He's awake, my lady," Starn replied.

Rosomon almost sobbed at the news, but she maintained her stoic reserve. Once again the guilt engulfed her. Why had she left his bedside at all? She had been exhausted, of course, but sleep was a selfish indulgence any decent mother would have forgone when her youngest son lay teetering on the brink of death.

Without waiting for Starn to lead the way, she left the room and rushed through the palace to the infirmary. The Titanguard were keeping vigil outside, and the place was more a prison than a place of healing, but they allowed her to pass without question. Inside there was only a single patient. Fulren lay in his bed as several apothecaries ministered to him. One was pouring some water into his mouth as another changed the dressing on his side. Rosomon snapped a hand over her mouth as she saw the wound beneath, the skin dark with bruising around an expertly stitched laceration.

She moved to her son's bedside and took his hand.

"Can you hear me?" Rosomon asked, feeling his hand clammy in hers. "Fulren, can you hear me?"

"Yes, Mother. I can hear you just fine," he said, drowsily. The first apothecary had finished helping Fulren drink and stepped away. The second one worked on the bandages at Fulren's side, and he winced as the dressings were laid over his wound.

"Fulren, what happened? You have to tell me what happened." Rosomon tried her best to remain calm, but all the desperation and fear she had bottled up over the last two days were beginning to boil to the surface.

"We were attacked," he breathed. "The emissary..."

"Who attacked you?" Rosomon asked. "Who did this?"

"They wore masks," Fulren replied. "I didn't see. We fought back...but the emissary? Where is Assenah?"

"She..." Rosomon didn't want to tell him but knew there was no choice. "She is dead, Fulren."

He let out a long sigh, clearly cut deeply by the news. "Did they find any of them? The men who attacked us?"

Rosomon didn't want to reveal the truth, but she had to get as much information from him as she could if she was to persuade Sullivar of her son's innocence.

"They found no one. No witnesses. Only you wounded and her dead. Fulren, they think you were the one who killed her."

Fulren's brow creased, and he fixed his mother with a confused stare. "I killed her? We were attacked. The library. There were custodians."

"There was no one," Rosomon answered. "The library staff were interrogated. Olstrum himself questioned them. They saw no one but you and the emissary. A disturbance was heard, and when they investigated, you were the only one left alive."

"Olstrum," Fulren breathed. "He came to me. Just before I met Assenah."

"What do you mean?" she asked desperately. If there was anything he could tell her that would help, she had to know.

"In my workshop," he replied groggily. "Olstrum came to talk about Assenah. He asked me...asked me to spy on her."

"Olstrum Garner? Are you sure?"

Fulren nodded, growing more groggy by the second. "Yes. But there is more." He gripped his mother's hand before he slipped away once again. "I saw one of them. One of the assassins. Before they murdered Assenah she conjured some power. Some magic. His face was burned. Here..."

Fulren gestured to his chin. Then his hand went limp and his eyes closed.

"What is wrong with him?" Rosomon demanded in a panic.

"It's all right, my lady," one of the apothecaries said. "He is merely sleeping. We have administered a powerful draught to his water. It will help him recover."

Rosomon looked back at her son lying helpless. She reached a hand to his feverish brow and moved the hair from his face. Then she stood, kissed his cheek gently, and made her way from the infirmary.

Starn followed close behind, struggling to keep up as Rosomon rushed through the corridors of the palace, her haste born of desperation. Her son lay gravely injured and falsely accused of murder. She had to do something.

Her brother's throne room was sickeningly opulent. A monument to his vanity and something that would never have been brooked during their father's time. Rosomon saw him sitting at the far end, two of his consuls leaning in, their voices lowered to a whisper. Sullivar looked troubled, and so he should. He had gambled much on the emissary's visit. Had banked on it being a success. There wasn't a much worse outcome than her ending up dead.

"Leave us," Rosomon said as she approached the throne.

Both consuls looked toward her, neither moving.

"I said leave us," she repeated, this time more forcefully.

Both men obeyed, scurrying off to some abandoned alcove in the labyrinthine throne room. Sullivar waited for her to speak. It was clear he had been anticipating this visit.

"He's awake," she said.

"So I hear," Sullivar replied.

"Well? Aren't you going to see him? To listen to what he has to say?"

"What good would it do now?" Sullivar replied.

Rosomon felt her jaw tighten. "How can you be so obtuse?" she said, struggling to control herself. "You have to know the truth. Your nephew has been attacked. Someone tried to assassinate him. He's your family. You must hear him out."

Sullivar rubbed at his beard. He looked tired, as though he had not slept, but that was only to be expected. His grand plan with the Maladorans was in tatters.

He fixed her with a grave expression. She had never seen her brother look so serious. Even with all his responsibilities, with the prosperity of Torwyn and the Guilds resting on his shoulders, he had never seemed so troubled as he did now.

"The evidence has been gathered," he said. "Witnesses questioned, testimonies examined. It is clear what happened. Fulren murdered the emissary and almost died in the act."

"No!" Rosomon shouted. "It's not true. You know Fulren. You know he could never—"

"I have seen the transcripts. I have read them all a dozen times, Rosomon. Don't you think I want to believe he's innocent? He is my blood, but the evidence is clear. A sword was found next to Fulren, a knife next to the emissary's body. It's obvious he attacked her and was wounded when she tried to defend herself."

Rosomon could feel her emotions boiling over, and she fought to hold back the tears.

"He told me there were masked men," she said, her words frantic. "They were the ones who attacked them. He told me one of them was wounded. Scarred. We must search for this man, Sullivar. We must find him."

Sullivar shook his head. "The custodians have been interrogated. Their statements verified. Fulren and the emissary were seen entering the library together. They were the only ones in the building. There were no assassins, Rosomon."

"Olstrum," she said. "Did Olstrum tell you this?"

"He has been leading the interrogations," Sullivar said incredulously. "But you can't mean to suggest my senior consul had anything to do with this?"

"Fulren told me Olstrum came to the workshop before he was due to meet the emissary. That he ordered Fulren to report anything he found out. To spy."

Sullivar shook his head. "But then why would he try and have them both killed? What purpose would that serve?"

"I don't know," Rosomon said. "But the least you can do is try and find out."

"I... It's too late, Rosomon."

Behind her there was the sound of someone entering the throne room. She turned to see six figures, faces hidden beneath cowls, their robes identifying them as the Justiciers. Each wore the colour of a Guild, but their identities were kept hidden. They were the highest judicial authority in Torwyn, called upon only when a grave matter of law was in question.

"No," Rosomon breathed. "Not this... not yet."

The Justiciers silently took their places, three on each side of the throne room. After them walked Rearden Corwen, Sanctan Egelrath and Wymar Ironfall. None of them spoke or dared to look at Rosomon.

Finally another figure entered that Rosomon barely recognised. She wore tight-fitting black, her face a mask of arrogance. It took some time before Rosomon realised this was the emissary's handmaid, if that was the proper description. She was followed by a dozen warriors who entered Sullivar's throne room fully armed with spears and swords at their sides. They surrounded the diminutive woman, each one scanning the room as though they expected trouble.

"Sullivar, what is this?" Rosomon asked. "What is going on?"

Her brother stood. If Rosomon hadn't known better she'd have thought him ashamed.

"Rosomon, we have to deal with this incident quickly if we are to repair the damage done to our relations with Nyrakkis."

"What are you talking about? Why does this woman have an armed guard in the throne room?"

"They are for my protection, my lady," the woman said before Sullivar could answer.

Rosomon turned on her. "Your protection? This is the imperial palace of Archwind."

"And Assenah Neskhon was merely visiting a library. Yet still she was murdered."

Rosomon turned back to her brother. "What is she doing here, Sullivar?"

"Fulren must answer for his crime," he said. She could tell he was trying to be officious. Trying to appear every inch the emperor, but failing.

"And you intend to judge him? Here and now? While he still lies bleeding in his sickbed?"

"The Maladorans are leaving," said Sullivar. "We need a quick conclusion to this if we are to have any chance—"

"Any chance of what?" she bellowed. "Any chance of preserving a supply of pyrestone for the Archwind Guild?"

Sullivar had no answer to that, but Rearden Corwen stepped forward.

"My lady. This treaty will aid all the Guilds."

"Damn you," Rosomon screamed. "And damn your Guilds. This is a sham. All of it. Fulren has been falsely accused. There is a conspiracy here, you're all just too blinded by greed to see it."

"Aunt Rosomon, please," said Sanctan, taking a step toward her. "I know Fulren can't have done this, but we have to comply with the verdict of the Justiciers."

She allowed him to take her by the arm. She felt suddenly weak, as though she might collapse. Sanctan was clearly her only ally here.

Another figure entered the throne room. Olstrum marched to stand before the throne, but he didn't deign to look at Rosomon.

"Well?" asked Sullivar.

"As we thought, my lord," Olstrum replied.

"What?" asked Rosomon. "As we thought what?"

Olstrum locked her in his gaze. She could tell he was reluctant to speak to her, but he managed it anyway. "Fulren was seen training for combat. He has been honing his martial skills since he arrived in the city. Witnesses have testified to this and to the identity of his tutors. Both are notorious mercenaries, both have fought against the Maladorans in several border skirmishes and are known agitators against any kind of accord between our nations."

"This is preposterous," Rosomon said. "Where are these mercenaries? I want to speak with them."

"They are...missing, at present. But rest assured they won't get far."

"You see," she spat. "More conspiracies. Where are these witnesses, Sullivar? All we have is unreliable testimony."

"The witnesses have been thoroughly interrogated," said Sullivar.

"By him!" she yelled, jabbing an accusing finger at Olstrum.

"The day of the murder he tried to have my son spy for him. He cannot be trusted."

"Please, Aunt Rosomon," said Sanctan, trying to calm her, but she was in no mood to be calm.

"This is a mockery," she shouted for all to hear.

"Rosomon," Sullivar said as calmly as he could.

"There are traitors in our midst."

"Rosomon!" Sullivar bellowed.

That was enough to silence her. His shout echoed through the throne room, and she was instantly reminded of their father. But Sullivar was only a pale imitation of Treon Archwind. It was not Sullivar who had built the Archwind Guild into such a dominant force. It was not Sullivar who had formed alliances with the most powerful families in the land. Their father had ruled with a wise head and a fair hand and would never have been arrogant enough to proclaim himself emperor of all Torwyn.

"The evidence has been presented to us all," Sullivar continued. "The Justiciers have reviewed it. Though it is irregular to call for a verdict without the accused being present, the circumstances dictate we resolve this quickly."

Rosomon wanted to yell that this was inhuman. That her son was innocent. That they did not have the right.

But they did have the right.

They were the highest lawgivers in the land, despite the brazen injustice of it, and to add insult, her own brother was presiding over this mockery of a trial.

Sullivar looked to the Justiciers, standing silently in their different-coloured robes. "In the matter of the murder of Assenah Neskhon of Jubara by Fulren Hawkspur, what say you?"

The green-robed Justicier representing the Radwinter Guild was the first to turn, then the red of Archwind. The others followed, until the only one left facing the centre of the room was in the blue of Hawkspur.

"It is done then," Sullivar said.

"No," Rosomon shouted. "It's not bloody done, Sullivar. We are not done."

Sullivar ignored her, and Sanctan had to tighten his grip on her arm to stop her from mounting the stairs to the throne and flinging herself at her brother.

"The sentence will be carried out," Sullivar said.

"What sentence?" Rosomon screamed. "What have you done, Sullivar? What have you condemned my son to?"

There was silence as Sullivar lowered his head, unable or unwilling to answer.

"Fulren is ours now, Lady of Hawkspur."

Rosomon turned to see the Maladoran woman smiling. She seemed to be garnering much satisfaction from this whole sorry charade.

"No," Rosomon said. "Sullivar, please. You cannot give my boy to these demon-worshipping bastards."

Sullivar sank back to his throne defeated. "It is already decided," he said. "As soon as he is able, the Maladorans will take him back to Nyrakkis to answer for his crime... in their own manner."

"What does that mean?" Rosomon shouted, turning to the Maladoran woman. "What does that mean?"

With a shrug the woman turned and left the throne room, closely shadowed by her bodyguards.

Rosomon shook Sanctan off, barely hearing his protest as he vainly tried to calm her. She would not be calmed, not now. Not ever.

"Hear me, Sullivar," she said, her fists balled, barely able to speak through her gritted teeth. "I will never forgive you for this. Do you hear me? On the souls of our mother and father I will never forgive you."

Sullivar did not answer. He just sat, head in hand, as though he hadn't heard a word of it.

Rosomon had seen enough. With Starn at her shoulder she marched from the throne room and back to her son. Fulren would need her. Now more than ever.

CONALL

He could hear the gulls outside screeching at one another like squabbling washerwomen. Didn't they know there was a man in here with one shitter of a hangover? Could they not give him just one morning in peace?

Conall heaved himself out of bed. His lodgings were comfortable enough, the best they could find him in the garrison, but still a far cry from his chambers in Wyke. Still, he'd have to get used to roughing it once he was sent to one of the forts at the edge of the Karna Frontier. So far, though, he'd heard nothing about his posting, which served him just fine. For so long he'd had to uphold his father's legacy and his mother's expectations, and for once he was free of that. He'd managed to occupy himself quite nicely at the port, frequenting the drinking holes that sprang up wherever there was an abundance of fighting men.

As he relieved himself in the bucket that stood in one corner of the room, Conall gazed through the window, feeling the morning breeze blow in, the linen curtain billowing gently. Agavere was the furthest he'd ever travelled, the hot climate a welcome relief from the cold of Wyke, and it hadn't taken him long to get used to it. There was a quality to the place he liked. Or maybe it was just the distance from his homeland. Either way, Conall thought this was somewhere he could make a reputation for himself. A place he could write his name in glory.

Though perhaps not right this second.

He collapsed back onto the bed. Maybe another hour or two asleep would clear his head. He could find some glory to write his name in a little later. All notion of that was thrown to the winds as his door burst open.

Sted walked in grinning her stain-toothed grin from ear to ear. In one hand she held two small tankards, in the other a full bottle of liquor.

"Captain Hawkspur," she said in that deep gravelly voice of hers. "Still in your pit, you lazy dog? This is no time for sleeping, there's drinking to be done."

Conall felt his stomach churn at the prospect. "You're an animal," he replied. "Can't you see it's first thing in the morning?"

Sted looked confused. "But you said we'd spend all day drinking."

Conall could vaguely remember making that promise during the previous night's revelry. "Yeah, I might have done."

"Then how are we supposed to drink all day if we don't start in the morning?"

As usual, Sted's logic brooked no argument.

Conall swung his legs over the bed, girding himself for what was to come. Stediana Walden was his first lieutenant, though no one would have realised from the way she called him out, often and loudly. Not that Conall gave a damn. She was whip smart and a better fighter than most men Conall had ever met. Her penchant for hard liquor and harder women made her better company than *any* man Conall had ever met.

Reluctantly he held out a hand for one of the tankards.

"That's the spirit," she said. "Would sir like a single or a double?"

"A bird can't fly with one wing, Lieutenant," he replied, knowing he'd regret it later, but there were no half measures where Sted was concerned.

She poured him a generous cupful and handed it over. Conall sniffed at the pungent spirit, feeling his insides twist before he took a drink. He almost gagged but managed to hold it down. The second swig was easier, as always.

While Sted took his cup to refill, Conall pulled on his clothes. The travelling shirt and trousers were grubby and unwashed and his boots covered in dust, but he was hardly going to don his dress blues to wander the grimy streets of Agavere. Hat in one hand and tankard in the other, he followed Sted out of the barracks and into the streets.

The sun was already stifling, and he put his hat on, pulling the brim down to shield his eyes. It didn't do much for his hangover, but hopefully another few measures of whatever grog Sted was carrying and he'd feel much better.

They made their way north from the garrison, past a few shoddily erected buildings. Agavere should have been a thriving port, a hub for trade from the great continent of Karna Uzan into Torwyn. Instead it was nothing more than a staging point from which the Armiger Battalions waged war on the durrga.

When the first prospectors of the Marrlock Guild had arrived here, they'd soon discovered rich seams of pyrestone. They had also found the indigenous creatures that inhabited the place none too pleased to see them. The prospectors were slaughtered, but the abundant resources had been too tempting for Treon Archwind to ignore. He had offered each of the Armiger Battalions a generous share of the profits were they to defend the Marrlock Guild's mines on the frontier, and their marshals had flocked to the south, eager to stake their claims. Ten years of war had been the result. Ten years of fighting the durrga tooth and nail for their pyrestone, and despite the military might of Torwyn, the durrga didn't look as if they were going to give it up anytime soon.

Sted snorted in a deep breath as they reached the harbour. "Look at that," she said. "Makes you proud, doesn't it?"

Conall looked out onto the bustling seafront. Crates of arms and armour were being offloaded, stormhulk parts winched ashore along with bags of grain and barrels of fresh water. In the other direction a few carts laden with pyrestone were lined up to be shipped back across the Ungulf Sea to Goodfleet. There wasn't much—a testament to how little was left in the mines of the Karna Frontier. Arms came in, stone went out, but the yield had been dropping for years, the battalions making few inroads into the territory of the durrga due to the stiff resistance they faced.

"Proud of what?" Conall answered, not seeing anything to be proud of.

"The wheels of industry turning," Sted said. "The spoils of war won through the might of Torwyn. That's why we're here, isn't it?"

"I thought we were here to get pissed," he replied, offering his empty tankard, which she dutifully filled.

"We are here to fuel the machine," she replied, reaching in her shirt pocket and pulling out a stick of redstalk. "To keep Torwyn breathing."

"If Sullivar secures a trade deal with Nyrakkis, none of this will matter."

"You think that will stop the battalions? They're hardly going to abandon the place when there's still a profit to be made."

"What profit? An abundant supply from Malador will only lower the value of pyrestone from the Karna. How long do you think the battalions will carry on this war when it stops being profitable? This won't last."

She grinned at him, chewing slowly on the stalk protruding from one side of her mouth. "Then we should make the best of it while we can."

She strolled away along the front toward the bawdy houses, and he followed her down into what had become known as the Pit. It should have been a trade district—the Ironfall Guild had constructed its own forges back when Agavere had held ambitions of becoming a bustling centre for trade. Now the abandoned buildings had been appropriated for drinking holes, gambling dens and whorehouses—anything that would glean a profit from the endless stream of soldiers who passed through Agavere's harbour.

Conall felt a sudden twinge of excitement. Despite the early hour, the Pit was already buzzing with activity. Troopers of the battalions played dice, drank their ale and were even in their cups enough to sing bawdy songs as he and Sted made their way down into the narrow alleys. It was a far cry from the inns and public houses of Wyke, where Conall's every move was observed and judged. Here he was free to do as he pleased, and he'd taken advantage of that freedom with gusto. He knew his mother would have been disappointed. As far as she was concerned he was every inch the responsible heir. But what Rosomon Hawkspur didn't know wouldn't hurt her. Not that he gave a shit about that.

Before they reached their usual spot at the Hog's Tusk, Conall heard a familiar voice.

"Is that who I think it is?" asked Sted at the sound of grunting and cursing.

The voice was suddenly drowned by the sound of cheering and yelling.

"Who else?" Conall replied.

They both followed the sound down an alley and into the backyard of an alehouse. A group of troopers from the Tigris Battalion were standing around a small stockade used for cockfighting. In the midst of the cajoling soldiers was a man on his knees, hands tied behind his back, face a bloody mess. Despite the gore it was a face Conall recognised.

Nevan Ulworth was an ape of a man. He was also one of Conall's scouts, which made the fact that he was on his knees killing rats with his teeth that much more disconcerting. Then again, boredom made fighting men do the oddest things, so this was only to be expected.

"Ulworth," Conall pronounced over the din of the battalion troopers.

Nevan had just sunk his teeth into another of the rats that teemed around the stockade. On seeing Conall he jumped to his feet, rat still clamped in his prominent jaw.

"Might I ask what in the Five Lairs you think you're doing?" Conall asked.

Nevan spat the rat out. "Gambling, Captain."

"Is that what it is? For a moment there I thought I might have to review your rations."

A chorus of sniggers from the surrounding troopers.

"Sorry, Captain. It won't happen again."

"You'd better come with us, Ulworth. Before you get yourself in any more trouble." With groans of disappointment from his audience, Sted cut Nevan's bonds and helped him wipe his bloody face with a rag.

Together they made their way to the Hog's Tusk. There was no sign to mark it as an alehouse, just the head of a massive Karna boar nailed above the entrance. The owner of the place hadn't even bothered to have the head preserved, hence its rank smell and the fact that the rotting head looked severely the worse for wear.

Inside they took seats as close to the window as they could get, taking advantage of what passed for fresh air blowing down from the dock. The place was almost empty, which was a surprise considering how busy the rest of the Pit was. A serving boy brought them a jug of ale and three flagons and waited expectantly for his money. Sted just raised her eyebrow at Conall, still chewing on her redstalk. Conall flicked the boy a couple of coins.

"It's not a bottomless pit," Conall said as he put his coin purse away.

"Can't be expecting me to get my hand in my pocket with what the Talon pays, and I doubt Nev here has two pennies to rub together, considering you just scuppered his payday. Besides, rumour has it one of us is heir to the Hawkspur Guild, and I'm sure as shit it ain't me."

Conall had never made a fuss of Sted's assumption he would always foot the bill. He'd have happily paid for her company anyway—even if it was just so she would watch his back.

Nevan took the liberty of filling the flagons, and they weren't long into drinking before the door was pushed open and a group of Armiger troopers entered. From the bull-head sigil on their uniforms, Conall could see they were from the Auroch Battalion out of Fort Nekron. Considering they fought at the vanguard of the frontier, they didn't look too much the worse for wear.

The troopers crowded in, occupying the rest of the tables in the Hog's Tusk, and the serving lad was at pains to keep them all watered—rushing back and forth between tables and bar as if his life depended on it. The drink flowed, and the atmosphere quickly switched from subdued to raucous. Someone started a song about the Auroch Battalion being the mightiest warriors in all Hyreme, which Conall thought was a bit of a stretch. For the most part the three of them were ignored, right up until Nevan made his way toward the back alley to take a leak.

"Look at that beast," one of the troopers called from the crowd.

"Yeah, that's a head needs mounting over the fireplace. Keep the kids away."

Conall felt the atmosphere suddenly darken as Nevan stopped, regarding the troopers with a black look. He'd seen that look before, and there was usually violence to follow it.

Three of the Auroch Battalion stood up, ready to face Nevan if he didn't back down, and Conall braced himself for a fight.

"Any sign of Captain Hawkspur's drink yet, lad?" Sted shouted across the crowded bar.

The alehouse quieted, and the three troopers glanced over at Conall, realising the big man they were berating was one of his scouts. It was clear Conall's highborn reputation preceded him.

"Drinks are on us, Captain," one of the troopers said quickly. "Let us welcome you to the Karna."

That was enough to relax the mood, and the three men came to sit at Conall's table, happy to buy the drinks. It was something of a relief that he didn't have to keep standing Sted's round. The three men introduced themselves, but Conall was too far into his cups to remember any names. They talked the usual talk of soldiers—of the fighting they'd done, of the things they'd seen. The conversation soon turned to the enemy they were facing, and Sted asked what the durrga were like, keen to find out what was in store for them once they reached the front.

"The goatheads are monsters," said one of the soldiers, a ragged scar running from his right eye to the corner of his mouth. "Beasts in mind and body that show no mercy and don't ask for none. Throw themselves at us like they're not afraid to die."

"They're thick as mince," said his comrade, his head shaved to the scalp, neck almost as thick as Nevan's. "No better than animals. If they had any sense, they'd just let us get on with mining this place. It's not like they've any use for the stone anyway."

It was useful to get the opinion of men who'd faced the "goatheads," but Conall couldn't help but feel there was more to it than that. Even the dumbest animal would retreat in the face of insurmountable odds, so it was clear the durrga were more than just beasts.

Years ago in Wyke, he'd seen the huge bestial skull of a durrga brought back by scouts of the Talon. It had frightened him then—that monstrous inhuman thing—and the fear still sat uneasily in his gut. He had been afraid of the creature when it was dead, and he could barely conceive of what a live one might do to his faculties, let alone a whole warband.

"Have you not interrogated any prisoners?" he asked. "Found out why they're so fixated on defending this place?"

Both men seemed to find that amusing. "Goatheads don't get taken easy. Those that do don't speak any language but for braying and screaming. But they've taken plenty of ours prisoner, and if you follow one bit of advice, follow this: don't let them take you alive."

Conall had no intention of being taken prisoner, but he still appreciated the trooper's warning.

Before long Nevan took to challenging the men to an arm wrestling contest, and Sted turned her attentions elsewhere.

"Look at that beauty," she said.

Conall glanced toward the bar. There were several men and women standing there. From their purple uniforms he could see they were members of the Hallowhill Guild, presumably seconded to the Auroch Battalion to power their artifice. One of them was glancing in Conall's direction. She was striking—dark eyes and long curly hair making her stand out in the crowd of weathered soldiers.

"I'm going in. Wish me good fortune." Sted pulled the dragon pendant from the top of her shirt and kissed it. It depicted Ammenodus Rex and was crafted from solid steel. Sted never went anywhere without it, and Conall had never been able to understand how someone with so few morals could be so pious at the same time.

He watched as Sted made her way to the bar. She stood beside the woman, and they spoke for some time. Sted's confident smile gradually waned, and it wasn't long before she left the woman and returned dolefully to the table.

"The Great Wyrm of War not on your side today, Sted? Or are you just losing your touch?" Conall could barely hide his delight at her failure.

"Nothing to do with that," Sted replied. "She just doesn't ride mares, is all."

Conall laughed. He was tempted to bait Sted further about her lack of prowess but could see she was annoyed enough.

"Best drink some more," he said. "It'll make us both more charming."

Sted didn't argue. For the rest of the afternoon they continued to drink. Spirits were high and they laughed and sang along with the Auroch Battalion. Every now and again Conall glanced toward the webwainer at the bar, and each time he caught her eye. When night began to fall and torches were lit in the drinking hole, Conall realised the past few days of excess were catching up with him.

"I'm away to my bed," he announced, rising to his feet.

"Already?" Sted said, squinting at him to help her focus. "Are you saving yourself so we can drink all day tomorrow?"

It seemed like a good idea, but then it always did when he was three sheets to the wind. "Sure. See you bright and early."

Conall walked out into the warm night as the sounds of the Pit buzzed all around. Before he could take three steps someone called to him.

"Leaving so soon, Captain Hawkspur?"

He turned to see the woman who had rebuffed Sted at the bar. She was smiling sweetly, one eyebrow raised.

"My duties as an officer of the Talon have called me away, I'm afraid," he replied, though in truth the only duty he had was to his bed.

"Perhaps you could escort me back to the garrison before you move on to more pressing matters?" she asked.

"I'm sure I can make the time," Conall said, offering his arm.

"How gallant." The woman took it, and they made their way out of the Pit and onto the main thoroughfare of Agavere.

"You're looking forward to returning to Torwyn?" he asked.

"I'm not sorry to leave this place behind," the woman said. "Besides, there are big things ahead for the Hallowhill Guild. I don't want to miss out."

Conall assumed she was talking about the impending treaty with Nyrakkis. The increased trade in pyrestone would see the webwainers in higher demand than they had ever been.

"Might I ask your name?" he said.

"You can ask," the woman replied before walking on in silence.

"Withholding information? Clearly I need to interrogate you further."

"You can interrogate me as thoroughly as you like," she replied. "I'll never tell."

Through the drink-addled cloud of his head, Conall desperately tried to think of a pithy comeback—something suggestive but not too crude. He needn't have bothered. The woman grabbed his face, pulling him close and kissing him firmly. He was suddenly lost in the feel of her, the smell of her. She was the sweetest thing he'd tasted since he got to Agavere.

Their journey back to the garrison turned from stroll to march, stopping every now and again for them to engage in a fevered kiss. Before he knew it Conall and the woman were outside his quarters. A bright pyrestone lamp lit the stairwell, and the sounds of laughing voices and footsteps came from above.

She pushed him against the wall, kissing him hard, and Conall felt a sudden panic at the prospect of being discovered in the garrison fraternising so vigorously. His fears melted away as the pyrestone light flickered, then dimmed, plunging them into darkness.

Was that her? Who else but a webwainer could do such a thing? Conall didn't question it as he fumbled at his door handle, keen to enter his quarters before they were spotted.

His chamber was dark, but before Conall had a chance to light a lantern they'd managed to expertly remove one another's clothes.

It was a night he'd later wish he could remember more of.

When he opened his eyes the next morning, he was alone. Conall smiled, still able to smell the honeyed scent of her on his pillow. His head was throbbing, but he didn't care, and the sound of the squabbling gulls was nowhere near as annoying as it had been the previous day. He sat up and stretched, seeing a note on the dresser by his bed.

Captain Hawkspur, my thanks for such a satisfying interrogation. May your gallantry know no bounds. Keara Hallowhill.

Conall breathed out a long sigh on reading the name. She was a genuine Hallowhill. An heir of her Guild.

Had Treon Archwind not exerted full control over the webwainers two decades before, the power of the Hallowhills might well rival that of the other major Guilds. There was still much animosity between them and the Archwinds, since their rise had been stifled so ruthlessly. Little wonder Keara hadn't wanted to mention who she was. And neither was it surprising that she was eager to return to Torwyn in these changing times.

Someone knocked at the door. Must be Sted, though why she was bothering to knock for once was beyond him. Time to start drinking again.

"Come in," Conall shouted. "But you'll have to wait while I wash this time, I smell like a—"

The man who opened the door was not his lieutenant, but he was a member of the Talon, a scout, his clothes dusty and weathered from the road.

"Captain Hawkspur," he said, standing to attention in the doorway. "I have a missive." The man held out a sealed letter.

Conall rose from the bed, grabbing a sheet to hide his modesty. "Just give me the gist."

The scout broke the seal and looked at what was written.

"Your orders, sir. Your unit has been posted with the Phoenix Battalion at Fort Tarkis. Under Frontier Marshal—"

"Beringer," Conall said. He knew who the commander of Fort Tarkis was. Everyone did. Of all the postings he could have received, it was the one he'd dreaded the most.

He dismissed the scout and returned to his bed. Resting his head on the duck-down pillow, he knew he'd best make the most of it. This was the most comfortable he was going to be for quite some time.

TYRETA

She'd never been much of an early riser, but today she was up with the birds as they sang their dawn refrain. Dressing swiftly just as the sun was peering over the distant jungle, Tyreta felt excitement boiling in her gut. Days of tutelage on the thankless details of Guild administration had left her in a stupor. Now she was to rise anew like a butterfly, squeezing its way free of a chrysalis of unfathomable mandates and statutes. Or something like that.

As Tyreta left the villa behind she raised a hand to her chest, feeling the nightstone on its pendant. She didn't even remember putting it on, but she was relieved she'd brought it. There had been no repeat of the burning sensation she'd felt when she first arrived in the Sundered Isles, but still it was special to her. A family heirloom. Tyreta wasn't one for sentimentality, but the gift meant a great deal. It made her current deception all the harder to bear, but bear it she would. Hopefully the release from the shackles of endless responsibility would be worth it, just for one day.

She threaded her way through the backstreets of New Flaym. The deserted alleyways were a welcome change from the usual bustle. Here and there lay the drunken remnants of the previous night's revelry—a snoring mariner hugging a mangy hound, one of the waterfront women stumbling home in bare feet. Tyreta made her way past them with all haste, and when she reached the end of the street containing their storehouse, she saw Wyllow already waiting for her.

"I'm surprised to see you up," she said as he greeted her with his usual grin.

"What did you expect?" he asked, suddenly looking incredulous.

"I expected to be waiting hours for you."

"That hurts," he replied, in a way that suggested he wasn't the least bit hurt.

She looked him up and down. "Do you have them?"

"Have what?" He opened his arms to show he wasn't carrying anything.

"Don't make me hurt you, Wyl."

"Like you'd have a chance," he replied.

She moved toward him threateningly and he backed away, skipping like a frightened deer.

"All right," he said, reaching behind him and producing the coin purse he'd been hiding, dangling it in his fingers. "It's all here."

"Show me," she said, not satisfied.

Wyllow rolled his eyes, loosening the drawstring on the purse and showing her the contents. Inside were four large pyrestones, two red and two yellow. Tyreta could feel their power pulsating. She wanted to reach out and touch them but stopped herself.

"I know," Wyllow said. "Pure grade. Best I could find."

"How did you get—?"

He held up a hand. "It's best if you don't know."

"Yeah, I'm sure it is," she replied.

With that they walked the rest of the way to the storehouse to find Crenn was already there. He had finished the restoration of both stormhulks and was buffing the pauldron of the largest one with an oily rag. Tyreta had to admit he had done an incredible job. The machines looked far from pristine, but they were still unrecognisable as the rusty relics they'd found so many days ago.

"Here we are," he said when Tyreta and Wyllow entered. "Good as you're gonna get." He jumped down from his makeshift scaffold with the agility of a much younger man.

"Good enough," said Wyllow, staring at the job Crenn had done.

"Good enough?" Tyreta said. "They're amazing."

It was obvious they weren't. She'd seen stormhulks in the Anvil twenty feet tall, polished to a mirror sheen, gold and chrome trim lining every panel, but they dulled in comparison to what stood before her now. These machines belonged to her and Wyllow. A way to escape, if only for a short time. They were more beautiful than anything she'd ever seen.

"Would you like to do the honours?" Wyllow asked, holding out two of the pyrestones to Tyreta. She looked at them, one red, one yellow, sitting in his palm.

"No," she replied. "I think Crenn deserves that honour."

Suddenly the artificer looked bashful.

"Oh, I don't—"

"Nonsense," she said before he could make any excuses. "You've earned this."

With a wide grin Crenn took the pyrestones in his hand, cradling them in his palm as if they were two delicate flowers that might blow away at any moment. He approached the first of the storm-hulks, a couple of feet shorter than the second and painted a deep shade of blue. Already Wyllow had provided him with a number of blue pyrestones to fit in the joints of the hulk, which would stimulate its main points of articulation. The ones Crenn held were larger, more powerful. They would be housed in the central capacitors and bring these beasts to life.

After flipping open a panel in the stormhulk's abdomen, Crenn placed the pyrestones in their conversion chambers with reverential care. Slowly he closed the panel and took a step back, saying a whispered prayer to the Wyrms for good luck.

"Superstitious, Crenn?" Tyreta asked as she moved past him and climbed into the open seat of the stormhulk, the old cracked leather creaking beneath her.

"You can't be too careful," he replied.

Tyreta didn't put much store in superstition. The only prayers she'd say were those before she had to tell Lady Isleen what she and Wyllow had been up to, once they returned from their outing.

Nevertheless, she was determined to take the stormhulk out of the city and explore the surrounding jungle. It might be the only chance she got, and one not to be squandered.

As Crenn placed pyrestones in the second stormhulk, Tyreta grasped the metal handles of the access hatch and pulled the cockpit closed. The hinges creaked as she shut herself in and was immediately plunged into darkness. She could feel the pyrestones pulsing with energy as they communed with the latent power of the stormhulk. They were just waiting to be ignited…and she was the spark.

Tyreta closed her eyes, reaching out, channelling her abilities into the machine. Every pyrestone was brought flaming into life as she connected with their essence, linking them by ephemeral threads into an intricate web of power. She and the stormhulk became as one—she could feel the strength of its limbs, the pneumatics and hydraulics, the gears and engines becoming part of her. When she opened her eyes she could now see through the viewing port of the stormhulk, and not only straight ahead but all around, as the machine gifted her with a panoramic view of her surroundings.

Crenn had finished with the second stormhulk now, and Wyllow was climbing inside. He reached up, grabbing the steel bars that lined the cockpit hatch, and shut himself in. As Wyllow convened with his stormhulk, Tyreta could feel it coming to life, the engine responding to Wyllow's powers, hydraulics whining as it raised itself to full height.

"Can you hear me?" Wyllow's voice echoed inside her cockpit.

"Are you kidding me?" Tyreta said. "How is that—?"

"These machines are twinned," he replied, his voice sounding fuzzy but still audible within the chamber. "We can channel the sound of our voices across a short distance."

"But how?"

"How do I know?" Wyl laughed. "I'm no artificer. Ask Crenn."

"Maybe later," Tyreta replied, already moving toward the door of the storehouse. "For now, let's see what these things can do."

She saluted Crenn as she walked by and could see him dancing from one foot to the other—overcome at finally seeing the fruits of his labours. Outside the streets were all but deserted, and Tyreta turned north, pausing for a moment to make sure Wyl was following. His stormhulk was the larger, and somewhat more lumbering than her own spry machine.

"Try and keep up," she said as she moved through the streets. The tread of her stormhulk made a thunderous noise, and any notion of stealth was all but forgotten.

"I would, but it looks like I've got the slower machine."

"Excuses," she replied, moving faster through the streets.

They passed a group of dockworkers making their way to the front for the early-morning shift. Half of them ignored her as she moved by, having seen more than one stormhulk working on the dockside. Others stared, clearly wondering how such ancient machines were still operational.

"We need to be less conspicuous," she said, and she heard Wyl laughing almost immediately.

"It's a bit late for that," he replied.

As they made their way farther north she could see the main gates leading out to the jungle beyond. They were heavily manned, although the huge iron doors stood open.

"We're never going to get through," she said.

"Why don't you have a little faith?" Wyl replied, quickening his pace.

She slowed, letting Wyl take over, and his stormhulk strode up to the gate as one of the guards put a hand up to stop them both.

"No unauthorised access beyond the perimeter," the guard said, his voice tinny through the receiver of the cockpit.

The front section of Wyl's stormhulk hissed as he loosed the couplings securing him inside and flipped open the cockpit. The gate guard's expression changed as he recognised the son of the emperor looking down at him.

"Apologies, my lord. Please proceed."

Wyl closed himself inside the stormhulk once more and carried on walking.

"Neatly done," Tyreta said, relieved she hadn't had to reveal her own identity.

"This face gets me all sorts of privileges," he replied.

"I suppose it has a lot of making up to do for being so butt ugly," she replied, quickening her pace again and moving past him into the jungle.

"Charming," Wyl replied, stomping after her through the lush green.

The main road north was well-worn, and the trees had been cleared, granting a wide path for them both to travel. As they walked, Tyreta could see animals scurrying away into the undergrowth, and it only made her feel more powerful—indestructible even—as they strode farther into the jungle.

"This is amazing," she said, beginning to feel more comfortable in the metal skin. The longer she channelled her power, the stronger the communion between flesh and steel and the more she was at one with this inhuman carapace.

"Feels good, doesn't it?" Wyl said, his voice somehow clearer.

"It's like I'm...part of the machine."

Wyl laughed again. "Maybe we should see exactly what these things are capable of?"

"Damn right," she answered as Wyl began to accelerate, the legs of his stormhulk pumping harder, churning up the ground and foliage beneath him.

She watched him for a moment as he sped ahead, marvelling at the power of the stormhulk. Then she was off, chasing him through the jungle, eyes wide as the dense foliage rushed past her viewing port. Tyreta extended one of the stormhulk's arms, reaching into the foliage as she ran. As she channelled the power of the machine she could almost feel the leaves brushing against her own hand, marvelling at the sensation, laughing at the power she held as she watched the branches of trees snap at her merest touch.

Wyl turned up ahead, moving from the well-trodden path to delve through the dense jungle.

"Where are you going?" she called after him, but all she heard was the sound of his distant laughter through the cockpit's receiver.

She sped up, excitement growing as she forgot all the pressure she had felt pile up on her in the previous days. She felt no fatigue as she piloted the stormhulk, accelerating to catch up with him, running faster and harder than she had ever run before. The rush of sensations was overwhelming, but still Tyreta pressed on, laughing at the experience, thrilled and terrified all at once.

Up ahead she could sense rather than see Wyl. Their twinned machines allowed her to feel where he was as he smashed through the dense jungle, leaving a ruined path for her to follow. As she burst out of the brush he was waiting for her in a clearing.

Tyreta stopped in front of him, feeling every sense on fire, her breath coming in short bursts from the excitement.

"How does that feel?" he asked, and she could sense the joy in his voice.

"I can't..."

"I know. There's just nothing like it. This is what we were born for."

Wyl turned, the arm of his stormhulk pointing up to the foothills that rose out of the jungle and grew into the mountains beyond.

"I'll race you to the top," he said.

Tyreta looked up, the mountain range huge in her viewport. "Up there?" she said. "But we can't—"

"I think you'll find we can," Wyl replied before setting off, his stormhulk loping into the brush once more.

Despite her doubts, Tyreta didn't hesitate. The stormhulk responded to her will as she piloted it after her cousin. A small herd of porcine creatures scattered in Wyl's path, and she squealed in delight as the brutes fled for shelter at his approach.

Up they went, crashing through the foliage. At times Tyreta had to use the stormhulk's powerful hands to grasp at a tree and pull herself up the steepening slope. The feet of the machine slipped on the thick layer of sodden leaves and mud, but still she followed, determined not to be left behind.

After some time, which might have been hours for all she could tell, Tyreta reached a ridge at the top of the hill. The ground levelled out, with a thick canopy of trees to her right and a sheer face of dark rock to her left. They were on a road that seemed well travelled, winding its way around the side of the mountain face.

Through the viewing port she could see far behind her. Over the treetops New Flaym was perched on the coast. It was tiny in the distance, and they had clearly run for miles without her even realising it.

"Where are we?" she asked.

"This is the main road to Crow Station," Wyl replied, his voice distant. "It's used as a supply route to the mining outposts."

He had slipped from her view now, too far ahead for her to see him around the edge of the rock face. She moved along the road after him, eager to catch up.

"Is that where we're—"

Something slammed into the side of the stormhulk before she could finish. It knocked her off balance, and she desperately tried to keep her footing. Through the viewport she could see rocks tumbling toward her from atop the sheer cliffs.

Tyreta tried to dodge aside, but the stormhulk would not respond quickly enough before she was hit again. The sound was deafening as the rocks clanged against the stormhulk's carapace. The light within the cockpit winked out as her connection to the pyrestones was momentarily broken. She heard the grinding of metal, the juddering of gears as she tumbled. All was darkness as she fell, spinning over and over until, with a final clank of steel, she came to rest.

Tyreta was alone in the blackness. She tried to cry for help, to use the communication device to shout to Wyl, but the pyrestones did not respond. The rockfall must have damaged something in the ancient machine's power core, and now she was trapped in a useless hunk of twisted metal.

Desperately she tried to push open the main hatch to the cockpit. It moved—but only a few inches, allowing sunlight to creep in, replacing darkness with dim shadows.

"Wyllow!" she cried. "Wyl, help me!"

The steady thumping sound of Wyl's approaching stormhulk made her sigh in relief. There was a grinding of metal hinges as his powerful machine wrenched open the access hatch and Tyreta was suddenly bathed in sunlight. She crawled out and climbed unsteadily to her feet. Her stormhulk lay useless among the rocks, dented and battered by their fall.

With a hiss of hydraulics, Wyl opened the hatch of his own engine. He looked down at her with an expression of rapt disappointment.

"Well, that was a bit clumsy of you," he said, grin breaking across his face.

"It was a rockfall," she replied, gesturing pathetically at the smashed machine and the huge rocks that lay all about.

His eyes followed the trail of destruction the stormhulk had left back up to the main road.

"That's not all," he said, pointing back up the hill. "There's a rope over there."

Tyreta squinted up the rise to the edge of the path. A rope had been tied between two trees, forming a trip wire at the base of the rock face.

"A trap," she said, feeling her stomach lurch with panic. "But who—?"

There was a rustle amid the tree canopy above them. A huge figure dropped down from the shadow of the foliage, landing atop the open hatch of Wyl's stormhulk.

Tyreta stared in awe at the powerfully muscled beast. He was almost seven feet tall, downy flesh a deep grey dappled with black, animal skins hanging from his waist, head adorned with the skull of some giant reptile.

"Wyl!" she screamed.

Her cry of warning was drowned out as the creature roared in fury, raising a huge spear with a wide, wickedly curved blade. Wyllow just had time to turn and face this monster before it scythed down with that weapon. Tyreta could only watch in horror as her cousin's head was hacked from his body.

Blood pumped from the headless corpse, spraying the killer in red, anointing him in his victory. Tyreta was frozen with terror, but only for a moment as the beast turned that lizard-skull mask toward her.

She ran.

Her legs felt heavy as she fled through the thick brush, no longer augmented by the power of the stormhulk. She didn't think what direction she was running in, she just had to move—to put as much distance between herself and Wyl's killer as she could. Behind her she could hear the monster roar again, but this time his victory cry was joined by others. More beasts in the jungle.

As the echo of their cries followed her, all she could do was keep running.

FULREN

He was done pacing. Fulren had walked every inch of the cramped cell a score of times and now he stood still, staring out of its small window. The evening sky looked beautiful, even to a man condemned. Or perhaps because he was condemned.

Fulren's side still throbbed, but it had healed well. The wound was neatly stitched, the bruise surrounding it had turned yellow, and at least now he could move without tearing himself open. The apothecaries had done a good job. Part of him wished they hadn't. Better he had died quietly in his bed than face the nightmare that was coming. Better he had drifted away than watched his mother's sorrow as she told him the verdict of the Justiciers.

Of course, Lady Rosomon had railed against it. Cried her heart out and cursed his Uncle Sullivar to the Five Lairs. Perhaps Fulren should have been angry too, but what good would raging do? Best he face what was to come with dignity. Anger wouldn't save him now.

The sound of a key in the door. Fulren's heart began to beat faster as he realised his time was up. The door opened, and he saw the solemn faces of the Titanguard beneath their open visors. They didn't have to speak, he knew what was coming.

Fulren walked out of the cell in silence and up through the

corridors of the palace, the Titanguard adopting a tight formation around him. No one wanted to say anything to him as he passed the courtiers and serfs and consuls, their necks craning to watch as he was paraded past. It was as though he were being led to an execution. Truth was, his fate might be much worse, the mystery of it unnerving him more than the thought of a swift death.

All the while he knew he had to face this with courage. He could not falter, could not let his rising panic overwhelm him.

The Titanguard had not placed him in irons, and they led him like an honour guard through the palace, up to the rotunda where he'd seen the arrival of the emissary so many days ago. If only he could go back to that now. He would have refused his uncle's request to show Assenah the city. Might even have left with Tyreta and Conall, and flown away across the sea as far from this place as he could get. But there was no going back.

They were waiting out on the long promenade, that huge black airship squatting at the far end, ready to take him away. His mother stood between two ranks of the Talon, the only person of any consequence to bid him farewell. Fulren's uncle was nowhere to be seen, and neither was Olstrum or any of the Guildmasters. It seemed he was to have a discreet send-off.

As he was marched toward the waiting airship, his mother moved into his path. She held up a hand and the Titanguard halted, taking a step back so she could say goodbye to her son.

Rosomon stood in front of him, reaching forward and straightening his collar as though she were sending him to his first day of tutelage at the academy. It looked as if she was in no mood to say goodbye.

"You can trust no one, Mother," Fulren said under his breath. "There is treachery here."

She looked up at him, and he could see she was fighting back tears.

"Do you understand?" he asked.

She nodded. "Yes..."

"You have to protect yourself."

She shook her head. "You have to protect yourself," she replied. "This is not the end. There is still hope."

"Forget that," he replied. "You must send word to Conall and Tyreta. There are traitors in the palace. Perhaps beyond the Anvil. I don't know how far this conspiracy might have spread."

"We'll be fine," she replied.

"No, you won't. Listen to me. Someone wants to stop the treaty between Torwyn and Nyrakkis. Someone is determined to break the accord. They will stop at nothing. If Uncle Sullivar will not listen, then you have to . . . you have to protect yourself."

She nodded. "I understand."

"Do you? Mother, no one is safe. You can't trust anyone. Go to my workshop. I have left a blade in the desk drawer. Take it and keep it with you at all times."

"I have no need for a knife, Fulren," she replied.

"Promise me you'll find it," he said firmly.

"Yes, yes," she replied, reaching a hand up to touch his cheek.

The guards moved closer to them. Their time was up. "I will see you again," he said.

"Yes, you will," she said, but he could tell she hardly believed her own words. "I will make sure of it."

The Titanguard took him by the arms.

"And tell my brother and sister . . . Well, you'll think of something."

She held on to his sleeve for as long as she could before the Titanguard pulled him away and marched him along the platform.

Fulren couldn't look back. Couldn't bear one last glance at his brokenhearted mother as they led him away. He had to forget her now. Had to find his own strength.

Up ahead, a small woman was waiting for him. She wore tight red leathers, her hair short and dark. As he drew closer she greeted him with an open smile. Surrounding her were the tall Maladoran warriors. They all looked identical with their shorn hair and painted flesh.

The Titanguard stopped some yards away. Fulren paused before he realised that from here he would have to walk alone. For a brief moment he glanced toward the edge of the promenade. Perhaps flinging himself into the void would be a better end than whatever awaited him in Nyrakkis. But that was never going to be an option, not with his mother watching at least.

He walked forward with as much courage as he could muster. There was no way he would falter so close to the end.

"Greetings, Prince of Torwyn," the woman said when he reached her. "So glad you could join us. I am Wenis of Jubara." She motioned to the huge ark behind them, which was already growling as though impatient to be away. "Your carriage awaits."

Fulren glanced at the guards surrounding her, each standing stock-still and emotionless. "Am I not to be clapped in irons?" he asked.

Wenis giggled. "I don't think that will be necessary. Unless of course it is your preference?"

Fulren didn't answer, he just stared up at the ark, its front hatch yawning open, waiting for him to enter and be devoured.

"Shall we?" Wenis asked, beckoning him inside.

Fulren took a breath before walking forward, stepping onto the gantry and entering the darkness. Wenis and her guardians followed him. The noise of the engines was louder inside, like a host of voices murmuring in a chorus of lamentation. Chains clanked against a pulley as the hatch was pulled up, and Fulren turned to look out along the runway. He could see his mother in the distance, standing tall, bravely watching as her son was shrouded in darkness. Fulren closed his eyes, unable to watch as they were finally shut inside with a resounding clang of metal.

When he opened them again, the bowels of the ark were dimly lit by red torches. Wenis was smiling up at him, her face taking on an eerie aspect.

"Let's move onto the upper deck," she said. "It's a much more pleasant view."

If Fulren had expected to be consigned to some dank cell for the journey west, it seemed he had been sorely mistaken.

He followed Wenis up a winding stairway and out onto the open deck of the ark. It was all but deserted—no crew making ready to set off, no captain to give any orders. Instead he found a deck of dark polished oak, the gunwales artfully wrought in black iron depicting a host of demonic faces. To the stern sat an aftcastle that leered over the deck like an ogre, and the forecastle was equally imposing.

At the centre of the deck a circular sigil was set in the same dark iron as the gunwales. It was wrought in an intricate pattern, some kind of arcane symbol Fulren didn't recognise.

"Impressive, isn't it?" Wenis said, gesturing about the deck. "One of only three in all Nyrakkis. Queen Meresankh granted it for Assenah's use personally. Though I suppose it's for my use now." She seemed to delight in the prospect.

"You don't look overly concerned that your mistress has perished," Fulren said. "Or that the man accused of murdering her is aboard your ship."

Wenis shrugged. "She had her time. All great arcanists perish in one way or another. At least her end was quick—but I suppose you know that already."

"You don't care?" Fulren asked.

"Care about what? It is all part of the Cycle. With the death of one arcanist comes the birth of another." She offered him a playful wink.

"So you were... her apprentice?"

Wenis raised an eyebrow at that. "You people use the most primitive of terms. Apprentice? No. I was merely an arcanist-in-waiting. And now, thanks to you, I am waiting no longer."

"If it makes any difference, I wasn't the one who killed Assenah."

Wenis stroked her chin as though pondering his words. Then she shook her head. "No. It makes no difference at all."

Before Fulren could protest his innocence any further, the doors to the forecastle opened. From within the dark iron structure walked a procession of hooded figures, faces hidden beneath dark-grey cowls, black sigils stitched into the linings of their robes.

"Looks like it's time to leave," Wenis said, stepping back from the iron symbol nailed to the centre of the deck. "You might enjoy this spectacle, Prince of Torwyn. I doubt you will have seen its like before."

Fulren moved back to the gunwale as the robed figures took their places, standing at seven equidistant points around the iron symbol. They faced inward, their heads bowed. Fulren could hear them chanting some kind of prayer, a quiet lament that gently increased in volume. As their voices rose, so did a feeling of nausea. The air around him grew thicker, as with the coming of a thunderstorm, pressure building in his head as though his ears were about to pop.

As one, the seven figures threw off their robes. They were a mix of men and women, all naked, heads shaved, emaciated bodies covered in an array of arcane markings. Their eyes were closed, lips still moving in a sorcerous canticle. Fulren's stomach started to churn as he witnessed the rite taking place before him.

The strange markings on one of the sorcerers began to glow with a sickly yellow light. Smoke ebbed from the fiendish sigil, and one by one the rest of the seven chanting figures began to display similar markings, some glowing blue, others red.

In response, the wailing of the ark's engines grew. It groaned as though some troubled beast were being disturbed in the bowels of the ship. The deck shuddered, and Fulren placed a hand to the gunwale to steady himself.

"Stunning, isn't it?" Wenis said, spellbound by the spectacle. "I was equally awestruck when I first witnessed it."

"What...what are those markings?" He pointed at the glowing runes on the flesh of the seven sorcerers.

"Necroglyphs," Wenis replied. "The source of their arcanist power. It's through necroglyphs that even mortals like these can convene with... Well, I'll show you later."

The ark grew more agitated, the deck trembling until, as one, the seven sorcerers opened their eyes, revealing solid black beneath. They stared, voices falling silent as the sound of the engines changed from scream to murmur and the vessel rose up from its perch at the end of the promenade.

Higher and higher they climbed until the ark slowly turned, pulling away from Archwind Palace and leaving it behind. Fulren could not resist taking a last look back, instantly regretting it as he spied his mother at the edge of the esplanade, a lone figure watching her son disappear into the distant horizon.

"Try not to think on your homeland too much, Prince of Torwyn," Wenis said. "That is in the past."

"So what now?" he replied. "Am I to be caged in a cell?"

Wenis laughed at the notion. "What need have we to cage you? Where would you go?" She opened her arms as though inviting him to try and escape. For a moment, falling a thousand feet seemed a tempting option, but just as before he dismissed the notion as soon as it came to him.

There was a sudden choking noise. Fulren turned back to the seven arcanists, seeing one of them convulsing where she stood. Bile seeped from the corner of her mouth and a stream of dark mist poured from her black eyes. With a last gasp, the woman fell, collapsing in a heap.

Fulren moved forward to help, but Wenis grabbed his arm to stop him.

"She is dead," Wenis said. "There is nothing you can do for her."

Two of the tattooed guardians came forward and dragged the corpse away from the iron circle. The other arcanists seemed not to have noticed.

"What about the rest of them?" Fulren asked.

"Most will suffer the same fate by the time we reach Nyrakkis," she replied matter-of-factly. "They are thralls, their arcanist power attuned to but a single task. Debtors, thieves, murderers. All are condemned to die, but rather than execution they are given a last chance to be... useful."

"They give their lives just to pilot this vessel?"

"It is an honour, Prince of Torwyn."

He turned to see the guards unceremoniously dragging the dead woman belowdecks. "Tell that to her," he said.

"Not convinced? Then I will show you," she said. "Perhaps if you see how the ship works, it will give you a better understanding of our ways."

Fulren followed her toward the rear of the ark. He was glad to leave the arcanist thralls behind him; their silent vigil was unnerving, and the more distance he put between them and himself the more his nausea abated.

Wenis led him into the aftcastle, down a ramp lined with a dozen iron carvings of leering gargoyle faces. More warriors guarded the way into the depths of the ship, standing in silent vigil. Fulren could hear the grumbling of the engines grow louder the deeper into the bowels of the ark they went, until they came to a chamber hunkered within the deepest bulkhead.

"The engine room, if you will," Wenis said.

Fulren saw a huge iron casket laid out in the centre of the room. It was vast, leering faces and clawing figures twisted into every facet. Iron tubes ran from its base, disappearing into the bulkheads surrounding it. The sound of growling came from within, an inhuman snarl that filled him with unease.

"This is the source of the airship's power?" Fulren asked.

Wenis smiled, reaching out a slender hand to gently touch the iron sarcophagus. "This is the beating heart of the ark. The spirit bound within imbues this vessel with life. The thralls you saw above give their lives so that it obeys their will. In turn, their will is bound to mine."

"Spirit within?" Fulren said, both enthralled and frightened by the power it contained. "You mean a demon?"

Wenis laughed. "If that is what you choose to call it, then yes."

"But... the dangers. If the thing inside were to escape."

"It is quite safe," she replied. "While I live."

Fulren shook his head. The nausea had returned, and he reached a hand to his top lip. Blood had run from his nose, and his head started to pound.

"I think I've seen enough," he said.

"Of course. You should rest. There is a long journey ahead."

She led him from the sarcophagus, and Fulren couldn't follow her away fast enough. They made their way back up through the aftcastle, almost to its summit, where Wenis opened the door to a chamber looking out from the ark's stern. Through the window he could see they had already left the Anvil many miles behind.

"I hope you will find these lodgings suitable?" she said.

Glancing around the room, Fulren realised it made for much more inviting surroundings than his room at the workshop. On a table by the window sat a number of trinkets. As he looked closer, he realised they were an assorted collection of artifice—old devices, some rusted, some gleaming in the light that shone through the window. Scattered about them were an assortment of pyrestones, blue and red and yellow. A quick calculation and he realised they were worth enough to buy an opulent manse in the Anvil.

"It will more than suffice," he replied.

"I thought providing you with these ornaments might help pass the time?"

"It will," he said, still staring at the array of devices. "These are some fascinating pieces."

"I'm sure. You'll have to educate me on how they work sometime."

"It's a fairly rudimentary concept," Fulren said, picking up one of the less rusted devices. "Affix a red pyrestone, which acts as a regulator, through which you can control a power source. Blue for electric charge, yellow for heat. It's really just—"

"Yes, I'm sure it is," Wenis interrupted, perhaps not that keen to be educated after all. "So I suggest you make the most of it. I cannot guarantee you will be so lavishly accommodated when we reach Jubara."

"What will happen to me?" he asked.

Wenis thought on that for a moment before offering a shrug of her slight shoulders. "Most likely you will die, Prince of Torwyn."

He nodded at her reply. But then, what had he been expecting? He was hardly going to be greeted with a parade and a feast.

"Call me Fulren," he said. "I'm no prince. Not now."

"As you wish, Fulren," she replied. "Now I suggest you rest. I will come check on you soon." With that she bowed and left him alone in the room.

He gazed after her, then at the room he was now imprisoned in. There were no bars, but neither was there any escape. He walked toward the table, picking up one of the broken devices and turning it over in his hand. One thing was for sure—he was prince of nothing now.

TYRETA

The jungle was alive. Without the armour of the stormhulk to protect her Tyreta was exposed to every aspect: every hiss, every chirrup, every low and hidden growl from deep within the brush. But more dangerous than any creature were the murderers who had slaughtered Wyllow.

He had been hacked down like an animal right in front of her, and what had she done? The only sane thing. She had run. Faster and farther than she'd ever run before, trying to leave the sound of the howling beasts behind, but no matter how far she fled, they were still there. She could hear their calls through the trees, sometimes far away, sometimes terrifyingly close. In the light of day, all this had been frightening enough, but now the sun was starting to set, and her panic was becoming almost too intense to control.

Wyl had told her about these things in the jungle. Kesh, he had called them. From his description Tyreta had envisioned docile creatures, too stupid to be dangerous. That assumption had turned out to be so much horseshit. It had gotten her cousin killed, and if she couldn't escape, it was pretty damn clear who would be next.

She paused, clinging to the trunk of a massive tree. Tyreta had to get a hold of herself. She couldn't succumb to the terror. The only way she would survive was by thinking. There had to be a way out of this.

Tyreta tried to focus. Her pursuers had fallen silent for now, but that didn't mean they weren't still hunting her. She had no clue where she was or which direction New Flaym was in, but that didn't matter anyway. There was no chance she would reach it before she was caught, even if she could work out which way to run.

She just had to keep going, ignore the fatigue, ignore the fear and the grief. Just escape, that was all that mattered.

Another roar bellowed from deep within the jungle. It was answered by a second call, farther away. Tyreta glanced around her, eyes wide, trying to discern from which direction the noise had come. The echoing calls seemed to resound all about, and she had no idea where her pursuers were, or more importantly which way to flee.

"Just pick a bloody direction and keep going," she said to herself through gritted teeth.

That's it. Anger. Just get angry. Just let the hate fuel you. Those bastards killed Wyl. Murdered him in cold blood, and now they want to do the same to you. Don't let them win.

The encroaching darkness was making it harder to see, but Tyreta didn't care about that now. She plunged farther into the jungle, running a headlong race between her and the animals coming after. Her tunic was already slick to her back, but she dared not take it off and fling it aside for fear it would give sign of her passing. The farther she went the more the dread feeling grew that she was simply becoming more lost in the dense jungle, but what other choice was there?

Gradually the darkness began to settle. Above she could just see through the canopy. A bright moon shone between the thick leaves, but it was obvious she'd soon be plunged into nothing but blackness. Her only hope was that with the coming of night her hunters would call off the chase. She just had to evade them for long enough.

But what if they didn't? What if they still kept coming? Again she cursed herself for not bringing a weapon. She didn't even have a knife, not that it would have done her much good against spear-wielding kesh. Nevertheless, she paused in her flight, checking the jungle floor. Amid the thick moss and ferns was an abundance of fallen branches. Tyreta picked one up and stripped some of the leaves from it. It felt heavy in her hand. Sure, it was no broadsword, but it would just have to do.

At the sound of another howl in the encroaching night, she ran on. This time the noise was closer. They were moving in on her, their echoing cries growing louder. It wouldn't be long before they tracked her down.

The sky turned from deep blue to black as she moved, revealing a carpet of bright stars above. She stopped again, breathing heavily. Her legs felt like withered stumps and she had to rest, if just for a moment. Tyreta gripped the branch she held, knuckles whitening as she tried to draw some kind of strength from it. Every time she closed her eyes she saw Wyl as he looked up at the skull-helmed kesh. Saw his head cut from his body before he could even try to defend himself and heard that animal cry of victory. It was all she could do to quell a sob, but this was no time for weeping. She had to keep running. Had to survive.

Before she could move on, something stirred in the undergrowth. She looked up, unable to suppress a gasp of fear. It was answered by a low growl, deep and sonorous and oh so close. Tyreta opened her eyes wide, brandishing the stick like a spear. She scanned the surrounding brush. Surely it wasn't one of the kesh—the growl had been too low, too inhuman for that. But then her pursuers were far from human.

Two baleful eyes shone from the dark. Tyreta backed away, pointing her stick at the beast that pawed its way from the foliage. Her heart sank as the panther revealed itself, ears pulled back, eyes focused on her. Its prey.

Tyreta took another step away, shaking the stick threateningly, not that it did any good. But of course it didn't, what was she expecting to achieve with a stick?

"Back off," she said, as much to herself as to the powerful-looking beast. "Just piss right off."

It took no notice, still moving toward her, stalking her inexorably across the jungle floor.

She'd read somewhere that when faced with a more powerful enemy with nowhere to run, the only option was to appear more fierce than you actually were. If she'd been holding a spear rather than a branch, that would have been a much more reassuring theory.

Tyreta screamed, raising the stick above her head and darting forward. To her amazement it worked, and the panther, startled by her yell, retreated into the jungle a few paces. It was only a moment of doubt, and the creature quickly worked out she was not the apex predator she pretended to be. Its face twisted into a snarl, as though it were insulted at her attempts to dupe it.

She backed away again, and this time she couldn't have screamed if she'd wanted to. Her throat tightened with fear, her hands trembling as they held on to that useless piece of wood.

Another howl echoed through the jungle, this one frighteningly close. The kesh voice was joined by another, then a third. The jungle cat flinched, spooked by the close proximity of yet more predators. Tyreta took her chance.

She plunged into the dark, not daring to look back as she raced once more through the jungle. Leaves and branches slapped against her face, the sound of pursuit close behind, but she dared not turn around. There was no hope to this, no logic, but it was all she could do. Instinct had taken over, the need to survive, to escape...to live. The scant moonlight lit a treacherous path ahead of her, but somehow Tyreta managed to navigate her way through the jungle without turning an ankle. The howls all around did not abate, only growing louder as though homing in on her position, attracted by her desperate flight.

A glance back. Through the shadows in her wake she saw the panther coming after her, paws silently churning up the undergrowth. It would be on her in seconds.

Tyreta felt the cold dread of certainty chill her to the bone. She could not escape the predator, not in its own environment. With a cry of anguish she leapt aside, rolling through the dirt, coming up on her feet, the stick raised to defend herself.

The panther scrabbled through the brush, adjusting its angle of attack as she dodged aside, then pounced at her.

It was all fangs and claws, but by some miracle Tyreta managed to raise the tree branch, lodging it in the beast's mouth before it could clamp its jaws to her throat. One of its paws raked at her shoulder and she cried out in pain, the wound fuelling her anger, dispelling her fear. With a feral cry of her own she wrenched the stick to one side, flinging the beast bodily through the air.

The panther pulled the stick from her grasp as it rolled across the jungle floor, then scrabbled to its feet. Now she had nothing to defend herself with. No way to fend off another attack. Tyreta backed away as the panther eyed her, dropping the branch from its jaws. She backed up to the trunk of a tree, nowhere else to run.

The ground churned beneath the beast as it came at her, but as it made to pounce there was a sudden rustle of leaves, a twang of a trip wire, and the panther's foot was caught in a snare. The creature howled, the snare pulling tight, holding it fast. It writhed, hissing in fury, clawing at the snare about its leg, but there was nothing it could do to free itself.

Tyreta let out a breath in relief, feeling the hot burn of the claw wound in her shoulder. Looking down she saw her tunic was torn to the elbow, her flesh laid open, blood running down to her wrist, black in the moonlight.

Before she could begin to wonder how she would stop the bleeding, a tall figure stepped out into the clearing. She held her breath, fear replacing relief as she saw the savage features of a kesh warrior. His feral eyes were fixed on her, spear held casually in his hand.

The kesh said something she didn't understand before stalking toward her, the moonlight casting strange shadows on his downy skin. He seemed to relish the moment, as though sensing her fear and feeding off it. This was not the one who had killed Wyllow—he was smaller and wore no skull helm, but his face was just as fearsome, bared teeth even more wicked than those of the panther.

He spoke again, this time sounding more urgent. She wanted to answer, perhaps to beg for mercy, to ask that he spare her life, but that would have been desperation talking. Tyreta would not grant such satisfaction.

"I don't understand," she said, feeling anger well up inside her. "I don't speak your language, you arsehole."

The kesh spat some more words in his guttural tongue, clearly annoyed that she was not displaying enough fear. It served only to make Tyreta more defiant. These bastards had murdered her cousin. She'd be damned if she'd die begging.

"Go on then," she said, staring at the tip of that cruel spear. "Do it. Kill me if you can."

It was a stupid thing to say. Of course he could kill her—not that he understood anyway. Nevertheless, the kesh took a step back, a cruel smile spreading across his brutish face.

He hefted the spear to shoulder height and drew it back for a throw that would impale her to that tree. Tyreta raised herself up, standing as tall as she could. If she was to die alone in the jungle she'd do it like a Hawkspur. Her mother would have been proud.

An arrow hissed out of the dark, embedding itself in the kesh's leg. He growled in pain, reaching down to pull the arrow from his thigh, but before he could grasp it a second arrow struck from the night, this time into his throat.

The spear fell from his hand and he stumbled before dropping to his knees, gurgling blood, eyes glazing as he looked around for the enemy who had killed him. With a last wheezing, bloody breath he collapsed.

Tyreta couldn't move. She just stared, transfixed by the corpse in the clearing, one hand clamped over the wound in her arm.

There was an inhuman yell some distance away, breaking her trance. Before Tyreta could think to run, another kesh appeared from the dark. This one was holding a bow…a woman, slighter than her male counterpart but still every inch as wild.

The female swiftly shouldered her bow and checked the body of the male she had killed, making sure he was dead. Then she noticed Tyreta, staring at her with feline eyes before moving closer.

The instinct to flee was overwhelming, but for some reason Tyreta didn't feel threatened. They looked at one another, the kesh tilting her head, regarding Tyreta curiously before another howl in the distance attracted her attention. The woman glared out into the dark as though searching for her next enemy. When no one came she looked back at Tyreta. It was as though she was appraising her, weighing her worth.

The panther struggled against the snare again, thrashing in the dark, sending loose leaves flying. The kesh turned, sliding a knife from a fur sheath at her belt. She approached the panther gingerly, and Tyreta watched her hold out a hand, making soothing noises that calmed the beast. Just when Tyreta thought she might plunge that knife into the panther's throat, the kesh grasped the snare and cut the beast free in a single swift motion.

"What are you doing?" Tyreta hissed into the night, gripped by panic once more.

The panther shook its head, looking at the kesh woman, then at Tyreta, before racing off into the shadows of the jungle. When the kesh turned back to her, Tyreta could see the trace of a smile on her bestial face. Without a word she motioned for Tyreta to follow.

Tyreta wasn't about to argue, and she kept up as best she could in the darkness. For all she knew this female might be leading her toward the rest of the pack, but the fact that she had just slain one of the males made Tyreta think her luck had changed. Besides, what choice did she have? She could carry on blundering through the jungle until one of the hunters found her, or she could follow this female to the Wyrms knew where. It wasn't much of a choice at all.

The female suddenly stopped in front of her, crouching down. Tyreta did likewise, her breath coming in sharp gasps as she stared into the dark jungle, gripping tight to the wound in her shoulder as blood continued to pour down her arm. There was no noise now, the distant shouts of the chasing kesh had fallen silent. Even the insects and other jungle creatures had become still.

Then she saw it, creeping across their path up ahead—the silhouette of a hulking kesh warrior, all but invisible in the dark shadows of the jungle, but somehow the female had sensed him. He paused, peering through the dark, and Tyreta knew it was only a matter of time before he saw them crouching in the undergrowth.

Slowly, ever so slowly, the female took the bow from her shoulder. She plucked an arrow from the quiver at her hip: two feet of solid wood, tip glinting in the moonlight. Tyreta watched in awe as the female nocked the arrow in one swift motion and let fly. The kesh hunter went down without a sound.

The female reached back, grasping Tyreta's arm and pulling her along behind. Tyreta almost screamed as the woman touched the claw wound in her shoulder. The female stopped, turning to examine the wound with no word of apology. She pulled a cloth bandage from her pack and methodically tied it around Tyreta's arm. Briefly she touched a finger to her lips to signal Tyreta should be silent before the pulling the bandage taut and tying it off. The pain was excruciating, but Tyreta managed not to make a sound.

Another howl pealed through the jungle. It seemed to instil some urgency in the female, and she beckoned for Tyreta to follow as she delved deeper into the trees. They moved on as silently as they were able, all the while expecting some monster to come charging from the night.

As much as she wanted to thank this female, Tyreta knew it was pointless. She doubted they would understand each other anyway. Better to get on with the job of survival and save the thanks for later. With luck she'd live long enough.

ROSOMON

She had stood at the end of the promenade for so long watching the ark disappear into the clear western sky. Not until night had fallen and that sky turned black did she force herself away from the edge, taking the long walk back to the rotunda. Deep in her heart, Rosomon had hoped the ark would return, the Maladorans realising their mistake and bringing her son back to her. They had not come. All she had faced was the cold wind, freezing her to the bone as she stood alone in the dark.

Rosomon entered the palace rotunda, refusing to return to her room. Refusing to eat or sleep. She simply sat in the round hall, staring at the fire that burned in its centre. Her boy had been torn from her. All the power of the Hawkspur Guild and she had to stand there and watch as those demon worshippers stole him away.

No one spoke to her as she sat before the fire. No one dared. But what would they have said? Empty words of condolence were worthless. Even genuine concern would only have fallen on deaf ears. But who would have voiced genuine concern for her? Rosomon had no friends here, that much was obvious. Even her own brother was more interested in matters of state and the coffers of his Guild than the well-being of his own kin.

If only Rosomon could be so single-minded. If only she could put the business of her Guild before all else. But that had never been Rosomon's way. She had inherited the Hawkspur Guild by marriage. She had not been born to it like Sullivar. Her children had always come first. Even now, even when Fulren had been tried and condemned, she could not accept it. There had to be something she could do. Some way she could fix this.

The fire suddenly crackled at her, spitting sparking wood onto the stone tiles at her feet, but still she felt cold to her core. There would be no answers in the dancing flames. Rosomon had to find her answers elsewhere.

She stood, pulling her shawl tight around her shoulders. It was her only protection against the cold…against anything. She had dismissed Starn hours ago, and suddenly she felt the need to have him close by. Fulren's words began to echo in her head.

Trust no one.

There could be enemies all around. Conspirators ready to do her as much harm as they had done her son. She would summon Starn later. For now she had to find answers on her own.

Rosomon left the rotunda. The hour was late—or perhaps early, she could not tell—and as she made her way down through the palace, the corridors and grand halls were all but deserted. None of the Titanguard paid her any heed as she walked down into the depths of the palace, past the kitchens preparing bread for the coming day, down to the sublevel workshops of the Archwind Guild. The pungent smell of the forges was still in the air, the heat that warmed the palace more palpable here.

A custodian dozed in a chair at the entrance, his gentle snoring the only sound. His red uniform was undone to the nipples, revealing his grey chest hairs, and a line of drool ran from his bottom lip down his chin.

"Show me to Fulren's workshop," she pronounced.

The old man snorted, sitting up in his seat as though he'd been awake all the time. In his stupor it took him some moments before he recognised Rosomon, after which he shot to his feet, wiping his chin and straightening his jacket.

"Yes, my lady. Of course," he said.

He plucked a lantern from its stanchion and fumbled with the bunch of keys at his side before opening the huge doors that led into the warren of workshops.

The forges burned low, but the main hall was still stiflingly hot. Row upon row of workbenches lined the room, disappearing off into the shadows. Rosomon followed the custodian, past the abandoned apparatus and half-finished metalwork. On any other night it would have fascinated her, but not this night. There were more pressing matters that required her attention.

At the far end of the hall, the custodian unlocked another door and led Rosomon through a maze of corridors. Finally he reached a single door in the deepest part of the burrow, unlocking it before beckoning Rosomon to follow him inside. When he had lit a pyrestone lamp and illuminated the cell-like chamber, Rosomon ordered him to wait for her outside.

For long moments she gazed at the room and its contents. Evidence of her son's labours lay all about—hastily scrawled workings, pieces of unfinished artifice. It was as though Rosomon might be able to absorb some part of him by standing here, as though a shade of her son still existed in the room. But he was gone, and all that remained were remnants—mechanical gewgaws of which she had little understanding.

She needed to focus. Rosomon had not come here to lament. There might be something here that would offer a clue as to who had really assassinated the emissary. Or at least direct her to one of the conspirators of whom Fulren had spoken.

Methodically she began to search through the drawers of every workbench and cabinet. Inside she found neatly stacked notes on the workings of artifice, on hydraulics and pneumatics, equations for calculating power inputs and outputs, treatises on the nature of pyrestone and the limits, or otherwise, of its use. Nothing that might lead her to the real killers.

Rosomon felt her heart sink as she searched on, her frustrations growing as all she found was more evidence of her son's diligence. Her eyes began to fill with tears, her anger growing until she wrenched open the final drawer in the final bureau.

Atop a pile of papers sat a small sheathed knife. The weapon he had told her about. Rosomon took it out of the drawer, unsheathing it and holding it up to the scant light. It looked like any other weapon—six inches of bare steel, the grip bound in black leather, the stub guard wrought of plain iron. An altogether unremarkable thing compared to the skilled works of artifice that filled the rest of the room.

Rosomon placed it back in the sheath and made to return it to the drawer before pausing. Fulren had asked her to take the weapon. It had been his last request. How could she refuse it now?

Secreting the knife beneath her shawl, Rosomon left the room. The waiting custodian guided her back through the workshops, and she thanked him for his help before making her way up through the palace. When finally she reached her chamber and closed herself in, she had to fight back the tears.

There would be a way to put this right. There had to be. She just had to keep searching.

A sharp knock on her door broke Rosomon's reflection. It was the dead of night. Who could be visiting at this hour?

She grasped Fulren's knife tightly beneath her shawl. He had warned that she was in danger, and Rosomon could not ignore her son's words. She wondered whether it would be wise to open her door at such an hour, but then Rosomon was not about to shy from confrontation. If it was someone come to murder her she would face them, and to the Lairs with the consequences.

She turned the handle, peering through the gap at the dark corridor beyond. The tall frame of Lancelin Jagdor stood silhouetted in the dim lantern light. The swordwright of the Archwind Guild.

The Hawkslayer himself.

Rosomon opened the door wide, turned without inviting him in, and placed the knife down on the dresser. She heard him enter, closing the door gently.

"It's late," she said, without turning.

"Yes," he replied. "My apologies. But I thought you would appreciate discretion."

"Of course you did," she replied.

The man who had slain her husband in ritual combat had nothing more to say. But then, words were not Lancelin's strong suit.

"You know about Fulren?" she asked.

"Of course. The whole city knows."

"And does the whole city think him guilty? Do you?"

"I... I cannot believe he would be involved," Lancelin said.

"And yet your lord and master still had him sent away with those monsters. Sullivar, my own brother, condemned his nephew to death."

"I'm sorry, Rosomon. For what it's worth, I doubt it was an easy decision for Sullivar to make."

She laughed humourlessly. "Still so loyal, aren't you, Lancelin. You're blinded by it, you always were."

Rosomon turned to see him looking awkwardly at the floor, unable to hold her gaze. He didn't have the sword he always carried at his hip and looked virtually naked without it.

"So why have you come here at such an hour, swordwright?"

He stared deep into her eyes as though steeling himself for what was to come. "You know why," he replied.

Rosomon rushed to him, throwing her arms around his neck and kissing him hard on the mouth. At first he stood there, letting her lips press firmly against his until he could resist no longer. He succumbed, grasping her firmly about the waist and lifting her, returning her kiss, their tongues entwined.

When they parted she was reeling, heart drumming in her chest. "I've been here for days, what kept you so bloody long?"

"There was never a right time," he replied.

It was a flimsy excuse, but Rosomon was done caring. He could have kept her waiting a hundred years and she would have forgiven him for it.

She kissed him again, pulling him toward her bed. They both fell on it, wrapped in each other's arms, breath coming fast and fevered. Rosomon began to tear at his clothes and Lancelin stopped her.

"Are you sure?" he said. "What about—?"

She silenced him by pressing her fingers to his lips. Typical Lancelin. Always the gallant one. Always thinking about her first. She had to admit she had missed it.

"Yes, I'm sure," she replied. "Now stop talking and kiss me."

He obeyed, and as they lost themselves in one another Rosomon began to forget about her son, about conspiracies, about the danger she was in. She needed this release, however momentary. Needed to drift away in her lover's arms, if only for one night.

Their lovemaking was as she'd always remembered it. Her urgent need tempered by Lancelin's patience. She had so missed his gentle touch, his strength and his passion.

When it was over, the sun was beginning to rise, and she gazed out at the bruised sky through her chamber window. Lancelin gently kissed her shoulder, his hand tracing a line of perspiration down her waist to her hip, where it lingered for a moment.

"I've missed you," he whispered.

That brought a smile to Rosomon's face. But then Lancelin had always made her smile no matter how deep her sadness.

She turned, rolling into his arms, her hand teasing the wispy hair of his chest. Some of it was turning to grey.

"It's been too long," she whispered.

"It can't be helped," he said.

And he was right. They were condemned to steal passing moments together, as they always had been.

Rosomon and Lancelin had met when they were not yet thirteen summers old. She had instantly fallen in love with the implacable youth. Though a commoner of no name, he had possessed more nobility than any Guild-born heir. She had pursued him despite his seeming disinterest in her. Or perhaps because of it. And eventually she had won him. It was a love they both knew was impossible, but they had persisted with their secret affair until her father had arranged a betrothal to Melrone. An expedient union between the Archwind and Hawkspur Guilds.

Of course, she had raged against it. Vowed to herself she would not marry Melrone, that she and her lover would run away together, but as always Lancelin had taken the principled stance. He could not flee with Rosomon. He would not ruin her future or dishonour her name. And so she had been sent to Wyke to become a Hawkspur, and Lancelin had joined the Seminarium to dedicate himself to the Archwinds as a swordwright.

Though they were parted by five hundred miles, their love had still endured, their need for one another never waning.

Rosomon rose from the bed, donning the nightgown that lay over the back of her chair. As she and Lancelin had made love she hadn't noticed the cold night air, but now the morning breeze chilled her. The respite her lover had given was over now. She was back to reality. Back to the prospect that she might never see her son again.

"He will be over the Drift by now," she said, staring out of the window, the distant horizon just visible against a dark sky.

She heard Lancelin moving from the bed. "You shouldn't torture yourself like this," he replied.

Rosomon turned on him, the spark of anger she had so long been quelling bursting into flame inside her. She knew she shouldn't take it out on him, but there was no one else. And he would endure it for her.

"What else am I supposed to do?" she spat. "He was innocent and they still took him. Sullivar stood by and did nothing and now my son is gone..." She took a breath. "Our son, Lancelin."

He closed his eyes, letting out a long sigh, and Rosomon instantly felt regret at her words. She had not meant to punish him for all this. He must have been hurting as much as she was.

"I don't need reminding, Ros."

Of course he didn't. He had to live every day knowing he had a son, their son, but he could never acknowledge it. They could never have told anyone, least of all Fulren.

Rosomon had done her duty, had wed Melrone and united the most powerful Guilds in Torwyn. But she had suffered for it. Her husband had been dutiful at first, though it was obvious he never loved her. When she had given him a son, Melrone had seemed joyous enough, pouring much attention on young Conall. But after Tyreta's birth he had lost all interest in Rosomon, in his family and even in the Guild. Melrone had been interested in nothing but hedonism, and Rosomon had endured his drunkenness, his abuse. She had turned a blind eye to his dalliances with every whore and handmaid he could find.

And neither had she cared.

She found herself living for the days when she could travel to the Anvil, could meet in secret with Lancelin. Those moments had been precious to her, and she had coveted them like a miser. Until she found herself with child once more.

There was no way to hide her infidelity from Melrone. He had not touched her since Tyreta's conception. His retribution for her betrayal had been swift. There was nothing Rosomon could do to quell her husband's rage, and he had beaten her almost to death, kicked her ripe belly and vowed to kill the child on the day it was born.

In her desperation Rosomon had told him who the real father was in the hope that Lancelin's reputation would subdue Melrone's rage. He had just laughed.

"Sullivar's attack dog," he had called Lancelin, and named her a whore for debasing herself with such lowborn scum. In the sober light of the next day Rosomon had hoped Melrone would see sense—would at least offer a divorce. Instead he had challenged the swordwright to ritual combat. Lancelin was powerless to refuse, not that he would have. Seeing the bruises still raw on Rosomon's face, he had accepted the challenge without question. The duel was held, and Melrone had fought with all the rage he could muster. But rage was not enough to defeat a swordwright, and Lancelin Jagdor earned himself the name Hawkslayer.

"You know if there was anything I could do..." Lancelin said.

Rosomon moved toward him, placing her hands on his strong chest, feeling the scars there. Scars he had earned fighting on the borders of Torwyn and duelling the enemies of an unworthy emperor. He looked back at her with those brown eyes she had fallen in love with so many years ago.

"There is something you can do," she replied.

As soon as she said it she felt the guilt bite hard at her heart. What she was about to ask he would not refuse, despite the fact that it would almost certainly lead to his death. But she had to ask it. If Fulren was to have any chance at all, Lancelin was the only hope.

"Name it," he said.

She closed her eyes, taking a breath before condemning the man she loved.

"Go to Nyrakkis," she said. "Find our son and bring him home."

Rosomon expected some reluctance, some doubt. Perhaps even refusal. After all, Lancelin's first duty was to Sullivar.

"Very well," he replied. "I'll do it."

Rosomon looked into her lover's eyes. He had already sacrificed so much. Already done all he could to protect her and her son, and never once asked for a thing in return.

"Are you sure?"

He kissed her one last time. A long and lingering kiss that Rosomon could have hung on to forever. But nothing was forever.

Without another word Lancelin dressed and left her room before the morning sun had risen over the distant horizon.

Rosomon sat back on the bed, running her hand across the sheets, feeling the warmth Lancelin had left behind. She wanted to weep, to give in to her pain and cover that bed in tears, but the time for tears was over.

Now it was time to discover the truth of all this.

TYRETA

Morning brought a welcome heat, turning the cold air humid. Tyreta's saviour walked ahead a few paces, every now and again pulling a leaf from a hanging vine and stuffing it in her mouth, chewing it in her powerful jaws like a cow at the cud. Watching the woman eat did nothing for Tyreta's appetite as she stumbled along behind, hand clamped tight to her shoulder. The claw wound stung intensely, the pain almost maddening, but she gritted her teeth against it. She had to keep moving, ignore the discomfort, survive.

There was no point trying to ask where they were going, the woman couldn't understand her. Tyreta could try explaining later that there would be a hefty reward for returning her to New Flaym. For now she just wanted to put as much distance between herself and the kesh hunters as possible.

They eventually left the jungle, coming out onto a rocky promontory. The huntress walked to the lip of the rock and peered over the edge, then back at Tyreta, beckoning her closer while still munching on those leaves.

Tyreta followed her to the edge, gazing at the endless green vista that surrounded them. From atop the high rock all she could see was jungle. No coastline and certainly no city. Whichever direction

New Flaym now lay in, it was miles away. For a fleeting moment, Tyreta wondered if she would ever see it again, but she expelled that notion from her head. She knew such thoughts would only lead to despair, and she had to stay hopeful. It wasn't easy, though, exhausted as she was, in pain as she was. Right now, all she wanted to do was curl up and die, but she couldn't let despair kill her where the kesh had failed.

The huntress spoke, the mashed-up leaf pulp still visible in her mouth. It would have turned Tyreta's stomach if she'd had anything in it to turn. The kesh motioned for Tyreta to sit on a rock beside her, and she obeyed, too fatigued to argue.

Gently the kesh removed the bandage covering Tyreta's wound. It was stupid to look, but Tyreta couldn't help herself, and the sight of the congealed blood and torn flesh immediately nauseated her. The kesh didn't seem to notice as she reached into her mouth and pulled out some of the mashed leaves she'd been chewing. Gently but firmly she pressed the mush against Tyreta's arm. It stung, and Tyreta had to grit her teeth against the pain, breathing in sharply as the female covered the wound in leafy slop.

Tyreta had to admit she was a good nursemaid, seeing to that wound as swiftly and painlessly as she could. She even made soothing noises as she administered the poultice and tied off a fresh bandage. When the kesh had finished, she smiled at Tyreta, clearly pleased with her work.

"Thank you," Tyreta said.

The kesh nodded with a fang-toothed grin. "Welcome," she replied.

That was unexpected. "You speak my language?" she asked in amazement.

The kesh woman raised finger and thumb an inch apart. "Little."

Tyreta pointed a finger to her chest. "I am Tyreta," she said. "Tyreta." She spoke the name slowly before realising she was not talking to an idiot.

The kesh nodded, pointing at her own chest. "Gelila," she replied.

"It's good to meet you, Gelila."

Before she could answer, the kesh's attention was drawn by

something in the distance. She stood, peering out across the jungle as though she had heard a noise, then quickly gathered her things, speaking more words in the kesh language that Tyreta couldn't comprehend. She got the idea: there was still danger close by and they had to keep moving.

They pressed on across the rocky ground. Gelila offered Tyreta a waterskin and she drank deeply from it, savouring the taste of the tepid water. The going was hard, the rocky ground no easier to navigate than the jungle, but still Tyreta made no word of complaint.

As they trekked in silence, the events of the previous day returned to her in terrifying flashbacks. The war cry of the kesh warrior, Wyllow's dazed look before he was so brutally beheaded, the splash of his blood.

They had set out from New Flaym so innocently. Had only meant to snatch a day's respite from their responsibilities, and where had it got them? Her cousin was dead, and she had barely escaped with her life. Not that she was in the clear yet.

Tyreta just had to survive. Everyone in New Flaym would know she had gone missing by now. Lady Isleen would have organised a search party, and it wouldn't be hard for it to locate the abandoned stormhulks. Surely it was only a matter of time before she was found and rescued?

But Tyreta could not rely on that. The jungle was huge and infested with all manner of dangers. Even if there was an army out searching, there was no guarantee she'd be found. She had to get herself out of this, it would be foolish to rely on anyone else.

The rocky terrain flattened out. Gelila skipped over it, as lithe as a panther. Tyreta followed as best she could, but she was like a floundering donkey by comparison. Out in the open she was a feast for flies and found herself slapping at her neck and forearms to slay the beasts before they could suck her dry. The scrub that curled from the rocky ground snaked around her legs, threatening to trip her with every step. Still she followed Gelila, determined not to succumb to the environment no matter how poorly it treated her.

This kesh seemed much better suited to the terrain. Tyreta noticed her body was scarred, but not just with wounds from battle, of which there were many. Her flesh was marked with twisting patterns from some kind of ritual scarification. Those whorls had long since healed into something quite beautiful.

They walked for most of the day, the heat becoming almost unbearable until eventually they reached the thick jungle once again. The shade of the canopy offered some relief, but Tyreta's strength was beginning to wane. She leaned against a tree, her legs shaking, and Gelila stopped, looking back at her curiously as though she couldn't understand why Tyreta was lagging.

"I just need to rest awhile," Tyreta said.

Gelila gestured up ahead. "Not far."

Tyreta hoped she was right, unsure of how much longer she could go on. She steeled herself, staggering after the kesh once again.

She didn't have to follow for long before they came out of the jungle. The ground rolled down to a shallow river, and Tyreta let out a murmur of relief when she saw more figures moving between crudely erected huts.

Gelila took Tyreta's arm, half guiding, half carrying her down the slope to the settlement. The smell of campfires carried on the wind, along with the aroma of fresh meat. When they reached the edge of the camp, she heard high-pitched laughter, and at the river's edge saw three kesh women washing in the water, children frolicking around them and splashing in the shallows.

As soon as Tyreta reached the edge of the settlement there were cries of warning. Figures appeared from some of the huts, approaching warily as Gelila helped her walk. An older kesh woman approached, and they exchanged brief words before she ran off to the far reaches of the village.

Gelila lowered Tyreta to the ground as a group of inquisitive youngsters gathered. They looked like any other group of children but for the feline aspect to their faces and the markings on their downy flesh. Each one seemed to regard Tyreta with a mixture of fear and curiosity, none of them getting too close. She wanted to smile at them, to show them she meant no harm, but there was no energy left to make pleasantries.

Before long a large kesh female appeared, walking toward them with purpose. She was surrounded by smaller females, each one carrying a weapon and covered in ritual scars, the patterns covering their bodies like the most intricate of tattoos. She spoke to Gelila, her words harsh as she gestured toward Tyreta. For her part, Gelila seemed at a loss to explain why she had brought this outsider into their midst. As they spoke, Tyreta realised there was a complete absence of males within the settlement but for a few small boys peering from behind their mothers' legs.

Before Tyreta could think how to explain herself, the lead female stepped forward, taking Tyreta by the arm and hauling her to her feet. The woman's strength was tremendous, and even had she not been exhausted, Tyreta doubted she could have done anything to resist her.

Unceremoniously she was marched through the village, the curious crowd growing with every step.

"There's no need to be so rough," Tyreta managed to say before the huge female bundled her into one of the huts at the far end of the settlement.

She fell to her knees, breathing in the deep, musky smell of the dwelling. Mud caked the walls, and trinkets of bone and shell hung from the ceiling on leather cords. Beneath her was a rug of animal skin, and the pelt of a panther hung from the wall.

Outside she heard the big kesh female quarrelling with Gelila. Their voices rose to a crescendo until all of a sudden they ceased their argument. All Tyreta could hear was the sound of her own breath until another voice spoke. This one was croaky and old and spoke their guttural tongue with purpose.

The hide that covered the hut entrance was pulled back. The big kesh woman ducked as she entered, glaring down at Tyreta with barely subdued fury. After her came an old woman, yellow-and-blue chiton covering her to the knee, gaudy golden brooches linked by tiny chains pinned all over the material. Gelila came in after, looking somewhat sheepish.

"It's my fault," Tyreta said, done with being silent. "It wasn't her fault. She saved me."

She gestured to Gelila, but it seemed to do little good. The big kesh said something to the old woman, who simply raised a hand for her to be silent. She motioned at Tyreta, speaking low and calmly in kesh, her voice like gravel.

"I don't understand," Tyreta said. "But if being here is a problem, I'll just leave."

She tried to stand, but the big woman moved forward threateningly, pulling a short axe from the fur-and-skin belt at her waist. Gelila rushed forward and the two struggled for a moment, shouting as though they might kill one another. A single word from the old woman and they instantly stopped their bickering.

"Look, I don't mean to cause any trouble." Tyreta held out her hands, trying to placate them.

Gelila said something, probably trying to explain that Tyreta was no threat. Ignoring her, the old woman moved forward and began poking Tyreta like a prize horse. The kesh took her chin in one leathery hand, raising Tyreta's head. Her eyes were rheumy and ancient, but they still seemed to look right into Tyreta's soul. Her breath was sweet like cloves, and Tyreta was starting to feel relaxed under her ministrations until she saw one of her gold brooches move of its own accord.

She squealed, pulling herself away from the old woman's grip when she realised they weren't brooches at all, but insects of varying size and shape. Each had been pinned to a gold carapace and fastened to the woman's chiton by a tiny chain.

In response to her sudden move, the powerful kesh woman lurched forward, axe raised.

"Wait!" All Tyreta could do was hold up her hands, closing her eyes as she prepared for the axe to strike. It didn't.

Opening one eye, she saw the old woman had raised a hand and her attacker was frozen. Her eyes still bored into Tyreta, but she dared not strike without the ancient kesh's permission.

The old woman spoke, only a couple of words, and immediately the two younger women left the hut. As the two of them waited alone in the silence, Tyreta was unsure whether to be grateful or fearful. The crone was staring at her chest, and Tyreta looked down to see the chain that held her nightstone was visible over the top of her shirt. Reluctantly she pulled it out, showing it to the old woman.

"It's a family heirloom," she said, letting it dangle between her fingers. "For what it's worth."

"Kiatta," said the old woman, gesturing to the black jewel.

"Yes, yes. Very shiny," Tyreta said.

With speed that belied her years, the woman's hand shot out and she snatched the gem.

"Hey!" Tyreta said, grasping the old woman's wrist before she could break the chain. "It's mine."

"Kiatta," the woman said again.

"I said it's mine," Tyreta snarled, wrenching the nightstone from the old woman's grip. "What's wrong with you people? If you're going to rob me, at least have the decency to do it once I'm dead."

The woman took a step back, a smile creeping across one side of her wrinkled face.

"Oh, did you find that funny?" Tyreta asked. "See how funny you find it when the search party gets here. Then you'll have some explaining to do."

The old woman shook her head. "They not find you," she said.

Tyreta gawped at the old woman, still holding tight to the nightstone. "You speak—?"

"Yes I do," she replied. "It is best to know much about your enemies." She fixed Tyreta with a questioning look. "Or friends?"

"I'm not your enemy," Tyreta replied.

"We see," said the woman, gesturing to the nightstone about Tyreta's neck. "Already you steal from us."

"This?" Tyreta dangled the nightstone in front of her. "It's just a trinket. My father's last gift to me."

"And from where you think he take it?"

It seemed that much was obvious. Nightstone wasn't found anywhere but the Sundered Isles.

"I get it," said Tyreta, struggling to her feet. "He took it from your land so it belongs to you. But you're not having it back. You'll have to take it from my rotting corpse."

The old woman smiled again, clearly unimpressed by Tyreta's defiance. "Not needed," she replied. "You keep. For now."

"How did you learn my language?" Tyreta asked.

"Years ago your people come across sea to trade. We gave fish and meat for gifts of metal. We learn your tongue. Then tribes begin to trade stone. Then we trade no more. Then your people just trick and trap and take. We not forget your tongue. That way we are never tricked again."

The shame of that hit Tyreta hard. The Guilds had treated these people like animals when it was obvious they weren't. But she had also seen the way the kesh had treated her cousin.

"I was attacked... We were attacked," she said. "My cousin was killed. I just—"

"The Chul show no mercy to your people. The Chul fight back. Your people will perish."

"What? What do you mean?"

"War is coming," said the old woman. "Much death."

"Much death? How do you know this?"

"Shabak of the Chul. He unite the tribes... most tribes. They gather for war. They will destroy your city on the sea. Push your people back into the water."

Though the notion seemed implausible, Tyreta had already witnessed the fierceness of the kesh. If there was to be an attack, she had to do something.

"You have to take me back," said Tyreta. "You have to let me warn them."

"Not safe," she replied. "Best you stay here. Rest."

"But I have to get back. To warn my... my people."

The old woman regarded her with those wrinkled eyes. She looked almost sorrowful. With a nod she said, "Very well. You warn them. But go alone."

She gestured to the door as though Tyreta could leave if she wanted to. It was suicide. If she was to survive the journey back she would need a guide.

"Gelila knows the way. She could take me."

"No. Gelila forbidden to leave. You get well. You grow strong. Then go."

It sounded like the best deal she was going to get.

"All right. Then I will leave tomorrow." The old woman seemed satisfied with that. "My name is Tyreta, by the way."

“Yeki of the Lokai,” said the old woman, prodding her withered chest.

“It is good to meet you, Yeki. Are you in charge here?”

“Yes,” the old woman replied.

“And when do your men return?” she asked, curious about the fact that there were only females within the village.

Yeki shook her head. “No men return. Just us.”

“Just you? What happened to your men?”

The old woman looked up at her sombrely. “Shabak of the Chul want to unite the tribes. To fight your people. Lokai refuse. They decide to not fight but talk. Shabak of the Chul saw weakness, not wisdom.” She made a cutting motion across her throat. “No more men.” She moved to the doorway before casting a final glance back. “Now rest. Then go.”

With that Yeki left Tyreta alone in the hut, and she collapsed back to the hide-covered floor.

“Like I’m going to get any rest in a place like this,” she grumbled, gripping the nightstone tight in her fist. She lay on her side and tried to get comfortable on the hard floor. In an instant she was asleep.

FULREN

The wind whipped across the deck of the ark as Fulren looked out on a clear sky. He'd grown used to the sound of the engine as it growled and moaned above the noise of the wind. Not that *engine* was the right word for the thing in its sarcophagus. It was a demon, an unearthly being that propelled the vessel across the sky. A beast from Fulren's darkest nightmares.

Best not to think on that too much. Better to just enjoy the journey while it lasted—things were only going to get worse from here. Right now, the sky was clear, the day beautiful. Though not for everyone.

Fulren glanced across the deck, seeing the dark-eyed arcanists still standing amid the iron sigil. There were four left alive, two more having already perished during the journey. The rest stood impassively, their necroglyphs glowing in sickly shades of yellow and green. Fulren could only pity them. They had been men and women once, with lives of their own. Now they were mindless thralls condemned to die, and for what? To fly this airship across hundreds of miles? What a waste. Fulren would gladly have released them, or at least done something for those damned souls, but what then? Without the arcanists keeping the ark aloft, they would all plummet to their deaths.

As Fulren gazed at them, he knew he should never have become embroiled with the Maladorans. They were steeped in fell magics, and he had been spellbound by Assenah's dark enchantments from the first moment he laid eyes on her. The more he thought on it, the more he realised that everyone around her had succumbed to that glamour. Whatever arcane web she had woven was gone now, and he could see it all clearly. He had been the victim of a ruse, some scheme by Nyrakkis to influence the Guilds, but something had gone wrong. Someone had murdered Assenah before she could complete whatever plot she was hatching, and he had been the perfect scapegoat to take the fall. Good for them... bad for Fulren Hawkspur.

His hand fumbled idly in his pocket, and he pulled out the tiny machine he'd been toying with in his cabin. He had no idea what the device was for, but he'd still managed to rig it with both a blue and a yellow pyrestone. The problem was how to activate the mechanism. There was no housing for the red pyrestone that would regulate its power, nor a switch to turn it on. It was a conundrum, but one that he was determined to get to the bottom of.

"A spectacular view," said Wenis. She'd appeared out of nowhere like a snake from its hole. Fulren was finding it an annoying trait of hers. "One that should be savoured, no?"

He looked out over the gunwale as he slipped the pyrestone device back in his pocket. They were passing over the Drift. Miles of blasted land extended as far as the eye could see in every direction, dead ground that separated the nations of Torwyn and Malador. Nothing had grown here for a thousand years, and many scholars theorised that nothing ever would.

"I'm not sure 'savoured' is the right way to put it," Fulren replied, looking down at the endless wastes.

"Ah, but what it lacks in aesthetic charm it more than compensates for in historical significance. This land denotes freedom for all of Malador. It speaks of sacrifice, rebirth. You can almost smell its legacy."

All Fulren could smell was the brimstone stench of the engine room.

"Rebirth? Hundreds of thousands perished. It was a betrayal."

"Ah yes," said Wenis with her usual wry grin. "Torwyn paints it in different colours. The Age of Insurrection, I believe they call it."

"It was the betrayal of our faith."

"Or the start of it?"

"Cornelium Obek was a traitor and a murderer."

That one knocked the wry smile from Wenis's face. Fulren couldn't help but feel a certain satisfaction.

"Very well, Fulren. How do the historians of Torwyn tell the tale?"

Fulren thought back to his earliest lessons on the war of Archmages. His old tutor had made him study it well. A cautionary tale if ever there was one, and the reason the practice of unregulated magic had been abolished throughout the nation.

"Obek was an Archmage. A trusted member of the Council of Nine. He was also a necromancer. Over years he built up his cabal in secret, performing fell rites, murdering his rivals, plotting his ultimate conquest of all Hyreme."

Wenis nodded her agreement. "A pioneer," she said.

"A degenerate," Fulren replied. "A traitor whose plot was almost discovered too late. By the time the Ministry uncovered his plans he had gathered support in every province of the old world."

"United a movement that stood against the tyranny of your Draconate Ministry." Wenis seemed to take some delight in correcting him on his interpretation of history. "A religious order whose influence is now thankfully waning."

Fulren couldn't argue with her point about the Ministry. "United at what cost?"

"Revolutions are never bloodless, Fulren."

That much was certain. Obek was said to have gathered about him a powerful army. It faced the might of the Ministry, and the five Great Wyrms of the Draconate were summoned to fight its demon magics. The war was devastating. It ended in a cataclysm that split Hyreme in two and left Obek's Drift in its wake—a vast expanse of wasteland where nothing could grow. All that existed there were twisted, misbegotten creatures and desperate exiles. To be banished to the Drift was the cruellest of executions.

"You would know that best of all," Fulren said. "Malador has seen more than its share of uprisings, has it not?"

"True enough. And how much do you know of that?"

Fulren shrugged. "Not much. I don't have to tell you that contact between our nations has been scant over the past few centuries. There are rumours, but it's obvious enough that the all-powerful empire Obek envisioned never came to pass. Now Malador is split—"

"Obek's mistake was to share his power," Wenis interrupted, clearly keen to fill in the details. "He chose allies to rule alongside him. The Nine were supposed to bring order to Malador, but their petty rivalries ultimately led to Malador's sundering." Wenis spoke with relish. Fulren had not seen her so enthused, not that he was about to complain. This was a story he did not know. "Huntan was the first to break from the Nine. He took his followers north to the tundra, so the Nine became Eight. Smelling betrayal on the air, Obek tried to seize back control from the others, he could foresee the tensions between them and their lust for power, but by then it was too late. Obek was murdered, though it is not known by whom. His loss created a rift among the remaining seven, a second civil war that ended with the division of Malador. The four great Scions still share dominion over Iperion Magna, while Nyrakkis has but one ruler."

"Your queen?" Fulren said. "Said to be one of those original Archmages, who slew her two remaining rivals to seize the throne for herself. A likely story."

"You doubt the truth of it?"

"I don't believe anyone could live for a thousand years."

Wenis laughed. "You think a small thing such as age would stop Queen Meresankh? You think it would stop the Scions?"

"Everybody dies," said Fulren.

"Do they?"

With that wry smile still firmly affixed to her face, Wenis beckoned Fulren to follow her. She led him back inside the aftcastle and down to what looked like a small storage chamber. When she motioned him inside, he realised it was anything but.

Countless bags of herbs had been strung from the ceiling, giving the room a pungent aroma. Laid out on a slab in the centre of the chamber was a body, tightly wrapped in strips of linen. One of its arms was missing.

"Assenah?" Fulren said.

"The very same," Wenis replied.

"But she's...Are you going to try and tell me she isn't dead?"

"Of course not. She's as dead as the Drift. But that doesn't mean it's the end."

"You can bring her back?"

"No. I cannot. But there may be some way the queen can still commune with her. And that could be good news for you, Fulren."

The prospect of dark magics being used on someone he had known and admired sickened Fulren somewhat, but if it might prove his innocence, he supposed he could suffer it. Before he could ask what such a rite would entail, a bell rang out on the deck.

Wenis rushed for the door. Fulren was surprised at her reaction—she approached pretty much everything with ambivalence, but the bell stoked a fire within her he'd never seen before. He followed her up through the aftcastle and out onto the deck. The bell was louder out in the open as one of the tattooed warriors stood at the forecastle ringing it for all he was worth. When Wenis appeared on deck, he pointed out over the larboard gunwale.

Fulren moved to the side of the ark, staring out into the abyss. In the distance he could see what looked like a flock of birds ascending from the wastes below. As he squinted at the dark silhouettes he could just make out a rider atop each one.

"Reavers," Wenis breathed before turning to the spearmen who had flooded the deck and bellowing, "Defensive positions!"

In response the warriors rushed to their places at the gunwales and at the fore and aft of the ark, arranging themselves into rows ready to repel the raiders.

Fulren watched on helplessly as the reavers came closer. He saw that the flying beasts they rode were not birds but hideous lizards, their leathery wings propelling them ever closer to the ark, stubby heads snaking forward on elongated necks. Each of the riders wore a dark hood and held a cruel spiked lance to the fore like a knight in a joust.

They rose up, flying high above the ark, before gathering into a tight formation. Then, after a shrill cry pealed out from the flock, they swooped to attack.

As the first of the reavers approached the ark, Wenis began to chant. She spoke dark words that issued from the back of her throat, hands forming intricate patterns as a ball of energy coalesced between them. Fulren took a step back as her conjuration reached its climax and she thrust her arms toward the enemy. The dark ball of energy she'd created howled through the sky, leaving a contrail of black mist. It hit a swooping lizard, exploding against its body, tearing off its wing. With a wail of pain the beast plummeted from the sky, bearing its rider into the abyss below.

The rest of the reavers fell upon the ark. As one, the warriors on the forecastle threw their spears in a deadly volley. One of the riders was taken in the chest, but his flying beast ignored the attack. It landed on the deck, half a dozen spears protruding from its hide. The creature's jaws snapped forward, catching one of the warriors in its maw, and with a growl it shook its head before pitching the man overboard. He made no sound as he fell to his death.

The rest of the Maladoran warriors darted forward, curved swords drawn, slashing at the creature, cutting great divots in its hide.

Wenis unleashed another ball of energy, but Fulren could see she was weakening, her second stream of dark magic much less powerful than the first. It still hit a target, but rider and beast absorbed the assault.

The reavers attacked the ark with venom, and the Maladorans fought back with equal zeal. Fulren watched, stunned, as they battled with relentless fury. Blood splashed across the deck, and though the tattooed warriors defended the ark heedless of any danger to themselves, it was obvious they were outmatched. Fulren couldn't just stand by and do nothing.

He rushed to the aftcastle, picking up a fallen blade as he ran. It was well balanced—four feet of curved steel, comfortable in his hand. Fulren took the stairs three at a time, reaching the top ready to face one of the reavers. A single raider awaited him, lance held in a clawlike grip, face hidden beneath his hood. At his feet were the bodies of half a dozen Maladorans surrounding the corpse of his riding beast.

With a hiss the reaver struck forward with his lance. Fulren parried, turning it aside and trying to step within the range of the spiked weapon. The reaver darted back and out of danger. A spear was a vastly superior weapon to a sword at distance, but if Fulren could close with the enemy, his advantage would be lost.

The reaver struck in again, and Fulren blocked, the head of the lance missing his face by inches. Spikes hooked Fulren's blade and the reaver pulled back, wrenching the sword from his grip. He didn't wait for the reaver to strike again, darting forward, ducking the thrusting lance and barging into his opponent at chest height. The reaver fell back against the gunwale with a grunt as Fulren grabbed his throat. He could smell the rotting stink as they struggled, and he squeezed that leathery neck for all he was worth. The reaver's hood fell back, revealing a grotesque face, twisted flesh pulled tight over a prominent skull. Fulren's enemy looked like a walking corpse, piercing red eyes staring at him with unadulterated hate.

With a squawk the reaver swung the butt of the spear, knocking Fulren back and off balance. He staggered, foot catching on the body of a fallen warrior, and he toppled onto his backside. The reaver raised his lance, eyes burning in triumph. Fulren managed to twist aside, rolling across the deck as the lance skewered the wood.

He bent low, picking up a fallen spear. As the reaver wrenched his lance from the deck, Fulren acted on instinct, letting fly with that spear without thinking. His arm was good, the spear impaling his enemy and pinning him to the gunwale.

In that moment Fulren was frozen, looking on in victory at his dead foe. His first kill. Whatever emotion he'd expected to feel after killing a man, this wasn't it. There was just emptiness—no regret, but no elation either.

The ark juddered, and Fulren staggered as the vessel lost altitude. Looking down at the deck, he saw that one of the four remaining arcanists was lying dead, run through by a reaver lance.

Fulren grabbed a fallen sword and vaulted from the aftcastle, dropping down onto the main deck. Violence raged across the ark as the warriors of Nyrakkis fought a losing battle against the raiders. He couldn't see Wenis anywhere. If someone didn't take charge, they would be slaughtered to the last.

"Form ranks. Rally to me," Fulren shouted at the warriors. "Protect the arcanists."

In response the remaining fighters disengaged from the reavers and rushed to the centre of the deck. Fulren had never commanded anyone in battle before, but he was relieved these men understood and obeyed his instructions.

Another of the flying beasts swooped down onto the deck with a thud. Fulren raced toward it, leaping high before the reaver on its back could bring his lance to bear. With a grunt of rage, he hacked through the neck of the beast, spilling black ichor onto the deck. As the creature fell, its rider pitched from the saddle. Fulren darted forward and ran the hooded reaver through before he could recover.

"Protect the ark," Wenis cried above the din.

Fulren saw her standing at the centre of the iron sigil, surrounded by her warriors. Their spears were facing outward, holding back the remaining reavers.

One of the flying beasts soared low overhead, and the rider flung his lance, impaling one of the Maladorans to the deck. Fulren hacked his way forward, cutting down a robed attacker as he charged at the circle of spear-wielding warriors. On seeing Fulren approach, the Maladorans opened up a gap, allowing him inside the iron ring.

There were only three arcanists left alive, and Wenis had joined with them in their chanting, bolstering the spell that kept the ark aloft.

"You have to do something," Fulren shouted over the din of battle.

She glared up at him, doubt in her eyes. "I... I don't know if I'm strong enough," she replied.

The reavers battered at the circle of spears, and another Maladoran warrior fell.

"We don't have time for this," Fulren growled. "You have to act. And act now."

Wenis nodded, heartened by his words, standing as tall and straight as she could. She closed her eyes, lips moving in a silent litany, hands forming arcane shapes in the air. With each new gesture Fulren saw sparks flare between her fingertips.

The atmosphere became heavy with the stink of copper, and as Fulren watched, Wenis began to rise from the deck. There she hovered, three feet above the iron sigil, held aloft by her arcane power. Her eyes sprang open—two dark pits of evil.

In his pocket the pyrestone device suddenly burned.

Fulren pulled the thing out, feeling the heat emanating from it. Something Wenis had unleashed was reacting with the pyrestone, activating the mechanism despite there being no red pyrestone to regulate it. The device trembled as Fulren twisted it in his hand, sliding the circular brace so the conduits lined up. Immediately it began to pulsate, reacting with deadly intent, the pyrestones ready to blow.

"Whatever you're doing," he yelled, "keep it up."

As Fulren flung the thing into the midst of the battling reavers, Wenis raised her hands and clapped them together.

A seismic wave engulfed the deck, blasting outward from the pyrestone device. Fulren was knocked off his feet by the hot wave of arcane energy. He looked up in time to see one of the winged beasts blown over the gunwale as the reaver beside it disintegrated into dust. The devastating wave consumed the raiders in a deathly squall, and Fulren watched in awe as everyone outside the iron sigil was immolated by Wenis's arcane retribution.

When he managed to rise to his feet, Fulren saw the remains of corpses littered the deck; every reaver had been destroyed or had fled. He turned to see Wenis lying in the centre of the arcane symbol. The only figures left standing were the three surviving thralls, still transfixed in their silent vigil.

Fulren helped Wenis to her feet as the rest of the surviving warriors rose gingerly.

"You saved us," he said as she leaned against him.

"I... I didn't know I could—"

"Well, I for one am glad you did."

He led her to the gunwale, where she could rest a moment and recover her senses. Clearly casting such powerful magics had taken its toll on the fledgling sorceress.

The rest of the crew began pitching corpses unceremoniously over the sides of the ark.

"You fought well, Fulren," Wenis said, when she'd got her breath back.

"Well enough to earn a reprieve?" he asked, only half joking.

"If only it were up to me," Wenis replied. "But I'll be sure to report your contribution."

"Why does that not fill me with confidence?"

Wenis could only shrug. "My word will count for little. But rest assured, you will have a chance to prove yourself."

With that she walked unsteadily to the aftcastle, leaving him among the corpses to wonder exactly what that meant.

CONALL

They'd left Agavere in good spirits. Six wagons pulled by teams of Karna bulls, packed with troopers of the Phoenix Battalion along with Conall's unit of Talon, all crammed in together for the long journey south. There had been a feeling of excitement—they were finally going to see the frontier and earn their pay. They'd even sung songs as they left the port behind them. After two days on the road the songs had fallen silent, and their good spirits had drifted away like an old man's memories.

"My throat's so dry I could drink my own—"

Conall handed Sted the dregs in his canteen before she could tell him exactly what. She took a sip and handed it back. He could understand how she felt; he'd never been so thirsty. South of Agavere was nothing but desert, and without the cool sea breeze to take the edge off it, the sun was relentless.

"We'll be there soon," he said, though in reality he had no clue if they were even close. The journey from Agavere to Fort Tarkis was supposed to take two days, but still there was no sign of their destination. Conall was heir to the Guild that organised transportation across the length and breadth of Torwyn, and here he was lost in the desert. Best keep that fact to himself lest he lose the respect of the men in his unit. Not that they'd hold much love for him after he'd led them across endless tracts of dust and sand with no sign of reprieve. He would have understood if they'd wanted to lynch him.

There was a shout from the front of the column. Conall stood up in the cart, squinting into the distance. Something was approaching from up ahead.

"Pull to the side," ordered one of the battalion sergeants, and the six drivers urged the bulls to move over as they dragged the wagons off the road. There they waited as another team of wagons approached.

When they drew level, Conall could see the wagons were packed with troopers. Every last man was wounded, some lying on their backs, flies dancing around their soiled bandages. Others sat with dressed head wounds, others had missing limbs. The stench of rot hit Conall as they passed by, and he fought the urge to gag. No one spoke as they watched the forlorn passengers, there was no word of greeting, no encouragement, no warnings.

"That what we've got to look forward to?" Sted asked as their wagons moved on once more.

Conall didn't have an answer. He'd known this wouldn't be easy, the violent reputation of the Karna Frontier was renowned, but he hadn't expected to be greeted by the reality of it so quickly.

Night was falling by the time they reached Fort Tarkis. It loomed ahead, black and indomitable against the star-filled sky. Though not as mighty as the ancient forts that defended Torwyn from the Drift, it was still an imposing sight. The flags of the Phoenix Battalion flew proudly, if a little tattered, atop the ramparts.

As the wagons pulled up to the main gate there were shouts of greeting from within. A row of troopers bearing splintbows watched them from the battlements as the gates were unbarred and the column of wagons trundled into the main courtyard.

Conall wasted no time jumping down, desperate to stretch his legs. Sted climbed down beside him, chewing on another piece of redstalk as they surveyed the fort.

"Looks secure enough," she said, taking in the forty-foot walls that surrounded them.

"It does. Didn't seem to do those men on the road much good, though, did it?"

Sted shrugged. "Guess we'll just have to be careful."

"I'm always careful."

She raised an eyebrow at that, and before Conall could protest they were approached by an officer of the battalion.

He was tall and surprisingly well turned out considering the remoteness of the fort and its lack of facilities. His uniform was black with red-and-yellow trim, a rising phoenix emblazoned on the chest. At his hip was holstered a pistol, its handle polished to a sheen and worked in intricate brass. A rare and precious weapon for a lowly captain of the Armiger to be carrying.

"Captain Hawkspur. I am Captain Westley Tarrien of the Phoenix Battalion. Good to have you with us."

"Good to be here," Conall lied.

"You and your men are billeted in the eastern barracks room. Apologies in advance for the smell, until recently we were using it as an infirmary."

"I assume that was for the men we passed on the road?" Conall asked, unable to get the vision of severed limbs and festering wounds out of his head.

"Yes. We suffered a lot of casualties recently. We've been waiting on reinforcements for a month now, so you can imagine our relief when we heard you were coming."

"You can rest easy now, Captain. I assume Frontier Marshal Beringer has my orders? Where can I find him?"

"The frontier marshal will speak to you later, I'm sure. For now you and your men should settle in." Tarrien gestured to the building that butted up to the eastern wall.

With that he saluted and marched back in the direction from which he'd come. Conall and Sted led the rest of the unit toward the barracks.

"What was that about?" Sted asked quietly. "I'd have thought Beringer would want to greet you personally. Highborn officer such as yourself."

"Maybe he's busy," Conall replied as he opened the door to the barracks room. "I'm sure we'll have time for a chat later—"

He stopped as the smell hit him in the face. The putrid stink of rot rushed out of the bunk room like a hot wind.

"By the Wyrms, that smells like death," said Nevan, clamping a meaty hand over his nose and mouth.

Death was exactly what it did smell like. The place was in disarray, the floor still stained with blood like an abandoned butcher's yard, bloated flies filling the air. It looked as if someone had made a half-hearted attempt at cleaning the place but given up when the task got to be too much for them.

"Ulworth," Conall said, "take some of the men and find mops, buckets, scrubbing brushes, anything you can. This place needs cleaning from top to bottom."

With a nod Nevan went and did as he was told. He returned in short order, and the Talon scouts set about cleaning the place as best they could. Water was in short supply, and the full buckets turned a dirt-red colour in no time. A couple of the men retched as they worked, and the flies plagued them relentlessly as Conall worked up a sweat mucking in. It was almost dawn by the time he deemed the room clean enough for them to rest. When the sun was starting to rise, someone sounded a horn outside to signal morning reveille.

"You have got to be kidding," Sted said, looking forlornly at Conall.

"All right," he said to the scouts. "I know we're exhausted, but we have to make an impression. Dress blues. Move it."

There was a sudden flurry of activity as the dozen Talon soldiers stripped off their desert jerkins and pulled on the uniforms marking them as soldiers of the Hawkspur Guild. When they were done, Conall had them stand to attention. He had to admit, his unit had looked better, and the stink of them was putrid, but it was the best they could do on short notice.

When they filed out of the room and into the courtyard, Conall saw the rest of the garrison was already waiting. Over three hundred men were arranged in neat ranks, their dark uniforms crisp, armour polished. The standard of the Phoenix Battalion stood proudly on the right flank, and on the left was Captain Tarrien, dressed immaculately.

"Get them in order, Lieutenant," Conall said under his breath.

Sted immediately started growling at the Talon soldiers, arranging them alongside the ordered ranks of battalion troopers. Conall moved to stand beside Tarrien, feeling awkward, as though all eyes were upon him, judging him for his tardiness.

"Glad you could join us, Captain Hawkspur," Tarrien said quietly. "I trust your accommodations are suitable?"

Conall could detect the sarcasm in his tone. "Most satisfactory. We had some issues with housekeeping, but nothing we couldn't resolve."

"Good to hear you're settling in."

Before Conall could reply, there was a noise from up on the mezzanine of the northern garrison building. The men visibly stiffened, and Conall glanced up, seeing a door swing wide. Frontier Marshal Beringer stepped out, pausing for a moment as he looked down on the courtyard. His features were broad, hair grey and cut squarely to his scalp. The man was a veteran of a dozen campaigns, that much was written all over his scarred and weathered face.

Beringer surveyed his troops for a moment, and Conall found himself suddenly staring forward rather than be caught in that gaze. Everyone stood to attention as Beringer made his way down the steps, his heavy tread the only sound echoing around the courtyard.

As the frontier marshal slowly inspected his troops Conall could feel the collar of his dress jacket tighten about his throat. The heat of the morning was stifling, and his body felt grimy beneath his clothes from days on the road. All he wanted to do was tear off his uniform and douse himself in a cold bucket of water. Instead he struggled against the discomfort as Beringer finally reached the rank of Talon scouts.

The marshal paused, sniffing at the stench of them. Hours of cleaning the barracks room had left them all stinking of sweat and grime and worse. Beringer stopped beside Nevan, looking up at the big man with disdain.

"What's that stench, trooper?" Beringer asked, his voice deep and resonant.

Nevan seemed at a loss. "It's…dirt, sir?"

"Dirt?

"Yes, sir."

"You've presented yourself for parade stinking like a latrine?"

Nevan looked around for help, and as much as Conall wanted to defend him, there was nothing he could say. He knew from his reputation that Beringer was not a man to accept excuses. "Yes, sir."

"Get that uniform off," Beringer ordered.

At first Nevan just stood, wondering if he'd heard right, but when it became clear Beringer was serious, he started to undress. They all stood in silence until Nevan had stripped down and stood naked as the day he was born in the middle of the courtyard.

One of Beringer's men appeared carrying a bucket, another had a broom. Before Conall could think to protest, Nevan had been doused in dirty water and was being vigorously scrubbed down. It was clearly a ritual that had been enacted before—a lesson the rest of the men had already learned. To his credit, Nevan stood there and took it all in silence.

"It seems we have new recruits among us," Beringer said, raising his voice for all to hear. "Lessons need to be learned about how we do things. Lessons you'd best learn quickly. But so there's no misunderstanding, let me be clear. Fort Tarkis is at the vanguard of the Karna Frontier. At any time we could be attacked and overrun by the enemy. To survive here you will need to adapt, and fast. Anyone who doesn't fit in won't last the week."

He left that last comment hanging there. Conall couldn't tell whether he was suggesting they'd be killed by the enemy or face some other fate. Either way, it didn't sound pleasant.

"Know this," Beringer continued. "My word is the only word." He fixed his gaze on Conall. "I don't give a damn what your name is or where you're from. I don't care what you've done or where you've been. From now on you serve under the banner of the Phoenix Battalion. You're mine."

There was little doubt what that meant. The Hawkspur name carried about as much weight around here as piss on a strong wind.

"Captain Tarrien."

"Yes, Frontier Marshal," the captain replied.

"Carry on."

With that Beringer turned and left his captain to dismiss the troops. They had finished scrubbing Nevan down now, and he stood naked, skin turning pink, as the rest of the Phoenix Battalion cleared the courtyard and started its daily duties.

Conall led the Talon scouts back to their bunkhouse. It still smelled bad, but nothing like the rotten-corpse stench that had greeted them the night before.

"Frontier marshal seems friendly enough," said Sted, looking at Nevan, his skin bruised and raw from the scrubbing he'd received.

"What were you expecting?" Conall replied. "Kiss and a hug? Beringer was just stamping his authority. Besides, he's right. Unless you want to end up with your head on top of a durrga spear, you'd best heed his words."

"Never thought I'd miss Agavere."

"Agavere's gone," Conall snapped. "Put it behind you. It's time we started acting like soldiers."

Sted nodded sheepishly, and the unit began to change from dress blues into scout uniforms. Conall hadn't meant to be so harsh, but he hadn't slept for two nights and he was already feeling the strain. Besides, they were going to be put to the test here. Their long nights of carousing were a thing of the past.

As his unit busied itself, Conall stepped out of the room. In the far corner of the courtyard an artificer was tinkering with the opened guts of a stormhulk. Up above, the walls were heavily patrolled, a tower in each corner of the complex manned by a spotter. Archers with splintbows guarded every walkway. Four great ballistae were mounted on the southern ramparts. Not even the walls of Archwind Palace were so well manned. The place looked impenetrable, and yet still Conall didn't feel safe. An air of tension surrounded the fortress. A feeling that at any moment they could come under attack.

He flinched as someone shouted, "Gate," from up on the parapet.

Two troopers slid aside the brace that held the gate shut, and as it slowly opened, the sound of drumming hooves heralded a rider. As he trotted into the courtyard Conall was surprised to see he wore a Talon uniform beneath the layer of dust that covered him.

"Captain Hawkspur," the man said, jumping down from his mount.

He breathed heavily, his horse panting, its hide slick with foam.

"Take a moment, man, catch your breath," Conall said.

The scout reached into his saddlebag and produced a note. "This missed you by a day at Agavere." The rider handed him the letter. It bore the winged-talon seal of Hawkspur.

With a nod of thanks, Conall left the rider to take some water and rest. He opened the note, immediately recognising his mother's handwriting. As he read the words, he felt his heart sink deep into his chest. Fulren had been accused and convicted of murdering the Maladoran emissary. Sullivar himself had condemned his brother to exile. What his fate was to be in Nyrakkis, none of them knew. To add insult, there was mention of conspiracy—a plot that Fulren had fallen foul of. Surely that could not be true?

His mother did not explicitly ask Conall to return home, but perhaps he would have to go back? His family had been torn apart. His mother needed him, though she would never have admitted it. But in reality what could he do? He could certainly return to the Anvil, but he did not have the power to see his brother returned to the bosom of Torwyn. Fulren was gone, and there was nothing Conall could do to change it.

He glanced up the stairs to the office of the frontier marshal, wondering if the best thing to do was resign his commission and return home immediately. It was hardly the first conversation he wanted to have with the man. Beringer had made his disdain for Conall's rank and title clear for everyone to hear. And now Conall had to ask the man leave to return to Torwyn, and he'd barely spent the night here.

Conall took the stairs to the frontier marshal's chamber. He paused at the door, considering how his news might be met, but dwelling on that would only make the event all the harder. He knocked.

There was a pause before Beringer's voice echoed from within the room. "Enter."

Conall walked in, standing to attention before the stout wooden desk Beringer sat behind. He saluted, briefly taking in the spartan nature of the chamber, no clutter, everything arranged neatly on shelves.

"Captain Hawkspur," Beringer said. "I wondered how long before you'd come for your assignments. No time at all, it seems. I must say this shows promise."

Not for long. "I received a missive from Torwyn, sir." Conall held out the letter for Beringer to read.

The frontier marshal took it, holding it a distance from his face like a man with failing eyesight and too much vanity to wear reading glasses.

He gave a sigh. "So you'll be leaving us already?"

"As you can see, it's important I return to the Anvil."

"To do what?" Beringer asked.

To do what indeed? To support his mother? To save his brother? Lady Rosomon was the strongest woman he'd ever known. She had never needed anyone's help. And according to the letter, his brother was already gone, there was nothing Conall could do for him now.

"If you look at the letter, my mother believes Fulren was the victim of a plot. There is danger in—"

"There is danger everywhere, Hawkspur. But if you need to run to the safety of your mother's skirts, then be my guest."

"That's not what—"

"When I heard they were sending me a highborn officer, I knew what to expect. Another noble sent to waste my time so he can do a few weeks on the frontier before running back to Torwyn to tell all his courtly friends what a real soldier he is. I just thought you might last a bit longer than one night. Looks like I should temper my expectations in future."

"I have a duty to my Guild, Frontier Marshal."

"And I have a duty to my men. So we both know where we stand. There'll be a consignment of stone running through here tomorrow. I'm sure they'll find room for you in a wagon back to Agavere."

With that Beringer went back to examining the manuscript on his table. The conversation was obviously done.

Conall closed the door behind him on his way out. When he made his way back down to the courtyard, he saw the rider was waiting with a fresh horse.

"Shall I inform Agavere ahead of your return, Captain Hawkspur?" he asked.

Conall gazed around the fort. The air of tension still hung thick. A sense of impending doom. It would have been so easy to leave all this behind. To return to the Anvil and console his mother in her hour of need.

But Conall had spent his life doing the easy thing.

"No," he replied. "Have a message sent back to Lady Rosomon that I have chosen to stay and complete my secondment to the Phoenix Battalion."

The rider nodded before mounting his horse. Conall watched as he galloped back north and the gate was closed in his wake.

He mounted the stairs to the parapet. The sun had risen fully now, and he wanted to view the desert—to take in what kind of place he had just condemned himself to.

Looking out over the battlements, he could see the endless wastes of the Karna Frontier rolling off into the distance. On the horizon, distant mountains crawled up to the red sky. As he scanned the surroundings, he caught sight of something littering the ground to the west. Stone markers were laid out on the ground on myriad mounds. More than he could count. Endless graves.

Had he made a mistake in staying here? It definitely wouldn't be his first. He'd just have to make sure it was his last.

FULREN

The Drift faded beyond the horizon as the ark flew within the borders of Nyrakkis. Fulren had expected a warped landscape, craggy valleys and baleful forests filled with twisted trees clawing at the skies. Something at least akin to the diabolical reputation of Nyrakkis and its demon-worshipping populace. Instead it was a beautiful country.

Green fields rolled off toward every horizon, spotted by verdant copses. Azure rivers meandered across the green, bisecting the distant villages and hamlets that dotted the landscape. If Fulren hadn't known better, he would have assumed he was back in Torwyn. It wasn't until their destination appeared on the skyline that he remembered he was a long way from home.

From his position at the prow, Fulren could see the city of Jubara clinging to the side of a distant mountain range. Its buildings were black like the mountain rock, minarets rising like clawed talons above the tips of the mountain peaks. It was as though the city were determined to prove its dominance over the surrounding land.

As they drew closer Fulren could see more towers spreading from the central spires, rising up to create a metropolis of dark stone. On the outskirts of the city the environment was treacherous. Deep gullies were carved into the earth, creating a system of natural channels that could be crossed only by means of the majestic bridges that spanned them. Fulren realised that Jubara, protected by the mountains to its back and with access limited at the front, would be nigh impossible to besiege.

Wenis leaned against the bulwark, staring down at her city with a look of wonder on her face.

"Have you missed this place?" Fulren asked, wondering how anyone could long to return to such a grim destination.

She turned her attention to him, eyebrow raised curiously. "Jubara is the most fearsome city in all Hyreme. Its queen the most powerful and cunning ruler Malador has ever bred. Treachery and death hide around every corner. To live here is a battle for survival, and you ask me if I have missed it?" That wistful grin crossed her face once more. "I have longed for it like an infant longs for her mother."

They were over the city streets now. Looking down, Fulren could see the black highways teeming with life. The roofs were topped with dark slate, all the buildings interconnected to form a tightly packed warren.

The ark approached the highest of the spires. It was built from what looked like a solid slab of granite hewn from the mountainside. As they soared closer to a huge circular platform, the ark's engine belched a beleaguered cough. Fulren saw another of the arcanists collapse on the deck. There were only two left now, both of them trembling in their effort to keep the vessel airborne.

As it landed, the ark bore none of the grace Fulren had seen when it arrived in the Anvil. Now it juddered, stuttering as though it were some dying bird about to plummet from the sky. He gripped tight to the prow as the ark skidded across the platform, churning the stone beneath it before finally coming to rest.

"You are truly honoured," Wenis said, gesturing toward the waiting procession.

Fulren could see a heavy military presence on the platform, a host of warriors surrounding a tall robed figure.

"Do they know?" he asked.

"That Assenah is dead? Of course. The Children of the Crimson Moon know everything."

"This is it then?" he asked, but he already knew the answer.

"It is," she replied. "But try not to look so glum. Your arrival is much anticipated, and you don't want to ruin such an auspicious event with your sad little face."

Wenis grinned as she led him down from the forecastle. The remaining arcanist thralls had collapsed, their duties now at an end, as well as their lives. Fulren should have felt at least some sorrow at their passing, but he did not pity them anymore. Their suffering was over. Best he think about himself now, and what awaited him within the dark tower.

The front of the ark yawned open, allowing them to walk out onto the platform as a hot wind whipped up the black-and-silver pennants that billowed all around them. Fulren could not discern what sigil they flew, but it looked like some diabolical symbol, similar to that within the iron circle on the ark's deck.

He followed Wenis to the waiting contingent, and the robed figure in its midst took a step forward. He was decked in black from head to foot, all that showed was his white-painted face peering from within a tightly drawn cowl.

"Lord Fulren," he said with a bow. "It is a pleasure to have you as our guest. I am Ak-Samtek, grand vizier to Queen Meresankh. I trust your journey was not too troublesome?"

"Your guest?" Fulren said. "I thought I was your prisoner?"

"He's just being polite," Wenis said. "That's what he does."

Ak-Samtek ignored her, forcing a black-toothed smile. "Your accommodations have been prepared. If you would like to follow me."

Before the grand vizier could lead him from the platform, a procession of tattooed warriors walked by, bearing the linen-bound corpse of Assenah Neskhon atop their shoulders. Ak-Samtek and his guards paused, bowing their heads in respect as the emissary was borne inside the huge tower. Once they had passed, Ak-Samtek and his guardians led the way inside. Fulren had no choice but to follow.

"See you soon, Lord of Hawkspur," Wenis said.

He offered her a curt nod, hoping she was right. Not much of a gesture, but it was all he had to offer right now with the fear that was twisting his gut into knots.

The interior of the tower was brightly lit with burning braziers, but it did little to penetrate the cavernous hall. Red marble columns soared up into the shadows, and Fulren couldn't shake the sense that he was being watched from the darkness as Ak-Samtek led him through the labyrinthine tower.

Eventually they reached an opulent chamber. The biggest bed Fulren had ever seen rested on a raised dais, and huge glass doors opened onto a wide veranda offering the most magnificent view of Jubara's soaring spires.

"I trust you will find this to your satisfaction?" asked the grand vizier.

Fulren could barely believe the lavishness of the place. He doubted Emperor Sullivar himself was privy to such grandeur. "Yes, absolutely."

"Fresh clothes and a meal will be brought for you later. I hope you will be able to rest well before tomorrow."

"Why, what happens tomorrow?" Fulren asked.

"Your judgement, Lord Fulren," the grand vizier replied, as though the answer were obvious. With another bow he left Fulren alone in the chamber.

Fulren opened the huge glass doors, walking out onto the veranda. The wind still blew, but in the shelter of the veranda it was little more than a warm breeze. He looked out onto the city, surrounded by every comfort he could wish for, and couldn't help but feel he was being lulled into a stupor, much like a pig before the slaughter. Whatever the Maladorans' motives, Fulren wasn't about to pass up the chance to rest. He might not get another.

His food was brought by silent servants dressed in simple togas of white and red. Fulren ate the platter of sweet meats and spiced vegetables. It was the most delicious thing he'd ever tasted.

Afterward he lay down exhausted on the huge bed. Sleep came easily, despite the prospect of what the next day might bring, and when he woke in the morning the same servants were filling a bathtub with steaming water. Once he'd bathed he found a pile of fresh clothes waiting for him—stout boots with a tunic and leggings of Hawkspur blue. At least if he was to be executed, it wouldn't be in rags.

When he'd dressed, there was a knock at the door. He opened it, surprised that it was not locked, to see Wenis standing in the hall.

"It's time," she said. There was no sign of her trademark grin.

Fulren took a deep breath before following her from the chamber. As they made their way through the brazier-lit corridors Fulren didn't spy any sentries. Neither were there any servants or slaves busying themselves with the drudgery of the tower's upkeep. It was as though the place were abandoned and they the only ones walking the vast tracts of its hallways.

When they finally reached the bowels of the tower, Fulren could hear distant music. The tempo of beating drums grew faster and louder the closer they got.

"What is that?" Fulren asked.

Wenis shrugged. "Looks like they've laid on a welcome for you."

"I thought this was a trial?"

"Who says it isn't?" she replied.

The dark corridor widened. Here the braziers burned brighter, and Fulren could see a row of sentries vigilantly lining the thoroughfare. Ahead the corridor opened out into a vast hall. He could see twisting, writhing figures just past the entrance, dancing to the rapidly beating drums.

Wenis led him out into the cavernous chamber. Burning braziers hung from the walls, bathing the place in warm, red light. The sound of the drums was almost deafening, the drummers arranged in two rows, stripped to the waist, sweating heavily as they beat their instruments as though their lives depended on it.

In the centre of the chamber half-naked figures writhed in a wild dance. They twisted and sidestepped around one another with precision, sheer red silks hanging from their bodies, leaving little to the imagination.

Beyond the dancers stood a huge throne of glimmering rock carved into the wall. Upon it sat a figure who caught Fulren's attention and held it in a steely grip.

She was rake thin but still beautiful, eyes white but for two black pupils that gazed at the dancers as they performed. Atop her head was a silver headdress, spikes splayed out like the tines of a fan, the cobalt blue of her gown contrasting starkly with the white of her flesh. This was undoubtedly Queen Meresankh, ruler of all Nyrakkis and the woman who would lay judgement on Fulren for his alleged crime.

Wenis leaned in to him as Fulren stood gawping at the woman on her throne.

"You are truly honoured," she said above the sound of the beating drums. "The great and good of Nyrakkis have come to witness your judgement."

Fulren dragged his eyes away from Meresankh, seeing the figures who stood at the foot of the throne. Wenis gestured to the man standing at the far left of the gathering.

"That is Bekis Katanen, the Overseer." Fulren saw a tall, athletic warrior bedecked in gold-plated armour. "He is the queen's bodyguard. A man whose influence on her is only challenged by the grand vizier himself."

Fulren could see Ak-Samtek standing next to Bekis Katanen. Surrounding him were a gaggle of what Fulren assumed were more viziers, all dressed identically in their black cowls, white faces peering uncomfortably at the dancing throng.

"Who's that?" Fulren asked when his eyes fell upon a brute of a warrior at the foot of the throne. He was thickly muscled, shaven head shining in the light of the braziers, a massive war maul strapped across his armoured back.

"Ah, Serapion. General of the Medjai—the standing army of Nyrakkis. There is a man with a temper as short as his hair. I would avoid him if I were you."

"And that one?" Fulren motioned to the end of the row. A woman stood there, modestly dressed in comparison to her fellow courtiers. Her black hair hung straight to her shoulders, dark eyes watching every part of the room apart from the performers in front of her.

"Amosis Makareth," said Wenis. "The Bearer of the Silent Key. Head of Meresankh's cabal of arcanists. If General Serapion is the queen's war wolf, Amosis is her venomous spider, ready to strike from the shadows. Her too I would avoid if you value your life... and your sanity."

"And what about you?" Fulren whispered, turning to face her. "What part do you play in all this?"

Wenis raised an eyebrow. "For now I am just your keeper, Fulren."

Before he could ask anything else, the drummers fell silent. As the echo of their last unified beat permeated the air, the dancers fell to the ground, sprawling in a heap, their breathing heavy, silks clinging to their moist bodies.

Ak-Samtek took a pace forward. "Approach, Lord of Torwyn," he said, beckoning Fulren closer. All the pleasantries the grand vizier had displayed the day before were now gone. Here he was nothing but a solemn judge.

Steeling himself for what was to come, Fulren marched toward him as the dancers and drummers scuttled past and out of the huge throne room. Wenis remained in the shadows—it was clear he was on his own now, not that he'd expected any help.

As he approached the throne, Meresankh regarded him with those piercing white eyes. She reminded him of a snake about to strike.

When Fulren was within twenty feet of the throne and the gathered courtiers, he stopped. He clenched his fists at his sides, trying to stop himself from trembling, but with so many auspicious eyes upon him it wasn't easy.

"You have been brought here to answer for the crime of murder," Ak-Samtek continued. "You are accused of killing Assenah Neskhon. Of wilfully attempting to disrupt an accord between the nations of Nyrakkis and Torwyn. How do you answer these accusations?"

Fulren tried to swallow before answering, but his mouth was too dry. "I am innocent," he said, as clearly as he could manage. "I am the victim of—"

"Very well," Ak-Samtek interrupted. "It is time to commune with the witness."

Somewhere behind Fulren a bell chimed. It rang out a monotonous beat, and when he turned he saw a group of warriors bearing a palanquin. At their fore a hooded priest swung a silver censer, wafting pungent smoke before them, but Fulren could still smell the stink of rot as they carried their burden to the foot of the throne. Laid out on the palanquin was what could only be the body of Assenah Neskhon, still wrapped in strips of linen.

Queen Meresankh stood, and the courtiers moved away from the foot of the stairs that led up to the throne. Slowly she descended, her bare feet taking one delicate step after the next. Fulren watched in awe as she moved—there was something ethereal about her, otherworldly. She was encased in an aura that was both alluring and sickening at the same time.

When she reached Assenah's body, Amosis Makareth moved forward. Several other women appeared with her from the shadows, surrounding the palanquin. They knelt, whispering into their hands, saying silent litanies as though praying over the body. Fulren saw necroglyphs spring to life on their flesh, felt the metallic tang in the air as though a storm were brewing inside the confines of the throne room.

Pressure began to fill his head, intensifying till it felt as though it might explode. Suddenly Meresankh thrust her arms forward and, with an agonised gasp, Assenah's corpse convulsed. As though lifted by invisible strings, the linen-wrapped body rose up into Meresankh's welcoming embrace.

Fulren watched in horror as the queen opened her mouth impossibly wide. A stream of glowing mist spewed from that vast maw into the mouth of Assenah's corpse, the two of them locked in some kind of unholy communion—a forbidden kiss of necromantic sorcery.

Then it was over. Meresankh released the body, staggering back as the corpse collapsed back onto the palanquin like a rag doll. Silence filled the throne room.

Bekis Katanen rushed to the queen's side before she could fall, holding her up as she wavered on unsteady legs. She looked into his eyes as though relaying an unspoken message, then he stood back, allowing her to regain her composure.

"Nothing," announced Bekis.

General Serapion took a step forward. "Enough of this," he said, voice deep and sonorous. He pointed an accusing finger at Fulren. "It is obvious this boy is guilty. Even his own people judged him so. Execute him now and we can be done with this—"

He fell silent as Meresankh's gaze fell upon him. It cowed the powerful general, and he stepped back like a scolded whelp. Then silently the queen made her way back up the stone stairs and took her place on the dark throne.

Ak-Samtek paced forward, his fellow viziers at his shoulders. "Lord of Torwyn," he began. "Your guilt is still in question. As such, you will be given the chance to prove your innocence." He then turned to the rest of the queen's court. "The Trial of Ghobeq. What say you?"

Bekis Katanen was the first to nod. "Aye," he replied.

Amosis Makareth was the second to agree, though from her demeanour Fulren doubted she cared one way or the other.

Then General Serapion laughed. "It would have been more merciful to let me crush the pup. Aye."

Ak-Samtek turned back to Fulren. "We are agreed, then. You will face the Trial of Ghobeq on the Night of the Black Moon. Praise Queen Meresankh in her mercy."

That seemed to be the end to it, but Fulren was none the wiser.

"What does that mean?" he asked, but Wenis was already at his shoulder, ushering him away.

As they left the throne room he could contain himself no longer. "What just happened?" he asked, pulling his arm free of her grip.

"You've been given a chance," she replied.

"A chance at what? Another trial?"

She shook her head, her expression solemn. "It's more of a..."

"More of a what?"

Wenis just shrugged. "More of an execution." With that she led him away along the dark corridor.

As thankful as Fulren was to leave the place behind him, he couldn't help but wonder if there was anything he could have done or said to better persuade the queen of his innocence. By the sound of it, things couldn't have gone much worse.

TYRETA

The air was stifling when she woke, and it was difficult to breathe in the confines of the hut. Sunlight lanced in through gaps in the hide sheet that covered the doorway, and she could hear the sound of children laughing outside. Tyreta gingerly wiped at the clammy sheen of sweat on the back of her neck, feeling her heart sink as she remembered all she had gone through to end up here.

Her wound still stung, but the pain had dulled from the day before. She shifted to a sitting position and carefully pulled back the bandage to examine the damage. The flesh of her shoulder was livid and blue, but there was no bleeding, no stink of rot. Whatever Gelila had chewed and stuck to her arm was working. One piece of good news at least.

Before she could think to rise and exit the fusty confines of the hut, the sheet was pulled back, the sun beaming in so brightly she had to shield her eyes. As Tyreta squinted in the blinding light, the diminutive figure of Yeki made her way inside. Despite the old woman's bestial features, there was a look of placid calm about her. If she'd been concerned that Tyreta might have died in the night, she didn't show it. Behind her came Gelila. The young kesh warrior looked much more concerned, but on seeing Tyreta her face softened and she smiled her greeting, prominent canines protruding over her bottom lip.

"Alive," Yeki said, her voice so loud within the confines of the hut it made Tyreta wince. "Good. You are survivor."

"So far," Tyreta replied under her breath as she made to stand.

Yeki pushed her back to the hard earthen floor. Her fingers probed at the bandage on Tyreta's arm before peeling back the dressing to examine the mulch beneath.

"Good," she said ponderously. "Heals well. Up now, come."

Despite having slept like the dead, Tyreta still felt exhausted.

"I think it's best if I rest a while longer."

Yeki shook her head, tutting with those wrinkled lips. "No. You go with Gelila."

With strength that belied her slight frame, the old woman grabbed Tyreta's arm and pulled her to her feet.

"Look, I appreciate what you've done for me, but—"

"You go with Gelila," the old woman repeated more firmly.

Gelila smiled enthusiastically, baring those big white teeth. It was obvious Tyreta had no choice in the matter.

"You're pushier than my mother," she grumbled as she followed the kesh outside into the bright morning light.

Gelila led her through the settlement. The place was alive with activity as children chased one another between the tightly packed huts and older women stoked fires and scraped at animal skins with bone tools. Kesh warriors stood at the periphery of the settlement, watching vigilantly, and some of them regarded Tyreta with suspicion as she made her way past. For the most part the very young and very old members of the tribe looked on with curiosity. It was obvious they had never had an outsider in their midst, and Tyreta began to feel somewhat out of place.

"Hungry?" Gelila asked, offering a green fruit that resembled an apple.

Tyreta hadn't realised just how starved she was and accepted the fruit with a nod of thanks, devouring it in three bites and letting the juices run down her chin. It did little to sate her hunger but she still appreciated the gesture.

As they moved further through the settlement, she couldn't help but marvel at Gelila, who walked ahead of her with a confident gait. An axe and dagger hung from the hide belt at her slim waist, a spear and bow slung across her back.

"Are you a warrior?" Tyreta asked, to break the silence if nothing else. "You don't really look old enough."

That seemed a stupid thing to say when she heard the words aloud. She'd already seen what Gelila could do with that bow. Besides, this was wild country, it was obvious you had to grow up quick to survive. Tyreta had learned as much already.

The kesh nodded, gesturing to the intricate marks on her downy flesh and running a finger down a scar on her forearm. "These marks young."

"You mean they're new," Tyreta replied, peering closer at the scars. But they didn't look it. The whorls and concentric patterns on Gelila's skin looked as if they had healed years before.

"They are *new*," Gelila replied, grinning in pleasure at learning the word.

Tyreta could only marvel at how she formed the words so easily. These kesh had bestial faces, little different from those of the panthers that roamed the jungle, but they could form words in the language of Torwyn with ease. If only the Guilds who had come to these islands had taken the time to befriend the kesh rather than exile them from their lands, things might be much different.

The pair approached the narrow river running by the settlement, where a group of women were beating hides with rocks. As Gelila knelt to cup water from the stream and drink deeply, one of the girls playing nearby stopped what she was doing and approached. She looked up at Tyreta with curious wonder before offering what she held in her hand—mashed-up yellow fruit, the juices dripping over her chubby fingers. For a moment Tyreta thought about accepting the gift, until she saw it was crawling with ants.

"No thank you," she said, forcing a smile. Her stomach protested, but there was no way she'd be putting that ant-infested slop near her mouth.

"Come," Gelila said, beckoning Tyreta closer. Beside her sat a pile of clothes, and Gelila sifted through them before holding up a clean chiton of red and green. "For you."

For a moment Tyreta considered refusing, but her own clothes were little more than muddy rags. As quickly as she could, she undressed and pulled off her boots. Gelila then helped her into the chiton, wrapping it around her waist and tying it deftly at the back. Immediately Tyreta felt more comfortable, no longer stifled by her tight-fitting Guild uniform.

"Are they going to wash my clothes in the river?" Tyreta asked when she'd finished admiring her new garb. "The tunic needs sewing up, but—"

Gelila furrowed her brow as though she struggled to understand. Tyreta turned to gesture at her uniform just as one of the kesh women dropped it onto a fire next to the riverbank.

"Guess not," Tyreta sighed.

She would have complained at their lack of respect for her Guild colours, but no one here would give a damn. For these people, survival was a daily struggle. What would they care about the symbolism of the Hawkspur uniform? Besides, that pressed tunic and those leggings were unsuited to this environment. She'd miss the boots, but Tyreta couldn't help but feel a little grateful. As her uniform burned it felt as if she'd been unshackled from chains that had bound her for months.

Tyreta watched as a couple of the youngsters stopped their splashing in the shallows and chased one another around Gelila's legs. The young warrior grinned as they played, and it gave a curiously human aspect to her face. Tyreta could have been watching a scene from anywhere in Torwyn.

It was clear these kesh were not the beasts they had been painted as. They felt the same emotions as anyone else. Still, Tyreta could not expel the memory of Wyllow's death. The way he had been killed was the most savage thing she had ever seen. The kesh might act human, but they were capable of horrific butchery. Tyreta knew she was in danger here, but she also knew her own countrymen were capable of equal acts of violence. Nevertheless, she had to find a way home, and soon.

"Come, come," Gelila called as she made her way along the riverside.

The children had grown bored with tormenting her and ran off to find other mischief. As Tyreta walked toward her, the kesh warrior took the spear and bow from her back, brandishing them with some enthusiasm before motioning to the thick jungle beyond the river.

"What?" Tyreta asked. "You want me to go hunting?"

The notion seemed ludicrous, but from the way Gelila was gesturing with the weapons, that was exactly what she was suggesting.

Strangely, the more Tyreta thought about it, the less ludicrous it seemed.

"All right, then," she said, taking the spear in her hand. "Why not?"

"I show," Gelila said, moving forward to demonstrate how to hold the weapon, but Tyreta took a step back, cradling it protectively.

"I know what I'm doing," she insisted. "When you found me, I might have looked as dangerous as a blind mule, but I've used one of these before."

Remembering those old lessons, Tyreta adopted a fighting stance.

"I trained alongside my brothers for a while." She thrust the weapon forward, straight and true, using her front arm for accuracy and the back arm for power. "Learned everything from the best weapon masters in Wyke." Taking a step back, she spun the spear in a dazzling defensive flurry. "Then my mother decided I had to abandon weapons and concentrate on matters more befitting a lady of my standing."

Tyreta finished the move with a flourish, wedging the spear in the crook of her arm, poised for another strike. It looked impressive if nothing else.

"Not that I've exactly excelled in that either," she said. "But then there's never been much pleasing my mother, the old hag."

Gelila let out a gruff guffaw and mimicked Tyreta's last dramatic gesture before repeating the phrase "old hag."

"No," Tyreta replied, not sure whether to laugh or feel ashamed. "That's not what that means. I was talking about my mother."

"Mother?" Gelila asked. "She…looks for Tyreta?"

Wouldn't that be a marvel. The great Lady Rosomon would have no idea what was going on yet. Tyreta could only imagine her fury when she finally learned what had happened.

"No," Tyreta replied. "My mother is not looking for me."

Gelila's bestial face took on a sad expression. "Father?"

"He is dead."

Gelila nodded her understanding. "My father also dead."

"I'm sorry," Tyreta said, wondering if he had been killed along with the other men of the Lokai tribe.

If Gelila appreciated her words, she didn't mention it. Instead she turned and made her way toward the jungle. Feeling somewhat awkward, Tyreta followed, gripping the spear tightly as they started their hunt.

It didn't take long for them to leave the settlement behind. They had to walk only a few dozen yards before they were enclosed beneath the thick jungle canopy, the sounds of chirruping, grunting and hissing from every shadow. The trickle of the river was soon lost, along with the high-pitched giggles of kesh children. Tyreta began to feel the environment closing in around her and struggled to fight back the panic.

"Where are we going?" she asked.

Gelila didn't respond, leading her farther through the dense foliage.

Tyreta knew she had to be braver if she was going to make it out of this. She couldn't balk at every unfamiliar noise, especially if she was to prove herself deserving of the help she had been given. There was no way her brothers would have shown any fear. The great Conall Hawkspur would face this adversity head-on and come out the other side with a sparkling grin and smelling of some woman's perfume.

"Do you have any brothers or sisters?" Tyreta asked, as much to distract herself from the fear as to spark conversation.

Gelila shook her head. "Only me."

"Count yourself lucky. Sometimes I wish I was an only child. Rather than being the one who was always ignored. They got all the attention. I might as well have been invisible as far as my mother was concerned. Conall and Fulren always had their roles, everything mapped out for them. I guess I was just the spare—"

A grunt from the foliage stopped her. Gelila dropped to a crouch, and Tyreta felt every muscle suddenly tense. Taking the lead from her guide, she lowered herself to one knee, peering through the jungle for any sign of danger—not that she would've known what to do if something came rushing out of the bushes.

Gelila's attention was focused through a gap in the trees. Slowly the hunter crept forward, taking the bow from over her shoulder and nocking an arrow with practised grace.

Tyreta followed, keen to stay close, wary of any danger. When she was almost level with Gelila's shoulder, she could see what had drawn the hunter's attention. Barely visible through the ferns was a hog snuffling in the underbrush. It dug in the earth feverishly with its tusks, determined to uproot whatever it could smell hidden beneath the carpet of leaves.

Gelila drew back her bowstring, eyes focused on the target. Tyreta could only marvel at her strength and poise, every muscle moving with skilful ease. As Tyreta leaned forward, eager to see the arrow strike, she heard the crunch of a branch beneath her foot.

It was barely audible, but the hog's keen senses picked up the sound, and it immediately scrambled away through the underbrush. Tyreta watched it disappear into the jungle, feeling an immediate sense of embarrassment.

Gelila let out the breath she'd been holding in a long despondent sigh.

"I'm sorry," Tyreta said. She expected Gelila to be angry, but the kesh hunter placed the arrow back in her quiver as though nothing had happened. "You shouldn't have brought me. I'm a bloody liability. I don't even belong here."

And until she'd said the words, she'd never understood how true that was. Of course she didn't belong here. No one but the kesh belonged here; not her, not the Guilds. None of them should ever have even come to this place.

Gelila suddenly growled a warning, snatching an arrow from her quiver and darting to one side.

Tyreta barely had time to reel back in fright as a sleek, feline beast leapt from the surrounding trees, barely missing her. The panther landed only a few feet away, turning quickly and regarding both women with emotionless green eyes.

Was this the one from before? The panther Gelila had set free from the snare? The one that had raked Tyreta's shoulder with its claws? Perhaps that wasn't important right now as the panther crouched, deciding which one of them to attack.

Tyreta already had her spear poised, the only thing between her and those jaws. Gelila had her bow nocked but seemed reluctant to loose.

"What are you waiting for?" Tyreta spat, fighting the urge to turn and flee into the jungle. "Shoot it."

"I cannot," Gelila replied as the beast began to pace the ground in front of them.

"What are you talking about? It's going to bloody eat us."

"Creature is sacred to Lokai. To kill brings bad luck. Much bad luck."

"What are you talking about? It'll be much worse luck when it rips your fucking throat out."

The panther was focused fully on Tyreta now. It looked wary of that spear tip, but she could tell it was fast overcoming its fear. As the beast tensed its haunches, preparing to leap, there was a sudden burning sensation against Tyreta's chest.

The nightstone inside her chiton heated up at a frightening rate. She fought the urge to grab hold of it and stop it burning her skin, keeping her eyes focused on the panther and her hands on the spear. Rather than strike, the creature seemed to relax as they stared at one another. Tyreta's vision began to blur at the edges as she focused on the one threat.

A rush of emotions overwhelmed her as she locked eyes with the beast. Hunger, pain... fear. Somehow she realised the panther was even more scared than she was, but it was fighting that fear. Desperation, its basic need to survive, was overcoming trepidation so it could hunt, so it could eat. Would it be able to bring these two women down and avoid being injured? Tyreta could feel the panther weighing the risk against the gain.

She braced herself, waiting for the inevitable attack, but instead the panther tilted its head, offering a final longing glance, before turning tail and disappearing into the brush.

Tyreta gasped, dropping to one knee and touching a hand to the nightstone beneath her chiton, now cooling against her flesh. She'd experienced that stinging heat before, but it had never offered such a strange sensation, such insight. This was magic she had never experienced, much different from her webwainer gift. And much more frightening.

Gelila offered her a hand, pulling her to her feet.

"We go back now," the kesh said, as though nothing had happened.

Tyreta felt sweat running from every pore. "Yeah. That's a good idea."

She couldn't follow Gelila closely enough as they made their way back. Every step she gripped tight to the nightstone, wondering what other strange magics it might harbour. With any luck she'd never have to find out.

ROSOMON

She had to go home—return to Wyke and wait for news of Fulren. Hope and pray that eventually Lancelin would return with her son and all would be well. Better still, she should travel to New Flaym and be with her daughter. She had already sent Conall a message telling him of what had happened. He had sent a brief reply to inform her he was staying in the Karna to complete his secondment in the Phoenix Battalion. Perhaps she should send another, more urgent missive? Demand that he return to her side during this crisis?

No. She had insisted both Tyreta and Conall become responsible for the Guild. What example would she set by asking them to abandon their duties and come help her deal with the grief?

Fulren was innocent, that much was without question, but Rosomon had little chance of discovering who was really guilty. Olstrum was at the top of her list; Fulren had mentioned him by name, but so far the consul had managed to avoid her. When she'd demanded an audience, Rosomon had met a wall of silence. It was as though her authority had been stripped, the name Hawkspur no longer carrying any weight in Archwind Palace, let alone the rest of the city.

She had no friends here in her brother's court. No one who could help her get to the bottom of this. Her only allies were back in Wyke, her home. There was no choice but to return.

Rosomon donned her blue gown and a cloak embroidered with the sigil of her Guild. It was barely sunrise as she left her chamber. It would be a long journey. Best she get started early.

As she passed the huge open terrace that looked out onto the Anvil she heard a solitary bell ringing. It was a single monotonous chime coming from the Mount. She had not heard that bell for many years. Not since the death of her father...

That sound unnerved Rosomon, and she moved down through the palace, passing courtiers and servants, all equally confused by the funerary bell. No one seemed to know the reason for the noise, and that uncertainty only caused her unease to grow. Was it Sullivar? Had he perished in the night? Rosomon had tried her best to warn him of the dangers, but now guilt suddenly took hold—had she done enough to stop this?

"My lady."

Rosomon saw Athelys, one of her handmaids, pushing her way through the growing throng of palace inhabitants. The slight-framed girl fought through the crowd as best she could until she reached Rosomon.

"What is it?" Rosomon asked, trying to hide the concern in her voice. "What has happened?"

Athelys seemed reluctant to speak, her doe eyes searching the ground while she wrung her hands, trying to find the words. "There's been a death, my lady."

"Who?" she snapped. "Is it my brother?"

"No. The emperor is well. It's... his son."

"Which one?" When Athelys didn't reply, Rosomon grasped her arms and shook her. "Which one, Athelys?"

"Wyllow, my lady. Wyllow Archwind is dead."

The implications of that struck Rosomon like a knife. Wyllow had been in New Flaym with Tyreta. Had her daughter met a similar fate?

"What about Tyreta?" Rosomon demanded.

Tears began to fill Athelys's eyes. "I'm sorry, my lady. I don't know."

Rosomon left the girl, joining the burgeoning crowd as the entire palace woke to the sound of the bell. She had to reach Sullivar. Had to find out what was going on.

When she approached the throne room, Starn Rivers was there waiting for her. He nodded at her approach.

"Lady Rosomon—"

"Where is my brother?" she demanded.

"He's not here, my lady. Word has it he has gone to the Mount."

"The Mount? But why?"

"They told me the emperor has gone to pray."

It seemed a preposterous notion. Sullivar had never been religious. He had only continued their father's legacy of dismantling the Draconate's power.

"Have you heard word of Tyreta?" she asked. "Do you know what happened?"

"A messenger arrived from the Karna this morning," Starn said. "Wyllow and Tyreta went missing from New Flaym some days ago. A search party was sent out to find them. Other than that, there has been no word."

"So no bodies have been found?" she asked, feeling a little relief despite the grave news. "They are missing, not dead?"

"That's what I heard, my lady. But still, Emperor Sullivar ordered the bell of the Mount to be rung."

"I have to see him," she said.

Starn nodded, leading Rosomon from the throne room. He pushed his way easily through the crowd, making a path for Rosomon. Once they were in the open she could hear the chime of the bell all the clearer, calling out across the Anvil.

They made their way over the Bridge of Saints. All the while Rosomon grew more anxious. She had not seen her brother since Fulren was condemned by the Justiciers. The memory of Sullivar's reluctance to help her son still burned within her. She remembered how she had cursed him. How she had vowed never to forgive him, but none of that seemed to matter now. She had to find Sullivar. They had to work out what to do together. Now that both their children were in peril, surely Sullivar would see sense. Perhaps now he would know a little of what she was feeling.

For an instant that seemed a selfish notion, but Rosomon had the right to be selfish. Sullivar had let her son be taken. If she believed in such things, she might see it as divine justice that Wyllow had gone missing. But her daughter was also gone. Where was the justice in that?

Rosomon knew Tyreta had to be all right. She was resourceful. Strong. If Wyllow and Tyreta had gotten lost in the jungles, been abducted even, then Rosomon was sure her daughter would find a way out of it. She just had to.

As they neared the Mount the crowd grew too dense for even Starn to push his way through. It was as though half the city wanted to reach the temple of the Ministry and join its emperor in his grief.

"There's another way," said Starn, leading Rosomon away from the growing multitude and along a side street. The way led down to the riverside, and Rosomon could smell the stink of sewage mixed with rotting fish as they picked their way through the back alleys.

From down the warren of streets ahead, Rosomon heard a commotion. Starn put up a hand to warn her, fearing danger, but she was not about to be stopped.

They turned a corner, and she saw the red-and-yellow hauberks of soldiers ahead. Rosomon recognised the livery of the Revocaters—the iron hand of the Corwen Guild, a cadre of agents who ensured the word and power of the Guilds was maintained as gospel. Three men were on their knees, and an interrogation of sorts was underway.

As Rosomon approached she saw words daubed on the wall in pitch, an overturned bucket lying beneath them. *The Wyrms Rise Again*, said the hastily scrawled statement. Rosomon had heard tell of Draconate zealots. They had resisted the growing power of the Guilds for years, yearning for a return to the days when the Ministry was in control of Torwyn. Sullivar had dismissed them as a harmless fringe group. Clearly Rearden Corwen did not think them so benign.

"I won't ask again—who's behind this?" one of the Revocaters asked—a captain, judging by the red plume on his half helm.

The three men on their knees seemed reluctant to answer. Rosomon could see they were barely older than boys, each one scared for his life. When they didn't answer, one of the soldiers stepped in, striking the nearest one with a notched club. The boy screamed, falling forward onto his face.

"Looks like we have to do this the hard way," said the captain, taking his own club from his belt.

"There'll be no need," said Rosomon, making her way toward them.

"My lady," said Starn, "this is not a good—"

She silenced him with a gesture and approached the Revocaters. As she stepped into the light, the three soldiers froze, recognising her Hawkspur garb. But then, they were the eyes and ears of the Corwen Guild—it was their job to know who she was.

"I think you've made your point," she said to the captain.

"My lady," he replied, bowing his head curtly. "These men are guilty of sedition. They need to be punished."

"For painting a wall?" Rosomon gestured to the hastily scrawled words daubed on the filthy brickwork. "And one that very few will see, from the looks of it."

"We have our orders, my lady."

"On whose authority?"

The Revocater shrugged. "Lord Rearden himself."

Of course Lord Rearden, who else would be so bold as to imbue their enforcers with the power to mete out justice on the streets of the capital? He had always coveted power, and his position at the head of the Corwen Guild afforded it to him.

"And would Rearden have you beat these men to death in the street?" Rosomon asked.

The captain shook his head. "No, my lady, but—"

"But what? Cutting off some fingers and toes perhaps? A public execution? Look at them." She gestured to the three cowering youths on their knees, one of them bleeding from the back of his head. "They're barely more than children."

"But Lord Rearden—"

"To the Five Lairs with Lord Rearden. You will let these boys go or I'll make sure the emperor hears you're abusing his citizens in the street, for nothing more than painting a wall."

She could see the captain wavering. Weighing up whether it served him best to argue or to turn a blind eye. Luckily he went for the latter.

"Of course, my lady."

He bowed one more time before gesturing for his men to retreat. With another bow he followed them away along the passage.

Rosomon glanced down at the young men. "Get up," she ordered.

They did so, one of them tugging at his forelock gratefully. He had keen blue eyes and wore a dark moustache waxed to rakish curls at the tips. It gave him more the look of a wealthy merchant than that of a religious zealot. "Thank you," he said.

Rosomon gestured to the message they had daubed. "What's the meaning of this?" she said.

"We meant no offence, my lady," he replied, bowing apologetically.

"I'm not offended," Rosomon replied. "But should I be?"

"No, milady. I mean..."

"Are things so bad that you want a return to the days of the Draconate? You would rather live under the harsh rule of a religious order than the Guilds?"

The boys didn't seem to know how to answer until the one with the bleeding head stepped forward. "What difference does it make who rules us?" he said. "Could it be any worse than this?"

He removed a hand from his head, and Rosomon could see the blood on it.

There was no arguing against his evidence. "Very well. You'd best be off. I suggest that way." She gestured in the opposite direction to the one the Revocaters had taken.

They didn't need telling twice, all three of them scampering off down the passage.

Rosomon gazed at the graffiti. "'The Wyrms Rise Again,'" she said. "Any ideas?"

Starn just shrugged. But then it was doubtful her loyal swordwright had many ideas about anything other than how to kill.

They continued through the stinking passageway, coming out just east of the Mount. The crowds were gathered in their hundreds, a vast throng congregated in a silent vigil. Starn pushed his way through, Rosomon close behind, until they eventually managed to reach the main doors of the vast temple.

Sullivar's Titanguard were standing at the entrance, their presence enough to deter anyone else from entering. They didn't try to hamper Rosomon as she made her way into the Mount.

It was eerily silent as Rosomon entered the vast temple. She was suddenly reminded of her father's funeral—of the packed interior, of the thousands who had come to pay their respects. It was a very different place now. Her footsteps echoed on the white marble floor. The dragon motifs that hung from the walls and leered down from the gantries seemed much more intimidating than they had all those years ago.

Inside were none of Sullivar's Titanguard. Instead the way was guarded by Drakes, the Knights of the Draconate, their steel armour and dragon helms luminous in the torchlight. They wore white tabards depicting a dragon rampant surrounded by five stars of differing hues, each representing one of the Great Wyrms. Every one of these knights was a devout warrior-priest, a statuesque reminder of the power the Ministry once held over Torwyn. None of them spoke or even acknowledged her, which made them seem more imposing. Rosomon had never felt intimidated by the Titanguard of Archwind nor the Talon of Hawkspur, but the Drakes were a different matter. They were trained from birth to be the protectors of the faith. All compassion and empathy were said to be bred from them so all they knew was how to obey. Any man who controlled the Drakes controlled the Draconate. Right now, that man was her nephew Sanctan, Archlegate of the Ministry, but it did little to stifle Rosomon's caution.

"My lady, you have come."

A figure moved to block her path. Rosomon stopped when she saw the pinched features of Consul Olstrum barring her way. Immediately she fought to control her anger. Fulren had implicated Olstrum in the plot against him before he was sent to Nyrakkis. So far Rosomon had failed to corner the man so that she might question him on the matter, but now was neither the time nor the place.

"Where is my brother?" she asked.

"Might I just take the opportunity to offer my condolences, Lady Rosomon."

"You may," she said. "Now where is my brother?"

"I'm afraid the emperor does not wish to be disturbed," Olstrum said.

Rosomon fought all the harder to control herself. "I will see Sullivar," she said. "And you will get out of my way, or Swordwright Rivers will make a mess of this floor with your brains."

As though on cue, Starn moved a little closer to her shoulder. It was enough to cow Olstrum, who bowed again.

"Of course, Lady Rosomon. He is at the Altar of Undometh." Olstrum gestured toward the far end of the huge temple.

The Mount was split into vestibules, each housing an altar devoted to one of Torwyn's Great Wyrms. Undometh was its god of vengeance.

As Rosomon moved past the consul she leaned in. "And don't think I've forgotten we are due a talk, Olstrum. The next time I demand an audience, I expect it to be answered."

The consul mumbled his assent as Rosomon left him in her wake. She made her way across the centre of the Mount, past the huge statue of all five Wyrms entwined in battle. Or were they engaged in some kind of carnal ritual? Rosomon had never really known or cared, all that mattered right now was talking to her brother.

She saw him kneeling before the crimson statue of Undometh. Sullivar was tiny before the huge effigy, and Rosomon had never seen him look so insignificant. The Drakes were standing in force here, as though ready to protect the emperor. It did little to assuage Rosomon's fear of them until she also saw Sanctan standing vigil to one side. He offered a nod of greeting as she approached.

"Aunt Rosomon," he said quietly.

"Sanctan," she replied, though perhaps here, in this holy place, she should use his title of Archlegate. "What is happening?"

Sanctan gestured to where Sullivar knelt a few feet away. "The emperor is at prayer. I am afraid he is overcome with grief at the news of his son."

"What news?" she asked. "What have you heard?"

"Wyllow's body was found some miles from New Flaym. He left the port with your daughter. Of her I'm afraid there is no news. I'm sorry."

Her heart would have sunk like a stone in her chest, but after the grief she had felt over Fulren, there seemed little sorrow left in her. A lack of news could mean anything. Rosomon was not about to give in to despair yet.

She looked back to Sullivar, kneeling before the altar. Rosomon had never seen her brother pray or known him to put any store by religious observance. It seemed odd to see him kneeling so devoutly, hands clasped, lips moving in a silent litany. Slowly she approached, stepping into the shadow of the huge red statue of Undometh.

"Sullivar," she said, laying a hand on her brother's shoulder.

When he looked up, his eyes were bloodshot, tears running freely down his cheeks, and she suddenly felt guilty for the way she had last spoken to him. It was a guilt she had to swallow down. Though she was sure Sullivar had not been involved in any plot, he had nonetheless stood by while Fulren was condemned. She had to remind herself she was not here to make amends.

"He's gone, Ros," whispered Sullivar.

Her brother looked so small. Rosomon now saw why it was imperative the city folk be kept away. It would not serve them well to see the man who had proclaimed himself their emperor suffering such anguish.

She knelt beside him, taking his head in her hands. He sobbed, grabbing hold of her cloak and resting his head against her chest. It reminded her of the many times in their childhood when their father had been in one of his rages and Sullivar had come to her for protection. He was that scared little boy all over again.

"I am sorry," she whispered. "I loved Wyllow too."

"You have to help me," he replied. "I can't do this without you."

All the resentment she had felt for her brother seemed to slough away as she held him close. But Rosomon knew she could not do as he asked when her daughter was still in danger.

"I know you need me, but I have to go to New Flaym. If there's any hope that Tyreta—"

"No," Sullivar said, sounding more beggar than emperor. She could see he was fighting back his sorrow. Trying his damnedest to wrest back his senses. "You will remain here with me. Where it's safe. I will have Rearden send someone to investigate what has happened. He will look for Tyreta."

"I have to find her, Sullivar," Rosomon said. The thought of Rearden's hounds being dispatched filled her with little confidence. "She's my daughter."

Sullivar gazed up at her with a look of anguish. He took her in his arms, squeezing her as though he couldn't let go.

"I need you here," Sullivar said. "By my side. I can't do it without you. Please don't leave."

In that moment Rosomon realised what was at stake. A conspiracy was afoot, though she had no idea of its nature or who was behind it. Her brother was responsible for the whole of Torwyn, and here he was, broken. There was no one else who could help him. No one else who could hold this machine together.

Even if she did seek passage to the Sundered Isles, what could she really do to help find Tyreta? She remembered how much she had hated her brother just a few days before, but now, as she looked at him, she realised that without her his empire might be lost. Their nation could collapse in a matter of days.

"All right," she replied. "I will stay."

Sullivar began to sob in gratitude, letting out all his grief, all his loss.

As they held each other in the silence of the temple, a monument to deities neither of them worshipped, Rosomon had never needed more faith.

FULREN

He was almost to a hundred, lowering himself till his chest brushed the tiled floor, raising himself till his shoulders and biceps burned, keeping the core of his body tensed all the while. Sweat dripped from his brow, forming a puddle on the floor. Once he reached his target, Fulren jumped nimbly to his feet, feeling the ache in his limbs. His chambers offered little in the way of functional apparatus for training, but he had adapted what there was. Hanging from the lintel of the door would work his back. Slow and measured squats would ensure his legs remained strong.

It was crucial that his body be as supple as his mind, but as he began his regimen of stretches Fulren wondered if it was worth the effort. He had been condemned to death. They had called it a trial, but from what he could gather there was little hope of a fair hearing. It would be nothing more than an execution. If he was to die, perhaps it would be better to spend his last days taking advantage of the hospitality he had been offered rather than punishing his body.

When his stretching was done, he considered running through some sword forms, but without a weapon to hand there was little point. Instead he took one of the cotton towels that had been left for him and wiped the sweat from his naked torso. A warm breeze blew in through the open patio, and he made his way outside, taking in a deep breath of the Jubaran air.

A haze hung over the city as if an evil mist had descended from the nearby mountains to consume all but the highest towers. It was beautiful. Somewhere a bird sang a jolly tune, its refrain echoing from the distant rooftops. A bell chimed dolorously in the distance, the relentless knell pealing from the roiling mist. And above it all, Fulren heard laughter. It was shrill and joyless, but this was the first time he had heard its like in this place. It served to remind him how far he was from home, but also how similar this place was to the Anvil or Wyke. These were just people, after all, and despite his imprisonment, they had treated him well.

Every night since his arrival Fulren had been gifted with a bath of hot water and perfumed oils. He had dried himself on the softest of towels and dined on food laced with such exotic spices his mouth watered at the thought of it. But despite the generous hospitality, he knew he was just a lamb awaiting the ceremonial knife.

An inclement breeze gusted across the balcony, and Fulren felt the sudden chill prickle his skin. He turned to go inside, and through the silken drapes that shifted gently in the gust he saw someone waiting for him.

Wenis was sitting in one of the great embroidered armchairs as he walked through the doors, her smile giving her the look of a mischievous child. She spoke no word of greeting, but at the sight of his naked torso her right eyebrow rose a full inch.

Fulren suddenly felt exposed. He snatched his shirt from where it lay over the back of a chair and donned it as quickly as he could. It clung to the moisture on his flesh, but it was all he had to cover his modesty.

"Are you well, Fulren?" Wenis asked. "You look well."

"I'm as well as can be expected," he replied.

"I hope you are enjoying the generosity of Queen Meresankh."

Fulren clenched his jaw. The notion that he should be grateful made him bristle with anger, but raging would do little to see him freed.

"Why are you here, Wenis?"

"No particular reason," she said, picking at a loose thread on the arm of the chair. "I merely desired to be in your company."

"My company? Why? Do you feel some kind of obligation because I saved your life?"

She giggled at that. "The question of whether you saved my life or I yours is still up for debate. Perhaps I am here because you fascinate me."

That seemed a little bit strong. Fulren had never considered himself fascinating.

"Do I fascinate you enough to get me out of here before my execution?"

Her brow creased for a moment before she let out a disappointed sigh. "I am afraid that is impossible."

He gazed at her, wondering whether she had merely come to torment him. But no. Despite her lack of concern for his fate, he doubted even Wenis was that cruel.

"If you won't help me, there's nothing I have to say to you."

She rose from her chair, an uncharacteristic look of sincerity crossing those delicate features. "Fulren, there is nothing I can do. I would help you if I could, but the judgement has been made."

"Nothing you can do? The least you can do is tell me how I will die."

Wenis let out another long sigh and turned away from him. He doubted she had been expecting an interrogation when she came to his chamber unannounced.

"On the Night of the Blooded Moon you will be taken to the arena," she said, speaking the words as though reciting from a script. "Along with other prisoners you will face Ghobeq, God of the Rivers, and be subjected to his judgement."

"By judgement, I assume you mean murder?"

Wenis nodded. "There will be no clemency."

"What is this Ghobeq? A demon? A beast?"

"Yes," she replied. There was a look of apprehension to her, as though she were reluctant to speak of it.

"But it can be killed?"

Wenis giggled as though Fulren had said something stupid. He felt anger well up inside him again. He was about to be slaughtered by some demonic creature, and all she could do was find humour in his plight.

"I'm going to fucking die," he spat.

That was enough to wipe the mirth from her face.

"I am sorry," she said. "Truly. But the notion that Ghobeq could be defeated in the arena is folly. The best you could hope for is a quick end." She took a step closer to him, laying a hand on his chest. "That feeling of despair inside you is a wasted emotion, Fulren. You still have time. Take your pleasure where you can."

She gazed at him expectantly, her hand still pressed to his chest. Surely she couldn't be suggesting...

But why shouldn't he? If Wenis spoke the truth, he was as good as dead. Perhaps he should heed her advice and take all the pleasures that were offered.

"No," he said, gently removing her hand from his chest. "I won't give in to this. There has to be a way to defeat this demon. Some way it can be killed."

Wenis rolled her eyes, not even trying to hide her disappointment.

"Killed, no. Defeated... perhaps. Weapons will be placed throughout the arena. The Nine Houses sponsor their chosen prisoner and offer them at least a fighting chance, but it is all for show. To excite the crowd. There are few weapons that could harm Ghobeq. The entire spectacle is designed to show the people of Nyrakkis how futile it is to resist the gods."

"Few weapons? So this beast can at least be harmed? There must be something that can hurt it. Something I could forge—"

"No," Wenis interrupted. "This is not something that can be defeated by your mechanical playthings. Its hide is thick as iron. Teeth sharp as razors. Ghobeq is swift as a snake and brutal as a lion."

"Then perhaps I can forge something that uses your magics? When we were aboard the ark bound for Jubara, we conjured devastating sorcery together, using artifice and your arcanist abilities."

Wenis shook her head. "Your artifice is forbidden in Nyrakkis. By Queen Meresankh's decree."

"But why? When there is such power in it? When it can be used for so much good?"

That brought another grin to Wenis's face. "Good for whom? Meresankh has watched from across the Drift as the Guilds of

Torwyn have crafted their machines and grown in power. Seen them gain the favour of your people and usurp the high seat of the Draconate. Your inventions have raised you higher than the gods themselves. Meresankh would not have the same here. She would not allow your artifice to threaten her position on the throne."

"I don't care what your queen thinks about it, or what she has forbidden. I care whether you think it could work." Wenis fell silent. It told Fulren all he needed to know. "If we could combine the power of a necroglyph with pyrestone weaponry, surely there'd be a chance of sending this demon back to where it came from?"

Wenis turned away as though she was done with the conversation.

"We have to do it," Fulren said. "I have to be marked with one of your necroglyphs. Then I can create a weapon—"

"You don't know what you're asking," she said, turning back to face him. Fulren saw that all her humour had gone now. Wenis looked odd with such a grave expression marring her features. She held up her arm to show the intricate sigils on her flesh. "These are not mere trifles, Fulren. Imbuing the body with a necroglyph has its price."

"Worse than dying?" he snapped.

"Have a care, Fulren. Bearing the mark of the necroglyph brings grave consequences. It will open a door that can never be closed."

"We have sorcerers in Torwyn," he replied with a dismissive shrug. "Webwainers convene with the web every day, and some are cursed by it. Madness. Affliction. I know everything has its price, Wenis. But what price is higher than death?"

"Your eastern magics are not the same as ours. The webwainers of Torwyn merely channel the latent energy of pyrestone. The sorcery of an arcanist requires a much more specific commitment of mind and body. To wield the power of a necroglyph requires a benefactor. A god. A demon. Why do you think your Ministry forbade the practice of sorcery so many centuries ago? Fulren, if you walk this path, you will risk not only your life but your soul as well."

He had never seen her look so serious. This was not some ruse to dissuade him from the notion. This was a dire warning of what would happen if he embarked on this journey. But there was no other option, other than to die in that arena, and to the Five Lairs with that. Even if marking himself with a necroglyph might damn his soul, he would take the chance.

"Will you help me or not?" he asked, done with arguing. Done with doubts. His mind was made up, and Wenis would either assist him in this or leave him to his fate.

"Even if you underwent the ritual to imbue a necroglyph, there are no guarantees it would work. If the ceremony failed, at best it would grant you no powers. At worst you would be driven insane by it. Besides, you would also need to craft a weapon of ingenious design, and who would there be to help you in a city where artifice is forbidden?"

"All you have to do is give me the mark and allow me access to a forge. I will do the rest. Nobody else need ever know."

Wenis barked a shrill laugh. "No one will ever know? Of course they will. Meresankh knows everything. Her spider, Amosis Makareth, is most likely listening to us right now. Reporting every word to her mistress."

Fulren cupped a hand to his ear. "And yet no one is here to break down the door. The queen's inquisitors have not come to drag us to the nearest dungeon. If Meresankh can hear, she is most likely looking forward to the spectacle I will give her in the arena. It will be a sight Jubara has never seen before. Just imagine how the crowd will roar on witnessing my glorious end."

He was getting carried away with the idea, but Wenis clearly did not share his enthusiasm for a magnificent death. Her eyes lowered to the ground and she took a step closer to him, almost resting her head against his chest. Fulren could smell the faint scent of lavender in her hair.

"I do not relish such an end for you," she whispered. "I was hoping we could steal these last few hours for ourselves. Think of the now, not what is to come."

As he looked down at her sullen expression and heard the sorrow in her words Fulren's immediate thought was whether he was being tricked. The longer they stood so close to one another, the less he thought that was the case.

Slowly Wenis looked up, and he could see something in her eyes. Was it concern? Was it need? Before he could decide, she raised herself on tiptoe and kissed him deeply. The sensation made his stomach lurch. Hardly what he had expected. Then, as though nothing had happened, she stepped away from him.

"I will try my best to do as you ask. But there are no guarantees."

He wanted to reply that he understood. That he already knew there were never any guarantees. Instead he watched as she turned on her heel and marched from his chamber.

What had just happened? He could still smell the scent of her on the air, his lips tingling from the sensation of her kiss. Was there some genuine affection between them?

Surely not. She was the one who had taken him from his home. An agent of the very institution that now imprisoned him. And yet she was the only person who seemed to care if he lived or died. His one salvation in this pit of demons.

Fulren shook his head, emptying it of any lingering sensation. Most likely he was reading too much into it. Besides, what did it matter if there was some deeper feeling behind that kiss? In a day or two either he would die or the necroglyph would save his life. And if it did, he might well have more trouble than death to contend with.

CONALL

The chair in his personal chamber was far from comfortable. Conall reckoned it had been made that way on purpose. He wouldn't put it past Beringer to make sure all his officers sat in discomfort so they never got used to shining their arses for too long. At least he had a chair and a desk. It was a small privilege, but one Conall appreciated out here in the desert, where luxuries were hard to come by.

His desk was sparsely covered, holding only a few reports and missives along with a single candlestick to see by at night. He had parchment and ink in his drawers, but so far there had been little need for him to write to anyone.

Conall knew that wasn't exactly true as he glanced at the letter on its own to the left of his official papers. A letter from his mother, sitting there as though goading him. The story of his brother's arrest and exile. The subtle intimation that he should return to the Anvil.

He should feel guilty for refusing, but every time he thought about her it only made him angry, filling him with spite, and the more he tried to put it from his mind the worse it plagued him. How dare she insinuate such demands? He owed her nothing.

Conall reached for the letter, fully intending to crumple it in his fist and set it alight, when Sted walked in. She didn't bother to knock, but he'd long since grown used to that.

"Frontier marshal wants to see you, Captain Hawkspur," she said, feigning an officious tone.

"What about?" he replied, standing up and feeling relief in his numb arse cheeks.

"No idea. I'm just a lowly lieutenant. No one tells me nothing."

Conall walked past her, out into the bunkroom. "This could be our chance," he said.

"Chance for what?"

"To prove our worth," he snapped. "Get the men ready."

Conall strode out into the dusty courtyard. He hadn't meant to snap at Sted, she didn't deserve that, but his frustration had only grown since his arrival. The boredom was unbearable, and he was desperate for some way to show Beringer he was more than a man of privilege. Maybe now he would have that opportunity.

He crossed the courtyard as the troopers of the Phoenix Battalion drilled, marching in an endless rhythm before practising defensive manoeuvres. Conall could only admire their discipline. If only his own men of the Talon showed such professionalism. But then he supposed that was his fault.

Perhaps if he spent less time wallowing in self-pity, he would find the time to get his scouts in order. Well, maybe now was the chance.

He saw the frontier marshal at the far end of the compound. Beringer was stripped to the waist, his barrel chest on view for all to see, but he had only one spectator as he trained with his sword. Captain Tarrien stood to one side, looking every bit the officer—uniform pristine, back straight as he stood at full attention. For a moment Conall felt conscious that his own appearance was not up to the same standard, but it was too late to have his uniform cleaned and pressed now.

"Tardy as ever, Captain Hawkspur," Beringer said as Conall approached.

The frontier marshal attacked the mannequin in front of him, dulled blade hacking divots in the wood. He was a powerful fighter, and Conall suddenly thought he would make a formidable opponent, even for the most prodigious swordwright.

"My apologies, Frontier Marshal. I only just received word of your summons."

Beringer did not answer as he attacked the wooden torso once more. Conall noticed a wry smile cross Tarrien's lips, which only served to annoy him further.

When he had completed a fierce combination of blows that almost left the mannequin in splinters, Beringer stood back, admiring his handiwork.

"We've lost contact with a mining outpost to the southwest," he said between breaths. "I need you to act as wayfinder and lead a contingent to find out what's happened."

Conall felt the excitement well up inside. This was what he'd been waiting for.

"The Talon are already prepared, Frontier Marshal," he said.

Beringer shook his broad head. "You won't need your entire squad," he replied. "Captain Tarrien will be leading a small patrol. You will accompany him. I doubt you'll need more than a couple of scouts."

"But surely this is a job for the Talon? This is why we're here."

Beringer took a step closer, and Conall thought that maybe he should have kept his mouth shut.

"This is dangerous country, Hawkspur. And you haven't yet proved to me you've got what it takes to survive in it, let alone lead men into enemy territory. You will accompany Captain Tarrien and follow his orders at all times. Am I clear?"

"Frontier Marshal, my men are—"

"I said, am I clear?" Beringer's threatening tone brooked no argument.

"As crystal," Conall replied.

"Good. Now we all know where we stand, I suggest you get prepared."

Conall swallowed down the humiliation as he made his way back to the barracks. He did his best not to catch Tarrien's eye as he walked across the courtyard, lest he say something he might regret.

The Talon were all but ready when he arrived at the bunkhouse, and he reluctantly stood them down. If he could take only a couple of scouts with him, it would have to be Sted and Nevan. He knew them the best, trusted them the most, and if he was going to be out in the desert for any length of time, he wanted them both watching his back.

By the time they prepared their arms and equipment and made their way back out into the courtyard, Tarrien and his unit of half a dozen men were mounted and ready to go. They looked every bit the disciplined squad, dark uniforms pristine despite the dust that swirled about them.

Conall still couldn't bring himself to look at his fellow captain and instead pulled the brim of his hat farther over his eyes before they mounted their waiting horses. He checked the breech of his longbarrel before sliding it into the saddle holster and nudging his steed through the gates.

Tarrien took the lead and they struck out to the west, the road eventually winding southward as they made their way through the desolate landscape. Conall thought he had grown used to the heat, but out here, exposed to the merciless sun, he was all but baking. The sweat on his arms dried quickly in the desert heat, but his hair was sodden beneath his hat. Tarrien's squad seemed unbothered by it, but Sted and Nevan grumbled most of the way. He could hear them chuntering their disquiet but thought it better to let them vent their displeasure than have them stew in silence.

When the column of riders had covered around five miles, Sted drew her horse up alongside him.

"You all right?" she asked.

It seemed odd that she'd be so concerned with his welfare. Usually she'd be laughing at his discomfort.

"Apart from the blistering heat? I'm dandy," he replied.

"Yeah, my bollocks are drenched in this saddle," she replied. "But that's not what I meant."

"Then what did you mean?" he asked, taking his flask from a saddlebag and uncorking it. He drank deep and offered it to her.

Sted shook her head in refusal. "I only... That letter. On your desk. The one from your mother. You must want to go home, but I guess it's a tough decision."

It wasn't, but she didn't need to know the whys and wherefores.

"You read the letter? I didn't realise your job as lieutenant was to read all my personal correspondence."

"My job as lieutenant is to make sure the men below me obey their orders and to look after the welfare of my superior officer. For that I need to know what's going on in his head, and if that means reading the odd letter I'm not supposed to, then so be it."

He should have berated her for that, dressed her down and put her on a charge, but what was the point? Sted was the only friend he had in this place, and besides—her heart was in the right place.

"So why did you choose to stay?" she asked.

"You think I should have gone back?" Conall replied, still unsure if he had made the right choice.

"She's your mother, Con. The only one you've got."

If Sted knew the secret Conall had lived with for so many years, she would think very differently. The great Lady Rosomon had betrayed him, betrayed the family, betrayed his father.

"There's nothing I can do to help her," he replied. "Going back to Torwyn will not bring my brother back."

"She's lost one son. Maybe she just needs the other one by her side."

"Why are you so bothered anyway?" Conall snapped. "What difference does it make?"

Sted shrugged. "All right. I just thought—"

"Well, don't think. That's not what you're good at. You don't know what you're talking about, so for once keep your mouth shut."

Sted said nothing else as Conall urged his steed to the front of the column. It was the most suitable place for him anyway—Beringer had appointed him the wayfinder, and so far all he'd done was follow.

The road wound to the west once more as the sun quested to its zenith. The farther they rode the more uncomfortable Conall felt at their straying so far from any form of civilisation. The Armiger Battalions had built six forts along the frontier, but they were heading away from them at an alarming rate.

"Are we close?" Conall asked Tarrien as he scanned the bleak horizon.

Tarrien shrugged. "I was hoping we'd be there by now. If we

don't find the place soon, we'll have to turn back. The last thing we need is to get caught out here at sundown. The goatheads could be patrolling the area, and we wouldn't see them until it was too late."

Conall had no idea how that could happen. The land was flat in every direction. Surely they'd see the durrga coming a mile away. Nevertheless, Tarrien's warning made him nervous. If it had been up to him he'd have turned back immediately, but he was damned if he'd look a coward in front of his rival captain.

His eyes fell on the pyrestone pistol at Tarrien's hip. It looked to have been made by a master artificer, fine enough to rival Conall's longbarrel. As they continued through the endless desert, Conall's curiosity got the better of him.

"That's a handsome weapon you're carrying," he said. "Family heirloom?"

That brought a wry smile to the corner of Tarrien's mouth. "Bought and paid for with my own hard-earned wages."

"Must have taken you a while to save enough gold to buy such a rare treasure."

Tarrien turned and nodded at the longbarrel slung from Conall's saddle. "How long did you save to buy yours?"

He felt suddenly embarrassed. The longbarrel had been a gift. One he had taken for granted, until now.

"With the money it cost to buy that pistol you could have bought a smallholding on the Sungem Coast. Got yourself away from this damned desert."

"Who says I want to?" Tarrien turned back toward the distant horizon. "We're not all here because we have to be."

"I don't *have* to be here," Conall said, quickly realising he was taking offence where none might have been offered.

"Then why are you?" Tarrien asked.

Conall had avoided giving it too much thought. Was he here because it was tradition? Because it was expected of him? Or did he have some point to prove?

Before he could even consider his excuses, Tarrien put heels to his horse's flanks and trotted on ahead. Conall was left to feel even more foolish. Even more alone.

It was with mixed feelings of relief and trepidation that they saw smoke in the distance. Tarrien ordered the column into a canter, and they rode their horses across the flat desert toward the drifting cloud. Eventually they reached the edge of a ridge, the land dropping away to the west. Half a mile along the canyon was the facility they'd come to find.

Conall could just see a collection of hastily built shacks. A mining frame stood at their centre, but the timbers were blackened and smouldering. There was no sign of life.

"Could still be survivors," Tarrien said, nudging his horse forward.

"Wait." Conall held a hand out for him to stop. "There could still be enemies too. If me and my scouts approach along the gully to the south, we can make sure it's safe. If we all go riding in, we'll be easy prey for an ambush."

Tarrien nodded. "All right. We'll wait for your signal."

Conall dismounted, signalling for Sted and Nevan to join him. As he unslung the longbarrel from its holster the implications of what he'd just volunteered to do began to hit him. If the goatheads were lying in wait, he'd just offered to flush them out—a dumb move by any measure. But that was why he had come here—to gain experience in enemy lands and hopefully gain respect. That would never happen if he hid behind other men.

The three of them donned their greatcoats. They would make them sweat like pigs, but they'd at least be offered some camouflage as they made their approach. Sted and Nevan loaded their splintbows and followed close behind as Conall made his way down the steep slope and dropped into the gully that ran toward the compound.

They kept their heads down as they moved. The closer they got to the smoking ruins the more uneasy he felt in his guts. He suddenly yearned for his sweaty chambers in Agavere but quickly put the thought from his mind. This was his chance to make himself invaluable and finally prove to Beringer that he wasn't deadweight. If he could manage not to literally end up dead, then all the better.

When they were a few yards south of the compound, Conall held up a hand for Sted and Nevan to stop. He peered over the lip of the gully. The devastation looked much worse from close up, and he could now see what looked like corpses abandoned in the dust. There was still no sign of life.

"What now?" Sted whispered.

Conall shook his head. "I can't see any sign of an ambush. From what I've heard the goatheads are hard to miss."

"That's not what Tarrien said."

"Bollocks to Tarrien. The durrga are eight-foot giants. Where the fuck could they be hiding?"

"So we going in?"

Conall looked over to see Nevan gripping tight to his splintbow. The big man was unusually quiet, but then fear did that to people.

"We can't hide here all day," Conall replied, and he pulled himself out of the gully.

With Sted and Nevan close behind him, he walked forward. His longbarrel was trained ahead as they approached the compound, and when he was within thirty yards he stopped.

They hadn't noticed from a distance, but the bodies weren't just littering the ground. Hanging from the mining frame were half a dozen corpses lashed and nailed to the woodwork. Each one had been eviscerated, their dried-up guts dangling in the sand.

Conall heard Nevan retch behind him, but the big man managed to keep his breakfast down. On the walls of the huts strange symbols had been daubed in blood. Conall couldn't read the goathead script, but he still got the message.

"Inhuman bastards," Sted said through gritted teeth.

"I think we've seen enough," Conall replied, lowering the longbarrel. "Signal Tarrien that—"

A sudden commotion made Conall almost drop the longbarrel, and they all spun to see something burst from beneath the wreckage of the nearest hut. Nevan levelled his splintbow, and Conall quickly slapped it down as he saw that what was coming was no fearsome durrga.

"Help me," said a small man as he rushed toward them. He staggered, the colour of his clothes unrecognisable for the dirt and dust that covered them. "Please, get me out of here."

He fell to his knees in front of them, hand grasping at the hem of Conall's greatcoat.

"All right, you're safe now," he said, pulling the man to his feet.

"They came out of nowhere. Those beasts. Slaughtered everyone."

That much was obvious.

Sted stepped forward, grabbing the man's dust-strewn shirt and shaking him in her usual sympathetic manner. "Not everyone," she said. "How did you manage to avoid..." She gestured at the mining frame and the grisly remains nailed on it.

"When the attack began, I hid." He motioned to the collapsed hut. "When they started destroying everything, I could only watch as they..."

His face screwed up and he began to weep, the tears leaving tracks in the dirt of his cheeks.

"You're safe now, friend," Conall said. "What's your name?"

"I'm Donan," he replied. "Donan Marrlock."

Conall had never heard of him, but if he carried the Marrlock name, he must be of some importance to the Guild.

"We have to get him out of here," Sted said. "And back to the fort before nightfall."

"I know," Conall replied, glancing about the ruined compound. "But not before we've checked the place out properly. There might be other survivors."

Sted frowned. "Are you serious? Look at this place."

"Just wait here and keep your eyes open. I won't be long."

There weren't many places still standing, and Conall headed toward the biggest building. It must have been a warehouse of sorts; a cart lay overturned just outside the entrance, its payload of ore splayed on the ground.

He paused at the door, nudging it open with the longbarrel before slowly walking inside. A lantern lay broken on the ground in front of him, and the interior was draped in shadow. Conall paused, letting his eyes adjust to the dark before he moved farther inside. He instantly regretted it.

More corpses were strung up from the rafters. All were hanged by the neck, bloated faces staring, some of their limbs hacked off in a seemingly random manner. As he got closer he could see bite marks, as though the goatheads had torn pieces of flesh away, most likely while these poor souls were still alive.

Gritting his teeth at the horror, he stepped farther into the warehouse. There was a door next to him leading into a small office. Papers were strewn all about the place from a needless act of vandalism, but there was no sign of life. When he turned to delve deeper into the warehouse, Conall almost fell over the body in front of him.

This one was no human. The durrga lay in a heap, huge and bestial. Conall finally realised what they were up against as he stared at the head of the creature, which reminded him of a bull's. Two horns curled from its colossal skull, and splintbolts peppered the thickly muscled body. At least these poor wretches had put up a fight before they were slaughtered.

He gave the thing a wide berth, conscious that time was running out. When he reached the centre of the warehouse, he mustered enough courage to shout, "Anyone alive in here?" before deciding this was a fool's errand. It was obvious everyone was dead.

Before turning to leave, he spied something else lying on the floor. The weapon glinted in the scant light, a glaive of the most intricate craft, but far too unwieldy for any human to use effectively. He knelt for a closer look, seeing it was finished with intricate ironwork, the grip bound in fine leather. Runic script had been carved into the blade, but this could not be the work of the goatheads. Conall had studied warcraft at the academy in Wyke and knew his weapons well. This glaive had been forged in Malador.

But how? The durrga were a savage species, or so he'd been led to believe. They did not craft or trade with other nations, though surely here was proof to the contrary. And if the Maladorans had gifted the durrga with weapons, what else might they be helping with? And why?

Conall stood, the implications racing through his mind as he turned back toward the door in time to see the beast rise. The sight froze him to his core when he should have pulled the trigger of his longbarrel. This durrga was over seven feet of monster, raising itself unsteadily on cloven hooves. Though it looked dazed, it was still fearsome to behold, shoulders broader than any man's he had ever seen, hands that could crack a skull without effort. Its eyes began to focus, and Conall knew then he had to act or die.

He raised the longbarrel, pointing it at the durrga's chest. It would have been a point-blank shot, but he was far too slow. Before he could pull the trigger, the beast slapped the weapon aside. It almost broke his fingers as the longbarrel went flying off into the shadows.

The durrga advanced a step, and Conall backed away, wrenching the sword from the sheath at his belt. He expected it to roar, to spit its hate at him, but the thing had an intelligence in those spiteful eyes. It regarded him with caution, weighing up its enemy before glancing to the ground where its weapon lay.

Conall took the initiative and dashed forward, swinging his sword down in an arc. Despite its wounds, the durrga dodged with animal agility, the sword sweeping wildly past its head. It countered with a backhand that caught Conall across the chest. It was like being hit with a lump of wood, and he was jettisoned across the warehouse and slammed into the wall.

Desperately he tried to heave in a breath, all the air knocked from his lungs. The sword had fallen from his grip, and by the time he regained his faculties the durrga had retrieved its weapon from the ground and was advancing.

Conall scrambled to his feet, looking around for anything he could use as a weapon…or a shield. The wheel of a mining cart lay discarded beside him, and he grasped it, hefting the thing up in time to parry the glaive. He felt the impact jolt through his arms as the weapon dented the metal rim, and he staggered backward.

The beast kicked out with a cloven hoof, catching him in the ribs, knocking him clear through the brittle wall and into the office beyond. The wheel was lost from his grip, and he lay on his back across the desk, surrounded by useless parchments.

As the durrga climbed through the gap in the wall, glaive raised, Conall rolled aside. The weapon smashed down, cleaving the desk in two. Frantically he scrambled from the office on hands and knees, desperate to escape, hearing the goathead clattering after him. His feet skidded in the dirt as he sprinted for the exit. Bursting through the main doors of the warehouse, he lost his footing and went sprawling in the dust. Conall rolled onto his back in time to see the huge durrga charging after him, the glaive glinting in the sun.

The rhythmic snap of splintbow fire cut the air. A volley of bolts struck the durrga in face and chest, one piercing its baleful eye. It let out a final, pitiful bellow before the glaive dropped from its fist and the beast collapsed beside him in a cloud of dirt.

As Conall tried to heave air into his bruised chest, Captain Tarrien casually strolled up beside him, looking down at the corpse of the goathead with an empty splintbow resting on one shoulder. He hadn't even bothered to draw the pyrestone pistol he'd invested so much of his wages in.

"We got bored up on that ridge," he said. "And fortunate for you that we did."

Conall struggled to his feet. Sted was some feet away with Nevan and Donan, and he shot her a withering glance. She just shrugged.

"The thing's glaive," Conall said, motioning to where the masterfully crafted weapon lay in the sand. "That wasn't made by any durrga."

"I think you might be right," Tarrien replied with disinterest.

"It's Maladoran. Do you know what that means?"

"It means the goatheads don't just slaughter the miners of Torwyn? They pillage indiscriminately?"

"Or they've formed an alliance with Iperion Magna. That weapon was crafted for durrga hands. This could change everything. This could mean we are effectively at war."

Tarrien smirked at the idea. "The durrga don't form alliances. They hunt and they kill and they eat. And if we don't get out of here now, we could be next on the menu."

"We have to find out," Conall said. "We have to follow this raiding party, see where they're going. If we leave now, we'll lose their trail."

"I'm in charge here, Captain Hawkspur. Or had you forgotten?"

Conall could hear the derision in his voice. Tarrien knew this was his command, and there'd be no persuading him otherwise. He wasn't about to let a Hawkspur question his authority.

"Let's clear out," Tarrien ordered, and his men obeyed.

Before they left, Conall retrieved the glaive from where it lay. It was the heaviest weapon he'd ever held; no one but a durrga warrior could have wielded it with any skill. This had not been pillaged from some Magnan pirates.

Tarrien was not about to listen, but perhaps Beringer would. The goatheads were being helped by someone, and Conall would not stop until he found out who.

FULREN

The forge was stiflingly hot, and Fulren's shirt clung to him so tightly he almost wanted to tear it from his back. Noise assailed his ears in a cacophony of rhythmic clangs, and the thick air clogged his lungs. Still he stood and watched as the smith went about his labours.

Fulren had given the burly giant his specifications. They had been precise in every detail, but as the smith smashed the weapon into shape it was obvious he was used to working to his own standards. The man was a brute, well over six feet of muscle, stripped to the waist, his entire body shaved smooth. He didn't even wear the thick leather apron necessary for his trade, and Fulren could see his chest and belly were peppered with burns.

It was pointless trying to explain any errors he might be making, the man was deaf, or so Fulren had been told. He also had no tongue, which made conversing all but impossible. Not that any of that mattered, it was too late to change anything now. Fulren would have to make do with what was crafted.

The smith hammered the final imperfections from the blade, the metal white-hot in his grip. Fulren marvelled at the man's strength and resilience—the hammer he wielded was bigger than any he'd ever seen. Even a man of the smith's gargantuan size should never have been able to raise a tool of such might. The anvil on which he worked was massive, easily a ton of iron.

Sweat poured from his brow, but he carried out his labours with vigour. He focused on the blade, at one with that giant hammer, and Fulren couldn't help but marvel at the synergy of it. The smith was a slave, but he went about his task not with resentment but with a deep affection for his work. There was something spiritual about the way he forged that weapon, and Fulren found himself envying the man. He was a master of his craft, the most peerless artisan Fulren had ever witnessed. Deep down Fulren knew that he could practise for a thousand years and never attain such a level of skill. Not that he had a thousand years. If the Maladorans had their way, he had only a day.

Wenis had told him what to expect in the trial ahead. There was little chance he would survive it; none ever had. He would be executed in the arena alongside other criminals and heretics by a demon known as Ghobeq. If such a thing put fear in Wenis, Fulren could only imagine the horror that awaited.

If he could give himself any advantage before the day of the trial, he would do so. That was why he was here, in this burning forge, watching the smith at his work. The sword was indeed a majestic weapon, but it was only one part of this. The hard part of the preparation was still to come, but Wenis had kept her word, given him access to a forge and hopefully more besides.

The hammering ceased, the last deafening ring echoing out through the forge. Glancing up from his work, the smith saw Fulren looking on with interest. There was a silent communication between them. Almost as though the smith were searching for some kind of approval. Then he raised a hand and beckoned Fulren closer.

He approached warily. The smith was a huge specimen and could most likely crush Fulren's skull in a single massive hand. Nevertheless, he did not spurn the opportunity to take a closer look.

The smith laid down his massive hammer, gesturing for Fulren to stand before the iron anvil. When he had positioned himself, the smith pointed eagerly at the sword, making a hammering gesture with one thickly muscled arm, before pulling one of the gloves from his meaty hands and offering it.

"You want me to finish it?" Fulren asked, glancing down at the smith's hammer. There was no chance he could even lift it, let alone strike the hot metal.

The smith raised a hand, an idea striking him, and he moved to one side of the anvil, producing a much smaller tool from its base.

Fulren took the hammer from him and the smith smiled, eager for Fulren to make his contribution to the forging. It was heavy, but he was sure with some effort he would be able to swing it true. Putting on the smith's glove he realised it was far too big, but better that than singe his flesh on the burning metal.

The sword lay on the anvil, but Fulren was reluctant to strike. The smith was a master craftsman, and the prospect of ruining this carefully honed weapon made Fulren balk.

Tentatively he took the cooler end of the metal and raised the hammer. With a single stroke he brought it down. The resulting clang of metal on metal almost made his ears burst. A tremor went up his arm, numbing his shoulder. Fulren had worked in a forge before, but never had he felt such potent energy. This was something visceral, and it filled him with a strange joy, the purity of the forge making him want to cry out in ecstasy.

Though the hammer was heavy, the sword in his hand was lighter than any he had ever held. It had been crafted from an alloy he was unfamiliar with, four feet of the most perfect steel folded and folded again more times than he could count. He raised the hammer and struck again, hearing the ringing echo like a symphony through the forge.

When he looked up, he saw the smile of pleasure on the smith's face. Fulren was relieved the man was impressed and not dismayed that Fulren had spoiled his work.

The smith took the sword from him, dousing it in a deep well of water, the steam rising with a hiss. When the metal was cooled, the smith walked toward a nearby worktable, beckoning Fulren to follow.

Before he reached the worktable, more figures appeared from the surrounding darkness, herded by a woman in dark robes. They took their places around the table, each with a different piece of equipment. No sooner had the smith laid the weapon down than they began.

It was a wonder to behold, and Fulren could only marvel at the industrious sight before him as the artisans began to buff and shine the metal. One honed the blade, his whetstone singing against the edge, as another kept the alloy moist. The grip was bound in leather, the solid metal cross-guard fixed in place with countless precise taps of a hammer.

Before Fulren's eyes, the raw hunk of metal was transformed into a magnificent weapon. His doubts about it not meeting the specifications he had outlined were dashed as he saw it gradually transform into exactly what he had sketched.

Holes were bored into the blade to reduce its weight yet further, and he saw there were chambers for him to insert the intricate wirework needed to connect the pyrestones he would eventually fit.

When the craftsmen had finished, they were ushered away by the robed slave master, and the smith eagerly beckoned for Fulren to take his place at the table. As he took his seat, the tools he had requested were brought forward. Fulren had not expected the city of Jubara to have half the artifice he needed for the task, but somehow Wenis had found everything he required.

Coils of wire, inductors, oscillators, tools of every gauge were laid out before him. Fulren could not manage to stifle a smile as he prepared to begin. This was his craft, and there was no one in this city who could rival his talent.

He looked up at the smith, who stood expectantly.

"Let me show you how we craft weapons in Torwyn," Fulren said to his silent spectator.

The smith watched with fascination as he went to work setting the coils. He inlaid a blue and a yellow pyrestone into the blade, tightening the clamps to hold them in place. The only things missing were the activation switch and the red regulator stone, but he would not need them. He and Wenis had planned an alternative method of bringing the pyrestones to life.

Fulren worked well into the night under the watchful eye of the smith, and when he was done, he sat back, marvelling at the sword they had created. It had the potential to be a devastating weapon. All he needed now was a way to make it sing.

As though she'd read his thoughts, Fulren looked up from the worktable to see Wenis standing in the shadows of the forge, watching him avidly.

"Impressive," she said, looking down at the newly crafted weapon.

"I can't take all the credit," Fulren replied. "Your smiths are the most skilled I have ever seen."

"I'm sure," she said, her expression turning grave. "But there is no time left for compliments. We have a pressing appointment."

Fulren had been dreading this moment, but he knew he could not turn back now. If he was to have any chance of surviving the trial, there was one more thing he had to do.

He stood from the worktable, nodding his gratitude to the smith, who bowed his acknowledgment.

As Wenis led him from the forge she said, "Are you sure this is what you want?"

Fulren was not sure. He had no idea if what he was about to do was the right thing, but what choice did he have?

"Yes," he replied.

"Once you walk this path there will be no turning back. The risks are great, for me as well as you."

"Are you having second thoughts?"

Wenis sighed. "Should anything happen to you during this ceremony, I will be held accountable. If you harbour any doubt about your commitment to this, you will not survive what we are about to do. You must be sure you have the conviction, the strength to go through with it."

"I know what has to be done," he said. "I won't falter."

She raised a questioning eyebrow. "We shall see, Prince of Torwyn. We shall see."

As she led him farther down through the tower, Fulren couldn't help but think on the seed she had planted in his mind. When they had discussed this previously, he had been only too eager, but now the reality of it gnawed at him. But if he did not go through with the ceremony, the weapon he had forged would be useless—little more than a pretty hunk of metal. This was the only way.

Wenis led him farther into the vast structure. He had thought the forge was the lowest level of this place, but corridors twisted down, boring deeper into the bare rock. It was a mournful place, and the farther they went the more he expected to hear the dolorous lamentations of prisoners and the screams of the damned. All that greeted them was silence. There was no echoing drip of moisture, no squeaking and scurrying of rats. All he had to focus on was the bright light of the torch Wenis carried as they delved into the bowels of the earth.

The corridor opened up into a vast chamber. It could have been a cavern for all Fulren could tell, but by the light of the torch, he could not see the full extent of the chamber. They might as well have been enclosed in a cell.

Before him candles burned on the floor, illuminating an intricate sigil carved into the stone. It reminded Fulren of the iron circle that had adorned the deck of the black ark, and he felt his stomach flip at the sight of it.

"Take your place," Wenis said, gesturing to the arcane symbol.

Fulren managed to take only a single step toward the candles before she said, "Wait. You must disrobe."

Reluctantly Fulren took off his shirt, boots and leggings. "Everything?" he asked.

Wenis nodded, and he removed his undergarments, leaving them in a pile. Now naked, he walked to the centre of the arcane symbol and dropped to his knees. As he waited he felt gooseflesh rise on his skin, but it was not from the cold. There was no chill to the air, but still the strange disquiet made his hairs stand on end.

From out of the dark surrounding him came a distant noise. At first it sounded like someone speaking in a guttural language, but as he listened he realised it was some kind of hymn. That single voice was soon joined by others, until he was being serenaded by an eerie chorus.

Eventually the singers stepped forward out of the shadows. Fulren was surrounded by a dozen of them, thin lustrous veils covering their naked bodies. In front of him a woman approached. Though her face was hidden by red silk, she was otherwise naked but for the whirling patterns that adorned her flesh. Every part of her body bore an intricate necroglyph, and Fulren found himself spellbound by the designs.

As she leaned in close he could smell her—a heady mix of incense and sweat. Unable to see the face beneath the veil, he could not tell how old she was. Her body was both lithe and youthful, but at the same time there was a facet to her that was old beyond imagining.

The woman bore a small golden jug in her hand. It was a simple thing, but she carried it with reverence, as though it was some precious relic.

She said something, and the words were in no language he had ever heard, as though she spoke with the tongue of an animal. He listened intently until she reached forward, tipped his head back gently and raised the jug in her hand.

Fulren opened his mouth, an instinctual gesture, as she poured the contents down his throat. It tasted bitter as he swallowed, leaving a rancid tang on his tongue.

Slowly the woman and her veiled entourage retreated into the dark, and Fulren was left to kneel. Their song faded to silence as he sat alone amid the carved sigil.

Time seemed to stretch out. All the while he concentrated on the winking candles, trying to measure the passage of time as they burned down to stubs, but he had no idea how long he knelt there in the dark. It was as though he were lost in a void.

"Wenis," he called out eventually. "Are you there?"

Fulren realised his voice was slurry as he tried to speak. There was no answer to his question.

This was foolish. The ritual had clearly failed. Whatever these arcanists had tried to do to him, it was not working. Damn this place, and damn him for believing some pointless ritual might save his life.

As he made to rise from the circle, his body was immediately racked with agony.

Fulren screamed as his flesh burned. Every nerve caught fire. His throat stung as if he had swallowed a nest of wasps, and he clasped his hands over his eyes as it felt as if they'd been skewered by white-hot pokers.

He writhed in agony at the centre of the circle, crying out for mercy, for some relief from the intensity of the pain. He was being eaten from the inside, his whole body consumed in a conflagration as he screamed.

Fulren's mind swam. Visions began to coalesce before him, and gradually the pain relented as a face solidified...

Assenah Neskhon walked forward from the dark. She was as beautiful and striking as the first day he had laid eyes on her, red hair flowing despite the still air. She looked down at him imperiously before the flesh began to crumble from her face. Her red hair turned white and brittle, eyes sinking back into her skull. Fulren wanted to scream, but the cry was caught in his throat as he watched Assenah reduced to a shambling corpse. As she crumbled, more figures stepped from the curtain of shadow around him.

His mother fell to her knees, weeping uncontrollably. She reached out for him, calling his name, and Fulren was overcome with grief at the sight. He held out his hand but could move no closer as she mourned the loss of him. He tried to tell her that he was not dead, that he was still trying to make his way home, but she could not hear.

His mother faded, to be replaced by his sister. Tyreta looked afraid, shrinking from the surrounding shadows. He called her name, but she too could not hear. As he watched, his brother moved from the darkness toward Tyreta.

Conall was no longer the loving sibling he had watched fly away on a great eagle. Now he looked cruel, imposing, and there was something inhuman about him. As Fulren watched helplessly, Conall fell on Tyreta, grasping her throat, squeezing and squeezing as his sister tried to cry out in terror, raking their brother with her nails...

Fulren opened his eyes. He still lay amid the intricate symbol. The candles had all but burned out. His breath was shallow, his flesh covered by a thick sheen of sweat. Slowly the veiled figures stalked from the dark once again. Fulren wanted to run, to stand and flee this place before they could torture him anymore, but he could not move.

The priestess, face still hidden behind the red veil, stepped close to him. In one hand she carried an array of needles, in the other a vial of liquid that roiled in the candlelight, the colour changing constantly from one strange hue to the next.

Fulren felt hands take hold of him as the veiled arcanists moved him into position. There was nothing he could do to resist them as he knelt, head bowed before the priestess. She touched the first needle to the back of his neck, and he felt the pain course through his spine. Gritting his teeth, he fought the urge to fight or scream or flee their attentions. Though the pain almost made him convulse, he endured it. If he did not see this through, he would surely die in the arena.

It seemed to last forever, the priestess taking her time while she worked. At first the sting of the needle was concentrated at the nape of Fulren's neck, but then she spread the tiny incisions. The necroglyph was cut into his skin along his spine and spread out to his shoulders. Though he could not see them, he knew those intricate patterns had been indelibly carved into his flesh. When finally she finished, Fulren was panting hard, his sweat forming a pool beneath him. Still shaking from the experience, he looked up to see that the priestess and her entourage had disappeared once more into the dark.

He shivered. His body felt weak, as though he were recovering from a fever. He tried to rise, but his limbs would not hold his weight. How could he face the arena if he could not even stand, let alone fight?

"How do you feel?" Wenis asked.

He turned gingerly to see her standing close by. From the look on her face she was relieved that he was still alive.

"Sick," he replied. "That's about it. How do I know if this even worked?"

Wenis giggled at him. "Of course it worked. If it hadn't you'd be dead. Or worse."

"But I feel no different."

"What were you expecting? To grow horns? A tail?"

He felt violated, humiliated. The fact that Wenis found that amusing made the anger boil within him.

"I was expecting more than to feel weak as a kitten. How am I supposed to fight in this state? I'll be the first to die."

"Somehow I doubt that. You are more powerful than you have ever been."

Fulren shook his head. "I find that hard to believe."

"Close your eyes," she said.

"What?"

"Just do it. Close your eyes... and feel."

This was foolish, but what choice did he have? Fulren closed his eyes and shivered in the dark. As he did so, he sensed something close by. It was calling to him, a disembodied whisper yearning for his attention. Fulren concentrated harder, trying to connect, and as he did so it felt as though he'd lit a spark with his thoughts alone. Something ignited in the distance, setting off a chain reaction, and Fulren felt as though he were at the centre of a network—a web of power in which he was the core.

"Now," Wenis said. "Open your eyes."

Fulren did as she asked. He was no longer in the dark. Now they were at the centre of a giant cavern, and studded into every facet was a pyrestone. Each one was shining brightly where before it had been dull and inactive. The myriad stones shone like stars, and every one had done so at his behest.

"Do you believe me now?" Wenis asked.

As he knelt in that glimmering cavern, Fulren began to laugh.

TYRETA

Gelila offered another arrow. As Tyreta took it from her, the tribeswoman said the word *ekko* once more.

"Echo," Tyreta said back to her, repeating the kesh word for *arrow*.

Gelila shook her head. "Ekko," she said more firmly.

It was a process they had repeated half a dozen times. On each occasion Tyreta had said the word back exactly the same. Clearly there was an inflection she was missing. It was starting to frustrate Gelila, but she persevered nevertheless. Tyreta appreciated her diligence, and it wasn't the only thing she was thankful for.

Though she had told Yeki she would stay only one night, determined to return to civilisation, Tyreta had remained. The wound in her shoulder had been worse than she thought, and despite Yeki's ministrations it was slow to heal, but she found herself being treated with care by the villagers, who all helped tend to her. She had inherited a strange affection from these women, who greeted her no longer as a stranger but as some curious pet. The warriors among them still gave Tyreta a wide berth, but Gelila and the rest treated her with kinship.

The settlement's children seemed to bear a particular fascination with her, and she with them. Within a couple of days she found herself being followed about the place by wide, smiling faces, and gradually Tyreta was made to feel part of the tribe. She walked around in bare feet, and one of the children had even gone so far as to tie feathers and bird bones in her hair. At first Tyreta had wanted to refuse the attention, but she didn't have the words to politely say no, so going along with it had been the most gracious choice.

Though she appreciated that they no longer treated her like a lost waif, Tyreta was still conscious that soon she would have to leave. Yeki had told her of the kesh warlord, Shabak. That he intended to rise up against her people. It would not be long before she was recovered enough to make the journey back to New Flaym, and with Gelila's help Tyreta was getting stronger every day.

Her target was a few yards away across the clearing, a small mound of straw roughly humanoid in shape. Archery was a lost art in Torwyn since the invention of the splintbow. Tyreta more than appreciated the chance to learn something of the old ways.

"Echo," she said once more before nocking the arrow to her bow and drawing to her shoulder. The muscle still ached, but still she managed to pull the string taut.

She followed everything Gelila had managed to teach her—as much as she understood from the woman's demonstrations anyway. Concentrate on the target. Feet shoulder width apart, three fingers on the bowstring. Keep her eyes fixed as she drew, and take a deep breath in. Target with the point of the arrow.

It was a lot to remember, and it hadn't done much good so far. Tyreta had missed with every shot.

"Echo," she said one last time before she loosed.

The arrow flew true, impaling the pile of straw and almost knocking it over.

Tyreta whooped with joy, ignoring the ache of her wound and leaping a foot in the air. It was loud enough to scare a flock of brightly coloured birds from a nearby tree, and when she looked around she saw a group of women and their children had stopped what they were doing to see what had caused such a commotion.

Gelila looked distinctly underwhelmed.

"Ekko," the woman said.

Before Tyreta could try again, she saw Yeki approaching from the nearby huts. She marvelled at how spry the woman was. Over the past couple of days Yeki had treated Tyreta's wound with utmost care, going about the task with more diligence than a woman of half her years. Tyreta could only hope she'd be as fit when she reached such a venerable age.

"You make progress," Yeki said as she came to join them. "Learn fast."

"Lia-kan," Tyreta replied, trying to approximate the kesh word for *thanks*, but when Gelila giggled she realised she had got it very wrong.

Yeki winced at her mangling of the word. "Language you learn not so fast," the old woman said. "Might take while longer."

"You're right," Tyreta said. "But I don't have a while longer. I appreciate all you have done for me, but soon I will have to leave. I have to go back to my own people. I have to warn them of what is coming."

"Of course," Yeki replied. "But before you do, there is something you should see. I wish you to witness."

"What is it?" Tyreta asked, hoping it was nothing sinister, but after spending some time here, she was no longer afraid of the strange customs of the kesh.

"In your language it is called rite of passage."

"A coming-of-age ceremony? You want me to witness someone's passage to adulthood?"

"Yes," said Yeki. "And you might understand us better."

"Of course," Tyreta said, unable to hide her excitement.

"Tonight then," Yeki said before leaving the two women to their training.

"Great honour," Gelila said once the old woman had left. Her grasp of Tyreta's language had improved greatly in just a couple of days. At least one of them was learning something.

"To witness such a ritual? I bet it is. But what does it involve?"

Gelila smiled her sharp-toothed grin. "You see. Now practise!"

"I get it... Echo?"

"No," Gelila replied. "Kelach."

She tossed a spear to Tyreta, who plucked it deftly from the air. Abandoning the bow, she turned to face Gelila, who bent her knees into a fighting stance.

Tyreta had experienced enough combat training to know what this entailed. She might not be as proficient as her brothers, but at least she knew one end of a weapon from the other.

The two practised long into the afternoon. Tyreta soon discovered that all the techniques she had learned from the weapon masters of Wyke were useless against the skills the Lokai had developed after years of hunting in the jungle. She also learned the hard way what the word *kelach* meant. Every time Gelila disarmed her or tripped her or struck her with the butt of the spear she would say it again. Kelach! Attack.

Eventually, as the sun began to set, Gelila dismissed Tyreta to her hut to rest before the rite of passage began. When she was within the dark confines, she stripped off the chiton, then lay down on the straw bed to rest for a few moments...

Fulren was calling to her. She couldn't see him through the murk, but still she ran through the thick mist to find him. It was humid, as though she were trapped within the bowels of some subterranean forge.

He called again, and she turned, seeing a figure through the cloying air. Tyreta pressed forward, feeling the smog fill her lungs. The ground beneath her was soft, the mud squeezing between her toes, but still she pressed on. She could see him right in front of her, but no matter how hard she ran to reach him, he remained some distance away.

"Fulren!" she shouted.

Her brother ignored her. She could see him more clearly now, looking upward, staring at something towering above him.

Her anger grew. Though she couldn't see what stood above her brother, she knew he was in danger and wrestled on through the gloom. When she had managed to fight her way to his side, he was still staring.

"Fulren," she said again. "What is it?"

She reached out to touch him but stopped. There was an ethereal aspect to him. Despite her being able to see him, he was still so very far away. Slowly he turned to face her.

"It's coming," he said.

There was a roar. Through the fog something lit up like a fire. Tyreta had only enough time to realise it was the burning eyes of some great beast, looming over them through the thick air...

She woke shivering.

Around her she could just see the shafts of light dissipating, a vision of the pyrestone web fading fast. Her chest burned.

Tyreta touched a hand to the nightstone still hanging around her neck, feeling the intense heat in her palm, but that too was fading. She took the chain and lifted it, seeing a squall of yellow light within the dark stone, but it went out before she could focus on it. As she sat in the dark hut, Tyreta began to wonder if she had even seen it at all, or if it had just been a trick of her dream.

The hide curtain that covered the entrance was pulled back, and the hut was illuminated by the bright light of a torch. As Tyreta's eyes began to focus, she could see Gelila standing in the doorway.

"Come," the woman said, beckoning Tyreta to follow. "Come. It starts."

Tyreta stood and slipped into a clean tunic before following Gelila out into the moonlight. The camp was deserted as they made their way across it, and in the distance Tyreta could hear a chorus of voices. She followed Gelila in silence to the edge of the camp. Ahead of them, gathered at the bottom of a nearby hill that rose to rocky peaks, the whole village had gathered.

As they got closer she could see part of the brush had been cleared to reveal stone carvings in the rock at the base of the hill. A stair of sorts rose up, strange images hewn into it. In the winking torchlight Tyreta couldn't make out any details, but it resembled the altars she had seen in the Mount back at the Anvil, only this did not depict ancient Wyrms. Instead concentric patterns wound around one another in a network of angular sigils. It reminded Tyreta of the pyrestone web she saw as she was about to commune—a visual representation of her webwainer gift carved into the rock face.

Closest to the altar were the female warriors of the tribe. Each stood tall in the torchlight, her face covered in white, chalky war paint, hair tied and braided and slick with mud. They reminded Tyreta of the fearsome men who had attacked her, murdered

Wyllow, and pursued her through the jungle, only these women bore a nobility that their male counterparts lacked.

Gelila guided her to the edge of the gathering as they quietly chanted in the kesh tongue. Tyreta could see they had crowded around a woman who waited on her knees. She was young, barely out of childhood, and she stared in a daze as though she had been drugged. Her eyes rolled within her head, unable to focus, and she swayed slightly. As a low moan came from the woman's throat, Tyreta felt a sense of foreboding well up within her.

The chanting grew louder, and the feeling in Tyreta's gut intensified. The warriors began to beat their spears against the ground, the children among them clacking sticks together to create a primal rhythm that Tyreta could feel as well as hear.

Some of the warriors strode forward, then picked the kneeling woman up and carried her toward the crude stone altar. There they laid her, shivering and writhing, all the while that steady beat playing out in the dark of the jungle.

Tyreta couldn't tell how long she watched before Yeki appeared from the shadows nearby. She no longer wore the chiton that usually covered her, nor the insects on their golden chains. Now she was dressed as a warrior, animal skins draped from her shoulders, war paint adorning almost every inch of exposed flesh.

The old woman raised a knife before speaking in kesh, the words flowing as though she had rehearsed them a hundred times. Tyreta was struck with fear of what Yeki might do with that blade, but surely they hadn't brought her here to witness some ritualised sacrifice?

The drumming of spears stopped, the jungle falling silent as Yeki finished her speech and turned her attention to the prone body before her. She leaned over the girl, blade striking out as she cut open the flesh of her face, twisting swiftly, carving a network of intricate patterns. Under the ministrations of Yeki's blade, the prone woman just stared, eyes fixed on nothing, showing no sign of pain as she was cut open.

When she was done, Yeki stood back, raising the knife. Swiftly she picked up a cup, letting the blood drip into it, the blade still shining slick in the torchlight. As she did so she chanted, her voice rising and lowering in pitch, the guttural noises reminding Tyreta of the jungle animals she had heard during her flight from the Chul.

An eerie silence had fallen on the place now. Tyreta could feel a strange power emanating from the earth. It reminded her of the rush she got when communing with pyrestone, the thrill of accessing her webwainer talent, only this was all around her, from the earth to the darkening sky above. Everyone stood in reverence; even the crickets and the nocturnal beasts of the undergrowth had fallen silent, watching, waiting in awe.

Yeki lowered the cup, lifting the woman's head so that she could drink of her own blood. No sooner had it passed her lips than she began to convulse, her body shuddering, those wide eyes rolling to the back of her head as she was consumed by a violent palsy.

The horror of it made Tyreta want to run forward and rescue the young woman from this foul rite, but she was rooted to the spot. All she could do was watch as the object of the ritual thrashed on the stone altar, hoping she had not been tricked into witnessing someone's murder.

It was with relief that she saw the girl's convulsions calm. The kesh woman breathed deep, and Yeki poured water onto her face, washing the blood that covered it, before helping her to stand.

As she did so the moon moved from beyond the clouds, bathing the clearing in a blue glow. Tyreta gasped as she saw the woman's face was no longer covered in lacerations. Now she bore scars, her flesh miraculously healed. Tyreta could barely believe her eyes as she watched the woman's naked flesh begin to darken in patches. Tribal markings appeared, reminiscent of those carved into the stone of the cliff face. It was as though she were being tattooed by an unseen hand, interlinking whorls of blue, black and red covering her naked flesh.

The kesh was out of her stupor now, eyes focusing on the crowd. Her breathing became less fevered, and as Tyreta watched she saw this young woman become a newborn warrior of her tribe.

Yeki took a step back into the shadows as this warrior raised her arms to the moon and howled. It was a feral cry of rapture, and Tyreta could feel its raw power. She felt imbued with all the latent energy of a thousand pyrestones, and she took a faltering step back in the face of such overwhelming strength.

The tribeswomen moved forward, embracing her and welcoming her like a long-lost sister. Gelila moved forward to pay her respects, and Tyreta was left to wonder what she had just witnessed.

"Wondrous, is it not?" said Yeki, now standing beside her.

Tyreta could not take her eyes from the woman as she embraced every member of the tribe. "What have I just watched?" she asked.

Yeki reached forward and grasped the nightstone. "Kiatta," she whispered, smiling widely.

Before Tyreta could question her further, a group of warriors came from the surrounding jungle. They were greeted by the villagers but seemed unconcerned about the rite that had just taken place. Something had them spooked, and one of them came to speak with Yeki in haste.

Immediately Yeki began to bark orders, and the rite was suddenly forgotten. Those warriors who had stood vigil during the ritual rushed to retrieve their weapons.

"What's happening?" Tyreta asked. "Are we under attack?"

"Not yet," Yeki replied. "Your people have been seen not far from here. Many men. Many weapons."

"They might be looking for me," Tyreta said, feeling a sudden wellspring of hope.

"Or hunting us," Yeki replied gravely.

Tyreta would not have admitted it, but the prospect of that was very real. Had she unwittingly placed everyone here in peril?

"Then I have to go. Show me where they are and I will lead them away."

"You might be in much danger," Yeki replied.

Tyreta cast her mind back to being pursued through the jungle and to Wyllow's gruesome end. There was a risk, but it was one she had to take. "You have to trust me. I am in no danger from my own people."

Yeki considered her words carefully, then slowly nodded.

"Very well. We will take you. But you must not return. We may not be able to protect you if you do."

"I understand," Tyreta replied.

And she did. As much as she was in danger from Shabak and his people, she understood these women had much more to fear from the Guilds. As much as she wanted to stay here, to learn more about the Lokai, she knew the best way to show her gratitude was to leave them behind and never come back.

FULREN

The Night of the Black Moon was aptly named. As Fulren was escorted across the raised plaza of the tower to a cell-like vestibule, he glimpsed the sky briefly through the thick cloud. The surface of the moon was matte black, visible only due to the iridescent ring around its edge. Seeing such an eclipse unnerved him. He knew from the astronomer's calculations in Torwyn that no such phenomenon was scheduled. This could only be the result of dark sorceries, but what else could he expect in such an unhallowed land?

Jubara was a place of much wonder, but also a seat of demonic power. Though his time here had proved that the savage reputation of Nyrakkis was overstated, it was still steeped in the arcane. Tonight, Fulren was to about to discover just how much.

"The Trial of Ghobeq will be sponsored by one of the Nine Houses of Nyrakkis," Wenis said, breaking the silence as Fulren was prepared for his execution.

He had been stripped of the clothes bearing his Guild colours and was now being helped into a leather tunic and leggings. The thrall who dressed him was silent, as Fulren had come to expect, and he allowed the old man to do his work without complaint.

"Before an event such as this," Wenis continued, "the Nine will bid for which House is to receive the resulting benefaction. A sacrifice such as this can yield great power, and the Houses will pay handsomely to receive it."

"So this is a rite rather than a gladiatorial contest? And my sacrifice to some demonic power will not be a total loss, because one of your great families will reap the benefit?"

"You grasp the concept perfectly."

"I also grasp the concept of armour," Fulren replied, looking down at the leather outfit he had donned. "And this is not it."

"Remember, this is no mere execution. This is also an opportunity for the Nine Houses of Nyrakkis to provide entertainment for the masses. And you will not be alone. You will fight alongside other condemned prisoners, and they want to live, just as you do."

"That comes as a great comfort," Fulren lied. "I look forward to making their acquaintance just before I'm torn to pieces."

Wenis did not see the funny side. If anything she had shed her smug exterior and now looked worried.

"You hide your fears well, Fulren. You should know I take no pleasure in this. I would rather we had found a way to spare your life."

"Talking like I'm already dead—that's just what I need right now."

There was no smart comment. No wry smile. Wenis just looked at him with resignation. "Your weapon awaits you in the arena. Keep your eyes open, and look for the winged talon. That is your sign."

With that she turned and left him alone. In the silence that followed he felt a strange calm come over him. He was about to be executed in a foreign land, far away from his family and everything he knew. There was fear, but his hands did not shake, his lip did not tremble. All he felt inside was a grim resignation. Even when the door to the chamber eventually opened and he saw the tall, tattooed warriors ready to take him to his death, he still did not succumb to panic.

As they surrounded him and walked out of the room, Fulren was reminded of the day he had been escorted from the Anvil. The day his uncle's Titanguard had conveyed him toward the demonic ark and he had been stolen away from his homeland. When the warriors of Jubara led him down a torchlit corridor, all thoughts of that disappeared as he heard the cheering.

It started as a rumble. A thousand voices united in the distance, growing louder the farther along the corridor he went. Soon the rumble drowned out the sound of the marching feet around him. By the time he saw light glimmering at the end of the tunnel it had become almost deafening.

The warriors led him out into the arena. Fulren had never seen a sight like it. For all the magnificence of Torwyn's great cities, they paled into insignificance against this vast structure.

Tiered seating rose up beyond the thirty-foot wall that surrounded him. It was as though he strode into the centre of a vast cavern, its walls mountainous, a starless sky overhead. The spectators were almost too small to distinguish, but the noise they made was cacophonous as it echoed around him.

In the centre of the arena was a scaffold, a structure of towers and bridges winding their way in and out of black stone obelisks. Flagpoles jutted from the structures, pennants of every colour hanging limp and bearing different sigils. Fulren remembered Wenis's words and tried to spot the winged-talon marker among them, but if it had been placed for him, it was not in plain view.

As the warriors surrounding him hastily retreated from the arena and an iron gate closed behind them, Fulren noticed a group already waiting up ahead. He made his way toward them, his fellow condemned, each of them similarly garbed in leathers.

Not one of them acknowledged him as he came to stand by their side. Each was gazing toward a ledge that overlooked the arena. Seated atop it on a throne of blue glass was Queen Meresankh. She watched the proceedings with that vacant glare, and even from a distance it sent a shiver through Fulren's spine. To her right stood her guardian, Bekis Katanen, grim and ever vigilant. There were more figures beside them, but Fulren had little time to distinguish them before Ak-Samtek walked to the fore, his black robes sweeping the brim of the ledge.

The grand vizier held up his arms, and the crowd was immediately quieted. Its noise echoed around the arena for a few short moments, and when finally the place fell silent, he spoke, his voice resonating throughout the rows of tiered stone.

"Jubara," he cried. "The great and good of Nyrakkis." The crowd cheered in approval, and Fulren could only think how easily pleased they were. "We are gathered for the Trial of Ghobeq at the behest of your queen." A portion of the crowd began to chant Meresankh's name, but it was a half-hearted display, fading into nothing as Ak-Samtek continued.

"The condemned stand before you. Ready to receive their judgement." His raised arm swept down, gesturing at a thin, dark-haired woman on the periphery of the gathered prisoners. "There, Tiaa Sakhopenra, witch of the Silent Key. Betrayer of her mistress Amosis Makareth."

Tiaa stared back at the vizier, disdain burning in her dark eyes.

"There." Ak-Samtek's arm swept toward a tall, square-jawed man, his shoulders broad, hands gripped tight into fists. "Gaddis Rekhmire, former centurion of the Medjai, condemned on the order of General Serapion himself."

The centurion gave little away, and Fulren could only admire this Rekhmire's resolve. He'd have liked to feel as brave as this man looked, but the longer the formalities went on the more he thought he might lose his nerve.

"There, Torrianus the Hydra. Infamous bandit leader, finally brought to justice."

The crowd booed and hissed as the grand vizier gestured to a squat, ugly man with filthy hair and a brutally scarred face.

Those boos turned to laughter as Ak-Samtek's arm pointed toward a portly figure, tears streaking his face. "There, Wenamun Surero. A man of influence and power, fallen to immorality."

Fulren could only wonder what might pass for immorality in a place such as this, but he had little time to think on it before the vizier's arm pointed right at him.

"And there." The crowd hissed and booed much more vocally than it had for any of the others, even the notorious bandit. It was clear who it had reserved most of its hatred for. "Fulren Hawkspur, Prince of Torwyn. Murderer. Deceiver. Heretic."

Perhaps a little bit strong, but what could he expect in the circumstances? He'd been painted as a killer and given little chance to prove his innocence. With any luck that chance was coming.

The booing lasted quite a while, and Ak-Samtek seemed in no mood to quiet the crowd, allowing it to express its contempt for the villain of the show. When eventually it finished, the grand vizier gestured to the far side of the arena, where another ledge overlooked the proceedings. There a corpulent figure sat beneath a roofed booth, surrounded by servile attendants and bronze-armoured women.

"Before we begin, join me in thanking the sponsor of this trial. Lord Nimlot of House Hamaket."

As though it had rehearsed, the crowd recited some kind of chant, and Nimlot rose unsteadily to his swollen feet to acknowledge its thanks. From what Wenis had told him, this man and his House would receive the benefit of the sacrifice to come. Fulren could only hope he appreciated the show.

The crowd slowly hushed once again. Fulren expected to hear more from Ak-Samtek, but when he looked back to the elevated podium, he saw the vizier had retreated out of sight. The silence was interrupted by the grinding of gears, and from the centre of the maze rose another black obelisk, much larger than the rest. Within the stone were glowing veins of gold and silver, intersecting in a beautiful pattern. Fulren would have been spellbound, but his eyes were drawn to the hooded figure chained to the obelisk's face.

If the prisoner was in discomfort, he made no sign of protest as the obelisk locked into place with a deep thud that shook the ground. Fulren glanced at his fellow condemned, but they were all staring at that black stone, some fearfully, some with grim looks of determination.

Sparks suddenly flashed along the gold and silver seams of the obelisk, and the chained prisoner convulsed as though an electric charge were coursing through his body. Fulren would have felt sympathy, but he had a feeling that worse was on its way for him and the rest of the prisoners.

With a final convulsion, the body chained to the obelisk began to break apart. Tears appeared in the flesh, blood running in rivulets until, with a sickening sound of cracking bone and bursting organs, his body exploded, showering the obelisk in gore.

The gold and silver veins glowed. A hairline crack appeared in the obsidian, spreading to break the smooth veneer apart. Torrianus took a nervous step away from the spectacle, and a squeal of terror escaped the throat of Wenamun Surero before he took flight.

With a deafening explosion the obelisk broke apart. Fulren staggered back, feeling a hot wind wash over him as dark rock was flung all about the arena. When he opened his eyes, he saw a sight from the depths of his worst nightmares.

A crocodilian giant stood where the obelisk had been. It was all of fifteen feet tall, forearms thickly muscled and ending in three-toed talons, hindquarters squat and powerful. Countless fangs lined its elongated mandibles, and its eyes regarded the arena with bestial familiarity. This was indeed no trial. It was an execution of the most diabolical kind. The demon Ghobeq had come to claim its sacrifice.

"By the Wyrms," Fulren breathed. If ever he had thought to pray, then now was most definitely the time.

Gaddis Rekhmire and the witch Tiaa were already sprinting toward the edge of the maze of towers and interlocking bridges. By the time Fulren had gathered himself enough to think, Ghobeq was advancing.

He backed away, unable to take his eyes from the creature. Ghobeq had him locked in its sights as it sprang forward on those powerful hind legs.

Fulren glanced around for somewhere to run. The maze of towers and bridges was some yards away. Would he ever reach it before this demon locked him in its jaws?

He ran, churning up the sand beneath him, hearing the demon's clawed feet drumming on the ground as it came for him. He managed to reach the bottom of one of the towers, the ladder leading up ten feet to a wooden platform. In that instant he knew he would never make it in time. Knew the beast would grasp him as he climbed and swallow him whole if it could.

Instead he dived to one side, hearing the panting breath of Ghobeq right behind him. The demon smashed into the scaffold, splintering wood as Fulren rolled to his feet.

Before he could dart toward the next tower, he heard a startled scream. Wenamun Surero had been cowering at the top of the tower, and as Ghobeq smashed into it the man lost his footing. Fulren just had time to see Surero hit the ground with a groan before Ghobeq came to its senses.

The demon reared. Surero screamed. Fulren ran for the next tower, unwilling to witness what was about to happen. Whatever Surero had done to find himself in the arena, Fulren doubted he deserved such a fate, but there was nothing he could do to save the man, even if he'd had the inclination.

As Ghobeq noisily gorged itself on Surero's limp body, Fulren reached the next tower. He climbed quickly, focusing as best he could despite the fear and panic. When he reached the platform, he saw the bandit king Torrianus and the witch Tiaa hunkering over something. Their backs were to him, and Tiaa crouched at the foot of a purple banner bearing an intricate sigil stitched in silver and black.

"Hurry, witch," Torrianus urged.

Tiaa said nothing as she reverently opened the casket at the foot of the banner. From within she plucked a curved dagger, beautifully wrought and bejewelled with amethyst and emerald.

"A knife?" Torrianus spat. "They gave you a knife against such a beast as this?"

Tiaa turned to him, her dark eyes regarding the bandit with amusement. "The knife is not for Ghobeq," she replied.

The blade flashed as she plunged it into Torrianus. Fulren could only stare in horror as it sank into his chest up to the hilt, and he barely had time to acknowledge what had happened before he collapsed. Tiaa leapt upon him, whispering an incantation as the bandit gurgled his last, not yet perished from the fatal wound. As his bubbling protest subsided, the necroglyphs that adorned Tiaa's arms began to glow yellow and red. The urge to flee and find the Hawkspur banner was overwhelming, but Fulren stayed to witness, utterly enthralled by the sight.

Torrianus had stopped twitching now, his eyes staring blankly at the dark sky. The witch rose to her feet, her eyes two pools of black. She regarded Fulren, reading the horror in his expression and smiling wickedly. For a moment he thought he might become her next victim, but instead she wrenched the knife free of her victim's chest and turned her attention to the demon running rampant in the arena.

"Witness the power of the Silent Key, son of Torwyn," she whispered before leaping from the platform.

Ghobeq saw her from the other side of the arena, where it had been trying to scale one of the platforms. It ceased its struggle, warily approaching the mortal who had dared to offer herself as the next sacrifice.

Tiaa began to recite an incantation, the necroglyphs on her flesh glowing as she channelled the power of the dagger in her grasp and the energy of the murdered bandit it had consumed. Ghobeq increased its stride, powering itself toward her, eating up the distance as Fulren held his breath.

Yellow light spewed from the outstretched dagger, dripping molten in the midst of the arena. The streak of energy smashed into Ghobeq's snout as it charged, halting the beast in its tracks. It howled, the noise filling the arena as the raw power of Tiaa's incantation struck it head-on.

Then that molten blast dissipated to nothing.

Tiaa was left standing at the centre of the arena as Ghobeq shook its powerful head, then focused its malevolent glare on her. Fulren had enough time to see the assured expression on her face fade to one of terror before the demon leapt forward to consume her.

Again Fulren could not watch as the beast devoured its victim, but the roar of the crowd told him all he needed to know.

"Are you just going to stand there, eastlander?" Fulren turned to see the former centurion, Gaddis Rekhmire, regarding him with grim focus. "Or are we going to kill this beast?"

He carried two swords. Where he had found them Fulren could only guess, but when Gaddis offered him one hilt-first, he took it without question.

Ghobeq had finished devouring the witch to the delight of the crowd. Fulren looked about the arena. Escape was impossible. As the demon looked up, mouth dripping crimson, he briefly thought that perhaps now would be a good time to find the winged-talon banner. But there was no time. Ghobeq had them in its sights. It could easily scale the platform and devour him where he stood. The weapon he had crafted was lost somewhere in the arena, if it had ever been here at all. Better he go down fighting. Better he honour the name of Hawkspur with a glorious death.

Both men dropped from the tower. This was madness and Fulren knew it, but then Nyrakkis was insanity personified, and if he was to die, he would do it his way.

Gaddis stepped to the side with practised grace, his sword held defensively. Seeing both men had weapons, the demon approached with caution.

"Take its other flank," Gaddis ordered.

Fulren obeyed, moving to the beast's left, gripping tight to the blade. It was perfectly balanced, keen edge glinting in the torchlight of the arena. At least he would get to die with a decent weapon in his hand.

Ghobeq regarded the two fighters with a keen intelligence. Nevertheless, Fulren recognised the hunger behind that eager glare; it could not hold itself back for long. Gaddis recognised it too.

"Come at me," he goaded. "Taste my steel, you stinking beast."

That was enough for Ghobeq, and it reared, snarling as it charged at the centurion.

Fulren darted forward as Ghobeq exposed its scaled flank. Gaddis leapt aside, the demon churning up the sand as it adjusted its approach. Fulren took his chance, raising the sword high and swinging it down against the creature's head. The strength of the blow jarred up his arm as the blade bounced off the creature's thick skull. It was enough to make the demon retreat a few paces, but there was no damage done.

"It seems our weapons might be useless, eastlander," Gaddis called as the crowd booed their momentary success. "We never had a chance. I hope you've made peace with your gods."

Just then something caught Fulren's eye—a pennant hung atop a distant tower. The winged talon.

He didn't wait, there was no time to explain himself as he set off at a sprint. Gaddis called something behind him, most likely cursing him for a coward. To Fulren's relief, Ghobeq seemed more intent on gorging itself on Gaddis's flesh than on chasing him down, and within moments he had reached the base of the tower to the hissing disapproval of the crowd. He pulled himself up one-handed, not yet willing to lose the only weapon he had, though it had proved useless so far.

At the top of the tower, Fulren pulled up short. Where he had expected to see his perfectly crafted sword there was nothing but the banner skewering the wooden platform. He cursed, glancing back to where Gaddis was dodging Ghobeq's attacks. So far the centurion had managed to avoid those ravenous jaws, but it wouldn't be long before he tired, and Fulren would be the last to die.

Looking back to the banner, he wondered if this had all been a ruse. If Wenis had tricked him, offering hope where there was none. But what would be the purpose in that? The weapon had to be here.

The base of the banner was driven into the wooden platform. The planks looked fragile, almost brittle. Fulren raised his sword and smashed it into them. The wood splintered, and through the gap he saw it glinting—his pyrestone blade.

Fulren dropped to his knees, tearing at the wooden planks with bare hands before grasping the hilt of the sword and wrenching it free. A more perfect weapon he had never seen. There was only one way to find out if it would grant him the power he needed to defeat this demon.

He leapt down from the platform, running toward where Gaddis still fought Ghobeq. The centurion was tiring as the creature snapped at him with those deadly jaws. As Fulren raced to join the fray, Ghobeq bit down on Gaddis's blade and wrenched it from his grip.

Fulren felt the necroglyph at the nape of his neck begin to burn. The vision at his periphery darkened, filling with dark tendrils as though he had been concussed. A disembodied voice whispered barely audible words in his head. He staggered, feeling the blade begin to vibrate in his hand as the necroglyph communed with the pyrestones mounted within. It whispered promises he could barely comprehend. Offering him power if only he would unleash its might.

Ghobeq was crouching now, ready to pounce. Gaddis breathed heavily, clutching a wound in his shoulder.

Before the demon could leap, Fulren raced forward and shouldered Gaddis aside, standing before the thing, his blade held aloft. The demon reared again, shielding its eyes from the blinding light of the pyrestones. Then it roared in anger before fixing Fulren with a baleful glare.

He should have been terrified, should have fled at the sound, but with this blade in his hand he felt invincible.

Ghobeq pounced. To Fulren's eye it was as though the thing leapt in slow motion. Time stretched out as Fulren raised the weapon, feeling the heat of the pyrestones hungering for Ghobeq's soul. Blue and yellow jewels flashed as the blade hummed with power.

The monster was upon him, those whispered promises of power screaming in his ears.

With a bellow of fury, Fulren hacked the demon from neck to belly, spilling its guts to the sand of the arena. Ghobeq landed in a heap, churning the dust in a cloying cloud and issuing a last gurgling breath before lying still. Fulren could only stare in awe as the necroglyph burned at his neck, his senses numb, hands still trembling from the thrill of violence. In his hand the hum of the sword had relented, the power of its pyrestones extinguished.

The arena fell silent as he felt his flesh prickling with energy, his teeth clenched lest he howl a victory cry to the bastard crowd. He looked up, seeing the shocked expressions on those distant faces, seeing Meresankh sitting, cold white eyes filled with fury.

Fulren Hawkspur had proved his innocence to the whole of Jubara. He had killed one of their gods. Surely they would have to release him now. At last he could go home.

"Eastlander!" Gaddis cried.

Fulren turned in time to see Ghobeq lurch toward him in a final death throe. He staggered back beyond its reach, but not far enough. The demon opened its jaws wide and a jet of green bile sprayed from its throat, hitting him in the face.

It was the last thing Fulren would see.

LANCELIN

For most men the prospect of travel on a war eagle would have thrilled. The feeling of freedom, the knowledge that death might be but one slip away, was enough to fill anyone with a sense of wonder. Not so for Lancelin Jagdor.

This was mere function. The beast beneath him was a means of travel, pure and simple. There was no thrill in this. The nearness to death at any moment gave him no pleasure. This was the quickest means of reaching his goal, and if anything a necessary inconvenience.

He had set out from Fort Karvan at dusk. That way he could cross the Drift and approach Jubara from the south under cover of dark before anyone would see he had travelled from Torwyn. He had to appear like an ordinary merchant from the southlands, of which there were many, plying their trade in rarities from the pirate coast of Iperion Magna and across the Ungulf Sea to the Karna Frontier.

Lancelin swallowed down his apprehension as he flew over Nyrakkis. At any moment he expected winged beasts to rise from the city, or one of their foul black arks to intercept his flight. Here were factors over which he had no control, and it did not sit well with him. Lancelin was a man who had long ago learned that control was power. It was a lesson he had learned the hard way. Now he was throwing himself into the jaws of the lion with no contingencies. But he had made a promise to Rosomon, and he would fulfil it at any cost.

When he drew closer to Jubara, his fears proved thankfully unfounded, and as the war eagle swooped closer he could see armoured figures atop the city's battlements directing him to an aerie clinging to the side of one of the black towers.

The beast set down heavily on the raised platform, panting for air as it finally rested. Lancelin unstrapped his thighs from the saddle, rubbing away some of the numbness before climbing down. Loping attendants had already made their way to the end of the jetty and were securing the war eagle to a mooring chain, wary of the beast's beak. They then began silently examining its payload. The baggage the eagle was laden with served to complement Lancelin's subterfuge. He had come as a trader, a dealer in foreign spices. If only the people of Nyrakkis had need of pyrestone, he could have brought that in abundance, but since the warlocks of this nation had little need for such commodities Lancelin had been forced to come up with a different resource.

Despite all official communication between Torwyn and Nyrakkis having been cut off for hundreds of years, it was common knowledge that clandestine routes of trade had been established for many decades. The Guilds had tried to stop such trade, and Lancelin had fought hard over the years to hamper this illegal black market, but now he was to turn it to his advantage.

It was not the only sacrifice he had been forced to make to embellish his masquerade. Gone was his Archwind uniform, replaced by drab travelling leathers. His swordwright's blade had been replaced with a well-used but functional weapon. His chin itched with the growth of a five-day beard, and though he couldn't smell it himself, he was sure he stank from lack of bathing.

As Lancelin began to think he might make his way from the aerie unchallenged, a short, wiry man limped from the small tower at the end of the jetty. Despite his ailment, he bore all the self-assured insouciance of a senior functionary. When the man reached him, he regarded Lancelin curiously.

"Here on business, eastlander?"

Now Lancelin would see if he could talk his way through this. Deception was not his strength, but he had practised this moment in his head all the way here.

"I am a trader, come to secure a new market for spices." He gestured back toward the sack-laden war eagle still being examined by the attendants. "You are free to check my goods should you wish."

The man shook his bald head. There was a triple-skull brand on his cheek that Lancelin assumed was a symbol of rank. Bifurcating tattoos crept up from his neck and along the sides of his shaven scalp. "Just your papers," the man said. "I assume you have a licence of marque from the Guilds of Torwyn? That should be enough to prove the truth of your words."

Lancelin reached into his leather jacket and took out the folded papers identifying him as a merchant with authorisation to trade within the borders of Torwyn.

"I have a freight concern based in Agavere," he said, gesturing to his steed. "A fleet of eagles just like this one."

The man looked down his nose at the papers. "The Guilds not paying you enough?"

"I am always keen to explore new avenues."

"Keen enough to risk swinging from a rope?" the functionary said, raising an eyebrow suspiciously. "The Guilds would execute you if they knew you were here."

"Then you had best not tell them," Lancelin replied, hoping to lighten the mood. He was a man unused to levity, but perhaps gallows humour was appropriate to a situation like this.

"The greater the risk, the greater the reward, eh?" the functionary said, his grin revealing a row of gold teeth. "Show me a man who never took a risk, and I'll show you a man who never achieved anything."

"Words I live by," Lancelin replied. It was a lie, he never took risks, everything was calculated. Until now.

"This all seems in order," the functionary said. "Who are you here to broker trade with?"

Lancelin had no idea. His knowledge of this place was scant, limited to what he had been told by his contacts in the Armiger Battalions. He would have to hide the truth within a lie.

"Perhaps you could advise me?" he replied, only half feigning his ignorance. "My spices have come from the Sundered Isles, and I have exclusive rights for the trade route across the Redwind. Who would you suggest I approach for the most lucrative contract?"

The functionary did not even need to consider it. "If I were you I'd arrange an audience with House Galavan. I could have my serfs escort you to their spire, if you so wished?"

"No need," Lancelin replied, eager to be away from this man and his prying eyes. "I will find them. Besides, it is the first time I have been to your city, and I would take in its delights at my leisure."

"Without a guide?" the functionary replied. "You are a brave one. But suit yourself." He handed the licence of marque back to Lancelin, adding papers of his own. "The slip is for ten days' upkeep of the eagle. There's also a chit with the warehouse ident where your goods will be stored. May the Black Moon guide you."

Lancelin took his leave with a nod of thanks, relieved the conversation was over. The longer he was forced to talk with the functionary the more chance he had of giving himself away. He left the jetty behind him, taking a steep flight of alabaster stairs down onto the street below.

He had to find his contact as soon as possible. There had been no official communication between Torwyn and the Maladoran nations for centuries. However, the Guilds were not without their spies within Nyrakkis. Lancelin was to meet with one such agent, and he had been given directions but no name. Now all he had to do was navigate the strange city of Jubara and find the man.

Before he left the Anvil he had committed the basic layout of the city to memory from a rough map that was years out of date. He had worked out the route to his contact based on the placement of Jubara's chief landmarks. Lancelin was relieved when he had not taken more than a dozen steps on the street before recognising a demonic-looking temple rising above the rest of the buildings. Still, there was a chance he would become hopelessly lost, and he could not shake the notion that this task might be beyond him.

As he walked the streets he was struck by the stark contrast in architecture between Jubara and the majestic cities of Torwyn. Where the Anvil was all marble and intricately hewn stone, here was alabaster and obsidian cast in curved and sweeping lines. Aesthetics over functionality, constructed to inspire awe and fear. But it was not the buildings that most held his attention, it was the outlandish characters he now found himself thrust among.

He passed a hooded and twisted figure bent in its labours as it carried a giant thurible that spewed incense. Behind the celebrant strode a woman dressed in black and white, her spiked headdress spiralling above the throng. Despite her freakish appearance, no one seemed to notice her as she strutted along the highway.

A group of dancing rogues, each one masked with a grotesque laughing face, frolicked on a walkway above him. Again nobody was taken aback by their strange revelry as they whooped joyously through the streets.

At the edge of a huge square stood a herald screaming in tongues. Crouching by his knees were two leashed slaves beating themselves with scourges as their master ranted.

If Lancelin had thought Assenah Neskhon struck an eccentric figure, then here was a veritable menagerie of the bizarre. Thankfully, his route was a simple one, and although the map he had memorised was outdated, the landmarks had not changed.

When finally he reached the brooding temple he had travelled so far to find, Lancelin paused at the threshold. Everything about the place struck him as blasphemous. Demonic gargoyles leered from every facet, each cobwebbed alcove housing the weathered depiction of some foul, forbidden rite. He could not pause, though, it was too late to reconsider his path. Though the situation might seem beyond his control, he had to grasp this opportunity. It was the only chance he had to save his son.

The door creaked open as he pushed it gently and stepped through. Inside, the air was musty, the interior only dimly lit by a few candles in their sconces. A young boy stood at the altar, lighting more candles with a pricket. He did not turn when Lancelin entered, and he carried on with his duties as the door closed with a noisy slam.

Lancelin walked down the aisle between rotted wooden pews, wary of the shadows, always on his guard as he came to stand before the altar. It was a squat, demonic figure carved from a solid block of obsidian and supporting a flat slab of onyx across its sculpted shoulders. When no one came rushing at him from the dark, he sat a couple of rows back from the altar, listening intently for any sign of life. There was nothing but the boy and his pricket.

When the last candle was lit, the boy disappeared behind a curtain beside the altar, leaving Lancelin alone. As he sat, he began to wonder if this had been a fool's errand after all. Rosomon had all but begged him to carry out this task, and he would have accepted even if it hadn't been his own son he was here to find. Now he had arrived, though, in this city full of enemies, he began to wonder if it had been a wise choice.

Choice.

What choice had he been given? He would have entered each of the Five Lairs for that woman just to see her smile. She had always been his one weakness.

Lancelin regarded the altar before him, and as he took in the sight he began to think how similar the idols of Nyrakkis were to those of Torwyn. The only difference was that the Draconate revered its dragons, and here they worshipped foul and evil gods. Perhaps in Nyrakkis they regarded the Great Wyrms as both foul and evil. Perhaps there was no difference at all.

A whisper of curtains alerted Lancelin to movement behind him. He made no sudden move, his hand slowly straying to the sword at his side as a robed figure came to sit at the pew in front of him. Pulling back a grey hood, the figure revealed a shaven head. Jet-studded rings adorned his ears and were pierced through the flesh of his scalp.

"Looks like you've come a long way, traveller," the man said, his high-pitched voice piercing the grim sanctity of the temple.

Lancelin had given no thought to how he stood out among the Maladorans, but then here, surrounded by such peculiar characters, he was the conspicuous one.

"Farther than you know, priest," he replied.

"Perhaps from a land where the serpents have fled?"

Lancelin felt the hairs prickle at the nape of his neck. Those were the words he had been told to listen for. Could this strange priest be his contact?

"And will return again," he replied.

The man turned to him, a smile crossing his face and revealing blackened teeth. "It's been a long time since I've spoken to someone from my own country, brother."

Lancelin would have relaxed, but he could not shake the ill feeling in his gut. "I am in the right place then?"

The man stood. "Indeed you are. My name is Kosma Khonos, custodian of the Temple of Soth."

It was obviously not the man's real name, and Lancelin felt no desire to share his own. He stood, regarding the priest's Maladoran garb. It was clear he had been here for many years and managed to deftly ensconce himself in Jubaran society.

"Not the talkative type," Khonos said. "I can understand that. Perhaps I should be more discreet, but it is rare I get to speak with one of my countrymen... Please, follow me."

He led the way from the main temple through a door to a vestibule at the rear. It was a small room, filled with piled texts, scrolls and random ornaments and lit by torches in finely wrought sconces. The young boy who had lit so many candles in the temple sat on a chair in the corner. His legs swung as he leafed through the yellow-paged tome that sat across his knees, not even bothering to raise his shaven head as the men entered.

Immediately Lancelin scanned the chamber for a secret entrance or curtain behind which someone could be hiding. Still this situation was out of his control, despite this man being his ally, and he would leave as little as possible to chance.

"I think I know why you're here," said Khonos. "It is not every day a prince of Torwyn arrives in the capital of Nyrakkis."

It seemed Fulren's arrival was common knowledge. Whether that would be an advantage or hindrance remained to be seen.

"Yes. And I am here to retrieve him," Lancelin said. "Do you know where he is?"

Khonos shuffled nervously, pulling at the embroidered sleeve of his robe. "I know where they are keeping him, yes."

"And what are you not telling me?" Lancelin asked impatiently.

"He was condemned," said Khonos, loosening a thread. "Sentenced to death in the arena."

Lancelin felt the bile rise in his throat. He had come too late.

"And where is his body?" he asked. If he could not bring Fulren to his mother alive, the least he could do was return his corpse for burial in his homeland. It would not do to leave him in this Wyrm-forsaken place.

"Oh, he survived. But..."

Lancelin felt an unexpected twinge of hope rising within. "But what?"

"He was gravely wounded, or so I hear."

Lancelin resisted the urge to reach forward and grab Khonos to shake the information from him. "How grave? Speak, man."

Khonos shook his head. "I do not know."

Lancelin clenched his jaw, fingers biting into his palms. This journey, this risk, would not be for nothing. If there was anything of Fulren Hawkspur left, he would find him and return him home, no matter how grievous his injuries.

"Where are they holding him?"

"He is somewhere in the Whispering Spire of Ak-Samtek. But even if I could identify the exact chamber, there is no way you could make your way inside, and certainly no way you could escape with the boy. No man could. Not even Lancelin Jagdor."

So this spy knew his name. Not much of a surprise. What concerned Lancelin more was the obstacles in his path. But he would not accept that this was an impossible task.

"So what do you suggest? There must be a way."

A sly grin appeared on Khonos's face. "Since I arrived here I have come to know these people. Come to adopt their ways and become one of them. I am a priest, and as such I am privy to their darkest fears and distant hopes. Though Meresankh holds this place in an iron fist, there are still some who dream of release. A disgruntled mob who hide their true feelings from her inquisition, awaiting their moment to rise. Perhaps now is the time for them to sacrifice themselves for a noble cause."

"Sacrifice themselves?"

"I am their conduit to Soth of the Deep. Many will do as I command, when I command it. They will gladly fall on their swords for a higher purpose."

Lancelin regarded the spy with some trepidation. For such a man to hide himself among his enemies for so long took an unparalleled determination. To rise so high among these demon-worshipping foreigners took cunning. Now Khonos was displaying a ruthlessness Lancelin had not anticipated. But could he trust this man? Did he have a choice?

"Very well, make your plans, Khonos. But be careful. Higher purposes are all well and good, but when it comes to facing the blade that will take their life, not all men are willing to yield to it."

"No, not all men," Khonos replied. "But you do not know the pious citizens of Nyrakkis as I do."

Of that there was no doubt. But Lancelin was sure he would get to meet plenty of them soon. He could only hope they were as keen to meet their gods as Khonos suggested.

TYRETA

For a night and a day they ploughed their way through the jungle. The eagerness with which Tyreta had set out after the patrol had waned within hours, and now she hated this place with as much venom as ever. Sweat was dripping from every crevice, and she'd lost count of the number of times she'd slapped at the menagerie of flying pests determined to suck her dry.

The spear she carried felt heavy in her grip, and at her side a sheathed dagger slapped relentlessly at her thigh. It was an annoyance, but Yeki had offered it reverently before she left the Lokai camp, and Tyreta appreciated the gift almost as much as the nightstone her mother had given her before this all began.

Gelila brought up the rear, and Tyreta felt reassured at her presence. She couldn't think of anyone she'd rather have watching her back. But for all the confidence Gelila inspired, it paled next to that granted by the other guides who travelled with her.

Tyreta had managed to learn their names, but none of them could speak the Torwyn language, so she just followed them faithfully in silence. Amanisa led the way, following the trail like a bloodhound, although how she was navigating the path Tyreta had no idea. There didn't seem to be any trail to follow, but Amanisa, with her long, lean stride, led them onward regardless.

Behind her followed Suma, hair braided in dark locks, temples shaved to reveal a twisting pattern of markings that ran down to her jaw. She was frightening to behold, but looked almost timid next to Ozoro. The last warrior of the Lokai was thickly muscled, an array of scars covering her grey flesh.

At times it was difficult to keep up with the nimble kesh, but Gelila was there to urge Tyreta on when she felt her strength flagging. Despite her lack of endurance, she was determined not to be a burden as they tracked down the patrol.

It was morning when they eventually reached a clearing in the trees, and Amanisa raised her hand, fingers making strange gestures as she ordered the hunters to spread out.

Gelila was at Tyreta's side, placing a hand on her shoulder to force her into a crouch.

"Something up ahead," she whispered.

The three other kesh warriors disappeared into the brush. Tyreta crouched, listening to her own breaths, feeling exposed. Despite having such experienced travelling companions, she was keenly aware of the danger she faced. When Amanisa appeared once more from the jungle, Tyreta sighed in relief.

The hunter gestured for them to follow, and Tyreta moved forward. In a clearing beyond the thick ferns, she could see the remains of a camp. She was hit by the sudden stench of burned and rotten meat, and as she peered through the darkness she could not stifle a gasp.

Bodies had been piled at the centre of the clearing. The charred remains of dozens of men were stacked atop one another. Even their hunting dogs had been slaughtered and added to the pyre. Surrounding the grim remains were discarded weapons and torn tents. Spears had been thrust into the ground and severed heads impaled atop them.

Suma snarled at a huge ratlike creature that was sniffing at the remains, and the beast scurried off into the jungle. Tyreta felt her head begin to spin at the overpowering stench.

"They fought," Gelila said, crouching in the clearing and scanning the ground.

Not well enough, Tyreta thought. But she had seen the ferocity of the Chul firsthand. She could only imagine the slaughter they had wrought on this unwary search party.

Ozoro called out to the women from across the clearing. Gelila approached as the tribeswoman pointed farther into the jungle.

"Chul that way," Gelila said.

Tyreta could only hope they were long gone. Now the search party had been murdered she had to work out what to do. Were they any closer to New Flaym? Would these women take her all the way to the port?

Before she could ask, Ozoro spoke again, and Gelila's expression turned grave.

"Chul take prisoners," she said.

"There were survivors?" Tyreta replied, thoughts of returning to New Flaym fading. Despite her fear, she suddenly felt a burden of guilt. She had made this happen, caused these men to come searching for her. This was all her fault, but maybe there was a way to redeem herself. "We have to follow them. We might be able to rescue someone."

Gelila shook her head. "Much danger," she replied. "We leave."

"No," Tyreta replied. "I can't just leave them. These men came to find me, I won't abandon them to..." She stopped short, unwilling to think on what the Chul might do to their captives.

Ozoro began to speak in the kesh tongue. Gelila replied, gesturing at Tyreta, and their conversation became heated. Tyreta caught only a few words she recognised, but it was clear Ozoro was none too keen to pursue the Chul.

"They not come," Gelila said eventually.

"They don't have to," Tyreta replied. She bit back the fear, letting her guilt and anger rise to the fore. "Just point me in the right direction. If they won't help, I will go alone."

Gelila looked to Ozoro, who let out a low growl. "You shame Lokai?" the warrior woman said. "You think us cowards?"

Tyreta was taken aback at realising Ozoro could speak her language but had chosen not to. "No. I understand. These are not your people. You shouldn't risk yourselves for them. But they are my people. I have to try and do something."

Amanisa, Ozoro and Suma shared a glance. Suma made a brief gesture before Amanisa shrugged.

"We go. But only to show the way," Ozoro said before leading them from the clearing.

Tyreta took up her position at the rear with Gelila close behind. She began to realise what she had asked and how much danger she was putting these warriors in.

"I did not mean to offend," she whispered. "They should not put themselves at risk for me."

Gelila shook her head. "Not for you."

"What do you mean?"

Gelila's expression grew serious. "Chul take from Lokai. Murder many men, send us to exile. One day we avenge dead."

Tyreta watched the women lead a trail through the jungle, barely able to imagine what they had been through. She could only hope they were not putting themselves in needless danger in their desire for revenge.

The foliage grew thicker, and she could not make out any sign the Chul had passed this way, even while dragging prisoners along with them. Nevertheless, Amanisa followed the invisible trail with confidence.

They travelled for most of the day, the bright sky above the canopy of trees gradually darkening. Tyreta gripped her spear tight, taking some comfort from it. The lessons she had learned from Gelila at least gave her some assurance, and she felt far from the desperate girl she had been days before when fleeing for her life.

As night fell and she picked her way through the brush, squinting in the dark, Tyreta saw Ozoro had stopped a few feet up ahead. She waited, staring at the tribeswoman's muscular back, the only thing she could make out against the black. Gelila moved past her, stalking toward her fellow hunters, and they exchanged brief words before disappearing.

Tyreta was alone with nothing but the eerie sound of the jungle for company. Insects chirruped all around, but as she listened she could hear other distant noises on the night breeze. The sound of voices, gruff and callous, carried through the jungle. They had found the Chul.

Her stomach suddenly churned, tightening into a knot. They had found their enemy. A savage band who would surely slaughter her if they found her cringing in the dark.

Tyreta gritted her teeth, twisting the shaft of the spear in her fists. She was a Hawkspur—a proud heir to the greatest Guild in all Torwyn. She was descended from warriors. If she was ever going to make her ancestors proud, she had to face this fear and defeat it.

Gelila appeared beside her, and Tyreta flinched, feeling the cold wave of terror subside. Without a word the hunter gestured for her to follow, and together they crept through the dense foliage.

There was light up ahead, the flames of a huge pyre just visible through the trees. Voices grew louder, cruel laughter blowing on the night air. Ozoro and Amanisa were crouched at the edge of the trees, looking down into a shallow valley. Both women were barely visible, blending into the foliage like panthers on the hunt. There was no sign of Suma.

Tyreta and Gelila moved up beside them. Crouching in the undergrowth, Tyreta could see warriors gathered below. They were some distance away, but Tyreta still felt fear clutching at her insides. There must have been two dozen of them, feline bodies glinting in the firelight, faces grim and fearsome.

They laughed and cajoled one another, one of them miming what he had done in the recent battle, demonstrating how he had hacked his enemy in two with his axe. It sickened Tyreta to think he was making light of such wanton murder.

Before she could grow angrier, more warriors came from the darkness beyond the fire. Between them they dragged a prisoner, and Tyreta had to stifle a gasp on seeing his swollen and beaten face.

The warriors dropped him in the centre of the clearing, barking at one another, stirring themselves into a frenzy. All their prisoner could do was flounder on the ground, his hands tied behind his back, face in the dirt.

One of the Chul shouted at his captive, bending closer to taunt the man, who could only mumble his protests. Tyreta felt tears well in her eyes. She knew what was coming, but she would not look away. All the guilt and anger welling up inside forced her to witness what she had caused.

Another of the Chul raised an axe. As the surrounding warriors barked their encouragement he brought the weapon down, taking the prisoner at the base of his neck. The blow didn't sever the head immediately, and Tyreta clapped a hand over her mouth as it took another two blows to part the head completely.

Tyreta felt Gelila's hand on her arm and saw that the other women were making their way around the perimeter of the Chul camp. Tyreta gripped her spear and followed, wary of the light from the huge pyre, swallowing back the bile that had risen in her throat. It was hard to comprehend the cruelty and hate she had just seen, but it made her all the more determined to find more survivors and rescue them if she could.

They worked their way around the camp to where smaller fires were lit. More warriors stood in the firelight, and there was no way to count how many of them were celebrating their recent victory.

Amanisa and Ozoro led them to the southernmost edge, where Suma crouched in wait. Tyreta was almost overcome by the realisation of what had happened. These men had struck out into the jungle to find her and Wyllow. They had died for their efforts, and she was responsible.

"No more survivors," Suma whispered, gesturing away from the camp. "But tracks go south."

In what little light there was, Tyreta could see a path had been flattened through the foliage. What must have been scores of warriors had already left the clearing. A war party was on the move, and there was only one place they could be headed.

"There's a mine," Tyreta whispered. "North of New Flaym. The Chul must be heading there. They'll murder everyone. We have to warn them."

"No," Suma replied with a cutting thrust of her hand. "Much danger."

"I did this," Tyreta said. "Those men came to find me and now they're dead. More people are going to die, I have to do something. Just take me there, and I will do the rest."

"Already too late," Gelila said, placing a hand on Tyreta's shoulder.

She shook it off, frustrated and angry and helpless all at once.

"I won't accept that. I can't accept that. If there's any chance I can make this right, I have to try."

Tears were welling in her eyes, and that made her even angrier. She was shaking with fear and hate. She wanted to murder these Chul, to kill Shabak for what he had done, but she knew that was impossible. If she could at least warn those miners, make them run before the kesh fell upon them, it might go some way to making up for what she had caused.

The four women exchanged glances that Tyreta struggled to read. She could see doubt in their eyes, but also determination. Eventually Gelila said, "Yes. We go."

Amanisa and Suma were already making their way through the thick foliage. Tyreta was quick to follow, with Ozoro and Gelila at her back. Their pace quickened, and she soon found herself racing through the jungle, spurred on by the urgency of her mission. Tyreta could not let the workers at the mine be slaughtered. Unless it was already too late.

LANCELIN

A narrow, cracked windowpane framed a view to the street below the Temple of Soth. Lancelin had watched hooded figures approach all morning, mingling with the scant traffic along the road before ducking inside the temple like rats scurrying from the light.

Behind him Khonos practised an array of garbled vocal exercises as the young boy dressed him in his vestments of priesthood. His drab grey robe had been swapped for a blue one the shade of the deepest ocean. It was embroidered with green thread, and incomprehensible script lined the hem and sleeves. Khonos had already painted his eyelids with a thick lining of kohl, a tear drawn at the corner of each eye.

"Are you sure we can trust these people?" Lancelin asked.

"As sure as I can be of anything in this cursed city," Khonos replied.

"And it sits well with you? Using them like this? They serve you faithfully, and you are about to betray each and every one."

Khonos shrugged. "They serve Soth of the Deep. He is their master, not Kosma Khonos."

"You're the one pulling their strings. Not Soth, or whatever you choose to call this demon."

Khonos spread his arms wide as the boy secured a thick leather belt about his waist. "The god Soth is very real. As are all the gods worshipped in Nyrakkis. You are right, though, I am the puppet master here. Only unlike the Nine Houses of Nyrakkis, I direct these marionettes toward a greater good."

"And yet you're still using them, whether it's for good or not. Still putting them in mortal danger. These people have learned to trust you."

"Strange that you of all people would have such qualms, Jagdor. A man raised from nothing to serve the Guilds. Taught to obey. To carry out the will of your masters, whether you agree with them or not. We are all used. We all serve a higher power, to one degree or another. In the end it is the cause that matters, whether you serve a god or a Guild."

"No, the two things are not the same. The Guilds exist to serve the people of Torwyn. For the betterment of the nation."

Khonos chuckled as he adjusted the belt at his waist. "You are right to some extent, Jagdor. Although even you must see that under the Guilds, some flourish more than others."

"Explain," Lancelin said, trying hard to quell his annoyance.

"Explain?" Khonos raised a dark eyebrow. "You serve the Archwinds. You are the emperor's trusted sword. A man raised from the gutter to high status, but in the end you are still a servant. As we all are. I once knew a farm labourer who served his Guildmaster faithfully. One day the Guildmaster came home with a new stallion, whiter than a snowcapped peak. The labourer said to him, 'My lord. This is the most magnificent beast I have ever laid eyes on.' And the Guildmaster replied, 'Yes. And if you work hard for me in the coming season, next year I will buy myself another that is even more magnificent.' You see my meaning?"

Lancelin didn't feel the need to answer. The point of the story was obvious. But everyone had their place, their role to play. There were always winners and losers. Questioning it would only lead to discontent. Or madness.

As the boy pulled thick leather gloves onto Khonos's outstretched hands, Lancelin began to wonder why a man like Khonos would put himself through such hardship, engineer such subterfuge, if he truly believed he was nothing more than a servant being used by his master.

"If you hold the Archwinds in such contempt, why continue to work for them? Why sink so low in this city of spite and devilry when you could simply apply your talents elsewhere? And perhaps even profit from them?"

"We all have our talents." Khonos flexed his fingers in those thick leather gloves. "I am merely applying mine in the most suitable way."

Watching Khonos standing there in his religious finery, Lancelin could only wonder just how loyal the man was. "So you are happy to serve Emperor Sullivar?"

Another enigmatic grin from Khonos. "It was Treon Archwind who tasked me with this mission. But even with a new emperor on the throne, I hold my faith in the Guilds. Have no fear where my loyalties lie, Jagdor."

Despite his doubts, Lancelin knew he had little choice but to take Khonos at his word. Still, there were so many questions to answer regarding how this man had managed to adapt so easily to Jubaran society and not be caught. Before he could ask any of them, Khonos made for the door to the vestibule.

"It is time," he said. Already his grin was gone and a solemn expression had fallen across his face. "You had best don a cloak before joining us."

Lancelin turned to see the boy holding up a suitable garment. As he threw it across his shoulders Lancelin couldn't help but screw his nose up at how bad the threadbare cloak stank. He donned it anyway, hoping it wouldn't leave him riddled with fleas.

The boy opened the door for Khonos and led the men down through the tower of the temple to Soth. When they reached the main sanctum, Lancelin was surprised to see it empty. Before he could ask where everyone was hiding, he noticed the hideous demonic altar stood askew on its dais. The statue of Soth had been moved aside on metal runners, revealing a dark opening. Age-worn stairs led down into the bowels of the temple.

Lancelin followed Khonos, who in turn followed the boy as he plucked a lit torch from a sconce on the wall and led the way down into a cellar. The sound of gentle whispering drifted up from the dark as they made their way deeper. When they reached the bottom of the stairs, flickering red torchlight revealed a vast subterranean chamber beneath the Temple of Soth, hewn from the black stone. It was filled with hooded figures kneeling in prayer, heads bowed.

As the gathered crowd continued with their prayers, Khonos grasped a rope dangling from above and pulled hard. With a squeak of pulleys the altar above grated on its metal runners before shutting them in.

"These things can sometimes get rowdy," Khonos whispered with a wink. "Less noise the better."

Lancelin saw the boy was already parading up the central walkway toward a granite slab at the far end of the chamber. In his hand he carried an old wooden bucket into which he dipped a brush before spattering the gathered flock. Some of them turned their faces toward him as he did so, keen to be anointed. The boy walked back up the aisle, his brush flicking to left and right. It wasn't until the young lad spattered Lancelin's filthy cloak that he realised the fluid was blood. Lancelin scowled his disdain, but the boy seemed oblivious to the slight he had given.

As Lancelin watched from the rear of the gathering with growing apprehension, Khonos strode forward to take his place before the kneeling crowd. He positioned himself behind the solid granite block of an altar, his demeanour transforming from one of amiable indifference to one of grim certitude.

"You have been patient, my friends," he said in a rumbling voice, richer and more commanding than the one Lancelin had heard before. "Oh so patient. But we have waited long enough." At that, some of the kneeling figures became agitated, nodding feverishly in their agreement. "Soth has heard your prayers, felt your yearning, and now the time of waiting is at an end. For too long we have suffered under the yoke of the undying Queen Meresankh, curse her name. Now is the time to rise up, to throw off the shackles in which she has chained us. Now is the time to shout the name of Soth so loud the whole of Nyrakkis will hear."

"Yes," screamed a voice, so suddenly Lancelin's hand went instinctively to the sword at his side.

One of the worshippers jumped to his feet, enthusiastically punching the air, but he was a lone figure among many. When the rest of the gathering failed to join in with his overenthusiasm, he gingerly sank back to his knees.

The air of fear and tension was palpable throughout the room. Despite Khonos's stirring words, there was little zeal for an uprising. These hooded figures might covet the favour of a demon god, but it was obvious they still valued their lives and had little stomach for standing in defiance of Meresankh. Lancelin began to wonder if this had been such a good idea after all. Nevertheless, Khonos was unperturbed, and he walked purposefully from behind the stone altar to stand among the gathering.

"I feel your apprehension," he said. "I taste your fear. And so does Soth." Khonos stopped beside one of the kneeling worshippers, a woman judging by the slightness of her physique. Gently he laid a hand on her hooded head. "I know what you have all suffered. I know what you have all lost. Especially you, Lyzanna." He tipped back the hood, and the woman looked up with tears in her eyes. "Now is the time for you to be redeemed."

As the woman began to sob uncontrollably, Khonos moved on. Lancelin could only wonder what this woman had suffered for the priest's words to affect her so intensely.

"And you, Berezhar," Khonos continued, his voice echoing through the cavern. "Soth only knows how hard you have laboured beneath the mantle of an unworthy queen." Another of the hooded men nodded enthusiastically as Khonos turned his attention elsewhere. "And you, Septagar. Soth of the Deep sees your sacrifice, knows what has been taken from you by the Nine Houses and how you have been left with nothing but your debts."

The mood was changing. More and more of the figures were sitting up and taking heed. Grumbles of discontent began to fill the cellar.

"Soth watches you all, but are you deserving of his attention?" Khonos continued. "What will you do, how far would you go to make yourselves worthy of his benefaction? Soth will not drag your pathetic souls to dwell by his side in the deep unless he deems you worthy."

"But how can we hope to defy the queen?" a small voice pealed out from the crowd. It was enough to silence the growing fervour in the room.

Khonos scanned the gathering as though searching for the source of that fearful voice. One eye glared madly, while the other twitched with a palsy. "Soth will be watching. Soth will aid us in our time of need. But there is one way to ensure he is with us in body as well as spirit."

The priest spun on his heel, marching back to the altar. Lancelin could see the boy was already laid out on the stone slab, eyes staring blankly at the ceiling. A sense of foreboding suddenly crept up within him, but he forced himself to stay at the back of the room.

The crowd immediately fell silent, bowing their heads as though this part of the ceremony had been rehearsed many times. They began to whisper once more, but this time their chants were not discordant. Now they spoke a single dark litany, their voices merged in worship.

Khonos joined in with their words, spoken in a language Lancelin had never heard before and would be happy to never hear again. From his robes the priest pulled out a flamboyant blade, its wicked edge glinting in the torchlight. The entire room took on a different aspect, the light seeming to cast baleful shadows against the wall. As the chanting became more feverish, Khonos raised his knife to the ceiling. Lancelin felt a fetid breeze blow through the room from somewhere, carrying with it the salt stink of the sea.

He knew what was about to happen and tried to take a step forward, but he was rooted to the spot. Lancelin would never know if it was some arcane power holding him there or the knowledge that if he interrupted this ritual, any chance he might have of rescuing Fulren would be lost.

With ruthless efficiency Khonos plunged the knife into the boy's chest. The sacrifice didn't move as the blade pierced him, but Lancelin flinched as though it were his own heart that had been run through.

The crowd surged to their feet, shouting and screaming approval at the deed. The noise shook Lancelin from his reverie, and he managed to step forward, adding his own voice in protest against the senseless horror he was witnessing. He bellowed at Khonos, but his voice was lost amid the noisome fervour of the crowd. All he could do was watch as the bloody ritual continued.

Khonos dragged the dagger from the boy's chest to his groin before discarding the weapon and reaching in with gloved hands. Grabbing a fistful of innards he wrenched them out, splaying them across the altar like the tentacles of some hideous sea beast. All the while the boy lay there unmoving, eyes staring at the ceiling in a diabolical trance while he was eviscerated in front of a baying mob.

Beside Lancelin, a hooded man was weeping uncontrollably. In front a woman had thrown back her hood and clawed at her scalp till it bled. Another woman bared her pendulous breasts to the altar, waiting for them to be anointed, screaming her desire across the chamber.

The crowd began to shuffle forward, gibbering hungrily, kneeling before that altar and throwing off their cloaks to bare flesh before the priest. Khonos began to bathe them in the boy's sacrificial blood, the chanting rising to a crescendo as Lancelin stood watching. His stomach churned, and he clenched his teeth against the bile rising in his throat. It was horror, plain and simple, but he forced himself to witness it, knowing that he was the cause.

Once the ceremony was done, and the crowd knelt quietly, Khonos leaned across the boy's corpse and whispered, "Tomorrow, you will all return here. Join me, and you will have your day. Remember, Soth awaits, and he is watching."

The gathered crowd remained silent as one by one they rose and made their way up the stairs from the underground chamber. Lancelin listened to the scraping of the altar above as someone moved it aside and those hooded figures fled the temple as furtively as they had arrived.

It was just him and Khonos, alone with the corpse of that wretched boy. Someone's son, gutted and cold on the slab. An innocent soul sacrificed so Lancelin's son could live. It was wrong, but he had known there would be corpses if he was ever to rescue Fulren from this place. He had just thought it would be him doing the killing, not some mad priest.

Khonos strolled toward him, peeling the bloody gloves from his hands and discarding them on the floor. "I think that went well, all things considered."

As much as he tried, Lancelin could not quell his anger. When Khonos came within reach, Lancelin's hand snapped forward and he grasped the priest by the throat.

"I should kill you. That boy was innocent and you cut him open like a pig."

"Calm, Jagdor," Khonos struggled to say, vainly trying to loosen Lancelin's grip. "It's not what you think."

Before he could ask Khonos what he was talking about, the boy's corpse stirred upon the altar. Lancelin felt a momentary pang of dread as the young lad sat bolt upright, hastily discarding the guts that were splayed across his body. Then he pulled the smock from his body, revealing the false bladder inside that had held the animal innards. Realising the boy was unharmed, Lancelin let go of the priest's throat.

"See," said Khonos. "No harm done. We've performed that ritual on a dozen occasions. Those fanatics have never realised it's been the same lad sacrificed each time."

With some relief Lancelin watched as the boy skipped nimbly from atop the altar, then went about stuffing the scattered offal into a bucket.

"You should rejoice, Jagdor. I have recruited your army for you. I only hope you're ready. The real sacrifice is yet to come."

"I'll do my part," Lancelin replied before turning his back on the blood-soaked temple and making his way up the stairs. "Just make sure you do yours."

FULREN

Darkness had become his constant companion. They said a man who lost his sight would compensate in other ways, his remaining senses heightening. So far Fulren had experienced nothing exceptional; he could hear and taste just the same, and all he could smell was the faint aroma of the venom extract they had used to dull his pain. Even that was fading, just as his pain had relented, leaving him with nothing but a dull ache about his face.

He stood at the balcony of his chamber, feeling the warm breeze play against his flesh. His eyes were bandaged, and he fought the urge to tear off the bindings and scratch at the raw wound beneath. It would have been stupid to disobey the apothecary's instructions, and he resisted the temptation, resigned to the fact that the itching at least meant his lesions were healing.

Fulren raised a hand, gently teasing the scarred flesh with his finger. Perhaps blindness was a mercy. At least it spared him the horror of seeing what Ghobeq's poisonous bile had done to his face. He could feel the uneven skin, the rawness of the wounds. If anyone had ever considered him handsome, it was obvious he was handsome no longer.

The door to his chamber opened, swinging wide with a creak of the hinge that heralded two sets of footsteps, one clacking confidently against the tiled floor, the other shuffling along in its wake. Wenis and the silent attendant. Perhaps his other senses were improving after all.

"Fulren," she said. "It is Wenis."

That brought a smile to his face. Since he had survived the Trial of Ghobeq she had become much more sympathetic to his plight, less arrogant, less cutting. It was the only good thing to come from all this.

"Nice to hear you again," he replied, turning to face her, despite the pointlessness of it.

"I have brought the apothecary. Perhaps your bindings can be removed today."

"Then let's get to it," Fulren replied, shuffling from the balcony.

As soon as he let go he felt a moment of panic. His arms were spread, but there was no wall to support him until he reached the archway. It was like being cast adrift at sea.

Before he could find the wall, he felt Wenis take his hand, gently guiding him to a chair. Though he would never have admitted it, he was relieved to sit down and anchor himself to something, anything.

The apothecary worked quickly, and Fulren heard the snip of scissors as his bandages were cut. With nimble fingers he unwrapped the binding from Fulren's eyes, gently pressing at the flesh. It was tender, and Fulren fought the urge to wince in pain.

"So how do I look?" he asked.

The immediate pause told him everything he needed to know.

"You are healing well," Wenis said eventually.

The apothecary pressed the lid of one eye, opening it up. Fulren gritted his teeth against the pain, but was more dismayed when he realised that even with his eye open the world around him was still black. Not even a smudge or an inky shadow.

"What about my sight?" he asked. "Will that return?"

Another pause. "It is . . . unlikely," Wenis replied.

Fulren sighed. "And I don't even have my good looks to fall back on anymore."

If no one else was willing to make light of this, then at least he could try.

"Such egotism is unbecoming, Fulren," Wenis said, missing the joke entirely. "We will leave the bandages off for now. Let the air into the wound so it will heal faster."

When the apothecary had finished applying some foul-smelling unguent to his open sores, Wenis continued, "You have to come with me now. They are waiting."

"Who is waiting?" Fulren asked as he stood unsteadily.

Wenis took him by the arm, leading him across the chamber and to the door. Of course she would not say—yet more surprises. Hopefully this one wouldn't end in a maiming.

Once they were outside, Wenis led him along the corridor. He could hear the footsteps of a group behind them, their tread heavy, and assumed they were the silent, tattooed warriors who now accompanied Wenis wherever she went. It seemed she had inherited Assenah Neskhon's bodyguards as well as her position.

Fulren stumbled more than once as he was led, despite Wenis doing her best to make the journey as smooth as possible. His irritation only grew as he missed the occasional step or bumped a shoulder into a wall, until he could take no more. Fulren had always relied on his wits and skill to see him through. Now that he was blind, all that was gone. The thought of having to learn everything anew cut him to the quick, and he was overcome by the injustice of it.

He pulled his arm free of Wenis's grip, stumbling for a moment as he was set adrift once more.

"What is this?" he demanded. "Where are you leading me?"

"Fulren, you must—"

"Enough games," he snapped. "Just tell me. I deserve that at least."

"You have been summoned for judgement, Fulren."

"For judgement? Is this some kind of sick joke? I've already been through your trial, and I won. What do I have to do to satisfy you people?"

"I understand your anger," Wenis replied. "But no one has ever survived the Trial of Ghobeq. This is unprecedented. Some have taken it as a sign."

"A sign of what? That I am innocent of what I was accused? That should be sign enough, but now the rules have been changed."

"We have no choice in this, Fulren," Wenis said.

He felt her lay a gentle hand on his arm, and he knew she was right. Even if he could see, even if he could run, there was nowhere for him to go.

Fulren let her lead him. As much as he strained his remaining senses, he was completely disoriented. He couldn't even calculate how far they walked or for how long before they reached their destination. The hot breeze of the open air was eventually replaced by a musty odour as they entered another building. Inside, the place was eerily silent, and they progressed through a complex of labyrinthine tunnels. Occasionally Fulren reached out a hand to guide himself along the wall, feeling the cold, smooth stone against his fingertips.

Soon their footsteps began to echo, suggesting they had entered a cavernous chamber, and Wenis came to a stop.

"I must leave you now," she whispered.

"Don't go far," Fulren replied, only half joking.

The echoing footsteps of Wenis and the warriors receded until he was left alone with only the sound of his breathing for company. He gritted his teeth, not knowing what to expect. Would he receive the swift stroke of the executioner's axe? Torture?

"Greetings, Prince of Torwyn."

Fulren recognised Ak-Samtek's silky brogue. There was a moment of relief at the familiar voice, but Fulren knew he was still in danger.

"Good to see you," he replied.

"Levity," Ak-Samtek said. "Even now. You are truly a remarkable man, Fulren Hawkspur."

Strange, he didn't feel particularly remarkable.

"Are we alone?" Fulren asked. "Or is there another jury for this trial?"

"I must commend you on your display in the arena," Ak-Samtek continued, ignoring his question. "It was thrilling to watch. You harnessed powerful magics to defeat Ghobeq. Something never seen before in Jubara. Tell me, how did you achieve such a feat?"

"How did I kill your beast? Wouldn't you like to know."

"We examined the weapon you crafted. So far none of our

arcanists have been able to activate its power. We must know how it was done."

"Keep guessing," Fulren said, trying hard to stifle his frustration. "I don't owe you shit."

Ak-Samtek let out a long sigh. "It would serve you well to cooperate in this. The rewards could be great."

"Can you give me back my sight?"

Fulren's words hung in the air for some moments.

"Anything is possible," Ak-Samtek replied.

"Do you think me a fool? Do you expect me to tell you everything? I know what you people are. I've seen it firsthand. Once I reveal my secrets, you'll have no further use for me."

A bluff, but a bluff was all he had. In reality Fulren had little idea how he'd managed to make his necroglyph connect with the pyrestone sword. Now he was blind it was unlikely he'd be able to replicate the ability.

"Your opinion of us is a harsh one, Fulren," said the grand vizier.

"Now who's quick with the levity?" he spat. "My opinion is harsh? I'm not the one sacrificing prisoners to demons. Executing them in front of a baying crowd. In Torwyn we don't use people as commodities. We don't chew them up and spit out the bones."

"Do you not?" Ak-Samtek replied. If Fulren didn't know better, he'd have thought the vizier was smiling. "I think your view of your homeland might be slightly skewed. Misted by your privileged upbringing. The history of our nations is not so different. You may not be as close to your gods, but the ordinary people of Torwyn are just as much a commodity as ours."

"Enough of the history lessons," Fulren said, his patience run dry. "Are you going to let me go or not? You've had your entertainment. I've proved my innocence in accordance with your laws. I'm done with you, so kill me or release me."

"Oh, we are not going to kill you, Prince of Torwyn. But neither can we let you go. You have proved yourself far too valuable. You will live out the rest of your days in the comfort of this city. And whether you like it or not, you will give us what we ask."

"You want me to teach you how to use artifice? Is that it?"

There was a pause as Ak-Samtek carefully chose his words. "There are those who believe it may be beneficial to the future of Nyrakkis."

"From what I know, Queen Meresankh isn't one of them. Not planning to betray her, are you?"

More silence. Fulren began to wonder if he'd gone too far, but what did it matter now? He was blind and imprisoned. The life he had known was over, and he would never get it back. Ak-Samtek could murder him right here for all he cared.

"Nyrakkis has enemies on every border," the vizier said eventually. "It serves us well to know the nature of those threats we face. Harnessing the weapons of our enemies is only one part of that. Overcome your stubborn resistance, and the rewards for your cooperation would be great indeed."

Despite the temptations Ak-Samtek was throwing at his feet, Fulren was done with being used.

"You'll get nothing from me."

"We shall see, Prince of Torwyn. We shall see."

Ak-Samtek's voice sounded distant as he spoke his final words. It made Fulren even angrier, he wanted to run after the vizier, to grab him by his stinking robes and shake him until he understood. He would never help these people, never give them the secrets of artifice.

As he stood helplessly, raging inside, the flesh at the nape of his neck suddenly grew hot and angry. The necroglyph burned furiously, so hot he had to clap a hand to it to stifle the pain.

"Come. We must leave."

Wenis's voice was close to his ear.

Suddenly the strange sensation given off by the necroglyph subsided, and he was led from the chamber and back through the labyrinthine tunnels. A sickening nausea overcame him as the pain relented, and he felt powerless to resist Wenis and her men as they led him away.

Once in the open, Fulren tried to catch his breath, but he couldn't suck in enough air to relieve the cloying sensation in his lungs.

"Come," said Wenis, leading him to a nearby balcony. "Lean against this."

Fulren gripped the balustrade, trying to calm himself, trying to acclimate to the warm wind. The air was humid and he was already perspiring. It took some moments before he could breathe freely.

"Are you all right?" Wenis asked.

Was he? With the nausea he was suffering he thought he might never be all right again.

"I'll live," he replied. "For now. Is this your job? Are you tasked with caring for a blind prince for the rest of your days?"

"I am no nursemaid," Wenis snapped. "And you are no longer a prince."

"I'm sorry," he replied, hearing the acrimony in her tone. "I didn't mean anything by it. I just... This is difficult to make peace with."

Before he could sink further into a malaise, he felt Wenis take his hand. It was an odd feeling; this woman who had once seemed so callous in her disregard of him was now his only comfort.

"Do not fear. I will do everything in my power to keep you safe."

Fulren stifled a laugh, resisting the temptation to point out what a terrible job she had done so far. Before he could reply, a distant noise was carried on the wind. Voices raised in a chant, drums being beaten, the clash of cymbals.

"What's that?" he asked, raising his head to better listen to the sound.

Wenis paused, assessing the situation. "Farther down the street, there is a gathering."

"A celebration?"

"No. This has not been sanctioned by the Houses or the Medjai."

"How can you tell?"

She grasped his arm, pulling him away from the balcony. "Because they carry weapons. Come, we must leave."

"What's going on?" Fulren asked as she ushered him away, surrounded by their guards. "Could this turn violent?"

"Unrest in the city has become more common of late. Sedition is rife in Jubara."

"Sedition? But Meresankh rules with an iron hand. How has it not been stamped out?"

He could hear the clash of cymbals grow louder now and thought that perhaps it might not be quite so melodic as he'd first thought. It could just as easily be the clash of steel on steel.

"No more questions," Wenis said as Fulren heard angry shouts far too close.

They moved with as much haste as they could, Fulren doing his best to hurry alongside Wenis and the guards. The noise had grown louder now, seeming to come from every avenue. Heavy footsteps tramped nearby, accompanied by the clanking of weapons and armour and shouts of rage.

"What's going on?" Fulren asked as something knocked into his shoulder, almost sending him sprawling in the street.

Wenis did not answer as someone grasped his other arm. This grip was tighter than Wenis's, most likely that of one of her silent guardians. Fulren was utterly disoriented, the noise echoing all about him. He could hear the clashing of steel nearby, voices raised in a single chant: "Soth! Soth! Soth!"

"Here," Wenis yelled before he was bustled along a narrow alley.

Eventually they came to a stop. The noise of the uprising was quieter here, but still echoed from across the rooftops.

"Are we safe?" Fulren asked.

"For now," Wenis replied, her breath coming in short gasps.

"What is going on?" Fulren demanded. His heart was pounding, and despite the guards surrounding him, he felt vulnerable, on the edge of panic.

"We just have to wait here awhile until the crowd is brought to heel," she replied. "Do not worry. All will be as it was."

Before Fulren could answer he heard the sound of spears being braced against shields. Wenis let go of his arm and once again he felt abandoned at sea.

"Step back," Wenis commanded. Fulren could detect a note of alarm in her tone.

"What is it?" Fulren asked.

"Step back," Wenis repeated. "Or my men will attack."

Fulren heard a slap, the thud of something hitting the ground. There was a hiss of steel, a grunt, the clash of metal on shield. Footsteps shuffled on the dry earth, followed by the unmistakable sound of someone collapsing in a heap. Ringing weapons, a snarl of rage or frustration or pain. The clack of a shield being dropped. The swift whip of a sword cutting the air. Hot fluid spattered against Fulren's cheek.

Then silence.

He held his breath, waiting for the inevitable, wondering if it might be a swift crack to the head or the slow impalement of a blade to the gut. There was nothing he could do to stop either.

"Who's there?" he spat. "If you're going to kill me, get on with it, damn you."

"There is nothing to fear." A man's voice, deep, imposing. "I am from Torwyn. I have come to take you home."

Fulren backed away, almost tripping over a fallen spear. "Who are you?" he asked, unable to shake the feeling there was something familiar about that voice.

There was no reply. Instead his arm was taken in a powerful grip, and he was almost wrenched off his feet. Fulren was helpless as he was led along, away from the sounds of violence, deeper into a labyrinth he could not even see. Whoever this man was, he was taking him away from Wenis, away from the only anchor Fulren had in this place. What fate awaited him now? Was it worse than the one he had already accepted?

That thought roiled within him, churning his mind into a panic, until eventually he grasped his would-be saviour's arm and dragged him to a stop.

"Who sent you?" Fulren asked. "Tell me, who sent you here?"

Fulren could sense the man leaning in close. He smelled of leather and weapon oil.

"Your mother sent me," he said. "Lady Rosomon Hawkspur."

Fulren barely registered the words as he suddenly recognised the voice that had uttered them.

"You," he whispered. "You're him."

"We don't have time for this."

"Lancelin bastard Jagdor," Fulren spat.

"We don't have time—"

"I don't believe you. I don't believe my mother would ever have sent you to find me. She would never ask anything of the man who murdered her husband. Where is Wenis? What have you done to her?"

He was shouting now, panic overwhelming him. Jagdor gripped his arms, trying to shake some sense into him.

"You have to be quiet. We're in danger here."

"No," Fulren spat, trying to break free of that iron grip. "Wenis!"

He shouted it with all his might, desperation confounding his sense. Jagdor shook him once more, and all the rage and fear and pain balled itself into Fulren's fist. He struck out, somehow managing to catch the swordwright in the face. That iron grip loosened for a moment and Fulren took his chance.

He turned, stumbled, but managed to stay on his feet. Then he ran, arms held out in front of him—it wouldn't do to escape so deftly and run straight into a wall.

Fulren hadn't taken three steps before he was wrestled to the ground. Jagdor was strong but also skilled. As Fulren flailed his arm was locked tight. He was defenceless. Before he could cry out, a firm hand clamped over his face. A cloth blocked his nose and mouth, infused with a smell he recognised.

The poppy essence was sickly sweet, and his remaining senses began to dull, fading to nothing…

ROSOMON

Days of ledgers, parchments, scrolls, deeds, charters and warrants. Rosomon's eyes were sore from the reading, her fingers ink-blackened, her neck aching, her backside numb from hours of sitting in the same uncomfortable chair. She had scaled a precipice of legislative papers, and there was still an entire mountain range yet to conquer. A revenant beast that she could never slay. And yet it was her salvation.

Rosomon had taken on this task for her brother and her nation. Sullivar had sunk further into his malaise at the loss of his son, and not even his wife Oriel could bring him out of it. Now the burden of running an empire fell to Rosomon, and she had allowed it to consume her. It was the only way she could divert her thoughts from her own tragedy. Fulren was gone. Tyreta was missing. Grief haunted her, but by allowing her thoughts to be dominated by the mundanity of work she could stave off its ghost, at least for a while.

Nights were the worst. There was no one to comfort her but the dark. She had sent her lover away in the faint hope that he would return with her son, but she knew that too was folly.

From her last chance at consolation there had been no word. Conall was still in the Karna, and her letters to him had been ignored. Or perhaps something had happened to him too. Perhaps he had received no word from her because he was also in danger.

No. Rosomon could not countenance such thoughts. That might be the final blow that broke her. She had to think on her current tasks, it was the only way to stave off the despair. And so she sat in a chamber at the heart of Archwind Palace and tried to hold together an empire.

The pyrestone lantern flickered above her. Rosomon reclined in her seat, pushing the ledger away across the table. She had not even registered what the last page said, so preoccupied was her mind. This was like navigating a maze; no wonder Sullivar had ceded so much administrative responsibility to the Corwen Guild. Before she had begun this mammoth task, Rosomon had thought everything was managed with precision, that each Guild was part of a whole, a cog in a well-oiled engine. The further she delved into the mire, the more Rosomon realised this was a bureaucratic labyrinth, that there were ledgers within ledgers, manifests within manifests, the left hand couldn't find the right, and the result was that Torwyn's prosperity was balanced on the edge of a blade.

Each major Guild took its annual stipend but contributed less each year, but then so did the minor Guilds and the Armiger Battalions. Commodities were dwindling, even on the Karna Frontier, but it was not just the supply of pyrestone that was in peril. Two bad harvests had meant food stocks supplied by the Radwinter Guild were low. In turn that meant insufficient supplies to the miners of the Marrlock Guild, which meant ore was dwindling, affecting manufacture in the forges of the Ironfall Guild.

Wheels within wheels within wheels, and one cracked spoke meant the entire machine failed. Rosomon had never needed her father more than right now. Even in her darkest moments, she had not relied on Treon Archwind. Now she would give anything to have him by her side for a day. The old warhorse would soon whip this administrative chaos into shape. But Treon was not here.

Rosomon glanced across the tiny chamber. Athelys sat in one corner, half-buried beneath a pile of papers. She squinted at the manifest in front of her, tongue poking from one side of her mouth. A poor substitute for her father, but the handmaid was all that Rosomon had. Her one ally in the fight against the might of the Corwen Guild.

Through an archway opposite, Rosomon could just spy the actuaries and scribes beavering away at their lecterns. Did they even understand the part they had to play in Torwyn's vast clerical machine? Did Rosomon?

For days she had been at this, and only now was she beginning to appreciate the immense task she had set herself. But she had to succeed, for her own sanity as well as the future prosperity of Torwyn.

She went back to the ledger, sliding it toward her so it was better illuminated by the pyrestone lamp. No sooner had she done so than a name in the creditors column all but leapt off the page.

Ossian Holder.

It was a name she had seen before. It shouldn't have bothered her—it was but one name in a list of many—but for some reason she could not seem to ignore it.

Standing, she moved to a shelf, finger tracing the spines of several more ledgers until she found the one she was looking for. After plucking it from the shelf and placing it beside the first, she licked her stained finger and began to flick through the pages...

There... Ossian Holder.

But both these ledgers detailed completely different accounts: one a shipping manifest, one a receipt from a weapons supplier. To provide finance for both would have taken a large source of equity, yet Ossian Holder was a member of no large organisation. His was but one name on a list of minor financiers.

Perhaps a clerical error? Perhaps he was an innocent investor with a large inheritance? Perhaps she should just ignore it and move on? After all, Rosomon had much more important matters to occupy her time with. But there was something to this she could not just let go.

She picked up both ledgers and rose from the chair, its legs scraping on the stone-tiled floor. She marched across the chamber and through the archway, where rows upon rows of lecterns were lined up along a great hall. There was no natural light here within the bowels of the palace, and the walls were dotted with pyrestone lamps, but Rosomon could not bring herself to feel sympathy for the scribes who were forced to strain their eyesight as they laboured in this warren. They had been a bane to her since she had started this endeavour, doing everything they could to be as obstructive as possible. If she didn't know better, she would have thought Rearden Corwen had ordered them to hamper her progress. But surely that could not be true. They were, after all, striving for the same goal.

Young Wachelm was squirreled away in the far corner of the hall. His booth backed onto a high shelf full of dusty codices where he sheltered, head bowed, face buried in a thick tome as his quill scratched a strident tune on the parchment.

Rosomon set the two ledgers down on Wachelm's desk, practically under his nose. He leaned back and looked up, his eyes appearing huge through the wire-rimmed eyeglasses perched on his nose.

The actuary was the only one of Rearden Corwen's administrators who had paid Rosomon so much as a glimmer of respect since she had arrived. Hopefully this time would be no exception.

"Who is Ossian Holder?" she asked.

Wachelm looked down at the ledgers, then back up at Rosomon, then back at the ledgers.

"Who?" Wachelm replied.

Was he playing dumb, or was he actually so ignorant? The jury was still out.

"Ossian Holder," Rosomon repeated, pointing to the entries in each ledger. "Who is he? He's attached to no agency of supply. There is no mention of him in any marque of trade. Yet he is named as creditor in the supply of goods to the Armiger Battalions and on a separate shipping manifest from the Karna."

"And?" Wachelm said.

"And that does not seem odd to you? That an individual with no apparent Guild affiliation should have access to enough funds to supply an Armiger Battalion and run ships outside the purview of the Hawkspur Guild?"

Wachelm looked back at the ledger, his finger tapping the side of his lectern as he thought on it. Finally he looked up once more.

"Perhaps a shadow company?"

Maybe Wachelm was not so ignorant after all.

Before she could continue, someone cleared their throat loudly enough for it to echo through the hall. Rosomon turned to see a pristinely dressed figure waiting at the far archway. Olstrum Garner raised an eyebrow expectantly.

"Look into it," she said to Wachelm. "Find out who or what Ossian Holder is."

Before the inevitable protest, Rosomon turned and left Wachelm with his task. Olstrum backed into her chamber as she approached, waiting patiently with his hands behind his back.

"Well?" she asked.

"We may have found something, my lady," Olstrum replied.

Rosomon felt a chill down her spine. All thoughts of administrative improprieties were gone.

She regarded Olstrum carefully. Over the past few days she had tasked him with finding information for her. It was an opportunity to prove his loyalty, one she had been reluctant to give him, but she had been left with no alternative. Even now she was unsure whether she could trust him or not, but there was no one else with his reach and influence throughout the Anvil, other than Rearden's Revocaters, and she was hardly going to trust the Corwen Guild with this. Olstrum might have been instrumental in Fulren's exile, but that was a task Sullivar had demanded he carry out. The man was a servant, loyal to his emperor. Now she would see if he held as much loyalty to her. Despite her disdain for him, Rosomon would rather have him close to her than free to go about his affairs unchecked.

"Tell me more," she said, guiding him out of the small chamber, away from Athelys and any other ears that might listen.

Once outside, Olstrum leaned in close. "I have found someone who may know of the man you described to me. But he is unwilling to speak to anyone but you. He will certainly not be seen talking openly about this matter."

"Which suggests I was right," Rosomon replied.

"It would certainly appear so."

"Take me to him. Now."

Olstrum nodded. "I took the liberty of setting up a meeting, my lady. You should probably wear something more discreet." He gestured to her gown of Hawkspur blue.

"I don't have time for that," she replied, grabbing a worn brown cloak from a peg and throwing it over her shoulders. "Lead the way."

Olstrum gave a curt nod, and together they made their way from the administrative dungeon and out through the palace. Olstrum was already in civilian garb, and they were both soon lost among the crowds of the Anvil. For a moment Rosomon wondered whether she should summon Starn Rivers to accompany them, but this required discretion. The fewer of them involved the less attention they would draw.

The consul led her across the Whitespin, down onto the esplanade that ran along one whole bank toward the fishing traders' drinking dens. The place stank, lobster baskets piled high against the wall that ran almost all the way to the city gates, fish carcasses and oyster shells rotting in the open air as the gulls and rats fought for scraps.

When finally Olstrum led her into one of the alehouses, Rosomon had time to glance up and read the hastily scrawled sign above the door: *The Drowned Lady.* She had never believed in portents, but she could only hope this was not a prophecy of what was to come.

Even at such an early hour the place was busy. Two serving boys scurried from table to table delivering full tankards and collecting empty ones. If Rosomon had thought the stink on the esplanade was powerful, then inside it was positively overwhelming.

Olstrum led them to a booth in one corner and Rosomon followed, pulling her cloak tight about her. To her relief no one offered so much as a second glance as they sat opposite a grimy-looking man staring deep into his tankard.

He looked up furtively, shifting in his seat as though he were sitting on ants. One of his eyes was glassed over like that of a dead fish. Rosomon struggled not to stare at it as he regarded her suspiciously.

"Well?" whispered Olstrum. "We are here."

"Pay first," the man said, the corner of his mouth twitching as he spoke.

Olstrum leaned over the table. "I've already given you more coin than you deserve," he hissed.

Rosomon laid a calming hand on Olstrum's arm before taking a purse from the pocket of her gown.

"I hope this is worth it," she said, sliding the purse across the table.

The man deftly slid it off the table edge before secreting it in his jacket. Rosomon was alarmed to notice some of his fingers were missing.

"Speak," Olstrum demanded.

The man glanced around the room. He didn't give his name, and Rosomon was in no mood to know it. All she wanted was his information.

"I know one of the serfs at the Mount," the man began, his mouth twitching once more. "Been bringing in supplies to him down the Whitespin. Fish, spices, and whatever. Those legates like a bit of flavour in their meals, you know what I mean?"

"Get to it," Olstrum said impatiently.

"Well, I took on what you told me those days back, and I asked him to keep an eye out. Lot of people coming and going at the Mount. Just yesterday he says he saw someone matches the description you gave me."

"In what way?" Rosomon asked.

"Flesh all black and burned." The man lifted a two-fingered hand to his face, clamping it over his mouth. "Just like this."

Rosomon's nails dug into the greasy tabletop. It was just as Fulren had described—a man burned about the face. But this was not proof of her son's innocence. Not yet.

"Who was it?" Rosomon asked. "A priest? A pilgrim? Where are they now?"

"No, my lady. My man said it was one of the Drakes. A Knight of the Draconate."

"You're sure?" she hissed, unable to believe what she was hearing.

"Why would I lie?" the man answered, raising his hands defensively. "Why would I make up such a thing? I'm not trying to get myself executed for heresy."

"Where is this knight now?"

The man shrugged. "That's all I know."

Rosomon rose to her feet. She was done with this. Done with

rumours and chasing dead ends. The notion that Fulren and the emissary had been attacked by a member of the Drakes was a ridiculous one. It could not be true.

She marched back through the tavern and out into the stinking air. Olstrum followed.

"I am sorry, my lady. I didn't know he would suggest something so preposterous. My apologies for wasting your time."

Rosomon looked out over the river. Two boats passed as they travelled the Whitespin, the boatmen greeting one another cheerily. It appeared as though they had few worries to speak of. What Rosomon would have given to swap places with them. To travel the waterways of Torwyn without a care.

"Thank you for your help, Olstrum," she said. "I will take it from here."

The consul took a step closer. "My lady, you're not thinking that this might be true?"

"I don't know," she replied. "But I have to find out."

"Then please, allow me to accompany you."

"This requires discretion, Olstrum. And besides, I am merely going to the Mount to pray. What possible danger could I be in?"

Olstrum sighed, considering his options. He nodded when he realised there were none.

"Very well, my lady." He turned to leave, but stopped himself. "Please take care."

With a discreet bow, Olstrum left her by the river. It was a small gesture from the consul, but one that meant much. At first Rosomon had blamed Olstrum for gathering evidence against her son. But the man had merely been playing the part he was tasked with. It was his job to carry out Sullivar's orders, no matter who was condemned as a result. Since Sullivar had become incapacitated, Olstrum had proved himself most useful. With Lancelin gone he was one of the only allies she had left in the Anvil, albeit one she would never completely trust.

Rosomon didn't tarry; the sooner she was finished with this business the better. Even if there was such a scarred warrior in the Mount, she had little hope of finding him. The place was vast and filled with Knights of the Draconate. What was she to do, interrogate them all?

She made her way up from the river and through the crowded streets. There was no plan, no rhyme or reason to this. Only a glimmer of hope that...

What? That she might find the real culprit? And then? Would she present this assassin to her brother? Would she order Sullivar to send heralds to Nyrakkis and have her son brought back to her?

There was no way this could end with Fulren being returned, Rosomon knew that. But she had to at least try to find out why this had happened. To discover who had been responsible and, if possible, snatch some morsel of justice from this hopeless situation.

The Mount loomed up ahead. Rosomon pulled the hood of her cloak tight about her head as she joined the throng filing into the vast temple. She was soon lost among the pious crowd. Many of them gripped talismans of the Great Wyrms as they marched inexorably toward their goal. A robed woman pressed a bluestone depiction of Vermitrix to her lips as she whispered prayers of peace, while beside her a young man held a steel amulet of Ammenodus Rex in his fist as he uttered devotions through gritted teeth.

Rosomon funnelled into the temple, moving silently past a circle of worshippers, their faces painted skull white, hands joined in praise of Ravenothrax the Unvanquished, Wyrm of Death.

Once within the lofty confines, she quickly realised the folly of her actions. Every member of the Drakes stood in grim vigil, faces hidden beneath their dragon helms. What was she to do now, order them all to remove their helms so that she might examine them for burns? Rosomon Hawkspur was a powerful woman, but even she could not breach the sacred dignity of the Drakes on the word of an anonymous source.

Nevertheless, she was not done yet. She owed it to her son to at least try, no matter how hopeless the task might seem. Rosomon walked up to the vast sweeping staircase that provided access to the main mezzanine. From up there she might at least get a better view of the crowd. She wandered up the stairs, passing the plate-glass windows depicting the legendary Wyrms alongside the heroes of the Draconate, their past battles and deeds, and the holy saints who had foreseen the return of their dragon gods.

Once at the carved balustrade she gazed down on the crowd, watching as it wended its way through the huge temple, paying its due to each of the five statues of the Great Wyrms. There were thousands of pilgrims, hooded legates among them. Rosomon made her way along the walkway, eyes scanning for any sign of a burned face, and the farther she wandered about the cavernous building the more foolish and out of place she felt. This was sanctified ground, and here she was creeping about the place like a ghoul.

Frustration got the better of her. This had been madness from the start. As she made her way back down the stairs to join the crowd once more, she could barely stifle a sob. All hope was gone, any chance of justice dashed. Even the sun on her face as she made her way out into the ornamental gardens at the rear of the Mount did little to lift her spirits.

At the far corner of the gardens sat a young High Legate. Her robes were the green of Saphenodon, her face smiling and open. At her feet were a group of children hanging on her every word as she preached the words of the Draconate, spouting the Ministry's litanies with soft and practised ease. The children were spellbound by her. Their innocent faces filled with hope.

Rosomon began to realise what the real power was in this place. It was not the might of the Drakes or the authority of the Archlegate. It was the quiet words of a religion that had ruled Torwyn for a thousand years. The Guilds might have brought prosperity to a privileged few, but the Ministry still provided for those who had slipped through that net. Still offered hope to the hopeless.

This had been foolish from the start, to come here and expect to exert her authority. Better she return to the palace. Better she bury herself in the menial labours of running this empire. Better she forget any notion of her son's salvation.

As she turned to exit through the vast archway, a figure moved to block her path. He was shorter than Rosomon, with a slender, pale face beneath a crop of corn-yellow hair. The young man was decked from neck to foot in the drab grey robe of a legate, and he looked at her dolefully.

"Lady Rosomon," he said quietly, as though not to attract attention.

At first she considered denying who she was, but that might only have drawn yet more attention. "What can I do for you?"

"I am Legate Kinloth, my lady. Willet. I... I must speak with you regarding a matter of great urgency."

She would have dismissed him, told him she did not have time for this, but there was a desperation in his eyes. A fear that he might suffer for what he was about to tell her.

"Then speak, Legate Kinloth."

His eyes darted around the gardens, which added to the sense of conspiracy. Had he learned of the man Rosomon sought? Did he have information regarding a Knight of the Draconate with a burned face? Rosomon held her breath as he began.

"I have recently returned from the Drift, my lady. The Ministry posted me at Fort Karvan and I was part of a patrol sent into the wastes. There we encountered..."

He paused, glancing about the gardens once more, as though what he had to say was somehow forbidden. Rosomon realised this had nothing to do with Fulren, nothing to do with who she was searching for, and her patience began to wane.

"My time is short, Legate Kinloth," she urged him. "I suggest you get to the point."

"We encountered something," he replied quickly, his lip starting to tremble. "Something evil. Something unholy. I was the only survivor. I have tried to tell them, tried to explain, but no one will listen."

"The Drift is filled with evil, Legate Kinloth. Both human and feral. This is not news—"

"This was not a beast, my lady. But neither was it human. It carried a weapon that thirsted for the souls of its victims. Its eye was red—"

"Control yourself," she snapped as he grew more hysterical. "You have obviously suffered a shock, Willet, but we are quite safe. The Armiger Battalions have defended our border with the Drift for centuries."

"Not from anything like this," he replied, his voice almost lost among the chatter of the gardens. "Something is coming that even the Armigers cannot stop. Please, my lady, you must listen to me. We have to—"

"Enough," she said. "I have an empire to oversee, Legate Kinloth. The last thing I need to hear is the feverish ranting of an anxious priest."

Willet bowed his head and took a step away. He looked ashamed of himself, and Rosomon almost felt sorry for the young man. She opened her mouth to apologise for reacting so harshly, but thought better of it. Perhaps she should have listened to what he had to say, if only to console him and make him realise he was in no danger.

Instead she turned her back, leaving Willet and the madness of the Ministry behind her.

CONALL

It leaned against the wall: five feet of tempered steel splaying into a six-inch-wide blade at one end. The killing end. Haft gilded in twisting patterns, handle enfolded in finely stitched leather. Conall was no weaponsmith, but even he could tell this was a blade of magnificent craftsmanship that even the metalworkers of the Ironfall Guild would have struggled to replicate.

So why was it in the possession of the goatheads?

It had been crafted specifically for durrga hands. Conall could barely lift it, let alone think about wielding it with any skill, and he was stronger than many. So where had they got it from?

Of course, there was a chance it had just been stolen. Pirates from Iperion Magna raided all along the coastline looking for slaves. It made sense that they would have travelled to the Karna Frontier, but why would they have crafted a weapon like this in the first place? The pirates of the Magna were fearsome warriors, but not bloody giants. There had to be some connection, and an alliance between the durrga and Malador was the only explanation. But to what end?

The Scions of Iperion Magna had no need for pyrestone, their demonic blood magics worked without such resources. They knew little of artifice. What could the durrga offer them in exchange for such glorious weapons? The more Conall thought on it, the more he was desperate to solve the mystery. He just had to pick the right moment to confront Beringer.

He had not seen the frontier marshal since returning from patrol, and if he was honest he couldn't think of a right time to ever approach his irascible commander, but he had to get to the bottom of this one way or another.

The creaking of cart wheels drew his attention from the glaive, and Conall stood up to peer from the window of his chamber, moving gingerly, feeling the ache of the bruises he'd suffered in his fight with the durrga warrior. A wagon was being loaded in the courtyard in preparation for its journey to Agavere.

Conall made his way outside, the heat striking him in an oppressive wave. Donan Marrlock was waiting patiently beside the wagon, shifting his weight from foot to foot in his eagerness to be away. When he saw Conall approaching, his expression brightened.

"Leaving us so soon?" Conall asked.

"I'm afraid so, my friend," Donan said, moving forward to embrace Conall, who could only grit his teeth as his bruises were squeezed.

"Safe journey," Conall said, patting the man on the back.

He was much different from the desperate survivor Conall had found a couple of days before. Now he had washed and been given fresh garb he almost looked respectable, but there was still a haunted look to his eyes. Hardly surprising after what they had witnessed.

"I cannot begin to thank you," Donan said.

He had already thanked Conall more than enough times, to the point that it was starting to get embarrassing.

"Don't mention it."

"I will mention it, my friend. I'll tell everyone what you did for me. And if there's any way I can return the favour, I will."

"Just stay out of trouble, Donan."

"Oh, I intend to. It's the quiet life for me from now on."

"Sounds sensible," Conall said. "I should try it one day."

Donan grinned. "I wouldn't have thought the quiet life would suit a man like you."

If only he knew. Conall would much have preferred his breezy chambers in Agavere to this place, but there was no way he could earn a reputation lying in a comfortable bed.

The wagon driver signalled he was ready to go.

"I'll see you in Torwyn when you get home," Donan said when he had climbed into the rear of the wagon. "We'll make a night of it."

"We'll make a week of it," Conall replied, waving as the wagon trundled away through the gates of the fort. No sooner had it left than one of Beringer's adjutants was at Conall's side.

"He wants to speak to you," the man said.

There was little doubt who he was referring to.

"Now?" Conall asked, glancing down at how dishevelled he was.

"Do you want to keep him waiting and find out?" the adjutant replied.

Conall glanced across the courtyard and up at Beringer's office, elevated above the rest of the fort. Tardy or messy. Not much of a choice. Messy it would have to be.

He marched across the courtyard, doing his best to dust down his shirt and leggings, stopping to rub each boot on the back of his calves, which served only to spread the dirt across the leather.

At the top of the stairs, Conall paused before knocking, listening for any sound from Beringer. What was he expecting? That the frontier marshal would be in a good mood? Singing to himself in his cups?

After a swift knock a deep voice ordered him to enter. Conall took a breath as he walked in, seeing Beringer standing behind his desk, glaring at missives and mining reports, his sunburned brow creased in consternation.

Conall stood for some moments, waiting for Beringer to acknowledge him. The temptation to noisily clear his throat was overwhelming, but even he wasn't so stupid as to aggravate the frontier marshal.

"I've read Captain Tarrien's report," Beringer said finally, still examining his papers. His words hung in the air as though they should bear some kind of significance before he looked up, fixing Conall with that condescending expression. "I haven't read yours."

"Apologies, Frontier Marshal." Conall hadn't realised a report was necessary. "I thought it best to relay my account in person." Conall was surprised at how convincing his own lie was.

"Then get on with it," Beringer replied.

Conall took a breath before he began. "We proceeded to the mining outpost as ordered. When we reached it there were obvious signs it had been attacked. I led my unit forward to scout out the area."

"With no objections from Captain Tarrien?" Beringer asked.

Conall tried to think back to the conversation. He could remember no argument from Tarrien.

"None, sir."

"So you took it on yourself to endanger your unit by striking forward alone?"

"With all due respect, sir, that's what the Talon is for."

"I hear Tarrien and his men had to pull your arse out of the fire when you were attacked. If they hadn't shown up when they did, you'd be speared on a goathead pole."

"I had the situation under control," Conall replied, remembering how he'd almost been torn to pieces.

"Reckless," Beringer said. "And arrogant. But what should I have expected?"

"Frontier Marshal, there's something you should know," Conall said, desperate to move on from the mention of his quite considerable flaws.

"Oh? Something that should perhaps have been written in a report?"

Conall ignored the further critique. "We discovered a weapon. One the durrga were using. But it was clearly crafted in an expert forge."

Beringer narrowed his eyes. "And?"

"And it could mean there is some kind of connection with Malador. The durrga might have formed a union with Iperion Magna. Or someone else."

"Or they could have looted it from any one of a dozen places."

"Frontier Marshal, if you look at the weapon—"

"I have pressing matters that require my attention, Hawkspur. I don't have time to look into every conspiracy theory some nobleman comes up with."

"Beringer, you have to take this seriously. We have to investigate."

Conall had experienced uncomfortable silences before, but the one that followed his final outburst was by far the worst.

The frontier marshal walked from behind his desk, fixing Conall with that contemptuous gaze of his. "Fort Tarkis stands as a last bastion of defence against an enemy that would slaughter us to the last man. I am responsible for its upkeep and for the men within it. I am also responsible for the mining outposts within its purview and the supply of stone that is funnelled back to Agavere. And you want me to assign men to a mission in enemy territory because you found a fancy spear?"

"It's a glaive," Conall corrected. Yes, arrogant, but he was in knee-deep now. Might as well wade in to his neck. "And yes, that's exactly what we should do. If the durrga and the Maladorans have formed an alliance, it could mean disaster for Torwyn and for this expedition into the Karna. I understand the pressure you are under, Frontier Marshal, but I am heir to the Hawkspur Guild. I insist you allow me to look into this."

Beringer raised his brow in surprise, creasing that tanned head of his. He nodded, as though appreciating Conall's candour.

"You're right, Hawkspur," he said, moving to the door of his office. "You are heir to one of the most powerful Guilds in Torwyn."

"I meant no disrespect," Conall said, as Beringer opened the door and beckoned to him to follow.

As they made their way down the wooden stair, he didn't know whether he was intimidated by Beringer's amiable aspect or would have preferred his red-faced rage.

"Disrespect?" Beringer said as he made his way toward the training station. "How could you disrespect me? I am, after all, a lowly marshal of the Armigers. You are veritable royalty."

Conall followed, a sinking feeling gripping his gut as he saw the racks of practice weapons and the wooden mannequins awaiting their attention.

"I assume you're sword trained?" Beringer asked. "You don't just hide behind that longbarrel?"

"I'm familiar with a blade," Conall replied. "I was instructed by the swordwright of the Hawkspur Guild."

"Starn Rivers?" Beringer said, picking two practice swords from a rack. "Deadly man. But boring as shit." He tossed one of the wooden swords to Conall, who managed to snatch it from the air. "Show me your defence."

Conall glanced across the courtyard. They were being watched by some of the troopers.

"I don't think this is necessary, sir."

Beringer lunged.

Conall barely had time to raise his sword, staggering back into a solid stance as their swords clacked noisily.

"Not bad," Beringer said. "I guess Starn is a better teacher than he is a talker."

Conall remembered the swordwright's lessons. How Starn had barely spoken in all those years of training. Now it seemed Beringer wanted to impart a lesson of his own.

"I learned a thing or two," Conall said.

"Then show me," Beringer replied, his amiable expression melting away.

If that's what this overbearing bastard wanted, then maybe it was time to demonstrate.

Conall danced forward, feet square, free hand behind his back. The practice swords flashed, and Beringer backed away as they struck one another. Conall could see in his peripheral vision that the tune they played had enticed more of an audience. Two dozen eyes were on them as they danced. The courtyard silent but for the sound of clacking swordplay.

Beringer seemed unimpressed with Conall's attack, moving forward relentlessly with a series of counters. His blows were strong, but his form was rudimentary. Conall met every swipe and thrust with an efficient parry.

He dodged back, out of range, settling into his form. It had been a while since he'd sparred, and he'd forgotten how much he enjoyed it. Rivulets of sweat ran down Beringer's creased brow, and it was clear he struggled in the heat.

As the marshal lumbered forward once more, Conall changed his stance, striking in low. He had the measure of Beringer now—strong but slow. One well-timed thrust and he would simulate a killing strike. Hopefully that would be enough to convince this ogre that he was more than just some privileged noble.

His practice sword lanced in. The thrust perfect.

Beringer moved like lighting, sidestepping and letting Conall dart within range. The marshal's free hand grasped Conall's wrist, wooden sword coming down to crack him on the side of the head.

The next thing Conall knew, he was on his arse in a cloud of dust, ear ringing a dinner bell in his head. He looked up to see Beringer regarding him dispassionately.

"Thank you for the demonstration, Frontier Marshal."

It seemed only right to make the compliment.

Beringer held out a hand to help him up. Conall was surprised at the gesture, but he took it. Perhaps now Beringer had established his superiority with a blade, they could start their relationship anew.

Conall was dragged to his feet, finding his balance for the briefest of moments before Beringer headbutted him back to the ground.

Not quite the response he'd been looking for.

Blood ran freely from his nose, and as he looked up through watering eyes, Conall could see Beringer's expression had changed to one of fury.

"The demonstration wasn't just for you, boy," he growled. "Every now and again a dog has to prove its dominance. When a new dog joins the pack, it needs to learn where it sits in the pecking order. So listen carefully. I don't give a slimy shit who your family is or where you come from. I rule the roost here. When I give an order, you obey. When I *say*, you fucking *do*. Am I understood?"

All Conall could do was stem the blood flowing from his nose and nod his agreement.

Beringer left him sitting in the dirt. As much as Conall tried to resist the temptation, he glanced up to see the troopers of the

Phoenix Battalion looking on with amusement. Westley Tarrien was among them, and if he was trying to stifle his grin of amusement, he wasn't doing a very good job.

Conall picked himself up, avoiding the spectators as he made his way back to the barracks room, gritting his teeth, clenching his fists, for all the good anger would do him now. He slammed the door behind him once he'd entered his chamber, glaring around the small office for something he could fling against the wall, but that would have been the most stupid move of all. What good would breaking his own belongings do?

Instead he slumped in his chair, looking for a cloth he could wipe his bloody face with. Before he could find it, the door to his chamber opened and in walked Sted.

"Did you see that?" he asked.

"Everybody saw that," she replied, perching on the edge of his desk.

"That's it," he said. "I'm done with this place. We leave tomorrow."

Sted went to a nearby shelf, plucking from it a half-drunk bottle of Agaveran brandy and a pair of mismatched cups.

"Far be it from me to speak out of turn." She placed a cup in front of Conall and poured. "But wouldn't that be a rather hasty move?"

"A hasty move?" he answered, still looking for a cloth in one of his desk drawers. "Look at my frigging face."

Sted plucked a kerchief from inside her shirt and waved it in front of his nose. Conall took it, wondering for a second if it was clean before realising he didn't care.

"If we leave tomorrow, you prove everyone right."

Conall dabbed at his nose. "Since when did you care a shit about proving people right? Or wrong for that matter?"

"So we're just going to run? Because someone hurt your pride?"

As Conall dabbed at his aching nose, he resisted the temptation to point out it wasn't just his pride that had been hurt.

"Beringer hates me," he said. "We're not welcome here. This is not what I had in mind when I decided we should come to the frontier."

"And what was the idea? Glory? 'Cause I've got news for you, in case you hadn't noticed: life on the frontier is pretty far from bloody glorious."

"He could at least show me some respect as an officer. But he can't see past my heritage. I can't change who I am."

Sted smiled that red-toothed grin of hers before taking a swig of brandy. "Beringer doesn't hate you 'cause you're highborn. He hates you 'cause you're trouble. He runs a tight ship, and you're here causing him problems."

Conall would have been offended if he didn't know Sted was right.

"And your suggestion is...?"

"Do as you're told, maybe? Don't upset the apple cart. Especially when the apples have a tendency to smash you in the face. We need to settle in, make ourselves invaluable, before we revert to type."

Conall glanced across the office at the glaive leaning against the wall. "Maybe you're right," he replied.

Sted looked more surprised than he'd ever seen. "Really? Blow me, that'll be a first. So we're gonna settle in and do as we're told?"

Conall flashed a grin of his own. "Not bloody likely. What we are going to do is prove our value. Just like you said."

"Hang on." Sted looked worried now. "I don't think I'm gonna like where this is going."

Conall pointed at the beautifully wrought glaive. "I'm going to find out where that came from. I'm going to get to the bottom of this, and if the Maladorans have formed an alliance with the goatheads, I'm going to report it. All right and proper, as a captain of the Talon should."

"So you're just going to head out into the desert and spy on the goatheads? Hope they don't spy you first and tear your guts out through your mouth?"

"That's pretty much the plan, yes."

She breathed out a long sigh and swigged the rest of her brandy. "Good luck with that," she said, wincing at the taste of the dregs.

"Oh, I won't need luck," Conall replied.

"Why's that?"

He finished his own brandy, then slammed the cup back down on the table and resisted the urge to pull a face at the foul taste.

"Because you'll be there to watch my back."

Sted had nothing to say to that. It looked like her good advice had all dried up.

LANCELIN

A balcony jutted from the summit of the Temple of Soth, looking out over the rooftops of Jubara. From behind its alabaster rampart, Lancelin watched the city beneath the dark skyline, its winking lights mirroring the star field above. As much as he hated to admit it, the sight was a beautiful one. It could have rivalled any view of the Anvil, and without the noise and dust of the forges, one might even have said Jubara surpassed it.

Lancelin dismissed the thought. He was a long way from home, and no matter the beauty of this place he knew how much danger he was in. It was a perilous move to become spellbound by aesthetics.

"It's time."

Lancelin peered through the dark to see Khonos standing in the shadows of the stairwell. Even in the darkness, the livid bruise surrounding his right eye was visible. He limped forward, cradling his arm gingerly. The riot he'd inspired had come at great cost. Hundreds had taken to the streets. Their diversion had been necessary, but it had taken its toll. Khonos had barely escaped with his life. Many others had not. More still were being interrogated in Jubara's dungeons, and it would not be long before someone came looking for the man who had instigated the uprising.

"I assume you've made arrangements to get out of here?" Lancelin asked.

A wry smile played across Khonos's lips. "I am not leaving," he replied.

"They will find you eventually."

The spy shook his head. "Their interrogations will certainly lead them to Kosma Khonos, high priest to Soth of the Deep. But when they do, he will no longer be here."

"Where will you hide?"

"Nowhere. Kosma Khonos will cease to exist, but I will have adopted a new life in another part of the city."

Lancelin would have liked to know more, but it was probably best if he didn't.

"Good luck," Lancelin replied, moving to the stairs and making his way down through the tower.

"Your path to the aerie should be clear. The route I gave you winds through the slums. I would have suggested the sewers, but they're crawling with Medjai looking for more insurrectionists."

"We'll be fine," Lancelin said, though he knew there were no guarantees. "You've done enough."

"I am a servant of Torwyn," Khonos said. "It will never be enough until our nation is safe from the predilections of its enemies."

Lancelin noted the fervour with which Khonos spoke. There was an almost religious zeal to the way he had arranged the riot. He had proved his loyalty was beyond question, and Lancelin resisted the temptation to point out how misplaced it was. Torwyn was unsettled, the Guilds fractious, the Draconate powerless, and all of it because of a weak ruler. As much as Lancelin was bound to serve and protect Sullivar, he could not help but think Torwyn would thrive under a stronger leader.

He made his way into the temple and down the secret entrance leading to the cellar. Candles were lit, casting a flickering yellow light on the walls, not that its occupant would appreciate the gesture.

Fulren was still tied to a chair and turned his head as Lancelin made his way down the stairs. His useless eyes darted about the room, vainly trying to focus. A milky film covered them, the livid welts on his face evidence of what he'd suffered. Lancelin could not help but feel sympathy.

"We have to go," Lancelin said.

Fulren had refused to speak to him before now, and it seemed he was willing to carry on the silence. Stubborn. Just like his mother.

"Are you ready?" Lancelin asked.

"I'm not going anywhere with you," Fulren snarled. His first words since Lancelin had drugged him with poppy essence. Progress at least.

"I will cut you free," Lancelin said. "You will not try to run. You will not shout or make a fuss."

"To the fucking Five Lairs with you," Fulren snapped.

Lancelin approached him, drawing a knife from its sheath. "Listen to me. We are both in a lot of danger. If you don't do exactly as I say, we'll end up dead. Or worse."

"I don't have to do a damn thing. I'm not the one in danger here. You're the one who's going to die. If I could see, I'd kill you myself."

Lancelin leaned in close. "I don't know what these people have said to make you believe they mean you no harm, but you have to think. They are not your friends. You're their prisoner and you're blind, Fulren. They did this to you."

"I would rather spend a decade imprisoned here than take a single step with you."

Khonos chuckled from the shadows. "That boy really does hate you."

"Hate doesn't begin to cover it," Fulren snapped. "This bastard murdered my father."

Lancelin gritted his teeth. The temptation to tell Fulren the truth was overwhelming, but the boy would never believe it, even if he tried to explain.

"Fulren, this is your chance to get home. Your mother is waiting for you."

That seemed to quiet his rage.

"You have a decision to make, boy," Khonos said. "Go home with this man, or put yourself back at the mercy of callous fanatics."

Fulren went silent as he thought on it, but Lancelin knew there was no real choice. One way or another, he was taking Fulren home. It was just a matter of how easy he would make it.

"He killed my father," Fulren whispered eventually. It was obvious he was fighting the tears, biting back his frustration.

"Listen," said Khonos, moving forward to stand in front of Fulren. "Jagdor's come a long way to help you. A lot of people have made sacrifices so you can go home. That's got to be worth something?"

Fulren nodded. "It makes sense, I guess."

Lancelin swiftly cut the rope tying Fulren to the chair. When he tried to help him to his feet, the boy snatched his arm away, stumbling before he found his balance.

"Follow my voice," Khonos said.

Fulren did his best, and the three of them moved from the cellar and up the stairs. Lancelin was encouraged by how Fulren used his instinct to navigate his way out. When they were in the main hall of the temple, Khonos fished something from inside his robe, wincing at the pain in his arm.

"You'll need this to get in the aerie," he said, presenting Lancelin with a wrought iron key, the grooves resembling feral teeth.

"You have my thanks," Lancelin said, stowing it in his jacket. "For everything. May the Wyrms protect."

"Let's hope so," Khonos replied.

From the shadows Khonos's young apprentice appeared. At first Lancelin didn't recognise him in his fine clothes and curly brown wig. Clearly he was joining his master in a new life somewhere else in the city.

Without a word, the young lad led them to the door and opened it a crack, peering out onto the street. When he was satisfied all was quiet, he opened it fully. Lancelin took hold of Fulren's arm to lead him outside, but instead Fulren grabbed his wrist.

"No," he said. "I hold you."

With that he grasped the belt at Lancelin's waist.

The two of them stole from the temple and made their way out into the night. It was eerily quiet after the upheaval the day before, the air still and humid.

Lancelin listened, but there was no sound. The streets were empty, no wandering patrols, not even the barking of a distant dog.

He clung to the shadows as they made their way from the temple. Fulren gripped on tight, doing his best to keep pace, but even with his best efforts they could manage only a fast march through the dark streets.

Khonos had shown Lancelin a circuitous route back to the aerie, and he had committed it to memory, confident he would not get lost in the labyrinthine slums. They ducked down a narrow alleyway, slinking past the arched doorways. Every now and again Lancelin would stop, listening for any sound of a wandering patrol, but all was silent.

Eventually the maze of back alleys came out onto a main thoroughfare overlooked by a series of towers that reached up into the starless night. Lancelin paused, peering up and down the street.

"We have to make a run for it," he whispered. When Fulren didn't answer, he said, "Are you with me?"

"Like I have a choice?" he hissed back.

If there had been any doubts this was Rosomon Hawkspur's son, they were convincingly dashed.

Lancelin took Fulren's arm and struck out, urging him faster along the street. There was scant light, the braziers set upon ten-foot posts casting intermittent shadows along their route. They were no more than halfway to the aerie when Lancelin heard the sound of marching feet.

He grabbed Fulren by his shirt, bundling him into a nearby doorway. It was poor cover, but if they stuck to the shadows they might not be seen. Both men squeezed themselves into the dark as the footsteps grew louder. Fulren's breathing became more fevered, as though he were resisting the temptation to cry out, and Lancelin clamped a hand over the boy's mouth.

Six warriors made their way past, spears held aloft as they hustled along the street. Lancelin held his breath. If they were discovered, it was likely he could eliminate the patrol, but if they raised the alarm, any chance of escape would be dashed.

As the sound of their footfalls receded, Lancelin let out his breath. Fulren wrenched the hand away from his mouth, sucking in air.

"Are you trying to suffocate me?" he hissed.

There was no time to apologise. He grabbed Fulren and dragged him along the thoroughfare as fast as he could. A metal gate stood at the end of the street, and Lancelin was already fumbling in his jacket for the key Khonos had given him. He slid it smoothly into the lock, relieved at the sound of tumblers clicking into place as he turned it.

The gate opened with a squeal of hinges, but it was too late for stealth now. As Lancelin pulled Fulren up the staircase toward the aerie, he could see the horizon was beginning to glow with orange light, the sun about to rise.

"We're almost there," he said, trying to reassure Fulren, or perhaps himself.

His heart was pounding, and he forced himself to control the panic and excitement. They rushed up through the tower, the smell of the aerie pungent, a mixture of dung and animal feed and stale straw. Symbols were written on a lintel in archaic script, corresponding to the ident he had been given by the functionary on his arrival.

By the time they finally reached the stable of eagles, the pale light of the sun was bright enough to light their way. His war eagle sat in its pen, hooded and resting. Lancelin opened the gate, making soothing noises so as not to startle the beast, relieved to find the saddle polished and waiting to be fitted.

He wrestled with the bulky tack, struggling to throw it across the war eagle's back. It was a two-man job, but it was doubtful Fulren would be any help.

"Why are you doing this?"

Lancelin paused at Fulren's question before going back to positioning the saddle.

"I told you," he replied as he buckled one of the girth straps. "Your mother sent me."

"But why the Hawkslayer? Why would she send the man who killed her husband?"

"It was a duel," Lancelin said. He had always hated the name Hawkslayer. Though few would ever have said it to his face, he knew the implication in that name: that he had murdered Melrone Hawkspur.

"You slew the man she loved," Fulren said. "You left me fatherless. Why would she send you of all people?"

The war eagle protested as Lancelin struggled with the breast collar. "Now is not the time," he said through gritted teeth. The notion that Rosomon had ever loved Melrone struck him like a knife to the gut.

"Now's exactly the time. I'll not take another step until I know what's going on."

Lancelin stopped, moving toward Fulren before curbing his anger. This was a desperate situation. He had to stay in control.

Before he could speak he saw movement in the corner of his eye.

The stable attendant was young, head shaved, eyes wide as he watched them from the other end of the stable. Before Lancelin could move, the attendant dropped the bucket he was carrying and sprinted away.

"Shit," Lancelin spat.

"What?" asked Fulren as Lancelin grasped the breast collar of the war eagle and began to pull the beast from the pen. The eagle struggled, but with some stern encouragement it began to move, the hood over its head making it docile enough to lead.

"What's happening?" Fulren asked.

"They're coming. We have to go."

The far side of the stable ended in a vast archway open to the morning sky—a perch from which they could launch their steed. He had not yet fitted the bridle, but it was a complex task. Who knew how long they had before the attendant alerted the guard?

The war eagle followed as Lancelin urged it closer to the vast arch looking out to the east. He risked a glance down from the precipice, seeing a drop hundreds of feet to the ground below.

"What's happening?" Fulren asked again as Lancelin grabbed him, pulling him to the war eagle.

"Get on," he urged, placing the boy's hands on the saddle.

With some difficulty Fulren climbed up. Lancelin grabbed a fistful of feathers at the beast's neck, dipping its head before he pulled the hood off. The bird blinked, beak opening wide as it let out a piercing screech.

Lancelin hastily climbed onto the eagle's back in front of Fulren, fumbling with the stirrups as he buckled them to his thighs.

"Hold on to something," he ordered, and Fulren wrapped his hands in the cargo straps.

With a kick the eagle stepped tentatively forward. Then, dipping its head, it leapt from the arch. Its wings spread wide, and there was a sudden lurch in Lancelin's stomach as it fell like a stone before catching the thermals.

He held on tight, grasping the thick feathers at the war eagle's neck, feeling the rush of wind in his face. Squinting in the bright rising sun, he was momentarily thankful Fulren was blind and couldn't see the imminent peril they were in.

The war eagle wheeled, finding its bearings. As much as Lancelin tried to use the fistfuls of feathers to urge the beast eastward, it swung about, soaring above the spires of Jubara, offering a brief glimpse of the city from the air. Then it rose.

Lancelin could hardly breathe as it gained altitude, rising through the scant cloud cover. The dawn air grew colder as they flew, and Lancelin's anger at his lack of control was soon replaced by dismay as he realised the beast was heading north.

There was nothing he could do to direct the eagle without bit and bridle. He was a helpless passenger, and Fulren along with him.

On it flew, high over the green fields. As time passed, the sun eventually rose in the blue skies. Always to his right, the far-flung outline of the Drift cut through the landscape like an ugly scar—a scar he was desperate to cross, but the war eagle had its own ideas. The sound of the wind in his ears was deafening, the chill of it countered by the blazing sun. They flew for hours, crossing rivers and dales, hill ranges and forests until Lancelin could spy mountains on the northern horizon.

A chill began to seep into his bones despite the warmth of the sun. Below them he could see smatterings of white. Fresh snowfall blotting the land in places. A glance back over his shoulder, and Lancelin's worries about where they were going suddenly faded.

Dark shapes were dogging them in the distant blue sky. Four winged beasts, their riders barely visible on their backs.

"Shit," Lancelin said.

Fulren shouted something that was lost on the wind before the war eagle swooped lower. The ground rushed up toward them before the beast adjusted its course, soaring above a dense forest of redwoods. Beyond the trees was a high mountain range, snow-capped peaks disappearing into the mist.

They were in the Huntan Reach.

Lancelin knew the dangers here. If the war eagle were to set down now, they'd be in as much trouble as they had been in Jubara. Maybe more. Before he could begin to formulate some kind of plan, any plan, a bolt of light streaked overhead. Lancelin felt the heat as it flew past and then hit the trees, setting the foliage aflame in a bright plume.

Fulren screamed again, and this time Lancelin could pretty much work out what he was asking, but there was no way to explain they were being pursued by Jubaran sorcerers.

The war eagle screeched, realising it was prey, banking to one side in a panic. There was no way to stop it.

An explosion of light and heat almost smashed Lancelin from the saddle.

The acrid stink of burning struck his nostrils, the beast beneath him shrieking as it quickly lost altitude. All he could do was hang on like grim death as it spun. His vision was a blur of trees and sky and singed feathers. Fulren grasped him tight about the waist as they plummeted toward the treetops.

The crack of a branch. Something sharp scratched his face. Lancelin reached to his belt, wrenching his knife free and cutting the stirrup straps that bound his thigh to the falling beast. He managed to free one, feeling himself lurch to one side before they struck the ground.

Silence.

Lancelin opened his eyes. The war eagle lay beneath him, the feathers of its belly smouldering, wings broken, body still tangled in the remains of the saddle. The knife was gone from his hand.

Gingerly Lancelin unbuckled the remaining stirrup strap, saying a quick prayer of thanks to Vermitrix that he had landed on top of the dying beast and not the other way around. As he released himself he looked around for Fulren, feeling himself begin to panic.

"Fulren?" he shouted.

His voice echoed through the forest as he glared past the thick trunks of redwood trees. At his feet was the knife he had dropped, and he quickly retrieved it and slipped it into the sheath at his sword belt.

"Fulren?" This time louder.

"Here," came the reply.

Lancelin staggered away from the creature still floundering in its death throes. When he saw Fulren leaning against the bole of a tree, he let out a sigh. He could see cuts on the boy's face, but otherwise he looked fine.

"Are you hurt?" he asked.

"Do I look hurt?" Fulren replied.

Another reminder of exactly whose son this was.

Before he could check on Fulren's condition, there was a howl from above the treetops. Their pursuers were not done yet.

"All right. On your feet." Lancelin grabbed Fulren and hauled him up.

They both groaned at the effort but managed to stand.

"Are we in Torwyn?" Fulren asked.

Lancelin looked up, seeing a dark shadow swoop overhead.

"Not exactly," he replied before dragging Fulren on through the trees.

"Then where are we?"

"I'll explain later," he replied as another shriek echoed from above. "For now we have to keep moving."

"Some kind of shit rescue this is," Fulren mumbled as they went.

Lancelin wasn't inclined to disagree.

TYRETA

Amanisa set a rigorous pace. Tyreta bounded through the jungle in her wake, managing to keep up and surprising herself into the bargain.

War cries echoed through the trees. The mine wasn't far ahead, along with the unmistakable sound of battle. They were too late to warn the miners, but perhaps not too late to help them. The thought of that struck fear into Tyreta's heart. What possible help could they be against an army?

Ozoro and Suma were already waiting as they reached a cliff edge. Amanisa slowed, ducking down to crawl up beside them. Tyreta did likewise, with Gelila right beside her. The noise from beyond the ledge was almost deafening, roars of anger and desperate shouts echoing as a battle raged. When she peered into the quarry, Tyreta saw a scene from her nightmares.

Bodies lay strewn all across the valley floor. A horde of Chul warriors were attacking a defensive position on a ridge the miners had boxed themselves into. Crates and wagons had been turned on their sides, over which the miners repelled hundreds of ferocious kesh. A few defenders had splintbows, but not enough to make a dent in the Chul numbers. It wouldn't be long before they were slaughtered to a man.

"We have to do something," Tyreta said as she witnessed the horror below.

"Too many," said Gelila.

"Those people need help," she replied, desperately.

Tyreta looked to Gelila and the other women. She could see Ozoro and Suma glaring at the battle, eager to join in and take their revenge on the Chul. Gelila looked less sure.

"There must be something we can do," Tyreta pleaded.

Gelila shook her head. "We cannot win."

Tyreta couldn't argue with the sentiment. The miners were putting up a valiant defence with little more than pickaxes and shovels, but it would ultimately be in vain against spears and bows. Bodies peppered the battlefield, limbs hacked and stuck with arrows, but as Tyreta scanned the bloody ground her eyes fell on a rusted machine standing in the shadow of a mine shaft.

"There," she said, pointing to the far end of the quarry. "A stormhulk."

It was a mining hulk rather than a military model, and old from the look of it.

"You can bring metal beast to life?" Gelila asked.

"I can try. I just need to reach it."

Gelila looked as though she was weighing up their chances, but Amanisa, Suma and Ozoro didn't seem to think it so outlandish an idea. The women talked briefly in kesh, becoming more animated as they did so.

"Yes," Gelila said. "We go. Quickly."

With that the women began moving along the edge of the ridge. Tyreta followed the warriors as they crept down into the quarry and picked their way over the fallen bodies. She could see the miners had not gone down easily, and there were Chul raiders among the dead. Blood was spattered on the ground, running in rivulets and drying fast on the dusty earth. Tyreta tried her best not to look at the slaughter lest she lose her nerve. Better to focus on the hulk up ahead, steel herself enough to try to make a difference.

Amanisa darted forward, Ozoro at her back. They had not covered more than ten yards of open ground before there was a roar to their left. One of the Chul came charging at them, spear raised. Gelila was swift to respond, drawing and nocking her bow in one swift motion. An arrow appeared in the Chul warrior's side and he grunted, stumbling to one knee, still vainly trying to raise his weapon.

With a vengeful howl Suma leapt for him, raising her axe high and bringing it down with ruthless fury. Tyreta looked away before the inevitable crack told her Suma had caved in the warrior's skull.

More raiders spotted them and began peeling off from the battle with the miners. As the first of them approached, Amanisa thrust her spear, jabbing at him as he charged. Ozoro raced ahead to meet another, twin axes spinning in a blur. Arrows thrummed from Gelila's bow. The spectacle would have been magnificent had Tyreta paused to witness it, but as the women fought she ran on, eyes fixed on the stormhulk, ignoring the carnage as best she could.

The entrance to the mine lay at the top of a steep ramp, and Tyreta felt her legs ache as she sprinted up it. Closer to the rusted hulk, she realised what a poor state the machine was in as it stood leaning against the cave wall. Its hatch was open, more a cage than a cockpit, with only steel bars to protect the pilot. Even if she was able to bring the hulk to life, it would offer little to shield against the weapons of the attacking Chul.

Tyreta ran past a corpse still bleeding into the dust, barely noticing the spider sigil of the Hallowhill Guild emblazoned on the purple tunic. She planted a foot on the bent leg of the hulk, pulled herself inside the cockpit and wrestled with the hatch. A low growl issued from her lips as she put all her strength into swinging the thing shut—a crisscrossing frame of steel that would be the only thing standing between her and the raiders.

"Please work," she growled, shutting out the sounds of battle around her. "Move, you bloody thing."

Tyreta closed her eyes. With her webwainer's vision she could already make out the threads of the web connecting the machine's engine; the pyrestones fitted into their conversion chambers were still live at least. She pushed further, shutting off the outside world, sinking deeper into a reverie, channelling the latent energy in those stones.

With a juddering of gears, the stormhulk ground to life. A hiss of pistons and the machine rose to full height. Opening her eyes, she could see the Chul were still assaulting the defensive position up on the ridge. More warriors had peeled off from the main group to attack Gelila and the other women, and Tyreta feverishly willed the hulk to move.

Smoke belched from ventilation ports, spewing a black cloud in her wake. Hydraulics whirred as those piston legs moved, propelling the cumbersome machine onward.

This was far from the ecstasy she had felt before, when Wyllow had led her into the jungle in their refitted stormhulks. This machine was a beast of burden designed for smashing rock and shifting earth. With a clenching of her fists, Tyreta raised the hulk's arms, two massive hinged shovels that instantly responded to her command. Now she would see if this had been as stupid an idea as she thought.

Suma backed away from two Chul attackers, swinging her axe to fend them off. Tyreta lumbered forward, seeing the look of surprise on one kesh face as she brought the shovel arm down.

It crushed the warrior to the ground, a bloody stain appearing beneath the hulk's shovel. A second raider had time to fling his spear wide of the mark before she swung the other arm, batting him yards across the quarry floor.

"Come on!" she yelled above the din of the fighting, as much to encourage herself as anything else.

Another warrior ran straight at her, axe raised high, as she brought both arms of the hulk crashing together. She heard bones crack, saw his face contort as his feline skull was pulverised. Tyreta should have been horrified at the sight, but it only served to spur her on, fuelling her rage, her lust for revenge.

The stormhulk lumbered toward the Chul as they attacked the ridge. Already the miners' defensive position was faltering, the raiders tearing down the carts and wagons and crawling all over the barricade. At her lumbering approach, some of the Chul turned to face her, the looks of surprise and fear on their faces only making her more determined. They had come here for murder. Tyreta would give it to them.

She screamed as she swung the hydraulic arms of the stormhulk, feeling its power, revelling in its strength. Those arms, intended to bore into solid rock, smashed a bloody swath through the ranks of the Chul. The impetus of her attack drove her into their midst, forcing many to retreat in the face of the unstoppable machine.

One of the Chul leapt at her, and she caught him in the grip of the digger's shovels, crushing him with a squeal of pneumatics. The ventilation ports coughed more black smoke as she pushed the hulk to its limits, raising one of its legs to stamp down on another attacker.

Fury overcame her, the power at her disposal driving her rage, and she felt as one with this devastating machine. With each sweep of those mechanical arms she screamed a curse, ploughing a path straight through her enemies.

A spear ricocheted off the hatch with a harsh clang. An arrow embedded in the leather backplate just beside her head. It only fed her determination. She was exposed, she might die here, but by the Wyrms she'd take these killers with her.

Seeing the Chul attack buckle, the barricade's defenders fought back with greater zeal, pushing the Chul from the ridge. The kesh raiders began to falter. Now as Tyreta manoeuvred the hulk to face them they fled before her, racing across the quarry to safety.

She breathed hard, blood running down her chin from a wound she hadn't noticed. Her eyes scanned for the next enemy, but the Chul were already routed. All she could do was laugh as she looked for Gelila and the other women, ready to celebrate her victory.

There was a shout of warning from up the ridge. An axe cracked against the cage in front of her, and the hydraulics whirred in protest as she staggered back.

When she could focus, Tyreta saw one of the Chul remained, ready to face her. As she recognised the lizard-skull helm he wore, it filled her with a sudden dread. The feelings of power and might she had absorbed from the stormhulk dissipated in a waterfall of fear.

Shabak stood amid the corpses, refusing to retreat. Tyreta looked for anyone to help, but the miners still waited fearfully up on the ridge, too frightened to rush into the fray. In the distance Gelila and the other Lokai were locked in combat with the fleeing raiders. There was no one to aid her.

The warchief of the Chul roared, snarling something in kesh. Before she could move, either to attack or to run, he plucked a spear from a bloody corpse and flung it at her. She tried to raise those machine arms but wasn't fast enough. The spear embedded itself in the exposed knee joint of the hulk and sent sparks flying. A whine issued as though the engine were in pain.

Shabak roared again, raising his blade, and Tyreta tried to shift the stormhulk in response. It was sluggish, slow to answer her commands. Whatever damage the spear had done was impairing the machine's performance. She barely had time to raise the hulk's arms and fend off his attack, the sound of clashing metal ringing in her ears.

Shabak leapt at her, grasping the cage that was her only shield. She could see fangs grinning beneath the skull helm, teeth dripping red as he raised his blade. Tyreta swung an arm in desperation, but it was not fast enough as the blade lanced down. She barely had a chance to shift her weight to one side before the weapon cut a deep tear in the leather of her pilot's headrest.

With a cry of frustration she lurched forward, willing the hulk to pivot at the waist, spinning it violently. Shabak couldn't hold on, leaping clear and rolling in the dirt.

The warchief came up on his feet, the helm lost from his head. Baleful eyes stared at her. Eyes fit for murder. He was not going to stop, and this lumbering machine was no match for such speed. It was not designed for combat.

Tyreta closed her eyes. She knew Shabak was about to attack, but this was her only chance. Her last chance.

The strands of the web connecting her to the stormhulk's pyrestones were nebulous in her subconscious. She dug deep, strengthening that connection, willing the stones to respond, overloading them with power. As she did so, the light of the web intensified, the pyrestones burning bright in her mind.

She felt the stormhulk begin to rumble. Its engine turbines roared as they were overloaded with energy, pistons hissing like furious serpents, vents spewing gouts of bright flame.

Tyreta opened her eyes in time to see Shabak charging, face furious, blade raised to spear her in the cockpit. The stormhulk jolted forward, moving with a speed that belied its metallic bulk. She met Shabak before he leapt, hydraulic arms screeching in protest as they swung faster than the kesh warrior could attack. He was caught a glancing blow on the edge of its crushing shovel, enough to fling him across the quarry.

There was a dull explosion as one of the pyrestones disintegrated in its chamber, a burning stink filling the air. The left leg of the hulk became unresponsive, and she could only limp to face Shabak. To wait for the final strike.

He rose unsteadily to his feet, weapon gone, yet he looked more fearsome than anyone she had ever seen. The warchief roared, shouting something at her, gesturing with his hand and crossing a clawed thumb across his heart.

Tyreta braced herself, ready to face his next attack, but she could feel the hulk's hydraulics failing, the light in the pyrestones dimming to nothing.

An arrow whistled past Shabak's head. He turned, seeing Gelila racing toward him, Amanisa and Suma following across the quarry. The rest of the Chul had all but fled, a few stragglers limping away into the trees.

With a last snarl of defiance, Shabak picked up his fallen helm and ran. Tyreta would have followed, would have ended his crusade here and now, but she knew it was impossible. The stormhulk juddered, its power source expended. There was nothing else she could do.

As she swung the battered cage of the cockpit open and nearly fell from the slashed pilot chair, a couple of surviving miners made their way down from the barricade. One of them approached, his face a bloody mess, the crossed-hammers symbol of the Marrlock Guild emblazoned on his filthy tunic.

"You have our thanks," he said. "We would have been slaughtered to the last if you hadn't come along."

Tyreta could see the shock in his eyes, his hands shaking by his sides. It was only to be expected. For her part, Tyreta was still trembling.

"The kesh won't accept defeat for long," she said. "You and your people need to get back to New Flaym."

The man shook his head. "It's too far. We're heading to Wolf Station while we can. That's closer."

"You're not safe at Wolf Station. That was only a raiding party. More than half the kesh tribes have united. Someone has to get to New Flaym and warn them of what's coming."

"Listen, I'm grateful," he said. "But if you think we're going to trek through miles of hostile jungle with the kesh waiting to hack us to pieces, you must be mad."

He turned, shouting at the rest of the miners to move out while they could. Tyreta should have grabbed him, shaken him, tried to make him understand, but he had seen scores of his fellow miners murdered. There was no persuading someone so desperate.

Turning, she saw Gelila, blood covered and panting hard. The warrior was her only hope. "You have to take me to New Flaym. The city by the sea? I have to warn them of what's coming."

Gelila looked unsure. "They not come."

She gestured across the quarry. Tyreta could see Suma and Amanisa kneeling over a body on the ground. Ozoro.

As she approached, Suma let out a wail of anguish that sounded like a wolf in pain. Amanisa looked up, anger in her eyes. Ozoro had been struck with a spear, the shaft still protruding from her ribs.

"They take Ozoro home," Gelila said. "Guide no more."

"Then I will go alone," Tyreta said. "I can find the way from here. You've all done enough. More than enough."

Gelila placed a hand on her shoulder. "I come," she said. "Keep safe."

Tyreta could have hugged her, but now was not the time. "Shabak said something to me at the end. He crossed his chest like this." She showed Gelila how the kesh warrior had gestured over his heart.

"He marks you," Gelila replied. "For death."

Tyreta turned south, toward New Flaym. Time was running out, and there was little daylight left. They would have to make their journey in the dark.

"He's too late," she replied through gritted teeth, remembering Shabak's howl of victory after he slaughtered Wyllow. "I marked him first."

ROSOMON

A gentle wind rustled through the trees, putting a pair of sparrows to fluttering flight. Rosomon glanced up, letting the sun bathe her face in warmth. The palace garden was a welcome change from the administrative dungeons she had been condemned to over the last few days, and she was determined to enjoy it while she could.

There was little enjoyment to be had, though. Were she alone, Rosomon was sure her thoughts would have plagued her, turning this idyllic setting into a nightmare as she continued to mourn her lost children. But Rosomon was not alone.

Becuma sat across the circular iron table from her. Was she an actual Radwinter or just one of their representatives? Rosomon had no idea. She probably should have ascertained the woman's family name before this began, but it wasn't important now. She certainly looked like one of the Radwinters, with her round face and those doe eyes staring with indolence. And not to forget the fact that she appeared very well-fed. Whatever her heritage, she spoke for the Guild, and that was all that mattered as far as this meeting was concerned. Rosomon was confident she could treat her just as she would Jarlath Radwinter himself if he were sitting there.

Athelys approached the table, seeing Becuma's glass was empty. She raised the decanter and filled it in silence before retreating a few yards to pretend she couldn't hear. A pointless gesture, but Rosomon was not here to discuss any secrets. In fact the more people who knew about this the better. The shame of it might even spur the Radwinters into action, though she doubted it. So far she'd exchanged niceties with Becuma, amiable chat about the capital, about the weather, about the cut of her green uniform. Now to get to the crux of things.

"Tough times for all of us," Rosomon said. Best not to go for the kill too soon. Better to offer the rope first rather than force it around Becuma's neck.

"Indeed," Becuma replied, taking a sip of the wine. Rosomon hadn't touched hers. "All our holdings are struggling at the moment. Poor winters. Poor summers."

Becuma's voice was high pitched, almost a squeak. Rosomon couldn't tell if it was because of nerves or not. She'd have hated to think the girl sounded like that all the time.

"Poor returns," Rosomon said.

"A natural result of the unseasonable climate, I'm afraid." Becuma took another mouthful of wine. It left red marks at the corners of her lips, giving her the look of a baby drinking grapewater.

"One might think." Rosomon turned to the girl, finger teasing the rim of her wineglass. "If one was to only take into account the tax ledgers your Guild has provided."

She paused, waiting to see if Becuma was in on this or if Jarlath had just sent an unwitting stooge. From the sudden look of panic in her eyes it was clear she was complicit.

"I can assure you, our records are all in order."

"Are they?" Rosomon said, gesturing to Athelys. The girl approached, placing a single ledger on the table. It bore the tree symbol of Radwinter. "Because I managed to come by this. It tells a very different story from the documents you've previously submitted. It shows tax revenues from your smallholdings are not quite as meagre as the principal records suggest."

"Where did you—?"

"Where, when, how? They're not the right questions. What you should be asking is: What else does Lady Rosomon know?"

Becuma put her glass back down on the table. Rosomon could almost hear the cogs whirring as she tried to work out the answer to that one. In the end she gave up.

"I'm sure you're going to tell me," Becuma replied.

As good an answer as any. At least she wasn't going to implicate herself further by trying to guess. Jarlath had definitely not sent an innocent stooge at all.

"As well as withholding tax revenue, the Radwinter Guild has also begun to stockpile—grain, dried goods, cured meat, lumber. Jarlath is trying to drive up prices. And it ends now."

Becuma swallowed. "My lady, I can assure you—"

"Assure me you've heard what I have to say. And assure me you will relay this message to Jarlath: I am in charge here, and I will not stand for this kind of underhand manipulation. There are other, younger Guilds to whom I can transfer Radwinter farming interests. Your monopoly will be torn up. If I see fit, you will end up with nothing but a fallow field to plough and an incontinent goat to milk."

"Sullivar will never—"

"Sullivar is not here!" Rosomon raised her voice. Lost control. Lancelin would have chided her for that, but then Lancelin was not here either. "If Jarlath doubts the power at my disposal, he is free to test me."

She took up her wineglass and drank. It tasted pleasant enough, but she would have preferred something more full bodied.

Becuma rose to her feet, and Rosomon could see her hands were shaking. Just the result she'd been looking for.

"They told me you were a bitch," Becuma said, the squeak in her voice oddly missing.

"They say a lot of things, don't they?" Rosomon replied, not deigning to look at the girl. "Now run along, you've got a message to deliver."

Becuma paused for a moment. If she had more to say, she didn't have the courage to say it.

Rosomon drained her glass once Becuma had left. As Athelys obediently filled it, she noticed two figures waiting patiently at the edge of the garden. Olstrum bore his usual amiable expression, the one that always put people at their ease. Or, if they knew him well enough, the one that made people mistrustful. Beside him stood Wachelm in his yellow tunic, looking distinctly uncomfortable outside his natural habitat, the administrative vault.

Once Becuma had left the garden, Olstrum led Wachelm forward. Both men stood patiently beside the iron table as Rosomon took another drink.

"My lady," Olstrum said with a bow. "I trust your meeting with the Radwinter Guild went well?"

"As well as I expected," she replied.

Olstrum gestured to the ledger with the Radwinter symbol embossed on the front. "A little light reading, I see."

Jokes were not Olstrum's strongpoint.

Rosomon reached out and opened the ledger, flicking through blank page after blank page.

"A bluff," she replied. "One that happily paid off. I knew that snake Jarlath was up to something. Now *he* knows *I* know."

"A sly move," he said.

High praise indeed, from a man like Olstrum. "So what do you have for me? I assume neither of you is here to shower me with compliments?"

"Young Wachelm here has learned something interesting about the mysterious Ossian Holder."

Rosomon placed her glass down. "Really?"

Wachelm bowed awkwardly. "Yes, my lady. I looked further into the matter as you requested, but unfortunately I could find no further instances of the name in any ledger, writ or licence of marque."

"That seems like disappointing news, Wachelm. I hope you haven't come to interrupt my enjoyment of this delightful garden just to tell me that."

Wachelm shook his head so vigorously Rosomon thought the eyeglasses might work their way free of his nose. "Indeed not, my lady. When not performing as an actuary for the Corwen Guild and navigating Torwyn's legislative departments, I am also a student of its history. Some might see it as an indulgence, a diversion if you will, but I find it relaxes me in the hours I am away from my bureaucratic chambers of office. I see myself as a scholar in all things, and the subject of Torwyn's labyrinthine history is a fascinating one to decipher. I can recommend a number of archival codices if you would like to know more on the subject."

"For now, Wachelm, I'd just like you to get to the point."

"Ah, yes. Of course. Apologies. Well, the point is, I recently came across a reference in an obscure codex detailing the annals of the Draconate, a hierarchical journal, so to speak. It listed the names of the original acolytes and minor celebrants said to have been involved in summoning the Great Wyrms during the Age of Anarchy. One of those names was Ossian Holder."

Not altogether revelatory information, but Wachelm was right—it was interesting.

"Coincidence?" she asked.

"No, my lady. Further investigation revealed other names from antiquity used in various ledgers of trade and supply. I could list the—"

"I assume all names linked to the Draconate?"

"Your assumption is correct, my lady," Wachelm replied, seeming somewhat pleased with himself.

"That's not all," said Olstrum. "I took the liberty of looking further into rumours of a scarred man seen in the Mount. I know your search yielded little fruit, but I've had people on the lookout nonetheless. They've reported an individual to me, said to be a knight commander of the Drakes."

"His name?" Rosomon asked.

"Ansell Beckenrike, my lady. One of the Archlegate's most trusted warriors, if my intelligence is accurate."

Rosomon suddenly had yet more desire for a stronger drink. The temptation to have Athelys fill her wineglass once more was almost overwhelming, but she resisted. This would call for a clear head.

Could her nephew really be the one behind this plot? That charming little boy she had watched grow to manhood? It seemed preposterous, but the evidence against him was mounting up. Perhaps she should have waited, gathered more information, but Rosomon was done with being patient.

She stood, brushing down her skirts. "It appears another visit to the Mount is in order. My nephew has some questions to answer."

"He is not at the Mount," Olstrum replied.

"Then where?"

"He was seen not an hour ago heading to the Guildhall with a contingent of Drakes."

"What business does he have there? I was not notified of any Guild meeting."

"I cannot say, my lady."

"Then best I find out. Wachelm, thank you for your diligence." She turned to Olstrum. "I will see you later."

"Should I not accompany you?"

Rosomon shook her head. "I am in no danger from Sanctan. After all, what harm could a polite conversation do?"

"I should at least have a unit of Titanguard come with you."

"No. If I approach him with a naked blade, Sanctan is unlikely to tell me the truth of the matter. Besides, this could all be a misunderstanding. Perhaps my nephew has a perfectly reasonable explanation."

As she made her way from the garden, Rosomon knew there was no excuse that could explain this away. Sanctan was involved in something, of that she had little doubt, but she had to question him herself. To see the look in his eyes when his guilt was unveiled. That was the only way she could be certain.

It was a short walk to the Guildhall, but Rosomon took no comfort in the familiarity of the place. She felt as though she were about to step into a nest of vipers. Perhaps she should have heeded Olstrum's warnings, but she had to put Sanctan at his ease if she was to reveal his deceit.

Two Knights of the Draconate stood at the entrance. When Rosomon approached, they stood to attention, crossing their spears over the archway.

"I am here to speak with my nephew," she announced with as much authority as she could muster.

Silence.

"Do you know who I am?" Rosomon said, hating the words even as she spoke them. She had never thought to use her position to gain favour or respect as other nobles did, but if there was ever a time, this was it.

"Apologies, Lady Rosomon," said one of the knights, voice sonorous within his full helm. "But the Archlegate is indisposed."

"I don't care if he's meeting with one of the Great Wyrms. I intend to enter the Guildhall and you will not stop me."

Neither of the Drakes moved in response. Rosomon felt her hackles rising. Perhaps she should have brought the Titanguard after all, but she doubted an armed battle on the streets of the Anvil would serve her purpose.

Before she could further insist, another warrior appeared from within the building.

"Lady Rosomon," he said as the two knights lifted their spears. "The Archlegate bids you enter."

"Does he indeed?" Rosomon replied before the knight led her along the corridor and into the main meeting chamber. For the briefest moment she wondered if this hulking warrior was Ansell Beckenrike. When she entered the main hall, she realised it was pointless wondering.

Knights of the Draconate stood to attention all around the huge circular chamber. At least a score of them, standing like statues, armoured and imposing. At the centre of the Guildhall, standing close together in the speaking circle, were Sanctan Egelrath and a young woman. She couldn't have been more than thirty, beautiful, with a head of hair Rosomon would have murdered for when she was a girl. Brown curls fell about her shoulders and ran down her back, adding to her youthful aspect, but there was definite steel in her eyes.

In the garden, when Rosomon had questioned Becuma, she had felt in control, the spider in her own web. Now she suddenly felt like the fly.

"Aunt Rosomon," Sanctan said as she approached. His smile was charm personified, his white vestments of office shouting their authority. "How good it is to see you."

"Sanctan," she replied with a nod, then to the woman, "I don't believe we've met."

"Allow me to introduce Keara Hallowhill. Newly returned from a spell on the Karna Frontier. After so long in such a Wyrm-forsaken country I was taking the opportunity to welcome her back into the open arms of the Ministry's benevolence."

A quick glance showed Rosomon no religious icons about the girl's neck. If she was religious in any way, she was certainly shy about demonstrating it.

"Would the Mount not be a more suitable venue for bestowing blessings?" Rosomon asked.

"It was my suggestion, my lady," Keara said. "As a member of the Hallowhill Guild, I find this as much consecrated ground as any other."

The Hallowhills were a minor Guild, though their importance as webwainers was definitely rising since Treon Archwind had reduced them to little more than vassals. Nevertheless, the Hallowhills had never had a seat at the Guildhall. Perhaps that was Keara's ambition? Certainly a conversation for another time.

"My son recently began a tour in the frontier," Rosomon replied. "Perhaps you were acquainted?"

"Conall? Yes, my lady, we met in Agavere before I returned to the Anvil. Alas, our meeting was disappointingly brief."

A twinkle in her eye perhaps? It suggested a conversation Rosomon was happy not to pursue.

"Sanctan, I need to speak with you in private."

Her nephew glanced at Keara, then smiled in that disarming fashion. "I'm sure there is nothing you have to say that a fellow member of the Guilds could not hear?"

Rosomon had not prepared for this. She had hoped a private conversation might better allow her to expose Sanctan's guilt. Now there was more than one spider to think about on the web.

"Very well," she replied. "The night the emissary was murdered, I have learned one of the assassins was wounded, leaving him with a distinctive scar. It has been suggested to me that this assassin is known to you."

If Sanctan was surprised by the allegation, he did not show it.

"Really, Aunt Rosomon? This matter is—"

"Ansell Beckenrike. One of your Drakes. Do you deny knowledge of him?"

Sanctan shrugged. "I am familiar with all the Knights of the Draconate."

"So you know the man?"

"Of course, but—"

"And you will bring him before me? I would see this man's face for myself."

Sanctan flashed another smile. "I am more than happy to oblige," he replied, then, raising his voice, "Ansell. Please present yourself before my aunt."

From behind him a Knight of the Draconate strode forward to stand at Sanctan's side. He was tall and broad, but then so were all these hallowed warriors. The Drakes only selected the most imposing of religious acolytes to join their ranks.

Ansell regarded her from behind his full helm. "I would see his face," Rosomon demanded.

"Of course. If you would, Ansell."

The knight reached up and removed his helmet. He was surprisingly young, blond hair shorn to tight curls about his head. He would have been handsome but for the ugliness of his broken nose. His square jaw showed no sign of scarring. Not so much as a blemish on his rugged flesh.

"Satisfied?" asked Sanctan.

She should have known it would not be this easy. "How do I know this is Beckenrike? He could be any one of these men."

"Very well." Sanctan turned to the silent warriors standing in vigil around him. "All of you. Show my aunt your faces."

The score of knights obeyed. As each helmet was removed and face revealed, Rosomon began to feel more foolish. Some bore scars, but none of them had the vicious burn she had been told of.

"Is there anything more I can do for you?" asked Sanctan. "To allay your suspicions?"

Rosomon wanted to mention Ossian Holder and the other links to the Draconate in the purchase ledgers and dockets, but she knew she had already made a fool of herself. She had played her hand too soon, and Sanctan now held the high cards. There was no real proof of anything, and both she and Sanctan knew it. Rosomon forced a smile onto her face.

"No," she replied. "That is all. My thanks for your assistance."

Both Sanctan and Keara offered a curt bow as Rosomon turned and walked from the Guildhall. Fury was building inside her, but she could not let it take hold.

Once outside she took a deep breath, the faint smell of the forge-works filling her nose. Was she going mad? Was she reading too much into coincidence? Should she just give up on this?

Leaving the Guildhall behind her, Rosomon knew she could never give up on Fulren, even if she was never to see him again. Today she had made sure Jarlath Radwinter knew she was onto his schemes. He had underestimated her and fallen into her trap.

Eventually Sanctan Egelrath would do the same.

PART TWO

UPRISING

CONALL

Sted stumbled groggily, stinking of liquor, but what had he expected? As she followed him through the barracks room, trying not to wake any of the other scouts, Conall wondered where she'd managed to find more booze out here in the middle of the desert since their brandy had run dry. He dismissed the thought, concentrating on the task at hand. Now wasn't the time to unravel Sted's talent for purloining contraband. They had a job to do.

Outside the temperature had dropped. Conall still couldn't get his head around how the desert was so stifling during the day but freezing at night. He pulled his greatcoat tighter about him as they both made their way to the stables. The horses were already saddled, and they unhitched them, whispering soothing words to try to keep them quiet, before leading them out of their pens. Conall turned to see someone standing in the stable entrance, an imposing silhouette framed against the light from the courtyard.

He froze, expecting Beringer's grim, admonishing visage to come leering at him from the dark. When he realised it was Nevan Ulworth standing there and not the frontier marshal, he let out an audible sigh.

"By the Wyrms," Sted hissed. "You big, dumb fucker. I almost shit myself."

"Where are you going?" Nevan asked.

"Mind your business," Sted replied.

"Are you on a mission?" he persisted.

"Yes," Conall said. "But we need to keep it quiet. So go back to bed and forget you saw us."

"Where are you going?" Nevan repeated. Stubborn as a bloody brick.

"Nevan, just go back to the barracks."

Ulworth seemed to find the concept confusing, and he turned to look out across the courtyard, then back at Conall.

"If you're going on a mission, I should go with you. We're the Talon. We have to stick together."

Sted opened her mouth to speak, most likely to chastise Nevan way too loud. Conall raised a hand for her to be quiet before she could mess this whole thing up. There was no use in arguing, that would only make it more likely they'd be discovered.

"All right. Saddle a horse, and do it quietly."

Sted shook her head as Nevan did as he was told. Conall stood at the gates of the stable, looking out for any sign they'd been heard, but it appeared their luck was in. For now.

"You know you're a captain of the Talon, right?" Sted whispered as Nevan fumbled around in the dark behind them.

"So I've been told," Conall answered.

"That you're supposed to act as a beacon of authority to your men?"

"I am aware of that."

"Well, maybe you should work on it a bit."

Nevan appeared from the dark, leading his horse. On its saddle he'd strapped the biggest axe Conall had ever seen.

"Are we all ready now?" Conall whispered.

Sted and Nevan nodded before he led them out across the courtyard. The sound of hooves on the dry sand was way too loud, but still they attracted little attention. The sentries up on the battlements looked down with disinterest. Conall even offered a friendly wave that wasn't reciprocated.

As they approached the gate, one of the troopers gave a knowing nod before sliding the brace to one side. Another push and the gate opened, allowing them to walk right out into the night.

"How was that for authority?" Conall asked as they mounted their steeds.

"They're probably just glad to see the back of you," Sted whispered in reply.

Conall had to agree. His presence as a privileged nobleman hadn't endeared him to anyone recently.

The three of them struck out at a walk. It was almost impossible to see the path ahead, but they managed to find the road south toward the mining facility without any of their horses turning an ankle. They rode in silence, keeping an ear out for any sound that might herald an ambush, but it seemed they were the only ones mad enough to be out in the desert before dawn.

As the sun began to rise, Conall was relieved to see that they were still on the road and still heading in the right direction. It wasn't until the hazy light of dawn had turned the desert red that any of them spoke.

"They'll know we've gone by now," said Sted.

"If you're worried they're going to come after us, I wouldn't fret too much," Conall replied.

"I'm not thinking Beringer's going to send someone to take care of our well-being. It's what he'll do when we get back that bothers me."

"You're obeying orders. Let me worry about the consequences."

"Excuse me if I'm not reassured by your confidence, Captain."

"Look, when I get to the bottom of this, Beringer will be grateful. There's more to that glaive than meets the eye, I'm sure of it."

"And if you're wrong?" Sted was chewing on a stick of redstalk with urgency. Always a sign she was nervous.

"Then I'll be suitably repentant. What's the worst thing that can happen?"

"I can think of a few things. I don't admit this often, but that man scares me."

"Right now, you should be scared of the goatheads. Let me worry about Beringer."

"We should all be worried about Beringer," she said, touching two fingers to the dragon pendant about her neck. "I heard he had an entire garrison flogged because one man had an unkempt uniform."

"Rumours, Sted. Don't believe everything you hear."

"Where that man's concerned, I reckon rumours are just the start of it."

They'd reached the ridge overlooking the mining outpost. It appeared as lifeless as the day they'd left it.

"Still looks abandoned," said Sted, chewing vigorously.

Conall unslung his longbarrel and made sure it was primed. "Let's take a look then."

They nudged their horses forward, trotting down the ridge to the outpost. The bodies they'd left strung up had been picked clean, little more than bones with strips of cloth and dried flesh holding them together. A soft breeze blew motes of dust across the ground, covering every structure in a layer of red dirt.

Conall climbed down from his horse, handing his reins to Sted. Nevan joined him, grabbing that big axe and sticking close to Conall's back. As they approached the warehouse, Conall saw the body of the durrga Tarrien's men had killed was missing. Not even a pool of blood to mark where it had died.

He pushed the door to the warehouse open, and it was caught on a sudden gust, swinging wide and slamming against the wall. Something growled inside, disturbed by the sudden movement, and Conall raised the longbarrel, stepping back, holding his breath.

A desert fox snarled at him from the dark before sprinting out into the open and making a dash for it. Conall let out a sigh, seeing it had been dining on the paltry remains of a corpse within the warehouse. There was nothing else alive.

Conall knelt, examining the ground. There were fresh tracks in the dirt, and by the look of them they weren't human.

"I've got goathead prints leading off to the southwest," he said.

"That's good," Sted replied. "At least we've got something interesting to tell Beringer when we get back."

Conall knew they shouldn't have come here. What was he hoping to find? What could putting himself and his scouts in more danger prove? But there was something going on. It niggled too much for him to let it go.

"Mount up," he said to Nevan. "We can at least see where they lead."

Nevan nodded, and they climbed on their horses. They hadn't struck out far from the outpost before Sted could hold her peace no longer.

"Do you want to tell me exactly what we're looking for?" she said.

"I'll know when I find it," Conall replied. "Beringer will thank me, you'll see."

"Beringer? Is that what this is all about? He gives you a fat lip and now you're desperate to please him like a scolded puppy?"

"Fuck Beringer," Conall snapped. "This could be important. An alliance between the durrga and Malador could have consequences for Torwyn. Should we just sit and wait to find out what's going on?"

"There could be nothing going on. And you're willing to chase this theory based on some weapon you found in the desert? Willing to risk our lives?"

"You can go back if you want. Me and Nevan will carry on alone."

He glanced at Nevan, hoping he wasn't overstating the man's loyalty, but the big scout didn't even seem to be listening. For her part, Sted spat out her masticated stick of redstalk and fished a fresh one out of her shirt pocket.

Conall kicked his horse a little too hard in his frustration. As they followed the tracks south he couldn't shake the doubt Sted had put in his mind. He'd convinced himself that he was right, that there was some kind of scheme to uncover. Now he wasn't so sure. He could be leading them into danger for nothing.

The sun began to cast its haze over the red sands, and as their horses plodded on through the midday heat, he got an uneasy feeling. They were riding off the beaten track, deeper into durrga country, if this could be called country at all. There was no one to help them if they encountered the enemy. More than once he thought about turning back, abandoning this fool's journey, but he couldn't expel the notion that this would lead them somewhere.

To their deaths, most likely.

"Does anyone get the feeling we're being watched?" whispered Nevan.

There was no one for miles in any direction, so whispering was probably pointless. Nevertheless, despite the flat desert stretching out around them, Conall had the same feeling.

He glanced over his shoulder, expecting Sted to continue her griping, but she was just glaring at the horizon, the pendant of Ammenodus Rex held tight between her lips. The Great Wyrms wouldn't help out here, but if it gave her comfort, then who was he to question it?

It wouldn't be long before the sun passed its zenith. Then not long until nightfall. The last thing they wanted was to be caught out here after dark.

Conall was about to admit defeat, to give in and abandon the trail, when he saw something through the heat haze, barely visible against the flat plain.

"See that," he said, pointing ahead.

Sted squinted across the desert. "Looks like a building."

"Can the goatheads build structures like that?" he replied.

"I have a sinking feeling we're about to find out."

Conall kicked his horse forward, and the three of them trotted toward their goal. There was still no sign of any durrga, but the tracks were leading directly to the structure. It looked out of place, and the closer they got the more curious it appeared, alone in the desert with nothing else for miles around.

"Some kind of temple?" Sted asked when they were within a dozen yards.

It was an open ruin that looked as though it had been hewn from the red desert rock a thousand years ago. A staircase bisected its centre, disappearing into darkness. Flanking it were stones that had once displayed intricate carvings but now were little more than worn granite.

"No idea what it is," Conall replied, jumping down from his horse and taking the longbarrel from its sling. "But I am curious enough to take a look inside."

"You must be joking," Sted replied. "There could be anything waiting for us down there."

"Goatheads, by the look of these tracks," Conall said, gesturing at the clear trail that led from the sand down the stone stairs. "But there's only one way to be sure."

Sted shook her head. He could see the mix of emotions on her face as she went from doubt to fear to anger to resignation.

"You're an arsehole," she said finally, dropping from her saddle and unstrapping the splintbow from her horse.

"I'm your captain," Conall reminded her.

"You're an arsehole, Captain."

At least she was right about something.

Nevan made to join them, pulling that big axe from his saddle, but Conall held up a hand.

"You're staying here," he said. "We might be coming out from there pretty soon, and at speed. If there's no horses waiting for us, we could be done for."

The big man looked as though he might argue, but then he glanced down into the darkness below. Even Ulworth must have realised he'd got the decent end of the deal, and he tightened his grip on the axe, nodding that he understood.

When Sted had loaded a full clip of bolts into the stock of her splintbow, they were ready to go. Conall checked the primer of the longbarrel as they made their way down the stairs, eyes scanning for any sign of life.

The staircase led down thirty feet before it flattened out to a wide tunnel. Someone had left torches conveniently placed along it, and Conall began to think this was going a bit too smoothly.

"Hear that?" Sted whispered as they started along the wide corridor of hewn rock.

"Water," Conall replied. The sound of it echoed from somewhere up ahead.

It started as a trickle, but the farther they went the louder it got.

The tunnel sloped downward, burrowing deeper under the earth until it came out into a natural cavern. Below them flowed a wide expanse of water that ran from a gabled construction at one end and fed into an underground tunnel.

"I didn't know the goatheads could build something like this," Sted said over the sound of rushing water.

"If these tunnels run throughout the Karna, it explains how they can come and go so easily."

"Beringer needs to know about this. We should head back."

Conall shook his head. "We're not done yet."

He led Sted down to the walkway that ran along the side of the river. It was wide enough for a horse and cart to drive on, and the whole complex must have required a huge feat of engineering to construct. They'd been underestimating the durrga from the start, and it made Conall all the more curious to discover what else they were up to.

The deeper they went, the more his trepidation fought against curiosity. As Conall came out onto a platform of rock looking down on a river, crisscrossed by a system of mechanical locks, he realised his persistence had paid off.

They were at the edge of a vast riverport, there was no other way to describe it. Barges were moored at its jetty, and both humans and durrga were busying themselves unloading cargo. It could have been a scene from any seaport in Torwyn were it not for the facts that they were in a cave and that there were giant man-eating beasts not a hundred yards away.

Conall and Sted crept to the lip of the rock and watched the activity below.

"I hate to say it," Sted whispered. "But you were bloody right."

The more Conall witnessed, the more right he realised he had been. The barges were crewed by pirates. From their outlandish hair, hanging in greasy locks and teased into spikes, they were from Iperion Magna. At the edge of the port a durrga, chieftain from the look of the rings and scars that marked it, was gesturing to a huge crate filled to the brim with pyrestone. In return the pirates were unloading food, supplies and weapons by the bundle.

"Pyrestone?" Sted hissed. "What in the hells would the Magnans want with pyrestone?"

Conall didn't have a clue. The Maladorans did not use artifice—not so far as anyone knew. If they had started to build their own machines, it could have dire consequences for Torwyn.

"Let's worry about that later," Conall said, already turning back the way they'd come. "I think we've seen enough for one trip."

Sted didn't argue as he made his way back through the archway and down the corridor. There was no need to tarry, the sound of the river rushing by hid the sound of their footfalls as they rushed back toward the surface. So eager was Conall to get back and report what he'd found that he almost didn't see the durrga warrior until it walked right into him.

There were two of them, both stepping out of an access tunnel, their looks of surprise immediately turning to grimaces of hatred. Conall raised the longbarrel without thinking, levelling it, taking aim in the instant before he pulled the trigger.

The sound was deafening. He'd almost forgotten how loud, it had been so long since he'd let off a shot. The first durrga's head exploded in a red spray.

Conall didn't have time to congratulate himself, as the second goathead came roaring at him. He heard the staccato thrum of Sted's splintbow unleashing its full volley, saw three of those four bolts embed themselves in the durrga's shoulder, chest, abdomen, but it barely slowed the beast down.

A sword was in Conall's hand, wrenched from his scabbard on instinct—an instinct that saved his life as he parried the goathead's war axe. It was enough to stop the monster burying that axe in his head, but not enough to keep him on his feet.

As he fell back, he heard Sted yell over the sound of the river. Saw her rush to attack. Saw her batted aside by the goathead's powerful arm.

The durrga ignored her, eyes focusing on Conall—baleful eyes full of fury and intelligence and evil intent. He'd lost his sword, lost his longbarrel, not that there would have been time to load it. This was it, torn apart by a beast from the desert. He could only hope Sted would live through this and lie about how bravely he'd died.

The durrga's head split with a sickening crack. Blood ran down the centre of its face as those callous eyes turned in on one another. The beast fell forward, and Conall rolled aside as it landed with a thud.

Nevan Ulworth stood there, looking pleased with himself now he'd had a chance to put that axe to use.

"Let's get the fuck out of here," Sted shouted in Conall's ear, dragging him to his feet.

Conall paused long enough to grab the longbarrel, no idea where his sword had gone, before the three of them raced back toward the stone staircase. Something echoed from down the tunnel as they ran, and it didn't take a genius to work out what. As a huge arrow swept past his head, Conall knew they had to keep moving, had to hope the horses were still waiting for them on the surface.

Another arrow soared past his ear, haft shattering as it smashed against the rock wall. He heard more snaps, not daring to look back and see how close the goatheads were. They just had to keep moving.

The bright desert sun bathed them in a welcome glow as they sprinted to the top of the stairs. Nevan had seen fit to hobble the horses so they didn't go wandering off. Conall could have kissed him, but there'd be time enough for that kind of thing later.

He slung the longbarrel, grabbed the reins and leapt into the saddle. Sted and Nevan weren't far behind him as he kicked his horse, reining it northward in a flurry of sand.

The three of them galloped, the sound of roaring in their wake louder than the drumming of hooves and the snorting of steeds. A two-foot arrow skewered the ground to his left, another flying overhead to pierce the red desert earth in front of him. A glance to the left and he could see Sted's face, windswept and desperate, that dragon pendant clenched in her teeth. He almost laughed at that, at their good bloody fortune, at the thrill of being alive. Conall's steed began to huff and froth, but he didn't give it any respite until they'd put at least a couple of miles between them and the goatheads.

As his horse panted, muscles spasming from the exertion, he

glanced back, seeing nothing but empty desert in their wake. Then he heard Sted laugh.

"That was too close," she said when she could get her breath back. "The Wyrms must be watching our arses like hawks for us to make it out so easy. Should have seen the look on your face when that goathead came round the corner. I thought you were gonna shit."

"Don't speak too soon," Conall replied. "I haven't checked my leggings yet."

The two of them laughed too long and too loud before Conall realised Nevan hadn't joined in. He turned to look at the big man, who had a curious look about him—all pale and confused.

"Nevan?" Conall said. "Ulworth, what's—?"

The big scout slumped forward in his saddle. A foot-long shaft of arrow sticking out the back of his rib cage.

Sted shouted something, jumping from her horse and rushing forward to help. Conall just sat there as the man under his command sat dying, but he had no idea what to do. All he could think was maybe the Wyrms weren't watching their arses after all.

FULREN

He gripped tight to the leather cord, legs pumping through the snow, breathing the chill air in short gasps as he desperately tried to match Lancelin's pace. A sheen of sweat covered his brow and dampened his shirt, and if he hadn't been blind, Fulren was sure he would have seen steam rising from his body with the exertion.

But he couldn't see. Everything was black. The lesions on his face stung as they were exposed to the cold air, and without that cord to hold on to he'd have been lost in an ocean of darkness.

A shriek echoed from above, filling Fulren's ears and making him shudder. They'd been dogged by that noise for so long now he should have been accustomed to it, but it filled him with as much terror as the first time.

Lancelin stopped, and Fulren almost ran right into him. They both drew in ragged breaths as the swordwright shoved him against a tree.

"Are they close?" Fulren asked.

"Can't see above the treetops," Lancelin answered. "It's almost nightfall. We need to find shelter."

Fulren could imagine him glancing around in the twilight for signs of danger. The Huntan Reach was no place to be caught after dark, if half the tales he'd heard were true. Let alone when you were being hunted by skyborne arcanists.

"Come on," Lancelin said, pulling Fulren along again. "I think I see something."

They ploughed on, moving uphill, the snow deepening as they struggled through knee-high drifts. The wind was picking up, masking the crunch of the snow underfoot and the gasp of every chill breath. It got so steep that he found himself reaching out a hand to keep his balance, the cold surface of the rock chilling his palm.

Eventually Lancelin was virtually dragging him over loose shale. Every time he thought he would fall, there was a strong hand to guide him, pulling him along like a helpless child. The indignity sat ill in Fulren's gut, but there was nothing to be done about it. Without Lancelin he'd be left to the elements, and no matter the hate that filled him, he knew there was no choice but to let himself be led by the man who had killed his father.

The cold gusts blowing in his face relented all of a sudden as the ground flattened out.

"We should be safe in here," Lancelin said, voice echoing as they entered a cave.

Fulren let himself be guided to the wall, where Lancelin let him go. He tried to catch his breath, to orient himself, but it was useless. In defeat he slid down the wall and sat his numb arse on the cold rock, waiting for whatever came next.

He heard footsteps, then silence. Lancelin left him alone for the Wyrms only knew how long. The howl of the wind outside was like a plague to his ears, but at least it wasn't the sound of some flying beast dogging their trail. He sat there in the black, trying to process what had happened. They had survived, but only just, and it seemed the more time passed the more danger they were in. The frustration was overwhelming—Fulren had always been able to look after himself. Blindness had robbed him of that.

Footsteps on the rock suddenly put him on edge.

"It's me," said Lancelin's now-familiar voice.

Fulren didn't know if he should be relieved or resentful. Maybe even grateful. He dismissed that thought before he felt tempted to thank the bastard for saving him.

There was more rustling, the sound of sticks being piled and stones clacking together as Lancelin built a fire. He blew on the embers as the crackle of flaming tinder filled the cave. Before long Fulren could feel a welcome heat.

"Move closer," Lancelin said. "The wood's wet so I can't build too big a fire. Smoke will—"

"Give away our position," Fulren interrupted, shuffling toward the sound of the meagre flames.

They sat in silence. Fulren's stomach grumbled, but there was no point griping about it. Even Lancelin wasn't about to run around the forest at night hunting rabbits. They'd just have to suffer it until...

What? Where were they even heading? The Huntan was leagues from home, and on the wrong side of the Drift. Lancelin Jagdor was a capable fighter, but could he guide a blind man across the wastes from here? Even if Fulren could see, their chances of survival would be slim.

He rubbed his hands together, blowing some warmth into them. The heat of the fire filled the cave quickly, and he began to appreciate just how cold he'd been.

"Why did she send you?" Fulren asked suddenly. He didn't even know where the question came from, but anything to break this silence.

Lancelin sighed. "There was no one else."

"No one else? In the whole of Torwyn there was no one else she could have sent after her son?"

"Can you think of anyone?"

"My brother for one."

"Conall is miles away in the Karna. And she would never have put him in such danger."

"So you're saying there was no one else my mother could have asked? Even if I do believe that's true, what made you say yes? You're not a Hawkspur. Not beholden to my mother in any way, unless..." The answer seemed an obvious one. "You came out of guilt? Lancelin Jagdor is ashamed of his dark deeds? Is that it? You're doing this to make amends for murdering my father?"

"Maybe," Lancelin said.

That brought a smile to Fulren's face. "Perhaps you're human after all. Maybe there is some good in that black heart of yours. So how's it working out for you? Doing the right thing?"

Fulren knew he was goading, and what might come with that, but what did he care now? Lancelin was a dangerous man, not the kind you poked unless you wanted to get poked right back in the jugular. He'd heard tales that Jagdor had killed a hundred men in a single day fighting invaders at the Drift. What difference was one blind man added to his tally? But it wasn't as if things could get any more desperate.

"Do you feel vindicated yet?" Fulren carried on when Lancelin didn't answer. "Have you made up for leaving my family fatherless?"

Still nothing. He may as well have raged at the wind, but he'd opened a floodgate now, there was no way to stop it. Fulren didn't care if no one was listening. He just wanted to fill the silence.

"They say you don't miss what you never had. It wasn't like that for me. Growing up, I always knew there was a void. An empty space where he should have been. There were other men who wanted to take on the job, and Mother could have taken her pick of suitors, but they were never entertained. It was as though she wanted to be alone. To take on the role of both mother and father and damn anyone who tried to get in the way."

"Rosomon is a remarkable woman," Lancelin said.

"And my father was a remarkable man."

Fulren could hear Lancelin shifting uncomfortably. "Melrone Hawkspur was not—"

"Don't speak his name," Fulren snapped, frustration building up in him. He had waited so long to be alone with Lancelin Jagdor, to be given the chance to avenge his father's memory, and now it felt as though all that had been stolen.

More silence but for the howling of the wind. Their pointless conversation was done.

He hunkered down next to the fire, lying on his side and hugging himself against the cold. Their flight had been desperate, and the strain was starting to catch up with him. He closed his eyes, though there was no difference to what he could see. Maybe he wouldn't even realise when he was asleep...

Fulren squinted at the sun. A beach stretched out below the yellow haze, the sound of waves. Gulls screeching. Footsteps in the sand.

His skin tingled with the feel of sea salt. He raised a hand to his face to shield his eyes from the sun—something was off about that, but he couldn't quite work out what. He turned his head, seeing a figure farther down the beach. Squinting through the brightness, he saw it was Tyreta. She was stripped down, bare flesh oiled, her skin bearing peculiar markings. She made no sign of acknowledgment, no wave, no smile. She just stood there on that beach, heedless of any danger, but something deep within made him realise she wasn't safe.

Fulren wanted to call out to her, to warn her of the danger neither of them could see, but no words would come.

He turned the other way. On the other side of the beach stood Conall. Though he couldn't make out his brother's face, he was sure it was him—tall, broad shouldered, dressed in black from head to foot. A shadow in the sun.

There was no danger there. His brother had nothing to fear. But the more Fulren looked the more the sense of menace grew. It took a while before he understood Conall was not in danger from anything... he was *the danger.*

Someone whispered his name. A voice he recognised. Imploring him with that one word. His mother.

Fulren wanted to turn, but he couldn't move. Wanted to cry out, but he couldn't speak. All the while a burning sensation grew at the back of his neck. He tried to raise a hand, but he was too fearful to touch it. As the intensity increased he thought he recognised the source of the pain, but he couldn't quite bring it to mind.

He had been stricken with something, like a disease. A malady whose source started at the top of his spine and infected him to his core. Burning him from the inside. Blackening his bones. Blackening his soul...

He opened his eyes, reaching instinctively to his neck. The dream was fading, but the pain still burned. It took him some moments to realise there was a dull light in his field of vision.

The fire had burned down to embers, the last of its heat dissipating in the chill of the cave... and Fulren could see it.

It glowed faintly against the black, little more than a yellow smudge, but his eyes were open and it was right there in front of him. He reached out, the outline of his hand silhouetted against the faint yellow.

Fulren concentrated. Feeling the necroglyph at the base of his neck tingling. Images began to coalesce, faint outlines, grey against the shadowy darkness. He could see the entrance to the cave, yawning open, the pale dawn light just a smear beyond. On the ground, a body lay next to the fire.

He sensed Lancelin's steady breathing, the outline of his body becoming more distinct as Fulren concentrated. Beside him was a sword, on the belt a knife in its sheath. It lay there untouched, just within his grasp. He could avenge his father right now. Just take that knife and finish this. Damn the consequences. The hunters of Nyrakkis were not intending to kill him. All he had to do was get rid of Jagdor and offer himself to them in surrender.

Before he knew it, he had risen to a crouch, stealing toward Jagdor's prone body. Silently he drew the knife from its sheath. The necroglyph was burning now, the tingling rising in intensity, coursing down his spine, whispering for him to act.

The well-balanced blade felt comfortable in his grip. He could kill Lancelin easily, the man would not even wake. And what purpose for a knife other than to kill?

But you are no murderer.

Fulren gritted his teeth as the necroglyph suddenly ignited. Fire flickered at the nape of his neck, every nerve caught alight and his back spasmed with the intensity of it. He lurched to his feet, his flesh burning, scorched white-hot as he cried out, reaching to his neck but feeling no flames.

His vision went black, but the burning only increased. He was blind once more, his body racked by a conflagration. The knife was still in his hand, and he knew the only way to stop this was to rid himself of the necroglyph.

Before he could begin to cut the flesh at his neck, his wrist was caught in a steely grip. Lancelin wrestled him to the ground. Fulren tried to fight, but he was no match for the man's strength. Before he knew it, the knife was gone from his fingers, but the pain only grew. He screamed, his howl echoing through the cave, before Lancelin clapped a hand over his mouth.

"Take the pain," growled the swordwright. "Endure it."

With his other hand, Lancelin grasped the back of Fulren's neck, squeezing the burning flesh. Gradually the pain subsided, and Fulren was left gasping in the cold of morning. Lancelin released him, leaving him floundering on the floor of the cave.

"The Maladorans have cursed you," Lancelin said eventually. "That mark is evil."

Fulren wasn't so sure. "I could... I could see," he breathed.

"And now?"

Fulren managed to sit up. Whatever blessing the necroglyph had bestowed was gone. The world was darkness once more. "Nothing."

Lancelin pulled him to his feet. "Then you still need me."

He pressed something into Fulren's hand. The knife he had taken.

"I was..." There was no way to explain.

"Keep it," Lancelin said. "If it makes you feel better."

It didn't. But he would keep it anyway.

"The sun's up," Lancelin said. "And we need to keep moving." He pressed the leather cord into Fulren's other hand and led him to the cave entrance. Fulren could feel the morning sun on his face, but he could see no welcoming glow. Whatever had happened to his eyesight was over. Whether it would happen again he could only wonder.

As he slipped the knife into his belt, he wondered if his urge to kill Lancelin Jagdor had passed. He guessed he would have to wonder on that too.

TYRETA

She could hear the bustle of New Flaym long before the gates appeared through the trees up ahead. Tyreta should have felt some relief on seeing the familiar palisade that surrounded the port and the rooftops of the tallest villas rising above it, but there was only a sinking sensation in the pit of her stomach. If she didn't warn them, if they didn't listen, this whole place would soon be ashes, every man, woman and child slaughtered.

Gelila slowed as they approached. She looked warily at those iron gates, and Tyreta realised this was a sight she had never seen before.

"It's okay," she said, placing a reassuring hand on Gelila's shoulder. "We're safe here."

It seemed to ease her fears a little, but Gelila still unslung the bow from her shoulder, her free hand not far from the quiver at her waist.

Before Tyreta reached the gates, one of the sentries on guard recognised her. That was a relief in itself—she looked much different from the day she'd left with Wyllow, and there had been as much chance the guards would confront them at the gate as welcome them.

The sudden thought of Wyllow stung her. After all this time she hadn't appreciated how she had been responsible, at least in part, for what happened to him. How she had persuaded him to take her out into the jungle on what should have been a harmless adventure. Now safety beckoned, the guilt of that came rushing over her like a wave.

One of the guards ran back into the port, shouting for someone to get help. The other came toward her, a look of concern on his grim features.

"My lady," he said. "We had all but given up hope."

"Lord Serrell," Tyreta replied. "I have to see him immediately."

The guard nodded, reaching out to help her, but she shrugged him off.

"Tell him now," she insisted.

Obediently he rushed off after the first guard.

As they walked the path to the port, past the villas and down through the shanties and tap houses that sat closer to the harbour, everything seemed so normal. No one realised the peril that was coming once the Chul turned their eyes south.

Workers and traders stared at the pair as they walked by. Gelila struck a proud but threatening figure, and Tyreta was not surprised it made the populace nervous.

Well, they should be nervous. What was coming for them through that jungle was more terrifying than one kesh warrior, and they had to learn the truth of it.

"Tyreta!"

She recognised the voice before she saw Isleen waddling her way up the street, the gate guards hustling along behind her.

"Thank the Wyrms," Isleen said breathlessly. "Everyone was certain you had perished... but not me. I never gave up hope."

"I must speak to Lord Serrell," Tyreta replied, keen to get this over with.

"Yes, yes," Isleen replied. "But first we have to get you..." Her eyes fell on Gelila. "What is this?"

"She is my friend," Tyreta said.

"Why have you brought this creature into the city?"

"This woman saved me," Tyreta said, fast losing patience. "She is a warrior of the Lokai and you will show her the respect she is due. Now take me to Lord Serrell."

Isleen briefly looked as though she'd had a glass of cheap wine thrown in her face before regaining her composure.

"All in good time. First we need to get you cleaned up and—"

"Fuck that!" Tyreta spat. "Wyllow is dead. The miners have been slaughtered by a kesh army that is now heading this way. Take me to Serrell or I'll bloody well find him myself."

"But...Lord Serrell is—"

"I don't care if he's summoning the Great Wyrms in his frigging underwear. If we don't evacuate the port right now, we'll all be slaughtered. So either lead me to him or move your arse out of my way."

Isleen would most likely have been furious if she weren't so shocked. With a faint nod she turned and led Tyreta down the street toward the harbourside. The Marrlock embassy loomed huge and white against the bright blue sky. A flag bearing the crossed hammers flew from its summit, two guards in grey uniforms standing vigilantly outside, splintbows braced across their chests. When they saw Isleen approaching, both men bowed.

"My lady," said one of them. "Lord Serrell is in a meeting with the chancellor. I am afraid—"

"He'll want to hear what I have to say," Tyreta said before Isleen could make any further excuses. "And he'll want to hear it now."

"I cannot let—"

"Cannot let me in? Tyreta Hawkspur? Heir to the Hawkspur Guild? Niece to the bloody emperor?"

She'd never used her name to open any doors before, but now seemed the right time to start.

The guards glanced at one another uncertainly before one of them said, "Of course, my lady. But that will have to stay outside." He gestured to Gelila with his splintbow.

"She goes where I go," Tyreta replied. "If you have a problem with that, I'll be sure to let my uncle know."

At the second mention of Emperor Sullivar, the guard's nerve seemed to give out altogether, and he pushed open the doors to the embassy and ushered the three of them through.

The entrance hall was more opulent a foyer than any Tyreta had seen at home in Wyke, or even in the Anvil. In the city of her birth they went for dark, polished oaken panels mounted with the stuffed animal heads their hunters brought from across the Guildlands. At the Anvil it was all solid granite and iron cogs. Here was white marble that must have cost a fortune to ship over from Torwyn. To the right of a wooden staircase stood a sculpture artfully depicting the symbols of the Guilds, to the left a statuette of the Great Wyrms twisted together atop an onyx plinth.

Tyreta ignored the spectacle as she followed Isleen up the stairs. On the landing she was faced with a row of portraits depicting luminaries of the Marrlock dynasty from bygone days. Grey-haired old men all glaring with a look of smug arrogance.

Isleen led them to double doors at one end of the corridor, pausing to listen for voices. Tyreta briefly got the impression that Isleen was well practised at such mischief, which explained why she was such a renowned source of frivolous gossip.

Pushing the woman out of the way, Tyreta grasped the handles and pushed the doors open, not bothering to knock. Inside stood Chancellor Eremand, pale, pockmarked face perched atop his high-collared jacket. Beside him was Lord Serrell Marrlock, tall and rangy but with thick forearms protruding from within his rolled-up shirt-sleeves. Both men looked up in surprise as Tyreta entered. Eremand appeared shocked at the disturbance, but Serrell's face opened up in a wide and beaming smile.

"Thank the Wyrms," he said. "We thought the worst had happened."

Tyreta could well believe his relief was genuine. Whether it was from concern for her or fear of what her mother would do if Tyreta had perished under his watch was anyone's guess.

"I tried to stop her, but she insisted on seeing you right away," crowed Isleen.

Tyreta ignored her, stepping into the room with Gelila at her side. From Eremand's frown it was clear he was unused to the sight of a kesh warrior. Serrell barely acknowledged her.

"You look like you've been through it, Tyreta," Serrell said.

"Gone native, more like," Eremand whispered, but they could all hear him.

"New Flaym is in danger," Tyreta said, keen to get to the point. "An army is on its way. We've just come from a mining outpost to the north. There was a massacre."

Eremand shook his head dismissively. "Nonsense. We would have received word—"

"The survivors were headed to Wolf Station. Have you heard from them?"

Eremand and Serrell shared a grave look before Serrell said, "We've heard nothing from Wolf Station for days. We were just discussing whether to dispatch a messenger."

"Don't bother. The place will have been overrun already. It's unlikely there are any survivors." Tyreta tried not to think of those men who had lived through the attack at the mine. She had done all she could to save them, but it seemed they had fled from one peril straight into the jaws of another. "There's an army of kesh looking for blood, and they are headed this way next."

"No," Eremand said, looking more sceptical by the moment. "We have received no such reports. We sent a scouting party to find you. They would have returned with word if they'd encountered such a large war party."

"They're dead," Tyreta snapped, fast losing patience with the chancellor's pigheadedness. "Wyllow is dead. The miners at Wolf Station are all dead, and we will be too if you don't do something. I've seen their army. The tribes of the Sundered Isles have come together under a single warlord, and he's coming for us."

"We are in no danger." Eremand waved a hand dismissively, but his voice had risen an octave. A tinge of doubt perhaps? "New Flaym has its own garrison. No number of kesh savages would be a match for them."

"A single garrison won't be enough." Tyreta began to feel she was fighting a losing battle, but she could not give in. "You have to evacuate the port. Get everyone you can on ships back to Torwyn."

"Impossible," said Serrell. "The Guilds have far too much invested in these islands to abandon them because of a few rebellious natives."

"Listen to me." She took a step forward, slamming her hand on the table that sat between them. "When the kesh get here, it doesn't matter how much you've got invested. Money and status and commodities won't stop Shabak. It won't matter how much wealth you've got when he spits you like a bloody pig."

Silence. Tyreta thought perhaps she had gone too far, but how far should you go when trying to rescue someone who refused to be saved?

"Lady Tyreta," Eremand said eventually. "I can assure you we are quite well defended here. You have obviously endured much over the last few days. It has more than likely inspired these hysterics. I think once you've calmed down and cleaned yourself up, you'll be able to see things much more clearly."

She had to stay calm. These men would not countenance her if she lost control again.

"Chancellor, I can assure you a bath and clean clothes will not calm me down. I've seen what they can do. I've watched them kill without mercy. If you don't listen to me, we're all going to die. Lord Serrell, please."

He couldn't look her in the eye at first, but eventually Serrell met her gaze. She could see the conflict in his expression as he weighed financial gains against mortal danger.

"Tyreta, we will heed your advice and bolster the port's defences. Thank you for bringing us this warning, and I'm sorry for what you've suffered. In the meantime, Lady Isleen will see that you're taken care of, and in the morning we'll have you on the first ship back to Goodfleet."

Isleen took a step toward her, but Tyreta flashed her a glance that stopped the old woman in her tracks. She had lost. No amount of raging, no further dire warnings were going to persuade these men of the threat that was coming.

"You've just condemned this place to the Five Lairs," she said. "You're both blinded by your greed. The Guilds don't belong on these islands. None of us do. You pushed the kesh aside to take what you want. Now they're going to push back, and there's nothing you can do to stop them."

Before any of them could reply, could tell her she was overreacting, she turned and left the room. Gelila was close behind her as she made her way back through the halls of the embassy, this monument to the might of Torwyn. Everything about it symbolised their arrogance, their complacency. Soon it would be turned to ash.

Out on the street, Tyreta sucked in the warm sea air, trying her best to stay calm.

"Come, dear," Isleen said, laying a gentle hand on her shoulder. "We'll get you all cleaned up and ready for the journey home."

"Get your hand off me," Tyreta whispered.

"What's that, dear?"

"Get your pissing hand off," she hissed. "And get away from me."

So much for staying calm.

If she'd slapped Isleen across the jowls it was doubtful she'd have looked more stunned. Her mouth opened, lips working to speak, but no words came out. Then, in a flourish of skirts, she marched up the street toward the villas.

Idiots. Tyreta was surrounded by idiots—blinded by avarice, too swollen with their own importance to comprehend what was coming for them. Maybe this place deserved to fall.

"Bad smell," Gelila said.

Tyreta saw she was staring down toward the dock. The stench of rotting fish and the tannery wafted up the wide, swollen street as effluent ran down it.

"Yes," Tyreta agreed. "This whole place stinks. But these people don't deserve to die."

As though on cue, two children raced one another across the street, barefooted and carefree. No one could know what was coming. No one would believe her if she screamed it from the dock, but Tyreta could not just abandon the place to Shabak and his horde.

"Will you help me?" she asked Gelila. "I... I don't have anyone else to ask."

At first she wondered whether Gelila understood. "You want help from Lokai?" she answered.

"If someone doesn't help me stop Shabak, everyone here will be murdered."

Gelila looked around at the place. Tyreta could only imagine how alien it must seem to this woman who had been raised in the jungle.

What stories she must have heard of how the Guilds had taken what they wanted and displaced the kesh to get it.

"I know what you're thinking," Tyreta said. "And you're right. We have done untold harm to this land. But we're not all monsters. There are some people here worth saving."

"No," Gelila replied. "None worth saving here." She fixed Tyreta with a grim look. "But Shabak and Chul. They worth killing."

"So you will help me?" Tyreta asked, wanting to sound less timid than she did.

"I help. But you fight for your people. Alone."

It sounded impossible, but what other choice was there? Tyreta gazed across the harbour, at the sea and toward her home beyond. She could leave here tomorrow if she wanted. Or stay and try to save these people, no matter how undeserving they were.

"I am no warrior," Tyreta said. "But yes, I will fight."

Gelila laid a strong hand on her shoulder, and with the other she grasped the nightstone about her neck and held it in her grey fist.

"Kiatta," she said.

Tyreta almost laughed. "I still don't know what that even means."

Gelila fixed her with those piercing eyes, and Tyreta was almost fearful of what she saw behind them.

"Not yet," Gelila said. "But soon."

ROSOMON

He was late. And no one kept her waiting. Well, perhaps Lancelin had on occasion, but his tardiness she had always forgiven. For Rearden Corwen she would offer no such absolution.

A breeze blew across the atrium, but the sun was shining bright. Another beautiful day. Not that Rosomon could appreciate it. The view from the summit of Archwind Palace was as majestic as any in Torwyn, but her days of admiring the beauty of things were long gone.

She glanced along the long stone jetty, remembering the last time she had been here. When she had watched as her son was taken from her in that ugly black airship. Perhaps it had been a mistake to meet here, the memories were still raw, but she needed neutral ground. Somewhere she could feel more at ease, and somewhere Rearden would not feel threatened. This was as good a place as any.

Wachelm stood by the entrance to the atrium, clutching a pile of ledgers to his chest. His discomfort was palpable as he gripped those books like a shield. She would have spared him this torment, but she needed him. He knew those ledgers inside out, understood them better than she ever could. He may have been an actuary of the Corwen Guild, but she still considered him part of her coterie, someone she could trust. Right now, she could count such people on one hand. Perhaps even just a couple of fingers.

They were here to confront Rearden, or at least to find out what he knew. The sense that something was afoot, something clandestine, lay heavy on her shoulders. Rosomon could find no clear evidence, but even the city seemed different, as though preparing itself for upheaval.

From the summit of the palace she could see stormhulks lumbering about the streets as the Armiger Battalions gathered. Had they been there all the while, or were they a new addition to the city? Was Rosomon just more sensitive to their presence after everything that had happened in the past few days?

Pilgrims were gathering from all over the Guildlands, and she could see the Mount in the distance, barely able to contain their numbers as they filed in and out through its vast archways. The halls of the palace were filled with delegates from every Guild both major and minor, as though they were crows awaiting the outcome of a battle. Could they smell blood? Did they see Sullivar's grief as some kind of opportunity? Were they readying to take advantage of his weakness?

And here she was, seemingly in charge. Cast into the centre of all this with no idea what was going on. It angered her to be cursed by so much doubt. Perhaps it would serve her best to abandon her brother and return to Wyke. She was Guildmaster of the Hawkspurs, not empress of Torwyn. She was not meant for this, but there was no way she could abandon her duties now.

Rosomon took a deep breath, tasting the faint acridity of the forge fires on the air. She had to forget her woes. This was a battle, of that she had no doubt. If she gave in to fear, succumbed to paranoia, it would only lead to weakness, and as her father Treon had always said, *Show weakness to the wolf, and you may as well offer your throat.*

She glanced over to the opposite side of the jetty. Starn Rivers leaned against the balustrade. Her one protection against any threats. Was she succumbing to her suspicions by having him here? It was, after all, his job to protect her, but what possible threat could there be to her life here in this seat of power?

Better to fortify your walls against friends than see them fall to your enemies.

Was that one of her father's too? Or had she just made that up? Before she could try to work that out, there was movement within the atrium.

Rearden Corwen wore a smug smile beneath his hooked nose as he strode into the open air. She seldom saw him in daylight, and she half expected him to shrivel like some ghoul in the sun.

He was alone, no bodyguards, no swordwright—but then the Guildmaster of Corwen had never submitted any warriors to train at the Seminarium. Instead Rearden had his Revocaters, though he clearly thought them unnecessary for this meeting. A man comfortable in his environment. Oh, how she envied him that luxury.

He opened his arms as though to embrace her, but stopped short a few feet away before offering a bow.

"Lady Rosomon," he said. "Please accept my apologies. I am laden with administrative matters and quite lost track of time."

She doubted that. Rearden was a meticulous man, no detail unresearched, no matter left unattended. He was merely testing her, pushing the boundaries, trying to prove who was really in charge. She should have admonished him for it, demonstrated who held the most power here.

"That's quite all right, Lord Rearden," she replied. "I completely understand."

She let the silence last just a little while. The smug smile on his face began to waver, and she wondered how long he might hold it there if she continued to say nothing.

"I imagine you're wondering why I summoned you?" she said finally.

He faltered just a little bit more at the word *summoned*. It insinuated she *was* in charge. That he *was* at her beck and call. Such suggestions would never sit well with Rearden Corwen, but he suppressed his indignation.

"I must admit I was curious," he replied, glancing toward Wachelm, who still stood clutching those ledgers.

"It's a trifle really." They both knew it wasn't. "Probably nothing to be concerned about." It most definitely was. "But I have discovered certain...irregularities within a number of trade ledgers, and

I wondered if you'd be able to address them for me. It won't take up much of your valuable time."

"Of course," said Rearden, unable to hide the doubt in his voice. "If we go to my chambers at the embassy I'm sure I can resolve the issue with little fuss."

"No need," Rosomon said, raising her hand toward Wachelm, who began to approach. "I have brought the relevant ledgers with me. To save time."

Rearden glared at Wachelm, who avoided that furrowed gaze and dutifully held out one of the ledgers for Rosomon. She took it and flicked through the passages until she found the relevant entry.

"I stumbled on the name of this creditor quite by chance," she said, opening up the ledger to show Rearden the name Ossian Holder. "I wondered if you recognise it?"

If Rearden was feigning ignorance, it was done masterfully. "I must admit I'm not familiar with the name," he replied innocently.

"No? Only it has appeared more than once in a number of ledgers and dockets of trade, along with others. All names linked to the Draconate. All ghosts from the past."

She tried to read his response, but Rearden gave nothing away.

"I'm afraid I am at a loss, Lady Rosomon."

"Trade arrangements have been made between these dead men and various organisations throughout Torwyn. Armiger Battalions, minor Guilds, city governors, chancellors, port executives. Letters of marque have been drafted, goods bought and sold with no reliable source for the investment. And every transaction has passed right under your nose."

The nose in question twitched slightly, like that of a mouse sniffing at cheese.

"May I?" Rearden asked, holding out a bony hand for the ledger.

Rosomon handed it over and watched as Rearden's beady eyes scanned the columns of accounting, the assets and balances and signatories. He reverently licked finger and thumb before leafing through the pages, flicking them over with a well-practised flourish. Eventually a crooked grin worked its way up one side of his mouth, and he peered back over the top of the ledger with a look of uncompromising victory.

"I think I've identified the issue," he said.

"Do tell," Rosomon replied, preparing herself for some trite or implausible excuse.

Rearden turned the ledger so she could see the entries, that bony finger pointing to the tiniest of marks in the bottom corner of the page.

"All these entries have been scribed by the same actuary. Arvus Rainham. You can see his mark here."

Rosomon peered closer, seeing a stylised monogram of an *A* and an *R*. "And the relevance of this?"

"Arvus was a particularly devout servant of the Corwen Guild. Given to spouting the odd pious lecture on occasion, but his talents as an actuary were incomparable, so I was happy to overlook his eccentricities."

"You're losing me, Rearden." She'd almost had enough of being led around by the nose. "What's the point?"

"The point is, at the Corwen Guild we have a number of clerical and administrative departments that are . . . innominate. Subdivisions within subdivisions that we use to provide finance, and which are given no official designation."

"You mean secret chambers of office to hide your improprieties?"

The accusation did not fluster Rearden, and a smile crept up the side of his gaunt face. "Not so secret that Emperor Sullivar is unaware of them. And no, their aim is not impropriety. They merely exist to relieve the burden of debt placed on your brother. As you know, the Archwind Guild has been suffering financially since the demise of your late father. Sullivar merely tasked me with massaging the appearance of Archwind debt. We can ask him about it if you doubt my word."

She'd never doubted anyone's word more, but there was little chance of getting sense from Sullivar at the moment.

"So these names—"

"Affectations chosen by Arvus." He flicked through the pages, pointing to another entry. "See, Miklosz Karvage. And here, Grius Lantion. These are just ways for Arvus to record the investments made by the Corwen Guild—on Sullivar's behalf, of course—and not reveal their source. All at your brother's request."

She stared at the ledger. The longer she did, the more it made sense. From what she had already uncovered she knew Sullivar was in dire financial straits. The Radwinter Guild had withheld taxes, the Armiger Battalions were taking an ever-increasing cut of profits from the pyrestone trade. If Sullivar had admitted to borrowing so heavily from the Corwen Guild, his reputation and position might well have been in jeopardy.

"And where is this Arvus Rainham now?" she asked.

"Sadly, no longer with us. I'm surprised young Wachelm was unable to shed any light on this. It is common knowledge within the embassy, but of course I do apologise for the misunderstanding."

Wachelm was looking wide eyed from behind his glass lenses. A lamb before the slaughter.

"I am sorry, Lady Rosomon," the young lad said. "Clearly an oversight on my part."

All this looked credible on the surface, but there was something that still did not sit right. Rosomon turned, looking down on the city, seeing the increased bustle below. A pyrestone-fuelled carriage trundled its way by on the skyway that encircled the city like a halo. Where before she had found the familiar sight reassuring, now it felt alien to her. Even the air was different, a sense of foreboding hanging on the breeze. In the distance she could see a patrol of dark-armoured troopers marching across the Bridge of Saints. From beyond the steepled roofs drifted the industrial rattle of Torwyn manufacturing its perpetual war machine.

"Tell me, Rearden," she said, trying to steady herself, trying to fend off the rising sense of dread. "Do you not think the city is on edge? Can you at least tell me there is a greater military presence, or am I just imagining that?"

Rearden joined her at the balcony, looking down on the view. "Not at all. But as you know, the festival is only a few days away."

Festival? She had been so preoccupied with all that had happened, with all she had to contend with, the thought of a celebration was the furthest thing from her mind.

"The Raising of Undometh," she breathed.

"Indeed," Rearden replied. "Representatives of all the Guilds and

Armiger Battalions will be here. Some have already arrived, as you can see."

Rosomon suddenly began to feel something of the fool. The Raising of Undometh was held every fifth year. Its main festival was always centred on the Mount, but even in Wyke it was celebrated by adherents of the Great Wyrm of Vengeance. How had she forgotten?

But she knew why. So much strife, so much pressure, had made paranoia cloud her judgement. These had been fraught times, and she the most fraught of all. Rosomon could not even remember the last time she had slept without waking in a cold sweat halfway through the night.

"Are you sure you're all right?" Rearden asked gently.

"Of course," she replied, turning on a smile. It would never do for Rearden to see she was mired in a swamp of anxiety. "Thank you so much for your help in this matter. It has certainly set my mind at ease."

"Your servant," Rearden said with a bow before turning back to the atrium.

On his way out he clicked his fingers at Wachelm, who dutifully followed him through the archway. A demonstration perhaps? Showing her who was really in charge of the administration?

How she would have loved to offer a demonstration of her own and have Starn club the wrinkly old weasel to death, but what would that have gained her? A brief moment of satisfaction certainly, but little long-term reward.

No sooner had Rearden disappeared into the atrium than Athelys came rushing out. She was furrow browed and nervous as ever. Rosomon had learned long ago that this could mean either good news or bad news; the expression that heralded both was identical.

"My lady," the girl sputtered, bowing as much like a lady's maid as she could manage, but she'd never gotten the hang of it despite years of trying. "Prince Lorens is here to see you."

Lorens Archwind. Sullivar's eldest and heir to the empire. A wellspring of hope suddenly washed through Rosomon's malaise as she saw her nephew appear at the archway to the atrium.

He bore a wide, toothy grin. The one she remembered from

his childhood, which would see him win over even the stoutest of Guildmasters. A black uniform adorned him from the stiff collar at his neck to his shiny leather boots. On one shoulder was an epaulette of black feathers, the crow symbol of the Corvus Battalion emblazoned proudly on his chest.

"Aunt Rosomon," he said, arms wide, just as Rearden had greeted her, only this time she was far from repulsed by the gesture.

She rushed to embrace him, pressing her head to his chest.

"Lorens," she said. "You don't know how good it is to see you."

"I can only imagine, Aunt Rosomon. These have been difficult times for all of us."

She looked up into those dark eyes, his hair tousled in a curly mop. It had been too long since she'd seen him, and in that time he had grown into rugged manhood. It did not seem more than a week since she had watched Conall and Lorens playing at warriors, whacking one another with sticks. Neither of them was playing anymore.

Rosomon took a step back, suddenly remembering propriety and bowing. "Apologies," she said. "It's not fitting for me to be so informal."

"Nonsense," Lorens replied. "You used to bounce me on your knee. Nothing formal about that, and little's changed apart from my size."

"I doubt it. They're calling you prince now. A warrior grown with an empire at your feet."

Lorens laughed. "I don't feel much like an emperor-in-waiting. But a year serving in the Armiger will keep anyone's feet on the ground."

"Have you returned for the festival?"

"The Raising of Undometh is close to my heart," he replied, raising a hand to touch the ruby amulet at his neck depicting the Great Wyrm of Vengeance. "But I would have come anyway. I should have come earlier, but my duties for the battalion kept me at Ravenscrag."

"Conall is likewise serving the Phoenix Battalion in the Karna."

"Then you should be proud of him," Lorens said.

She should have been, but she'd heard no word from him in days. No acknowledgment of Fulren's exile or Tyreta's disappearance. Nothing.

"Are you all right, Aunt Rosomon?" Lorens asked.

She realised she had been staring into space and forced a smile. "Of course. I was so sorry to hear about Wyllow."

Lorens's jaw tightened, the vein pulsing at his temple as he thought on his lost brother. "And I was sorry to hear of Tyreta. And Fulren. If only I had been here..."

Rosomon felt a sudden darkness cloud her as she remembered the old days, remembered how her brother's family had been so close to her own, and how both had now been torn apart.

"There is nothing you could have done," she said, wondering if that was true. Had Fulren had an ally here as powerful as Lorens, perhaps he would not have been offered up to those demon lovers as a sacrifice.

"I tried to speak with my father earlier, but he is still at his bed. My mother is inconsolable. Their chambers stink of poppy essence."

"It has been a difficult time for all of us. I have overseen Guild matters as best I could."

"Not an easy task for anyone. Let alone a grieving mother."

"I have survived," she said, trying to sound as though it had been an easy task and not the withering burden it was.

Lorens took a step forward, laying his hands on her shoulders. "Rest assured, you won't have to endure it alone from now on. If one day I am to take my father's seat in the Guildhall, I had better start taking on some of his responsibilities. There seems no better time than now, and I will need someone to guide me."

She laid a hand on his, feeling the weight lift from her for the briefest of moments.

"Then let's begin, Prince Lorens."

CONALL

The shirt clung to his back as he dug the hole, the sun not caring a damn about his discomfort. It was hard work, the ground dried solid, his shovel doing its best to clear away the earth before Sted went at it with her pickaxe.

Conall took a step back, letting her hack away, lump of redstalk still dangling from her mouth. They were surrounded by grave markers, but he hadn't bothered to count how many. Each one was a little reminder that they were in a hostile land, death waiting for them at every turn. Maybe if Conall had heeded that warning sooner, they wouldn't be digging this hole.

The fact that this was all his fault hung over him like the vultures that circled above. He might as well have fired that arrow into Nevan himself.

When Sted finished, he bent his aching back once more and shovelled the dirt onto the pile. They were up to their waists now, covered in dust, sweating like pigs, but they weren't done yet. He at least owed Nevan a grave deep enough to rest in.

Conall watched again as Sted went at the ground like she hated it. Sound of the pick echoing through the mortuary quiet of the desert. She'd not said a thing to him since they got back. Did she blame him too? Was she thinking what a stupid bastard he'd been to lead them out into durrga country, just the three of them?

Before he'd come to the Karna, Conall had been told about the honour of command. He didn't feel very honourable now, standing in a four-foot hole burying a man who'd died because he'd been too bloody loyal to stay behind.

Sted stood back, tossing her pick out of the hole and stretching her aching shoulders.

"Can we put him in now?" she asked. "He's starting to smell riper by the minute."

Conall glanced over at the body. They'd wrapped him as best they could in sheets of linen cloth. Sted had stuffed his pockets with desert weeds to hide the stench of rot, but nothing sweet lasted long in the Karna.

"I guess we've dug deep enough," he replied, throwing the shovel aside and climbing out. He helped Sted from the hole, and they both patted down clothes so dusty it barely made a difference.

Somewhere he'd heard a grave was supposed to be six feet deep. Four would have to do for Nevan Ulworth.

Sted took the legs and Conall grabbed the shoulders. She was right, the big man's corpse stank. Another reminder of the indignity of death. As they dropped him in the hole, Conall wondered if Nevan had ever thought what his grave would be like or where he'd end up buried. Whether he'd be interred reverently in a mausoleum or dumped in a hole in the desert with such a sickening thud. Too late to ask him now.

Despite the urge to fill the hole in straightaway, Conall stood by the graveside with the silence and the stink.

"One of us should say something." There was no legate at the fort, no one to deliver the proper rites. Every man who had died here had been sent to his final rest without the observance of the Draconate.

"Be my guest," Sted replied, chewing on her redstalk.

"You're the religious one." Conall gestured to the dragon pendant hanging loose on her sweaty chest.

"And you're in charge."

For all the good it had done him so far.

"Just say some bloody words so we can get this hole filled in."

Sted sighed, taking hold of the pendant and bowing her head. "Here lies Nevan Ulworth. A more stubborn idiot you'll never have met. May Great Ravenothrax convey him to his lair. Hope the big fucker has more luck in the next life than he did in this one."

With that she made the crossed-wings sign of the Great Wyrms.

"Is that it?" Conall asked.

"If you'd wanted more you should have brought a priest," she replied. "Now can we fill in the hole?"

Conall wanted more for Nevan, but sometimes you just had to make do.

Picking up the shovel, he began to fill the grave, watching as the big man gradually disappeared beneath the earth. He could see Sted glaring at him as he worked, pick slung over her shoulder, working the redstalk around her mouth. It made him wonder what she thought of this. Whether she blamed him as much as he blamed himself. There'd been no *I told you so*, but that wasn't Sted's way. Not until she was drunk at least. Conall couldn't wait for that conversation.

When he was done, he placed a stone on the grave. Not much to mark a man's passing, but it was all they had. Conall would have written a letter to the Ulworth family, telling them about their son's bravery, lying to them about his glorious demise, but he didn't even know if Nevan had a family.

Some leader of men he was.

They walked back into the fort in silence. Two ghosts amid a sea of strangers. Everyone knew what he'd done, he could sense them judging him. Beringer hadn't even deigned to emerge from his lofty office yet, and Conall was dreading that meeting. Maybe he'd have to fight him again. This time Conall would be sure to give a better account of himself.

The barracks were empty as he entered and headed toward his chamber. A glance back over one shoulder showed him Sted was gone, disappeared somewhere to find liquor, maybe? Not that he could blame her. Conall blew out a long sigh, feeling more alone than ever.

When he closed the door to his chamber, he realised his hands were shaking. It was cooler inside, but he still felt claustrophobic. Suddenly he wanted to run to the stables, saddle a horse and not stop till he was back in Agavere, or on a ship back to Torwyn. How many letters had he received from his mother now? There was one still lying unopened on his desk. She needed him, of that there was little doubt, but if he left, he wouldn't be going for her, he'd be going for him. To escape this. To turn his back on what he'd done and how he'd failed.

But he hadn't failed. What he'd seen in that underground harbour could be significant. He at least had a duty to report it. Maybe it was time to write a letter of his own?

Before he could sit at that uncomfortable chair behind that uncomfortable desk, he caught sight of the glaive leaning against the wall. It taunted him with its silence but still asked so many questions. The main one being: What in the Lairs did the pirates of Iperion Magna want with pyrestone?

Conall grabbed parchment and stylus and cracked open a pot of ink. He had to write his account, had to remember everything, had to record it in duplicate so he could send a copy to his uncle at the Anvil.

His hand hovered over the vellum, still shaking. Conall took another deep breath. What was wrong with him? Maybe he was just hungry or thirsty, but since he'd returned from the desert there'd been no time to fill his belly.

Gritting his teeth, he dipped the stylus and prepared to write. Two spots of ink dripped onto the paper as his hand shook. Dark black droplets, like blood on the desert sand. Nevan's last gasps. His eyes dulling.

A glance to the side and the glaive was still sitting there, still accusing him. That bastard thing.

He dropped the stylus, smearing the paper with ink. His chair fell back as he rushed at the weapon, a growl in his throat as he picked it up. Damn it was heavy, but in his rage he managed to heft it overhead, slamming it down on the desk and driving the blade into the wood, desktop cracking as he grunted in feral rage. The outburst did nothing to stop the shaking in his hands, and as the door to his chamber opened he took a breath to bellow for whoever it was to get the fuck out.

Beringer stood regarding him blankly. His head was well below the lintel, shoulders almost touching the frame, accentuating the not-too-tall-, far-too-wide-ness of the man.

"Am I interrupting?" he asked, with uncharacteristic politeness.

It was obvious he was. "No, Frontier Marshal," Conall replied, standing to attention.

Beringer stepped into the room, eyes taking in the disorder.

"You should be more careful, Hawkspur. We have no carpenter at the fort."

With some effort Beringer wrenched the glaive from the desk and leaned it back against the wall. Conall waited for him to turn in a fury. For his calm exterior to be shed, replaced by a muscular ball of rage, but it didn't come.

"You've buried your scout? What was his name?"

News travelled fast, but it was unlikely anything went on at Fort Tarkis that Beringer did not know about.

"Nevan Ulworth. And yes, we've buried him, Frontier Marshal."

Beringer nodded knowingly. "The first man you've lost?"

"It is."

A strange, distant look overcame Beringer. "Always the hardest, losing your first. There's no easy way to deal with it. But hacking apart your quarters is probably as good as any."

"Apologies, Frontier Marshal. I..." Should he try to make an excuse? Should he try to explain while Beringer was being so sympathetic? "I was about to write my report."

"Will it explain why you led an unsanctioned expedition into the heart of the Karna? Will it explain how you expressly disobeyed me after I took such great pains to explain how things work here?"

"Great pains" was definitely the right way of putting it.

"I have discovered something—"

"Will it explain how you got your man killed because you were too stupid and arrogant to do as you're told?"

The fact that Beringer was not raging was the most surprising thing of all. He seemed calm, almost resigned to this.

"Frontier Marshal, my report will explain my findings in full. Despite the casualty, my mission was a success. I can explain—"

"Save it for dispatches," Beringer said. "For now you have more important things to worry about."

"Such as?" Conall asked, feeling something change in the air, a sense of rising dread.

Beringer regarded him closely, his quiet manner more intimidating than his anger.

"You disobeyed me, Hawkspur. While you're here, under my command, you will take the same punishment as any other trooper. But because of your status as a Guild heir, you have the option to leave rather than suffer what's due."

"Marshal Beringer, I—"

"I suggest you consider those options carefully. If you want to stay here, if you want to prove you're not just some highborn arsehole, you'll take the punishment. Otherwise just piss off. Today. Don't take too long to decide."

With that he turned and walked out of the door, not even bothering to close it behind him. Conall watched him disappear, wanting to shout after him, to make him understand that there was something going on in the desert more important than any of this. More important than he or Beringer or some petty antagonism. But he would just have been wailing against the wind.

Conall was not just alone in his chamber, he was alone in this whole desert. He had come here to prove...what? That he was better than everyone thought? That he was a leader of men? That he was worthy of the Hawkspur name? What did that even mean anyway?

Whatever the reason, he had come to the desert and failed. And in his hubris he'd got a man killed. Nevan Ulworth had been loyal to him, and now he was buried in the desert with only a stone to mark his passing. And the thing that hurt Conall the most was the realisation that he couldn't give two shits.

His hands weren't shaking from grief or guilt. They were shaking because he was worried about himself, about his own reputation. About his position and what people would think.

Clenching his fists, he closed his eyes and took a breath. Looking down, he saw the shakes had stopped. With that one revelation he was whole again. At least he was true to himself.

Conall Hawkspur—arsehole. Always had been, perhaps always would be. Only decision now was whether to take his punishment or leave. It was the easiest decision he'd ever had to make.

Fuck Beringer, fuck Fort Tarkis and fuck the Karna Frontier. He was Conall Hawkspur, he didn't need this place or to prove himself to anyone.

He walked to the chest in one corner of his room. Inside were his meagre, worthless belongings. A greatcoat, a bag with a spare shirt and missives from the Talon. All bullshit. He could burn them now and it wouldn't make a difference to anything. He was heir to the Hawkspur legacy no matter what happened here. He'd been kidding himself all this time that serving on the Karna Frontier mattered.

Shouldering his bag, he reached for the longbarrel resting on its wall bracket.

"Going somewhere?"

Westley Tarrien was leaning against the doorframe to the barracks room, striking a much less imposing figure than Beringer as he took a bite of jerky.

"As pleasurable as it's been, I think my time here is at an end," Conall replied.

Tarrien nodded as though he'd known that was the answer all along.

"Hardly the biggest surprise. Not everyone's cut out for the frontier."

Conall should have let it go. Should have disregarded the snide dig in his ribs, but sometimes shit stank too much to be ignored.

"What's your problem, Tarrien? Have I done something to offend you? Is there some wrong I've inflicted in a past life?"

"I'm just curious. Why did you come here in the first place?"

That was a question Conall had struggled to answer since he'd left Agavere.

"I have a duty to my Guild."

Tarrien smirked at that one. "Duty? You don't have duty to shit. You're here because it's something you can impress all your high-born friends with back in Torwyn. You don't need to be here."

"None of us *need* to be here," he snapped, feeling his hands shaking once more.

"Don't we? Do you think I was just handed this captain's uniform like you were handed yours? I was born in the gutter. My mother cleaned the floors at a Ministry temple for pennies. I never knew my father. I had to eat shit to reach this position. Unlike you, I've worked for what I have. Beringer never handed me anything."

"I never knew my father either," Conall replied, desperate not to sound desperate. "Not for long anyway."

"But he left you a legacy. All mine left me was a cleft chin and an empty belly."

"Then I'm sorry for your shit luck," Conall replied, and he meant it.

"I'm sure. But then you can afford to be sorry. Enjoy your trip back to Agavere." He tore another strip of dried meat from the stalk before leaving Conall alone.

A tragic story if ever Conall had heard one. Still didn't explain why Tarrien had to be such an arsehole about it. Jealous perhaps? But why was that Conall's problem? He hadn't abandoned the man's mother, and neither did he have any choice about his own, admittedly substantial, birthright. If he'd had the choice, he might even have offered Tarrien some of his wealth and balanced the scales a bit. Then again, maybe not.

His hands were shaking again, but why now? Was it that he knew Tarrien was right? Back in Wyke he would be able to tell his friends anything he wanted. They wouldn't know if he'd been a hero or a coward, nor would they care. He wasn't here for them. And neither was he here for stories.

Conall Hawkspur had come to prove he was worthy of the name. Not to his mother, not to his friends or the Guilds. But to himself.

He flung the sack back into the chest and pushed it shut with his foot. Outside he breathed in the dry air, hearing the sound of Beringer talking to his men. Ranks of them stood in their dark uniforms flashed with red and yellow. As soon as Conall appeared, Beringer ceased his lecture and gazed across the courtyard.

"Captain Hawkspur," he said. "So good of you to join us. Have you made your decision?"

Conall felt the cold chill of panic tease the hairs at the back of his neck. He glanced across the parade square, desperately looking to see if Sted was watching. Any friend would do. She was nowhere to be seen.

"I will take whatever punishment you see fit, Frontier Marshal," Conall said, as loud and as confidently as he could.

There was a ripple of disquiet through the gathered soldiers—was it from amusement? It definitely wasn't from concern or respect.

"Very well, Captain Hawkspur. Then you shall have it. Captain Tarrien, if you would do the honours."

Tarrien was trying and failing to look less pleased than he was as he commanded his men to clear the yard. They moved aside as he beckoned Conall to come closer. With a practised gesture he signalled for two of his men to step forward.

"If you wouldn't mind removing your shirt, Captain," Tarrien said, more politely than Conall would have expected under the circumstances.

He pulled his shirt over his head and dropped it in the dirt. A trooper stood to either side of him, each binding a wrist. As they pulled tight, spreading Conall's arms wide, a third tossed something to Tarrien, who deftly snatched it from the air.

A whip, snaking long and slender to end in a mess of leather thongs.

Conall glanced up at Beringer, panic rising. For the briefest of moments, he wanted to cry out for this to stop, that he had changed his mind, that he would take a horse to Agavere after all.

Instead he stood in silence as Beringer said, "You may proceed, Captain."

Tarrien leaned in close behind Conall, wedging a leather strap into his mouth and buckling its clasp at the back of his head. Conall bit down, waiting for the inevitable.

"Are you sorry for my shit luck now?" Tarrien whispered.

Conall couldn't have answered if he'd wanted to. Before he could even think what his smart reply would be, a crack echoed through the courtyard.

It felt for a moment as though he'd been struck with a stick across the shoulder blades before the white-hot sting flared. He grunted at the pain, a throaty and pathetic squeal.

Another lash, this time the burning more immediate, tearing into him as though he were being flayed alive. Now the scream hurt his throat and he bit down tighter, feeling the leather give slightly as his teeth dug in.

His vision went blurry at the edges. Sweat beaded on his brow as he strained against the ropes binding his wrists, but those troopers held on tight.

At the third stroke, the courtyard went black.

LANCELIN

The dark-grey sky above the trees made it impossible to navigate the forest. They could have been running south back to Nyrakkis for all Lancelin knew.

So far Fulren had not complained once about the elements or the hectic pace, easily matching Lancelin's endurance. The boy certainly had a warrior's will. Any father would have been proud.

Lancelin put that thought out of his mind. He could let nothing cloud his judgement, not here. He had been set a task, an impossible one for most men, and he could not let sentimentality hamper his focus.

The howling calls of their pursuers had grown more distant and less frequent since the morning, but Lancelin knew they were still up there somewhere. One misstep and they were done for, and that was not taking into account the beasts of the forest that might even now be setting their eyes on two desperate fugitives alone among the trees. That was something else he had to put far from his mind. Take each foe as it came. That was the best Lancelin could hope for.

Up ahead he could see the forest beginning to thin out. He slowed the pace to a walk, Fulren still gripping the leather strap behind him. Beyond the tree line was open ground, snow whipping across it, blown by the rising winds. Through the white haze he could see a narrow valley on the far side.

"What's happening?" Fulren asked between deep gasps of air.

"We're at the edge of the forest," Lancelin replied. "There's no cover from here."

"So what do we do?"

Lançelin looked up through the swirling snowfall. There was no sign of their pursuers, but that didn't mean they weren't still being hunted.

"We'll have to make a run for it," he said.

The sudden madness of it struck him. He had no idea where they were or where they were headed. If they stayed in the forest, they'd starve. If they carried on, they could be attacked by howling beasts from the skies. Even if they weren't, they might still succumb to the elements. But Lancelin could not stand and wait for the end. He had to keep going, keep moving. Meet what was coming head-on.

"Are you ready?" he asked. "We need to move fast."

"I'm right behind you," Fulren replied.

It sparked a rush of pride and brought an unexpected smile to Lancelin's face. He was glad the boy couldn't see it.

With a sharp tug on the leather strap, they both set off. Lancelin's eyes scanned the dull skies, looking for any sign they'd been spotted, but there was nothing to see through the grey. The snowfall was growing heavier, chilling his face, forcing him to squint as they ran.

Out from beneath the shelter of the trees, the snow had settled in drifts, and the pair soon found themselves wading, hauling one leg after the other. Fulren stumbled, falling face-first into the white, and Lancelin dragged him up, the wind beginning to buffet them as they slogged toward the narrow valley.

By the time they reached the edge of the rocks, both men were panting, breath coming in misty gasps. Here the snow was lighter underfoot, the sides of the gorge shielding it from the worst of the squall.

"We need to keep moving," Lancelin called over the sound of the rising storm. "There'll be shelter farther on."

He was trying to convince himself as much as Fulren. By the look of the sky there was a blizzard on its way, but he had to stay confident they would find some cover. He'd hate to suffer all this just to freeze to death on the side of a mountain.

They pushed on along the valley floor, Lancelin shielding his eyes from the flurry. He almost didn't see the dark shadow that passed overhead, almost didn't have time to react before he heard the beat of leather wings.

"Get down," he barked, pushing Fulren to one side, wrenching his sword from its sheath.

No sooner had it rung clear than the beast landed not twenty feet in front of him. If those flying lizards had looked monstrous as they circled overhead, up close they were truly fearsome.

A reptilian head curled forward, sickly maw opening wide, roaring its fury across the valley. The noise was deafening, but Lancelin pushed back the fear, willing himself to stand and face it.

The creature dipped its head, and Lancelin saw the rider, black armour stark against the snow. He expected the beast to attack, to snap at him with those wide jaws, but instead it crouched, allowing the armoured behemoth on its back to slide from the saddle. Curling its wings, the lizard hunkered back, seeming fearful of the dark knight as he strode forward.

Lancelin was unarmoured. Never a good start when facing a foe bedecked in plate, but there was no use trying to escape now. The running was done.

There was a sword at the knight's belt, encased in a scabbard of obsidian, but instead of drawing it, he grasped the black gauntlet on his left hand and pulled it free. As he discarded it in the snow, that pale, exposed hand began to glow with eldritch light.

Lancelin pushed back the fear, quelling every emotion as he prepared to fight. There could be no anger, no desperation, despite what he faced. He had been taught his trade in the Seminarium, trained to detach himself from everything but his opponent.

The knight drew his blade, and Lancelin darted forward, taking the initiative. His first strike was high, the knight parrying with frightening speed. His second jabbed low, again the knight deflected it with precision. A final thrust and the knight met his blade, turning it with inhuman speed, trapping Lancelin's sword in the crook of his arm before reaching forward with that sickly, glowing hand.

It struck Lancelin in the chest. He felt as though he'd been hit with a tree trunk and staggered back, falling to his knee. The sword was still in his hand, he had that to be thankful for as a wave of nausea overwhelmed him. He tried to take a breath, but his lungs felt as if they'd been crushed. All he managed was a strangled cough, spitting blood into the snow.

In the corner of his eye he saw Fulren, back against the wall of the gorge, blind eyes flitting uselessly as he held out his knife defensively. If Lancelin fell, the boy would be at the mercy of this sorcerous warrior.

Spitting more blood, he struggled to his feet, raising his sword as the knight's shadow crossed his vision. He had to stay in control, let his training take over. Rashness would be his end.

Blades clashed, once, twice, the knight countering with a massive swipe of the black blade—a devastating attack but easy to read. Lancelin rolled to the side through the snow, rising to his feet and forcing air into his bruised lungs.

The knight followed, steel-tipped boots trudging relentlessly after him. His left hand glowed with that vomit-green light, the pressure of its magic pulsing in Lancelin's ears. He had never faced such an opponent before, nor encountered such magics. This enemy bore an advantage that might well defeat Lancelin's martial prowess. He had to level the field.

Charging forward, he raised his blade high, offering an easy target. The knight took the bait, sword cutting down as that infernal hand was poised to strike again. Lancelin easily read the move and sidestepped, bringing his blade up in an arc, slicing the knight's unarmoured hand from the wrist.

A hollow growl pealed from the hideous helm as his opponent staggered back, barely holding on to his sword, blood spraying in a gout from the stump of his wrist. He tipped his head back—enough of a gap above the gorget. Lancelin's blade struck through the snowfall, inch perfect, piercing deep into the knight's throat.

Blood flooded out, shining black against the dark armour, running down the breastplate and pattering in the snow. Lancelin staggered back, wondering for a moment if this armoured behemoth could even be killed. The flying beast roared into the storm as its master collapsed in the snow.

Lancelin braced himself, expecting the creature to attack on seeing its rider defeated. Instead it spread those leathern wings, brushing the sides of the canyon before, with a powerful beat, it took flight.

He heaved breath into bruised lungs, seeing that severed hand on the ground begin to necrotise, snow melting around it in a plume of steam.

"Jagdor," Fulren shouted.

The boy looked desperate, helpless, but before Lancelin could tell him he was fine, the snow around them billowed in a furious gust.

Another of the beasts landed behind him, a second in front. Above, on the lip of the narrow gorge, he saw a third, its beastly head craning down to stare with malevolent eyes.

One of the riders dismounted, but this was no knight. Through the snow Lancelin recognised her pinched face and the dark hair about her head, blowing in a flurry—the Jubaran witch who had held Fulren prisoner. The bruise on her face where he had hit her with the pommel of his sword was still yellow and livid.

"There's nowhere left to run," she shouted above the worsening blizzard. The woman was unarmed, but she walked through the snow with all the confidence of a seasoned warrior. "Give Fulren back to us, or you'll die here in the snow."

Surrender was never an option. He had come too far, endured too much to give up. Dying in the cold was always a better prospect than giving in, but he doubted there was much point trying to explain that.

The second knight had dismounted, and the one up on the ridge glared down from the back of his flying beast. Lancelin planted his feet, steadying himself, trying to get enough air in his bruised lungs for the fight to come. Whatever these devils were about to do, he would face it.

"Wenis, wait," yelled Fulren, pushing himself away from the wall and stumbling toward the sound of her voice. "I'll come with you. Nobody else has to die."

Wenis raised a cynical eyebrow. "It seems your friend disagrees."

"He's no friend of mine."

"And yet he is so eager to protect you. He risked much to liberate you from the bosom of Nyrakkis."

"I didn't leave willingly. But I'll come back with you. Just let him live."

Lancelin took a step toward the woman, keeping an eye on the knight standing silently behind him. "That's not for you to decide, Fulren," he said.

Wenis grinned as though she had been hoping that would be the answer.

"Brave and stubborn," she said. "Sure you two aren't related?"

Before he could answer there was a flurry of activity from above. The beast on the ridge howled, a strangled cry of pain rather than fury. A bellow rose above the sound of the storm as something dropped into the valley with a sickening thud.

A reptilian head lay in the snow. Its jaws twitched for a moment, green eyes dulling as blood pooled from the stump of its neck and stained the ground red.

Lancelin dashed in front of Fulren, pushing him back against the wall as the black-armoured knight drew his sword. He barely had a chance to turn toward their unseen enemy before a spear flew from the midst of the storm, piercing the obsidian breastplate dead centre. The knight sank to his knees, the spear shaft propping up his body, head dipping as the life ebbed out of him.

Arrows hissed through the storm, impaling the ground all around them. One of the flying beasts took wing, the other turned, legs churning the snow, as it plunged into the blizzard to face whatever was coming. Through the white haze, Lancelin could see the hack and slash of violence and the beast thrashing against some unseen foe.

Another spear impaled the ground at Wenis's feet, her confident expression draining away as she desperately looked for somewhere to flee. The markings on her bare arms began to glow with a bilious green light, but there was no one to direct her sorcery at.

As fast as it began, the sounds of violence ebbed to nothing. All that remained was the howl of the storm. Wenis glanced up and down the gorge, eyes wide with fear. Her knights were gone, the flying lizards defeated or fled. It was just the three of them left.

"What's going on?" Fulren snarled.

"Just stay calm," Lancelin replied. Maybe not the best advice. Maybe they should be trying to run.

From both sides of the gorge Lancelin could make out bulky shadows approaching. Crunching through the snow were a score of figures, each face hidden behind a steel helm, furs about their shoulders, spears reaching eight feet or more into the snowy air. First from the storm stepped a huge warrior, axe slung over one shoulder, a helmet of bone atop his head, steel-tipped antlers rising from it. The newcomers stood in silence, letting the snow whip their cloaks as Lancelin tightened his grip on the sword. He could feel the chill begin to infest his bones. If they stood and waited long enough, he'd be too frozen to fight.

Then that huge antlered helm tipped back, and a laugh echoed along the valley. Piercing blue eyes stared madly from within the helm's sockets.

When he'd finished bellowing, the warrior reached up a meaty hand and removed his helmet, handing it to one of his men. It was a face of beaten meat, half the nose cut off, scars driven deep into the flesh. His greying hair was whipped by the wind as he regarded Wenis, then turned to Lancelin.

"You look cold, eastlander," he said with a smile, though it wasn't obvious what was so bloody amusing. "All that fighting not make your blood boil?"

He spat the last word like he hated it.

"We've been in the cold awhile," Lancelin replied.

The warrior nodded. "I know. Been following you for a day. Was wondering whether you'd make good meat, but you make better bait. Thought they'd kill you, but you fight without fear." He turned to Wenis, his eyes going wild like an attack dog's. "And any enemy of Nyrakkis. Eh, witch?"

The sorceress stared back with determination, but Lancelin could tell she was scared. Witch she might be, but it was doubtful her magic would save her from these barbarians. One of them had already removed the dead knight's helmet and decapitated the corpse with a wicked-looking knife. Another hefted the severed head of the flying beast and was making its mouth open and close to the chuckles of his fellow warriors. Lancelin could only hope their trophy hunting ended there.

"Come," said the leader, gesturing to Wenis. "Finish her, and we'll be on our way."

Lancelin could see her lip tremble, hands balled into fists to stop them shaking.

"No," Fulren yelled, staggering forward in the snow to the amusement of all around. "Don't kill her."

Lancelin tried to restrain him, but Fulren shook off his hand. The Huntan warrior peered at Fulren, raising one of his bushy grey eyebrows.

"Spare her, blind man? So she is not your enemy?"

"She is our enemy," said Lancelin, desperate not to antagonise their new allies. It was obvious Wenis meant something to Fulren, though he had no idea what. "But she must be worth more to you alive than dead?"

The warrior's brow creased. "She is yours to kill, eastlander. But if you offer her as a gift to Saranor the Bleeder, he will accept. The Night of the Blooded Star comes soon, and she will make a fine offering. What say you?"

It sounded like a poor fate, but at least it would keep her alive, for now.

"She is yours," Lancelin said, grabbing hold of Fulren before he could object. "All I ask in return is that you give us shelter. At least until the storm is past."

Saranor smiled, showing teeth whiter than the blizzard, canines big as a wolf's.

"A witch of Nyrakkis in return for shelter? A small price to pay. Come. Saranor the Bleeder will show you the hospitality of the Huntan."

Hopefully it was an improvement on what they'd received so far.

Wenis was quickly bound, the warriors wary of the tattoos on her arms. She didn't resist as they tied her hands and secured a rope about her neck. She offered a swift glance Lancelin's way as she was dragged off, but he couldn't tell if it was one of gratitude or not. It made no difference. He'd saved her for now, but whenever this Night of the Blooded Star came along, she'd most likely wish he'd killed her here.

The Huntan warriors led them on through the valley until it opened out into a vast gorge. Lancelin led Fulren close behind as they skirted the lip of a steep drop that fell hundreds of feet. With every step the blizzard got worse until eventually one of the warriors offered Lancelin the fur of some animal. He placed it over Fulren's shoulders. If the boy was grateful, he didn't mention it.

Eventually the pathway led up onto a wide plain stretching to the foot of mountains in the distance. Through the snowstorm Lancelin could see the outline of a settlement nestled in the shadow of the distant range.

"Tonight there will be much feasting," Saranor shouted above the blizzard. "Henakor the Butcher carves the most tender meat." He gestured to the limbless torso of one of the flying beasts being dragged on a sled.

Lancelin nodded in feigned enthusiasm. Such endearing names these Huntans had, though a man called Hawkslayer could hardly make comment on that.

As the settlement loomed large through the snow ahead, Fulren grasped his arm and pulled him close.

"What are we doing?" he hissed.

"For now we're biding our time," Lancelin replied, keen not to be heard above the storm.

"This is madness. We have to figure a way out of here."

Lancelin couldn't argue about the madness part. These barbarians were clearly insane. But for now he and Fulren were alive and seemed to have found allies in a place that so far had only tried to kill them.

"I'll think of something," Lancelin replied, gripping Fulren's arm.

"What about Wenis? They'll murder her if we don't do something to help."

Lancelin squinted through the storm, seeing her being dragged along with less care than they gave the meat for the coming feast.

"I'm more concerned that they'll murder *us* unless we're very careful."

"I won't leave her here," Fulren said, pulling Lancelin to a stop. His face looked determined, though his eyes still darted about blindly, seemingly impervious to the whipping snow. Whatever hold she had over the boy was a strong one. More Maladoran sorcery? Or was it genuine affection?

"I'll do what I can," Lancelin said, urging Fulren on once more.

They followed the warriors toward their settlement, and Lancelin felt some relief that they were at last to be offered shelter. In front of him Wenis stumbled, only to be dragged roughly to her feet by the rope around her neck.

As the stormy sky began to darken, Lancelin could only hope he'd think of a plan before this Night of the Blooded Star.

ROSOMON

The Cogwheel was elevated above the streets of the Anvil, a circular plaza from which the whole city could be viewed. It had been constructed during the earliest days of Treon Archwind's reign, a symbol of his Guild's dominance. Rosomon had always considered it a bombastic and unnecessary construction, but now as she stood waiting at the centre of it she appreciated the full significance of her father's legacy.

The sound of hammers and saws drowned out the lively noise of the city. Behind her, at the northern side of the Cogwheel, craftsmen were constructing a huge wooden podium from which the coming festivities could be officiated. The Raising of Undometh would include a lengthy parade through the centre of the city, and where in previous decades it had been a purely religious ceremony, now it was used as a demonstration of the might of Torwyn. Every Guild would be represented, every Armiger Battalion would march its troopers. Of course the Draconate would still observe its rites, but that ceremony had long since been overshadowed by the powers that now ruled over an empire.

A demonstration of that power was approaching even now, and as Rosomon watched along the Parade of Builders she got some sense of how vulgar and imposing those celebrations would be. Scores of dark-uniformed troopers were marching in disciplined ranks, the sun glinting from their wolf-shaped helms. Flanking them were a dozen stormhulks, dwarfing the strutting soldiers.

Beside her Lorens shuffled uncomfortably, loosening his stiff collar with one finger. He had abandoned the black uniform of the Corvus Battalion for Archwind red, now representing his Guild rather than the Armiger.

"You'll be fine," she whispered to him, laying a reassuring hand on his arm.

"Only days ago I was taking orders from men like this. Now I'm to stand here as an equal."

"I know it seems a daunting prospect, but remember, they are not your equals. One day you will be their emperor."

"I don't have the training for this," Lorens said, staring at the column of warriors making their way ever closer to the Cogwheel.

Rosomon had to stifle a laugh. "There is no training for this, Lorens. You are born to it. But don't worry, I'll be here to guide you, should you need it."

Her reassurance didn't seem to help much as Lorens fidgeted with the cuffs of his jacket, flattened his unruly mop of hair and cleared his throat several times. All the while the unrelenting might of the Bloodwolf Battalion made its way along the Parade of Builders. The sound of its marching grew louder, echoing across the Cogwheel and drowning out the sound of hammer and saw.

With a final stamp of attention, the column came to a standstill. Three officers at the front made their way forward, one of them carrying the battalion's black standard with a red wolf head emblazoned, surrounded by the names and dates of its distinguished victories. When the officers had mounted the stairs to the plaza, the warrior at their centre walked forward to present himself. A wolf helm was held in the crook of his arm, a ceremonial sword at his side. He was young for a man of such esteemed rank, but his eyes were careworn, face scarred, hair prematurely greying at the temples.

"Prince Lorens," he said with a curt bow.

Lorens offered an awkward bow in return. "Drift Marshal Rawlin. It is an honour."

"My lady," Rawlin said, offering a much less officious nod to Rosomon.

"Welcome to the Anvil, Drift Marshal," she replied.

Rawlin glanced about the plaza, taking in the sight of workers labouring at the podium.

"I would have expected Sullivar to be here to greet us. Is the emperor unwell?"

Lorens opened his mouth to speak but couldn't find the words. Rosomon smiled at Rawlin, as contrite a gesture as she could manage.

"He sends his apologies. My brother would have welcomed you personally, but he is mired in Guild matters. It has not been an easy time for any of us after what happened to his son Wyllow."

"Of course," Rawlin replied. "He has the sympathies of the battalion. As do you, Prince Lorens."

No mention of sympathies for the loss of Tyreta or Fulren, but Rosomon would not have expected any. Why would a man like Rawlin care for the loss of one girl and a lowly artificer, no matter their heritage?

"Your sympathy is appreciated, Drift Marshal," Lorens said.

"Nevertheless. His absence is still a slight. The Bloodwolf Battalion has served on the borders of the Drift for decades. We have bled for the Guilds. Bled for Torwyn."

Perhaps not so sympathetic after all. Lorens stood, mouth agape, unsure how to respond. If she'd had the chance, Rosomon would have told her nephew to explain how he too had bled for Torwyn. How he was heir to an empire and deserving of respect from every Armiger Battalion on every battlefront, no matter its pedigree.

"Perhaps a gesture to satisfy your honour, Drift Marshal?" she said.

Rawlin's brow creased with suspicion. "A gesture?"

"I have taken the liberty of arranging the banners for the Raising of Undometh. I hope this is to your satisfaction."

She turned, signalled to men standing below a score of flagpoles on the far side of the Cogwheel. At her command they unfurled a pennant on each one, displaying the sigils of the Guilds and Armiger Battalions side by side. The slavering head of the Bloodwolf Battalion was right beside the cog of Archwind.

"As you can see, Emperor Sullivar has chosen your battalion to take pride of place. A symbol of his appreciation for all you have done for the empire."

She could sense Rawlin looking for an excuse to remain affronted, but he could hardly argue with such a show of Sullivar's esteem. To be regaled beside the most powerful organisation in Torwyn was an honour not even the Drift marshal could dismiss.

"Very well," he said. "I will look forward to standing at the emperor's right hand during the ceremony."

"The honour will be ours," Rosomon replied, offering a bow of respect.

Rawlin's stern expression did not change as he curtly offered a nod to Rosomon and Lorens before turning on his heel and marching his men back down the stairs of the Cogwheel.

They watched as the Bloodwolf Battalion marched off toward its garrison, and Lorens let out a long sigh of relief.

"That was artfully done, Aunt Rosomon."

"A temporary obfuscation," she replied, turning back to the attendants at the flagpoles. With a gesture they began to take down the Bloodwolf pennant.

Lorens looked mystified. "The Bloodwolf won't be flying next to the cog, will it?"

"Of course not. The flag of Hawkspur will fly next to Archwind during the ceremony, as it always has. If Rawlin makes an issue of it, he can take that up with me later. For now, he need not be any the wiser."

Lorens chuckled. "Risking the ire of a Drift marshal? You're much braver than I am, Aunt."

"Nonsense," she replied, squeezing her nephew's hand. "Just more experienced at this kind of thing. Now, there is much to prepare. I trust I can leave you in charge of the stage construction?"

"I'm sure I can handle it," Lorens replied, unbuttoning his tight collar.

Rosomon left her nephew to oversee preparations at the Cogwheel, and Starn forged a path through the crowd as she made her way across the city toward the palace. All around, civilians and city functionaries were preparing for the festival. The Raising of Undometh was a time for celebration as well as worship, and the Anvil was buzzing with anticipation.

Stalls were being erected along the length of the parade. Vendors prepared their wares, food stands already traded beneath lines of brightly coloured bunting. There was a good-natured bustle to the city, an atmosphere of excitement. As she walked, Rosomon began to wonder how she could possibly have mistaken anticipation for the festival as a sign that something was amiss. But then she had been working herself to the bone, trying her best to drown in her duties rather than wallow in her grief. Perhaps it was time to be less hard on herself.

She tried not to think on Fulren, on Tyreta, on Lancelin—the man she had sent to his doom on a whim. Better that she stay focused on the tasks at hand, keep her mind occupied with matters of state, for her brother's sake if no one else's.

As she followed the parade route wending its way north toward its final destination at the Mount, Rosomon heard the steady beat of hammer on chisel. When Starn had cleared a path for her, she saw a statue was being hewn upon a raised dais at the side of the road. Already it looked magnificent—a rendering of one of the Great Wyrms, roaring its granite might to the sky. It would make an imposing fixture on the main route of the parade, but who might have sanctioned such a thing? Rosomon had certainly not been informed, and she doubted Sullivar would have approved of such a permanent reminder of the Draconate's influence.

Sanctan.

Of course, Sanctan. Clearly he had taken advantage of Sullivar's absence and ordered the thing erected in the Ministry's honour. She glanced to Starn, who stared up at the statue in silence. No point asking what he thought about it, she had never seen him moved by anything in all the years he had served her Guild. Perhaps later she would have to pay a visit to her eldest nephew and chastise him, despite their last meeting having ended in humiliation. On second thought, better to allow him this one indulgence, at least until the festival was over. Then she would have it torn down, just to demonstrate who was really in charge.

"Lady Rosomon."

Olstrum appeared from the bustling crowd looking quite out of breath. A sheen of sweat beaded on his brow and he looked uncharacteristically shabby in his dress reds.

"Taking a brisk stroll, Olstrum? I would have suggested more suitable attire."

"I came to find you as quickly as I could, my lady. I have been approached by someone with information you must hear."

"More rumours?" she asked. There was a wedge of anticipation in her gut, but she tried to quell it, remembering the disappointment Olstrum's previous contacts had yielded.

"I can assure you this is more than rumour. Someone has information on the night Fulren was attacked. A very reliable source."

"Where?"

"I had him conveyed to your chambers, my lady. This contact asked for privacy. He considers himself in much danger."

"From whom?"

"He would not say." Olstrum lowered his voice. "But he is a most dependable source. I think it would be wise to speak with him."

"Very well. I will hear what this dependable source has to say."

"I hope this time it yields fruit, my lady." Olstrum bowed before retreating back into the crowd.

Starn led the way toward the palace, Rosomon sticking close to his back, moving easily though the path he made. The anticipation inside her grew as they got closer to the palace.

She ignored acknowledgments from the guards and servants in the palace, trying to steady herself as she made her way up to her chambers. If there was any way she might exonerate Fulren, she had to pursue it. Try as she might to quell her rising hopes, she could not help but grasp the tiny hope this gave her. By the time she reached the door to her chamber her heart was racing. Rosomon willed herself to calm down as she turned the handle, so that as the door swung wide, she looked calm, collected... in command.

Inside waited a small, unassuming figure. Pale robes covered a slight paunch. A round, bespectacled face sat beneath a mess of wispy grey hair. The man stood as she entered, his hands clenched together as though he were holding some precious jewel between them.

Starn closed the door behind her, and she could see the man was holding his breath, unsure if he had done the right thing in coming here.

"Please, sit," she ordered.

He stared at her for a moment before obeying her instruction. "Lady Rosomon," he said in a surprisingly deep and commanding voice for such a mousy figure. "Please pardon the intrusion."

"Not at all. I am told you have information about my son. Although you have me at a distinct advantage."

"My apologies." He made to stand again, but sank back, changing his mind. "My name is Ailin. I am the Senior Bibliosoph of the Annalium."

A chief custodian of the Great Library. Here was a more reliable source of information than some anonymous fence in a backstreet dive. Perhaps this time Olstrum had outdone himself.

"May I offer you a drink, Ailin?" Rosomon gestured to the tray on her dresser holding a half-full decanter of spirit and two glasses.

"I'm afraid I don't partake, my lady," Ailin replied. "My duties require I retain a clear head and a keen eye at all times." He glanced at Starn, standing silent and imposing behind her. "I was hoping we might speak in private."

Ailin didn't look dangerous, but Rosomon would take no chances. "This is as private as we're going to get, so please, speak freely."

He shifted uncomfortably in his seat, adjusting his robe as though it had suddenly grown stifling in the airy chamber.

"I have information pertinent to the night of the Maladoran emissary's assassination."

"I was assured all avenues were investigated," Rosomon replied. "Every custodian questioned."

"Indeed, they were, my lady. And all protocols followed to the letter." She could see his left hand suddenly start to tremble before he grasped it with the right. "Protocols I put in place. Because I was ordered to do so. I ensured the library would be empty at the appointed hour of the assassination. I made sure all the doors would be locked but for one—allowing the real assassins to gain entry to the library."

Rosomon felt the hairs on the back of her neck begin to prickle.

"You were ordered to do so?"

"Indeed, my lady." The voice that came from this little man no longer sounded so assured.

"And who held such a position of power to command the Senior Bibliosoph of the Annalium?"

Ailin's eyes went wide behind the lenses of his spectacles as Starn pushed past Rosomon. She staggered, almost falling as the swordwright fell upon the librarian. Ailin managed to give off a strangled yelp as Starn grasped him by the throat, raising him from his seat and smashing his head against the dresser, once, twice, three times, until the yelping stopped.

She should have run, but she was frozen with rising horror as Starn let his victim drop, raising his booted foot and bringing it down on Ailin's head. The crack was sickening. When Starn stamped down for a second time, Rosomon screamed a wordless cry of anguish.

The swordwright turned on her, eyes rabid. She made a dash for the door, but he snatched her neck in one meaty hand before she'd covered five feet. As he squeezed tighter, she felt her throat close up, the air cut off, panic enveloping her like a shroud.

Starn raised a meaty hand and slapped her. The blow sent her reeling backward onto the bed, stark bright pain replacing the dread panic of suffocation. She was dazed, stars sparking in her left eye, a debilitating nausea overcoming every sense.

"Fucking years I've listened to your shit," Starn growled. "Watched you parade yourself around like a queen. Watched you get fucked by Jagdor like a whore. Protected you and your dumb pig spawn while you all treated me like some kind of fucking joke."

Rosomon managed to raise a hand to ward him off as he took a step toward her. "Starn, please, I—"

He slapped her hand away, taking her by the throat once more.

"I should do this slow." He began to squeeze. She grabbed his wrist, but it might as well have been made of iron. "Take my time."

The room began to darken at the edges, swallowing her whole. "Take my pleasure."

Rosomon's arms fell to her sides, her strength abandoning her. The palm of her right hand touched something solid in a fold of her skirts. Starn kept squeezing as she fumbled at her side, fingers closing around the handle of the vendetta blade. The one Fulren had been so adamant she find.

The room grew smaller as she willed herself to pull the blade free of its hidden sheath. She could hear herself choking pathetically in Starn's grip as she screamed inside, drawing on one last ounce of energy.

Rosomon plunged the blade into Starn's shoulder up to the hilt. He grunted, staggering backward, snarling as he clamped a hand to his wounded arm.

She scrambled back across the bed, gasping for air. There was something cold and hard in her right hand.

"Fucking bitch," Starn growled.

Rosomon looked down to see the handle of the vendetta blade in her open palm.

Starn removed his hand from the wound at his shoulder. The blade still protruded from it, blood trickling down his arm in dark rivulets. At the end of the exposed blade was a single tiny pyrestone, glowing yellow and furious.

"You fucking bi—"

He was cut off by a dull boom as the pyrestone exploded.

Rosomon covered her eyes as she was showered with blood and flesh. It peppered her clothes, spattering the pure-white sheets with red. Her ears rang, but she forced herself to look, seeing Starn still standing there. His torso was blackened, head and left arm nothing but smouldering stumps. Then the body collapsed like a smoking lump of meat fallen from the pyre.

She could hardly breathe, barely comprehending what had just happened, but through the fog of confusion, as she looked at the hilt of the vendetta blade in her hand, she knew one thing...

...Fulren had just saved her life.

TYRETA

Gelila knelt among the foliage as the wind hissed gently through the leaves. Tyreta hunkered beside her, listening to the birds tweeting and crickets chirruping from the long grass. In the far distance she could see the sky beginning to prematurely darken, ominous clouds rolling toward them to obscure the bright northern horizon.

Placing a hand over her mouth, Gelila made a sound like one of the yellow songbirds that were perched all around this part of the jungle. Tyreta could have sworn she heard an equally tuneful answer somewhere nearby.

When a kesh warrior stepped from the trees not ten feet to her right, Tyreta almost leapt up in fright. More appeared from the ferns and grasses, as though they'd been hiding there all the time. Gelila stepped forward to greet them and embraced them affectionately, and Tyreta recognised Amanisa and Suma among them.

As she watched the women hug one another, she barely noticed that Yeki had appeared from the jungle right beside her. The old woman still wore the animal skins she had donned for the ritual some nights before.

"You not return to your people?" Yeki asked.

Tyreta shook her head. "I tried to warn them, but they wouldn't listen to me. They've doomed the whole port."

Yeki nodded, as if she'd known that would be the answer. "Then you are wise to leave that place."

"No. I have to go back. I have to do something to stop Shabak, and Gelila said you could help me."

Yeki glanced to Gelila, who offered a shrug in return. "No. Much danger."

Tyreta stooped, staring the old woman in the face. "I've faced danger before and I'm still here. How much worse could it get?"

That brought a wry smile to Yeki's face. "Much," she replied. "But why should we help you? Why help your people, who came here to steal our lands from us?"

There was no reason. Tyreta didn't have any right to demand help from the Lokai or any of the kesh tribes, but she had to at least try. If she succeeded, there might be a way she could right the wrongs the Guilds of Torwyn had inflicted on the Sundered Isles.

"I'm not asking for you to come with me. You've already lost so much." She avoided looking at Amanisa and Suma, remembering their grief at the death of Ozoro. "But if I can defeat Shabak, there might be a way I can persuade the rest of my people to leave. To sail back to Torwyn and never return. I know we don't belong here, I've known since I first met you. But the only way you can be free of us is to help me. If Shabak destroys New Flaym, more of my people will come. And they will come in greater numbers. They will bring powerful weapons and they will not stop until they have wiped out every last kesh on these islands. There must be something you can do to help me. There must be some way of defeating Shabak?"

"Maybe," Yeki said, rubbing her chin with a wrinkled hand. "But only with sacrifice."

"Whatever the price, I'll pay it," Tyreta said, without even thinking what that might mean.

Yeki peered at her, as though wondering how much conviction was behind her words. The rest of the Lokai had gone silent now, watching their leader think on what to do.

"You do not know what you ask," Yeki said.

"Then just tell me," Tyreta said defiantly. "I am not afraid."

Yeki placed a hand to Tyreta's chest, and the nightstone beneath suddenly burned. "Kiatta."

"Kiatta," Tyreta spat, taking a step back and pulling out the stone on its chain. "Kiatta. It's all you say. If this thing is important then use it. Just do what you have to, but I'm running out of time, so do it now or stop all this talk."

Silence.

A bird cawed loudly in a tree as the women of the Lokai continued to stare at her with grave resignation.

"Come," said Yeki.

She led the way through the trees. Tyreta felt a sudden tug of apprehension holding her back. But she had asked for this. There was no turning away from it.

The old woman set a brisk pace. Behind Tyreta the warriors of the Lokai followed in silence. It was almost ceremonial, the hush doing little to calm her nerves. She would have asked what was coming, but it was doubtful she'd get an answer she could understand.

She didn't have to follow for long before Yeki led her to a clearing. Sprawled in the centre was a fallen standing stone, half-reclaimed by the jungle. It jutted from the earth aslant, surface worn smooth, vines and moss snaking their way across every inch.

"What is this place?" Tyreta asked.

The birds had gone quiet and there was an eerie stillness to the jungle. Even the crickets were silent.

"In this place you will find your strength," Yeki replied. "Only if you give yourself to it."

The urge to run was overwhelming. Tyreta could see the rest of the kesh had solemn expressions fixed on their faces. Even Gelila had lost her usual cheeriness and looked apprehensive at what was coming.

"What do I have to do?"

"What you think?" Yeki said.

"Do you answer every question with a question? Why can't you give me a straight answer to anything?"

Yeki shrugged. "You want to save your people?"

Tyreta fought the urge to scream. "Yes, I do."

Yeki offered a final nod and turned toward the fallen stone. Tyreta watched as the old woman began to sniff at its base, as though she were a dog searching for scraps.

Whatever was going on here, she knew she would have to endure it. So far she had trusted these kesh women, and they had rescued her, protected her. Now she had to put her trust in them one last time.

Yeki found what she was looking for and began to dig at the base of the fallen stone, pulling at the earth and sodden clods of grass with her hands. After a short and frantic dig, she unearthed something buried in the stone's shadow. Wrenching it from the ground, she gave a triumphant yelp.

"Knew it was here," said the old woman.

"What is it?" Tyreta asked, not even expecting a straight answer.

Yeki wiped some of the soil away to reveal a copper bowl. "It will help you," she said. "And you will not be same after. Last chance."

Last chance for what? To run? To live out her days with the Lokai? No, she was out of chances now.

"Let's get on with this," she replied.

Yeki grinned, revealing her gums and the scant teeth protruding from them. "I know you would say that."

Tyreta could only wait and watch, those far-distant clouds rolling ever closer, as Amanisa and Gelila climbed the stone and began to rip away the vines clinging to its surface. Other warriors of the Lokai brought kindling, and they built a small pyre in a wide indentation hewn into the stone as the sky prematurely darkened. When dusk finally drew in and the smell of the approaching storm freshened the air, they lit a fire that began to rage at the centre of the fallen stone.

The warriors surrounded the ancient shrine, standing in vigil as Amanisa and Gelila helped Tyreta out of her clothes. She should have felt awkward, no one had undressed her since she was a child, but there was a ritual aspect to this whole thing that she forced herself to accept.

When she eventually stood naked amid the clearing, there was no embarrassment to it. She felt no humiliation under the eyes of the kesh, just an odd sense of approval.

Yeki stood atop the fallen stone, the light of the flames illuminating her in a bright flickering glow. When she beckoned Tyreta forward, there was no doubt, no apprehension. She climbed up and stood opposite the old woman, feeling the furnace heat of the fire against her flesh. As Yeki placed the copper bowl over the flames there was a flash in the distance, a rumble of thunder only seconds in its wake.

The old woman held out her hand. "Kiatta."

Tyreta placed a hand to the nightstone still hanging about her neck. It was the last gift her mother had given her before she came to this place. The only keepsake of her father's she would ever own. As she gripped that stone in her fist, she suddenly felt light-headed.

Everything was about to change, and she clung to the nightstone as though clinging to her old life.

Yeki's solemn expression softened. She lifted her hand gently, and before Tyreta realised what she was doing she had taken the pendant from around her neck and placed it in the old woman's palm.

A strong sense of relief overwhelmed her as she watched Yeki pull the chain from the stone and cast it aside before laying a hand on Tyreta's shoulder. The old woman gestured to her to kneel in front of the fire and held the nightstone up to the ominous sky, staring through it with one eye.

Another flash of light in her periphery, another rumble, much closer than the first. Yeki cast the stone into the bowl. The flames of the fire sparked before immediately receding. Yeki held out the bowl, and Tyreta could see the black stone turn pale, glowing yellow, then white. Still she felt no fear, still she did not move as Yeki raised a curved dagger, kneeling before the bowl and striking down.

The knife pierced the heart of the nightstone.

Tyreta was struck by blinding light. The jungle was suddenly brought to life. She could sense the activity around her in all its crawling, scurrying, stalking, billowing forms. She could hear a rodent nearby, the bird of prey that watched it from above, the wind that blew its feathers. She saw the sway of trees on the breeze, heard the sap as it moved within their boughs, felt snakes slither among the branches.

And within and around and through all this, she could see the web. The strands of its power connecting all things. It was in everything, binding, connecting, until it reached its foundation...the nightstone.

Tyreta should have been awed, should have been terrified, but all she felt was at peace with that unimaginable source of power. She felt a part of it.

Yeki lifted the bowl from atop the fire. The searing heat should have turned her hand to a charred ember, but she ignored any pain, raising the curved blade again and stabbing down. The stone shattered, sending dark wispy clouds into the air. Again the old woman struck, again and again, pulverising the stone, scratching the knife along the base of the bowl, scraping patterns with its dust.

A droplet of rain struck Tyreta's face as Yeki lifted the bowl up to the dark clouds. The patter of raindrops started as a slow, lulling tune, growing in tempo, its drumbeat quickening. As the shower turned to a torrent, drenching Tyreta where she knelt, Gelila and Amanisa stepped up beside her, grasping her arms, raising her.

Yeki was chanting, a lament that filled Tyreta's head, clouding her senses. Still she could see the strands of the web all around her, but its essence was dulled. All she could do was give herself to this—to the rain, to the ritual.

The knife scratched her arm, making a track mark from shoulder to wrist, twisting its way along her flesh. She looked down to see Yeki through the rain, curved dagger in hand, caught up in the ritual, lips moving feverishly as the deluge beat down. Tyreta's flesh was being stained black, the essence of the nightstone marking her forever, but there was no pain. All she felt was the reverie, the ecstasy of being at one with the web. With every stroke of the blade it filled her. Every new mark on her skin uniting her more closely with the power of the stone, now mashed to pulp in that bowl.

Her head lolled to one side and she saw the jungle, spattered with rain, drenched with life from the clouds. Eyes watched from the foliage, the fauna as enrapt at this ceremony as she was. With every drop of her blood washed away by the rain she felt more imbued, alive, fulfilled.

But with that new strength, there was an ebbing... a loss.

She heard a whisper. Closing her eyes, she focused, still feeling the knife against her flesh...

The words were muted, but someone was calling for her in the distance.

A strand of the web led off into the darkness beyond her vision, and Tyreta followed. She was swept up in it, following strand after concentric strand, winding, circling, falling and rising on the winds.

Through the dark she caught sight of a kneeling figure... her brother, Fulren. He tinkered with something, fingers moving deftly though his eyes searched blindly for focus.

Then in an instant he was gone.

A scream of anguish. Her mother, racked by grief, bellowing her rage and hurt, her insides twisting and breaking.

Then she too was gone.

The strands of the web began to break. No longer was Tyreta borne on the winds. Now she was falling, the void sweeping her along. Lost. Alone.

He stood before her, tall and ugly. Not as she remembered him. This beast stared down. One eye she recognised, a look of longing in it. Sadness. Loss.

The other shone red, baleful, hunting, searching, its core glowing with absolute evil. An evil that would ultimately consume her...

Tyreta opened her eyes, sucking in a wheezing breath and sitting up sharply.

The dawn light cast the jungle in a warm glow, raindrops still falling from the trees, playing a tune in the muddy puddles that surrounded her. From atop the ancient shrine she could see the sky was clear; there was no sign of the storm that had soaked the land.

She lifted an arm to see the wounds of her ordeal, but all that remained were intricate markings, black against her flesh, a labyrinthine web of patterns already fading in the light. Scars that looked long healed.

The warriors of the Lokai were gone.

Tyreta rose to her feet, feeling anxious at their loss, but there was no trace of them, not even a footprint in the sodden ground. She would have called out, but she knew that was pointless. They were gone. This last task was hers alone. If they had intended to offer her any more help than the ritual, they would have been here waiting for her.

When she jumped down from the standing stone, her feet landed deftly, perfectly balanced on the uneven ground. Clenching a fist, she felt stronger, invigorated. Had it not felt so natural, the change in her body might have panicked her. Instead it brought a smile to her face.

In a pile at the base of the stone the Lokai had left clothes, an outfit crafted from cloth and animal skins. Atop them were a bow, a quiver of arrows, a knife. Leaning against the fallen stone was a spear.

More gifts from the Lokai. She would have to thank them if she ever saw them again. As she dressed in clothes that days ago she would have scoffed at, Tyreta began to realise she was a webwainer no more. That power had been replaced by something different. Something stronger. If she reached out with her ability, she could not just sense the latent energy of the pyrestone beneath the ground. Now she could feel the energy from the land itself, its flowers, its trees, its insects and birds.

A growl from the trees nearby put her every sense on edge. The spear was in her hand instinctually, feeling so natural in her grip.

She sensed it through the brush before she saw that feline head appear, those eyes she remembered from days ago. The panther snarled at her, lips curling as it watched warily, only now Tyreta was not afraid. She could see its apprehension. Feel its fear as it regarded her from across the clearing.

She ran toward it at a sprint, bounding across the open ground, covering the distance in no time, as the panther disappeared in a flurry of grass and leaves. By the time she burst through the tree line in pursuit of the animal it had already disappeared from sight, but its scent was still on the air—the stink of fear.

Tyreta raced through the brush, feet sure on the boggy ground, jumping lithely over the tree roots snaking across her path. The thrill of the chase made her tingle with excitement, the need to corner her prey the only thing that mattered.

The panther led her on a trail uphill, and she pushed herself, unable to reach the limit of her endurance, covering the ground as though she were being swept along by an unseen hand, lips curling back from her teeth in a grin of pure delight.

Up they ran, predator and prey, where days before those roles had been reversed. On they went, up they climbed, until Tyreta darted from the trees onto a wide cliff edge. Beyond was a sea of jungle spreading toward the ocean in the distance. At the edge of the sheer drop was the panther, pacing warily, nowhere left to run.

Tyreta came to a stop, breathing in the new dawn air. She had never felt more alive, her emotions stirred by the ecstasy of the hunt.

The panther's ears were drawn back. Its fight-or-flight instincts heightened, and there was nowhere left to fly.

Tyreta felt the weight of the spear in her hand, the heft, the balance. It would take but a single throw...

She raised the spear high and skewered it into the earth.

The panther snarled as it scratched the air with its paw. Tyreta held out a hand, but still the beast hissed, glancing back to the ledge and the fatal drop beyond.

Slowly she lowered herself to one knee, and the panther regarded her with curiosity. Perhaps this was not the end it had expected.

"Your move," Tyreta whispered.

In that moment she could once again feel the land, its energy. A hawk screeched a mile above, and she heard its cry on the wind. A butterfly burst from the brush, wings sending waves of vibration she could feel brush her cheek.

The panther padded toward her to sit no more than a foot away before lowering its head. Tyreta reached out, touching the fur, ruffling its ears before it looked up and nuzzled her chin.

"Good choice."

Slowly she stood as the panther rolled onto its back in the morning heat. Looking out across the jungle, she knew the time for making friends was over. Now she had to save a city.

LANCELIN

The feasting hall was in chaos. He sat amid the maelstrom as warriors of the Huntan bellowed their revelry to the redwood timbers, singing ancient war cants as they drank their ale. So much ale.

A full tankard sat in front of Lancelin, but so far he'd managed to avoid drinking. His tolerance for alcohol had never been the best, and he needed his wits about him now more than ever. Though he and Fulren had been accepted into this tribe of barbarians, it was still no guarantee of safety—there had already been two vicious brawls between warriors who had been laughing like brothers moments earlier. One of them had been carried out of the hall a bloody mess, and Lancelin had no way of telling if he was dead or alive. No one else seemed to give a damn.

"Not thirsty, lad?" Saranor growled, slapping a meaty hand on Fulren's shoulder.

The boy sat between them, given pride of place at Saranor's table—a tradition to do with blind men being lucky or some nonsense. Clearly it had been an invention of someone who could see, there was nothing lucky about being blind.

To Lancelin's right was an old warrior Saranor had introduced as Indoneth the Flayer. Thankfully he didn't look in a fit state to skin anyone as he sat in a drunken stupor, glazed eyes staring across the feast hall.

The chieftain placed a tankard in Fulren's hand. To his credit, the boy feigned a smile, blind eyes flitting vainly as he raised the tankard in thanks before glugging down as much as he could.

"That's the spirit," Saranor barked.

The hulking blue-eyed warrior turned expectantly to Lancelin, who quickly took up his own tankard, gulping as much as he could. It tasted sour on the way down, and he almost gagged, managing to hold it in without vomiting. It was doubtful it would taste any better on the way back up.

A cheer resounded from the far side of the hall as the doors opened and a gust of snowy air blew in. Saranor climbed atop the thick wooden table, screaming his approval as a blackened lump of spitted meat was carried toward them. It was secured on a metal prop at the centre of the hall as a burly woman with a shaved head glared up at Saranor.

"Henakor," he roared. "In the name of Obek the Father... carve!"

Lancelin watched as Henakor the Butcher began to slice great hunks of lizard onto a platter with a wicked-looking blade. She went at the carcass with relish, tongue lolling hungrily as slabs of bloody meat were distributed through the hall.

Sallow-eyed vassals carried the food and drink, but Lancelin had little pity to spare them as he watched the brutal merriment all around him, wondering how in the Five Lairs he was going to get them out of this.

"Here, eastlanders," Saranor said, placing wooden trenchers of meat in front of them both with surprising reverence. "Guests of honour eat first."

Lancelin nodded his appreciation, in no mood to refuse. The thought of tucking into lizard meat would have turned his stomach were it not so empty, but Fulren did not even balk at the plate before him, tearing off a piece with his teeth and chewing with gusto. As Lancelin tore off a bite he was surprised at how tender it was. He'd certainly eaten much worse while serving on the edge of the Drift.

"Tasty, eh?" Saranor said. "Dark meat is good. But tomorrow is the Night of the Blooded Star. Then we will feast on white meat."

"On what?" Fulren asked.

Saranor clapped a hand on his shoulder. "The witch. What better way to appease the gods than to dine on the flesh of their enemies, blind man?"

Fulren had stopped eating, and Lancelin felt his appetite wane despite his nagging hunger. Before either of them could begin to consider Saranor's words, the huge warrior rose to his feet and climbed back on the table.

"Hear me," he shouted. "I see you gorging yourselves, you greedy bastards." A cheer in reply. "Don't forget to be grateful for the bounty. Tomorrow we also eat for the gods. Tomorrow we celebrate the rite of the Blooded Star, and we have here a gift." He gestured to Fulren, who received an appreciative cheer of his own. "The blind man is a good omen. It was he who brought us the witch of the south. Our sacrifice will be in his honour, and we will feast on that bitch till we are glutted. I, Saranor the Bleeder, warchief of the Skull Kin, decree it so."

Another cheer, this one turning raucous as the horde began to bang on their tables, chanting for the blind man, smashing their tankards together as they chewed meat and quaffed more ale.

Saranor climbed down from the table, slapping a hand on Lancelin's and Fulren's backs.

"You shall both stay here, as my guests. There is a place for you at my table for as long as you wish it."

Lancelin glanced around the room. The prospect of spending more time here than was needed was not an attractive one. To drive the thought home, another fight spontaneously broke out in the far corner.

"We appreciate the offer, Saranor," he said. "But we must return to Torwyn as soon as we are able."

The warchief shrugged. "Very well, my friend. After we have sacrificed the witch to the Blooded Star, I will have my best guide lead you to the edge of the Drift. From there you will have to find your own way."

"You've already done more than enough," Lancelin said, rising to his feet. "But your help is much appreciated. You have the thanks of the emperor of Torwyn."

Saranor laughed, then fixed Lancelin with those mad blue eyes. "I need no thanks from emperors. But you . . . are welcome."

Lancelin bowed, for what it was worth. "Now we must rest. The boy has been through much."

"Of course," Saranor said, beckoning one of the vassals closer. "You will be given shelter for the night. A dwelling fit for kings."

Lancelin grabbed Fulren and pulled him to his feet. The boy swayed slightly, either from fatigue or from too much Huntan ale. Together they followed the vassal out into the night and across the huge compound. The vassal's torch blew frantically in the wind, but the blizzard had mostly passed, and now only scant snowflakes floated down from the night sky. Despite the hour, there was still light dancing above the northern peaks, and Lancelin caught sight of war eagles wheeling about the summits of the nearby mountaintops.

As they slogged through the foot-deep snow he heard the snarling and barking of dogs in the distance. Peering through the dark, Lancelin saw warriors taunting someone in a cage within the shadow of the settlement's palisade. It was easy to guess who was unlucky enough to be inside.

The vassal stopped at a rickety-looking hut, unlatching the door and offering the torch. As he slogged away miserably, Lancelin led Fulren inside. A fire was glowing in the hearth, but the rest of the place looked as if it had been recently ransacked by a savage burglar. Fit for kings indeed; it was barely fit for rats.

No sooner had Lancelin closed the door than Fulren grabbed his coat.

"We cannot leave her here," he said. "We have to get Wenis out. They're going to bloody eat her."

Lancelin pulled Fulren's hand free and made him sit in a nearby chair.

"Would she offer you the same mercy?" he said. "We have to think of ourselves. I doubt that witch—"

"You don't know her," Fulren snapped. "She's no witch."

"I don't care what she is. She's none of my concern. I was sent here to bring you home, and that's what I'm going to do."

Fulren rose from his chair, gripping the back of it to steady himself. "I'll go nowhere with you until I know she's safe."

"You're going to get us both killed," Lancelin said.

"Then leave if you want. Run back to Torwyn. But I'm going nowhere without Wenis."

Running back to Torwyn was the most sensible option, but Lancelin knew Rosomon would never forgive him if he turned up at the Anvil alone. This boy was as stubborn as his mother, and he was turning out to be just as much of a pain in the arse.

"All right," he replied. "I'll do what I can. But I hope she's worth it."

He turned to the door and Fulren shuffled after him.

"You need to stay here," Lancelin demanded. "This will be hard enough as it is without having to keep you out of trouble too."

"If we both—"

"I said no. I'm not going to argue with you on this, boy. Learn to pick your battles, and know when you've lost."

Fulren sank back into the chair. "I'm no boy."

He'd never looked more like one.

When Lancelin opened the door to the shack, the wind had picked up outside. A good thing. Perhaps his luck was changing, but best not rely on that yet. Better to rely on his skills, not that they'd do him much good against an entire tribe of Huntan barbarians.

In the distance he could hear the sound of singing still resounding from the feast hall. There was a ringing of steel and a crash of wood amid the ruckus. The longer they fought among themselves the better.

He headed toward the cage, hugging close to the shadows of the tightly packed shacks. The wind whipped up, shaking the rafters and sending snow billowing. When he heard deep voices approaching, Lancelin flattened himself against a barn.

Two warriors walked by, oblivious to him hunkering in the dark as they made their way toward the feast hall. He watched them, hand on the hilt of his sword until they disappeared into the night.

When the way was clear, he stole across the open space. The cage was just beyond a long, flat outhouse, and he almost cursed the crunch of snow underfoot as he rushed to close the gap. No sooner was he in the shadow of the building than he sensed something in his periphery. Leaping aside, he was suddenly assailed by the deafening bark of a huge hound.

He landed on his arse in the snow, sword half out of the sheath, but the muscular beast stopped short of mauling him, its neck tethered by a thick chain. It strained against the studded iron collar at its neck, teeth gnashing, ears pinned back to its wide head.

Lancelin scrambled to his feet, glancing about in panic, expecting one of the huge, bearded warriors to heed the noise. All he heard was the distant sound of revelry from across the settlement.

He backed away as the dog continued to bark its frustration, making his way past the outhouse and through the mess of shacks until he reached the palisade. In its shadow sat a row of iron cages.

The first two were empty, but in the third he could see a figure hunched in the shadows. She clutched her knees tight to her chest, shivering in the dark and the cold. Before he could call to her, Wenis looked up, her doleful eyes narrowing.

"Come to gloat?" she managed to say through chattering teeth.

He almost felt pity for her. Hunkered there in the dirt, she looked pathetic. It would have taken a heart colder than his to not feel at least some sympathy.

"I don't know what spell you've cast on Fulren, but he's adamant we can't leave you here."

Her eyes narrowed further. "Is this some kind of trick?"

"No trick. But you have to vow, if I let you out of here, you'll release Fulren from this enchantment you've cast over him."

She rose gingerly, head dipped below the top of the cage as she moved closer.

"I have cast no spell on Fulren. I swear it by all the gods."

"I don't give a damn about your gods. Just make the vow and let's get out of here."

She regarded him with a wry look. "What's your name?"

He was reluctant to tell her. Knowing his name might give her some kind of dark power over him. Who knew what curses this witch might be able to cast with the knowledge of a man's name?

With time to think on it, maybe he wouldn't have told her, but time was not a luxury he had.

"I am Lancelin Jagdor. Now make the vow."

Some people hid their subterfuge behind a veil of sincerity. From the look on this woman's face, she didn't care a shit whether Lancelin thought her genuine or not.

"Very well, Lancelin Jagdor. I vow on all the gods of Nyrakkis to release Fulren from my spell."

The words seemed to amuse her. For a moment he thought it might be better for them both if he just left her in the cage and took his chances dragging Fulren out of here against his will. Instead he drew his sword. One precise stroke and the padlock to the cage fell away with a dull ringing of metal.

"Stay close," he ordered as he led her back across the compound.

He took a different route back, avoiding the attentions of the hound. Still the sounds of singing drifted across the rooftops. Lancelin caught sight of someone patrolling the palisade in the distance, but the guard seemed more focused on what lay over the wall than on what was sneaking about within. As they moved through the snow, he spied two warriors guarding the main gate, hunkered within their bear skins as they shared a tankard of ale.

By the time he and Wenis entered the tiny shack, Fulren was waiting by the embers of the fire. His eyes darted about in a panic as he heard them. Wenis approached him, taking him by the arms.

"It seems I owe you my life, Prince of Torwyn," she said.

"Are you hurt?" Fulren asked.

"I will survive. Though my pride has taken something of a beating."

"When you've both finished," Lancelin said. "We have to get out of here before they check those cages."

"How?" Wenis asked. "The gate is guarded. The wall too high to climb."

With Fulren blind, Lancelin had to come up with another way.

"You're both going to walk right out of the front gate, once I've distracted the guards."

"No," said Fulren. "We need to stick together."

Lancelin was struck by Fulren's concern for him, but he pushed the sudden emotion back down into the pit of his stomach.

"There's no way we can all go together. Wenis will lead you out through the gate. I'll catch up with you after."

"Agreed," Wenis said quickly.

Her eyes locked on Lancelin. That wry look was gone now, replaced by something else. Respect perhaps?

Fulren had nothing else to say. He knew he was beaten, knew he was helpless without someone to get him out of here. Maybe he had taken Lancelin's advice about picking his battles. Not so stubborn after all.

"You'll know what to do. Once the guards are clear of the gate, head north toward the mountains. When you hit the high ground, wait for me there. If I don't arrive by sunrise, or if you see anyone else, move east and don't stop till you're across the Drift."

It was so easy to say the words, but they all knew crossing the Drift would be the most dangerous part of all this. Nevertheless, both Fulren and Wenis murmured their agreement.

Lancelin took the torch that still burned on the wall and some kindling from beside the fire and stole out into the night.

The thatched roofs were too wet from the snowfall to catch alight, but there were plenty of stores of wood at the backs of the dwellings. He found one at the centre of the settlement that looked as good as any. It took only a little encouragement, some teasing from the brittle kindling and a flame from the torch, before the woodpile was smouldering.

Lancelin stole away from the scene as smoke began to billow. As he passed an open-sided barn full of straw he tossed the torch inside and made his way back toward the gate. The singing from the feast hall had grown louder, angrier, as though the celebrations had reached some kind of frenzied peak. He could only imagine how that fury would intensify when they discovered what he'd done.

Before he was halfway to the gate, he heard a cry of warning. Over the rooftops flames licked at the night sky as the fire he had started blazed. A bell rang. Dogs barked in a furious chorus. All at once the sound of singing stopped, and angry voices called out into the frigid air.

From the shadow of a hut, Lancelin saw the guards from the gate rushing past, bellowing warnings at anyone in earshot. No sooner had they trudged by than he broke from the cover of darkness and sprinted toward the gate.

Up ahead, he saw the gate stood open, Wenis and Fulren already gone through. The realisation that his plan had worked filled him with a sudden thrill, but he fought it back. He had to stay focused, had to keep a clear head until they were miles from here.

There was twenty feet of open ground to cover, and he focused on the gate, hoping he wouldn't be spotted in the confusion. The wooden bar that held the gate shut lay discarded in the snow. He was almost there.

Lancelin ducked on instinct as an axe slammed into the gate just in front of him, barring his escape. He lurched back as a huge warrior wrenched the weapon free, sending splinters flying, before taking another swing. It was a deadly blow, but easy enough to duck, and Lancelin lurched for the gap in the gate, squeezing through as the warrior cursed in his wake.

Fresh tracks in the snow ran from the compound and into the darkness beyond. All Lancelin could do was concentrate on them as he waded through the drift. A glance back and he saw the warrior heaving the door wider so he could shift his bulk through. He roared an incoherent curse, blue eyes shining in the dark.

By a gibbous moon Lancelin managed to follow the tracks, more than aware he was being pursued, more than aware his trail would be an easy one to follow. He should have stopped, should have slain his pursuer, but better to lose him in the night than kill him and give Saranor more reason to hunt them all down.

The ground steadily rose underfoot, the mountains looming ahead. He eventually managed to find purchase, feeling rocky ground replace thick snow. More voices called out behind him, the distant barking of dogs giving him the impetus to carry on, despite his lungs almost bursting from the effort.

Craggy rocks rose all around, and he came to a staggering stop, hands on knees, sucking in the chill air.

Silence as he glared back into the blackness of night.

The Huntan warrior loomed from the dark.

Lancelin had time to wrench his sword free of its sheath before their weapons crashed together. He almost buckled under the warrior's immense strength but managed to hold that axe at bay, inches from his face.

The barbarian roared, filed teeth shining in the moonlight. He wrenched his axe free, raising it again, and Lancelin thrust forward, throwing himself into the strike. His blade pierced the warrior's abdomen, punching through leather and flesh and organs. There was enough time to see his foe's eyes go wide before he pitched forward.

Lancelin couldn't pull his weapon free in time, his foot slipping on the slick ground as the warrior collapsed on top of him. It was like being buried beneath the corpse of a bear, and he floundered in panic, struggling to crawl from beneath the hulking body. As he did so, another huge figure came striding from the dark.

This one was bigger than the first, beard black, eyes shining blue in the light of the moon. Lancelin could only watch as he raised a massive hammer, the steel of its head winking in the starlight.

Someone jumped from the rocks above, landing on the warrior's shoulders. They were tiny by comparison, an imp fighting a giant, but what they lacked in size they made up for in speed. Two tattooed hands clamped down against the giant's jaw, a sickly green light emanating from those palms. Lancelin heard a hiss, suddenly drowned out by the high-pitched screech of the warrior as his face burned with corrosive sorcery.

He dropped the hammer, staggering back, grasping hold of his attacker, but she would not relent. As the warrior's face began to smoke, his flesh blacken, he dropped to his knees and the life ebbed out of him. His eyes stared into the night, turning from blue to grey to black before eventually he pitched forward on the rocks.

Wenis rolled clear of the corpse, her hands still smoking from the infernal power she had summoned, as Lancelin crawled from beneath the barbarian's corpse.

"It seems we are even, Lancelin Jagdor," she said with a self-satisfied grin.

Farther up the path, Lancelin spied Fulren waiting in the shadows.

Back toward the settlement he heard the howling of dogs, and the bellowing voice of Saranor the Bleeder carried on the wind.

"Let's not tally up what we owe just yet," said Lancelin, planting a foot on the dead warrior and wrenching his sword free of his guts. "This is a long way from over."

ROSOMON

The key to her chamber door sat on the dresser. Rosomon kept glancing toward it, trying to remind herself she was safe now. But even with the door locked and members of the Talon guarding it, she knew she was not safe here.

Blood still stained the floor, despite the ministrations of the palace maids. The rugs, sheets and curtains had all been replaced, the chamber scrubbed to a mirror sheen, but still she could see the discolouration on the floorboards. Perhaps she should have requisitioned another chamber somewhere else in the palace. Perhaps she should have fled this place altogether and returned to her stronghold in Wyke. But that would have been too easy. Rosomon had endured too much to run now. She would see this through till the end.

"A little powder will hide the bruising, mistress," Athelys said.

The girl had been fussing all morning—doing her best to tidy the already pristine chamber, desperate to be useful. It was admirable but also annoying.

"Perhaps just a little around the eye?" Athelys approached with her brush.

Rosomon pushed her away. "By the Wyrms, girl, stop threatening me with that thing. Can you not sit in silence for more than a minute?"

Athelys placed the powder and brush back on the dresser. "I'm sorry, mistress."

She was almost in tears. Most likely afraid she would share Rosomon's fate should assassins make another attempt on her life. The wood of the dresser was still cracked where a head had been smashed against it. Poor Ailin had become embroiled in this, had bravely tried to tell her...some secret. Tried to tell her who was behind this. It had cost him his life.

"Just take a seat," Rosomon said softly. "Read a book or something."

Athelys did as she was told. She was poor company, but she was the only person Rosomon could trust not to try to kill her.

There was no sign of Olstrum. She had dispatched scouts to find him, but he had disappeared. Fulren's words came back to her in a rush—*You can trust no one, Mother.* Was Olstrum in on this too? He was, after all, the one who'd sent her to this chamber. The one who'd made Ailin wait for her. Was he part of the conspiracy? Had the consul sent Ailin to be killed at Starn's hand, and Rosomon after him?

Her eyes drifted back to the stain on the floor. All that remained of Starn. For years he had lived within her household. One of her husband's most trusted retainers, a man who had taught martial prowess to her children, whose job it had been to protect her.

She truly could trust no one.

A firm knock at her door. Athelys drew a sharp breath, grasping at her skirts with nervous fingers. Rosomon rose from the edge of the bed and approached the door.

"Who is it?" she asked, trying her best to not sound afraid. Most likely failing.

"It is Prince Lorens, my lady," replied one of her guards. "He has asked to see you."

Rosomon grasped the key from the dresser and unlocked the door, opening it slightly. Beyond she could see Lorens in the hallway, a look of concern marring his handsome brow.

She opened the door. "Come in, Lorens."

He stepped past the guard and into the room. Rosomon quickly locked it after him.

"I have only just heard," he said. "I was dealing with business on the other side of the city. How are you?" He winced as he took in the full extent of the bruising to her face.

"I am as well as can be expected, Lorens. Thank you for coming to see me."

"But your face, Aunt. It must have been a horrific thing for you to suffer."

Rosomon thought back to years before, when her own husband had beaten her so badly she could barely speak. By comparison, this was easy to endure.

"I'll live," she replied, placing a calming hand on his arm.

"Why would he do this? Starn was a swordwright. A trusted servant."

"You have to listen to me, Lorens. There is something happening. Something dire and poisonous within the Anvil. If I am to stop it, I will need your help."

"Anything," Lorens said. That one simple word brought a smile to her face. It seemed she had at least one ally left in the Anvil. And a powerful one at that. "Please, tell me what this is about. I will do all I can."

"It all has something to do with the Draconate Ministry. The attack on me, the assassination of the Maladoran emissary, Fulren's exile. It all leads back to Sanctan Egelrath."

Lorens furrowed his brow, desperately trying to take it all in. "But how? He is the Archlegate of the Ministry. He is your damned nephew, as I am."

"I struggled to believe it myself at first. I have already uncovered financial irregularities involving the Ministry. Rearden Corwen is most likely involved too. Who knows how many others? I don't know what his ultimate aim is, but your father needs to be warned. He must be kept safe."

"But how can we know for sure Sanctan is part of this?"

Rage built up in her, frustration that the Archlegate had sidestepped her at every turn. He would evade her no longer.

"He must be arrested," she said. "Today."

Lorens looked stunned at the suggestion. His hand strayed to the ruby pendant at his neck, as though seeking guidance from Undometh himself.

"Arrest the Archlegate?" he breathed.

"He is not worthy of the title, Lorens. He plots against the empire, and if we wait, it could be too late. You must put him in a cell, at least until we can get to the bottom of this."

The madness of it struck her all at once, but Rosomon knew it was the only way. They could delay no longer.

Lorens nodded, as though the idea was not such a mad one after all. "Very well, Aunt Rosomon. If that is what you believe, then I will do it."

"You will need help. Men you can trust."

Lorens nodded. "I will take a contingent of Titanguard. Sanctan's Drakes will not stand against us. I could also enlist the Armigers."

"No," said Rosomon. "Best they are left out of this for now. There's no telling where their loyalties lie. This must be done with discretion."

"I understand."

Rosomon could only hope he did. Their lives might well depend on it.

"I must see your father. I have to warn him of what is happening. To make him listen. He has to understand what is at stake and rally himself from his grief."

"He has taken to praying in the chapel, north of the palace garden. You'll most likely find him there."

She grabbed Lorens by the hand. "Then go. Gather your men. I will speak to Sullivar and meet you at the Mount."

"Be careful, Aunt Rosomon," Lorens said.

She could see the fear in him, but the bravery too. It reminded her of Fulren before he had been condemned to that infernal airship and sent away in chains. The words caught in her throat, and all she could do was nod her reply.

As she unlocked her chamber and watched Lorens leave, she wanted to call after him, to tell him he had to be careful too, but it was all she could do to stifle a sob.

"Wait here," she said to Athelys. "Don't open this door for anyone but me."

The girl nodded obediently. She had heard every word and must be terrified. Rosomon would have spared her all of this, but there was no time now. Athelys would have to fend for herself as best she could. With any luck, whatever Sanctan had planned would be stopped without a drop of blood being shed. A final glance at that dull stain on the floor and Rosomon was reminded it was already too late for that.

The guards of the Talon followed her through the guest quarters. Their company would have made her feel safe, but then Starn had proved the folly of being so complacent. The palace servants were busying themselves with preparations for the coming festival as she made her way past—cleaning, polishing, hanging sigils of the Guilds and Armigers and Ministry. On seeing her, many bowed their heads, and others looked shocked, raising hands to mouths when they saw the livid bruises on the face of such a powerful woman.

Rosomon ignored them all.

The Titanguard grew more numerous the closer she got to the chapel. By the time she reached the archway that led to the garden she was all but surrounded by the hulking, armoured warriors, their bronze plates shining, giving them the look of automatons with little trace of humanity. None of them made a move to stop her until she reached the edge of the ornamental garden.

A bronze-armoured behemoth barred her way, red plume on his helm denoting his seniority as imperator of the guard.

"Apologies, my lady, but your men will have to remain outside." The voice resonated from within his helmet, giving him an inhuman quality, but then that was the point.

Rosomon was in no mood to argue, signalling for the Talon to wait outside before she made her way through the archway.

Slumped on a reclining chair in one corner of the garden was Sullivar. His beard was an unkempt bush, shirt hanging limp from his shoulders, an embroidered blanket across his knees. Behind the scent of fresh blooms, Rosomon could smell the unmistakable musk of poppy essence hanging heavy in the air.

Before she could approach her brother, Oriel stepped from beneath an awning. Her sister-in-law looked exhausted, dark shadows beneath glassy eyes, her former immaculate appearance little more than a memory.

"Rosomon," she said. "We weren't expecting you."

Of that there was little doubt. And not so much as a word about the attack she had suffered the day before.

"I have to speak with my brother," Rosomon replied.

Oriel shook her head. "He is not to be disturbed. The emperor is still unwell."

Sullivar barely looked up from his stupor. "Unwell? He is inebriated."

"He is grieving, Rosomon," Oriel insisted. "He cannot be troubled."

Rosomon ignored her, approaching Sullivar and kneeling before his chair. Her brother's head lolled to one side, eyes barely focusing.

"Who has ordered this? Which apothecary decided dosing him with essence of poppy was the best remedy?"

"It wasn't the apothecaries..." Oriel's voice withered to nothing.

"Then who?"

Rosomon turned to see the last face she had expected.

"I'm afraid that was me, Aunt Rosomon."

Sanctan Egelrath stood at the entrance to the garden. At his side was the woman she had met in the Guildhall, Keara. With her were three other members of the Hallowhill Guild, the spider emblem on their purple tunics marking them all as webwainers.

"What are you doing here?" Rosomon asked, suddenly feeling exposed despite the heavy presence of the Titanguard.

Sanctan smiled that charming smile, the one that made it so easy to like him.

"I heard you were looking for me. I thought I'd save you the trouble of searching."

Rosomon fought back the panic. There should be no threat, it was only Sanctan and four webwainers. What trouble could they cause without a troop of stormhulks? But so far Sanctan had been a step ahead of her at every turn.

"I also heard about the attack in your chamber," Sanctan said, charming smile switching instantly to a look of concern. "I hope you're all right. If something happened to you, I would never forgive myself."

She'd had enough of his games. Enough dancing about one another. It was time for this to be over one way or the other. "What have you done, Sanctan?"

He glanced toward Sullivar. "I saw a man in pain. I had the legates of Saphenodon relieve his burden. Is it not the purpose of the Ministry to offer solace where there is grief?"

"I don't mean what you've done to Sullivar. I mean what you did to my son. What you're planning to do with the empire. I know something is going on, Sanctan, and I will not stop until I find out what it is. I will expose you, whether we are kin or not."

Sanctan sighed, bowing his head, like a child caught stealing biscuits from the kitchens. "Aunt Rosomon. You have no idea the lengths I've gone to in order to keep you out of this. To keep you safe." He looked up, all pretence of charm sloughed away. "If we weren't blood, you'd be dead by now."

"What are you talking about?"

Sanctan moved toward one of the rosebushes, teasing a bright red flower with his fingers. "Starn Rivers was one of my faithful, if a little too zealous for his own good. But he understood, as I do, that it's time for things to change." He stared at her, and she had never seen him look so serious. "This empire has become profligate. Wasteful. Neglectful. It has forgotten the tenets on which it was built. Has cast down its idols in favour of profit. And I say, no more."

"Sanctan, are you mad? You speak treason. And in front of your emperor."

He almost laughed, stopping short as he regarded Sullivar with a look of disdain. "And what an emperor we have. Slovenly. Useless. Incompetent. He would have allied us with a nation dead set on our destruction, just to see his coffers swell. No, Aunt Rosomon, I do not speak treason. I speak prophecy. The new order has been tried, and it has failed. Now is the time for the old order to reclaim its rightful place."

Rosomon turned to see Sullivar still sitting in his chair. Beside him was Oriel, grasping her husband protectively.

"Sullivar." Nothing, just a hazy look about his eyes. "By the Five Lairs, Sullivar, get up and command your men to arrest this traitor." Still he sat in his stupor, as though Sanctan had been right about him all along.

The Titanguard were still standing immobile, not even the red-plumed imperator making a move.

"You've heard what this damned priest has said," Rosomon shouted at them. "He speaks treason. He threatens your emperor. Arrest him."

With a hiss of pneumatics, the imperator stepped forward. Likewise, his men came to life, pyrestone-powered armour buzzing with energy, glaives braced to attack.

As they approached him, Sanctan sighed. "I was hoping to avoid any unpleasantness."

He stepped into the centre of the garden as the Titanguard bore down on him, one clanking step after another. Before they were within ten feet, Keara Hallowhill stepped forward. The three other webwainers had spread out, watching the proceedings from the periphery.

Rosomon felt the air grow heavy, a calm before the storm. Before any of the Titanguard could take another step toward Sanctan, there was a tinny explosion. One of the bronze-armoured giants fell to his knees with a grunt, smoke billowing from within the backplate of his armour. Another cried out in pain as the pyrestones powering his mechanical suit burst into shards. Blood ran down his breastplate as he fell.

As the webwainers unleashed their power, overriding the pyrestones in the Titanguards' armour, Rosomon saw her only defenders begin to fall. Minute explosions went off within their plating. Joints burst apart, oil mixing with blood as the warriors fell. Their towering might was laid low in an instant, and the air filled with the stink of burning pyrestones and the cries of men in pain.

Rosomon took a step toward the archway. She was about to summon the guards of the Talon, but before she could take another step, she heard a dull ringing of steel from beyond the garden.

The violence was brief, the ensuing quiet stretching out as she realised her men were not coming. As though to drive the fact home, a huge Knight of the Draconate made his way through the archway, blade in hand, his white surcoat stained red. He wore no helmet, and as Rosomon gazed at his face, she suddenly felt sick to her stomach. Across the warrior's mouth and chin was a faded black welt. Despite the beard he had vainly tried to grow to mask the scarring, it was still a discernible handprint.

More Drakes entered the garden behind him as the last of the Titanguard collapsed to the grass with a whine of hydraulics. Rosomon saw there was no one else to help her. Oriel knelt beside Sullivar, gripping him tightly as he sat in a torpor.

The huge, scarred knight seized Rosomon's arm in an iron grasp, and Sanctan gazed at her. There was no triumph in that look, only sorrow.

"I would have avoided this if I could, Aunt Rosomon. Please believe me."

She struggled in that grip, wanting to strike the Drake, to spit in Sanctan's face, but she knew she was beaten, at least for now.

"You have damned yourself, Sanctan. Lorens will not stand for this. He will raise an army and crush the Ministry and all its traitorous allies."

"Lorens?" Sanctan said. "I wouldn't rely too much on him. How do you think I knew where to find you?"

Rosomon let the words sink in, struggling to comprehend how deep this conspiracy went. "No. I don't believe you. He would never betray his own father."

"Brother Lorens has been a devoted member of the Draconate's brood for some years. And he will make a fine Guildmaster. A most faithful one."

Rosomon wanted to scream, to rage, to fight.

When Sanctan nodded at the scarred knight holding her, all she could do was let herself be dragged away. The last thing she saw as she was pulled through the arch was her brother Sullivar, sitting in that chair, powerless to defend himself or his empire.

FULREN

He gripped tight to that leather cord, his one lifeline. Wenis all but dragged him up the steep incline, shale slipping beneath his feet. Above the sound of the wind gusting in his ears, threatening to send him toppling from the mountain, Fulren heard the dogs.

They had started as a distant yelp, hounds eager for the chase. Now they were so much closer, their barking more resolute as they chased the scent of their quarry. It was more than enough motivation to keep Fulren running despite his exhaustion.

The air was getting thinner, and every other breath he tried to force into his aching lungs was snatched away by an errant gust. At least the blizzard had stopped, replaced by bright sunshine. He could feel it on his face, countering the chill of the wind. Had he been able to see, no doubt the vista would have taken his breath away. Instead he was fleeing in darkness, helplessly dragged along, relentlessly pursued. All he had to hold on to was a thin leather cord and his anger, his determination that this not be the end. He was not going to die on this rock on the arse end of the continent.

His foot snagged an outcrop and he went sprawling. For a moment the wind was knocked out of him, sharp pain lancing up his arm as it struck a rock on the way down. He let go of the cord, lost in that sea of darkness, floundering for a moment before he tried scrambling to his feet.

Dizziness hit him, his hands questing for purchase, feet slipping on the slick surface. He was falling.

A hand gripped his, steadying him. "I'm here, Fulren."

Wenis held him as his hands shook from the lack of air and the pain of the fall. They both panted at one another before she pressed the cord into his hand once more.

"Are you with me?" she asked.

"I'm going nowhere without you," he replied.

He felt her hand in his, the sensation almost bringing a smile to his face. A connection, fleeting, but one he needed just to prove he was still alive, that there was still hope.

"Keep moving!" Lancelin shouted from farther along the pass.

Wenis made sure the cord was wrapped tight about Fulren's fist before urging him up the mountain.

"Do you even know where you're taking us, Jagdor?" she called ahead as they struggled on.

No answer as a gust of howling wind threatened to knock Fulren off his feet again.

"Only I'd hate to think you brought us up here without a plan."

"I saw war eagles roosting at the top of the mountain," Lancelin called back. "They could be our only chance."

Fulren heard Wenis curse beneath her breath. "So you know how to tame wild eagles, Jagdor?"

They came to a sudden stop, all three heaving breath into their lungs.

"Do you have a better idea? Something you haven't told us? Maybe you could turn us all into crows so we can fly off this mountain."

Her silence told him all he needed to know.

Fulren raised his head toward the mountaintop. Through the dark he was sure he could sense a squall at the summit. As he watched, images began to solidify, streams of light wheeling about the silhouette of a rugged peak. The more the vision coalesced, the more he felt the sting of the necroglyph at the nape of his neck.

Turning back the way they had come, he saw only darkness, but there was something malevolent hidden within it—a sinister essence, the malice on their trail, manifesting as a deep fog in his mind's eye. A pall of death relentlessly pursuing them.

"We have to keep moving," Lancelin urged.

Fulren felt the tug of the cord in his hand as Wenis dragged him on once more. This time as he turned his head to the summit the image was less nebulous. The shape of the mountain was distinct against a pale sky, the silhouettes of soaring eagles outlined in dull gold.

He had opened his mouth to tell Wenis that by some miracle he could see when he was cut off by the snarl of a hound.

Wenis yelled a cry of warning, and on instinct Fulren ducked. He felt hot breath tease his ear, heard the sound of a sword being pulled from its sheath. The cord in his hand suddenly went slack as Wenis released it.

There was a thud, a yelp of pain, before Fulren heard the sound of more heavy paws scrabbling up the rocks toward them. He was helpless, unable to run, unable to defend himself.

Through the darkness he saw light begin to emerge, beads of gold gathering about one another in a tight vortex, swirling like distant stars forming a nebula. A hiss like hot steel in water, light forming a distinct figure before him.

As Wenis channelled power through her necroglyphs he could see her all too vividly against the darkness, a vision of sorcerous energy. She darted forward, leaving a wispy contrail in her wake. Fulren was almost overcome by the beauty of it.

A beast growled as it fell on him.

He was knocked on his back, the vision expelled, his hands blindly grasping at snapping jaws, grabbing the hound by the ear before it could tear out his throat. Its hot breath stank, the snap of its fangs too close to his face. Fulren grabbed the hound's studded collar, and it took all his strength to stop it clamping those jaws to his face. He gasped, rolling on the cold ground, wrestling with the hound for his life.

The beast snarled, paws tearing at Fulren's coat, desperate to find purchase, muscles bunching as it struggled in his grip. He managed to get a second hand on that collar, pulling its vicious head away from his vitals, but he could not struggle forever against the beast's superior strength.

Another coalescence of light.

This time he could see the hound's baleful eyes glaring all too close in his mind's eye. But there was something else, a feeling, a sense of this creature's spirit. Fulren focused on it, grasping it tight, concentrating on it like a beacon in the dark.

For the briefest moment he was overwhelmed by the hound's anger. Its fierceness battling with its nature. It obeyed without question, enacting the will of its master. It had been abused, forced into servitude and taught unrelenting loyalty to its keeper.

A vision struck him, a memory that wasn't his. The hound had been beaten, starved, forced to obey. And as he looked into those wicked orbs framed against the shadow, Fulren felt its sorrow.

For a moment the hound ceased its struggle. Its muscles relaxed and it stopped its frantic attack, as though Fulren were no longer its prey. Man and beast regarded one another—a blind man and a dog. Two victims, abused, afraid.

Fulren heard the sweep of the blade, the hound going limp in his hands, the unmistakable spray of hot blood on his face. In an instant he was consumed in blackness, as though the hound no longer existed.

"Get up," Lancelin growled.

The carcass of the hound was shoved to one side, and Fulren felt Lancelin dragging him to his feet. He could barely comprehend what he'd just experienced. The shade of the hound's memory was still imprinted in his mind, as though he had awoken from a vivid dream.

"Keep moving," urged Wenis. "They're not far behind."

With that they were on the move again, a frantic dash to the summit, their panting breaths rising above the sound of the wind. Over the howling gale, Fulren could hear their pursuers shouting curses in their wake. Something clattered against a rock behind him. Arrows.

It served to spur them on to greater effort, and before long the mountain path began to level out. Fulren could feel the pathway closing in on both sides until they were eventually forced to squeeze through a narrow ravine. Once they made it through to the other side they stopped, suddenly sheltered from the wind.

"We could hold them here," Lancelin said. "That's the only way through."

"Hold them until when, Jagdor?" Wenis snapped. "I doubt help is coming. They can just wait us out if they want. We'll starve to death up here."

A screech cut the air, the cry of a giant eagle tantalisingly close. Fulren raised his head again, blind eyes straining through the dark until he willed them to see. In the sky golden trails were painted against the grey as the eagles wheeled in flight above their heads.

"There might not be another defensible position on this mountain," said Lancelin. "If we carry on up to the summit, we might have nowhere left to run. Here we at least have a fighting chance."

Fulren barely heard him, too intent on those shapes in the sky. He could feel their essence as they soared above, as though he might reach out and touch them, could sense their urges, their alarm at strangers advancing on their nesting ground. Their fear for their young, but also their sense of freedom, their soaring grace, their need to hunt. It came to him in a glut of emotion, filling him with the sudden urge to vomit.

"Eastlander!"

The call echoed through the narrow pass. The resonant voice of Saranor the Bleeder.

Wenis cursed beneath her breath, a foul tirade that surprised Fulren enough to bring him out of his malaise.

"You have run us ragged. Killed my hunting pack. But there is nowhere left to go. There's nothing on top of that mountain but the wind. Surrender yourself to us. We will take the witch and keep your blind man, but you can live."

"I told you this was a stupid plan," Wenis hissed.

Silence from Lancelin.

"Don't take too long to decide, eastlander," called Saranor, his voice frighteningly close. "If I have to come through there and reclaim my prize, the deal is off."

"Fuck you, Huntan pig," Wenis yelled back through the ravine.

They heard Saranor's laugh echo back in reply. "Very well. It seems the decision is made for you."

Another screech from the sky. Another shock to his system as Fulren was bombarded by a wave of the eagle's fear.

"We have to go," Fulren whispered.

"What?" Wenis said.

"Trust me, we can make it."

"Shit," Lancelin said. "They're coming."

"Come on," Fulren barked, already moving, already fleeing blindly, following the gentle slope up to the summit.

He stumbled and fell to one knee before pushing himself up. With no one to guide him, with the wind howling and threatening to toss him from the mountainside, he could hardly get his bearings, but on he rushed, feeling the presence of those eagles above him, following them upward to the peak.

"Fulren, stop," he heard Wenis shout.

There was a clash of steel behind, but he pressed on, pushing himself through another narrow pass, crawling up a steep rise until he was suddenly out in the open, cast adrift again as he had been so many times. Only now he was not surrounded by black. Now the darkness was fading, and he could sense the eagles above, watching from the skies, seeing him... feeling him.

He reached out an arm. The necroglyph at his neck began to itch, then burn as he opened his mind, straining with every sense but sight, locking his focus on to one of the giant birds. Immediately he was awash with alien feelings, filled with emotions he had never felt before and would never understand. Just as he had felt a moment of connection with the hound, now he was linked to one of the eagles, its will becoming one with his, their goals entwining into a single purpose.

Fulren felt the creature wheel in the air, altering its course before swooping down to land on the summit of the mountain not twenty feet away. Behind him he heard distant sounds of violence, the staccato clash of swords, the hiss of sorcery as Wenis and Lancelin held the way, but he forced himself to put their struggle from his thoughts.

Slowly he approached the eagle, arm still held out. He could sense its unease, but he focused his mind as the necroglyph seared his flesh. The creature had to understand he meant it no harm. He closed the distance, and the eagle took a faltering step forward. Through the shadows he could see the majestic creature as a golden outline, huge and imposing in his vision.

Fulren's fingers touched the eagle's beak as it dipped its head, hard against his numb flesh. He would have said words to soothe it, to make it trust him, but knew there was no need. They were as one. Accepting each other, confident that they were on the same path.

He grasped a bunch of feathers at the eagle's neck. In response it dipped its head, hunching down as he climbed up onto its back. Across the summit he could still hear the ringing of steel and the dull blast of arcane energy.

"Let's go," he cried over the wind. "Come on!"

As he did so he felt a swell of emotion from the eagle, and it tilted its head back, letting out a piercing screech.

The whip of an arrow flew past his head, and there was another blast in the distance, a flash in the periphery of his blinded sight. Someone grasped the eagle's wing, pulling themselves up, and as Fulren helped them climb onto the beast's back, he realised it was Lancelin.

"Where's Wenis?" Fulren shouted.

Suddenly his vision lit up with incandescence as sorcery shattered his senses. Beneath him the eagle bucked, their connection momentarily severed. The frightened animal spread its wings, hopping once, twice, before leaping into the air with a straining of its muscles.

Fulren's stomach lurched and he grasped a handful of feathers, feeling Lancelin grab him tight around the waist, both of them desperate not to fall. The eagle took flight, dropping from the summit at a frightening velocity before it caught the thermals and began to rise.

"Where is she?" Fulren screamed, his voice lost on the wind.

Another flash of light in his periphery, and he realised she was still on the mountaintop, still facing Saranor and his horde. Despite the wind rushing in his face, Fulren glared through the gale, desperate for any sign of her. The eagle wheeled around the summit, and he caught sight of her silhouetted against the black, the necroglyph that fed her power coursing through her body, filling it with the light of a thousand golden stars.

She was running toward the edge of the mountain, and pursuing her was nothing but shadow, a mist of terror in her wake. He wanted to cry out, wanted to force the eagle back so he could help her, but his voice was caught in his throat, any power he had manifested over the creature now gone. All he could do was watch as she reached the edge of the mountain, nowhere left to run.

Wenis leapt, high into the air, far from the edge, where the shadow of malevolence could not follow. She would plummet to her death rather than face the fate Saranor had condemned her to.

Fulren felt a dull ache in his chest, his vision fading, but before the blackness overcame him once more, he saw a golden trail streak toward that falling silhouette. An eagle, bright against the dark, caught Wenis in its grip and swooped away from the mountainside. It was the last thing Fulren saw before blackness consumed his sight.

Had she summoned the creature herself? Or had it simply plucked her from the air for its own ends? As he and Lancelin gripped tight to the eagle beneath them, he had to accept he might never know.

Fulren closed his eyes against the wind, hoping against hope that the eagle shared his longing for home.

CONALL

He sucked air through his teeth as Sted dabbed at the raw welts with a liniment-soaked rag. She hadn't bothered to tell him what kind of salve she was using, but it smelled worse than the latrines during high heat.

"I wish you'd stop your bloody whinging," Sted said, sympathetic as ever.

It had been a couple of days since his flogging, but his back still stung. The pain had dulled for sure, but not by much. He'd passed out after only three lashes, but the reminder of his punishment would be there for days to come.

"I'd like to see you put up with—"

He hissed again as she dabbed at another laceration, and none too gently. Her way of repeating the request for him to stop whinging.

"If you had a drink, this would hurt a lot less," she said.

Conall glanced toward the half-empty bottle sitting beside his bunk. Despite the temptation, he shook his head.

"Now's not the time," he replied.

And it wasn't. He was suffering from the pain, that was for sure, but he had to keep a clear head. Had to atone, and there was no way of doing that by sinking into a drunken stupor. He'd messed up. Badly. A man had died because of it, and there was no one who could make amends for that other than him.

At least Sted was talking to him now. When he'd come round after his punishment, hers had been the first face he'd seen. They hadn't said another word about Nevan yet, and he had no idea if she still blamed him for the big man's death, but that didn't matter now.

"Don't even know what we're doing here," Sted grumbled to herself in that way that ensured everyone could hear.

"Now who's whinging?" Conall replied.

"Well I don't. We get treated like shit. You've been pretty thoroughly disrespected, and it's no secret we're not wanted here. Why don't we just leave? Get back to Torwyn. Start fucking drinking."

Conall had asked himself that very question so many times. Fought with his desire to take the easy road against his need to keep walking the difficult one.

"We can't leave. Not yet."

Sted made a growling noise in her throat, and Conall managed to stifle another wince as she dabbed at his back again, even harder than before.

"Might I ask why?" she said through gritted teeth.

"Because I haven't persuaded Beringer that I'm right."

Silence. Sted stopped ministering to him. He turned to see her staring with her brows in a V. That was never a good sign.

"With all due respect, Captain Hawkspur. How do you think you're going to do that without pissing him off again?"

"I'll think of something. And if he won't listen to me about the glaive, about what we've seen, then I'll just have to go over his head."

"A cunning plan, Captain," she said, voice dripping with cynicism. "But how will you accomplish that without making more trouble for yourself?"

Conall shook his head. "That I haven't worked out yet."

"I see." Sted nodded as if she didn't see at all. "More to the point, how are you going to accomplish that without making more trouble for me?"

Her last word was bellowed from the depths of her throat. Good old Sted, you could always rely on her to voice her concerns with aplomb.

Before he could even begin to deal with that one, a pristinely uniformed trooper entered the small garrison building. He didn't even bother to knock or salute as he came to stand before Conall.

"The frontier marshal will be mustering the troops in the courtyard this morning," the trooper said. "Captain Tarrien thought it prudent to inform you well in advance."

Without another word he spun on his heel and marched back through the door.

"Arsehole," Sted said.

Conall rose gingerly to his feet. "Gather the men. Get them ready."

"You need to rest, Con."

"I need to be on parade with everyone else. Let's not give Beringer any more reasons to treat us like shit."

Sted shrugged, moving off to gather the rest of the Talon. Conall grabbed his shirt and pulled it over his throbbing shoulders. The touch of the cotton against his flesh was excruciating, but he gritted his teeth against the pain. Putting on his dress jacket hurt more, but he endured it, buttoning it to the neck, feeling as if he were trapped in some torture device. Sweat beaded down his forehead, and he resisted the temptation to wipe it on his sleeve. Strapping his sword belt around his waist did little to help him feel like an officer, but he had to at least give the appearance of being worthy of his rank.

No sooner had he donned the uniform than the bell clanged outside. Conall marched out into the sunlight, relieved to see the Talon were already standing to attention. His relief didn't last long when he saw the entire garrison was also waiting for him to arrive. Late again.

As he walked to join his men, he could see Beringer waiting atop the platform leading to his office. It was all Conall could do to avoid his gaze as he marched across the courtyard, refusing to rush. He'd already made enough of a fool of himself without scurrying like a shithouse rat to join his column.

Tarrien stood at the end of one column, his sly grin unmistakable. Conall made a point of staring straight ahead.

When he finally stood to attention with the rest of the Talon, he waited for the inevitable jibe from Beringer, but the frontier marshal merely watched the troopers below him, his expression grim as always. Was there something else to that serious visage? Some concern weighing heavy on his grey brow?

"I've received a missive," Beringer began, deep voice cutting through the silence. "From the Anvil."

Conall immediately felt the hairs prickle at the nape of his neck. Was his mother still at the Anvil?

"I have been informed," Beringer continued, "that the Draconate Ministry has assumed both military and administrative control of the capital. The authoritative power of the Guilds has been relinquished, and the city is now under the martial control of the Drakes, with the support of the Hallowhills. I am assured that so far there has been no violence, and Emperor Sullivar is safely confined to the palace."

Conall began to feel sick, the sweat pouring from him now. This could change everything. Suddenly all thought of proving himself was gone. The need to find answers in the Karna replaced by his sudden urge to get home.

"As far as we know, the Ministry intends to take full control of other cities within the Guildlands of Torwyn. We don't know yet how that will play out. Some Armiger Battalions have thrown in with the Ministry. Others have already expressed their support for the Guilds. As far as the Phoenix Battalion is concerned, we remain neutral. For now. So that means for every one of you it's business as usual. Nothing changes until you're told otherwise. Is that understood?"

Beringer's question was met with a resounding, "Yes, Frontier Marshal," from his obedient troopers. Conall's mind was racing too much for him to speak.

With a nod to his captain, Beringer turned and walked back into his office. Tarrien called for the garrison to fall out, and immediately every man at attention moved to retake his post.

Conall likewise dismissed the Talon, but he could see not all the men of the Phoenix Battalion were at their duties. Pockets of troopers stood discussing Beringer's news. There was a fraught atmosphere taking hold of the fort, a heightened sense of tension in the air.

When he was back in his chamber, Sted at his side, all Conall could do was stare at his storage chest. It would be so easy to run. To pack his belongings and leave all this behind.

"What are you going to do?" Sted asked.

Conall shook his head. "I don't even know if my mother is still at the Anvil."

"So don't you think you ought to find out? This could mean war between the Guilds and the Ministry. Do you really want to be hundreds of miles away when it starts? She needs you now more than ever."

"She's never needed me." Conall almost spat the words.

"Are you fucking dumb?" Sted moved to stand before him. She was a head shorter, but her fierce expression more than compensated for her lack of height. "You're a Hawkspur. Whatever you thought you were going to accomplish by being here means shit all now. Your Guild needs you."

"We could be walking straight into danger."

"By the fucking Five Lairs, Con. We're in danger here. If you were worried about danger, you wouldn't have come to the frontier in the first place. What's wrong with you? What is this shit between you and your mother?"

Conall shook his head, trying to dispel the memories. "Who says there's anything—"

"Are you kidding me? The look on your face whenever she's mentioned. The way you've ignored every one of her letters even after your brother was exiled. What is wrong with you?"

"She doesn't need my help. I'll only be a burden to her." A last-gasp attempt to justify himself.

"Don't you think you ought to find out if that's true, rather than guessing?"

There was no escaping this. He was heir to the Hawkspur Guild.

A legacy that had now been put in jeopardy. If he could help, even in a small way, he had to at least try.

"All right. I'll speak to Beringer. We leave today."

"About bloody time," Sted replied, walking past him to the gun rack on the wall. "And take this." She plucked the longbarrel from the rack and tossed it to him. "Just in case."

"Why would I—?"

"Just in case," she repeated. "Better to have it and not need it. I'll round up the men."

It made sense. Fort Tarkis had already proved itself a hostile environment. With such grave news from the Anvil it wasn't going to get any safer.

Conall made sure the chamber of his longbarrel was primed as he walked through the garrison building and out into the courtyard. The ache in his back had dulled, and he suddenly felt lighter of foot at the prospect of leaving this place. The dark-uniformed troopers of the Phoenix Battalion still spoke in hushed groups. Some of them even shot him wary glances as he made his way past, confirming he was making the right decision. Tensions were growing, and the farther away he got from here the better.

Before he reached the bottom of the stairs to Beringer's office, someone stepped into his path. Tarrien had a suspicious look to him as he blocked the stairwell. Conall wasn't sure what he hated most—his usual smug expression or this look of obvious disdain.

"Going somewhere, Hawkspur?"

Conall would have taken great pleasure in introducing Tarrien to the butt of his longbarrel, but he was surrounded by Armiger troopers. Probably not the best move to take on their captain with no backup.

"I need to speak to the frontier marshal," he replied, struggling to hold his anger at bay.

Tarrien glanced at the longbarrel. "And you're going armed?" he said.

Conall had to admit that probably wasn't the best look. "For my own protection. But if it makes you feel better, why don't you come along?"

"Yes, I think it would. Shall we?" Tarrien gestured for him to lead the way.

Conall made his way up the stairs, conscious of Tarrien practically breathing down his neck as he rapped a fist against the door. At Beringer's command to enter, both men stepped inside and stood to attention before the frontier marshal's desk. Tarrien took a step to the side, keeping his eyes fixed on Conall. Not that it mattered. Let him observe, it made no difference now.

"I'll admit," Beringer said, "I was expecting this visit, Hawkspur."

"I'm sorry, Frontier Marshal, but with everything that's happening back at the Anvil I will have to make a formal request to retire my secondment to the battalion and return to Torwyn, with immediate effect. I hope you can understand that considering my mother's position, it's the only option I have."

Beringer lowered his eyes, scanning the scrolls and missives that covered his desk. Conall half expected him to refuse the request.

"Very well, Hawkspur. You have my permission to leave."

Conall struggled to hide his surprise. "My thanks, Frontier Marshal. I appreciate it." He was about to turn and leave when he stopped himself. "If I might ask... why was that such an easy decision?"

Beringer looked up at him, those cold eyes softening for a moment. "I understand family comes first, son. You have to do what's right, and I appreciate this isn't an easy choice for you. I believe you were determined to make this commission work, and that's why you took your punishment like an officer should. I'll be sorry to see you go."

Beringer rose to his feet, straightening his jacket.

"Besides. This whole situation is fucked. Who knows what's going to happen? If the Ministry is enacting a nationwide coup, and I think they are, it could mean war. We've all got to choose our side now, and you have no choice about yours."

"And yours?" Conall asked, not even expecting an answer.

Beringer's mouth turned up in a grin. "I put no store by religious fanatics. The Guilds may be venal, but they've done right by the Phoenix Battalion. When I'm called upon to make the decision, I'll recommend we stand with the Guilds."

An all-too-rare sense of relief washed over Conall. "Thank you,

Frontier Marshal. I know my uncle will be glad to know he has your support."

"Take care of yourself, son," Beringer said, offering Conall his hand.

Before he could think to take it, the room exploded with noise.

Conall ducked, covering his head as he staggered back, smelling the stench of burning pyrestone. He opened his eyes to see a thick pall of smoke, his ears ringing in the aftermath of the noise.

Tarrien stood by the window, the pyrestone pistol smoking in his grip. Beringer was slumped in his chair, a blackened hole burned into his chest. The frontier marshal tried to take a breath, but all he could do was wheeze blood through punctured lungs before pitching forward, his head thudding against the tabletop.

"Alarm!" Tarrien screamed, discarding his pistol and reaching for his sword.

There was no time to think, to process what had happened or why. Conall fumbled with the longbarrel, trying to aim, but Tarrien was already charging forward. He managed to let off a shot, but it missed its mark, blowing a hole in the ceiling, before he was forced to parry Tarrien's blade. Anger ignited in him as he swung the butt of the longbarrel at Tarrien's head and missed. At such close quarters there was no time for another swing, and Conall was grappling for the sword, trying to wrench it from Tarrien's grip. They both went crashing into a bookshelf, papers and scrolls sent tumbling.

Tarrien grabbed Conall's head, shoving him into the window. The sound of smashing glass rang in his ear as his head broke the windowpane. He gritted his teeth, sending an uppercut into Tarrien's jaw and rocking him backward. His hand went to his own sword, but Tarrien quickly shook his head and darted forward before Conall could draw.

He ducked the first swing of Tarrien's fist, dodging away from a second.

"Help me," Tarrien screamed. "He's killed Beringer!"

Conall swung a fist of his own, silencing Tarrien, who staggered back into the wall. There came the sound of heavy footsteps approaching up the stairs, but Conall didn't care. He just wanted to kill this bastard as quick as he could.

He rushed forward, pummelling with his fists, but this time Tarrien covered his head with his arms, letting Conall rain blow after blow. Conall barely noticed as the door was kicked open and half a dozen troopers rushed inside.

They overwhelmed him in a second, but still he fought like a lion, teeth gnashing. He was wrestled to the floor, arm locked behind him, a knee pressed into his back sending searing pain through his wounded flesh.

"It was him," Conall screamed.

A fist to the jaw and he went dizzy.

As they dragged him from Beringer's office and down the stairs he saw Tarrien following, face a bleeding mask of innocence. Someone began ringing the courtyard bell, and as Conall was forced to the ground and held there by three troopers, the entire garrison came to see what the commotion was about.

"Captain Hawkspur has murdered the frontier marshal," Tarrien announced, taking a kerchief from his pocket and dabbing at his bloody lip. "He and the Talon are to be taken into custody immediately, pending trial. Hawkspur is a traitor and a heretic. We'll not be exposed to similar betrayal from his men."

Conall tried to look around for Sted, but with someone's knee on his head it was a tough ask.

"He's lying," he spat into the dust. "Tarrien shot him. He's the fucking traitor."

"Gag that man," came the order.

In an instant one of the troopers had secured a leather strap around Conall's mouth. He was dragged to his feet and his hands bound. Before they pulled a sack over his head, Conall saw the Talon being rounded up at the business end of a dozen splintbows. Sted raised her hands in surrender, though she looked none too happy about it.

Then all he saw was darkness.

ROSOMON

She was locked away like a common criminal. A bare room half the size of her bedchamber, a single window letting in the tepid light of a grey day, and nothing to sit on but a bare wooden pallet. The humiliation of it would have filled her with shame, but Rosomon was too enraged to consider the indignity.

Perhaps this was the cell Fulren had been caged in before being forced into that ark bound for Nyrakkis. That thought served only to fuel her anger. Whatever fate awaited her, whatever foulness she was destined to meet, she would greet it with all the fury of her bloodline. She was a daughter of kings, and her captors would know it before the end.

At the sound of jangling keys, Rosomon realised she might have to prove that sooner than expected. She suppressed the sudden fear that tried to rise in her gut. Gritting her teeth, she stood in the middle of that cell, waiting for the executioner to come. Let them humiliate her. Let them parade her before the baying crowd, then hang her from the highest gibbet. Rosomon Hawkspur would show no dread in the face of it.

Sanctan Egelrath stood in the doorway. He smiled his Archlegate's smile, as though he weren't the most devious bastard in all of Torwyn. He could have been ministering to his faithful, laying blessings on the heads of children. Rosomon knew only too well it was a mask he wore to hide his true visage. There was a devil beneath that fake smile.

When he stepped into the room, it was all she could do to hold herself back, to not leap forward and scratch those smiling eyes from his head. But she remained still, forcing a veneer of dignity over her fury, just as Sanctan wore a coat of virtue over his wickedness.

Behind him, ducking below the lintel, entered the scarred knight. Ansell Beckenrike regarded her, devoid of any warmth. His eyes looked almost sad in that granite face, and for the briefest moment it reminded her of the way Lancelin often looked. Eyes that had seen too much strife. Eyes that evoked empathy but could so quickly turn furious when the killing began.

"Come, Aunt Rosomon," Sanctan said. "It is time."

She waited for a moment, her feet unable or unwilling to move. "Time for what?" she asked, relieved at the calmness in her voice. She would have hated for him to think her afraid.

"The festival is about to begin. I wouldn't want you to miss the Raising of Undometh. Not on such an auspicious year."

With that he led the way from the cell. Ansell stood aside, allowing her to walk after Sanctan. Outside the cell Rosomon expected to see more guards awaiting her, but there was no one. She could have run, fled along the corridors and looked for some way to escape, but she knew that would only serve to make her look foolish.

Instead she followed close behind Sanctan, wishing she had another pyrestone weapon concealed in her gown so he could share the same fate as Starn Rivers. The corridors of the palace were deserted as they made their way from the cells, their footsteps echoing through the empty halls.

"You will never get away with this, Sanctan," Rosomon said eventually, unable to hold her tongue lest it ignite with rage.

Sanctan slowed his pace, turning his head toward her, that smile still playing on his lips.

"Oh, but I already have." They passed an open balcony, the Anvil suddenly framed within a soaring arch. From beyond, Rosomon could hear the sounds of the city gathering in celebration, joyous voices rising from the streets.

"Can't you hear them? The people cheering in thanks for their deliverance?"

"They don't see you as the tyrant you are. They don't yet know what you've done. That you've overthrown their emperor. And when word spreads through the city, they will rise against you."

Sanctan pursed his lips in thought. "Doubtful. I have the support of almost every Armiger Battalion in the city. Those who still bear loyalty to the Guilds will join me when they see which way the wind is blowing. The Ministry's devotees grow more numerous by the day."

"Somehow I doubt that. You can't control the masses with zealotry, Sanctan. The Armigers will not stay loyal for long. Not once they see your true colours. Your treachery."

"That hurts, Aunt Rosomon. You call me a traitor, and yet you haven't even given me a chance to prove my virtue. And please, don't underestimate the devotion of my followers. The Guilds may have usurped the influence of the Draconate over many years, but we have never left the hearts of the people."

Rosomon suddenly thought about Olstrum, now nowhere to be seen. About Lorens, who had seemingly betrayed his own father in favour of his faith. Perhaps Sanctan was right—the Guilds had grown blind with power and not seen the true conviction in the hearts of their subjects. Now they were about to pay the price for that arrogance.

"So my son was just a sacrifice on your altar?" she asked, clenching her fists. Remembering that day she had watched as Fulren was condemned.

Sanctan sighed, and for a moment she thought there was a brief flash of remorse in his expression. A genuine emotion beneath the mask.

"I was always fond of Fulren. What happened to him was unfortunate, but unavoidable. I would have spared him his fate, but he was simply in the wrong place at the wrong time. The emissary had to be dealt with. In the aftermath Fulren simply became a convenient scapegoat."

"But why?" Rosomon heard the anguish in her own voice and immediately regretted the demonstration of weakness.

Sanctan's brow creased and he regarded her with an earnest stare. "Because if Sullivar had succeeded in his bargain with Nyrakkis, it could have meant a new age of prosperity. The Guilds might have become even more powerful. Perhaps too powerful to fall."

"So that's what all this is about? Power?"

Sanctan barked a laugh. "You think I crave power like some miserly robber baron? You think I care for the trinkets of office like your brother? What I do is for the good of the faithful. For the good of Torwyn." Suddenly his eyes shone with a zeal Rosomon had never witnessed before. Despite the anger burning inside her, for the first time she began to fear Sanctan and the madness he harboured. "I mean to restore order, to restore faith to these lands. To return this nation to the way it was always intended to be. And the Guilds, the Armiger Battalions, every last citizen in every city and town, will fall in line and worship before the sanctity of the Draconate. Or they will burn in the breath of the Great Wyrms."

Rosomon swallowed down her fear, realising how far her nephew had fallen. This was no longer the boy she remembered. All that stood before her was a fanatic.

"And how many will burn until you are satisfied, Sanctan? Will Sullivar be the first?"

His hard expression softened, that smile playing across his lips, though now she saw it for the affectation it was.

"Sullivar will not burn. He has become part of my brood. The scales have fallen from his eyes. I will not have to make an example of the emperor, but merely allow him to speak, to willingly hand over these lands to me. Where do you think we are going, Aunt Rosomon?"

"I have no idea," she replied.

"To the Cogwheel. The Raising of Undometh will be celebrated there, and Sullivar will make his announcement to the whole city. I have merely asked him to hand his control to the Ministry, and he will do so gladly."

"You won't get away with this. I will not be party to this charade. You will have to kill me to keep me silent, Sanctan."

"No, I don't think I will." He moved toward the vast archway that opened onto a staircase running down to street level and the parade that led straight to the Cogwheel. "You have your family to think on. Conall is still on the Karna Frontier. Your one remaining heir. I would hate for anything to happen to him. A son should never pay the price for the sins of his mother."

Ansell moved close behind her, donning his dragon helm and silently urging her to follow Sanctan from the hall. The three of them made their way down the stairs, Rosomon unable to speak, her mind racing, panic rising as she heard the raucous sound of the crowd below.

When they reached the bottom, a column of Drakes were waiting, pennants of the Five Wyrms flapping in the breeze. Sanctan led the way, joined by more High Legates in the five colours of the Great Wyrms, and they pressed on through the palace grounds and out onto the main promenade.

The crowd was dense, lining the street on both sides, held back by troopers of the Armiger Battalions. For the most part Rosomon could see the citizens of the Anvil cheering for the Archlegate, an overwhelming expression of approval from the masses. But within that crowd was some dissent. Angry faces were dotted among the flock, shouting abuse, only to be berated by their neighbours.

Rosomon endured the march in silence, her thoughts writhing in a tumult, stomach lurching at the implications of what was happening. And she was powerless to stop it. There was no doubt Sanctan would murder Conall were she to offer any dissent. For now she would have to go along with this travesty.

By the time they reached the Cogwheel, there was an air of frenzy about the crowd. The noise was deafening, as though the entire populace of the Anvil had gathered in this one spot to worship at the feet of the Ministry.

The stage had been fully constructed, rising high above the crowd, and Rosomon had no choice but to follow Sanctan as he made his way onto the raised platform. The first person she saw was Rearden Corwen, waving graciously at the crowd, surrounded by his Revocaters. She stared at him as Ansell herded her past, but the old snake kept his eyes locked on the crowd.

There were no representatives of any other Guild present, the platform instead filled with towering Knights of the Draconate. Sanctan had surrounded himself with his most loyal—perhaps he was not expecting proceedings to go so smoothly after all. She looked for Lorens, for Olstrum, for anyone she might turn to, but there was no one here she could call a friend.

Ansell guided her to the edge of the stage, and Rosomon found herself standing beside Lady Darina. Of course she was here, come to share in the glory her son had stolen. Her eyes were fixed dead ahead, unable to even glance in Rosomon's direction.

Sanctan took his place on the central podium, raising his arms to the frantic crowd, and their cheers of support grew even louder. As she watched this vulgar display, Sanctan drinking in the approval, Rosomon could hold her tongue no longer.

"I hope you're proud of what your son has achieved," she hissed at Darina, raising her voice above the cacophony.

Darina continued to stare blankly ahead. "I had nothing to do with any of this," she replied.

"You expect me to believe you didn't see this coming? Sanctan is your son, Archlegate or not."

"I had no idea of the depths of his ambition, Rosomon. You think I would approve of this show? I would gladly see you brought low, but do you honestly think I would let the nation burn to achieve it?"

Rosomon was about to reply that she wouldn't put anything past the old witch when Sanctan spread his arms, gesturing for the crowd to be silent. A gradual hush settled over the city, the deafening voices dying in unison, all eyes on the Archlegate.

"People of the Anvil," Sanctan shouted. "Citizens of Torwyn. You have once again shown your devotion by gathering for the Raising of Undometh. But this is a most auspicious time. As you must know, a change has been brought about. The yoke under which you have toiled for decades broken." Some sparse shouts of agreement from the crowd. "The greed and avarice that infested this great seat of power have been eradicated. The Guilds that have ruled over you for so long have been brought into the light of the five Great Wyrms, and now those of you who never benefited from their covetous deeds will be emancipated. Now in the eyes of the Wyrms we are all their children, all equally valued. All equally precious."

More cheering, but this time a couple of isolated voices shouted in opposition. A hiss of discontent rippled through the crowd, but Sanctan focused on the dissenters, raising his hands for calm.

"I know some of you doubt me when I say this empire has achieved salvation. And I can understand that. Trust is not always easy to come by. So if my words do not convince you, then perhaps those of your emperor will."

There was movement across the platform. Two Knights of the Draconate stepped up onto the dais, Sullivar walking between them. Rosomon felt an ache inside as she saw her brother. He looked pristine in the red and gold regalia of Archwind, his beard and hair trimmed and flawless, but his eyes looked dead: heavy shadows beneath, the light in them extinguished.

Sullivar was guided to the podium, and Sanctan stood aside to let the emperor take his place before the crowd. Rosomon had witnessed the people cheer for her brother whenever he appeared before them. This time he was met by silence.

He stood watching the crowd, this man who had never been short of words but who was now mute. She could see his hand shaking at his side until he clenched a fist to stop it. As the silence became awkward, Sanctan took a step forward.

"Emperor Sullivar has seen the folly of his ways. The penury wrought by the Guilds can no longer be tolerated. He has learned from the Draconate Prophesies themselves, a scripture which dictates that only with the greatest of sacrifices can Undometh truly be raised." He looked to Sullivar, that false smile conveying fellowship. "Tell them of your rebirth, my son."

Sullivar gazed across the crowd, turning his head until he saw Rosomon standing to the side of the platform. For a moment his eyes regained some of their former spark, his mouth twitching at one corner in the vain attempt at a smile. Then his focus was back on the crowd.

"It is true," Sullivar announced. His voice was far from strong, but it was loud enough to carry across the mass of staring faces. "I...I have been blessed. Both with a clear view of the past, of my misdeeds, but also... also a vision of the future. It is..." The strength in his voice faded. "We must... There has to be a peace. The Ministry..."

His words failed him, as if he were an actor who had forgotten his lines. Sanctan placed a hand on Sullivar's shoulder, whispering words of encouragement, smiling as though to comfort the man now entirely under his control.

"No," Sullivar growled, shaking off Sanctan's hand. "No, I will not do this."

Rosomon felt the Drakes flinch around her. A murmur of disquiet rippled through the crowd. Sanctan's confidence drained in an instant, his smiling mask now discarded.

"I denounce the Draconate Ministry," Sullivar bellowed at the crowd. "They are usurpers. Do not let them take—"

Sanctan grabbed Sullivar's arm, vainly trying to drag him from the podium. Rosomon watched with growing horror as her brother reached into his sleeve, and she saw the glint of a blade in the sunlight.

The world seemed to slow as Sullivar lashed out, slicing a red line across Sanctan's forearm. The Archlegate fell backward, the silent air defiled by Sullivar's bellow of rage. His eyes were cowed no more. Now he glared with a ferocity that reminded Rosomon of their father in his most furious of rages.

As her brother bore down on Sanctan, blade high and poised to strike, there was a ringing of steel. Ansell Beckenrike drew his sword, darting forward, covering the distance before Sullivar could deal his death blow.

The huge knight hacked Sullivar down with a single stroke, blood spattering the white robes of the Archlegate as he cowered on the ground.

Rosomon heard the piercing trill of a scream before she realised it was her own voice. It was immediately drowned out by the roar of the crowd—some baying in approval, others screaming in horror at the death of their emperor.

Something landed a few feet away from her as she stood staring at her brother's hacked corpse. The ringing of a missile hitting a helmet made Rosomon look up to see rocks being flung by the crowd.

As more projectiles rained, the Drakes raised their shields against the deluge.

"Get the Archlegate to safety," Ansell growled.

His men responded, dragging Sanctan to his feet, covering him with a wall of tower shields before they rushed him from the podium. Two more grabbed hold of Lady Darina, sheltering her between them as they followed the Archlegate.

Angry screams cut the air. More missiles struck the platform, violence erupting among the crowd. Rosomon watched with growing horror as isolated pockets of fighting began to spread, the disorder rising like a storm. A wave of bodies rushed toward the Cogwheel, each face twisted in fury, before they were met by the swords and shields of the Armiger troopers guarding the platform.

Confusion took hold, panic sweeping across the dais in a wave.

"Get me to safety, you fucking idiots," Rearden crowed before his Revocaters bundled him away. Rosomon watched him go, standing in a daze, viewing everything as though it were through a looking glass.

Ansell knelt over the body of the emperor he had just slain, but there was no way to discern his expression beneath the dragon helm as he ignored the missiles bouncing off his armour.

This was her chance. She had to run.

Stones hammered the platform as she raced across it, one hitting her arm. Rosomon ignored the pain as she nearly tumbled down the stairs. Surrounding the Cogwheel were ranks of troopers, shields blocking the crowd, but the sheer weight of numbers was too much. As a mass of bodies burst through the faltering shield wall, Rosomon heard the piston hiss of stormhulks on the move, screams of terror pealing out as the vast machines waded through the tightly packed mass of bodies.

As soon as she reached the edge of the Cogwheel she was consumed by the angry crowd. Someone bellowed in her ear, his words indiscernible. She saw a man go down, head pouring blood. Just a few feet away, the foot of a stormhulk carved its way through the mass of bodies, screams of horror ringing out as bones were crushed beneath its lumbering tread.

Rosomon was carried along, fighting, struggling through the

press. She had no idea where she was going, but it didn't matter as long as she was away from the Drakes, away from Sanctan. The crowd was sweeping her along as though she were being dragged on a strong current.

Someone pulled at her hair. Her dress tore at the sleeve, but still she battled with the crowd. In the chaos she struggled to breathe and fought to quell her panic, lost amid the turmoil. Her legs suddenly gave out and she stumbled, the horde threatening to crush the air from her lungs. If she fell, she would be trampled to death beneath the riot.

A gauntleted hand grabbed her arm. She felt the swing of a weapon pass close to her face, and the crowd suddenly spread out, allowing her to take a breath. Through the fog of her vision she saw Ansell, his helmet lost, blood trickling from below his dark hairline. He didn't even look at her as he dragged her from the throng, battling his way inch by inch along the parade and toward the palace. Through the crowd came more of the Drakes, hacking a bloody path into the city folk of the Anvil. Rosomon was quickly surrounded by a wall of shields carving an oasis in the midst of the violence.

No words were spoken as they pushed on, up the main thoroughfare, across the bridge, until they were met by a line of defenders guarding the way to the palace. Stormhulks stood to the fore, troopers of the Armiger taking potshots with their splintbows to hold back the crowd. Ansell didn't let go of her arm until they were safely beyond the defensive line and within the sanctuary of the palace grounds.

Rosomon snatched her arm from his grip, staggering away and glaring up into the face of the man who had just cut down her brother. The man who had just saved her life.

There was nothing there—no sorrow, no victory or even relief. He was as cold a monument as any that lined the Bridge of Saints. She would have spit her fury and grief in his face, but what good would it do her now?

Silently she turned toward the palace and walked back to her prison cell.

TYRETA

She leapt a fallen tree trunk, bare feet brushing through the ferns, eating up the yards to the palisade surrounding the port. The wall was just visible through the trees, smoke rising from beyond its whitewashed surface.

Screams echoed from within the port. The terrified cries of civilians mixed with the guttural barks of the kesh and the desperate yell of fighting men trying to bring order in the chaos.

The iron gates of New Flaym lay open, one of them hanging limp from its hinges. The body of a huge mastodon lay dead across the threshold, peppered with splintbow bolts, but it had done its work before it perished. Bodies lay scattered in the road as she rushed through the open gate, and she tried not to look at the hacked corpses of both kesh and human. Vultures were already feasting, and they were put to flight as she raced past them into the port.

Tyreta had no idea where she would go, how she would help, but there had to be something she could do, some way she could stop this. When she spied the distant harbour, already ablaze, she realised she was too late.

The main thoroughfare was strewn with bodies. Most were ordinary civilians: dockworkers, tanners, mariners. Among them were the scattered bodies of Marrlock Guild guardsmen, but they hadn't put up much of a fight. There were no barricades, no burned-out defences. They'd barely had time to grab their weapons before the warriors of the Chul fell upon them.

Damn Serrell for not listening to her. Damn them all.

She stopped, breathing hard from the run, eyes wide as she took in the devastation. To her right the timbers of a blazing house suddenly collapsed, sending flames gusting higher into the sky. To her left she could hear someone weeping. Toward the port more screams pealed out. She should run, should flee this carnage, but Tyreta was done with running.

She moved toward the dock, eyes darting left and right, looking for any sign of enemies in the shadows. A squeal nearby made her tense every muscle, and she pulled an arrow from her quiver, nocking and aiming in one smooth motion. Before she could loose, a pig squealed its way from the terror, a broken arrow protruding from its haunches.

Tyreta stalked toward the raging battle until she reached the end of the thoroughfare that led down onto the docklands. With openmouthed horror she saw the remaining defenders were all but defeated. The kesh were slaughtering the wounded as the last of the valiant defenders were pushed into the sea. A solitary stormhulk floundered in the midst of the horde, pistons hissing, hydraulics whirring as it swept its metal arms in great scything arcs, but even as it fought, the kesh were securing ropes about its rusted chassis, a score of them surrounding the great machine. She could only watch helplessly as it toppled, the kesh swarming all over it, prising open the cockpit with their spears and dragging out the hapless webwainer. Tyreta averted her eyes rather than witness what came next.

A scream alerted her to danger close by. Down an alleyway there was a struggle. Two kesh warriors were dragging a guardsman along the street, a look of relish on their faces. The sight filled her with disgust and ignited a scorching furnace of hate within her.

She moved toward them, arrow drawn, aiming at one of the fearsome warriors as he raised his axe to take the guard's head as his prize. As the bowstring was loosed, singing in her ear, she breathed out just as Gelila had taught her, watching the arrow fly past its target to embed itself in the wall of the alley.

The axe came down, hacking into the head of the hapless victim. He died because of her poor aim, but Tyreta had no time for remorse, no time for guilt as the kesh warriors turned toward her. One of them roared in challenge, the other already charging along the alley.

All her bravery, all her confidence, all the determination she had mustered to come here abandoned her in that instant.

Tyreta ran, legs powering her around a bend and down a narrow passage, desperate to lose her pursuers in the maze of backstreets. She had no idea where she was going, all she knew was that she had to keep running. The kesh were not far behind, the sound of their pursuit echoing along the tightly packed alleyway.

Before she turned another corner, she chanced a glance over her shoulder. They were gaining on her, those painted faces wearing a mix of fury and glee as they hunted. There would be nowhere to run, nowhere to hide. Eventually they would fall upon her with all their savagery. If she was to die, so be it, but she would do it fighting.

Still running, she stripped another arrow from her quiver and nocked it to the bow. This time she forced herself to concentrate, to control her breathing as she came to a stop in the middle of the street and turned, pulling, aiming. She loosed as the first of the kesh rounded the corner. He was greeted by the arrow, straight in the centre of his chest.

Tyreta did not pause, nocking a second arrow in one smooth motion as the first kesh fell. She had loosed before he hit the ground, but this arrow swept wide of the mark.

Too late to nock a third, she dropped her bow, pulling the spear from over her shoulder and bracing it to face the onslaught. The second kesh ducked her wild jab, his axe hacking toward her, but she danced back, sure-footed in the mud of the alleyway. Another thrust, but the kesh met her spear with his axe, knocking it aside.

She ducked a vicious swipe of the weapon, then leaned away from the backswing. The kesh was frenzied now, fangs clenched, eyes glaring. Tyreta spun, the butt of the spear aimed at his head, but he grabbed it in his free hand, wrenching it from her grip.

Another swipe of the axe and Tyreta stumbled back, feet catching on the uneven ground before she went tumbling. The kesh warrior roared his victory, standing over her, gripping his axe in both hands as he raised it for the final strike.

A dull thud echoed through the alleyway, the head of the warrior snapping to one side. His furious eyes dulled before he collapsed to the mud. When she looked up, Tyreta recognised the old man who stood there with a desperate look on his face, heavy wrench gripped in both hands.

"Crenn," she gasped.

"That's my name," said the old artificer, glaring down at the corpse he had made.

Tyreta scrambled to her feet, wrapping her arms around him, never so relieved to see a friendly face in her life.

"We have to go," Crenn whispered as she released him from her bear hug. "It's not safe here."

Tyreta picked up her bow and spear. "You don't have to tell me that. Are there more survivors?"

Crenn nodded. "Follow me."

He led her through the back alleys, and Tyreta began to get her bearings as they made their way toward Crenn's workshop. The savage roar of the Chul warriors had died down somewhat, but the odd scream of pain and terror could be heard above the sound of crackling fires.

Crenn pulled open his workshop door before slipping into the dark confines, and Tyreta followed close behind. Beyond the shadows and the oil stink, figures were hiding in the dark, and she could practically taste their fear in the air.

As her eyes quickly adjusted to the gloom, Tyreta saw faces she recognised among the survivors. Lavren and Edana Larkin, those wealthy merchants she had met at Isleen's dinner party, hugged one another for comfort in one corner. Even their great wealth had not spared them from the anarchy running rampant throughout the port. Not far from them hunkered Chancellor Eremand, his eyes staring in shock and horror at what they had seen. Tyreta would have chastised him for his earlier arrogance, his dismissal of her warning, but it was too late to do any good now.

Surrounding them were other dirty, shocked faces, men and women from every stratum of New Flaym's society, from dock labourers to trading magnates.

"Is it over?" murmured a voice from the dark.

Tyreta shook her head. "It won't be over till the kesh have slaughtered everyone in the port. We have to get as far away from here as we can."

Chancellor Eremand rose unsteadily to his feet. "No. We have to stay where we are. Help will be coming. It has to."

Tyreta took a step toward him, and he shied away from her. "I warned you. Everyone else is dead. Every mine and outpost overrun. No one is coming to save you. Stay here if you want, but the only ones who will find you whimpering in the dark are the kesh."

The chancellor had nothing else to say as she turned to Crenn. "The gate's not far from here. It's unguarded. We need to get everyone moving, now."

The artificer nodded in agreement. "You heard her," he said as Tyreta moved to the workshop door to check the way was clear. When she saw there was no one awaiting them, she led the way north, a dozen bedraggled survivors following in her wake. Crenn was right behind her, that wrench gripped in a white-knuckled fist.

Once they had made their way past the burning villas, Tyreta could see the wall looming beyond. She slowed her pace, a sense of unnatural foreboding creeping up inside her gut. She raised a hand, halting the survivors as she crept to the edge of a building, hugging tight to the soot-blackened whitewash. Peering around the corner she saw four kesh warriors. Two were busying themselves dragging down the pennants of the Guilds that flew proudly beside the gate. Another two were smashing open the crates from an upturned cart, strewing their contents across the road.

Tyreta felt the burgeoning power of the pyrestone they had spilled onto the path. Back in Torwyn those discarded stones would have commanded a fortune. Here they were worthless baubles twinkling in the dirt.

"What now?" whispered Crenn, who had snuck up behind her, peering at the scene of carnage with a woeful expression.

"I'm working on it," Tyreta replied, eyes focusing on that pyrestone, feeling its energy calling to her from across the path.

Again she saw the web appear to her in vivid yellows, blues, reds, the strands extending to encompass everything in her field of vision. She was at the centre of it, connected to every living thing, feeling it pulsate, feeling it breathe.

The more she concentrated, the more that connection grew. Through the arcane imprint of the web she saw the pyrestone begin to shimmer, shining, winking in the sunlight. It burned, igniting and trembling on the ground.

Tyreta raised a hand, clenching her fist tight, and the discarded stones rose inches into the air at her unspoken command. She quelled her excitement as she took control, using her will to move the stones. All her life she had been able to manipulate pyrestone, increasing and decreasing the power it possessed, harnessing its energy, but never before had she been able to physically move it with her mind. A swipe of her open palm and the stones scattered at the feet of the kesh.

Immediately they stopped what they were doing, alerted to the movement, looking down curiously at the stones at their feet.

Tyreta stepped out from cover, hearing Crenn hiss a word of warning, but she ignored him. She was almost boiling inside, feeling the latent energy of the stones as she fuelled them, igniting their cores, overloading them with her power.

One of the kesh spotted her, barking a warning to the other three warriors. He barely had a chance to snarl his challenge before the pyrestone at his feet exploded. It set off a chain reaction, the other stones bursting apart in flaming shards, cutting through the warriors, shredding them like straw mannequins, burning them in her rage.

She stood trembling for a moment, staring at the scorched remains, before Crenn took her by the arm.

"What have I just watched?" he managed to say. "How did you...?"

"When I work it out, I'll let you know," Tyreta replied, blinking away the miasma, forcing herself back from the fugue. "Right now, we have to run."

Crenn didn't argue, and together they urged the rest of the survivors to make their way through the gate. They fled north, veering into the jungle, rushing through the thick foliage and leaving the port to burn behind them.

At any moment Tyreta expected to see the Chul pursuing them through the jungle, but by some miracle they managed to flee unmolested. As they ran, some of the beleaguered refugees faltered, but Tyreta was there to pull them to their feet, urging them on, determined they would all survive. It wasn't until the sun started to creep toward the horizon that they stopped.

The survivors finally dropped down exhausted, but Tyreta felt no fatigue as she stood and watched the black cloud that had risen over the sea. Most of their tiny band were silent, still in shock from what they had suffered. Others wondered what they would do, where they would go, who would come to rescue them. Tyreta had no answers. They were alive for now. It would have to be enough.

As the sun set, she heard a rustling in the undergrowth and braced her spear against the threat. Before she even saw who it was, she knew they were in no danger. Her senses did not scream at her to defend herself—this was no kesh hunting party.

Tyreta lowered the spear as a guardsman came stumbling into the clearing, his face a bloody mess. The man fell into Tyreta's arms, and she gently lowered him to the ground. Crenn and some others came forward to help, and eventually he was made comfortable enough to speak.

"The whole place is in flames," he whispered, eyes haunted. "We tried to run, only a few of us made it out, I don't know how I managed to follow your trail."

"Are there any more survivors?" Crenn asked.

The wounded man nodded. "Scores of them. The kesh took a host of prisoners. Men, women, children. They slaughtered the wounded, strung them up at the dock."

"What are they going to do to them?" one woman asked Tyreta, as though she might know.

She glanced at Crenn. "Nothing good," said the old artificer. "We just have to pray for their souls, I guess."

Tyreta stood. Praying wouldn't get them anywhere. There had to be something they could do. Something *she* could do.

The memory of the power she'd felt when igniting the pyrestones was at the forefront of her mind. The Lokai had granted her a gift, and there was no way she could spurn it.

Tyreta checked her quiver. There were eight arrows left, for all the good they had done her so far. She was an average shot at best, but perhaps there was a way to make every arrow count.

"I need pyrestone," she said to the survivors. "As much as you have."

Some shrugged, shaking their heads, as others looked to one another in confusion.

"I know some of you carry it," she said, more insistently, sensing the latent energy of the stone close by. Edana Larkin had a jewelled necklace that gave off a particularly powerful aura. "Now's not the time to covet your trinkets. If this man managed to follow our trail through the brush, then it'll be easy enough for the kesh to follow it too. I need your pyrestone. Give it to me."

Still no one moved.

Before she had to force them, a feline head appeared from beyond the tree line. Some of the survivors scattered as the panther made her way forward, brushing her haunches against Tyreta's legs.

"Now," Tyreta growled.

Edana practically tore the jewels from around her neck as Chancellor Eremand fumbled with the cufflinks at his wrists. Within seconds Tyreta had a dozen small pyrestones in the palm of her hand. They were a mixture of yellow and blue—fire and lightning. Tyreta was sure they'd do the job.

Drawing one of the arrows from her quiver, she turned to Crenn.

"I need one of these"—she held up one of the pyrestones between finger and thumb—"at the end of each one of these." She showed him the arrow.

Crenn nodded, a knowing smile crossing his face. "I can do that."

CONALL

The night had become an exercise in shivering like a shitting dog. Blindfolded and tied to a post in the centre of the courtyard, Conall had little option but to suffer it.

When the sun finally came up, he began to feel some respite from the cold, but the relief was never going to last. The morning wore on, and the warm sun turned to burning heat. Sweat ran from him in rivulets, his mouth drying till his tongue felt like a desiccated twig. Occasionally he licked at his top lip, letting the salty tang of sweat run into his mouth, for all the good it did. He was desperate for water, but he'd be damned if he'd beg.

The sound of troopers busying themselves within the fort was his only company. No one spoke, and there was a mournful atmosphere to the place. Beringer had been feared but also respected, and his passing left a tangible breach. Conall could only imagine what these men thought of him, the prisoner they believed had murdered their beloved commander. Luckily none of them had acted on their grief, and so far he'd been left unmolested. He was sure that wouldn't last.

When the sun was at its most intense, he heard the battalion mustering, scuffling feet organising into disciplined rows. Then Tarrien's voice, the sound of it making Conall flinch in anger.

He called to his men, voice sombre as he ordered them to convey the frontier marshal's body through the fort. Conall heard them file out of the main gate, toward the graveyard where he'd buried Nevan not too long ago.

In the quiet he could make out that distant voice spouting pious words as they laid Beringer to rest in his pauper's grave. One more body alongside his men. If only the troopers of the Phoenix Battalion knew the truth—that it was one of their own who'd murdered the frontier marshal. As it was, Conall was the one who would suffer for it, and he doubted there was anything he could say to persuade them of his innocence.

And how would he suffer? Tarrien would want him silenced as quickly as possible; surely a flogging was the least of his worries. Conall had no doubt that before the day was done there'd be one more hole dug alongside Beringer's, and he'd be the one filling it.

When the burial was over, the Phoenix Battalion returned to the fort. There was more movement, horses being brought from the stables, a wagon being hitched, angry words urging haste. In the midst of it, Conall heard a voice he recognised.

"I don't give a shit," Sted snarled. "What you gonna do, shoot me in the fucking back?"

Murmurs of disquiet. A stream of curses from Sted. He could still hear her mumbling profanities under her breath as she moved closer to him.

The blindfold was wrenched from his face, and Conall squinted against the brightness of the sun. The courtyard was alive with activity, but he tried to focus on Sted's frowning face.

"Drink," she said, pressing a waterskin to his lips.

At first he wondered if it might be some kind of liquor she'd pilfered, but as he felt it moisten his lips he didn't care. Greedily he swallowed it down, a little relieved it was only water.

"I hope you've got a plan, Con," she said under her breath. "These fuckers are ready to string you up from the nearest rafter."

Conall stopped drinking, gasping as the cold water ran down his throat. "If it makes any difference, I didn't kill him."

"I know that. But it's not me you need to convince."

"I'm working on it," he said.

She raised the waterskin to his lips once more. "Well, work fast. Tarrien's ordered us from the fort. We're leaving right away."

Conall glanced over her shoulder, seeing the wagon hitched and ready to go. The last of the Talon secured their gear on horses under the watchful eye of Phoenix Battalion troopers.

"They've confiscated all our arms and ammunition. We've got to travel the road back to Agavere with nothing but our bollocks in our hands."

Conall almost spat the precious water from his mouth at that. "You'll be fine," he whispered. "You've got a more dangerous pair of bollocks than any man I've known."

The trace of a smile crept up one side of her mouth before it vanished. Her frown deepened and she looked into his eyes. Was that a tremble to her lip?

"May the Wyrms protect you, Conall Hawkspur," she whispered.

Even in their gravest moments, he'd never seen this kind of emotion from Sted. She knew just as well as he did there was no getting out of this. He was all out of options, and no talk of plans and escape was going to save him.

A battalion trooper approached. "That's enough," he said, barely masking his contempt. "Time for you to be on your way."

"Why don't you fuck off?" Sted snapped. "Before I stick that spear up your arse and write my name in the sand with it."

The trooper's confident air wavered before he took a step back. Sted raised the waterskin to Conall's lips one final time, making sure it was empty. He gulped down what he could, no idea when there'd be a chance to drink again.

"Wish this could have been wine," she whispered.

"When I get back to Torwyn, we'll split a whole barrel," he replied. "The finest Wyke has to offer."

Sted nodded, forcing a smile on her lips, eyes moistening before she turned and walked back toward the rest of the Talon. She'd never been comfortable with goodbyes.

They mounted their horses, and Sted climbed atop the wagon, grabbing the reins. The gates were already open, the long road to Agavere stretching beyond. As his only allies trundled through the gate, Conall watched each of his scouts turn, giving a brisk salute to their captain as they left him behind to face whatever fate the Phoenix Battalion had in store. Sted didn't offer him a second glance.

The gate slammed behind them ominously. No sooner had the bars been secured than Tarrien mounted the stairs to Beringer's office and called for reveille. The troopers gathered, standing in their rows, silent as they crossed arms behind backs and looked up to their new commander.

"This morning was tough," Tarrien said. "I share your sorrow. Frontier Marshal Beringer was a father to us all. Tough but fair. His murder was a crime that shall not go unpunished, but take solace in the fact that I will take charge of his duties, just as he would have instructed. You all know me. You know I'm one of you, and I'll look to be as evenhanded as he was."

Conall could have laughed at that one, but his stomach was too tied up in knots and his mouth too dry for him to make a sound.

"You heard Beringer speak," Tarrien continued. "Heard him say how we'd stay neutral in the conflict to come until we heard different. Well, I think his murder proves one thing—we can wait no longer. Now is the time to pick a side." There was not a flicker of emotion from the men of Fort Tarkis. Every last one of them gazed up at Tarrien, listening intently.

"I know many of you follow the Ministry's faith. Many of you don't. I've never made a secret of where my loyalties lie." Tarrien raised a hand to the dragon amulet that hung around his neck. "I'll bear no grudge against any man for his beliefs. But from this day, Fort Tarkis stands with the Draconate. To any man that doesn't sit right with, you're free to leave. I won't hold it against you. But it's best you get your things and prepare to go now. There's no telling what will happen in the next few days. How things will change. So you're free to go, no one will stop you."

He paused, giving anyone who wanted it the opportunity to leave. Conall watched with rising dread as not a single man moved. Everyone stood to attention, focused on their new frontier marshal.

Tarrien nodded his approval. "You are all my brothers in blood. In war. Now we are brothers in faith. Let us pray."

Over two hundred men dropped to one knee, hands on hearts, heads bowed. Conall had only seen such disciplined piety in the Mount when the Drakes knelt to pray. It was impressive and terrifying all at once.

"Great Wyrms protect us in the battles to come. May Ammenodus Rex strengthen our arms and Undometh grant us the zeal to avenge our fallen. May Saphenodon gift us the wisdom to know our enemies and Vermitrix the nobility to show them mercy. May Ravenothrax bless us with the breath of the eternal flame should we fall."

"By the Five Lairs," his men answered in unison, their voices echoing throughout the fort.

"Rise," Tarrien said, and as one the battalion stood. "Now, on to other matters."

Tarrien regarded Conall tied to that post, barely hiding his contempt. With a gesture from him two of the troopers broke ranks and approached Conall. One took out a knife and cut the binding securing him to the pole. Immediately he felt relief at being able to lower his arms, but his wrists were still bound tight.

The troopers dragged Conall forward, the rest of the battalion moving aside until he was standing in front of the staircase.

"Conall Hawkspur," Tarrien said. "You stand accused of murder. Would you like an advocate to speak on your behalf?"

If there was anyone in the fort who'd speak for him, it was doubtful they'd do him justice.

"I can speak for myself," he replied. His fists were clenched before him, the best he could do to fight back the fear.

"Then I put it to you that in front of a witness you murdered Frontier Marshal Beringer without reason or provocation. What say you to the charge?"

"You know exactly who killed him," Conall spat. "And it wasn't me."

"As the sole witness, I can testify it was you. We both stood in his office as you demanded he forsake his faith in the Draconate to throw his support behind the Guilds. When he refused, you took your longbarrel and shot him dead. I imagine I would have faced the same fate if you'd had more than one charge in the breech."

"Bullshit," Conall said, trying and failing to hold in his anger. "Do you think I'm insane? What would I have to gain by killing Beringer? And in a fort surrounded by his loyal men?"

"I cannot speak for your motives. All I know is what I saw. You hated Beringer, showed him nothing but disrespect from the day you arrived at this fort. When he tried to show you the error of your ways, he was met with disloyalty and insubordination. After he was forced to discipline you, it was only a matter of time before you took your revenge."

Conall should have shouted his innocence to the four walls of the fort, but he knew it was pointless. It was his word against Tarrien's. How would he persuade the battalion of his innocence without a reliable witness?

"Nothing more to say?" Tarrien asked.

He was doomed and he knew it. Best not waste his breath railing against the injustice.

"Then I put it to the Phoenix Battalion. All those who find Conall Hawkspur guilty of murder, say aye."

Their answer was resounding and final—a chorus of ayes echoing off the walls of the fortress. If any disagreed with the verdict, they didn't feel the need to speak up.

Tarrien glared down without emotion. Conall guessed he was fighting the urge to display a self-satisfied grin. "Then I will pass the sentence—"

"No," Conall shouted, remembering the laws of Torwyn and the honour of the Guilds. Remembering his father. "I demand a trial by combat."

Tarrien laughed. The troopers surrounding Conall laughed along with him.

"Look around you, Hawkspur. Does this look like the court of some lofty Guild palace? We're not in Torwyn now, and we're not bound by Guild traditions. You will abide by the laws of the Armiger. The block and the axe are the only justice you'll get here."

With a wave of Tarrien's hand, Conall was grabbed and dragged back to the pole, his arms lofted high and secured once more. There he was left under the baking sun until the water Sted had given him was just a distant memory.

As the day wore on, he watched as a trooper struggled to carry a square wooden block from one of the storehouses before dropping it in the centre of the courtyard. Another trooper soon followed him, a wide-bladed axe slung over one shoulder. This one slammed the axe down onto the block in a mockery of Conall's fate and left them both in plain sight for him to ponder as the day darkened.

Just before nightfall another trooper walked right past him, not stopping as he casually gobbed a sticky ball of phlegm into Conall's face. Had it been wetter, Conall might have considered trying to lick it off, but instead he let it roll down his cheek, where it eventually dried to a crust.

When darkness and cold finally fell over the fort, he was left to think on his folly. Left to consider all the mistakes that had led him here and what he should have done differently. How he should have left when he heard of Fulren's exile. His family were the only people in the world who truly loved him, who would have given a shit about his fate, and he had ignored their strife in favour of his own indulgence.

And what of his mother? Lady Rosomon Hawkspur, alone, childless, trapped in a city besieged by fanatics. What of her fate? Conall guessed he would never know. He could only hope that despite all the ills he had dealt her, despite all the ills she had dealt him, she would still mourn her eldest son as much as she did her youngest.

The sky eventually blackened, revealing the myriad constellations above. As a trained scout of the Talon, Conall could name them all, but the last thing on his mind was stargazing. Navel-gazing might have done him as much good. He shivered. The first of the long night. The best he could look forward to now was the warmth of the sun in the morning before they hacked the head from his shoulders.

His legs started to give way beneath him as fatigue took over, pulling his arms tight and jolting him from the release of slumber. As he jerked himself awake for the dozenth time, someone shouted a call of warning at the gate. The alarm bell rang—there was someone approaching from the north.

Conall allowed a sliver of hope to cut through his despair. Was it the Talon? Returned armed and armoured to rescue him? When the gate was hastily pulled open and a covered wagon rolled in flanked by mounted troopers of the Auroch Battalion, he allowed that sliver of hope to fade in despair.

Tarrien rushed down the stairs from his chambers as one of the troopers opened the door to the wagon. In the torchlight Conall saw a robed woman step from within. The troopers of the Auroch Battalion lowered their heads in fealty as they helped her, and in the light of those torches Conall recognised the blue robes of a High Legate of Vermitrix.

Tarrien hurried across the courtyard before he dropped to one knee in front of her.

"We were not expecting such holy and honoured visitors," Tarrien said. "Certainly not at this hour. I am Westley Tarrien, acting frontier marshal of Fort Tarkis. To what do we owe—?"

"It's been a long journey," the woman said, gesturing for Tarrien to rise. "And I have no desire to spend any more time here than is necessary. I am High Legate Hisolda, and this is for you." She handed over a scroll.

Tarrien broke the seal, unfurled it, and read in the light of a torch one of his men held aloft. Through the dark Conall could see his expression turn grave.

"This is irregular," Tarrien said, brandishing the scroll in his fist. "This man is a murderer. Tried by the laws of the Armiger. He has already been condemned to death."

Hisolda took the scroll from Tarrien's trembling hand. "None of which is any of my concern. Are you going to hand him over, or do I have to report back to the Archlegate that Acting Frontier Marshal Westley Tarrien defied his explicit command?"

Tarrien glanced over one shoulder toward Conall. It was obvious that despite all his talk of piety, he was now conflicted about obeying the order of the Draconate.

"Of course, High Legate," he said finally, turning on his heel and marching toward Conall.

He pulled a knife as he approached, and Conall couldn't take his eyes off the blade glinting in the flickering torchlight.

"Seems you've got friends in high places, Hawkspur," he said through gritted teeth before cutting the rope that bound Conall to the post. He grabbed Conall by the arm and marched him toward the wagon. "But don't think this is over. I'll see you again."

The troopers of the Auroch Battalion took hold of him and guided him toward the back of the wagon. Hisolda was already waiting inside.

Before he climbed in to join the priestess, Conall turned to Tarrien.

"I'll look forward to it," he said.

Then he was bustled into the wagon, and the door slammed shut behind him.

Hisolda sat in silence, not even deigning to look Conall's way as the wagon began to trundle through the gate. He couldn't help but think he'd been released from the clutches of a war eagle only to fall into the mouth of a dragon.

As he succumbed to the sleep he'd been denied for too long, he resigned himself to dealing with this new problem much later.

LANCELIN

He clung to Fulren's waist, trusting that the boy's hold on those eagle feathers was a strong one. The flight across the wastes of the Drift had been long and treacherous, and Lancelin was more than aware of the dangers that lurked below. Mercifully they had made the journey safely, and once they crossed the peaks of the Dolur toward the distant city of the Anvil, he finally allowed himself to breathe easier.

How Fulren was controlling the beast with no bit or bridle, Lancelin could only wonder. More than likely it was something to do with the markings on his neck that had burned his flesh back in the cave so many days ago. Marks put there by the Maladorans, some kind of arcane gift. Lancelin could only hope they would not become a curse.

As the great spires became more distinct, the Whitespin visible as it wended its way south, he patted the boy on the back.

"We're close," he shouted above the rush of wind in their ears.

Fulren nodded. "I'll set us down at the palace aerie," he called back over his shoulder.

They eventually soared over the city walls, the labyrinth of streets tiny beneath them. As they approached Archwind Palace, Lancelin squinted at the vast monolith, air rushing into his face. Through the tears streaming from his eyes he spotted something that immediately unnerved him.

The flags of the Guilds had been removed from pride of place. Every last one had been exchanged for a pennant of the Draconate, and they were flanked by those of some Armiger Battalions—the crow of Corvus, the bear of Ursus, the bull head of Auroch. Only one Guild flag flew, one that had never been displayed on the palace before—the spider of Hallowhill.

"Wait," Lancelin shouted, patting Fulren on his shoulder once more. "Something's wrong."

"What is it?" Fulren replied. Beneath them he could feel the war eagle shudder, as though mimicking Fulren's apprehension.

"We have to land somewhere else."

"What? Why?"

Lancelin scanned the city below, spotting an aerie on the side of a municipal tower. "There," he shouted, pointing to it before remembering Fulren couldn't see the gesture.

Nevertheless the eagle banked, swooping toward the lonely aerie that jutted from the side of the tower. Lancelin's stomach lurched as they lost altitude, then flipped as the eagle spread its wings to halt their descent. Huge talons clacked and scraped against the stone surface of the jetty as the beast scrabbled for purchase, eventually coming to a stop.

The eagle gasped as they dismounted, and Lancelin fought back trepidation at being home. Something was wrong, he just didn't know what yet.

No sooner had their feet touched the jetty than the eagle reared. It issued a mighty screech before tensing its legs and powering itself into the sky once again. Lancelin watched as it swooped toward the streets before climbing, its piercing shriek of freedom echoing across the city. Though they darted from side to side, Fulren's blind eyes also followed the creature as it disappeared into the distant sky.

Lancelin took Fulren's arm, guiding him toward the tower of the landing jetty. At any moment he expected someone to come out and greet them, but the door to the tower remained shut.

"What's going on?" Fulren asked as Lancelin opened the door. "Why did we not land at the palace?"

"Something's not right. The Guild flags have been removed and replaced by symbols of the Draconate or Armigers. The only Guild flag flying is that of the Hallowhills."

"What could that mean?"

"It means we need to watch our step, and you'd better let me do the talking. For now, we're just two travellers newly arrived in the city."

They entered the tower and made their way up a dimly lit flight of stairs to a wide chamber at the top. Lancelin would have expected some administrator from the Hawkspur Guild to be waiting to log their arrival. Instead a young functionary sat at a desk, dressed in the sickly yellow of the Corwen Guild.

He looked up in surprise as Lancelin reached the top of the stairs, the stylus he had been using to scratch on a piece of parchment dropping from his hand. He was only a youth, barely fifteen at a guess.

"What's going on here?" Lancelin asked, possibly too harshly, but his patience was already worn thin. "Where are the Hawkspur administrators?"

The boy stood, shaking his head. "I...I should..."

Before Lancelin could stop him, he darted for the door.

"You really do have a way with people," Fulren breathed in frustration.

"We have to get out of here," Lancelin replied. "I have a feeling we've arrived at just the wrong time."

Fulren didn't argue as he was guided to the door. The corridor beyond led them through the abandoned building and down a set of stairs toward the skyway that ringed the city. Before Lancelin could guide Fulren to the freedom of the public streets he saw their way was blocked.

The Corwen scribe was talking with three Revocaters, gesturing frantically with his arm. Before Lancelin could even think about escape they saw him, ignoring the functionary and walking toward him with purpose.

"We've been spotted," he whispered to Fulren as they approached. "Just follow my lead."

"Of course," Fulren replied. "That's worked out so well up to now."

Lancelin stepped out onto the bridge that led to the skyway. He could hear a train of carriages trundling along its tracks, accompanied by the hum of pyrestone energy.

The three Revocaters bore that suspicious air Lancelin had come to expect from Rearden Corwen's inquisitors.

"What's your business here?" said the one wearing a red officer's plume in his helm. "How did you get onto the aerie?"

Lancelin saw one of the men eyeing Fulren suspiciously and tried to step into his line of sight. He only hoped that with his unkempt appearance and weather-beaten garb, the officer would not recognise the swordwright of the Archwind Guild either.

"We are merchants, new in from Goodfleet. Our eagle was injured and we were forced to set down at this aerie."

"Where is your letter of marque?" demanded the Revocater.

Lancelin shrugged, wary of the men eyeing him and his weapon suspiciously. "Lost. But if there's a representative of the Hawkspur Guild on hand, I'm sure we can clear this up."

The officer was not convinced, his hand moving to his sword. "Hand over your weapon."

Lancelin held his hands out in a gesture of contrition. "I don't think that's necessary."

One of the Revocaters leaned in toward his officer. "That's Lancelin Jagdor," he whispered.

The officer's eyes widened in concern. With a ring of steel his sword was clear of its scabbard. Lancelin took a step back, pushing Fulren to one side as the rest drew their weapons. The wide-eyed functionary backed away toward the edge of the bridge, a look of fear on his face at the prospect of violence.

"I said hand over the fucking weapon," the officer repeated.

"You don't want to do this," Lancelin replied.

"I'll tell you what I want," the officer spat. "I want your sword, and I want you both on your knees right now."

They were bristling for a fight, desperate to wet their blades. Maybe he could threaten them, tell them what danger they were in by confronting a swordwright, but what then? There was no way they would stay silent, no way that he and Fulren would be able to disappear into the city.

Lancelin pulled his sword free of his scabbard as the first Revocater rushed forward. It was a clumsy attack, and Lancelin ducked the wayward swing, bringing his blade up on instinct and slicing open the man's midriff. The second Revocater had barely raised his sword before Lancelin thrust the tip of his blade into his throat. He stepped aside as the man staggered back, clutching his neck, trying to stem the tide now spilling through his fingers, and the officer took his swing. This was more precise, he was well trained, but he could never be skilled enough to take on a swordwright.

Lancelin deflected the strike, knocking the blade from his hand. His backswing took the officer in the side of his neck almost deep enough to sever the head.

It all happened in less time than it took to blink, and the Revocaters fell to the ground at the same time. He had killed three of the Corwen Guild's finest, but there was no time to consider the consequences.

As Lancelin approached him, the functionary began to sob. He was only a boy, knees trembling as he dropped to the ground, holding up his hands mimicking a gesture of prayer.

"What's going on here?" Lancelin demanded.

Credit to the boy, he tried to answer, but all he could manage was a strangled sob, those hands trembling as though they might stop a sword blow with fear alone.

Lancelin crouched down, trying to stay calm, trying to appear as though he hadn't just slaughtered three men in an instant. "Tell me what has happened to the city."

More sobs. He would get no sense out of this one. Lancelin rose to his feet still glaring at the boy.

"Is there any chance you'll let us get away from here before you raise the alarm?" he asked.

The boy nodded vigorously, snot dripping from his nose, spit dribbling down his lip. Lancelin thought it unlikely—as soon as he moved on, this boy would be screaming bloody murder across the rooftops. Had he been a different kind of man he would have covered his tracks and silenced the only witness. But that had never been his way.

"We have to move," Lancelin said, grabbing Fulren by the arm and urging him across the bridge toward the skyway.

"By the bloody Lairs, what's going on?" Fulren replied as he was pulled through the gate at the end of the bridge.

"No time." Lancelin was all too aware of the urgency.

They raced down a flight of stairs and out onto the main thoroughfare. A few people were going about their business, but no one gave them a second look. Lancelin realised he had a naked blade in his hand, evidence of what he'd just done dripping from it onto the paved thoroughfare, and he used his sleeve to wipe the blood clear before sheathing it.

He pulled Fulren close beside him, walking toward the skyway platform in the distance, making sure not to draw attention to himself by making eye contact with anyone. There was a subdued atmosphere when they reached the wide platform. Silence replaced the usual bustle and verve of the Anvil.

As they waited, more people began to gather around them. Lancelin kept his head down, relieved when he eventually heard the distant clack of the rails. With a screech of brakes and a hiss of pistons, the skycarriage came to a standstill in front of them. He grabbed Fulren's arm and walked to an empty carriage, then wrenched open the door and stepped inside.

He only allowed himself to take a purging breath once they were alone. The skyway was used exclusively by Guild representatives—administrators, bureaucrats, functionaries—and it took them about their business across the Anvil. Today it seemed that business mattered little, and there was barely a soul aboard.

"Are we safe?" Fulren asked as the carriage juddered away from the platform.

Lancelin looked out of the circular porthole and down onto the city below. There was hardly any activity; no wagons, no bustle, no trade of any kind. Even the distant Whitespin River was devoid of traffic.

"No," he replied. "We are not safe. I don't know what's going on, but we need to get out of the city as quickly as we can."

The skycarriage descended on its rails to street level as it headed toward the next platform. If they stayed on board, they would eventually come to the city's landship terminal. Perhaps from there they would even be able to slip out of the city altogether. If Lancelin could get Fulren back to Wyke, they could plan their next move from there. But what of Rosomon? Where was she in all this mess? Could he really flee the city and leave her behind? At least then the boy would be safe. But as the hiss of pistons heralded their arrival at the next platform, all those ideas drifted away like piss on the wind.

Alarm bells clanged in the distance, growing louder the closer they got to the platform. By the time the carriage screeched to a stop, Lancelin could hear those bells chiming like a Guild wedding.

He drew his sword, wrenching open the door and pulling Fulren out onto the platform. Bells reverberated all around them. The rest of the debarking passengers, panicked by the noise, gasped in fright and moved from Lancelin's path when they saw the blade in his hand. If there'd been any hope of them getting lost in the crowd, it was gone now.

He rushed across the platform, desperate to reach the safety of an alleyway or the door to some nearby building before they were seen. Before he could reach the exit from the platform he heard an ominous cry for them to "Stop!"

A glance over his shoulder and he saw the dark uniforms of Armiger troopers, bear helms marking them as belonging to the Ursus Battalion. A dozen of them pushed their way through the crowd, calling for everyone to make way, yelling for Lancelin to halt.

Fulren kept pace alongside him as they rushed up a nearby staircase, across the thoroughfare at the summit and down an alleyway opposite. In the distance the alarm bells grew quieter, but the stamp of pursuing feet followed them all the way.

The alley was short, opening out onto a wide promenade. Lancelin came to a sudden stop, at a loss for which way to run. The Anvil was a huge city, wide boulevards linked by dark alleys. A hundred ways to escape, but which one to take?

Another alleyway led off into the dark, and Lancelin dragged Fulren down it. When they turned a corner, he realised his mistake. A dead end.

Rising up on three sides was nothing but sheer brickwork. Open windows overlooked the alley, and he saw faces glaring down, keen to see what all the commotion was about. He doubted any of them would be willing to help as he heard the troopers following in their wake.

"What do we do?" Fulren asked, his breath ragged, his eyes desperate.

A good question.

Perhaps they should just surrender. Offer themselves to the new overlords of the city. But Lancelin Jagdor could never surrender. He had come too far, suffered too much for that.

"There's nowhere left to run," Lancelin said. "So you'll have to give yourself up. Hopefully your mother has taken a stand against whatever has happened here. If so, she'll find you no matter what."

"What do you mean?" Fulren said. "What are you going to do?"

"I have to fight."

"What are you talking about, you mad bastard?" Fulren spat. "Does every problem you face have to end in dead bodies? We can both surrender. At least that way we'll live."

He could see the concern in the young man's face, and for a moment it almost gave him hope. When Fulren first realised who had come to his rescue, he had displayed nothing but contempt. Now there was only sorrow in his blind eyes.

The sound of tramping feet grew louder as it echoed down the alleyway beyond. Not long now.

"There's something you have to know," Lancelin said just as the troopers turned the corner. There were more than a dozen of them, blades drawn. "I'm—"

Lancelin was cut off by the sharp report of a splintbow. Four snaps echoed along the alleyway. The first volley was followed by a crescendo, the staccato thrum of a score of bowstrings, bolts thudding into the charging warriors.

Looking up, Lancelin could see archers positioned along the row of windows, hoods drawn up over their heads. Three of the troopers went down, riddled with splintbolts. The others stopped in their tracks, unable to defend themselves against the missile fire.

From behind the bear-helmed troopers charged five hooded warriors, their weapons striking with controlled ferocity. A head was struck from its shoulders by the mighty swing of a double-headed axe. Another was knocked to the ground by the powerful blow of a greatsword, its wielder remorseless, hacking down again and again until his prone victim lay butchered.

Lancelin pulled Fulren close behind him, sword held defensively, trying to work out what was happening. He would have joined the attack on the Armiger troopers, but he had no idea who these brutal warriors were, or whether he and Fulren would be next to suffer their wrath.

The sudden attack took the Ursus troopers by surprise, and they were overwhelmed by the hulking fighters who showed no mercy, each one fighting with hateful fury. In seconds the alley was a butcher's yard, the attack over as quickly as it had begun.

As the rest of the hooded warriors took the fallen weapons of the dead, one of them approached, axe held loosely in his hand, blood still dripping from its edge. When he pulled back his hood, Lancelin saw a face he recognised. Finally someone he knew he could trust.

The Imperator Dominus of the Titanguard nodded his shaved head grimly. "Jagdor," he said.

"Mallum Kairns," Lancelin replied. "I never thought I'd say this, but you're a sight for sore eyes."

The huge Titanguard raised an eyebrow on his wide, ugly face. "I never thought I'd say this, but where the fuck were you when we needed you?"

"I was sent on a mission," Lancelin replied, stepping aside and gesturing to Fulren. "One I couldn't say no to."

As Mallum saw the heir to the Hawkspur Guild, he raised his brow in surprise. Then he nodded his understanding.

"My lord Fulren. It is good to see you home. But we need to get off the streets. Armiger Battalions loyal to the Ministry are everywhere, and Corwen Revocaters won't be far behind."

"Then let's get out of here," said Lancelin, taking hold of Fulren.

With a nod Mallum and his hooded warriors led them out of the alley. Hopefully, he'd be able to tell Lancelin what in the Five Lairs was going on.

FULREN

They moved down through the streets and back alleys in silence, eventually squeezing into dank, dripping tunnels. Fulren strained his senses, desperate to use the necroglyph so that he might at least see what lay in front of him, but he was still plagued by blindness, urged on by unseen figures, wondering where Lancelin was and hoping he was close.

Wasn't that ironic? A man he had hated, had planned to kill, was now the only friend he had in all the world. His only protector in the darkness.

Nevertheless, Fulren fought back the panic, allowing himself to be led. There were many figures surrounding him, of that he was certain. There was no way to count them, but their footfalls echoed through the subterranean tunnels. Judging by the stink, they were most likely the sewer systems beneath the Anvil. A labyrinth easy to get lost in.

Deeper they went, slopping ankle-deep though the effluent, until Fulren could hear the river flowing nearby. A cool breeze brushed against his face, and he could only imagine the majesty of that vast waterway as it flowed by, heedless of what was going on in the city around it.

The men surrounding him slowed to a stop, and he heard the

sound of rusted hinges and the creak of an ancient door opening before he was urged on. The ground was suddenly firm beneath his feet as the door was closed with an ominous slam.

"We'll be safe here for now." Fulren recognised the voice of Mallum Kairns, and knew the Imperator Dominus was one of his uncle's most loyal warriors. His voice was deep, commanding, but Fulren could still sense his apprehension. "The others will arrive soon. Take a seat, Lord Fulren."

Fulren felt the man take him by the shoulder, guiding him to a chair. Despite the discomfort of the hard, rickety wood, Fulren was sure he could easily fall asleep right there.

"What others?" Lancelin's voice. Fulren could barely quell the relief at hearing it.

"The Titanguard are not the only ones who have taken a stand against the Draconate," said Mallum. "Egelrath has not whispered his poison into every ear in the Anvil. Not yet, at least."

"What is happening?" Fulren asked, trying not to sound as scared as he was.

Mallum sighed. "Apologies, Lord Fulren. But much has changed since you..."

"Since I was banished," Fulren finished for him, wondering if Mallum himself had been among the Titanguard who had taken him to the demon ark and handed him over to Wenis.

"Lord Fulren, if there was anything I could have done—"

"That's in the past," Lancelin said. "We have to focus on what's happening now."

"Indeed," Mallum replied. "The Draconate Ministry has initiated a coup against the Guilds. They control the city, and their poison is spreading throughout Torwyn. We hear that other cities of the Guildlands are ready to declare themselves for the Draconate."

"But how?" Fulren asked. "How could this happen so quickly, and right under the nose of the emperor?"

"I can only assume the Archlegate has been planning this for some time. He has the Hallowhills and half the Armiger Battalions behind him. With their help he overcame most of the Titanguard. Half my men have been slaughtered or imprisoned, the rest of us only just managed to escape. Emperor Sullivar... was murdered. In front of the entire city. His son Lorens has declared himself for the Ministry."

"This is madness," Lancelin breathed.

"Madness or not," said Mallum, "that is the truth of it."

"What about my mother?" Fulren asked, steeling himself for the answer.

"As far as I know, she is still Egelrath's prisoner."

"So she lives?"

"For now, confined to the palace. A hostage of the Ministry. There are still many men and women loyal to the Guilds, but as long as the Archlegate holds his captives they are powerless to organise an uprising."

"What about my brother and sister?"

"We have received no word, Lord Fulren."

Someone knocked at the door before Fulren could press further. At the creak of hinges and the sound of footsteps entering the chamber, Fulren rose to his feet, keen to know who these newcomers were.

"Greetings," Mallum said to whoever had arrived. "You both know Lancelin Jagdor and Lord Fulren Hawkspur?"

"I do," said a man's voice.

No word from the second newcomer. Instead Fulren felt himself being embraced; a woman. Though there was an essence of mustiness to her garb, her hair smelled like summer flowers.

"I thought I'd never see you again," she whispered.

"Emony?" Fulren asked.

He hugged her back until he felt her hand gently touch his face. "What have they done to you?"

He had always watched Emony Marrlock from afar. Always wondered what it might be like to be the object of her attention. Now, blind and broken, he suddenly wished he weren't.

"It's a long story," Fulren replied, taking her by the hand.

"One for another time," Mallum said. "Lord Fulren, this is Drift Marshal Rawlin of the Bloodwolf Battalion. He is loyal to the Guilds and their rightful masters and has chosen to stand with us against the usurper."

Fulren nodded, though he could not see the man. "You have my thanks, Marshal Rawlin."

"Don't thank me yet," Rawlin replied. "We are vastly outnumbered and trapped in enemy territory. As far as I know, every Armiger Battalion in the city stands against us. If it were up to me, we'd get as far from here as we could."

"No," said Mallum. "We have to strike back now. If we leave the city, we might not get the chance to return. Egelrath will only tighten his hold on the Anvil and its people."

"I have less than a thousand men," said Rawlin. "How many Titanguard do you have, Mallum? And how effective are they without their pyrestone battle armour?"

"I will not leave here while Lady Rosomon is still a prisoner of the Ministry," said Lancelin.

"And how do you seek to rescue her, Jagdor?" asked Rawlin. "Will you stroll up to the palace and take on the Drakes alone?"

"If I have to."

As they argued, Fulren could feel the pressure building in his head. There was power nearby, something sorcerous he could sense in his bones. The necroglyph at his neck began to tingle, and he tightened his grip on Emony's hand.

The door opened again, this time swinging wide as someone was bundled inside. Fulren caught the sound of a sword being half-drawn from its scabbard and assumed it was Lancelin reacting in his usual measured fashion. As soon as the newcomer entered, Fulren was almost overwhelmed by an intense light in his field of vision.

He raised a hand to shield his eyes on instinct, but it did little to stifle the brightness. This was arcane energy, a burning light emanating from a single figure. They were all but carried into the room and dumped in a chair at its centre.

"What's this?" asked Marshal Rawlin.

In the arcane glow given off by the newcomer, Fulren could see the shadows of everyone surrounding them—the tall outline of Rawlin, Mallum's huge, imposing bulk, Lancelin's athletic physique, even Emony standing beside him, the contours of her face just distinguishable against the dark.

"We grabbed this one off the streets yesterday," said Mallum. "She put up a hell of a struggle too."

"Well, she's not struggling now," Rawlin replied. "A lowly webwainer of the Hallowhills if my guess is right. Was this the best you could do?"

"Under the circumstances, yes." Mallum moved forward, looming over the prisoner in her chair. "She's not had much to say so far. I was hoping we might change that now. The more we know, the more chance we'll have of—"

"Of what?" snapped Rawlin. "Of retaking the city? That's still a bloody mad idea."

"When you have a better one, let me know." Mallum crouched down beside the webwainer in the chair. Fulren could see she was conscious, but barely. Emony gripped his hand tighter at the sight, and he squeezed it back as reassuringly as he could.

"How many webwainers have the Hallowhills brought to the city?" Mallum asked.

The prisoner looked up, staring at him but making no sound. Fulren could see the latent energy within her begin to spark. Was it fear? Anger?

"Why have you done this?" Mallum asked, his voice growing more frustrated. "You are a Guild of Torwyn, yet you've thrown your lot in with the Ministry. They will burn down this country and everything the Guilds stand for. They must be defeated. Give me something, anything, and I promise you will live."

The webwainer smiled. Though Fulren could not make out her eyes, he knew she was staring straight at Mallum.

"You think I would betray my Guild? The Ministry? For what, the old ways? So you can take back what was yours and continue your avarice and lust for power? I will tell you nothing. And soon you will kneel before the Draconate or be consumed in the breath of the Wyrms."

Fulren heard Mallum sigh. "This is pointless," he said.

"No, it isn't," insisted Lancelin. "Give me some time and I'll get the information we need."

"Wait," said Fulren, letting go of Emony's hand and taking a faltering step forward. "I think...I think I can get her to talk."

He had previously managed to exert some kind of power over a hound and a war eagle. What difference a webwainer?

"Lord Fulren." Mallum sounded unsure. "I think it best if you—"

"Let him try," Lancelin said. "What do we have to lose?"

Fulren moved toward the webwainer. He could see the power of her sorcery rushing through every fibre. As he regarded her, he could sense her feelings—a raw mix of fear and determination. She was powerful in her webwainer gifts, but as Fulren's necroglyph began to burn with anticipation he knew she would not be powerful enough to resist him.

"Where is my mother?" Fulren asked, the first question that came to his head. "Is Lady Rosomon safe?"

Resistance, cold and stark, as the webwainer tried to remain silent. Fulren persisted, pressing his will, forcing her to trust him, to open her soul to him. He felt the necroglyph begin to sear, exerting its darkness over the light of her webwainer gift. There was a distant whisper in his ear, someone urging him on from across a sea of blackness.

"She is at the palace," the woman gasped. "Under the protection of the Archlegate."

"Why have the Hallowhills betrayed the Guilds?"

"Because you have ignored us," the webwainer spat, and Fulren could feel her disdain, the truth and ignominy of it pouring out of her. "You have treated us as little more than servants for too long. Ingelram Hallowhill will stand for it no longer. We will take our rightful place as rulers of Torwyn, no longer slaves to merchants and farmers."

"Where is Sanctan Egelrath?"

The webwainer shook her head. "I don't know...but there will be a meeting at the palace two nights from now. They will all be there. Egelrath, the marshals of the Armigers, Keara Hallowhill. The Archlegate has summoned them all to plan the next stage of our blessed restoration."

As she spoke, Fulren could feel her dedication to the cause wavering. When she mentioned the Archlegate there was no respect there. No worship. She was not the religious fanatic she professed to be, just a sorceress faithful to her Guild.

Fulren took a step back, feeling the necroglyph immediately cool as he cut off his link with the woman. "We need to kill Egelrath," he said. "This whole thing centres on him. He might control the Drakes with his faith, but the rest are just in it for the power he can offer them. Cut that bastard's head off and this whole uprising falls."

"How can you be so sure?" asked Mallum.

"I can feel it. This is no fanatic, she's just a soldier doing her duty. Killing Egelrath is the only chance there is to end this quickly. You heard her—in two nights we have all the conspirators in one place. We might not have legions at our command, but an assault on the palace is the best option."

"It's a gamble," said Mallum.

"It's suicide," Rawlin spat. "We'll all be slaughtered."

"Not all of us," Lancelin said. "Begin a full frontal assault, bring out their forces, then take up a defensive position across the river from the palace. Hold the Bridge of Saints. I can get into the palace and execute Egelrath during the confusion. Once he's gone... Well. We'll see."

"And if you're wrong?" said Rawlin. "What if we cut the head from the serpent and two more grow back? What if the Hallowhills and the Drakes and the other battalions carry on the fight?"

"Then we withdraw," said Fulren. "Regroup and find allies elsewhere." He turned to Emony. "Does the Marrlock Guild still have barges in the city, and men loyal enough to pilot them?"

"Of course," she replied.

"Then we'll need you to station them at the Riveryard. If something goes wrong, we can retreat there and make our way out of the city along the Whitespin."

"Fighting for our lives every step of the way," Rawlin said.

"Perhaps not," said Mallum. "We don't just have men at our disposal. There could be a way to form a strong tactical withdrawal."

"Explain," Rawlin demanded.

"I can do better than that."

Mallum led them from the room. Fulren spared a glance back to the webwainer as they left, still captive in the chair. He should have shown pity, should have asked for mercy, but who was he to make such demands? She had made her own choice in joining Egelrath and would have to face the consequences of that decision.

They walked toward the water's edge, the sound of it growing louder, overwhelming Fulren's senses as he was plunged into darkness once more. He felt Emony take his hand, leading him on along the riverside. The smell of it brought back memories of those long days he had spent training with the Kartias in the old warehouse. Days he had loved and would never get back. Not that it mattered anymore—the man he had been striving to kill was now his saviour, and the city he'd thought he would grow old in had become a hostile pit of vipers. How quickly things changed.

Before long he heard the sound of another door being opened, this one on well-oiled hinges, and they were swiftly led inside. Immediately Fulren was overcome by the essence of pyrestone magic that saturated the vast warehouse.

"What is this place?" he heard Rawlin ask. The gruff certainty was gone from his voice. Fulren could imagine him gazing around in amazement.

"The palace is not the only centre of artifice in the Anvil," Mallum replied. "This warehouse has been used by the Titanguard for decades. And we have our own order of artificers. Men and women dedicated to developing weaponries and armaments outside the purview of the Guilds."

Fulren could hear the artificers quietly going about their labours. The more he stood and took in the atmosphere, the more he could see the strands of power threaded throughout the room amid the shadowy silhouettes of artificers working on their machinery.

"All this was done in secret?" Fulren asked. "Without the knowledge of the Archwind Guild? Or Emperor Sullivar?"

"It was," Mallum said. "Since the days of Treon Archwind, I have overseen this place. The Titanguard has always been loyal to Torwyn. We are this nation's true custodians, and sometimes that means acting in the shadows for the good of its people, without the knowledge of its rulers. And it's a good job we did—no one knows this place even exists, especially not Egelrath. I only wish you could see it, Lord Fulren."

"I see enough," he replied. His own experiments with pyrestone weaponry had borne encouraging results, but as he approached one of the workstations, his fingers tracing the outline of the devices on the table, he began to realise what he could yet achieve. "And I understand. We can use what pyrestone we have to cover our escape. You're crafting munitions. I've worked on detonators like these myself, though the results were mixed. We can plant them to cover our retreat. Perhaps even to help us assault the palace."

"I won't pretend to understand any of this," Rawlin said. "But didn't the Hallowhill Guild already render your pyrestone armour useless? Surely they can disable anything you throw at them?"

"They won't be a problem," Fulren replied. "There's enough munitions here to keep them occupied while Lancelin does his work. And if we rig the right mechanism on the bridge, the pyrestone will remain inert until it's time to ignite it. The Hallowhills won't know what's hit them."

He felt a strong hand pat him on the shoulder. "They told me you were a naturally gifted artificer," Mallum said. "But now you are blind—"

"I told you, I see enough, Mallum. Trust me. I can rig us a detonator that will blow the Bridge of Saints into the Whitespin."

"Then we have much to prepare, and little time to do it."

With that Mallum ordered his men to gather, and he and Rawlin began working out their plan of attack. As they did so, Fulren approached Lancelin, who was lingering at the door to the warehouse.

"May we speak?" he asked.

Lancelin silently took his arm and led him outside, just the two of them and the river for company.

"You've accomplished what you set out to do," Fulren said. "You have brought me home, for good or ill."

"My task is not accomplished until you're safely miles away from here," Lancelin replied.

"I am as safe as I can be. From now on, whatever debt you think you owe is paid. I don't know if you did this out of responsibility or guilt or something else. But you should know I bear you no ill will. Not anymore."

Anyone else would probably have appreciated the words and acknowledged them. Not so Lancelin Jagdor, who merely stood in silence.

"Back in the city," Fulren continued. "When you were about to give your life for mine. You said you had to tell me something. What was it?"

Lancelin took a deep breath. "It can wait," he replied.

"Then I would ask you this: Did you mean what you said about not leaving this place until my mother was freed?"

"You have my word on it, Lord Fulren," Lancelin replied.

"Then I can't ask anything else of you. Good luck, Jagdor."

Fulren held out his hand. It was there for some moments, long enough for him to think Lancelin might ignore the gesture, before he took it in his iron grip.

"Good luck to you, son," Lancelin said. "Now let's end this uprising."

CONALL

He opened his eyes to bright sunlight lancing in through a small square window. The wagon trundled along, rocking gently, one wheel creaking with each rotation.

Conall stretched as best he could with his hands still tied in front of him, taking a breath of the stifling air as he sat up on the wooden seat. His throat was parched, neck clammy, shirt sodden from the oppressive heat. Hisolda sat opposite, fanning herself with a folded piece of parchment. Silently she reached to her side then threw Conall a waterskin.

Hastily he uncorked it with his teeth, raising the spout to his mouth and letting the tepid water moisten his throat before glugging down the entirety of its contents.

"Thank you," he said, after squeezing out the last drop. "Have I been asleep long?"

"Long enough for us to almost be at Agavere," Hisolda replied. "Your snoring has made for the most scintillating of company."

Conall was almost certain he didn't snore, but there was no point arguing about it.

"Any chance you'll tell me what's going on?"

"I can only tell you what I know. That we are bound for Torwyn."

The many implications of that raced through Conall's mind. If the Draconate had truly subjugated the Guilds, he was being taken as a prisoner straight into the dragon's lair. But he was alive, at least. If they wanted him dead, surely they would have let Tarrien execute him at Fort Tarkis.

"Before we left the fort, the frontier marshal told me I must have friends in high places. What was he talking about?"

Hisolda shrugged. "All I know is what I was ordered to do. Locate Conall Hawkspur and return him to the Anvil. A directive from the Ministry. From that I think we can safely assume you now live at the pleasure of the Archlegate himself."

"What does he want with me?" Conall asked, feeling himself begin to panic. Sanctan was his cousin, which should have put him at his ease. But they had never been close. By all accounts Sanctan had started a coup that would undermine the power of the Guilds. Family counted for nothing any longer.

"What he wants from all of us." A knowing smile crept up Hisolda's face. "Unyielding devotion to the Draconate."

Fat chance, but Conall wasn't about to make that feeling known.

From outside the wagon he could hear the distant screech of gulls. It didn't take long for that to mix with the sounds of bustle and raised voices. The road became smoother as they approached Agavere, and when they eventually reached the city, the wagon driver spoke briefly to whoever held the gate. Conall couldn't make out the exact words, but it was a terse exchange.

The wagon rolled on, and Conall could see the whitewashed buildings standing alongside rickety hovels through the small window. Agavere's muddle of architecture rolled by to the sound of aggravation. The disquiet did nothing to calm his already frayed nerves.

The salt tang of the sea was in the air as the wagon came to its final stop. It rocked as the guards jumped down, and when they opened the rear doors, the wagon's interior was assailed by a cacophony of light and noise. Conall squinted in the bright daylight.

"If you would," said Hisolda, gesturing for him to climb out.

Conall did as he was bid, though it was a struggle with his hands still tied. Outside the wagon, the oppressive air that hung over

Agavere was even more intense. Troopers of the Armiger roamed the streets in disparate groups, the animosity palpable as they eyed one another warily. He spied the livery of the Griffin, Viper, Tigris and Raptor Battalions, but there was no way to tell which were still loyal to the Guilds and which had thrown their lot in with the Draconate. Those civilians who had previously gone about the place without a care now looked on with fear and derision.

Toward the harbour the streets were filled by an unruly mob, and it looked as if a riot might break out at any moment. The crowd desperately tried to push its way toward the seafront, some of them waving transit papers in the air as troopers and harbour security held them back. The whole place was like a tinderbox ready to ignite.

A man in a bright shirt pushed his way through the crowd to greet Hisolda, and Conall recognised him as one of the harbour-master's officials.

"High Legate," he said with a sycophantic bow. "I was not expecting you back so soon."

"Is our ship ready to leave?" Hisolda asked.

The man shook his head, a worried look on his face. "I'm afraid not, High Legate. Three frontier marshals have declared that all transit is to be halted until clear lines have been drawn."

"Clear lines?" snapped Hisolda.

"Until all the Armiger Battalions have declared what side they are on, High Legate."

"The rivalry of the battalions does not interest me. I must return to Torwyn immediately, on the Archlegate's order."

The official fidgeted with the hem of his shirt, caught between Torwyn's military and its ecclesiastics. Not a comfortable place to be for anyone.

"I'm sorry, but I can do nothing," he said pathetically.

Before Hisolda could chide him further, the man backed away into the crowd, disappearing into the throng as he fought his way back toward the dock.

"Shit," Hisolda breathed, trying to suppress her temper.

"Looks like we're stuck here," Conall said with a grin. "At least for now."

"We'll see about that," Hisolda replied. "Come."

She pushed on through the crowded street toward the harbour. Two troopers took Conall by the arms and dragged him along after. The closer they got to the seafront the thicker the press became. He could barely see Hisolda up ahead as she struggled through the mass, the brightness of her blue robes standing out starkly against the drab garb of the crowd.

"Make way," she shouted.

For the most part she was ignored, but when some of the mob saw the approach of a High Legate, they took pains to move from her path. Someone shouted angrily in Conall's ear. The shout was answered by another, even louder cry. Profanities were exchanged. Then fists.

Conall was buffeted by the mob as the violence began to spread like an infection. The troopers holding Conall's arms did their best to hang on, but amid the ensuing violence he was torn from their grip. They shouted in alarm as Conall was dragged away, cursing at him, as though he were intentionally trying to escape. In an instant they and Hisolda disappeared among the fray.

Something hit Conall in the side of the head. He heard a smashing of glass, felt something moist and tepid run down his face. More glass shattered as a hail of bottles were thrown. A woman screamed next to him as she was hit in the face by a missile, blood pouring from her head.

A glance over one shoulder and he saw the Auroch troopers desperately fighting their way through the crowd. One of them had drawn a weapon, but he was quickly dragged to the ground by the angry mob, squealing as he was relentlessly kicked in the balls by some furious woman.

Was this the good luck he was owed? Conall couldn't quite believe he had managed to escape so deftly, with little effort on his own part. But then, he hadn't quite escaped yet.

He shouldered his way past the press of bodies, away from the harbour. The more he fought his way through the crowd toward the periphery of the dock, the less violence there was, until eventually he managed to reach the edge of the harbourside. The darkness of an alleyway beckoned, sweet freedom drawing him closer. He stopped, looking over his shoulder, seeing the extent of the ensuing riot as it began to spread all across the seafront. Windows were being smashed, and more troopers of the Armiger rushed up the main street to quell the angry crowd.

He smiled at his good fortune just as someone reached from the alleyway and grabbed him from behind. His instinct was to fight them off, but his hands were tied. Whoever had grabbed him was wiry but strong, and his feet skittered on the cobbles as he was dragged into the alley, away from the mob, away from any witnesses and into the shadows.

"Get the fuck off me," Conall snarled as he was slammed up against the alley wall.

His assailant took a step back. Sted looked at him with a grim mixture of relief and amusement.

"You really have the Wyrms' own bloody luck, Captain," she said.

Conall almost slumped to his knees in relief.

"What the fuck are you doing here?" he asked.

She pulled a knife and cut the bonds at his wrists.

"Can we save the soppy reunions for later?" she said. "And put some distance between us and everyone who wants to kill you?"

A good idea on reflection, and Conall followed Sted as she led him through the fish-stinking streets of the harbourside and down into the shadowy alleys of the Pit. The place was familiar but much changed since he'd last been here. Where men used to lie drunk outside one notorious bawdy house, now there was a corpse left to rot. Windows had been smashed, the words *The Wyrms Rise Again* painted in hastily daubed script.

Eventually Sted was leading him through streets he didn't recognise. The clangour of the harbourside receded as they entered a mess of shanties. They stopped at a door, salt weathered and all but hanging off its hinges, and Sted knocked three times in succession, paused, then twice again. It opened a crack, and Conall saw a wary eye he recognised glaring from within.

Donan Marrlock opened the door and feverishly beckoned them

inside. The interior of the room was neat and relatively clean considering the state of the exterior. Donan looked like a frightened rabbit, his wits almost as threadbare as the day they'd found him at that mine in the desert.

"I was starting to get worried," he said.

Donan was clearly a man used to worrying, and Sted offered him a reassuring pat on the shoulder.

"Is someone going to tell me what's going on?" Conall asked. He was starting to calm down in the relative safety of the little house, but his heart was still clanging a raucous tune in his chest.

"Please sit," said Donan. "You must be exhausted. I'll get you some food."

Conall gladly took a seat at the table in the centre of the room as Donan left. Sted took the chair opposite. "When we got here, the place was in uproar," she said. "Rioting, looting. The Armigers didn't seem to give a damn at first, but eventually they brought some order to the streets. Whatever's happening on the mainland, it's spreading. This whole place is about to catch fire. When we couldn't get passage out of here, I found Donan. Thought he might be grateful for the help we gave him."

"For saving my life," Donan said, walking back into the room. He was carrying bread and a hunk of pungent cheese, and he placed them on the table. Conall hadn't realised how hungry he was and began to demolish them as Donan placed a ewer of water and a cup on the table.

"We managed to get the rest of the Talon on a boat bound for Goodfleet," said Sted. "But I thought I'd hang around. See if there was anything I could do."

"For me?" Conall asked, still chewing the dry bread. "I'm touched."

"Should have known you'd come up stinking of roses. We got word the Ministry was bringing you back from the fort. Lucky that riot broke out and I was waiting for you."

"We were due some luck," Conall replied before taking a drink of the water. It was warm but still refreshing, and he let out a sigh as he put the cup back down and refilled it from the ewer. "What's the situation now? Any chance we can get a ship out of here?"

"The harbour has been shut down by the battalion marshals," Donan replied. "Until they can come to some accord, all transit permits are revoked. Worse news is storms are brewing across the Ungulf. Even when they've resolved their issues and ships can sail, you'll struggle to find a captain willing to cross the sea until the weather has passed. But there is—"

"How long will that take?"

Donan shrugged. "We could be stuck here for days. However, I—"

"What's the situation on the streets? Who are the battalions putting their loyalty behind?"

"They're split straight down the middle," said Sted. "The Auroch and Phoenix Battalions have declared for the Ministry. The Griffin and Viper Battalions still support the Guilds, for now. That street riot was just a small slice of what's gonna happen if my guess is right. The Armigers have been kept in order for years by the Guilds, but old feuds are bubbling up. The whole port is just about ready to blow."

"Maybe we can use that to our advantage. I have to get back to Torwyn. If the authorities here are distracted by infighting, maybe we can slip away unnoticed. What about the port's aerie?"

Sted shook her head. "Last eagle was dispatched back to Torwyn two days ago. Aerie is shut down."

Donan raised his hand. "I might be able—"

"Maybe the safer bet is to just wait it out," Sted interrupted. "The Ministry's looking for you. We don't know who we can trust. What if we just sit tight and let everyone fight it out? Then we make our move when it's safe."

"No. I have to go now," said Conall. "Who knows what's happening back in the Anvil, in Wyke. There's a war coming, and I can't be stuck here sweating my arse off in some shack."

Sted leaned across the table. "So what you gonna do? Sprout wings and fly home? There's a sea to cross, and you ain't that strong a swimmer."

Donan lifted a finger one last time, as though asking for his turn to speak. Sted and Conall both glared at him expectantly.

"I might be able to help," he said.

A twitchy smile played at the side of Donan's mouth, as though he wasn't sure if he'd spoken out of turn.

"I mean, I might be able to," he continued. "There's a ship chartered by the Marrlock Guild sitting in port right now. I have some sway, I'm sure I could persuade the captain to get us out of here, despite the blockade."

Conall reclined in his seat. "See? Where there's a will..."

"There's generally fucking danger," Sted replied. "There could be open warfare on Agavere's streets at any moment. We might have to sneak back to the docks. Then hope no one tries to stop us boarding that ship. Are we gonna fight our way through every Armiger Battalion in the Karna?"

"I for one have had enough of this place," Donan sputtered unexpectedly. "I've had enough of the sand. The shitty food. The bastard goatheads. I want to go home." He picked up a knife lying on the kitchen side. "I'll bloody well fight with you, Hawkspur. Let's get out of here."

Sted let out a long, unimpressed sigh. "Put the knife down, Donan, before you do yourself a mischief."

Reluctantly Donan did as he was told. He began to look a little embarrassed, but Conall wasn't so sure it was a bad idea.

"If we have to fight, we'll fight," he said. "Hopefully it won't come to that, but I can't wait out the storm, and I definitely can't wait until this war's been fought and lost."

Sted shook her head. "And there was me thinking that being accused of murder and arrested by the Ministry might make you a little more cautious."

"I think the time for caution has passed, don't you?"

Sted rolled her eyes, picking out a piece of redstalk from her pocket and shoving it in her mouth.

"I'd best go and make the arrangements," said Donan. "Ensure the ship is ready to sail."

"Be careful," Conall said as he reached the door.

Donan offered him a nod of reassurance, but he looked almost as terrified as the day he'd come rushing toward them at the mining outpost, reeking of muck and death.

When he'd gone, Conall finished the food and emptied the ewer. He should have been exhausted, but he was almost shaking with the anticipation of getting away from this place. Or was it trepidation at what might be waiting for him in Torwyn?

Sted lit some candles as the afternoon drew on and the room began to darken. She was quiet, uncharacteristically so, and Conall wondered if she was hankering for a drink or a fuck or just troubled by the air of tension hanging over the port. No, she was never troubled by the prospect of violence. More likely she'd be relishing it.

"Are you going to tell me what's bothering you?" Conall asked when she eventually sat down opposite him.

"What do you mean?" she asked.

"You've been wandering around like a sullen pup all afternoon. What's the problem with you? Thirsty for some wine?"

"Fuck wine. Even I know now's not the time, and we need to keep clear bloody heads. It's you that's bothering me."

"What do you mean?"

She narrowed her eyes at him. "Since we landed in the frontier all you've done is go out of your way to stay put. You've never once given a shit about going home, even after your brother... Well, you know what. Now at the first sign of trouble we're risking our lives to get back there. What's going on in that head?"

"It's just what I have to do. My mother—"

"Your mother shit!" she spat. "You hate that witch, for some mysterious reason. You've been avoiding her for years, and now you have to get back and rescue her? Like you're some one-man army? What's with the sudden devotion to family?"

All his doubt began to creep back in. Was this the right thing to do? Did he even care? Was he just being swept up in some newfound need to prove his loyalty to the Guild?

"My mother and I have had our differences. But I have to—"

"Bollocks. What differences? What's the big frigging problem?"

He'd never told anyone. Barely even admitted it to himself. But maybe if he opened up it might settle some things in his head. A burden shared, and all that.

"All right, since you asked. When I was a boy, can't have been much older than four or five, my father was killed in a duel."

"We all know the story, Con," Sted replied.

"Right. So you know the man who killed him was swordwright of the Archwind Guild? Lancelin Jagdor?"

"That's not news either."

"No. What might be news is that a few years after we'd laid my father in the sepulchre at Wyke, I was visiting the Anvil with my mother. Some diplomatic thing, I don't know, I was only young. One night I couldn't sleep, strange place, strange bed. I got up to do something, go somewhere, I can't remember. And that's when I saw them."

Even the memory of it made him pause, gave him shivers. Just speaking the words was painful.

"Saw who?" Sted asked.

"Jagdor. And my mother. Together."

Sted wrinkled her nose. "You saw your mother fucking the man who killed your father?"

Conall shook the thought from his head. "Not fucking, but they were obviously together, in an embrace, an intimate moment in each other's arms. I didn't hang around for what came next, but I do remember the way they looked at each other. They were in love. So what if she had something to do with it?"

"With what?" Sted asked.

"With my father's death. What if she'd planned it? My mother persuaded her lover to murder my father."

Sted didn't seem at all surprised by the revelation. In fact, he could just as easily have been talking about the weather.

"So that's the reason we're here in the Karna then?" she said. "That's what all this has been about? Your need to prove yourself? Or your need to punish her? Or fucking whatever. We're here in the shit end of fucktown because you saw your mother getting wet over the man who killed your daddy? You put our lives at risk? You got Nevan killed? Because your mother might not have loved your father?"

"It's not as simple as—"

She slapped him hard across the face before rising to her feet. The sting of it shocked Conall out of his malaise, and he stared at her in disbelief.

"Since we're sharing, how about this," she spat through gritted teeth. "When I was a little girl, I watched my father beat my mother to death because she couldn't get a stain out of his shirt. Just beat her head in with a hammer, then sat back down and carried on eating his breakfast. Things got tough for me after that, but do I sit around fucking crying about it?" Conall shook his head in the face of her rage. "Of course I don't, because I'm a fucking grown-up."

With that she spun on her heel and left him sitting in his chair.

One of the candles sputtered. A cat yowled somewhere down the street.

Conall drew in a long breath, his face still stinging.

"Fuck."

TYRETA

New Flaym's perimeter wall ran into the sea, protecting the port from the jungle fauna. Tyreta followed it to the shore, gazing out across the water, the reflection of the moon dancing on its calm surface. Beyond the wall there was no sound, no screaming, no tortured voices from within the city. It could have been any other normal night.

Turning her head, she saw the panther sitting at the tree line, watching her curiously. She was reluctant to enter the water, not that Tyreta could blame her.

"I'll be back soon," she whispered, hoping against hope it was a promise she would keep.

As she walked into the sea it was shockingly cold—ankle-deep, knee-deep, up to her waist, almost taking her breath away. She paused, teetering on the point of no return. Plunge in or turn back. Forget this madness. Run. Hide.

One deep breath and she eased herself forward. The wall extended twenty yards into the water, and she easily covered the distance with a few powerful strokes. At the edge of the wall she paused, peering at the dockside. One of the jetties was burned and half-collapsed. She could see the huge whitewashed embassy of the Marrlock Guild, now a ruin, in the distance. There was no sign of movement.

No roaming kesh warriors waiting for her on the harbour. All was quiet... as if she was heading right into a trap.

Every instinct told her to turn back, but she fought the impulse. There were people who needed her. Just the smallest chance she could save someone spurred her on, and she pushed herself away from the wall, swimming the short distance to the nearest jetty.

Pulling herself from the water, she paused again, squinting into the night. Tyreta had expected to see bodies scattering the seafront, but there was nothing. The only signs that a battle had been fought were bloodstains in the dirt, black in the light of the few pyrestone lanterns that winked intermittently from their posts.

Quickly she moved along the jetty to the dockside, every sense straining. She crept into the shadow of the nearest building, its windows smashed, door hanging limp and useless from its broken hinges.

Peering around the corner toward the main market square, she was confronted with the true horror of the kesh raid.

In the distance a fire glowed bright from beyond the rooftops, and in the light of those flames bodies were hanging from ropes lashed between the gables. More corpses than she could count, strung up and left to rot: a grim monument to the victory of Shabak and his Chul.

Tyreta slowly made her way across the square, moving beneath the corpses strewn like grim festival garlands, a lump catching in her throat as she fought back the tears. Was she too late? Had the whole of New Flaym been butchered?

As she unslung the bow from her shoulder, Tyreta swallowed down the lump in her throat, teeth grinding together. So what if there was no one left? She was here, and so were the Chul. So was Shabak. That monster from the jungle who had slaughtered her cousin and so many others. He would pay for this, even if it cost her life.

She pulled an arrow from her quiver and gazed at the arrowhead and the tiny pyrestone set within. It pulsed in response to her attention, her arcane gifts igniting its core. Could the pyrestone sense her rage? Tyreta had never felt such hate before. Now all she wanted was a reckoning. To avenge herself on the beasts who had murdered these people.

Leaving the market behind, she let the shadows consume her as she stalked toward the distant fire. Despite straining her ears for any sound, she could hear nothing. She would have expected the bellowing voices of the kesh to rise above the rooftops, for them to be singing their victory, but all was silent when she reached the end of the street.

Peering around the corner, she saw the centre of the thoroughfare was cleared of debris. The buildings that flanked it were nothing but embers, and in the middle of the street a massive pyre had been erected. It rose thirty feet in the air, every inch consumed by flame. The stench of it hit her in an acrid wave of burning meat and charred wood. Through the haze she could see the corpses of fallen kesh stacked within the funeral pyre.

Surrounding the furnace was an army. Each kesh warrior stood in silent vigil, honouring the dead with their silence. It would have been so easy to unleash her pyrestone arrows upon them, but she had only eight. Better that she pick her targets with discretion.

When a figure walked into the light of the fire, tall and powerful against the flames, she remembered there was only one target she was interested in.

Shabak was bareheaded, the lizard skull he wore as a helm discarded, as he walked proudly among his followers. As soon as he appeared they began to kneel, one by one, showing fealty to the chieftain who had led them to such a resounding victory. In his hand he carried the long-tipped spear he'd used to sever Wyllow's head, and he raised it high, its blade flashing in the light of the pyre.

His howl filled the port, a feral cry of triumph but also of loss. Behind Shabak burned the bodies of a hundred warriors, his kinfolk, and Tyreta could sense his grief as well as his pride.

No sooner had the echo of Shabak's roar faded than it was answered by the cries of his followers, so loud they were almost deafening. Tyreta felt her resolve suddenly buckle, but she willed herself to focus on her enemy.

She raised her bow as their roars faded. Shabak began to speak, snarling in the guttural kesh language as she nocked the pyrestone arrow. With her rudimentary understanding of the kesh language she heard him praising his men, their bravery and their savagery.

Tyreta drew back the string, visualising that arrow cutting the air to its mark as he continued to speak. She should have been shaking, terrified, but she had never been more determined to succeed. Never more certain she would strike her target.

Holding her breath, she began to reach out with her powers, opening up her senses to the web. In response the pyrestone arrowhead glowed—hungering, thirsting to bury itself in Shabak's heart. Her fingers twitched as she prepared to release the bowstring...

A mournful feeling overwhelmed her before she could loose. Her bow hand began to tremble as she was assailed by feelings of hopelessness and loss. It took a moment before she realised those feelings were not hers.

Tyreta lowered the bow, retreating into the shadows, closing her eyes, pressing with her senses. Some yards away she could feel the despair...the terror.

Moving away from the pyre, she shrouded herself in darkness, hunting, following that feeling of bleak helplessness, until she reached the next street. Cages lined the darkened avenue—row upon row, filled with the cowering figures of the port's survivors. Some were sobbing, others staring into the dark with hollow eyes, resigned to their fate.

Tyreta darted to the first cage. The occupants moved away in fear, thinking she was one of the kesh come to drag them from their captivity and slaughter them as so many others had been slaughtered. Moving along the rows, cage after cage, she saw men, women and children, filth covered and soot blackened, clothes torn, many bearing crudely bandaged wounds.

"Tyreta," a familiar voice whispered.

She moved closer, peering inside the cage to see Isleen shuffle forward. The woman grasped the bars, her tear-streaked face mournful in the moonlight.

"You have to run, girl," she hissed. "You have to get away. They'll kill you."

Tyreta shook her head. "Not until I've got you all out of here," she replied, reaching for the knife at her waist.

A startled cry from one of the cages alerted her to movement farther up the avenue. Four kesh warriors strode from the dark, one of them barking in alarm when he saw her by the cage. Another of them raced toward her, pulling an axe free of his belt.

Tyreta rose to her feet, bringing her bow level, free hand already plucking an arrow from the quiver to nock in one fluid move. She pulled the bowstring on instinct and loosed, forgetting about her breathing, about aiming, about anything.

As the arrow left the bow she could already sense it was pulling wide of the target. In that instant her mind ignited the pyrestone, communing with its power, and it flared, shedding light that filled the street. She focused, forcing the arrow to swerve, altering its trajectory to find its mark. The shaft hissed into the warrior's chest, its impetus knocking him back into the dirt.

A second warrior charged past the corpse of the first. Tyreta already had another arrow nocked, loosed, focused. Another corpse.

The last two charged at her, mouths spitting their vile fury. No time for two shots. Tyreta pulled two arrows, nocking both to her string, pulling, loosing.

As the arrows flew she unleashed the power of their pyrestones, overloading them, fuelling them with her furious will.

Both exploded as they reached the kesh. One warrior was blown back by the detonation, his chest a mass of charred flesh. The other stood for a moment, his head blown clean from his shoulders, before he collapsed to the muddy street.

Tyreta tore the knife from her belt, slicing through the ropes that secured the first cage. Isleen staggered from within, unable to take her eyes from the dead kesh that littered the street.

"You have to get away from here," Tyreta said, grabbing the woman by the arm and squeezing hard. "Lead everyone north to the gate."

"But—"

"We don't have time," Tyreta hissed before moving to the next cage and hacking through the rope that secured it.

Within moments she had opened every cage and urged the prisoners to run, taking up the rear as a score of them followed Isleen up the street toward the gate. The funeral pyre still rose high above New Flaym, but it would not keep the kesh distracted forever.

Before they had covered a hundred yards, Tyreta heard guttural voices close by.

She should have run with the prisoners, should have fled this place and its dangers, but there was no way they would all make it if she did. Instead she stopped, watching as the people of New Flaym escaped into the dark.

When the first of the kesh appeared from the shadows she already had an arrow nocked. He didn't even have time to snarl a challenge before she raised the bow. The arrow left a trail of bright-yellow fire behind it. The kesh fell without a sound.

Two more came racing after the first, but still she stood her ground. Nocking. Aiming.

Before she could loose there was movement from the darkness to her right. Another warrior, axe raised.

She managed to duck the blow, the arrow falling from her grip. He struck again and she instinctually raised her bow to parry it. The steel blade hacked the bow in two, and she danced away, reaching for the spear strapped to her back.

More kesh were coming. So many of them rushing at her from the dark, but she had to give those people time. Had to fight till the end.

Tyreta thrust her spear at the first attacker, holding him at bay. He stumbled back, feet slipping in the muck to avoid the spearhead. A second warrior came at her, and she swept the spear to the right to hold him off. Instinct took over, her breath coming in desperate gasps as she swiped wildly from left to right. Everywhere she looked, she was surrounded by eyes staring at her with hate.

Gasps turned to snarls of rage as she fended off every attacker. The tip of the spear caught one of the kesh in the arm, and he growled as he retreated from her. She spun, weapon coming up in time to clash against a kesh spear. It deflected his attack, but her guard was down…

She hardly felt the blow that struck her from behind.

Next thing she was facedown in the dirt, her arms grabbed, a knee pressed to her back. She wanted to scream, to rage, but with the weight on top of her she could barely breathe. Tyreta was helpless to resist as she was swiftly dragged along the street, out into the main thoroughfare, and brought into the light of the funeral pyre.

Warm moisture ran down the back of her neck as she tried to raise her head. Her vision was blurry, focusing in the light of the flames in time to see one of the kesh standing before her, eyes burning in the light of the pyre as he raised an axe.

A bark of command halted the death blow and made her executioner flinch before taking a step away.

Tyreta squinted against the heat of the fire as he approached. A figure silhouetted by flame, lithe and powerful. Shabak was terrifying up close, that lizard skull now firmly atop his head, making him appear like the monster he was.

He knelt by her as she was held by the arms, helpless.

"Get on with it," she spat, forcing herself to stare into those animal eyes as they peered from within the skull.

Reverently the kesh warchief reached up, lifting the skull helm from his head and placing it down in the dirt. His eyes shone with fearsome light as his lips turned up into a smile. She could see his incisors, sharp and deadly. If he wanted to rip her throat out with his teeth it would be an easy job.

"You are brave," he said, accent so clipped and perfect he could have been raised in any city of Torwyn. Voice soft and gentle as though he were lulling a child to sleep.

One of his warriors came and handed him the three arrows she had left. Shabak gazed at the pyrestone arrowheads in wonder.

"And you are skilled in the magic of your homeland," he continued before snapping one of the arrows in two and discarding it without a care.

"How do you speak my language?" Tyreta asked, trying to buy time, trying to clear her senses.

Shabak shrugged. "Did you think me some animal from the

wild? Some savage warlord no better than a beast?" His smile grew wider. "Of course you did. That is how all you people think. You have always underestimated us. It is how we were finally able to defeat you." His eyes glistened in the firelight as he snapped another arrow in two and flung it over his shoulder. "I was not always leader of the Chul. Years ago I was taken in by your people. Taught your language. Cheated. Cast aside. Exiled from my own land. But I returned to lead my people and free this island. I was not made a warrior by the dangers of the jungle. You created me."

There was movement farther up the street. Shabak's warriors had captured some of the escaped prisoners and were dragging them back, into the light of the funeral pyre. Tyreta could see Isleen among their number, her face streaked with tears as she and the rest were driven to their knees.

Shabak tapped the final arrowhead against his pursed lips. "It is fitting that these former conquerors will soon be a sacrifice to our fallen. They will honour them in death as they never did in life. And when they are nothing but ash, this place will finally forget them. Forget you. This land will not even remember your names."

Tyreta's vision was clear enough for her to focus on the arrow. The pyrestone at its head pulsated, speaking to her in an arcane tongue only she could understand. She called back, filling it with all her anger and vitriol. Her hate for Shabak fuelling its volatile core.

Before the pyrestone could ignite, Shabak shot to his feet, flinging the arrow toward the fire. It exploded in a bright conflagration, sending a wave of panic through the kesh.

Tyreta shook off the startled warriors who held her arms. She could have drawn her knife, could have thrown herself at Shabak in a last attempt to end him, but instead she stood her ground.

"My name is Tyreta Hawkspur," she snarled, staring down Shabak as he squinted at her through the smoke. "And I challenge you."

As soon as the words left her mouth she began to wonder what she had just done. What she had condemned herself to. Two of the kesh rushed at her, but Shabak held up a hand to stop them.

"You challenge me?" he said. "Do you even understand what that means?"

Tyreta raised a hand, drawing her thumb across her chest in a cross, mimicking the gesture he had made to her back at the mine.

"I'm sure I'll find out," she said. "But if I win, you will release my people."

Shabak considered her words for a moment before showing his fangs. "I accept your challenge. Tonight we honour the dead with silence. Tomorrow, when I have slain you in front of these witnesses, they will join you in sacrifice. You may choose one weapon with which to face me. I suggest you think hard on what that weapon will be."

At his dismissive wave, Shabak's men grabbed her, dragging her away from the light of the pyre before dumping her in the shadow of a burned-out building.

There she sat, wondering what she had done and how she might ever defeat this brutal warrior. Whatever weapon she chose to do it with, it had best be a damned powerful one.

CONALL

They waited till the small hours for Donan to return. Conall was starting to worry, and even Sted thought that sending him off into the volatile streets of Agavere might have been a mistake. When he finally came back, panting like a racehorse and shaking like a leaf, they both had to admit it was a relief to see him.

Donan had good news, and the Wyrms knew they were due some. The Marrlock ship was ready to go, still waiting in the dock, and if they moved fast they could be on board before it left. He also brought them civilian dress so they could blend in with the ordinary folk of Agavere. Conall looked shabby in a cloth jacket and weathered boots, but there was something liberating about abandoning his Talon uniform.

They had one splintbow between them, and Sted decided it was best she carry it. Conall wasn't going to complain—the last thing he intended to do was fight. Hopefully they wouldn't have to, but from the sounds of it there was already trouble waiting for them on the streets.

As the night wore on the sound of shouting had gotten closer with every passing hour. Soon it had turned to the ring of clashing steel and the intermittent sound of splintbows clapping in response to one another. Isolated skirmishes had become more frequent, but luckily they were still a few streets away from the trouble.

"Are we ready?" Conall asked as he stood by the door. Part of him was hoping the others wouldn't be. Part of him was hoping neither of them wanted to throw themselves into the madness outside and they'd changed their minds about leaving.

Sted checked the breech of the splintbow and gave him a nod. She had a spare clip of bolts at her waist and patted it reassuringly.

"I'm ready," said Donan. He sounded anything but.

"You're willing to stake our lives on this, Donan? If we get to the seafront and that ship—"

"It's crewed and ready, I swear it," Donan said. "When I left the dock, there were only a few Armiger troopers on patrol. The rest have been called to defend their holdings in the port."

Conall could well believe it. From the sounds of it the battalion marshals had failed to come to any kind of accord, and now their ingrained feuds were boiling over. He could only hope those old animosities kept them occupied long enough for the three of them to reach the dockside unnoticed.

They slipped through the door and into the alleyway. Donan quietly closed the door behind them, not even bothering to lock it; there was no point now. With any luck Agavere would be little more than a memory before the night was out.

Sted led them up the street. It sounded as if they were heading toward the violence, but as they progressed along the labyrinthine back alleys it became obvious they were already surrounded by it. Ahead he could see the alley opened up onto one of the main thoroughfares. Sted slowed her pace, creeping toward the edge of the building. Beyond, the sounds of battle were cacophonous—the snap of splintbow fire, the furious shouts of commanders ordering their men into lines.

As Conall neared the end of the alley there was a flash of light and the muted crack of a longbarrel. He peered around the corner in time to see a row of tower shields behind which sheltered ranks of Armiger troopers. A hail of splintbolts rained down on their position. One of them went down, creating a breach in the shield wall, which was hastily plugged. Glancing up the other way, Conall saw a barricade—barrels and carts overturned, ranks of archers firing in disciplined volleys from behind it.

"What now?" Sted asked.

"We'll have to retrace our steps," Conall said. "Find another way around."

"There's no time," Donan hissed from the rear. "The ship won't wait all night. Especially not now this whole place is going up in flames."

In response to a bellowed shout of command, a gap appeared in the shield wall. Conall watched in dismay as Armiger troopers wheeled a cannon forward. Two of them frantically secured the props as another primed the barrel.

Conall just had time to cover his ears as the charge began to whine, the pyrestone flashing bright as it fuelled the cannon. There was a deafening boom and a breath of hot air as fire streaked along the thoroughfare, smashing into the barricade and sending wood and men flying in a blanket of black fog.

Another order was bellowed, this one from behind the barricade, and as one the defenders leapt over the smashed defences, charging toward the shield wall before the cannon could be primed again.

"Fuck this," Conall snarled, bursting from cover.

As the two battalions clashed together he raced through the fray. Conall kept his head down, Sted close on his heels. He barged past a charging trooper, dodging another who went down screaming, a splintbolt transfixing his eye. Donan brought up the rear, cursing over and over as he did his best to keep up.

Halfway across the street, Conall could see there were no alleyways to duck into, nowhere to run but through the violence. He turned toward the barricade, desperate to push his way through the charging ranks. In their civilian garb, the three of them weren't seen as a threat, just an inconvenience. So intent were the Armiger troopers on attacking their rivals that they ran straight past.

Before they'd gotten within thirty yards of the barricade, Conall heard a roar. Reinforcements were climbing over the defences, ranks of armoured warriors heading straight toward them. Even if they weren't seen as the enemy, they'd be trampled in the onslaught before they reached any semblance of safety.

"We're dead," whined Donan above the ruckus.

"This way," Conall bellowed, running toward a shop front.

He barged into the door with his shoulder, hearing the satisfying ring of the lock breaking as he fell headlong inside. Sted and Donan ran in after him, then slammed the door closed, instantly dulling the sound of battle raging outside.

They were plunged into darkness. All he could hear was the sound of their frantic breaths and the clacking report of splintbows on the other side of the door, punctuated by the snap of longbarrel fire. Then something moved in the dark.

Conall flinched at the sound, straining his eyes to see whoever was hiding in the dark. A gas lamp hissed as it was ignited, the brightness of the flame making him squint.

When his eyes adjusted to the glare, he saw a face outlined in the flickering illumination. It was a young lad, expression all fearful in the dark. He raised the lamp, casting shadows across the room and revealing more figures hunkering for safety.

"Who the fuck is it?" hissed a woman's voice.

"They're not from the battalions." A man, his voice gruff but wary.

Conall could make out more details now. There were around a dozen civilians, all taking refuge in the room. They looked bedraggled, wan, half-starved. Some of those faces he recognised—here a barman from one of the drinking dens, there a woman who ran a bawdy house just south of the Pit.

"Look," he said. "We're only sheltering from the battle. Just like you. If there's a back way out of here we'll take it and be out of your hair."

The boy with the lamp opened his mouth to speak, but the woman from the whorehouse rose to her feet, brow creasing as she looked him over.

"Hang on," she said. "I know you."

Shit. That was the last thing he needed.

"You're Hawkspur," said a man who looked decently dressed, all things considered. Conall didn't recognise the face, but clearly his reputation preceded him.

"I'm just trying to get out of this in one piece," Conall said. "We're all in the same boat here."

Sted was slowly raising her splintbow, and Conall gently laid a hand on her arm.

"This is all your doing," said the woman. "You and the bloody Guilds."

"I can assure you—"

"They're looking for him," said the man, pointing an unnecessarily accusing finger. "If we take him to the Armigers, this could all be over. They'll reward us. See us to safety."

"Hang on," said Conall, desperate to be the voice of reason. "This has nothing to do with me."

"Grab him," said the woman.

Sted took a step forward, and Conall was of no mind to stop her this time. "Sit your fucking arse down, bitch," she ordered.

The woman's eyes flicked to the splintbow before she did as she was told.

Conall took a step forward, raising his arms to try to calm the situation. "Look, I can get us all out of here. You just have to trust me."

"How?" asked a voice in the dark. "This whole place has gone to shit."

"There's a ship waiting in the dock. Fuelled and ready to take us back to Torwyn. All we need to do is get to the harbour." The silence of the dozen civilians spoke volumes. "Tell them," he said to Donan.

"It's true," he said quickly. "I swear on the Wyrms. Room for everyone. All we have to do is make it to the dockside and we can leave this dump in our wake."

"Now," Conall said. "Is there a back way out of here or not?"

The boy with the gas lamp nodded enthusiastically as the woman stood. "It's this way," she said, moving to the back of the room and opening an adjoining door.

"Then what are we waiting for?" Conall said, marching across the room as if he knew what he was doing.

There was a short corridor. At the end of it another door, bolted shut. He slid back the bolts, opened it slightly and peered through the gap. The back alley was empty, and Conall led his bedraggled group of refugees from the safety of the building.

The air was peppered by the distant reports of more cannon fire as they moved in silence up the backstreet. At the end they reached a street he recognised, and beyond it was the dock. He paused, glancing back, reassured that Sted was right at his shoulder, Donan just behind.

"Whereabouts is the ship?" he whispered.

"East side," Donan replied. "We need to hurry."

Conall needed no encouragement, and he began to cover the short distance through the empty streets. The smell of cordite and burned pyrestone was replaced by the stink of the dock as they crossed the street to the north. Ahead he could see the jetties stretching out into the sea, a dozen ships moored and waiting. There was no sign of life on any of them.

"Where the fuck is it?" Conall asked.

Donan gestured further east. There stood a walled-off anchorage—an area closed in by a huge gate, where trading vessels had their cargo checked for the relevant customs dockets and marques of trade before being allowed to set sail. Enclosed within it was a single ship.

"It's in the bloody tithe dock?" Conall spat.

"I…I thought the gate would be open," Donan said helplessly. "They told me—"

"You fucking idiot," Sted said. "As soon as we start tampering with the gate there'll be a hundred Armiger troopers swarming all over us."

"Well, someone needs to open it," Conall said. As soon as he opened his mouth he knew who that someone would be. He had led these people here on the promise that they would find a ship to get them out of Agavere. For once he would keep his word. "Get everyone on board and fire up the engines. As soon as the gate starts to move, launch the ship."

"What about you?" Sted asked. "How you gonna get on board if you're in the frigging gate tower?"

Conall shrugged. "I'll think of something," he replied, already moving toward the stone staircase that led up the side of the wall.

As Donan and Sted led the civilians across the cobbled dock toward the moored ship, Conall made his way up a set of weathered stone stairs to the top of the walled tithe dock. From the summit he could see all across the rooftops of Agavere. Fires were burning sporadically, and the noise of battle drifted toward him, framed by flashes of light and a layer of cannon smoke.

On the far horizon the sun was starting to rise. In the light of morning Conall could just make out a distant thunderhead rolling in toward the coast.

A walkway ran across the top of the wall toward the gatehouse, and as he made his way across he heard the sudden rumble of the ship's engines being fired. Smoke billowed from its outlet funnels, and water began to swell at the stern as turbines roared into life. Mariners unfastened mooring ropes at the jetty, and as Conall finally reached the gatehouse the ship began to move away from the dock.

The dawn light shone through a portal in the wall, illuminating the mechanical wizardry that controlled the dock's gate. Pulleys, levers, cogs large and small, belts and sprockets, all surrounding a central mechanism that wound its way down through the bottom of the gatehouse like a giant screw. The whole chamber was an artificer's wet dream. For a moment Conall thought about his brother, and how much Fulren would have loved the place, before he started wondering how all this shit worked.

He pulled a random lever. Nothing. Turned a circular handle. Still nothing. Outside, the chugging sound of the ship's engines grew louder as it neared the gate.

"This is bollocks," he snarled, pulling two more levers.

Nothing.

"What kind of mad bastard comes up with this shite?"

One last lever set in the floor. He grabbed it with both hands, squeezing the brake lock to release it before wrenching the lever backward.

Chains moved in unison, and the clacking sound of gears filled the chamber as the central mechanism began to revolve. The gate was opening.

Breathing a long sigh, Conall made his way outside. Down in the tithe dock the ship had almost reached the vast gates that were now sliding open, water rushing in a torrent as tonnes of wood and iron opened up a fifty-foot passage. He would have marvelled at the sight, taken satisfaction in his deciphering of the mechanism, but instead his attention was drawn away from the ship as several figures made their way along the walkway toward him.

Half a dozen troopers of the Auroch Battalion levelled their splintbows at him. With no other option Conall raised his hands, breathing a curse as someone stepped past the troopers.

High Legate Hisolda was framed in the dawn sun, its warm light playing off the deep blue of her robes.

"Mischief is a gateway to damnation, Conall," she said. There was a smile on her face that didn't reach her eyes. "Saphenodon teaches us that only by putting aside mischievous things can we protect ourselves from the path to wickedness. For even the most innocent child—"

"By all means fucking shoot me," Conall said. "But please, spare me the sermon."

Her brow darkened. "There's nowhere for you to run," she proclaimed above the noise of the ship's pumping engines as it cruised toward the open gate. "You cannot elude the Ministry's embrace, no matter how reluctant you are to feel its arms about you."

He glanced over the edge of the walkway to the choppy waters a good forty feet below. It seemed she was right. But would a watery grave be better than whatever fate Sanctan Egelrath had in store?

"Come," she shouted above the din. "Enough of this futile procrastination."

As she spoke a sound rose above the clank of the engines. Smoke billowed around them as a massive sail unfurled aboard the passing ship. It heralded a sharp clack from below as a volley of splintbow bolts soared past the Armiger troopers. They ducked, lowering their bows for a moment.

Conall was already moving, sprinting toward the edge of the walkway, blinded by the rising sun, hoping against hope that this wasn't a leap to his death.

His stomach lurched as he flung himself at the ship. The sail was hoisted high, the unsecured canvas still billowing as he fell against it. For a moment he was consumed by darkness, falling, slipping, hearing the zip of friction as he fell. At the bottom the sail spat him out with little ceremony, and he went sprawling onto the deck.

Sted was there to help him to his feet. He could see her laughing, splintbow still in hand, but he couldn't hear a thing above the raging of the ship's engines.

Looking up, he saw Hisolda glaring down, her hand still raised to stop the troopers from firing on them. Conall staggered to the bow, unable to stifle the smile crossing his face, unable to resist one last gesture.

As the sun came up over Agavere, and he left it in his wake forever, he raised a hand to his lips and blew the place one last kiss.

LANCELIN

He waded knee-deep through fetid water. The sluice outlets from the many palace workshops drained directly into the Whitespin via a labyrinthine system of tunnels built in the days of Treon Archwind. They were no secret, and this was a risk. Sanctan could have posted sentries at any point along their path, expecting resistance to come from below. So far it appeared the Archlegate's focus was on the full frontal attack raging outside the palace.

Lancelin could hear the distant sound of thunder echoing along the circular passage as warriors loyal to Sullivar engaged the traitorous palace defenders. The Titanguard had lost their emperor, but they still risked their lives to avenge him with blood, steel and artifice.

It took all Lancelin's will to quell the guilt at his own failure. He should have been there to protect the emperor in his hour of need. If he had been by Sullivar's side, none of this would have happened. But he had not been by his emperor's side. Instead he had travelled a thousand miles across the Drift, abandoning his duty, and now the people of Torwyn would suffer for it.

All that remained was to enact his vengeance, but he could not allow anger to fog his mind. He had to focus.

Cullum Kairns was right behind him, along with a dozen other

Titanguard. The young imperator was Mallum's younger brother, much less ugly but equally imposing. He had volunteered to join Lancelin despite how little hope they had of succeeding, while his elder brother led the attack on the front of the palace. Lancelin knew each of his men by name, though he was unused to seeing them without their mighty battle armour. Nevertheless, it was not steel plate and pyrestone artifice that made the Titanguard exceptional. Each man was a paragon of war, a peerless fighter with or without arms and armour. Lancelin would have had no other warriors join him in this.

At the end of the passage an iron grille blocked their path to the outlet from one of the workshops. Lancelin stood back as Cullum ordered two of the Titanguard to move it aside. Every one of the Archwind elite was a thickly muscled brute, but Arten and Dagamir were the strongest of their peers, and they made short work of lifting the grille and moving it from their path. Lancelin was the first to climb through, checking the way was clear before helping the men behind him.

The workshop was dark, the fading pyrestone lights casting grim shadows as the Titanguard stole across the empty chamber. The main door to the workshop led out onto the bottom landing, and they hurried across it to mount the stairs, moving up flight after flight, the sound of the battle outside growing louder as they neared the surface.

Lancelin ordered the men to stop before they reached the ground level. Above the lip of the stairs he spied a unit of Armiger troopers standing guard over the rear of the palace, their Corvus Battalion uniforms marking them as traitors. Before he could plan how to take them down quickly, Cullum and his men raced past, eager to bring vengeance in the emperor's name.

They fought in disciplined silence, Cullum the first to hack down an unwary enemy, the trooper barely having a chance to raise his blade. Dagamir's greatsword swept the head from another, his backswing hacking off the arm of the next. The Titanguard took to the task like demons, slaughtering without mercy, and by the time Lancelin had joined them, the deed was done. Blood and corpses marred the marble floor, and not a single Titanguard had been wounded in the fray. He could only hope Sanctan died as easily.

There was no time to congratulate themselves on first blood as they took the northern staircase upward. It ran its way through the rear of the palace, but they could still hear the dirge of battle at the other side of the monolithic building. As they ascended, Lancelin saw evidence of how the Draconate had begun to tear down the symbols of the Guilds. The great stone carvings of cogs were smashed and had already been replaced with the dragon idols and pennants of the Ministry.

It angered him to see such desecration, and made him yet more determined to find the man responsible. He had to kill Sanctan quickly and end his reign before it began.

They reached the top of the stair, coming out onto a huge landing. It cut through the midst of the citadel, opening up on both sides to give a panoramic view of the Anvil. Vast columns soared a hundred feet, row upon row of pillars carved in intricate detail to resemble a forest of mighty oaks that supported the upper levels of the palace.

A hundred yards across the vast hall, Lancelin spied their target. The Archlegate had his back to them, surrounded by a score of his Drakes as he viewed the attack through a huge stained-glass window.

"Ranks," Cullum snarled.

His men quickly formed into two rows. Most carried shields along with swords and axes. A poor substitute for the battle armour and glaives of their order, but Lancelin still felt as though he had an army at his back as they advanced across the hall. They were within forty yards when the first of the Drakes turned to see their approach.

In silent discipline the Archlegate's honour guard took up their tower shields, forming a wall of iron in front of him. Sanctan stood behind them, his face emotionless. There was no fear in him, but why would there be? He was defended by an impregnable shield of his most faithful.

"Cover," Cullum growled when they had advanced to within twenty yards.

Lancelin and the rest peeled off, seeking shelter behind the vast pillars as Cullum took an apple-size device from the pack at his waist. He twisted the switch at its top and the contraption, constructed by the artificers of the Titanguard, began to whine and shudder.

Cullum sent it skating across the polished floor, and Lancelin watched it slide toward the Drake shield wall before he concealed himself behind the nearest marble column.

A blast of searing light burst throughout the hall, followed by a deafening boom. The floor shook, and Lancelin felt the seismic vibration rock through his entire body before he raced from cover. The Drake shield wall had been consumed by a grey cloud of dust, and he rushed headlong into it, expecting to see their armoured bodies cut to pieces along with the Archlegate's.

Through the choking smog he spied Sanctan, on his knees, coughing up the dust in his lungs. Lancelin tightened his grip on his sword, eager to spill blood, eager to enact Sullivar's vengeance.

A shield slammed down in front of him, a hulking armoured warrior behind it, dragon helm leering from the dust cloud. Lancelin's sword lashed out on instinct, bouncing off the shield, and before he could reach Sanctan, the Drakes rallied.

"Defend the Archlegate," came the cry. "Kill these heretics."

As the dust cleared, it revealed a huge crack in the marble floor. The corpses of dead Drakes were strewn along it, but more than a dozen were still on their feet.

Lancelin ducked the swing of a sword, darting back, trying to focus on Sanctan. As the shield wall reformed and the Titanguard threw themselves against it, Lancelin spotted him. The Archlegate's nerve had given out, and he was fleeing the chamber, rushing past the mighty pillars in his eagerness to leave the violence behind him.

As the Titanguard charged at the Drakes, melee turned to slaughter all about him. Lancelin would have fought with these men till the end, but he had to abandon them. The only way he could finish this was by killing Sanctan.

He ran from the battle, the sound of steel on steel ringing behind him. Cullum's voice was raised above the din as he barked at his men to avenge their emperor.

Lancelin ate up the ground in Sanctan's wake, feeling the blood coursing through his veins as he tracked his prey. A short corridor led from the hall, and he was immediately plunged into darkness. Unable to see Sanctan ahead of him, he slowed his pace, wary of attack from the shadows. All he could hear was his own breathing and the distant battle behind him as he paced along the corridor. At the far end he came to a vast chamber. Sullivar's throne room.

It was wreathed in shadow, its majestic pyrestone chandelier torn down and replaced by torches and braziers. Now the throne room more resembled a cave... the lair of the wyrm.

At the far end of the chamber, Sanctan stood by the throne. There was nowhere left to flee, and he waited with one hand on the throne's headrest. Not a care in the world.

Lancelin would make him care.

"Did you think you could take it so easily?" he asked as he walked down the centre of the throne room. The shadows were oppressive, but there was no sign of anyone else here but Sanctan. "That throne was never meant for you."

A smile crossed the Archlegate's face and he chuckled, patting the granite throne. "You think I did all this so I can sit in a chair, Jagdor?"

"Then why?"

Sanctan's mirth fled as quickly as it had come. "Because there should be no throne at all," he screamed.

Lancelin was within feet of the Archlegate, but he slowed his approach. There would still be a reckoning, but first he would hear what Sanctan had to say.

"Do you even believe your own lies? Whether you sit on the throne of the Archwinds or stand atop a lectern at the Mount, you have still usurped the rightful authority of the Guilds."

"Still can't see beyond your own prejudice, can you, Jagdor. You were Sullivar's loyal dog for too long. You refuse to understand that I don't care about authority. All I want is to bring the people of this nation back beneath the gaze of the Great Wyrms. They have lost their faith. And I will be the one to find it again."

"You really believe that, don't you. You can't see what you've become. A fanatic. You are a tyrant, Sanctan, no matter how you try and wrap your motives in lofty ideals of salvation. You murdered the rightful emperor of Torwyn."

A flicker of doubt troubled Sanctan's brow. "He was never meant to die. I tried to deliver him from his avarice, but..."

"It doesn't matter," said Lancelin. "It's too late now. I cannot let you live. You know that."

Sanctan met his gaze without fear and nodded. "I know. And I feel the same."

A hulking figure loomed from the shadows to Lancelin's right. He barely had time to duck as a blade swept by where his head had been. He dodged back, bringing up his blade as a huge Knight of the Draconate blocked his path to the Archlegate.

Lancelin silently cursed his stupidity. Sanctan had kept him talking, diverting his attention long enough for his protector to arrive. There would be no more words.

He lunged forward, sword striking at the armoured knight, but it was easily blocked by his tower shield. The knight countered, a sweeping blow of his huge blade that could have cut a man in two. He wielded the weapon as though it weighed nothing, and Lancelin ducked back, ready to counter, but the tower shield was up before he had a chance.

Sanctan was already backing away into the shadows of the throne room. If this fight lasted too long, he would escape again. Lancelin had to end it quickly.

He swallowed down his fury, focusing on the tower shield, and attacked with all his might. The knight handled the shield as though it were light as a feather, and every swing of Lancelin's sword rang off it. His attacks were devastating, the noise filling the chamber as he gave the knight no chance to fight back. All the while he searched for an opening, anything that might give him an opportunity to take his huge opponent down.

The knight was not slowing, and in desperation Lancelin kicked out, all his weight behind the blow as he smashed his boot into the centre of the shield. The knight staggered, almost losing his footing on the stairs to the throne. Lancelin brought his sword down on the knight's exposed leg, blade crashing into his brigandine. The huge warrior grunted, falling to one knee.

In the corner of his eye Lancelin could see Sanctan fleeing the throne room by a side entrance that led to the eastern staircase. He could not let him go. There was no time to finish the kneeling Drake.

He abandoned the fight, sprinting after the Archlegate. His blood was up, and he tried to quell his battle fury, desperate not to let emotion cloud his focus.

Lancelin raced out onto the landing, where two sets of stairs ran down to the north and up to the south. There was no sign of Sanctan, and Lancelin listened for the sound of desperate footfalls, but there was nothing, no sound of flight, no cries for help.

Before he could curse his ill luck there approached a faltering footstep behind him. Lancelin managed to turn in time to see the knight bearing down, sword raised. He ducked the blow, dodging aside as the blade clashed against the granite balustrade, sending sparks flying.

Relentlessly the knight swung again, this time off balance, favouring his right leg. Lancelin charged in beneath the blow, grabbing the edge of the tower shield and wrenching it from the knight's grip. His blade sliced in, but the knight parried, their swords ringing together furiously.

Lancelin pressed his initiative, backing his enemy against the stone banister. A snarl of fury issued from within the knight's helm as he countered with frustration, his attacks desperate, gaps beginning to show in his defence. Lancelin picked his mark, dodging a swing before drawing his blade across the knight's sword arm just below the pauldron. It cut a gash through the hauberk to the flesh beneath, and the knight grunted, clamping a hand to the wound. He staggered back, struggling to keep his sword up in a neutral guard.

"Yield," said Lancelin. "You can't win this. Sanctan is not worth your life."

He could hear the knight's heavy breaths, see his eyes gazing with fury. For a moment they softened, as though he was considering the possibility of surrender. Then he lurched forward for one final attack.

Lancelin sidestepped the downward swing, driving his cross-guard up and smashing it into the side of the dragon helm. The knight staggered, his helmet falling to the ground with a clatter.

Still he stood, dazed, barely registering he was in the fight but stubbornly refusing to give in. Lancelin noted the dark burn that marred the knight's chin before he grasped the blade of his sword and swung again. This time the pommel struck a final blow to the knight's head and he staggered, foot slipping on the top step, before he tumbled down the staircase.

All was quiet but for the dull boom of artillery on the south side of the palace.

Sanctan was gone.

Lancelin had failed to kill his enemy. But there was one last task he needed to complete before he threw himself back into the fray.

ROSOMON

The room was more a prison cell than a bedchamber. A simple mattress, a jug of water, a table and a chair. This was not the kind of chamber she had envisioned herself dying in, but it appeared that was a very real prospect.

Outside she could hear the dirge of battle as an army assaulted the palace. Occasionally the walls would shake their anger in time to the cacophony, and Rosomon took solace in the fact that an uprising had begun. Those loyal to the Guilds and the emperor had risen up to scream their fury. Sanctan's plans for dominance were finally being opposed.

Another explosion. Another tremble of the chamber, this time dislodging dust from the rafters. Rosomon's nerve almost gave out as she walked to the door and rapped on it with the heel of her hand.

"Is anyone there?" she called. "Will someone tell me what's going on?"

Nothing. She had been exiled to her lofty prison, all but forgotten by her captors.

She didn't know what made her angrier—the prospect of dying alone in this chamber or the fact that she was being ignored. She would have cursed Sanctan till her tongue grew dry and broke off, but what good would it do? For now she would have to resign herself to the mercy of the Great Wyrms. That was a more frightening prospect than that of the palace collapsing about her ears.

The sound of a key being fumbled in the lock made her stand back suddenly. Rosomon stood tall to receive her visitor, raising her chin, flattening the creases in her skirts. She might be a prisoner in this chamber, but she would be damned if she'd look anything but regal.

When the door swung open, it was all she could do not to scream from the bottom of her lungs. Olstrum smiled as he walked in the room. In his hands he held a pewter jug and a single goblet.

"I'm glad to see you are unharmed, Lady Rosomon," he said, placing the jug and goblet down on the table.

"You've got some nerve showing your face, Olstrum," she replied, almost snarling the words. "You should be hiding in your pit."

"And yet I'm here," he said. "Your only friend in this place."

"Listen to that," she said, cocking an ear to the tumult outside. "My friends will be here soon enough."

"Somehow I doubt that," he replied.

She took a step forward and slapped him hard across the face. One of the Armiger troopers outside made to step into the room, but Olstrum held a hand up for him to wait where he was.

"Fucking traitor," she said.

That brought a smile to his face. "Whether or not I'm a traitor is purely relative."

"Relative to what?"

He shrugged. "To who ends up winning this war."

"You are finished, Olstrum. No matter what side wins, you will be damned to the Lairs. You betrayed Sullivar. A man you served for years. Do you think Sanctan will trust someone who so easily deceives his master?"

"As long as I am useful to the Archlegate my position is quite safe. And I intend to be valuable to him for a very long time."

"You're playing a dangerous game, Olstrum. Sooner or later you will lose."

"Please," he said, raising a hand to calm her. It made her even more enraged, but she resisted the temptation to slap him again. "Why don't you pour yourself a drink?"

Rosomon glanced toward the jug. She could see wine filled it almost to the brim. The urge to pour herself a goblet and forget her anger, accept her defeat, was overwhelming.

"Why are you here?" she asked.

"I merely wanted to ensure you were safe."

As though on cue, another explosion rang out in the distance, a shower of light sparking outside the window.

"You wanted to make sure I was still caged like an animal, you mean. Still here to ensure the obedience of the Hawkspur Guild. Let me assure you, there will be no compliance. I will not be played like my brother was. I refuse to be used by you, or Sanctan, or any of his fanatics."

Olstrum nodded thoughtfully. "And I believe you, Lady Rosomon. I believe every word." He gestured to the jug once more. "Please, take a drink. And rest assured, you are *not* safe here."

With that he gave her a final, curious look. One of urgency. One of deep concern.

When he had gone, and the key turned in the lock once more, Rosomon tried to work out what that last sentence meant. Of course she was not safe here, the palace felt as if it might shake from its foundations at any moment. If the uprising was quelled, she would then be at the mercy of the Archlegate.

Rosomon clenched her fists at her sides, silently cursing her stupidity, desperately suppressing the urge to throw the wine across the room. What a waste that would be. What did it matter now if she drank or not?

She picked up the jug and filled the goblet before raising it to her lips. It smelled good, drawn from the best of her brother's cellar, no doubt. She downed the goblet in one mouthful, a dribble of the wine pouring down the side of her lips. With the back of one hand she wiped her chin before filling the cup again. As she poured, something plopped into the goblet, followed by a soft tinny sound as it hit the bottom.

With two fingers she fished in the wine, and when she removed her hand, she held an iron key.

Damn Olstrum. He was sly as any snake. More cunning than

Rearden or even Sanctan. And yet, even after he had given her the key to her freedom, she still didn't know whose side he was on. She could only hope she'd live long enough to find out.

Rosomon pressed her ear against the door. No sound of any guards. No sound at all other than the dull boom of artillery outside. Carefully she inserted the key and heard the satisfying click as it turned. She opened the door, seeing the dull light of the corridor beyond. Peering out, she let out a breath when she saw no one there.

As she made her way along the passageway, she passed open doors to left and right, each revealing a tiny set of quarters. This was where the palace servants resided, but each room was abandoned, a stark reminder of what the Draconate had done to this once-vibrant place.

A staircase at the end of the corridor led down to a lower level. More of the same empty rooms until she saw a light flickering through an open door ahead. Rosomon slowed, peering round the corner, unable to stifle a gasp at who she saw.

Athelys sat, quietly reading a book by candlelight. Her handmaid looked so lost and alone, Rosomon couldn't stop herself from rushing in.

"What are you doing here?" she asked, scooping the girl up and holding her in a tight embrace. When she was done, she could see that Athelys was almost stupefied with fright.

"I...I was just left here," the girl replied. "I didn't know what to do, or where to go. They told me you were here but wouldn't say where. I couldn't leave without you."

Rosomon felt grateful she had at least one ally left in Archwind Palace. She hugged Athelys once more.

"We have to get out of here," she said. "We have to get as far away from here as we can."

She took Athelys by the hand and led her from the room. The two of them all but ran along the corridor, and every moment Rosomon expected someone to step from the shadows and bar their way. The farther through the servants' quarters they went, the louder the sound of the attack from outside.

The route led down to the kitchens, and beyond that the dining and reception halls. At every turn Rosomon expected to be stopped by one of the Draconate's warriors, but in each new part of the palace there was nothing but empty chambers and the ever-increasing sound of battle echoing through the corridors.

"Where are we going?" Athelys asked.

Rosomon was about to tell her she had no idea when the sound of raised voices echoed from up ahead. She pressed Athelys against the wall, creeping up to the edge of the corridor. Before she looked around the corner, she recognised one of those voices.

"Where in the fucking Lairs has he gone?" Lorens shouted. She could hear the panic in her nephew's voice, the fear.

"We haven't been able to find him, my lord," replied another voice. "But it is clear the palace defences have been breached. We must get you to safety."

"Safety?" said Lorens. "You think I should run and hide at the first sign of trouble?"

"My lord, our forces are concentrated at the southern perimeter of the palace. If the enemy has managed to gain entry, we cannot protect—"

"Here!" another voice shouted. A woman's voice.

It took Rosomon a moment to realise it was Athelys. The girl had walked out from their hiding place, and her hand was raised in a frantic wave. "She is here."

"Athelys," Rosomon hissed, but she realised it was already too late as footsteps made their way toward her.

She stepped out from the corridor to see four Armiger troopers approaching. They wore the crow helms of the Corvus Battalion, naked swords held in their hands.

From beyond them Lorens watched with a confused look on his face.

One of the troopers made to grab her, and Rosomon shook off his hand. Her stare was enough that the rest of them left her unmolested. No one touched her as she marched toward Lorens. She didn't deign to look back at Athelys. The girl had made her loyalties clear.

Rosomon stopped when she was within five feet of her nephew. She should have scratched out his pretty eyes for this betrayal, for his stupidity, but instead she held him in her gaze, taking some satisfaction from his discomfort.

"I only have one question, Lorens," she said, struggling not to scream at this wayward boy. "Why?"

His hands were shaking, and he had to clench his fists to stop them trembling. "Faith, Aunt Rosomon. I did this out of faith. To return this nation to—"

"Your father was murdered, Lorens. In front of his people. In the name of faith. And yet you still follow Sanctan blindly. I can see your doubt, how this weighs on you. I know this is not the boy I knew. Don't betray your father's memory as you have his—"

"You will come with me," he said, his sorrow turning to anger. She could still see the regret behind his eyes, but also the zeal quashing it to nothing. "Bring my aunt," he said to his men.

Two of the troopers took a step toward her.

"Don't touch me," she spat, relieved when they did as she demanded and glanced uncertainly toward Lorens.

Before her nephew could make further demands, the sound of footsteps caught their attention. A tall figure was approaching them along the corridor, one Rosomon recognised as he appeared from the shadows. Lancelin strode with purpose, sword drawn, eyes focused. A killer on the hunt.

Lorens shielded himself behind her as the four troopers stepped forward. A flash of steel and one of them fell. A clash of metal, a sidestep, a riposte, and a second one collapsed.

Athelys fled when another body dropped, spraying the wall with his blood. Lorens grabbed Rosomon, holding her for protection, and when the last of the troopers was skewered through the neck, she could feel her nephew trembling in terror.

Lancelin was not finished. His eyes focused on Lorens.

"Wait," Rosomon said.

But Lancelin had already grabbed her arm and pulled her aside. Lorens fell to his knees before the unstoppable swordwright.

"It wasn't me," her nephew screamed. "It wasn't me."

Lancelin paused, glaring down at this boy, a child he had watched grow to a man. The wayward son who had betrayed his father.

Rosomon laid a gentle hand on Lancelin's arm. She wanted to grab him, to hold him, to ask so many questions, but the noise of an explosion all too close made those urges dissipate.

"We have to go," she said gently.

Lancelin turned to look at her, those eyes of his, so filled with hateful intent, gradually softening. He reached out and took her hand, pulling her away from Lorens and back along the corridor.

They ran in silence, so much left unsaid as she followed him. Had he managed to find Fulren? Had he brought him home to her?

The pyrestone lanterns that lit their way flickered in protest at the barrage of artillery propelled against the palace. On they fled, racing down a flight of stairs, dodging past the fallen masonry and the smashed remnants of her father's hallowed palace.

When they reached the vast entrance hall, every window lay smashed and shattered, the great iron doors blown off their hinges. Mangled bodies littered the ground, a testament to the ferocity of the assault. Through the arch Rosomon could see the bruised darkness of the predawn sky, lights flaring as burning missiles rained toward the great citadel.

Lancelin didn't stop, urging her onward, and they ran across the shattered hall and through the arch. Outside, the battle came to life all too vividly.

The defenders were in disarray, their barricades smashed and peppered with the metal carcasses of stormhulks. Orders were being screamed, ranks of Drakes crouching behind their tower shields as field surgeons desperately tried to stanch the wounds of the fallen. Dozens of Armiger troopers yelled at one another, desperate to organise themselves against the onslaught.

Rosomon held tight to Lancelin's hand as they raced down the stairs toward the onslaught. She ignored the insanity of it, the madness of rushing through the enemy ranks, toward the torrent that soared in their direction.

From the Bridge of Saints came another volley of artillery—splintbolts, ballista fire and glowing pyrestone devices. A nearby explosion threw masonry and a wave of heat in their wake. All the while Lancelin did not stop, focused, implacable.

At the foot of the stairs the Armigers were rallying, readying themselves to charge forward. In the distance Rosomon could see a wall of shields across the centre of the bridge, behind which hunkered the attackers. Scores of corpses littered the ground in front of them, and two stormhulks had been brought down, lying smashed and burning on the bridge.

Lancelin paused behind an abandoned barricade. The walkways to left and right were packed with troopers cowering behind their defences, shielding themselves from the torrent that poured across from the bridge.

"We have to make a run for it," Lancelin shouted above the din.

Even as he said it, Rosomon heard the whine of pneumatics as a battered stormhulk limped its way from east of their position, making its way toward the bridge. Its arm began to whir, clacking as it pumped ammunition into the breech of its heavy splintbow.

Lancelin grabbed her wrist, pulling her from cover, sprinting toward the distant shield wall. As they ran she heard the staccato snap of the stormhulk's weaponry. Bolts flew over their heads, showering the wall of shields in front of them.

Rosomon watched in horror as the attackers fell, almost losing hope as she heard the stormhulk's footfalls clanking ever closer behind them.

Something landed nearby, winking in the dawn light. As it began to whine with rising discordance, she grabbed Lancelin, pushing him away from the device before it exploded in a blinding corona.

Rosomon's shoulder hit the wall of the bridge, and she came to rest in a heap. Her ears rang from the blast, and smoke filled the air, along with the stink of burning. Lancelin was already forcing himself to his feet, sword still in his hand, his face marred by soot and dirt.

He pulled her up, holding her tight in his arms and asking if she was hurt, but she struggled to hear his words above the ringing in her head. As the dust cleared, she saw the stormhulk looming at them from the night. Its hydraulic arm began to rotate once more, and now she could hear the click, click, click of splintbolts being funnelled into the rotary breech.

There was nowhere to run. Nothing they could do but face this behemoth. And still Lancelin stepped in front of her, raising his sword, yelling a defiant cry at the steel colossus that bore down on them.

At least he had returned to her before the end. At least they would face it together…

FULREN

The sky was alive with fire. Lights streaked toward him, flashing bright as pyrestones ignited. Explosions assaulted his ears with dull booming echoes, the stink of an inferno assailing his nostrils. He could taste the slaughter in the back of his throat. Feel the death in his gut.

Beyond the wall of shields fifty yards across the bridge, the palace burned. The power of his necroglyph brought the flames alive in blue and red and yellow. Though he couldn't see the masonry fall, he could hear it smashing on the vast stairway that led up to the broken palace doors. Glass shattered, iron bent and groaned under the strain.

Bodies lay all around him. He could hear their groans of pain and sense the light within each warrior dimming. The stormhulks of the Hallowhills had attacked in numbers, striding across the bridge to annihilate them, but Mallum's artificers had done their job. Artillery had been fired in volleys. Mortar and cannon flinging one explosive after another to bring down the clanking behemoths as they relentlessly strode across the Bridge of Saints. The enemy webwainers had done their best to stifle the deluge, but they had faced an overwhelming barrage of munitions. Though the attack had taken the palace defenders by surprise, its success was only fleeting. It was becoming obvious they could not hold this position for much longer.

Fulren turned his head to view their escape route. Charges had been placed along each side of the bridge. Through the dark haze of his vision he could see the pyrestones glowing within each ingenious machine, lighting a pathway along the bridge. Twenty yards away, one device had been placed in the centre, its pyrestone shining red in the dark. It was the central detonator—the device that would set off a chain reaction, kindling the pyrestone charges to bring the bridge crashing down. It was their last desperate line of defence. As more of Mallum's men fell under a volley of splintbolts, Fulren realised the time to use it was drawing nearer.

"We have to withdraw," Mallum bellowed above the din.

"No," Fulren yelled. "We have to give Lancelin more time."

The shield wall braced itself in the face of another fusillade of missile fire.

"There is no more time," Mallum growled.

Fulren turned his attention back to the palace. From within the smashed facade of the vast citadel he could sense two figures rushing through the carnage.

"Look!" He grabbed Mallum by the shoulder, pointing across the bridge.

"It's them," the warrior replied, then raised his voice to his men. "Covering fire!"

Fulren's senses were suddenly overwhelmed as the defenders on the bridge, Armiger and Titanguard alike, sent volley after volley of missiles streaking toward the palace. In the distance he could sense those two vague silhouettes rushing through the storm, dodging the missile fire as they raced from the palace and onto the bridge.

From beyond the enemy's front line he felt sudden movement. Above the din of battle, Fulren could hear the grinding of gears, the whining of hydraulics as a stormhulk moved in pursuit of the fleeing figures.

His mother and Lancelin had reached the bridge, still running despite the sheer weight of missile fire, until a pyrestone device exploded in their path. The bridge erupted, and he lost sight of them amid the carnage. Fulren could not stand and watch any longer.

He grabbed one of the mag-charges from the hands of the nearest artificer and rushed forward, barging through the shield wall. Someone shouted in his wake as he burst from cover, but their warning was lost amid the deafening sound of artillery.

Streaks of fire soared through the sky. Splintbow bolts and arrows crisscrossed inches above his head. All around him echoed the clacking report of bolts striking the bridge as he ran headlong into the salvo. All he could focus on was the stormhulk as it stomped toward the last place he had seen his mother.

Lancelin rose to his feet just yards ahead, helping Rosomon from the rubble just as the stormhulk bore down on their position. Fulren twisted the circular charge in his hand, feeling it whir in response, clockwork mechanisms activating the conversion chamber. The blue pyrestone within began to pulsate with energy.

As he advanced to within ten yards of the stormhulk he drew back his arm and threw.

The mag-charge left a contrail of blue light, stark in his vision, as it flew toward its target. A heavy magnet attached to its base clamped the device to the steel chassis of the stormhulk with a resounding clank.

Immediately the charge burst, the blue voltaic light of the pyrestone igniting, spreading electricity in a sparking web across the hull of the vast machine. He could hear the scream of the webwainer pilot as fulminous energy pulsated through the stormhulk, jamming her connection to the web and rendering the machine inoperable.

"Come on," Fulren yelled.

Lancelin needed no further encouragement, grabbing Rosomon by the hand and pulling her away from the slaughter.

The three of them rushed back toward the defensive line of shields. In their wake the palace defenders fired more ordnance, shattering the last statue that stood along the bridge. Fulren could hear the shouts of encouragement from the Titanguard as they ran closer. He stumbled, but Lancelin and his mother were there, one at each arm, dragging him to the relative safety of the shield wall.

"Retreat," shouted Mallum as soon as they were safely behind the row of shields. "By ranks, we have to withdraw."

As one, Fulren could hear the Titanguard begin to march back across the bridge. His mother gripped tightly to his hand, leading him back amid the snap of splintbows as Rawlin's troopers covered their retreat. At the far entrance to the bridge was another hastily erected barricade. Back across the span of the bridge, Fulren could make out the palace defenders taking advantage of the retreat, already advancing toward them.

"Blow it now," Mallum ordered.

Through the haze Fulren could sense one of the artificers begin to manipulate a brightly glowing detonator. He twisted the device, sending effulgent energy sparking through its innards. Blue light flared before he heard an ominous hiss. Where there should have been blinding light as the pyrestone charges detonated, there was only blackness.

"What's happened?" demanded Mallum.

"The pyrestone has overloaded," the artificer replied in a panicked tone. "I don't have enough power."

"What the fuck does that mean?"

Fulren stepped forward. "It means we can't detonate the charges on the bridge. At least not from here."

The enemy were approaching with caution. Two huge stormhulks stomped their way at the vanguard, slow and relentless.

"We have to run then," said Mallum.

"No," Fulren replied. "We won't make it to the Riveryard before they catch us. Those hulks will hunt us down—"

"There's no other way. We don't have enough ordnance left to bring down the bridge."

Fulren could see the red light of the detonator glowing dully halfway across the bridge. At his neck the necroglyph suddenly tingled. He knew there was another way.

"I can set off the charges," he said to Mallum. "But I need to get close to the detonator."

"No," his mother cried. He could feel her arms enfold him, holding him close. Fulren felt the urge to embrace her, to tell her everything was going to be all right, but he knew that would be a lie.

"Don't be an idiot," said Mallum. "You'll be killed. Besides, you can't see."

Fulren gazed over the bridge, watching the pyrestone lights dance amid the blackness of his vision, blazing a path toward the detonator. "I can tonight," he replied.

"You can't go," Rosomon said, holding him tighter. "I won't let you—"

"Mother, there's no time. And no other way."

"I've only just got you back," she said, reaching up to touch his cheek, tracing the mess of scars on his face. Her touch was so gentle it made his flesh tingle. "I won't let you leave me again."

"If I don't do this, we'll all die." He could see the outline of his mother's face, faintly illuminated by the ambient energy. Tears ran down her cheeks in golden rivulets.

"It doesn't have to be you," she said gently.

"There's no one else." He took her by the arms, pulling her grip free. "Lancelin, see my mother to safety."

The swordwright stepped forward, pulling her away and holding her in a firm embrace. "You have to go with him," she said to Lancelin. "You swore you would see him safe."

"And he's fulfilled that vow, Mother," said Fulren. "Now he must fulfil the promise he made to me."

There was a sudden lull in the noise, an ominous hush that fell over the bridge. Fulren could hear the clank of the approaching stormhulks, smell the smoke on the wind. In that moment every doubt and fear was swept away on the breeze.

He set off at a sprint. If he could reach the centre of the bridge, there was a chance he could ignite those pyrestone charges. It was a small chance, but as the necroglyph began to burn at his neck, he knew it was the only one they had. He just had to cover fifty yards of broken bridge without being killed.

A stormhulk already had him in its sights, levelling one arm, the light of its heavy longbarrel igniting as the breech flared with pyrestone magic. Fulren dodged to the side at the last moment, feeling the air above his head superheat as the missile streaked past. Splintbolts rained all around, ricocheting off the stone of the bridge. His breath came in ragged gasps, and at any moment he expected the inevitable thump of a bolt through his chest as he ran through the storm.

He was almost at the centre of the bridge, seeing the red light of the detonator's pyrestone shining only a few yards away. Another volley of missile fire and he dived for cover, a lump of masonry all that shielded him from the approaching army.

Fulren placed his hands on the cold ground, summoning the power of the necroglyph, feeling it begin to agitate, an itch turning to a burn turning to hot searing pain. He heard that dread whisper as his senses heightened, his consciousness dancing along the web, every fibre straining as he felt the latent power of a score of pyrestones spark to life at his command. Each one began to tremble as he imbued it with energy, building to a tumult before it...

A searing pain brought him from his trance, his thigh suddenly burning with white-hot agony. He clamped a hand to the wound, feeling the shaft of a splintbolt protruding from his thigh. Fulren gritted his teeth, stifling his cry of pain as blood poured from his leg.

In front of him he saw more glistening silhouettes framed against the darkness. Ranks of Armiger troopers, splintbows aimed at his position, towering Knights of the Draconate stalking ever closer.

Someone bellowed the order to fire and was answered with the high-pitched twang of bolts being loosed. Fulren could not see the volley, but he knew it was coming right for him. His meagre barricade would not be enough to halt the barrage of missiles.

Before the bolts could land, a shield slammed down in front of him, followed by the staccato drumming of missiles. A dozen bolts smashed into the shield, the rest falling wide of their target.

"Whatever you're going to do, Hawkspur, do it now," growled Mallum.

Fulren could see his dark bulk hunkering behind the shield, the scant outline of his face fixed with grim resolve.

"You should have let me do this alone, Mallum," Fulren snapped. "Now we'll both die."

The grim Titanguard barked a mirthless laugh. "I should have perished with my emperor, boy. To die avenging him is a poor substitute, but it's all I have left. Now fucking blow this thing."

Fulren squeezed his eyes closed, an unnecessary action but anything to help him focus. He concentrated, suddenly fuelled by rage, by Mallum's bravery, by the desire to protect his mother.

The web sparked to life in his field of vision, threads dancing across the bridge to connect him with each of the pyrestone charges. In response they burst into life, shining brightly as he fuelled them with his arcane power. The necroglyph scorched the flesh at his neck. He gritted his teeth against the pain, a growl issuing from his throat and rising to a shout, then a scream as he was consumed by the necroglyph's demonic power.

The nearest pyrestone charge exploded, sending the bulwark of the bridge collapsing into the river. It set off a chain reaction as charge after charge ignited, dazzling explosions lighting up the night.

It was beautiful.

Fulren had time to see one of the stormhulks topple to a watery end, lit up in a blinding conflagration, before he too was consumed by light.

TYRETA

The captured survivors were back in their cages. She had listened to them sobbing through the night, but as the sun rose behind a grey sky all was silent.

Tyreta sat in the centre of the main street. To the south she could see the dock and hear the sea lapping against burned timbers. There was no cage for her—she had been left alone to prepare herself for the fight to come. It would have been so easy for her to make a run for it, to leave this battle behind and flee into the jungle. But she had stayed.

Across her lap lay a spear—a simple wooden shaft tipped with a poorly tempered head of steel. Tyreta had torn strips from the hide tunic she wore and laid them neatly on the ground. She glanced about her to see if there was anyone watching, but the warriors of the Chul paid her no attention.

From the belt at her waist she took the last pyrestone in her arsenal. It glimmered yellow in the morning light, and she felt it trembling in her fist. Hardly the most potent source of energy, but it was all she had left.

Carefully she folded it in one of the hide strips, using the others to lash it to the head of the spear before fastening the knot tight. No sooner had she finished than she heard an ominous rumble on the far horizon. A storm was coming, making slow progress across the Redwind Straits. For a moment she wondered if she would live long enough to see it arrive on the shores of the Sundered Isles and feel the torrent wash across her body. More likely it would anoint her corpse.

No, she couldn't think like that. To contemplate defeat meant she had already lost. Though she faced Shabak, the most fearsome warrior she had ever seen, there was no way she would succumb without a fight.

The funeral pyre had burned down to embers overnight. All that remained of Shabak's fallen warriors was a pile of blackened bone in the centre of the port. Tyreta rose to her feet, letting the final wisps of the pyre's smoke blow past her on the sea breeze. She was ready. At least as ready as she ever could be.

The warriors of the Chul approached, creeping from the wreckage of the town, advancing to watch the spectacle. Tyreta had never felt so vulnerable, but strangely her fear was easy to quell. Her hand did not shake as she hefted the spear, taking a breath, calming herself and letting the grim atmosphere wash over her.

She felt the sweep of a gull flying overhead before it screeched at the sea, heard the rummaging of a rat in its burrow nearby. Even when Shabak appeared, his skull helm discarded, huge spear in his grip, she did not balk.

"You are ready?" Shabak asked, his soothing voice sounding strange coming from such a beast.

Before Tyreta could answer there was movement from up the main street. Someone was approaching, their arrival spreading disquiet through the ranks of the kesh. Shabak's warriors brandished their weapons, adopting defensive stances. Through the mass of warriors that blocked the street, Tyreta could see a group drawing closer. Her heart almost stopped as she recognised the faces of Lokai tribeswomen making their way through New Flaym as though they owned these streets.

Shabak barked an order, and his warriors warily opened a gap, allowing the women to walk through. Yeki was at their fore, Gelila, Amanisa, Suma and a dozen more at her back.

The Chul warriors held their spears threateningly, but the arrival of the women only seemed to amuse Shabak, and he called for his men to lower their weapons.

"Your Lokai friends have come to watch you die," Shabak said.

He walked toward Yeki, standing some feet away from her. Tyreta could see the look of amusement on his face waver slightly when Yeki stared back, holding his gaze as an equal. He spoke to her in the kesh tongue, but still the old woman did not answer. At the moment Tyreta thought he might strike Yeki down, the chieftain turned his back on her, his expression grim.

"Let them watch," he said. "Let them be reminded of what happens to those who stand against me."

The Chul and the Lokai, along with the other kesh warriors, formed a rough circle around them both. Shabak spun his weapon in his hand before rolling his shoulders. It seemed there would be no ceremony. Just a simple execution.

Tyreta gripped her spear, sensing the power of the pyrestone at its tip, hoping it would be enough to give her an edge. Briefly her eyes scanned the crowd, falling on Yeki. The old woman offered her a respectful nod.

"Remember," she said. "You are never alone."

Tyreta wasn't sure if that was supposed to reassure her. It didn't look as if any of the Lokai were going to lend a hand. As she looked at the imposing figure of Shabak, eyes staring like a wild beast, she had never felt more alone in her life.

"Begin, girl," Shabak said. "I promise this will be over quickly."

He almost sounded sympathetic, but it only served to make her more determined. She would not go down easily.

Tyreta gripped her spear in both fists, and they began to circle one another. Shabak held his own weapon in one hand, tip pointed at the ground, as though goading her to attack. It was an opening she could have exploited, but if she'd learned one thing from her time in the jungle, it was to spot a trap when she saw one. Nevertheless, they couldn't just walk around one another forever.

She reached out with her senses, fuelling the pyrestone, feeling its warmth glowing like a beacon. Then she dashed toward him, spear tip aimed at Shabak's heart. His look of confidence wavered at the speed of her attack, and he was at pains to bring his spear up in time to block the thrust. He almost lost his balance but gathered himself, sure-footed in the muddy circle as he danced away from a second jab of her spear.

Shabak's brow furrowed. He had not expected that. Now he held his spear in both hands, eyes focused. She had rattled his confidence if nothing else, made him take her seriously, but now she would have to endure his wrath.

He danced to one side, then the other, spearhead flashing faster than her eyes could follow. Tyreta backed away, feet much less nimble than his on the boggy ground. He cut back in and she barely had time to dodge aside, feeling the breath of the spear as it sliced the air in front of her.

She retreated to the edge of the circle, feeling warm moisture run down her face. Lifting a hand, she dabbed at the blood on her cheek. He had cut her, and she hadn't even realised.

At the tip of her spear the pyrestone burned, fuelled by her sudden anger. Shabak's doubt was gone now, she could read it in his eyes and in the smile that crept up one side of his face.

As she gripped her spear tighter it began to shudder as the pyrestone reacted to her will. She felt its warmth imbue her with strength, with speed, and as she rushed to attack again a snarl issued from her throat.

Shabak met her thrust with the haft of his weapon, turning it aside before countering with a thrust to her thigh. She was faster, stepping aside, slicing down with the spear, forcing him to back away.

Tyreta did not relent, could not allow him the space to recover, and she darted after him. Their spears clacked together, filling the quiet air with the sound of clashing wood. With a scream she thrust above his guard, scoring a red stripe across his chest that provoked sudden yells of approval from the warriors of the Lokai.

Shabak darted back, glancing down in disbelief at the wound. When he looked back at her, all amusement had fled. There was only fury, but measured, controlled. He bared his fangs, spinning the spear again before bringing the fight back to her.

Tyreta had enough time to note the pyrestone smoking at the end of her spear, its power causing the hide strips to smoulder, before she was forced to defend herself.

His weapon scythed past her head, but she managed to dodge his furious attack. He drew back for a final thrust, and she raised her spear to parry, but he twisted his weapon at the last moment, their hafts cracking together. The blow jarred her arm and sent her spear spinning from her grip to land a few feet away.

She ducked as Shabak thrust at her throat, dancing away from the death blow, desperate to reach her weapon.

Shabak darted into her path, standing between her and the spear, his own weapon held out menacingly. Her eyes locked on that spear tip poised to strike at her heart.

Tyreta's spear was only feet away as Shabak drew back his arm for the killing thrust.

She held out her hand, drawing the energy of the pyrestone, willing it to move at her command. Before Shabak's blow could land, her spear soared through the air, forcing him to dodge aside or be struck by the weapon. The haft slapped against her palm, and she darted forward to attack, fuelling the pyrestone with all her rage. Shabak planted his feet, raising his blade to block her sweeping strike.

No sooner had their weapons connected than the pyrestone overloaded. Light blinded her, flinging her backward into the mud as the stone exploded.

When she opened her eyes, she saw Shabak rising groggily some yards away. The crowd looked on, stupefied by what they had seen, some still shielding their eyes from the sudden blast. Tyreta scrambled to her knees, glancing around, desperate to find a weapon, but both spears were little more than matchwood scattered about the fighting circle.

Shabak staggered, barking an order to his men, holding out his hand for another weapon. As Tyreta stood, managing to maintain her balance, one of the Chul threw a spear to his warchief.

She was helpless. None of the Lokai made a move to intervene. Shabak stared, ready to attack once more, but he held himself back.

"You need a weapon, girl," he said, unwilling to show he was a coward in front of his men by striking down this unarmed foe.

"You don't need to do this," Tyreta said.

Shabak grunted a laugh from the back of his throat. "Of course I do. This is what you asked for. This is what all your people asked for."

"I can make them leave. We will take our ships and never return. The killing can end here. No one else has to die."

"Of course they do. Someone always has to die. And now it is your turn."

Perhaps she should have said more. Made him understand that she only wanted to help the kesh. But Tyreta could see the look in his eyes. That certainty that he was in the right. That the only way to end this was with her death. There would never be any reasoning with him or his followers.

With a nod from Shabak, one of the Chul threw a spear at her feet. Tyreta knelt and picked up the weapon. It would be less than useless against him. Without the pyrestone to give her an advantage, Shabak would kill her in an instant. She threw the spear back to the warrior.

"You have to choose a weapon," Shabak said. "That is the way."

Tyreta stared back at him. You are never alone, Yeki had said. She knew now that was true. Her senses told her as much. This place was alive—Tyreta could hear every heartbeat, feel every rapt emotion. She would never be alone again.

"Choose a weapon," Shabak repeated, growing frustrated with her silence.

"I already have," Tyreta replied.

Shabak furrowed his brow as she let out a cleansing breath. There was no fear now. No anger. She was as emotionless as the storm wind. As unfeeling as a wave that engulfs the ship at sea.

Yeki took a small step forward from the circle surrounding them. The old woman laid a hand to her chest, closing her eyes before she breathed a single word: "Kiatta."

As one, the women of the Lokai whispered it in reply. "Kiatta. Kiatta. Kiatta."

Shabak snarled a warning, hands shaking in fury at their impudence. He turned his eyes to Tyreta, and she saw in that moment his hate, his doubt... his fear.

She closed her eyes, spreading her arms wide, inviting him to strike. Even with her eyes closed her senses were alive, assailed by her surroundings, the sea and sky, the jungle beyond the walls of the port. She heard his first footstep as he advanced toward her, sensed him raise that spear, fuelling his thrust with all his anger.

Her eyes opened. The face of Shabak leered through a smog of arcane reverie, the world slowing around her. His spear was aimed at her heart, but still she felt no desire to move. Tyreta had already summoned her weapon, and she was swifter than any spear.

A roar cut the air as the panther leapt above the heads of the warriors. Its paws padded down in the circle before it propelled itself toward Shabak. The chieftain tried to dodge, to bring his spear to bear, but he would always be too slow. The panther was on him before he could even try to defend himself.

Tyreta watched emotionless as the panther clamped those powerful jaws onto Shabak's arm. He screamed, caught in that deadly maw, snarling his defiance and clawing at the beast's hide. Blood spurted as the panther twisted her muscular neck. The sickening sound of tearing flesh and cracking bone heralded Shabak's cry of agony as his arm was torn off at the shoulder.

The panther reared back, shaking her prize in those vicious jaws before discarding the arm. She stared at Shabak, muscles tensing to finish the job, before looking up at Tyreta expectantly.

Shabak's hand was clamped to the stump of his arm, his eyes wide as he struggled to stanch the blood pouring from the wound. Even in shock he fought to retain his wits, but he could not manage to stand.

"Witch of the sea," he breathed, staring around at no one. "I should have known you would use your cursed magics to cheat me of victory."

Tyreta could sense every eye on her. Each spectator waiting expectantly for her to show mercy.

"I never understood before," she said, as much to herself as to her defeated enemy. "But it's all so clear now." He gazed up at her, and in his eyes she saw only defiance. Saw the man he had once been. Saw the warrior he had become. Saw the monster he would always be. She stared back, and in that moment Shabak realised his fate. There would be no mercy here.

"I will not go unavenged," he whispered. "In my place will rise—"

"Kelach!" Tyreta screamed.

In an instant the panther fell on Shabak. He had no time to cry out as the beast went straight for his throat.

As their chieftain died, Tyreta turned to the gathered crowd, seeing the faces of the Chul, their horror, their defeat, their hate.

"Return to your homes," she commanded. "Keep to your lands and your hunting grounds, and this I swear to you: my people and I will leave these islands forever. And I promise we will never return."

At first they stared, still standing in a circle around her, but Tyreta knew they had heard. Murmurs of disquiet spread through the kesh ranks, and those who spoke the language of Torwyn relayed her vow in solemn whispers.

One of the Chul stepped forward. He looked to be the biggest among them, even bigger than Shabak. He spat a guttural threat, shaking his spear, eyes darting toward the panther.

Another challenger. One Tyreta didn't know if she had the spirit to face. Should she pick up a spear and fight? Should she summon the help of the panther once again? Could she?

A grunt from behind heralded a spear flung through the air. It struck the warrior full in the chest. He stared at it for a moment before staggering back and falling to the mud.

Gelila strode forward from the surrounding wall of onlookers to stand at Tyreta's side. Other warriors from the Lokai did likewise, staring down the Chul as though daring another warrior to step forward. None of them took up the challenge.

Once the first of their spears was dropped to the ground, Tyreta knew she had won.

The Chul and their allies abandoned their dead leader. Every one of them walked the path north through the town, back to their homes. Back to the wilds.

She watched as they went, feeling no relief, no sense of victory. All she had left was exhaustion.

When they had gone, Yeki offered Tyreta a final nod of respect before turning and leading the Lokai after the other kesh. Gelila was the last to leave, turning to Tyreta and regarding her with solemn reverence before grasping her and holding her tight.

"I hope you can keep promise," she whispered.

With that she turned and followed the rest of the kesh north from the burned port.

"So do I," Tyreta whispered after her. The words were lost on a sudden gust of wind as the storm continued to roll in.

ROSOMON

She fought back the tears as she ran. Fought back the pain and the loss. Rosomon wanted to stop, to howl her grief and fury, but the instinct to survive forced her onward.

Fulren had sacrificed himself so the rest of them could escape. And all she could do was stand and watch. Scream herself hoarse as she witnessed the Bridge of Saints collapse and her boy plummet into the dark waters of the Whitespin. If she stopped running now and gave in to her anguish, that sacrifice would have been for nothing. Instead she gripped tight to Lancelin's hand. He was all she had left, the only man she could trust, her one solace amid all this madness.

They were surrounded by a host of fleeing warriors. Titanguard led the way through the early-morning streets as Armiger troopers of the Bloodwolf Battalion ran in disciplined ranks. They had covered no more than half a district before Rosomon heard the first clap of splintbow fire and the desperate shouting for men to take cover. Along the street, rival battalions loyal to the Ministry were already attempting to halt their flight. The crow helms of the Corvus and bear helms of the Ursus marked them as the enemy.

"Keep moving," Lancelin said, ducking his head as he pulled her along.

"Where are we going?" Rosomon asked, desperate to know how they could escape.

"Emony Marrlock has boats waiting at the Riveryard docks. If we can reach them, they'll take us out of the city."

To her left Rosomon heard the dull thud of splintbolts embedding themselves in masonry. The fearsome shriek of a cannon being primed howled from across the street.

They were almost at the Cogwheel. From there they could double back toward the river, but as they rushed onto the avenue that ran down to the centre of the city, Lancelin pulled up short.

The way ahead was alive with frenzied activity. It looked as though every last civilian had taken to the streets, and the Cogwheel was more crowded than the day Sullivar had been slain. A wall of noise echoed along the avenue, and already missiles were being thrown by the mob as sporadic fights broke out between separate factions.

Banners were held aloft, some reading *The Wyrms Will Rise*, others *The Guilds Protect Us*, *Long Live Sullivar.* It heartened Rosomon to know that a large part of the populace still supported the Guilds, but there was no way they could make their way through that crowd without bloodshed.

Drift Marshal Rawlin was at their side, his men at his back, heaving in breath after their frantic flight across the city. "We have to go around," he said, glaring at the riot in front of them. "Come on, this way."

"No," Lancelin said. "We have to split up. There's no way we can all get to the river without encountering resistance. We need to break into smaller groups, at least then some of us will make it."

"All right," Rawlin replied. "But you should both come with me."

"No," Rosomon said, unwilling to trust anyone but Lancelin. "We can make our own way."

Rawlin looked as if he might argue but thought better of it. "Very well, Lady Rosomon. Then I wish you good luck."

With that he barked orders for his men to take the western side street toward the riverside.

"Maybe we should—" Lancelin began, but Rosomon shook her head.

"I don't trust anyone but you," she said, locking him in her gaze. "Only you."

Lancelin nodded, taking her hand once more. "Then let's get out of here."

They raced away from the Cogwheel and the rioting, rushing down the alleyways that ran parallel to the main thoroughfare. Lancelin suddenly pulled her to one side, pressing them both against a wall as the sound of smashing glass echoed up the passage. Looters were busy taking advantage of the chaos, and several buildings were already ablaze.

"You there," came a deep cry from down the street.

Rosomon couldn't tell whether the cry was directed at her or the torch-wielding looters, but Lancelin had already taken her by the arm, and he crossed the street and planted a booted foot against a closed door. The lock shattered, door swinging inward before he pulled her inside and slammed it shut behind them.

She had just enough time to see a family hunkering for safety in the shadows given off by a nest of candles before Lancelin had taken her arm once more, pulling her through the dwelling to a door on the other side.

He unbolted it, leading her out into the morning light. This air was quieter as they moved down another alley, ducking beneath a row of dirty sheets hanging like ragged pennants across their path.

Before they reached the end of the passage, there was a bellowed chant as more fire-wielding rioters paraded across the street in front of them. Rosomon gripped Lancelin tight as they squeezed themselves into the nearest alcove. Water dripped from the drainpipe above, plopping in time to the chant that rang out from the street beyond.

She looked up at him, at that face she had yearned to see for so many days. Grabbing his shirt, she pulled him close, feeling the firmness of his chest, taking some comfort from having him near. But she knew there would be no comfort now. The son she had sent him to rescue was gone. Their boy was dead.

"I'm sorry," she whispered.

He touched her chin, raising her head to look at him. "What would you have to be sorry for?"

"I should never have sent you away. If you'd never left, Fulren would still be alive. Sullivar might still be alive. This is all my—"

"None of this is your fault," he said, staring into her eyes, and she knew he meant every word. But then Rosomon could commit murder right in front of him, and Lancelin would still swear on his honour she was innocent.

"I had him," she whispered. "I had him in my arms for just a moment."

She stifled a sob as he held her close. Rosomon had always felt safe in Lancelin's arms, but now all she felt was emptiness.

"Here!" barked a voice from the alleyway.

Rosomon saw someone standing at the mouth of the alley, glaring toward their hiding place. He held a wooden bat in his hand, the kind children used to play games with, but she doubted he was about to propose a round of stickball.

Lancelin's hand strayed to the blade at his hip, but Rosomon reached out to stop him as another civilian joined the first and squinted down the alley to where they hid in the shadows.

"Who've you found?" a voice asked from farther up the side street. A crowd was forming. A mob.

"If it's one of those Guild bastards, drag them the fuck out," snarled another angry voice.

Someone pushed his way to the front of the growing crowd. Lancelin strained against her grip to pull the sword free, but Rosomon held on tightly. If they tried to fight, they'd be killed, no matter how good Lancelin was with that blade.

The newcomer peered into the alcove, then took a step forward, and Rosomon saw his face. She recognised those blue eyes and the well-kept moustache that curled across his lip. Days ago, on her way to the Mount, she had witnessed a group of youths being abused by the Revocaters. This one had seemed so harmless then, a disgruntled young man scrawling graffiti on the city walls. He didn't look harmless now.

Silently they regarded one another. The man...the boy gazed into her eyes, and in that moment she knew he recognised her too.

"It's nobody," he said before turning back toward the mob. "Just a couple hiding from the fight."

"Shouldn't we question them?" asked a voice from the crowd.

"What are you, a fucking Revocater? We need to get to the Cogwheel, not abuse every innocent person we meet. So let's move."

With that Rosomon heard the crowd begin to leave.

They held one another until they were alone once more, and only then did Lancelin let his hand slide from the hilt of his sword. He took her hand, leading her from the alcove, and peered out into the street.

"We have to hurry," he said before heading toward the river.

Rosomon began to feel the knot tighten in her stomach as she heard the Whitespin flowing. A pall of smoke from a burning building was drifting over the rooftops, rolling down to the river. When they finally reached the stone bank, there was no one waiting for them. No boats to take them to safety.

"Come on, we can't wait here in the open," Lancelin said.

"No." Now it was her turn to grab his arm. "Look."

She pointed to the north. Up the Whitespin, the prow of a trading skiff was drifting through the smog. They gripped tight to one another's hand as the boat approached. Only when Rosomon recognised young Emony standing at the prow did she allow herself to breathe.

"Quickly," the girl said. "Jump aboard."

Neither of them needed any encouragement, not waiting for the boat to slow before they jumped from the esplanade and onto the deck. On board were troopers of the Bloodwolf Battalion whom Emony had picked up farther along the river. Many were wounded, all looked relieved to be travelling to safety, but they were not safe yet.

Behind their boat came a convoy of others, sputtering along at little more than walking speed. Squinting through the smoke, Rosomon could see Titanguard and Armiger troopers hunkering on deck. The tension as they progressed down the river was almost unbearable; they would easily be picked off from the shore if the Ministry's loyal followers caught them in such a vulnerable position.

The farther they progressed toward the Rivergate, the louder the sounds of violence became. The city was in uproar, the crowds on the streets determined to show their love of the Ministry or their zeal to defend the Guilds.

"Where is Fulren?" Emony asked as she joined Rosomon at the prow's bulwark.

Her words made the breath catch in Rosomon's throat. She took the girl in her arms, holding her tight as they were carried on the current toward the Rivergate and through the greatest city in Torwyn, now aflame and riven with hate.

"We're almost there," Lancelin whispered, glaring forward through the smoke.

The great barbican that led out onto the flat plains of the Guildlands towered proudly ahead of them. Rosomon gripped the prow, gritted her teeth, willing the steel portcullis to be open.

As they cleared the haze that washed across the river, she saw the way was clear. Emony looked up at the barbican, seeing a group of city guard standing atop it. Slowly the girl raised her hand.

Rosomon expected them to sound the alarm. To take up their bows and fire down volley after volley. When instead they returned Emony's wave, Rosomon almost fell to the deck in relief.

It took too long for the convoy to pass beneath the shadow of the barbican, but when finally they were heading south and away from the city, Rosomon allowed herself to breathe more easily.

She bit back the tears, forcing herself to look back at the Anvil, to her brother's seat of power, now usurped by a madman. All that was gone. Sullivar was dead. Fulren dead. Tyreta missing. Of Conall's fate she had no clue. All she had was Lancelin and a beaten army of loyal men. In the days to come, she knew that loyalty would be tested to the full.

She could only tell herself that this was not over. Rosomon Hawkspur would not run and hide for long. She would return with an army at her back, no matter what she had to do to raise it. No matter the sacrifice.

Let Sanctan have his victory. Let him preach to his faithful. He would not sit easily on the throne he had stolen. Not as long as she lived.

CONALL

The cabin rocked in response to another wave lashing the side of the ship. A flash of light through the porthole and the single pyrestone light sputtered fretfully in its precarious housing. If there was a rumble of thunder to follow, it was lost in the din of the howling wind and furious waves.

"So what's the plan when we get back?" Sted asked.

She was sitting across the table from him, holding tight to the cup in front of her in case it slid off the table and spilled her rum all over the wet cabin floor.

Before Conall could answer, the sound of dry heaving filled the room as Donan retched into a bucket for the dozenth time. The poor sop hadn't quite found his sea legs yet, and from the sound of him he never would. The first time they'd hit a wave he'd puked his guts out. Now there was nothing left in him but air, and still his body was trying to empty itself. Conall would have felt sorry for him if he didn't have more pressing problems than seasickness to deal with.

"It depends where we manage to dock," he replied, gazing up at the porthole, seeing the waves rising to block out the dark-grey sky. "There's no telling where might be a safe port to land. Windstone? Candlehope? Maybe Wyke's our only safe bet."

Donan managed to stagger away from the bucket and gingerly

seat himself in an empty chair. His face was cabbage green, and a string of vomit had dried to a crust on his chin.

"Maybe this will all have blown over by the time we get home," he said, convincing no one.

"Sounds like you've pretty much puked your brains out if that's what you're hoping for," Sted snapped. "This shit's only just begun."

Trust Sted to be the voice of reason, in her own subtle way.

"We should try and persuade the captain to make his way up the coast rather than stop at Goodfleet," Conall said. "The closer we can land to Wyke the better. It's the only place we can guarantee we won't be handed straight to the Ministry. There'll be allies there still loyal to the Guild."

"What about your mother?" Sted asked. "What if she's been captured? Or..."

She stopped herself before finishing the sentence, but it was obvious what she meant.

"Whatever's happened to her, she'll want me to take the fight to the Ministry. The Hawkspurs will never give up. I will lead them if necessary."

"And you're sure you're up to that?"

"If not me, then who else?" he asked, fast losing patience. Maybe Sted was trying to help, trying to get him to admit he was no substitute for the great Lady Rosomon. That he should just surrender and save himself the trouble. "I have to fight."

Before he could slam his hand down on the table to affirm his position, a huge wave hit the side of the boat. It tipped the cabin, Donan almost fell from his chair, and the pyrestone light was sent swinging, casting frantic shadows up and down the walls.

"But we don't know how many of the Guilds have fallen or gone over to the Archlegate," Donan said when he'd managed to right himself. "Sullivar is dead, if the rumours are true. Surely we have to negotiate rather than fight?"

"Don't underestimate the strength of a single Guild," Conall replied. "If my uncle is dead, it's a blow, but he was not the Guilds. He was head of the Archwinds, but even a single Guild has enough power to rival the Ministry. We command the nation's resources."

"But Sanctan holds their faith," Donan said. He looked scared, and the weather wasn't doing his nerves any good. "He holds people's hearts. And what if the Guilds have already surrendered to him?"

"I don't believe that for a second. My mother would never surrender. I won't surrender. We won't give in to a tyrant."

Another wave smashed against the bow of the ship, just as the door to the cabin burst open. The captain entered, hair soaked, eyes wide and desperate.

"We're turning back," he gasped. "We can't make it through this storm."

Conall rose to his feet, wishing he'd bothered to learn the man's name, but in all the excitement of jumping on board from a forty-foot wall he'd quite forgotten to make the necessary introductions.

"What are you talking about?" he said. "We can't turn back now."

"We'll not make it through this damned storm. The ship will be torn apart."

As though on cue, there was a sound of cracking timbers and the creak of iron bending under immense strain.

Conall crossed the room, pushing his way past the beleaguered captain and into the hallway. Water was washing down the stairs, and the wooden boards were slick underfoot. He managed to grab the banister and pull himself up, salt water splashing in his face at every step.

As he dragged himself out onto the deck, Conall saw what the panic was about. The ship was surrounded by fifty-foot waves, a lone piece of flotsam amid a raging torrent. Overhead the clouds billowed thick and black, the air heavy with static.

Mariners rushed around like madmen, desperate to secure rigging in the violent winds. Already cargo straps had come loose, spilling crates across the deck. Above the raging storm Conall heard the engines straining against the elements, desperate to keep the ship moving, smoke billowing from the twin funnels to be immediately whipped away by the winds.

Sted staggered up the stairs after him, pulling Donan close behind. The crew was working frantically to bring in the sails, one already flapping, shredded and useless.

"The captain's right," Sted shouted above the wind. "We can't go on through this."

Before Conall could even consider the implications, the sky lit up. A bolt of lightning concertinaed from the black billowing cloud, striking the forecastle and spitting sparks across the deck.

The next thing he knew, Conall was sprawled on his back, the stench of scorched wood wafting across his nostrils. He looked up in time to see the mast falling and hear the sound of timbers cracking.

As he scrambled to his feet, he looked across the ship to see one of the huge funnels had split, half of it already dropped away into the sea, the black smoke it had been pumping now replaced by rampant flames.

A mariner staggered from the engine room in a billow of black smoke, his face a mass of soot already washed into streaks by the rain. He grabbed the captain, hauling him to his feet.

"The engine's toast," the man screamed above the lashing wind. "We have to abandon ship."

The captain looked as if he was in shock, staring in horror at the carnage across his deck. Eventually he nodded as his wits returned to him.

"All right, gather the crew and passengers," he cried, then, to his men. "Prepare the lifeboat!"

At his order the men ran to starboard, where a long rowboat was secured to the rigging.

"Come on," Conall shouted to Sted. "We have to help."

He staggered across the slick boards, a wave hitting him and threatening to knock him off his feet. He hadn't covered ten feet before he was blinded by another streak of lightning and a second galvanic shock wave coursed through the ship. This time Conall managed to stay on his feet, and he looked up in time to see the mizzenmast begin to fall, timbers cracking over the sound of the wind.

It came down hard, smashing the port-side bulwark. Someone screamed, and it took Conall a moment to realise he recognised that wail of fear.

"Con," Sted screamed over the tempest.

She was already picking her way across the deck to where Donan was trapped beneath the fallen mast. Conall followed as Donan flailed in the rainstorm. His lower leg was held fast, bone just visible through his leggings. From the looks of it he'd struggle to ever walk again, if they could manage to free him.

"Help me," Sted said, putting her weight beneath the mast and struggling to lift it.

Conall braced his shoulder underneath, straining to push it free. It didn't take him long to realise they'd never be able to move the thing.

"Leave me," Donan screamed. It was the bravest thing Conall had heard him say, but he'd be damned if he was going to let this man drown.

He squinted through the squall, spying an axe wedged in the wood of the quarterdeck. Another great wave almost took him off his feet as he slid across the deck, grasping the axe and wrenching it free. In the corner of his eye he could see the crew struggling to lower the rowboat from the side of the ship as he rushed back to the fallen mast.

"Are you a fucking lumberjack now?" Sted screamed at him. "By the time you've hacked through that mast we'll be at the bottom of the ocean."

She had a point. Donan had gone quiet now, almost passed out from the pain.

"What about his leg?" Conall said.

"What about it?"

"If we cut it off we can get him on the rowboat."

"And he'll have bled to death by the time we've rowed three bloody strokes."

Conall grabbed her by the shirt, staring into that drenched face. "Have you got a fucking better idea?"

It was clear from her expression that she hadn't.

"No," Donan cried when it was obvious what their only option was. "Just leave me. Just leave me."

"Take off your belt," Conall growled at Sted.

She got the idea, unbuckling the belt at her waist and kneeling next to Donan. He continued to protest as she wrapped it around his leg just above the knee, pulling it tight like a tourniquet. Donan screamed in fear as Conall raised the axe high.

Sted grabbed him, holding him still as Conall brought the axe down clean, shearing off Donan's leg just below the knee. That scream of his rose in pitch and volume, pealing out above the storm.

As they both dragged him from beneath the mast, he went limp, the shock and the pain making him pass out. Conall could only think it a mercy. Together he and Sted stumbled across the slick boards of the deck, dragging Donan's unconscious body toward the lifeboat. The ship lurched, and Conall saw someone pitched over the side into the sea. Salt water splashed onto his face, almost blinding him, and through the squall he could see mariners desperately holding on to the support ropes as they lowered the boat.

"Get him in," Conall shouted, hauling Donan to the edge of the lifeboat.

He heard Sted grunting as they lifted the flaccid body. Two passengers already in the boat helped pull the unconscious Donan on board. No sooner was he safely in the rowboat than another massive wave hit.

Sted's feet were swept from under her as the lifeboat lurched, dropping several feet from the side of the ship. Above the screams of the passengers, Conall heard Sted's familiar cursing.

He managed to rise to his feet, seeing her gripping the bulwark, hand slipping from the slick metal. He leapt, grasping her wrist before she lost her grip.

There she swung above the churning waters eager to consume her if she fell. The lifeboat hung just beneath them before dropping the last few feet to splash into the water.

"Don't fucking let go," Sted screamed.

He was already losing his hold on her, their hands slipping apart. With a cry of rage he swung her toward the lifeboat, their hands sliding free of one another as he did so. He could only watch as she fell ten feet to the boat below, landing amid the passengers in a heap.

Conall crawled to his feet in time to be blinded by another flash of light. Sparks flew, more timbers cracked, but above the noise of the storm rose a dread rumble.

"The engines have overloaded," screamed one of the mariners before pitching himself over the side.

Fire was licking up through the timbers of the deck. Black smoke churning from the funnels at the forecastle. The grinding of the engines rose in pitch, the scream of the turbines rising to a torturous crescendo.

Conall barely had time to leap over the bulwark before the engines blew, the deck erupting, the force of the blast pitching him far into the sea.

As he hit the icy waters his breath escaped him just when he needed it most. Down he went, pulled under by the tempest as fire rained all around, broken pieces of the hull hissing through the dark waters.

He fought, kicking, struggling, but still he was dragged down into the black depths until he could resist no longer, his lungs bursting, throat filling with water. The surface seemed so far away.

Conall Hawkspur could only give in to the storm, to the sea, to the endless dark…

TYRETA

The dawn brought peace. A clear sky on the horizon above a calm blue sea. It was as if the night's storm had been nothing more than a bad dream.

Tyreta sat at the edge of the dock, watching as the sun came up, bathing her in its light and warmth. She closed her eyes, letting it wash over her. By her side the panther stirred in the warm morning air, rolling over like a faithful hound wanting its tummy tickled. She could only smile at the beast, once so vicious, now nothing more than a docile pet.

No one came anywhere near them. Tyreta first thought it was the panther at her side that kept everyone at bay, but she realised that wasn't the only thing. She was different now. Not just in the way she looked or held herself, but in an aura that hung about her. A sense of the unnatural. She wasn't exactly sure how she felt about that. Before, she'd been nothing remarkable, apart from her name and her webwainer gift. Now she had defeated a champion and learned to wield magics beyond her understanding.

Strange how things worked out.

Behind her the town began to stir. They'd done their best the previous day to pull themselves from their cages, to hug and weep and look for survivors. There hadn't been many. Those few who'd fled to the jungle returned at nightfall and began working despite the storm to repair what had been burned and smashed by the kesh. Even as the storm raged they still worked for as long as they could. Tyreta could only admire them for that.

She should have helped them, but she knew it was all for nothing. Tyreta had made a vow to the kesh that they would all leave these islands. Eventually she would have to tell these people their old lives were over and they had to go back to Torwyn. As she saw the first ship approaching the harbour across the clear blue waters, she knew that time would be soon.

Three ships had docked by the time the sun cleared the horizon. Tyreta continued to sit and watch as the crews discovered what was going on in the port. There were frantic discussions, panicked survivors demanding safe passage. None of the captains could refuse, and before long the ships had a steady stream of bodies making their way on board. One set off within an hour; Tyreta watched it leave as the panther began to stir. A butterfly danced past her whiskers, and she tried to catch it in her mouth before lazily swiping at it with those giant paws.

A second boat made ready to leave, and Tyreta saw Isleen among the passengers making their way up the gangplank. Their eyes met across the dock, but Isleen didn't deign to offer so much as a wave of acknowledgment. She hadn't even stayed long enough to see if they'd given her cousin, Lord Serrell, a decent burial.

No sooner had her vessel left the dock than Tyreta rose to her feet. Another ship was already making its way to port. Perhaps it was time to see that her vow was fulfilled. The people of New Flaym had to be told.

She made her way back toward the centre of the town, the panther rising and following at her knee like a loyal hunting hound. The port survivors watched her suspiciously as she passed them, every one giving her a wide berth while Tyreta and her new friend made their way up the main street.

The harbour square had been cleared of hanged bodies and the ground dug up, the market now little more than a mass grave. Bodies lay within it, some hastily wrapped in muslin, others left exposed. Already the stench was ripe, and Tyreta ignored it, trying not to look into that grave lest she spy a face she recognised looking back accusingly. No sooner had she skirted the square than she heard someone speaking farther up the main street.

"We can rebuild," said Chancellor Eremand. "There is no need for you to leave. New Flaym can be born anew."

She could see a crowd had gathered around him. Eremand was standing on a porch, raising himself above them.

"We have beaten the kesh," he continued. "Put them in their place. There is nothing to fear. As soon as we get more workers and supplies across the Redwind this place will be as great as it ever was. We cannot just give in. We cannot abandon everything we've worked so hard to build."

Tyreta stepped up onto the porch. Eremand's speech came to a stumbling halt as he saw her, glancing to the panther at her side.

"Step away, Eremand," Tyreta demanded.

He opened his mouth to speak, then thought better of it. His eyes shifted to the crowd. His thoughts were obvious: Should he step aside and concede to this girl, or try to affirm his authority?

"I am still chancellor," he said. "I still have the—"

"Step aside, Eremand," Tyreta repeated as the panther issued a low growl from her throat.

That was enough for the chancellor, and he took a stumbling step backward. Tyreta turned to the gathered crowd of no more than thirty souls. They looked as if they'd suffered enough.

"I understand what you've gone through," Tyreta said. "We've been through the mill and back again. But the fact is, you all need to get on a ship and leave this place to the jungle."

There was a slight rumble of discontent, a couple of people shaking their heads. Tyreta could understand—many of them had made their lives here. New Flaym had been a mining outpost for ten years. It was likely many of them barely remembered Torwyn.

"If you stay here, there will be no one to protect you. You need to go back to Torwyn. These islands belong to the kesh, whether you like it or not. They've gone back to their villages for now, but they won't stay gone for long. We were never supposed to be here in the first place. We have no rights to strip this place down for profit. You can agree with me or not, but believe one thing—if you stay here, you'll die."

She expected more dissent, but the fight was gone from them. There were no arguments, not even from Eremand. When Tyreta walked away, she was pleased that the chancellor had kept his mouth shut, and the crowd began to disperse. She could only hope those people would listen to her and not his empty promises.

As she made her way back toward the dock, she saw Crenn making his way toward her. The old artificer looked wary of the panther, but he still moved close enough to speak.

"Captain of one of the ships been asking after you by name," he said.

"Me? What does he want?"

Crenn just shrugged. "I think it's best if you hear it from him." He turned and gestured toward the dock. A mariner stood by the jetty in Hawkspur colours marking him as the captain of a Guild trading vessel.

She nodded her thanks to the artificer. "All right then. Must be important if they've sent the captain of a ship."

As she approached the mariner, Tyreta laid her hand flat, gesturing for the panther to sit and wait for her. She half expected the wild beast to ignore her, but instead she sat in the middle of the street, watching Tyreta walk away.

"Captain, I've been told you wish to see me?" she said.

The mariner turned, a look of relief washing over his grim features. "Tyreta. It's good to see you safe. When we saw the state of the port, we thought the worst."

"It's been a tough few days," she replied.

"I have grave news from Torwyn," he continued, raising a hand to scratch at the wispy beard on his chin. "The Anvil has fallen. The Draconate Ministry has risen against the Guilds. The emperor is... slain."

Her uncle Sullivar? Dead? But what about... "My mother? What is the news from my mother? My brothers? Is Fulren safe? Has Conall left the Karna?"

The captain shook his head. "I'm afraid I don't know about your mother. But Fulren... You did not hear he was exiled for murder?"

Tyreta felt her heart sink at the words. She had been away so long, it seemed as much madness had descended on Torwyn as had on these islands. But Fulren a murderer? She couldn't believe it was true.

"What about Conall?"

The captain shook his head. "I'm sorry, but we've had no news from the Karna Frontier since the insurrection began. We only received word you were alive a few days ago. As soon as we heard, my ship set off from Goodfleet to bring you home, but under the circumstances it might be safer if you remain here. The Draconate Ministry has usurped the Guilds' power and imprisoned any dissenters. It is not safe for you in Torwyn."

"But I..." She had just told the people of New Flaym they would have to leave. How could she stay here? Then again, she knew the jungle, knew its people. If anyone was going to survive here, then it would be her.

"My ship is moored and ready to leave immediately. The decision is yours if you wish to return home."

She nodded her thanks as the captain headed back to prepare his ship.

There was no soul-searching to do, no decision to make. Tyreta had to go home, had to find her mother and brother and stand alongside them to face what was coming. Besides, she had made a promise to the kesh that they would all leave this place. There was no way she could remain after she had gone through so much to make the others go home.

"You've heard about the Guilds?" Crenn asked. She nodded absently, staring out to sea. "And are you going to stay?"

She turned to face him. The old artificer looked as if he'd weathered the recent strife pretty well, all things considered. "No. I'm going home. And I could use a man who knows how to make things. Someone who can keep their head in a crisis. How are you fixed?"

Crenn shrugged as though considering the proposition. "Well, I was heading that way anyhow."

"Good," she replied. "So let's get out of here before either of us changes our mind."

They both walked to the jetty where the Hawkspur vessel sat ready and waiting. There was nothing to think on, no looking back.

The captain and crew welcomed her aboard, wasting no time before they pulled up the gangplank and cast off the mooring ropes. As they were about to push off from the dock, Tyreta gazed back toward New Flaym. At the harbourside the panther sat watching her, wondering where she was headed. It was a jungle beast. It belonged here. But with a curious tilt of its head, the panther reminded her of a...

"Cat," she called.

The panther sprang into action, racing along the jetty and leaping the gap to the ship, scrabbling with its claws as it pulled itself over the bulwark and onto the deck. Several mariners leapt out of the way as the panther came to her side and sat on the wooden boards.

"That's a wild animal," Crenn said matter-of-factly.

"It is," she replied. "But I have a feeling when we get home, I'm gonna need all the help I can get."

No sooner had she spoken than the sail was unfurled and they were on their way.

ROSOMON

It was approaching dusk before they finally moored somewhere along a tributary of the Whitespin. The river twisted its way through the Eastern Marches, feeding countless tiny settlements as it made its way to the Dargulf Sea. The day had seen them pass by towns and hamlets without incident. It gave Rosomon hope that the people of Torwyn still supported the Guilds and not the Ministry. More likely they were reluctant to declare their support either way until a true victor had risen to dominance.

She sat alone in the shadow of an old mill, which in turn sat beneath the shadow of Ayan Tarn, the lone mountain in a flat sea of green. Legend claimed that Saphenodon herself lay beneath that mountain, but if she did, she was not stirring. Even the rise of the Draconate Ministry was not enough to rouse her from slumber.

The miller—a minor member of the Storlock Guild—had greeted her with appreciation and offered as much bed and board to their small army as he could. He was scared like the rest of them, unsure who to trust in these tumultuous times. Rosomon had ordered her ragtag band to camp here for the night, then move on. No need to put the miller in danger. There was no telling what reprisals the Ministry might have in store for a man who helped those resisting Sanctan's tyranny.

In the hazy twilight she watched the waterwheel turn, listening to the peaceful trickle of the river and the creak of old timbers. It was soothing. So much so that she could comfortably have sat here forever. But Rosomon knew such peace was never going to last.

There was much to do, but still she sat. She would have wept, but there were no tears left. The least she deserved was some respite, if only for a little while, if only to plan their next move. And what would they do now? How would they begin their fight? Was there even a chance they could prevail?

After everything she had seen and suffered, Rosomon's instinct was to resist, but was that even the right way forward? Perhaps she should seek a truce. Perhaps if they surrendered, accepted the Archlegate's terms, she might be able to save some lives. Avoid a needless conflict she could never win.

Sanctan was her nephew, after all. They were kin. Surely that must stand for something? Or perhaps nothing. She had seen the zeal in his eyes, watched as he had commanded the attention of thousands at the Cogwheel. Sanctan was a man obsessed, if not with power then with the authority of his faith—no matter how malevolent it was.

Rosomon dismissed any thought of peace. Even had she sought it, there was every chance she'd just be leading her rebels to slaughter. Her father would certainly never have entertained such a notion. Treon Archwind would have fought back with all the fury of his name. Rosomon Hawkspur would do the same.

She rose to her feet. Despite the fatigue in her legs and the ache all over her body, she was done with resting. She walked out from beneath the shadow of the mill. The field stretching from the river led to a flat meadow next to a wide spinney. They had made their camp there, if it could even be called that. There were no tents for this army, but they had pooled their talents enough to erect wooden shelters above shallow ditches. The speed with which they had adapted to their situation gave Rosomon some hope, but without guidance even the most disciplined army would fail. With no one else to take the lead she would have to be that guide.

The boatmen tended to their barges as she passed by. They had been indispensable, and Rosomon knew how much she owed young

Emony Marrlock and her band of traders. How loyal they would remain was anyone's guess.

The girl was standing beside the boatmen, observing their labours, and Rosomon raised a hand to summon her. Emony hurried closer.

"Yes, my lady?" she asked.

"I need you by my side," Rosomon said. "It's time to begin."

Emony asked no questions, and Rosomon was relieved at that. Had she asked what the plan was, there would have been no answer to give. She was making this up as she went.

As they neared the edge of the camp, Lancelin was sitting with those few Titanguard who had survived the battle. They were huge warriors, rivalling even the Drakes for stature and martial prowess. If only she had more of them, but this was the army she had been given. It would have to suffice for now.

He saw her as she passed by and made his excuses before coming to walk by her side.

"They are keen to strike back quickly," Lancelin said. "I would like to tell them when and where."

The weight of expectation in his words made Rosomon realise how much belief these warriors had placed in her. She was all they had, the only beacon of authority left now their emperor was dead.

"Am I expected to come up with a strategy now?" she replied, immediately regretting her words. She would need a cooler head if they were to have any chance of resisting the power of the Ministry.

"We have to at least work out our next move. Where we will go, who we will recruit and how."

Rosomon spied Rawlin talking with senior officers of the Bloodwolf Battalion. His voice was quiet, but it was clear he was urging them to join him in this crusade, if that was the right term for an uprising of no more than a hundred fighters.

"It looks like someone is already formulating a plan of their own," she said, making her way toward the Drift marshal.

Rawlin and his men fell quiet as she approached, and Rawlin offered a curt nod. It was as much respect as she'd get from him for now. A decent enough start, she supposed.

"Now we're all gathered, it's time to find out just how far-reaching the Ministry's coup is," Rosomon said. "We need to learn exactly who's on our side. Who we can trust to help us strike back."

She paused, expecting Rawlin or one of his men to question her, but instead they waited for her to continue. Best she come up with something good.

"Emony, you will visit with your father at the Rock. Find out if this insurrection has spread throughout the Marrlock Guildlands and if we can rely on Oleksig's support. Meet us at Wyke in fifteen days. If you don't come by then, I'll know the answer."

Emony nodded her agreement. The easy part was done.

"Lancelin, you will go to the Forge. See which side Lord Wymar Ironfall is backing, and persuade him that joining us is in his best interest. He will listen to the word of a swordwright."

"Yes, my lady," Lancelin said. "But what about the other Guilds?"

Rosomon shook her head. "The Radwinter Guild cannot be trusted. I suspect Jarlath already supports the Ministry, and Rearden Corwen is little more than Sanctan's pet. Marrlock and Ironfall are the only ones we can trust."

"I can guarantee the support of the Bloodwolf Battalion," Rawlin said. "As for the rest of the Armigers..." He shrugged.

"That is why I have to give you the most difficult task of all, Drift Marshal. I need you to gather an army. Find out which of the Armigers support the Guilds and which have fallen to the empty promises of the Ministry. Discover what kind of numbers we can expect when we fight back."

It would have been a challenge for any of them, but judging by Rawlin's expression he relished the opportunity to prove he was up to the task. "I will do as you ask, my lady, and relay any support back to you in Wyke."

Before she could thank him, they heard the steel-shod hooves of a horse approaching. Lancelin instinctively moved closer to Rosomon, his hand on his sword, but when only a single rider made his way from the trees, dressed in the blue livery of a Talon scout, they relaxed.

"Lady Rosomon," the rider said, reining in his horse and sliding deftly from the saddle. "Thank the Guilds I have found you."

It was a new expression none of them had heard, but Rosomon was heartened by it. It appeared the Talon at least had abandoned the Ministry altogether, instead putting their faith in the Guilds.

"I have ridden from Goodfleet, my lady. We received a message from the Sundered Isles. Lord Serrell sent a missive regarding your daughter."

"Tyreta?" Rosomon said, the name almost catching in her throat.

"Yes, my lady. Tyreta is alive. A Hawkspur ship was dispatched across the straits to bring her home days ago. If they have weathered the storm, she could be heading to Torwyn as we speak."

One tiny shred of hope. It was all Rosomon needed to finally believe there was some way they might prevail. But she could not show it. She could not let it be known how much this affected her.

"Ride back to Goodfleet," she said. "Find Tyreta and see her safely to Wyke. That's where we will form our bastion."

"Of course, Lady Rosomon, but...word reached us yesterday that the Ministry has set its eye on Wyke already. It will be the first city outside the Anvil to fall."

"No," Rosomon replied. "Wyke will not fall. Let them come. I will show them that the Guilds are not so easily brought to heel."

The rider bowed his head, then jumped back on his horse and set off south toward Goodfleet.

"You all know what you have to do," Rosomon said, looking at those faces—Rawlin, Emony, Lancelin. Hardly much of an army to bring down an entire religion. But what other choice was there?

Rosomon watched them go, to prepare themselves for their journeys, before she would make her own way back home to Wyke, her adopted city, and what might serve as a last beacon of resistance. If it had not already fallen.

The sun was starting to drop behind the flat green horizon. The end of a day that had brought so much loss. Tomorrow the real fight would begin.

EPILOGUE

The storm had passed the previous day. The Ungulf stretched out to each horizon, calm, placid. Wispy clouds hung in the blue above, as though that raging torrent had never happened. Any ship caught in that storm would have been ripped apart and dragged beneath the waves, and now all evidence of such murder was gone. It was a reminder of what a treacherous bitch the sea could be. And of all the men who plied their trade on her, Mortivern Keelrunner knew all too well just how treacherous she was.

He raised a hand to scratch at the scarred flesh above his well-oiled beard. Another reminder of treachery he wore with pride. It was how he'd gained his name: by being dragged along the hull, feeling those barnacles tear at his flesh. A storm of his own he had survived.

The *Grimhide* cut through the waves, making fast progress. There was not another ship that could match her for pace on these seas, and as the breeze whipped his dark locks, Mortivern felt that familiar thrill. The taste of the salt air, the cooling of his butchered flesh, the sound of the mainsail snapping in the wind. Despite the hardships he had suffered, the horrors he had seen, he would not have swapped this life for any other.

They were two days out of Argon Kyne. The vast seaport squatted on the southern coast of Iperion Magna, the only place he would have called home, other than the ocean. Not that Mortivern missed it too much. It held its delights—its fleshpots, drinking dens and fighting pits—but he would have abandoned every land-born pleasure for the open wave, and he knew his men felt the same.

Mortivern glanced back over his shoulder, seeing his crew at their labours. Tulsen stood at the wheel, a man he trusted above all the others, which was the reason he held a position of highest honour. He was a hulking beast, a mass of hard and scarred flesh—bare chested and frightening in repose. Mortivern had met him slaughtering foe after foe in the death pits of Tallus Rann. He remembered well the day Tulsen's handler had grown tired of his insubordinate slave and arranged for him to face half a dozen fighters in the pit. Mortivern had leapt into that blood-soaked arena himself to fight alongside Tulsen. They had earned a fearsome reputation that day, and Mortivern had earned Tulsen's undying loyalty along with it.

Up in the crow's hung Hasdrubal the Longeye, peering out to the far horizon. There was a man almost as loyal as Tulsen, though not quite. He could be relied upon in a fix, a fierce fighter when needed and a cunning mariner besides. Unlike Tulsen, Hasdrubal would forever be swayed by coin, and Mortivern knew full well that if a richer paymaster came along his loyalty would be tested. But then coin was always the great leveller. Though his crew might shed blood together, they were not in it for the love of brotherhood. Gold was their only mistress. As long as they were paid handsomely they would sail and fight and serve at Mortivern Keelrunner's pleasure. And for now they were earning more than a handsome wage.

The *Grimhide* had been the first ship commissioned to run stones out of the Karna. Why such a commission had been ordered, Mortivern had no idea, but who was he to question the motives of the Scions? They had decreed it, given contracts to a few select pirate lords—weapons and armour to the durrga in exchange for as much stone as could be brought back to Magnan shores. Maybe they wanted to stifle the supply to Torwyn. To make it harder for the eastlanders to construct their metal monsters and their cannons. Maybe there was something more sinister afoot. Whatever they had planned was of no concern to Mortivern.

He had received his commission from Ekediah the Betrayer, albeit through an intermediary. No one had received an audience with Ekediah himself for over two hundred years, and Mortivern did not envy anyone called to the court of a Scion. Meeting one of them in the flesh was said to test the sanity of even the most stalwart lord of Iperion Magna.

Senmonthis had also commissioned her own privateers to trade on the Karna coast. All had been generously compensated for their time, now they weren't reaving the coast of Torwyn and hunting for spoils on the eastern trade routes. That was two of the Four gathering a stock of stone. Mortivern wondered how long it would take the other two to offer contracts of their own.

"Flotsam," came the cry from the crow's.

Mortivern dispensed with further thought of what those Scions might be plotting and looked up to see the Longeye pointing out to the east. He signalled for Tulsen to adjust their course, moving to the prow and shielding his eyes from the sun as its reflection danced across the flat blue sea.

As the *Grimhide* ploughed its way east, Mortivern caught sight of the first piece of wreckage floating on the waves. He recognised the timber, the polished wood of a Torwyn trader. Most likely the rest of the ship was at the bottom of the Ungulf. The heavy trading vessels of Torwyn were crafted from oak and iron, leaving little to salvage once they'd been ravaged by a storm. They were not sleek and manoeuvrable like Magnan brigantines, which made them easy pickings as long as they weren't too heavily armed.

Mortivern squinted through the glare as they sailed, eyes scanning for anything they might pluck from the waves. There was nothing but flotsam scattered across miles of open sea. He quickly grew weary of the search, and these days his time was a precious commodity. Better they make sail for home now before another storm struck than waste their time on this folly.

"Salvage larboard side!" came the cry from above.

Mortivern moved to larboard, squinting past the sun. In the distance he could see something bobbing in the water. A wave of his hand and Tulsen brought them about. The closer they got the easier it was to see this was no salvage. More like a survivor. Or just a corpse.

Mortivern cursed under his breath. Damn his ill luck. He glanced up to the crow's.

"What do you think?" he asked Hasdrubal.

The Longeye shrugged. "Better than nothing," he replied. "If he's alive."

Only one way to find out. With another wave of the hand, Mortivern signalled his men to retrieve the body. They adjusted sail, slowing the ship as they passed by, and one of the crew dangled over the bulwark with a pike pole. Mortivern watched as he hooked the flotsam the body was draped over, pulling it closer to the bow. Another one of the crew climbed down with a rope and secured it to the body before they were both pulled back on board.

The pirates dumped the drowned man on the deck like a landed fish. He wasn't moving. Waste of bloody time.

"All right then, throw him back," Mortivern said.

"Hang on," Tulsen replied before the crew could rid the ship of its useless salvage.

Mortivern's first mate strode across the deck, the rest of the crew keeping a respectful distance as the savage Tulsen approached their salvage and knelt down.

He turned the body over, none too gently, sticking a finger in its mouth. Mortivern could see the corpse was a young lad, broad at the shoulder and fit, when he was alive. He would have brought a decent price at the Argon slave market, but for the fact that he was drowned.

Tulsen tilted the lad's head back, then blew a deep breath right into his mouth. Without pausing he then beat on the chest of that corpse like he was banging a drum.

"You're not gonna get much of a tune out of that bastard," came the booming voice of Broad Yon, to the guffaws of his fellow mariners.

Tulsen carried on regardless, breathing, punching, breathing, massaging, breathing, pressing hard, once, twice, three times.

Just when Mortivern thought Tulsen might give up, the corpse sputtered to life, puking water out of his lungs before taking a massive, wheezing gasp of air.

"See," Tulsen said, rising to his feet. There was a self-satisfied grin on that battle-ruined face. "Not quite ready for the deep yet."

The lad turned on his side, sucking in more air, looking as surprised as any of them that he was still alive.

"Where the fuck am I?" he eventually managed to say.

Mortivern knelt down beside him. "You're on board the *Grimhide*, son. Bound for Argon Kyne."

"No," he replied. "I have to get back to Torwyn."

"Torwyn?" Mortivern grinned, and his crew laughed at the notion. "Boy, this ain't no passenger vessel and you ain't no passenger. When we get back to port I'm gonna sell your arse and we're all gonna drink the profits."

"Wait," the lad said, rising unsteadily to his feet. "I have money. I can pay you for safe passage."

Mortivern rose to his feet. "That's what they all say, son. That's what they all say."

The bewildered expression on the lad's face faded, and there was sudden steel in his eyes. Quick as a snake he snatched the cutlass from Mortivern's belt and held it out like a duellist in a pantomime.

"Take me back to Torwyn, or I'll gut you where you stand," he proclaimed.

He could act tough at least. And he was fast. Whether he could wield that cutlass as well as he talked was another question.

"Go on then," Mortivern said. "Fucking gut away. Gut us all, if you've got the skill. But then what? Sail a ship on your own, can you? Do you even know which way Torwyn is?"

That look of steel on the lad's face faded till he looked forlorn enough to pitch himself back over the side. Slowly he lowered the cutlass before handing it over.

"Don't be too sad," Mortivern said, putting the cutlass back where it belonged. "At least you're alive. For now."

With that he gestured dismissively to his men, who grabbed the boy and began dragging him off to the brig.

Poor lad. Plucked from a sea grave to be sold on a Magnan slave market. Mortivern wasn't sure which fate was worse. With any luck he'd never find out.

The story continues in...

Engines of Chaos

CREDITS

Writer
R. S. Ford
Publisher
Tim Holman
Editorial
Bradley Englert
Hillary Sames
Agent
John Jarrold
Production Editor
Rachel Goldstein
Copyeditor
S. B. Kleinman
Proofreaders
Roland Ottewell
Janine Barlow
Production
Xian Lee
Design
Mike Heath/Magnus Creative
Marketing
Laura Fitzgerald
Paola Crespo
Amanda Melfi
Publicity
Angela Man
Audio
Thomas Mis
Alison Campbell
Ciaran Saward
Phoebe McIntosh
Ewan Goddard
Andrew Kingston
Martin Reeve
Stephen Perring
Early Reader
Claire Rowe

extras

meet the author

R. S. Ford is a writer of fantasy from Leeds in the heartland of Yorkshire. To find out more, and to download FREE exclusive content, go online at wordhog.co.uk.

Find out more about R. S. Ford and other Orbit authors by registering for the free monthly newsletter at orbitbooks.net.

if you enjoyed

ENGINES OF EMPIRE

look out for

ENGINES OF CHAOS

Book Two of The Age of Uprising

by

R. S. Ford

The empire has fallen.

Torwyn lies in the grip of the Archlegate as battles rage across the Guildlands. The Armiger Battalions engage in a vicious civil war, and the Guilds take their stand against the tyranny of the Draconate Ministry.

Rosomon Hawkspur must lead her ragtag band of rebels against the might of the Great Wyrms. With no one to trust, she must put her faith in her daughter Tyreta, her lover Lancelin, and those few allies she can find in a land riven by war.

Meanwhile, across the blasted landscape of the Drift, her son Conall must fight to survive in the dread nation of Iperion Magna. But he will soon discover that to throw off the chains that bind him in slavery, he may have to embrace the demon he harbours within…

Prologue

The needle dug deep into his forearm, his right hand steady as he carved the last letter into his flesh. He gritted his teeth against the pain, but there was no way he'd show an ounce of discomfort in front of this gathering.

Every now and then he dipped the needle into a well of ink that pooled on top of a rock. The mark had to be permanent, had to show his commitment to this gang. Every eye watched intently as the final letter formed on his arm and the name they'd given him stood out stark against his bare skin.

Stone. It was the only word he could spell with any accuracy. This adopted family had picked it on account of his stubborn head and stout fists. His own family were dead and gone. His mother before he could remember her. His father not three winters ago. Stone could remember those last days; his father coughing up oily shit from the manufactories, looking and sounding older than his years. But the blacklung came for everyone who worked the forges and refineries sooner or later. Even now, the smog hung over them, clinging to the sky above the Burrows.

When finally he'd finished, his arm bleeding like fuck, Stone put the needle back down. Coins wiped his arm for him, round face grinning, more of a leer than a smile. Queen Clariss rose to her feet. She was the oldest and best dressed of all of them, though that wasn't saying much. The girl wore a blue velvet jacket, frayed about the hem, stained about the sleeve, but still a sight better than what anyone else wore. Her boots were black and muddy, hair tied in a bright red band instead of a crown.

"Stone," she said, voice making a little whistle on account of her missing front tooth. "Welcome to the Clan of Bastards."

Someone started clapping and the rest joined in. Stone stood up to a cacophony of whoops and cheers, and everyone was looking at him with pride. He could put a name to every dirty face—Diamond Tooth, Jaffer Threetoes, Mad Dog Mace, Claiburn the Jester, Ranley Scars, Henny the Razor, Lysa Smokes, Vic the Shark. Now there was Stone to join those names. Another member of the Clan of Bastards, the wiliest street gang in the whole of the Anvil. Or so they told themselves. Stone knew it wasn't true. There were plenty of wilier gangs besides this, but it wouldn't do to point that out.

As he looked around at the mob standing in that old crumbling building, the skeleton of what might once have been an artisan's school or a Guild embassy, Stone felt a part of something, no longer looking in like a stranger. Now he was one of them.

Queen Clariss took her place on the cracked dais of some missing statue. There was a serious look to her youthful features.

"Now we've got that shit out of the way let's get onto the first order of business," she said. "Our next job's gonna be big. We're gonna hit a Marrlock warehouse. There's one sitting right on the Riveryard and it's too tempting to ignore."

"Fucking Marrlock Guild?" replied Diamond Tooth through those teeth that were conspicuously bereft of diamonds. Stone could hear the fear in his voice. "That is big. How are we supposed to rip that place off?"

"I've got it all planned out," Clariss said. "Won't be nothing to it. As long as you all do your bit we can be in and out with enough pyrestone to see us all living like Guildmasters. Them Marrlocks won't even see us coming."

Stone could see some of them were up for it, their faces greedy and needy. Others weren't so sure. Least of all Coins.

"Never mind the fucking Marrlock Guild," he said in his little voice. "We all know what's waiting down at the Riveryard. And I'm not so sure I want to go strolling around in there, especially after dark."

That put a dampener on the enthusiasm. They all knew the rumours and the truth that went along with them. People had been going missing, and not the highfalutin citizens of the Anvil—the movers and shakers, the well-dressed and well-moneyed. It was people like them: the underclass, the needy and the dirty living in their hovels.

No one had a clue who was behind it. Could have been Revocaters, picking off the poor. Could have been something else. Stone had heard more than one tale about the Ghost. The spectre that haunted the Riveryard. A man or a beast that stalked the empty warehouses in the dark, picking off its prey and eating their flesh. Maybe it was just some madman getting his kicks from killing the poor. Maybe it was another gang doing its best to rid itself of competition. Whatever it was, neither the Ministry nor the Guilds seemed too keen to stop it.

"Not afraid of bedtime stories, are you, Coins?" Queen Clariss said. "We all thought you were made of tougher stuff." Giggles from the surrounding gang made Coins's round face start to redden like a tomato. "Let me worry about monsters in the dark, brother. You concentrate on not getting spotted by the guards."

They were all looking at him now, and Coins turned a deeper shade of red. It wouldn't do to show cowardice in front of this gang. That was as likely to get you cast out as anything else.

As they carried on giggling at Coins's discomfort, Stone turned his attention to something shifting in the shadows of the old building. Movement in the dark. A flash of red and yellow. Before he could shout a warning, the clacking report of splintbow fire echoed across the room.

Queen Clariss went down. She grabbed her leg, splintbolt sticking out like a broken bone, blood pouring between her fingers as she rolled off the dais. More splintbows fired their payloads across the room, but their sound was drowned out by a piercing scream.

Stone had heard people yelling before but it never sounded so pained, like foxes fucking in the woods. Mad Dog Mace went down but didn't make a sound, body stuck with two bolts in the chest. Stone was already moving, Coins right by his side, bare feet slapping against the loose floorboards as they fled for cover.

"Revocaters!" someone shouted. Could have been Ranley Scars, could have been Jaffer Threetoes, they both sounded much the same. Whoever it was, they were stating the bloody obvious.

Chaos spread throughout the derelict building. Revocaters burst from out of the shadows and through doorless archways. They'd been harrying the street gangs of the Anvil for years, but Stone had never seen them so determined, never known them kill with such merciless intent.

He ducked at the sound of a splintbow close by. Heard the snapping ricochet of bolts hitting the wall beside his head. Another of his gang went down with a yelp, but Stone had no mind to stop and see who. He and Coins raced for a gap in the floor that dropped down to the level below. Stone's feet crunched against the bricks below, the marble floor having long since been carved up and sold for pennies.

A deep voice shouted for them to stop, but after what he'd just seen there was no way that was happening. Stone had never been able to work out why they always shouted "Stop!" It wasn't like you were gonna just give yourself up. Instinct, he supposed, just like running when someone was trying to kill you.

He and Coins sprinted across the ground level, fleeing the ruckus above, until they came out on the street. Another Revocater was waiting behind the wall opposite, looking for runners just like them, but Stone surprised him so much he shot his payload of splintbolts without thinking to aim. As the bolts clattered harmlessly around them, they raced down the street.

More shouts followed them, drowned out by the sound of the steelworks pounding, sheets of metal rolling off conveyor belts, bound for the manufactories. They raced past a wagon surrounded by workers. A couple of them glanced up with disinterest as the boys sprinted by, too preoccupied with their own drudgery to care about a couple of urchins being chased down by Revocaters.

Stone risked a glance over his shoulder. Three of them were still in pursuit, those yellow-and-red uniforms standing out starkly against the drab buildings of the Burrows. There was plenty of distance between them though. All they had to do was reach the fish market and they'd lose them easy enough. Stone could already smell it in the distance—the pungent stink of fish cutting through the acrid smell of the steelworks.

Coins went down with a yelp. Stone stumbled to a stop as his friend floundered on the ground, grasping his twisted ankle. There was a slapping report in the distance, another volley of splintbolts skittering along the ground toward them, just out of range.

Stone reached down to pull Coins up, but he could already see his friend wasn't gonna be able to run.

"Help me," Coins whimpered.

Stone saw those Revocaters gaining. He could help Coins, of course he could, but then they'd both be caught. And it didn't look like the Revocaters were gonna let them off with a slapped wrist. Most likely it would be a gallows rope.

Stone offered one last look at his friend's big round eyes in his big round head. There wasn't even enough time for him to say sorry before he set off again at a run.

If Coins shouted anything in his wake, it was lost in the noise of the manufactories. If the Revocaters were gaining on him, Stone didn't dare look back to see as he raced toward the relative safety of the fish market.

He almost stumbled as he rushed across the Parade of Builders, the Cogwheel to his right, the Whitespin up ahead. The sound of grinding machinery was quickly replaced by the hubbub of market vendors bellowing across the open plaza.

Stone tried to lose himself amid the crowd, squeezing through the press of bodies. Another shout for him to stop resounded across the marketplace, catching the attention of stallholders and punters alike. These fucking Revocaters were relentless. Didn't they know he was barely worth their time?

His way was suddenly barred by a broad-shouldered fishmonger. Stone barely had time to notice the stains on his apron before he ran right into him, the reek of fish guts on the man's clothing. He grabbed hold of Stone's shirt, the sleeve tearing as he held it in a meaty fist.

"I've got him," the fishmonger shouted. Twatting do-gooder.

Stone wasn't yet into his teens, but the Clan of Bastards hadn't given him that name for nothing. He balled a fist, planting his feet for purchase before he swung at the fishmonger's chin. The man was taller, wider, stronger, but a punch to the jaw would put anyone on their arse if you hit them right.

The fishmonger went down, still holding Stone's shirt and ripping off the sleeve. No time to gloat. Stone was off again and this time the crowd was moving out of his way, giving him a clear path out the other side of the market, the tramping feet of the Revocaters following close behind.

Up ahead he could see the edge of the plaza dropped away to the warehouses that crowded the shores of the Whitespin. When he reached the edge he took a breath, then used the edge of the wall to propel himself forward. Stone cleared a good ten feet of nothing to land on the roof opposite. Something whistled past his ear. Didn't take a genius to know it was a splintbolt, not that he needed any encouragement to keep moving.

His feet made a racket on the roof as he raced to the far side. A quick look over his shoulder and he could see the Revocaters were none too keen to follow him. He slowed, heaving in air, in two minds whether or not to throw them a crude gesture, but the instinct to find safety won out.

Stone clambered down the drainpipe at the other side of the roof, heart still racing when his feet touched the ground. The riverside was busy but it wouldn't take long before those Revocaters caught up. He had to find somewhere to hide.

No one paid him much mind as he walked past the fishermen and bargemasters on the quay. He slipped into a back alley, hoping to lose himself in the thick press of warehouses. The buildings got more ramshackle the further he delved into the maze of passages until eventually he found himself outside an old storehouse. The main doors were chained shut, but if he could get inside it would at least give him a chance to think on his next move.

At the back of the building were some boarded-up windows, and it took little effort to prise one open and squeeze inside. Stone was hit by how dark and dusty it was. A musty stench hung heavy in the air—that fusty stink of rotting wood and decay. He took a moment to gather his thoughts, trying not to think on Coins lying there in the street or what might have happened to the rest of the Clan. His arm stung, and he looked down to see blood running in rivulets down to his hand before he remembered he wasn't injured—it was just the tattoo he'd given himself.

The sleeve of his shirt was hanging on by a thread, and he pulled it free, tying it around his forearm and tightening the knot with his teeth. As his eyes adjusted to the gloom, Stone could see the place was cavernous. Crossbeams had rotted away and fallen from the roof, lying aslant across the floor of the warehouse, giving it the look of a shadowy forest. As he picked his way through the enclosed space, he was forced to battle through the dusty remains of spiderwebs that made it impossible to see more than a few feet in front of him.

He could hear the sound of running water and eventually saw light up ahead. As he made his way through the forest of beams he began to hear a dull thud above the sound of the river. It was rhythmic, drumming a slow monotonous beat.

Eventually he struggled from the mass of fallen beams, seeing one side of the structure had fallen away into the Whitespin. A gap in the wall showed the river flowing past, and framed within it was a single figure stripped to the waist. He was hulking, his broad back showing pockmarks on bare flesh. With a muscular arm he reached down and plucked something from the floor before flinging it through the open gap and into the river beyond. It seemed a curious way to fish. The man didn't even attach a line to his bait.

It was then Stone saw the cleaver in the brute's hand.

Gore clung to the steel. The thing must have weighed a tonne, but in that huge ham fist it looked little heavier than a knife. Stone stood frozen as he dragged his eyes away from the dull steel to what was on the floor. Hunks of meat lay discarded like loose offal. As his eyes focused he realised this butcher wasn't carving any pig. A human hand lay grey and desiccated on the ground. Next to it was a lump of thigh. Not far from that, a human head.

Before Stone could think on what to do the butcher turned to face him. He must have sensed someone watching, must have known his game was up. Stone should have run, but he was trapped in the butcher's gaze. Those eyes were so small Stone could hardly see the whites.

Neither of them moved. Just stared at one another across the derelict storehouse. They were only a few feet apart. If Stone made a run for it maybe he'd get away, but his feet wouldn't move.

"Seen enough, little piggy?" said the butcher. "You should be careful where you tread."

Stone shook his head. Should he have nodded instead? He had no idea what the fuck to do. His feet wouldn't move and all of a sudden he needed to piss like he'd never needed it before.

"You're the Ghost," he managed to whisper.

That brought a grin to the butcher's face that didn't reach his tiny eyes.

Stone knew if he didn't get a grip on himself and run the fuck away, he was done.

He turned, racing across the storehouse, jumping a fallen beam, webs catching against his face. Heavy boots slammed down in his wake. He'd already run for his life once today, but this time there was terror to his desperation. At least with the Revocaters there was a slim chance of mercy. With the Ghost he knew there'd be none.

Ahead he could see a door hanging badly in its frame. Light shone beneath the lintel. Open air. Escape.

Stone focused on it, bare feet padding across the splintered boards. Could he wrench it open in time and fling himself into the freedom of the outdoors?

He heard the crunch of snapping wood. Felt his foot break the floorboard and slip into the gap. Stone shrieked in pain as he went down, face slamming against the ground. Dragging his foot out of the hole he saw how mangled it was, the flesh torn almost to the bone. He tried to stand, but the pain in his ankle was agonising.

Solid footsteps drew nearer. The Ghost was taking his time. No need to rush. Stone wasn't going anywhere.

He turned to see that cleaver hanging from the butcher's meaty grip. Those eyes filled with hunger.

"I warned you, little piggy. Be careful where you tread," the Ghost said. He licked his lips, as though he might take a bite of Stone's flesh before he cut him into chunks and flung him in the river.

This was it. Nowhere to run, even if he could have. All Stone could do was crawl on his back, trying to put distance between him and this killer. The urge to piss was overwhelming, his bladder felt like it would burst, and he gritted his teeth against the pain.

"Come on then, you fucker," Stone spat. Maybe if he goaded this killer he'd end it quick with his cleaver. At least then he wouldn't have to worry about pissing himself...

The door to the storehouse burst inward, rusted hinges springing from the wood. The light from outside was blocked by a huge figure who stooped beneath the lintel. The Ghost took a step back, looking like he might flee, but he stood his ground, gripping tight to that big old cleaver.

Stone squinted through the dark, watching as the intruder made his way in. Almost seven feet of armoured might, winged helm reflecting the sun that shone through the door, white surcoat bearing a rearing dragon.

The Drake glanced at Stone lying there on the floor, then at the Ghost. A huge sword hung from the gilded scabbard at his side, but he made no move to draw it. Stone willed him to reach for that blade, to hack down the Ghost where he stood, but he made no move, silent like a statue.

The Ghost's tiny eyes displayed a flicker of doubt where previously they'd shown nothing but malice. Then he squealed like a cornered animal, raising that cleaver high and lumbering forward to attack. Stone held his breath as the Drake just stood waiting, like he wanted this butcher to hack him to pieces. At the last moment, as the Ghost sliced down with his cleaver, the Drake raised an arm. The sound of the weapon clanging off armour rang through the storehouse. One of the Drake's gauntleted hands snapped forward, taking hold of the Ghost's meaty neck. His other grasped the wrist holding the cleaver. The butcher gave off a squeak as the air was caught in his throat. He didn't look menacing anymore. As the

Drake's grip tightened, the cleaver fell from the Ghost's stumpy fingers to clatter on the floor, and he grasped the armoured hand clamped tight about his neck.

"Did you think you could elude the justice of Undometh forever?" the Drake snarled from within his helm. The words were terrifying. Hate and might mixed into a single breathy voice. "Ammenodus grant me the strength to slay this villain."

The Ghost's eyes began to roll back in his head as he choked, spitting what little breath he could from his pale lips.

"Ravenothrax comes for you this day," growled the Drake. "Can you see him? Do you feel those black wings embracing you?"

The choking had stopped. The Ghost's thick arms hung limp at his side, his tiny eyes wide and staring at nothing up in the broken rafters.

"To the Lairs with you, murderer." The Drake was whispering now, his grip still tight around the throat of the corpse. "May Vermitrix grant eternal peace to your victims."

Stone had seen enough. He flipped over onto his belly, trying his best to crawl away out of the light. With any luck the Drake would ignore him and not decide to send another sinner to the Five Lairs.

There was a thud as the body of the Ghost was discarded. Stone froze where he lay, gritting his teeth, still trying his best not to piss. Footsteps drew nearer and he braced himself, ready to feel those armoured hands clamp around his own throat.

The Drake grasped his arm, and with incredible strength pulled Stone to his feet. He stumbled, hobbling on his injured leg as the Drake regarded him, eyes barely visible within that huge helmet.

"Rejoice, child. By the grace of the Wyrms, you have been spared a most grisly fate."

Stone glanced at the body of the Ghost. He didn't look so scary now. Just another hunk of dead meat.

"Can…can I go then?" Stone asked. Still wondering if his luck was about to change.

The Drake stared, still holding him up by one arm. "Go where, boy?"

Now there was a question. "Home," Stone replied, surprised at how small his own voice was.

The Drake reached down, grasping Stone's forearm before sliding back the shirt sleeve he'd tied around his bleeding arm. The letters there stood out stark and livid, marking him as a ganger from the Burrows.

"Do you even have a home, child?"

Another fine question Stone wasn't sure how to answer. If anyone in the Clan of Bastards had survived, they'd be scattered across the Anvil. Their home was empty lofts and cellars. How long before they were found by the Revocaters again? The answer was obvious, and Stone wasn't in any mood to lie about it.

"No," he replied. "I haven't."

Again the Drake regarded him in silence, as though weighing him, measuring him. Before the presence of this armoured behemoth, Stone could only stand and wait to be judged.

"I can offer you shelter, child. Come with me to the Mount. There will be a roof over your head and food in your belly. And perhaps you may yet gain the favour of the Wyrms."

"What would I want that for?" Stone snapped. The Wyrms had never done anything for him up to now.

"Perhaps in time you will see," the Drake replied, bearing Stone's weight as he guided him toward the light of day. "But first, let's get you home."

if you enjoyed
ENGINES OF EMPIRE
look out for
THE JUSTICE OF KINGS
Book One of Empire of the Wolf
by
Richard Swan

The Justice of Kings, *the first in an epic new fantasy trilogy, follows the tale of Sir Konrad Vonvalt, an Emperor's Justice—a detective, judge, and executioner all in one. As he unravels a web of secrets and lies, Vonvalt discovers a plot that might destroy his order once and for all—and bring down the entire Empire.*

As an Emperor's Justice, Sir Konrad Vonvalt always has the last word. His duty is to uphold the law of the empire using whatever tools he has at his disposal: his blade, the arcane secrets passed down from Justice to Justice, or his wealth of knowledge of the laws of the empire. But his reputation as one of the most revered—and hated—Justices is enough to get most any job done.

When Vonvalt investigates the murder of a noblewoman, he finds his authority being challenged like never before. As the simple case becomes more complex and convoluted, he begins to unravel the threads of a conspiracy that could see an end to all Justices and a beginning to lawless chaos across the Empire.

I

The Witch of Rill

'Beware the idiot, the zealot, and the tyrant; each clothes himself in the armour of ignorance.'

From Caterhauser's *The Sovan Criminal Code: Advice to Practitioners*

It is a strange thing to think that the end of the Empire of the Wolf, and all the death and devastation that came with it, traced its long roots back to the tiny and insignificant village of Rill. That as we drew closer to it, we were not just plodding through a rainy, cold country twenty miles east of the Tolsburg Marches; we were approaching the precipice of the Great Decline, its steep and treacherous slope falling away from us like a cliff face of glassy obsidian.

Rill. How to describe it? The birthplace of our misfortune was so plain. For its isolation, it was typical for the Northmark of Tolsburg. It was formed of a large communal square of churned mud and straw, and a ring of twenty buildings with wattle-and-daub walls and thatched roofs. The manor was distinguishable only by its size, being perhaps twice as big as the biggest cottage, but there the differences ended. It was as tumbledown as the rest of them. An inn lay off to one side, and livestock and peasants moved haphazardly through the public space. One benefit of the cold was that the smell wasn't so bad, but Vonvalt still held a kerchief filled with dried lavender to his nose. He could be fussy like that.

I should have been in a good mood. Rill was the first village we had come across since we had left the Imperial wayfort on the Jägeland border, and it marked the beginning of a crescent of settlements that ended in the Hauner fortress of Seaguard fifty miles to the north-east. Our arrival here meant we were probably only a few weeks away from turning south again to complete the eastern half of our circuit – and that meant better weather, larger cities and something approaching civilisation.

Instead, anxiety gnawed at me. My attention was fixed on the vast, ancient forest that bordered the village and stretched for a hundred miles north and west of us, all the way to the coast. It was home, according to the rumours we had been fed along the way, to an old Draedist witch.

'You think she is in there?' Patria Bartholomew Claver asked from next to me. Claver was one of four people who made up our caravan, a Neman priest who had imposed himself on us at the Jägeland border. Ostensibly it was for protection against bandits, though the Northmark was infamously desolate – and by his own account, he travelled almost everywhere alone.

'Who?' I asked.

Claver smiled without warmth. 'The witch,' he said.

'No,' I said curtly. I found Claver very irritating – everyone did. Our itinerant lives were difficult enough, but Claver's incessant questioning over the last few weeks of every aspect of Vonvalt's practice and powers had worn us all down to the nub.

'I do.'

I turned. Dubine Bressinger – Vonvalt's taskman – was approaching, cheerfully eating an onion. He winked at me as his horse trotted past. Behind him was our employer, Sir Konrad Vonvalt, and at the very back was our donkey, disrespectfully named the Duke of Brondsey, which pulled a cart loaded with all our accoutrements.

We had come to Rill for the same reason we went anywhere: to ensure that the Emperor's justice was done, even out here on the fringes of the Sovan Empire. For all their faults, the Sovans were great believers in justice for all, and they dispatched Imperial Magistrates like Vonvalt to tour the distant villages and towns of the Empire as itinerant courts.

'I'm looking for Sir Otmar Frost,' I heard Vonvalt call out from the rear of our caravan. Bressinger had already dismounted and was summoning a local boy to make arrangements for our horses.

One of the peasants pointed wordlessly at the manor. Vonvalt grunted and dismounted. Patria Claver and I did the same. The mud was iron-hard beneath my feet.

'Helena,' Vonvalt called to me. 'The ledger.'

I nodded and retrieved the ledger from the cart. It was a heavy tome, with a thick leather jacket clad in iron and with a lockable clasp. It would be used to record any legal issues which arose, and Vonvalt's considered judgments. Once it was full, it would be sent back to the Law Library in distant Sova, where clerks would review the judgments and make sure that the common law was being applied consistently.

I brought the ledger to Vonvalt, who bade me keep hold of it with an irritated wave, and all four of us made for the manor. I could see now that it had a heraldic device hanging over the door, a plain blue shield overlaid by a boar's head mounted on a broken lance. The manor was otherwise unremarkable, and a far cry from the sprawling town houses and country fortresses of the Imperial aristocracy in Sova.

Vonvalt hammered a gloved fist against the door. It opened quickly. A maid, perhaps a year or two younger than me, stood in the doorway. She looked frightened.

'I am Justice Sir Konrad Vonvalt of the Imperial Magistratum,' Vonvalt said in what I knew to be an affected Sovan accent. His native Jägeland inflection marked him out as an upstart, notwithstanding his station, and embarrassed him.

The maid curtseyed clumsily. 'I—'

'Who is it?' Sir Otmar Frost called from somewhere inside. It was dark beyond the threshold and smelled like woodsmoke and livestock. I could see Vonvalt's hand absently reach for his lavender kerchief.

'Justice Sir Konrad Vonvalt of the Imperial Magistratum,' he announced again, impatiently.

'Bloody faith,' Sir Otmar muttered, and appeared in the doorway a few moments later. He thrust the maid aside without ceremony. 'My lord, come in, come in; come out of the damp and warm yourselves at the fire.'

We entered. Inside it was dingy. At one end of the room was a bed covered in furs and woollen blankets, as well as personal effects which suggested an absent wife. In the centre was an open log fire, surrounded by charred and muddy rugs that were also mouldering thanks to the rain that dripped down from the open smoke hole. At the other end was a long trestle table with seating for ten, and a door that led to a separate kitchen. The walls were draped with mildewed tapestries that were faded and smoked near-black, and the floor was piled thick with rugs and skins. A pair of big, wolf-like dogs warmed themselves next to the fire.

'I was told that a Justice was moving north through the Tolsburg Marches,' Sir Otmar said as he fussed. As a Tollish knight and lord, he had been elevated to the Imperial aristocracy – "taking the Highmark", as it was known, for the payoffs they had all received in exchange for submitting to the Legions – but he was a far cry from the powdered and pampered lords of Sova. He was an old man, clad in a grubby tunic bearing his device and a pair of homespun trousers. His face was grimy and careworn and framed by white hair and a white beard. A large dent marred his forehead, probably earned as a younger man when the Reichskrieg had swept through and the Sovan armies had vassalised Tolsburg twenty-five years before. Both Vonvalt and Bressinger, too, bore the scars of the Imperial expansion.

'The last visit was from Justice August?' Vonvalt asked.

Sir Otmar nodded. 'Aye. A long time ago. Used to be that we saw a Justice a few times a year. Please, all of you, sit. Food, ale? Wine? I was just about to eat.'

'Yes, thank you,' Vonvalt said, sitting at the table. We followed suit.

'My predecessor left a logbook?' Vonvalt asked.

'Yes, yes,' Sir Otmar replied, and sent the maid scurrying off again. I heard the sounds of a strongbox being raided.

'Any trouble from the north?'

Sir Otmar shook his head. 'No; we have a sliver of the Westmark of Haunersheim between us and the sea. Maybe ten or twenty miles' worth, enough to absorb a raiding party. Though I daresay the sea is too rough this time of year anyway to tempt the northerners down.'

'Quite right,' Vonvalt said. I could tell he was annoyed for having forgotten his geography. Still, one could be forgiven the occasional slip of the mind. The Empire, now over fifty years old, had absorbed so many nations so quickly the cartographers redrew the maps yearly. 'And I suppose with Seaguard rebuilt,' he added.

'Aye, that the Autun did. A new curtain wall, a new garrison, and enough money and provender to allow for daily ranges during fighting season. Weekly, in winter, by order of the margrave.'

The Autun. The Two-Headed Wolf. It was evens on whether the man had meant the term as a pejorative. It was one of those strange monikers for the Sovan Empire that the conquered used either in deference or as an insult. Either way, Vonvalt ignored it.

'The man has a reputation,' Vonvalt remarked.

'Margrave Westenholtz?' the priest, Claver, chipped in. 'A good man. A pious man. The northerners are a godless folk who cleave to the old Draedist ways.' He shrugged. 'You should not mourn them, Justice.'

Vonvalt smiled thinly. 'I do not mourn dead northern raiders, Patria,' he said with more restraint than the man was due. Claver was a young man, too young to bear the authority of a priest.

Over the course of our short time together we had all had grown to dislike him immensely. He was zealous and a bore, quick to anger and judge. He spoke at great length about his cause – that of recruiting Templars for the southern Frontier – and his lordly contacts. Bressinger generally refused to talk to him, but Vonvalt, out of professional courtesy, had been engaging with the man for weeks.

Sir Otmar cleared his throat. He was about to make the error of engaging with Claver when the food arrived, and instead he ate. It was hearty, simple fare of meat, bread and thick gravy, but then in these circumstances we rarely went hungry. Vonvalt's power and authority tended to inspire generosity in his hosts.

'You said the last Justice passed through a while ago?' Vonvalt asked.

'Aye,' Sir Otmar replied.

'You have been following the Imperial statutes in the interim?'

Sir Otmar nodded vigorously, but he was almost certainly lying. These far-flung villages and towns, months' worth of travel from distant Sova even by the fastest means, rarely practised Imperial law. It was a shame. The Reichskrieg had brought death and misery to thousands, but the system of common law was one of the few rubies to come out of an otherwise enormous shit.

'Good. Then I shouldn't imagine there will be much to do. Except investigate the woods,' Vonvalt said. Sir Otmar looked confused by the addendum. Vonvalt drained the last of his ale. 'On our way here,' he explained, 'we were told a number of times about a witch, living in the woods just to the north of Rill. I don't suppose you know anything about it?'

Sir Otmar delayed with a long draw of wine and then ostensibly to pick something out of his teeth. 'Not that I have heard of, sire. No.'

Vonvalt nodded thoughtfully. *'Who is she?'*

Bressinger swore in Grozodan. Sir Otmar and I leapt halfway out of our skin. The table and all the platters and cutlery on it were jolted as three pairs of thighs hit it. Goblets and tankards were spilled. Sir Otmar clutched his heart, his eyes wide, his mouth working to expel the words that Vonvalt had commanded him to.

The Emperor's Voice: the arcane power of a Justice to compel a person to speak the truth. It had its limitations – it did not work on other Justices, for example, and a strong-willed person could frustrate it if on their guard – but Sir Otmar was old and meek and not well-versed in the ways of the Order. The power hit him like a psychic thunderclap and turned his mind inside out.

'A priestess... a member of the Draeda,' Sir Otmar gasped. He looked horrified as his mouth spoke against his mind's will.

'Is she from Rill?' Vonvalt pressed.

'Yes!'

'Are there others who practice Draedism?'

Sir Otmar writhed in his chair. He gripped the table to steady himself.

'Many – of the villagers!'

'Sir Konrad,' Bressinger murmured. He was watching Sir Otmar with a slight wince. I saw that Claver was relishing in the man's torment.

'All right, Sir Otmar,' Vonvalt said. 'All right. Calm yourself. Here, take some ale. I'll not press you any further.'

We sat in silence as Sir Otmar summoned the terrified maid with a trembling hand and wheezed for some ale. She left and reappeared a moment later, handing him a tankard. Sir Otmar drained it greedily.

'The practice of Draedism is illegal,' Vonvalt remarked.

Sir Otmar looked at his plate. His expression was somewhere between anger, horror and shame, and was a common look for those who had been hit by the Voice.

'The laws are new. The religion is old,' he said hoarsely.

'The laws have been in place for two and a half decades.'

'The religion has been in place for two and a half millennia,' Sir Otmar snapped.

There was an uncomfortable pause. 'Is there anyone in Rill that is not a practising member of Draedism?' Vonvalt asked.

Sir Otmar inspected his drink. 'I couldn't say,' he mumbled.

'Justice.' There was genuine disgust in Claver's voice. 'At the very least they will have to renounce it. The official religion of the Empire is the holy Nema Creed.' He practically spat as he looked the old baron up and down. 'If I had my way they'd all burn.'

'These are good folk here,' Sir Otmar said, alarmed. 'Good, law-abiding folk. They work the land and they pay their tithes. We've never been a burden on the Autun.'

Vonvalt shot Claver an irritated look. 'With respect, Sir Otmar, if these people are practising Draedists, then they cannot, by definition, be law-abiding. I am sorry to say that Patria Claver is right – at least in part. They will have to renounce it. You have a list of those who practice?'

'I do not.'

The logs smoked and crackled and spat. Ale and wine dripped and pattered through the cracks in the table planks.

'The charge is minor,' Vonvalt said. 'A small fine, a penny per head, if they recant. As their lord you may even shoulder it on their behalf. Do you have a shrine to any of the Imperial gods? Nema? Savare?'

'No.' Sir Otmar all but spat out the word. It was becoming increasingly difficult to ignore the fact that Sir Otmar was a practising Draedist himself.

'The official religion of the Sovan Empire is the Nema Creed. Enshrined in scripture and in both the common and canon law. Come now, there are parallels. The Book of Lorn is essentially Draedism, no? It has the same parables, mandates the same holy days. You could adopt it without difficulty.'

It was true, the Book of Lorn did bear remarkable parallels to Draedism. That was because the Book of Lorn *was* Draedism. The Sovan religion was remarkably flexible, and rather than replacing the many religious practices it encountered during the

Reichskrieg, it simply subsumed them, like a wave engulfing an island. It was why the Nema Creed was simultaneously the most widely practised and least-respected religion in the known world.

I looked over to Claver. The man's face was aghast at Vonvalt's easy equivocation. Of course, Vonvalt was no more a believer in the Nema Creed than Sir Otmar. Like the old baron, he had had the religion forced on him. But he went to temple, and he put himself through the motions like most of the Imperial aristocracy. Claver, on the other hand, was young enough to have known no other religion. A true believer. Such men had their uses, but more often than not their inflexibility made them dangerous.

'The Empire requires that you practise the teachings of the Nema Creed. The law allows for nothing else,' Vonvalt said.

'If I refuse?'

Vonvalt drew himself up. 'If you refuse you become a heretic. If you refuse to *me* you become an avowed heretic. But you won't do something as silly and wasteful as that.'

'And what is the punishment for avowed heresy?' Sir Otmar asked, though he knew the answer.

'You will be burned.' It was Claver who spoke. There was savage glee in his voice.

'No one will be burned,' Vonvalt said irritably, 'because no one is an avowed heretic. Yet.'

I looked back and forth between Vonvalt and Sir Otmar. I had sympathy for Sir Otmar's position. He was right to say that Draedism was harmless, and right to disrespect the Nema Creed as worthless. Furthermore, he was an old man, being lectured and threatened with death. But the fact of the matter was, the Sovan Empire ruled the Tolsburg Marches. Their laws applied, and, actually, their laws were robust and fairly applied. Most everyone else got on with it, so why couldn't he?

Sir Otmar seemed to sag slightly.

'There is an old watchtower on Gabler's Mount, a few hours'

ride north-east of here. The Draedists gather there to worship. You will find your witch there.'

Vonvalt paused for a moment. He took a long draw of ale. Then he carefully set the tankard down.

'Thank you,' he said, and stood. 'We'll go there now, while there is an hour or two of daylight left.'

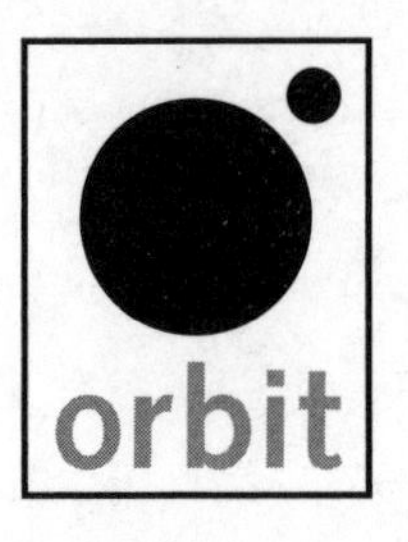
orbit